THE POETICAL WORKS

OF

CHRISTINA GEORGINA ROSSETTI

WITH MEMOIR AND NOTES &c

BY

WILLIAM MICHAEL ROSSETTI

London
MACMILLAN AND CO., Limited
NEW YORK: THE MACMILLAN COMPANY
1904

All rights reserved

PREFACE

CHRISTINA ROSSETTI'S first published poetic volume, which had been preceded by some poems issued in a more scattered shape, was produced in 1862; she died in 1894. It seems now to be time that her Poetical Works should be brought out in a duly co-ordinated form, practically though not in the most absolute possible sense) complete.

Her poetic volumes appeared as follows :—

1. *Verses,* privately printed, 1847. This volume has been reissued to the public at a recent date, but without any authority obtained, nor I suppose legally needed, from the representatives of the writer.

2. *Goblin Market and other Poems,* 1862 (Macmillan).

3. *The Prince's Progress and other Poems,* 1866 (Macmillan).

4. *Sing-Song,* 1872 (Routledge, now Macmillan).

5. *A Pageant and other Poems,* 1881 (Macmillan). The volumes 2, 3, and 5, have been reissued in a collected form, introducing a moderate number of additional poems.

6. *Verses,* 1893 (Society for Promoting Christian Knowledge). These poems are reprinted in the volume here named from three earlier volumes of combined prose and verse.

7. *New Poems,* 1896 (Macmillan). Collected and edited by myself after Christina's death.

From this list it will be seen that the Firm of Macmillan & Co., Limited, has now and heretofore been in a position to deal with all Christina Rossetti's poems, except only the *Verses,* 1893, No. 6 on the list. Those *Verses* include many of the finest devotional poems that she ever wrote; and to bring out, without including these, an edition of her poems professedly or proximately complete, would have been a fallacious attempt. By an arrangement made with the Society for Promoting Christian Knowledge, we are enabled to include the *Verses* in the present edition.

The division of my sister's writings in this edition runs thus: 7 Longer Poems, Juvenilia, Devotional Poems, General Poems, Poems Children and Minor Verse, and Italian Poems. Each of these sections arranged in order of date, so far as the conditions (as to which so details are given in my Notes) reasonably allow. I think that read already interested in Christina Rossetti's poetry will find some pleasure tracing the sequence of dates. They will learn that some of her b poems were written at a very early period of her youth. Her own arran ment of her poems in the latest collected edition (which, as alrea indicated, includes only the volumes that I have numbered 2, 3, and and not the other four volumes) may also be regarded as a point of so interest; I give that Table of Contents in an Appendix (A). That I arrangement in all instances was not merely haphazard may be taken granted—she consulted her brother Dante Gabriel a good deal, w regard at any rate to No. 3; at the same time, I do not perceive that a very definite plan has been followed in the latest collected edition. O clear distinction is made—that of separating the poems which first appear in vol. 5 from those which are proper to vols. 2 and 3; the contents 2 and 3 are fused together without any regard to dates of composition of first publication, and perhaps even with some inclination to keep tl point in a haze.

As to the few Italian poems, I have had before now occasion remark that they appear to me to be in essentials as good as those English, although I could readily suppose that in some points of dictio etc. they are not up to the standard of verse written by a native Italia Later on I was somewhat surprised to find, in an Italian literary pap named *Il Marzocco*, a criticism expressed in the following very adven terms: 'She wrote also some Italian verses; but, if I am to judge them from the specimens I know, they not only do not add anything to h fame as a poet, but rather detract from it, so formless and inept do the seem to me. It might almost be thought that the writer of those verse did not, as we know she did, speak from early childhood her paterni language.' This criticism is signed 'Th. Neal,' an English-seemin name which is used (as I have been informed) by an Italian writer. quote the observation for whatever it may be worth, and for candour' sake, but can hardly help thinking that it must be harsher than th circumstances warrant. Recently I have had occasion to converse with literary Italian, well versed in English: he considers that Christina's Italia

rses are not undeserving of commendation, and assimilate to native work
ore nearly than those of Dante Gabriel Rossetti.

With regard to the volume above-mentioned entitled *New Poems*, which
edited in 1896 after my sister's death, it has been alleged by some critics
at I raked together all that I could find, however indifferent in several
stances, and presented all to the public, who would gladly have dispensed
ith many. As a statement of fact, I know this to be incorrect; and, as a
atter of opinion, I consider it mistaken. So far from raking together all
at I could find, I left unused a considerable number of compositions that
ere at my disposal; and in the present edition I still leave these unused.
add in an Appendix (B) a list of them; this is perhaps not of much
oncern to any one, but it serves to confirm my assertion, and may perhaps
e regarded with favour by some future editor, who might really be
inded to carry to its utmost limit the 'raking-together' process. And
will not pretend to deny that, in the case of a writer who has attained a
ertain standard (it must be a high one) of fame and popularity, I consider
at that process has a good deal to say for itself.

The contents of the volume named *New Poems* are of course re-
roduced, in their due order of date, etc., in the present edition. In
refacing that volume I made the remark: 'I conceive *some* of the
compositions herein contained to be up to the level of Christina Rossetti's
est work,[1] and the great majority of them to be well up to her average.'
This is an opinion which I still entertain, although aware that several
tics of the *New Poems* formed and expressed a very different judgment.
They seemed to find little to commend in the volume, and much to object
, both in the poems themselves and in my action as their editor. Those
tics and I must apparently agree to differ as to the general ratio of

---

[1] It is possible that some readers might like to know which are the compositions here
ferred to. I will therefore give a list of them (which follows the order of their
tation in the *New Poems*, not in the present edition). They are twenty-six in number,
: *The Summer is Ended, A Pause, Restive* (which is now reprinted as Section 3 of
hree Stages), *Long Looked for, Let Patience have her Perfect Work, In an Artist's
dio, Meeting* (if we shall live, we live), *Under Willows, A Sketch, If I had Words,
o They Desire, Not Yours but You, By the Waters of Babylon, Birds of Paradise, Il
eggiar dell'Oriente;* and (more especially) *A Soul, Cobwebs, A Chilly Night, Acme,
rspective, To-day and To-morrow, En Route, By Way of Remembrance, Sleeping at
st, There remaineth therefore a Rest for the People of God* (Come, blessed sleep, most
ll, most perfect, come), and *The Heart knoweth its own Bitterness* (When all the over-
rk of life).

ment of the compositions in this edition, deserve to be borne in mind by her readers; and among the readers there may be some who would like to be furnished with a clue for following out, as the inclination prompts them at the moment, one or other of these trains of sentiment. It may perhaps be said that the two ideas most prevalent of all are the strenuous and onerous effort to attain to the salvation of the soul in heaven, and the ardent absorbing devotion to the work and the very person of the Saviour Jesus Christ. These ideas are diffused over the whole area of the authoress's Devotional Poems, and are to be traced in other compositions as well. It would, I think, be superfluous to call attention to particular poems embodying those paramount ideas, and I therefore limit myself to other ideas, subordinate, yet still marked and dominant,—some of them of much importance in themselves, others not thus important but highly characteristic of Christina Rossetti. I will define them thus: (1) Personal Experiences and Emotions; (2) Death; (3) The Aspiration for Rest (and her ideal of bliss appears to have consisted in ultimate rest, only less absolutely than in the promised fruition of heaven); (4) Vanity of Vanities; (5) A Love of Animals, and more especially such animals as are frequently regarded as odd or uncouth, rather than obviously attractive; (6) Winter—almost invariably contemplated as dismal and repugnant; (7) The loveliness of the Rose. In the Appendix (C) I give a reference to the principal instances (not by any means to all instances) in which these themes are prominently brought forward.

In my Notes at the end of the volume many details will be found bearing upon the occasions which gave rise to particular poems, the significance of the poems, etc. For such compositions as appeared in the volume of *New Poems* the Notes appended to that volume are here re-used, with modifications and omissions.

Brief though the foregoing remarks are, they may perhaps serve as being all that I need personally say about the Poems of my Sister. To puff them is neither my business nor my inclination. To analyse them in any painstaking manner is outside my editorial scope—many of them in fact have already sunk deep into the feelings and the memory, and I might say the conscience, of poetic readers. I think it well, however, to add to my Preface a condensed Memoir of Christina Rossetti. Up to the date of her death little was publicly known about her, as she had led an extremely quiet and even a secluded life. Since then the Biography by my friend, Mr. Mackenzie Bell, has appeared—January 1898. When that work came out some very erroneous opinions were expressed about it in the press, not of course in all the critiques, but in two or three of the most influent[ial]. The view thus propounded, and propounded in a very confident tone, w[as] that I had been a main performer in Mr. Bell's book: the voice might [be] the voice of Jacob, but the hands were the hands of Esau. The critics m[ust] permit me to tell them that this was totally untrue. Their semi-omniscier[ce] was at fault. The simple facts of the case are as follows:—Mr. Bell, so[on] after Christina's death, formed the project of writing a biographical a[nd] critical study of her. As he had known nothing personally of Christi[na] except during some thirteen months preceding her death, he was necessar[ily] aware that his biographical materials must be obtained from some one els[e,] and he very correctly opined that I knew much more about her than a[ny] other person living, and that therefore it would be expedient to apply [to] me for a large majority of his information. He asked whether I wou[ld] furnish such information, and I said yes; and in the course of his wo[rk] he addressed to me a great number of questions, mostly in writing, [to] which I replied, also mostly in writing. At one stage of the matter I p[ut] it very plainly to Mr. Bell that, while I was happy to return a direct an[d] full reply to most of his inquiries, I neither expected nor intended [to] regulate in any way the use he might make of my answers; and on th[is] plan I acted throughout, except that in some very few instances I foun[d,] when he sent me the proofs of his book, that he had reproduced in m[y] own off-hand terms some details (generally affecting outsiders) which [I] thought not fitted to be published in the same terms. These few instance[s] I pointed out to Mr. Bell, and he, with the right feeling which invariabl[y] marked his treatment of such matters, at once conformed to my view[s.] I observed in the proofs a great number of other instances in which h[e] had quoted my precise phrases. In several of these cases my opinion wa[s] that it would have been better, on literary or other grounds, if he ha[d] simply worked up into his own narrative the facts which I placed at hi[s] disposal (without quoting my precise words, or even naming me as th[e] informant), or if he had merely utilized my details so far as tacitly to avoi[d] making any mis-statement: but, faithful to my view that the book ough[t] to be his in the fullest sense, and in no sense mine, I advisedly abstaine[d] from raising any objection or demur on this point. The critics to whom I have referred, while treating Mr. Bell and his book with some favou[r] in the comparative if not the positive degree, fell foul of me in something not unlike the superlative degree—and this mainly on the ground, erroneously imagined by themselves, that most of the things which they disliked in the book had been foisted into it by me in a spirit of dictation at once arrogant and obtuse, and had by Mr. Bell been too tamely permitted to appear. Both Mr. Bell and I had reason to complain of these critics: Mr. Bell for being falsely credited with a degree of sheepish acquiescence which had tended to spoil his book, and I for being falsely arraigned of an offence not enacted by me but invented by my censors, who thereupon abused me for doing what I had not done, and for defects of mind and character evidenced by the imputed doing of it.

But all this is an old story, and barely worth referring to now. I glance at it chiefly because it has constituted one of my reasons for preferring on the present occasion to write something—a very little—about my sister in the way of biography. Mr. Bell's treatment of the subject is in many respects meritorious, but need not prevent a relative from stating a few facts in his own way. A reader of the poems ought to know who and what their authoress was. I propose to put him in possession of that amount of knowledge, and of little beyond that.

W. M. ROSSETTI.

LONDON, *September* 1903.

CONTENTS

PORTRAIT OF CHRISTINA ROSSETTI		*Frontispiece*
		Page.
PREFACE		v
APPENDIX A.—Contents of the Collected Edition issued by Christina Rossetti		xxxix
APPENDIX B.—Poems by Christina Rossetti extant in MS., etc.		xli
APPENDIX C.—Some leading Themes, or Key-notes of Feeling, in the Poems of Christina Rossetti		xliii
MEMOIR		xlv

No.	Title.	Year.	
1.	Dedicatory Sonnet	C. 1881	lxxiii

THE LONGER POEMS

2.	Goblin Market	1859	1
3.	Repining	1847	9
4.	Three Nuns	1849-50	12
5.	The Lowest Room (Like flowers sequestered from the sun)	1856	16
6.	From House to Home	1858	20
7.	The Prince's Progress	1861-65	26
8.	A Royal Princess	1861	35
9.	Maiden-Song	1863	38
10.	'The Iniquity of the Fathers upon the Children'	1865	41
11.	The Months : A Pageant	1879	48
12.	A Ballad of Boding	B. 1882	55
13.	Monna Innominata : A Sonnet of Sonnets	B. ,,	58
14.	An Old-World Thicket	B. ,,	64
15.	All Thy Works praise Thee, O Lord : A Processional of Creation	B. ,,	68
16.	Later Life : A Double Sonnet of Sonnets	B. ,,	73

JUVENILIA

17.	To my Mother on the Anniversary of her Birth	1842	82
18.	The Chinaman	,,	82
19.	Hymn	1843	83
20.	Love and Hope	,,	83

No.	Title.	Year.	Page
	JUVENILIA, *continued*—		
21.	On Albina	1844	
22.	Forget Me Not	,,	
23.	Charity	,,	
24.	Earth and Heaven	,,	
25.	Love Ephemeral	1845	
26.	Burial Anthem	,,	
27.	Lines to my Grandfather	,,	
28.	Summer (Hark to the song of greeting! The tall trees)	,,	
29.	Serenade	,,	
30.	The End of Time	,,	
31.	Couplet	C. ,,	8
32.	Amore e Dovere	1845-47	8
33.	Mother and Child	1846	8
34.	Mary Magdalene	,,	8
35.	On the Death of a Cat, a Friend of mine .	,,	8
36.	To Elizabeth Read, with some Postage-Stamps for a Collection	,,	9
37.	Love Attacked	,,	9
38.	Love Defended	,,	9
39.	The Martyr (See, the sun hath risen) . .	,,	9
40.	The Dying Man to his Betrothed . .	,,	9
41.	Lisetta all' Amante	,,	9
42.	The Dead Bride	,,	9
43.	Will these Hands ne'er be clean? . .	,,	94
44.	Gone for Ever	,,	95
45.	Present and Future	,,	95
46.	The Time of Waiting	,,	95
47.	Tasso and Leonora	,,	96
48.	Love	1847	97
49.	The Solitary Rose	,,	97
50.	The Song of the Star	,,	97
51.	Resurrection Eve	,,	98
52.	The Dead City	,,	99
53.	The Rose	,,	103
54.	Spring Quiet	,,	103
55.	I have fought a Good Fight . . .	,,	103
56.	Wishes	,,	104
57.	The Dream (Rest, rest; the troubled breast) .	,,	104
58.	Eleanor	,,	105
59.	Isidora	,,	106
60.	Zara	,,	107
61.	The Novice	,,	108
62.	Immalee	,,	108
63.	Heart's Chill Between	,,	109
64.	Lady Isabella	,,	109

No.	Title.	Year.	Page.
	JUVENILIA, *continued*—		
65.	Night and Death	1847	109
66.	Death's Chill Between	,,	110
67.	The Lotus-Eaters—Ulysses to Penelope	,,	111
68.	Sonnet: From the Psalms	,,	112
69.	Song (The stream moaneth as it floweth)	,,	112
70.	The World's Harmonies	,,	112
71.	The Last Answer (Written to Bouts-rimés)	,,	113

DEVOTIONAL POEMS

72.	I do set my Bow in the Cloud	,,	114
73.	Death is Swallowed up in Victory	1848	114
74.	Symbols	1849	116
75.	Sweet Death	,,	116
76.	A Christmas Carol (Thank God, thank God, we do believe)	,,	117
77.	For Advent (Sweet sweet sound of distant waters, falling)	,,	117
78.	Two Pursuits	,,	118
79.	One Certainty	,,	119
80.	A Testimony	,,	119

SONGS FOR STRANGERS AND PILGRIMS

81.	'Her seed: It shall bruise thy head'	B. 1887	120
82.	Judge nothing before the Time	B. 1886	121
83.	How great is little Man	B. 1893	121
84.	Man's Life is but a Working Day	1864	121
85.	If not with hope of Life	B. 1893	121
86.	The Day is at hand	B. 1886	121
87.	Endure Hardness	,,	122
88.	'Whither the Tribes go up, even the Tribes of the Lord'	B. 1882	122
89.	Where never Tempest heaveth	B. 1893	122
90.	Marvel of Marvels, if I myself shall behold	,,	122
91.	What is that to thee? Follow thou Me	B. 1886	123
92.	'Worship God'	B. 1893	123
93.	'Afterward he repented, and went'	B. 1886	123
94.	'Are they not all Ministering Spirits'?	B. 1893	124
95.	Our Life is long. Not so, wise Angels say	B. 1886	124
96.	Lord, what have I to offer? Sickening fear	,,	124
97.	Joy is but Sorrow	,,	125
98.	'Can I know it?'—'Nay'	B. 1893	125
99.	'When my Heart is vexed I will Complain' (The fields are white to harvest, look and see)	B. 1886	125
100.	'Praying Always'	,,	126
101.	'As thy Days, so shall thy Strength be'	B. 1893	126

No.	Title.	Year.	Page
	SONGS FOR STRANGERS AND PILGRIMS, *continued*—		
102.	A heavy Heart, if ever Heart was heavy	B. 1886	128
103.	If Love is not worth Loving, then Life is not worth Living	B. ,,	128
104.	What is it Jesus saith unto the Soul?	1850, etc.	128
105.	They lie at rest, our blessed Dead	B. 1886	128
106.	'Ye that fear Him, both small and great'	B. 1882	128
107.	Called to be Saints	B. 1886	128
108.	The Sinner's own Fault? So it was	B. ,,	128
109.	Who cries for earthly Bread tho' white!	B. ,,	128
110.	Laughing Life cries at the Feast	B. ,,	128
111.	The End is not yet	B. ,,	128
112.	Who would wish back the Saints upon our rough	1861	128
113.	'That which hath been is named already, and it is known that it is Man'	B. 1886	129
114.	Of each sad Word which is more sorrowful	B. ,,	129
115.	I see that all Things come to an end	B. ,,	130
116.	But Thy Commandment is exceeding broad	B. ,,	130
117.	Sursum Corda	B. ,,	130
118.	O ye, who are not dead and fit	B. ,,	131
119.	Where shall I find a white Rose blowing?	C. 1884	131
120.	Redeeming the Time	B. 1886	131
121.	Now they desire a better Country (Love said nay, while Hope kept saying)	B. ,,	132
122.	A Castle-builder's World	B. ,,	132
123.	These all wait upon Thee	1853	132
124.	'Doeth well . . . doeth better'	B. 1886	132
125.	Our Heaven must be within ourselves	B. ,,	133
126.	Vanity of Vanities (Of all the downfalls in the world)	1858	133
127.	The Hills are tipped with Sunshine, while I walk	B. 1893	133
128.	Scarce tolerable Life, which all life long	C. 1884	133
129.	All Heaven is blazing yet	B. 1886	134
130.	Balm in Gilead	B. ,,	134
131.	'In the Day of his Espousals'	B. ,,	134
132.	'She came from the uttermost part of the Earth'	B. ,,	134
133.	Alleluia! or Alas! my Heart is crying	B. 1893	135
134.	The Passion Flower hath sprung up tall	B. ,,	135
135.	God's Acre	B. ,,	135
136.	The Flowers appear on the Earth	1855	135
137.	'Thou knewest . . . thou oughtest therefore'	B. 1893	136
138.	Go in Peace	B. ,,	136
139.	Half Dead	B. ,,	136
140.	'One of the Soldiers with a Spear pierced His Side'	B. ,,	137
141.	Where Love is, there comes Sorrow	B. 1886	137
142.	Bury Hope out of sight	B. ,,	137
143.	A Churchyard Song of Patient Hope	B. 1893	138

№.	Title.	Year.	Page.
	SONGS FOR STRANGERS AND PILGRIMS, *continued*—		
144.	One Woe is past. Come what come will .	B. 1893	138
145.	Take no Thought for the Morrow .	B. ,,	138
146.	Consider the Lilies of the Field (Solomon most glorious in array)	B. ,,	138
147.	'Son, remember'.	B. ,,	139
148.	Heaviness may endure for a Night, but Joy cometh in the Morning	B. 1886	139
149.	The Will of the Lord be done .	B. 1893	140
150.	Lay up for yourselves Treasures in Heaven .	B. 1886	140
151.	Whom the Lord loveth He chasteneth .	B. ,,	140
152.	'Then shall ye shout' .	B. ,,	140
153.	Everything that is born must die .	B. ,,	141
154.	Lord, grant us Calm, if Calm can set forth Thee .	B. 1893	141
155.	Changing Chimes .	B. ,,	141
156.	Thy Servant will go and fight with this Philistine .	B. ,,	141
157.	Thro' burden and heat of the Day .	B. 1886	142
158.	Then I commended Mirth .	B. ,,	142
159.	Sorrow hath a double Voice .	B. ,,	142
160.	Shadows to-day while Shadows show God's Will .	B. 1893	142
161.	Truly the Light is Sweet .	B. ,,	143
162.	Are ye not much better than they? .	B. ,,	143
163.	Yea the Sparrow hath found her an House .	B. ,,	143
164.	I am small and of no Reputation .	B. ,,	144
165.	O Christ my God Who seest the Unseen .	B. 1886	144
166.	Yea, if Thou wilt, Thou canst put up Thy Sword .	B. ,,	144
167.	Sweetness of Rest when Thou sheddest Rest .	B. 1893	144
168.	O Foolish Soul! to make thy Count .	B. ,,	144
169.	Before the Beginning Thou hast foreknown the End .	B. ,,	145
170.	The Goal in sight! Look up and sing .	B. 1886	145
171.	Looking back along Life's Trodden Way .	B. ,,	145
	(*Close of Songs for Strangers and Pilgrims*)		
172.	The Watchers .	1850	145
173.	The Three Enemies .	1851	146
174.	Behold, I stand at the Door and Knock .	,,	147
175.	Advent ('Come,' Thou dost say to Angels) .	,,	148
176.	All Saints (They have brought gold and spices to my King) .	1852	148
177.	Eye hath not Seen .	,,	148
178.	A bruised Reed shall He not break .	,,	150
179.	St. Elizabeth of Hungary .	,,	150
180.	Moonshine .	,,	150
181.	I look for the Lord .	,,	151
182.	The Heart knoweth its own Bitterness (Weep yet awhile) .	,,	152
183.	Whitsun Eve (The white dove cooeth in her downy nest) .	1853	152
184.	There remaineth therefore a Rest for the People of God (Come, blessed sleep, most full, most perfect, come) .	,,	153
185.	A Harvest .	,,	153

No.	Title.	Year.	Page
	DEVOTIONAL POEMS, *continued*—		
186.	The Eleventh Hour	1853	15
187.	Sleep at Sea	,,	15
188.	Consider the Lilies of the Field (Flowers preach to us if we will hear)	,,	15
189.	Who have a Form of Godliness	,,	15

SOME FEASTS AND FASTS

No.	Title.	Year.	Page
190.	Advent Sunday	B. 1886	15
191.	Advent (Earth grown old, yet still so green) . .	B. ,,	15
192.	Sooner or later, yet at last	B. 1882	15
193.	Christmas Eve	B. 1886	15
194.	Christmas Day	B. ,,	15
195.	Christmastide	B. ,,	15
196.	St. John, Apostle	B. 1893	15
197.	'Beloved, let us love one another,' says St. John .	B. 1886	159
198.	Holy Innocents (They scarcely waked before they slept) .	B. 1882	159
199.	Unspotted Lambs to follow the one Lamb .	B. 1893	160
200.	Epiphany	B. 1886	160
201.	Epiphany-tide	B. 1893	161
202.	Septuagesima	B. 1886	161
203.	Sexagesima	B. 1893	161
204.	That Eden of Earth's Sunrise cannot vie . .	B. ,,	162
205.	Quinquagesima	B. ,,	162
206.	Piteous my Rhyme is	B. 1886	163
207.	Ash Wednesday (My God, my God, have mercy on my sin)	B. ,,	163
208.	Good Lord, to-day	B. 1893	163
209.	Lent	B. 1886	163
210.	Embertide	B. 1893	163
211.	Mid-Lent	B. 1886	164
212.	Passiontide	B. 1893	164
213.	Palm Sunday	B. ,,	164
214.	Monday in Holy Week	B. 1886	165
215.	Tuesday in Holy Week	B. ,,	165
216.	Wednesday in Holy Week	B. ,,	166
217.	Maundy Thursday	B. ,,	166
218.	Good Friday Morning	B. 1893	166
219.	Good Friday (Lord Jesus Christ, grown faint upon the Cross)	B. 1886	167
220.	Good Friday Evening	B. 1893	167
221.	'A Bundle of Myrrh is my Well-beloved unto Me' .	B. ,,	167
222.	Easter Even (The Tempest over and gone, the Calm begun)	B. 1886	167
223.	While Christ lay dead the widowed World . .	B. 1893	168
224.	Easter Day	B. 1886	168
225.	Easter Monday	B. ,,	168

CONTENTS

No.	Title.	Year.	Page.
	SOME FEASTS AND FASTS, *continued*—		
226.	Easter Tuesday	B. 1893	169
227.	Rogationtide	B. 1886	169
228.	Ascension Eve	B. 1893	169
229.	Ascension Day	B. 1886	170
230.	Whitsun Eve ('As many as I love'—Ah Lord who lovest all)	B. 1893	170
231.	Whitsun Day	B. 1886	170
232.	Whitsun Monday	B. 1893	171
233.	Whitsun Tuesday	B. 1886	171
234.	Trinity Sunday	B. 1893	171
235.	Conversion of St. Paul	B. 1886	172
236.	In Weariness and Painfulness St. Paul	B. ,,	172
237.	Vigil of the Presentation	B. 1893	172
238.	Feast of the Presentation	B. 1882	172
239.	The Purification of St. Mary the Virgin	B. 1886	173
240.	Vigil of the Annunciation	B. 1893	173
241.	Feast of the Annunciation	B. 1886	173
242.	Herself a Rose who bore the Rose	B. 1882	174
243.	St. Mark	B. ,,	174
244.	St. Barnabas	B. ,,	174
245.	Vigil of St. Peter	B. 1893	175
246.	St. Peter	B. ,,	175
247.	St. Peter once : 'Lord, dost Thou wash my Feet?'	B. ,,	175
248.	I followed Thee, my God, I followed Thee	B. 1882	176
249.	Vigil of St. Bartholomew	B. 1893	177
250.	St. Bartholomew	B. 1886	177
251.	St. Michael and all Angels	B. 1882	177
252.	Vigil of All Saints	B. 1886	178
253.	All Saints (as grains of Sand, as Stars, as drops of Dew)	B. ,,	178
254.	All Saints : Martyrs	B. 1893	178
255.	'I gave a sweet Smell'	B. 1886	179
256.	Hark ! the Alleluias of the great Salvation	B. 1893	179
257.	A Song for the Least of all Saints	B. ,,	179
258.	Sunday before Advent	B. ,,	179
	(*Close of Some Feasts and Fasts*)		
259.	There remaineth therefore a Rest (In the grave will be no space)	1854	180
260.	Paradise	,,	180
261.	Ye have forgotten the Exhortation	,,	181
262.	The World	,,	182
263.	Unforgotten	1855	182
264.	Zion Said	,,	183
265.	Hymn after Gabriele Rossetti—Two Versions	C. ,,	183
266.	I will lift up mine Eyes unto the Hills	1856	184
267.	How Long?	,,	185
268.	Amen	,,	186

No.	Title.	Year.	Page
	DEVOTIONAL POEMS, *continued*—		
269.	A Martyr (It is over, the horrible pain)	1856	186
270.	Now they desire (There is a sleep we have not slept)	,,	186
271.	A Christmas Carol, for my Godchildren (The Shepherds had an Angel)	,,	187
272.	Not Yours but You	,,	188
273.	After this the Judgment	,,	188
274-5-6.	Old and New Year Ditties	1856-58-60	190
277.	A Better Resurrection	1857	191
278.	The Heart knoweth its own Bitterness (when all the over-work of life)	,,	192

DIVERS WORLDS. TIME AND ETERNITY

No.	Title.	Year.	Page
279.	Earth has clear Call of Daily Bells	1858	193
280.	Escape to the Mountain	B. 1893	193
281.	I lift mine Eyes to see: Earth vanisheth	B. ,,	193
282.	Yet a Little While (Heaven is not far, tho' far the sky)	B. ,,	193
283.	Behold, it was very Good	B. ,,	194
284.	'Whatsoever is right, that shall ye receive'	1857	194
285.	This near-at-hand Land breeds Pain by Measure	B. 1882	194
286.	Was Thy Wrath against the Sea?	B. 1893	195
287.	And there was no more Sea	B. ,,	195
288.	Roses on a Brier	B. 1886	196
289.	We are of those who tremble at Thy Word	B. 1893	196
290.	Awake, thou that sleepest	B. ,,	196
291.	We know not when, we know not where	B. 1886	196
292.	I will lift up mine Eyes unto the Hills	B. ,,	197
293.	Then whose shall those Things be?	B. ,,	197
294.	His Banner over me was Love	B. ,,	197
295.	Beloved, yield thy Time to God, for He	B. 1893	197
296.	Time seems not short	B. ,,	198
297.	The Half Moon shows a Face of plaintive Sweetness	B. ,,	198
298.	As the Doves to their Windows	B. ,,	198
299.	Oh Knell of a passing Time	B. ,,	199
300.	Time passeth away with its Pleasure and Pain	B. ,,	199
301.	The Earth shall tremble at the Look of Him	B. ,,	199
302.	Time lengthening, in the lengthening seemeth long	B. ,,	199
303.	All Flesh is Grass	B. ,,	200
304.	Heaven's Chimes are slow but sure to strike at last	B. 1886	200
305.	There remaineth therefore a Rest to the people of God (Rest remains when all is done)	B. ,,	200
306.	Parting after Parting	1858-64	200
307.	They put their Trust in Thee and were not confounded	B. 1886	201
308.	Short is Time and only Time is bleak	B. 1893	201
309.	For Each	B. ,,	201
310.	For All	B. ,,	202
	(*Close of Divers Worlds*)		

No.	Title.	Year.	Page.

DEVOTIONAL POEMS, *continued*—

311.	Advent (This Advent moon shines cold and clear)	1858	202
312.	Christian and Jew—A Dialogue	,,	203
313.	A Burden	,,	204
314.	Only Believe	,,	205

NEW JERUSALEM AND ITS CITIZENS

315.	The Holy City, New Jerusalem	B. 1882	206
316.	When Wickedness is broken as a Tree	B. 1893	206
317.	Jerusalem of Fire	B. ,,	207
318.	She shall be brought unto the King	B. ,,	207
319.	Who is this that cometh up not alone	B. 1886	207
320.	Who sits with the King in His Throne? Not a Slave but a Bride	B. 1893	207
321.	Antipas	B. ,,	208
322.	Beautiful for Situation	B. ,,	208
323.	Lord, by what inconceivable dim Road	B. ,,	208
324.	As cold Waters to a thirsty Soul, so is good News from a far Country	B. 1886	209
325.	Cast down but not destroyed, chastened not slain	B. 1893	209
326.	Lift up thine Eyes to seek the Invisible	B. ,,	209
327.	Love is strong as Death (as flames that consume the mountains, as winds that coerce the sea)	B. ,,	210
328.	'Let them rejoice in their Beds'	B. ,,	210
329.	Slain in their high Places: fallen on Rest	B. ,,	210
330.	'What hath God wrought!'	B. ,,	210
331.	'Before the Throne and before the Lamb'	B. ,,	211
332.	'He shall go no more out'	B. ,,	211
333.	Yea blessed and holy is he that hath part in the First Resurrection	,,	211
334.	The Joy of Saints like Incense turned to Fire	B. ,,	212
335.	What are these lovely ones, yea what are these?	B. ,,	212
336.	The General Assembly and Church of the Firstborn	B. ,,	212
337.	Every One that is Perfect shall be as his Master	B. 1886	213
338.	As dying, and behold we live	B. 1893	213
339.	So great a Cloud of Witnesses	B. ,,	213
340.	Our Mothers, lovely Women pitiful	B. ,,	214
341.	Safe where I cannot lie yet	B. ,,	214
342.	'Is it well with the Child?'	1865	214
343.	Dear Angels and dear disembodied Saints	B. 1893	214
344.	'To every Seed his own Body'	B. ,,	215
345.	'What good shall my Life do me?'	1858	215

(*Close of New Jerusalem and its Citizens*)

346.	The Love of Christ which passeth Knowledge	,,	215
347.	A Shadow of Dorothea	,,	216
348.	For Henrietta Polydore	1859	217
349.	Ash Wednesday (Jesus, do I love Thee?)	,,	217
350.	A Christmas Carol (Before the paling of the Stars)	,,	217

No.	Title.	Year.	Page
	CHRIST OUR ALL IN ALL		
351.	'The Ransomed of the Lord'	B. 1893	218
352.	Lord, we are Rivers running to Thy Sea	B. ,,	218
353.	'An exceeding bitter Cry'	B. ,,	218
354.	O Lord, when Thou didst call me didst Thou know	B. ,,	218
355.	Thou, God, seest me	B. ,,	219
356.	Lord Jesus, who would think that I am Thine?	B. 1886	219
357.	The Name of Jesus	B. ,,	220
358.	Lord God of Hosts, most Holy and most High	B. ,,	220
359.	Lord, what have I that I may offer Thee?	B. ,,	220
360.	If I should say 'my Heart is in my Home'	B. ,,	220
361.	Leaf from Leaf Christ knows	B. 1882	221
362.	Lord, carry me.—Nay but I grant thee Strength	B. 1893	221
363.	Lord, I am here.—But, Child, I look for thee	B. ,,	221
364.	New Creatures, the Creator still the same	B. ,,	222
365.	King of Kings and Lord of Lords	B. ,,	222
366.	Thy Name, O Christ, as Incense streaming forth	B. ,,	222
367.	The Good Shepherd	B. ,,	223
368.	'Rejoice with Me'	B. ,,	223
369.	Shall not the Judge of all the Earth do right?	B. 1886	223
370.	Me and my Gift—Kind Lord, Behold	B. 1893	223
371.	'He cannot deny Himself'	B. ,,	223
372.	Slain from the Foundation of the World	B. ,,	224
373.	Lord Jesu, Thou art Sweetness to my Soul	B. ,,	224
374.	I, Lord, Thy foolish Sinner low and small	B. ,,	224
375.	'Because He first loved us'	B. ,,	225
376.	Lord, hast Thou so loved us, and will not we	B. ,,	225
377.	As the Dove which found no Rest	B. ,,	226
378.	Thou art fairer than the Children of Men	B. 1886	226
379.	'As the Apple-tree among the Trees of the Wood'	B. 1893	226
380.	None other Lamb, none other Name	B. ,,	226
381.	Thy Friend and thy Father's Friend forget not	1859	226
382.	Surely He hath borne our Griefs	B. 1886	227
383.	They toil not neither do they spin	B. 1893	227
384.	Darkness and Light are both alike to Thee	B. 1886	227
385.	'And now why tarriest thou?'	B. 1893	228
386.	Have I not striven, my God, and watched and prayed?	1863	228
387.	God is our Hope and Strength	B. 1893	229
388.	Day and Night the Accuser makes no pause	B. ,,	229
389.	O mine Enemy	B. ,,	229
390.	Lord, dost Thou look on me, and will not I	B. ,,	229
391.	Peace I leave with you	B. ,,	230
392.	O Christ our All in Each, our All in All	B. 1886	230
393.	Because Thy Love hath sought me	B. 1893	230

No.	Title.	Year.	Page.
	CHRIST OUR ALL IN ALL, *continued*—		
394.	Thy fainting Spouse, yet still Thy Spouse .	B. 1893	230
395.	Like as the Hart desireth the Water Brooks	B. ,,	231
396.	That where I am, there ye may be also .	B. ,,	231
397.	Judge not according to the Appearance .	B. ,,	231
398.	My God, wilt Thou accept, and will not we	B. ,,	231
399.	A chill blank World. Yet over the utmost Sea .	B. ,,	232
400.	The Chiefest among Ten Thousand	B. ,,	232
	(*Close of Christ our All in All*)		
401.	Easter Even (There is nothing more that they can do)	1861	232
402.	The Offering of the New Law	,,	233
403.	By the Waters of Babylon (By the waters of Babylon)	,,	233
404.	Within the Veil .	,,	234
405.	Good Friday (Am I a stone, and not a sheep)	1862	234
406.	Out of the Deep .	,,	234
407.	For a Mercy Received	1863	235
408.	Martyrs' Song	,,	236
409.	Consider .	,,	237
410.	The Lowest Place (Give me the lowest place ; not that I dare)	,,	237
411.	Come unto Me .	1864	237
412.	Who shall Deliver me? .	,,	238
413.	In Patience	,,	238
414.	None with Him .	,,	238
415.	By the Waters of Babylon (Here where I dwell I waste to skin and bone) .	,,	239
416.	Despised and Rejected	,,	241
417.	Weary in Well-doing	,,	242
418.	Birds of Paradise .	,,	242
419.	Dost Thou not care?	,,	242
420.	I know you not .	C. ,,	243
421.	If Only .	1865	244
422.	Long Barren	,,	244
423.	Young Death	,,	244
424.	Mother Country .	1866	245
425.	After Communion	,,	246
426.	A Christmas Carol (In the bleak mid-winter)	B. 1872	246
427.	Wrestling	B. 1875	247
428.	The Master is come, and calleth for Thee	B. 1876	248
429.	When my Heart is vexed, I will complain (O Lord, how canst Thou say Thou lovest me) .	B. ,,	248
430.	Saints and Angels	B. ,,	249
431.	A Rose Plant in Jericho .	,,	250
432.	Patience of Hope .	C. 1880	250
433.	I will arise	B. 1882	251
434.	A Prodigal Son .	B. ,,	251

No.	Title.	Year.	P.
	DEVOTIONAL POEMS, continued—		
435.	For Thine own Sake, O my God	B. 1882	
436.	Until the Day Break	B. ,,	
437.	Of him that was ready to Perish	B. ,,	
438.	Behold the Man	B. ,,	
439.	The Descent from the Cross	B. ,,	
440.	It is Finished	B. ,,	2
441.	An Easter Carol	B. ,,	2
442.	Behold a Shaking	B. ,,	25
443.	All Saints (They are flocking from the East)	B. ,,	25
444.	'Take care of Him'	B. ,,	25
445.	A Martyr—The Vigil of the Feast (Inner not outer, without gnash of teeth)	B. ,,	25
446.	Why?	B. ,,	26
447.	Love is strong as Death (I have not sought Thee, I have not found Thee)	B. ,,	26
448.	'If thou sayest, Behold, we knew it not'	B. ,,	261
449.	The Thread of Life	B. ,,	261
450.	A Sick Child's Meditation	C. 1885	263

OUT OF THE DEEP HAVE I CALLED UNTO THEE, O LORD

No.	Title.	Year.	P.
451.	Alone Lord God, in Whom our Trust and Peace	B. 1893	264
452.	Seven Vials hold Thy Wrath, but what can hold	B. ,,	264
453.	Where neither Rust nor Moth doth corrupt	B. ,,	264
454.	As the Sparks fly upwards	B. ,,	265
455.	Lord, make us all love all, that when we meet	B. ,,	265
456.	O Lord, I am ashamed to seek Thy Face	B. ,,	265
457.	It is not Death, O Christ, to die for Thee	B. ,,	266
458.	Lord, grant us Eyes to See and Ears to Hear	B. ,,	266
459.	'Cried out with Tears'	B. ,,	266
460.	O Lord on Whom we gaze and dare not gaze	B. ,,	267
461.	'I will come and heal him'	B. ,,	267
462.	Ah Lord, Lord, if my Heart were right with Thine	B. ,,	267
463.	The Gold of that Land is good	B. ,,	268
464.	Weigh all my Faults and Follies righteously	B. 1886	268
465.	Lord, grant me Grace to love Thee in my pain	B. ,,	268
466.	Lord, make me one with Thine own Faithful Ones	B. 1893	269
467.	Light of Light	B. ,,	269
	(Close of Out of the Deep have I called unto thee, O Lord)		

GIFTS AND GRACES

No.	Title.	Year.	P.
468.	Love loveth Thee, and Wisdom loveth Thee	B. ,,	270
469.	Lord, give me Love that I may love Thee much	B. ,,	70
470.	'As a King . . . unto the King'	B. 1886	270

No.	Title.	Year.	Page.
	GIFTS AND GRACES, *continued*—		
471.	O ye who love To-day	B. 1893	270
472.	Life that was born to-day	B. ,,	271
473.	Perfect Love casteth out Fear	B. ,,	271
474.	Hope is the Counterpoise of Fear	B. ,,	271
475.	Subject to like Passions as we are	B. ,,	271
476.	Experience bows a sweet contented Face	B. ,,	272
477.	Charity never Faileth	B. ,,	272
478.	The Greatest of these is Charity	B. ,,	272
479.	All beneath the Sun hasteth	B. ,,	273
480.	If thou be Dead, forgive and thou shalt Live	B. ,,	273
481.	Let Patience have her perfect Work (Can man rejoice who lives in hourly fear?)	B. ,,	273
482.	Patience must dwell with Love, for Love and Sorrow	B. ,,	274
483.	Let everything that hath Breath praise the Lord	B. ,,	274
484.	What is the Beginning? Love. What the Course? Love still	B. ,,	274
485.	Lord, make me Pure	B. ,,	274
486.	Love, to be Love, must walk Thy way	B. ,,	274
487.	Lord, I am Feeble and of Mean Account	B. ,,	275
488.	Tune me, O Lord, into one Harmony	B. ,,	275
489.	They shall be as white as Snow	B. ,,	275
490.	Thy Lilies drink the Dew	B. 1886	275
491.	When I was in Trouble I called upon the Lord	B. ,,	276
492.	Grant us such Grace that we may work Thy Will	B. 1893	276
493.	Who hath despised the Day of Small Things?	B. ,,	276
494.	'Do this, and he doeth it'	B. ,,	277
495.	'That no Man take thy Crown'	B. ,,	277
496.	Ye are come unto Mount Sion	B. ,,	277
497.	Sit down in the Lowest Room	B. ,,	278
498.	Lord, it is good for us to be here	B. ,,	278
499.	Lord, grant us Grace to rest upon Thy Word	B. ,,	278
	(*Close of Gifts and Graces*)		
500. 501. 502.	Christmas Carols (1. Whoso hears a Chiming for Christmas at the Nighest. 2. A holy heavenly Chime. 3. Lo Newborn Jesus)	C. 1887	278
503.	A Hope Carol	B. 1889	280
504.	Cardinal Newman	1890	280
505.	Yea I have a Goodly Heritage	C. ,,	280
506.	A Candlemas Dialogue	B. 1891	281
507.	Mary Magdalene and the other Mary	B. ,,	281
508.	A Death of a First-born	1892	282
509.	Faint yet Pursuing	C. ,,	282

No.	Title.	Year.	P.
	THE WORLD. SELF-DESTRUCTION		
510.	A Vain Shadow	B. 1893	
511.	Lord, save Us, We Perish	B. ,,	
512.	What is this above thy Head	B. ,,	
513.	Babylon the Great	B. ,,	28
514.	Standing afar off for the Fear of her Torment	B. ,,	28
515.	O Lucifer, Son of the Morning	B. ,,	28
516.	Alas alas for the Self-destroyed	B. ,,	28
517.	As Froth on the Face of the Deep	B. ,,	28
518.	Where their Worm dieth not, and the Fire is not quenched	B. ,,	28
519.	Toll, Bell, toll—for Hope is flying	B. ,,	28
	(*Close of the World. Self-destruction*)		
520.	All Things	B. ,,	28
521.	Heaven Overarches	C. ,,	28

GENERAL POEMS

522.	A Portrait	1847-50	286
523.	The whole Head is Sick and the whole Heart Faint	1847	287
524.	Vanity of Vanities (Ah woe is me for pleasure that is vain)	,,	287
525.	Three Stages—1. A Pause of Thought	1848	288
526.	2. The End of the First Part	1849	288
527.	3. I thought to deal the Death-stroke at a Blow	1854	289
528.	Lady Montrevor	1848	290
529.	Song (She sat and sang alway)	,,	290
530.	Bitter for Sweet	,,	290
531.	Song (When I am dead, my dearest)	,,	290
532.	On Keats	1849	291
533.	Have Patience	,,	291
534.	Song (Oh roses for the flush of youth)	,,	292
535.	An End	,,	292
536.	Dream Land	,,	292
537.	After Death	,,	293
538.	Rest	,,	293
539.	Looking Forward	,,	293
540.	Life Hidden	,,	294
541.	Remember	,,	294
542.	Sound Sleep	,,	295
543.	Queen Rose	,,	295
544.	How one Chose	,,	295
545.	Seeking Rest	,,	296
546.	Endurance	C. 1850	297
547.	Withering	C. ,,	297
548.	Twilight Calm	,,	297

No.	Title.	Year.	Page.
	GENERAL POEMS, *continued*—		
	Two Thoughts of Death	1850	298
	Three Moments	,,	299
	Is and Was	,,	300
	Song (We buried her among the flowers)	,,	300
	Annie	,,	301
564.	A Dirge (She was as sweet as violets in the Spring)	1851	301
565.	A Summer Wish	,,	302
	Song (It is not for her even brow)	,,	302
567.	A Fair World though a Fallen	,,	302
568.	Books in the Running Brooks	1852	303
569.	The Summer is Ended	,,	304
	After All	,,	304
561.	From the Antique (The wind shall lull us yet)	,,	304
562.	To what Purpose is this Waste?	1853	305
563.	Next of Kin	,,	307
564.	For Rosaline's Album	,,	307
565.	What?	,,	308
566.	A Pause	,,	308
567.	Three Seasons	,,	308
568.	Holy Innocents (Sleep, little Baby, sleep)	,,	309
569.	Seasons (In Springtime when the leaves are young)	,,	309
570.	Buried	,,	309
571.	A Wish	,,	309
572.	Two Parted	,,	309
573.	Autumn (Care flieth)	,,	310
574.	Seasons (Crocuses and snowdrops wither)	,,	310
575.	Ballad	1854	310
576.	A Soul	,,	311
577.	The Bourne	,,	311
578.	Dream-love	,,	312
579.	From the Antique (It's a weary life, it is, she said)	,,	312
580.	Long Looked For	,,	313
581.	Listening	,,	313
582.	Dead before Death	,,	313
583.	Echo	,,	314
584.	The First Spring Day	1855	314
585.	My Dream (Hear now a curious dream I dreamed last night)	,,	315
586.	The Last Look	,,	316
587.	I have a Message unto Thee	,,	316
588.	Cobwebs	,,	317
589.	May (I cannot tell you how it was)	,,	318
590.	An After-thought	,,	318
591.	To the End	,,	319
592.	May ('Sweet Life is dead'—'Not so')	,,	320

No.	Title.	Year.
	GENERAL POEMS, continued—	
593.	Shut out	1856
594.	By the Water	,,
595.	A Chilly Night	,,
596.	Let Patience have her perfect Work (I saw a bird alone)	,,
597.	In the Lane	,,
598.	Acme	,,
599.	A Bed of Forget-me-nots	,,
600.	Look on This Picture and on This	,,
601.	Gone Before	,,
602.	The Hour and the Ghost	,,
603.	Light Love	,,
604.	Downcast	,,
605.	A Triad	,,
606.	Love from the North	,,
607.	In an Artist's Studio	,,
608.	Fata Morgana	1857
609.	One Day	,,
610.	Introspective	,,
611.	A Peal of Bells	,,
612.	In the Round Tower at Jhansi	,,
613.	Day-dreams	,,
614.	A Nightmare (Fragment)	,,
	...other Spring	,,
	...r One Sake	,,
	...emory	1857-65
	Birthday	1857
	...n Apple Gathering	,,
	Winter : My Secret (I tell my secret ? No indeed, not I)	,,
	My Friend	,,
	Maude Clare	C. 1858
	Autumn (I dwell alone—I dwell alone, alone)	1858
	Up-hill	,,
	At Home	,,
	To-day and To-morrow	,,
	The Convent Threshold	,,
628.	Yet a Little While	,,
629.	Father and Lover	C. ,,
630.	By the Sea	1858
631.	Winter Rain	1859
632.	L. E. L.	,,
633.	Spring	,,
634.	What Good shall my Life do me ?	,,
635.	Cousin Kate	,,
636.	Sister Maude	C. 1860

	Title.	Year.	Page.
	GENERAL POEMS, *continued*—		
17.	Noble Sisters	1860	348
18.	No, thank you, John	,,	349
19.	Mirage	,,	350
20.	The Lambs of Grasmere, 1860	,,	350
41.	Promises like Pie-crust	1861	350
42.	Wife to Husband	,,	351
43.	Better so	,,	351
44.	Our Widowed Queen	,,	352
45.	In Progress	1862	352
46.	On the Wing	,,	352
47.	Song (Two doves upon the self-same branch)	B. 1863	353
48.	The Queen of Hearts	1863	353
649.	Seasons (Oh the cheerful Budding-time)	,,	354
650.	June	,,	354
651.	A Ring Posy	,,	354
652.	Helen Grey	,,	355
653.	A Year's Windfalls	,,	355
654.	A Bird's-Eye View	,,	357
655.	A Dumb Friend	,,	358
656.	Life and Death	,,	358
657.	Twilight Night	1863-64	359
658.	The Poor Ghost	1863	359
659.	Margery	,,	360
660.	Last Night	,,	361
661.	Somewhere or other	,,	362
662.	A Chill	,,	362
663.	Summer (Winter is cold-hearted)	1864	363
664.	Beauty is Vain	,,	363
665.	What would I give!	,,	363
666.	The Ghost's Petition	,,	364
667.	Hoping against Hope	,,	365
668.	Sunshine	,,	366
669.	Meeting (If we shall live, we live)	,,	366
670.	Twice	,,	366
671.	A Farm Walk	,,	367
672.	Under Willows	,,	368
673.	A Sketch	,,	368
674.	Bird or Beast?	,,	369
675.	Songs in a Cornfield	,,	369
676.	If I had Words	,,	371
677.	Jessie Cameron	,,	371
678.	Grown and Flown	,,	373
679.	Eve	1865	373
680.	Shall I forget?	,,	374

No.	Title.		Year.	P
	GENERAL POEMS, *continued*—			
681.	Amor Mundi	.	1865	
682.	From Sunset to Star Rise	.	,,	
683.	Maggie a Lady	.	,,	
684.	Dead Hope	.	,,	
685.	En Route	.	,,	
686.	Enrica, 1865	.	,,	
687.	Husband and Wife	.	,,	
688.	Italia, io ti Saluto	.	,,	3?
689.	What to do?	.	,,	3?
690.	A Daughter of Eve	.	,,	3?
691.	A Dirge (Why were you born when the snow was falling?)	.	,,	3?
692.	An 'Immurata' Sister	C.	,,	38
693.	Once for all (Margaret)	.	1866	38
694.	A Smile and a Sigh	.	,,	38
695.	In a certain Place	.	,,	38
696.	Cannot Sweeten	.	,,	38
697.	Of my Life	.	,,	38
698.	Song (Oh what comes over the sea)	.	,,	38
699.	From Metastasio	C.	1868	38
700.	Autumn Violets	B.	1869	38
701.	They desire a Better Country (I would not if I could undo my past)	B.	1870	38
702.	By Way of Remembrance	.	1870	384
703.	An Echo from Willow-wood	C.	,,	385
704-705.	The German-French Campaign, 1870-71. 1. Thy Brother's Blood crieth. 2. To-day for me	.	1871	386
706.	Venus's Looking-glass	.	1872	387
707.	Love lies Bleeding	C.	,,	388
708.	Days of Vanity	B.	1873	388
709.	A Bird Song	B.	,,	388
710.	Cor Mio (Still sometimes in my secret heart of hearts)	C.	1875	389
711.	Meeting (I said good-bye in hope)	C.	,,	389
712.	A Green Cornfield	B.	1876	389
713.	A Bride Song	B.	,,	390
714.	Confluents	B.	,,	390
715.	Bird Raptures	B.	,,	391
716-726.	Valentines to my Mother		1876-86	391
727.	Mirrors of Life and Death	B.	1878	393
728.	An October Garden	B.	,,	395
729.	Freaks of Fashion	C.	,,	395
730.	Yet a Little While (I dreamed and did not seek: to-day I seek)	B.	1879	397
731.	Parted	C.	1880	397
732.	To-day's Burden	C.	1881	397
733.	The Key-note	B.	1882	397
734.	He and She	B.	,,	398

№.	Title.	Year.	Page.
	GENERAL POEMS, continued—		
735.	Luscious and Sorrowful (Beautiful, tender, wasting away for sorrow)	B. 1882	398
736.	De Profundis	B. ,,	398
737.	Tempus Fugit	B. ,,	398
738.	Golden Glories	B. ,,	399
739.	Johnny (Johnny had a golden head)	B. ,,	399
740.	'Hollow-sounding and Mysterious'	B. ,,	400
741.	Maiden May	B. ,,	401
742.	Till To-morrow (Long have I longed till I am tired)	B. ,,	402
743.	Death-watches	B. ,,	402
744.	Touching 'Never'	B. ,,	403
745.	Brandons Both	B. ,,	403
746.	A Life's Parallels	B. ,,	405
747.	At Last	B. ,,	405
748.	Golden Silences	B. ,,	406
749.	In the Willow Shade	B. ,,	406
750.	Fluttered Wings	B. ,,	407
751.	A Fisher-Wife	B. ,,	408
752.	What's in a Name?	B. ,,	408
753.	Mariana	B. ,,	408
754.	Memento Mori	B. ,,	409
755.	One foot on Sea and one on Shore	B. ,,	409
756.	A Song of Flight	B. ,,	409
757.	Buds and Babies	B. ,,	410
758.	Boy Johnny (If you'll busk you as a Bride)	B. ,,	410
759.	Summer is ended	B. ,,	410
760.	Passing and Glassing	B. ,,	410
761.	Sœur Louise de la Miséricorde, 1674	B. ,,	411
762.	Pastime	B. ,,	411
763.	Birchington Churchyard	April ,,	412
764.	Resurgam	B. 1883	412
765.	Michael F. M. Rossetti	,,	412
766.	A Wintry Sonnet	B. 1884	413
767.	One Seaside Grave	,,	413
768.	Who shall say?	C. 1884	414
769.	One Swallow does not make a Summer	B. 1886	414
770.	A Frog's Fate	B. ,,	414
771.	'There is a Budding Morrow in Midnight'	B. 1890	415
772.	The Way of the World	C. 1890	415
773.	Brother Bruin	B. 1891	415
774.	A Helpmeet for Him	B. ,,	416
775.	Exultate Deo	B. ,,	416
776.	To my Fior-di-Lisa	1892	417
777.	To-morrow (Passing away the bliss)	B. 1893	417
778.	Sleeping at Last	C. ,,	417

No.	Title.	Year.	Page

POEMS FOR CHILDREN, AND MINOR VERSE

779.	Sonnets: written to Bouts-rimés (1 to 8) .	1848	421
780.	,, ,, ,, (9) The Plague .	,,	422
781.	,, ,, ,, (10a to c) .	C. ,,	422
782.	To Lalla, reading my Verses Topsy-turvy	1849	422
783.	Two Enigmas .	,,	422
784.	Two Charades .	,,	423
785.	A Bouts-rimés Sonnet .	,,	423
786.	Portraits .	1853	423
787.	Charon .	,,	423
788.	The P. R. B.—1 .	,,	424
789.	The P. R. B.—2 .	,,	424
790.	Child's Talk in April .	1855	424
791.	Winter (Sweet Blackbird is silenced with chaffinch and thrush)	1856	425
792.	Love's Name .	C. 1869	425
793.	Golden Holly .	C. 1872	426

SING-SONG—A NURSERY RHYME-BOOK

794.	Angels at the Foot	B. 1873	426
795.	Love me—I love you	B. ,,	426
796.	My Baby has a Father and a Mother	B. ,,	426
797.	Our little Baby fell asleep .	B. ,,	426
798.	Kookoorookoo! kookoorookoo! .	B. ,,	426
799.	Baby cry .	B. ,,	426
800.	Eight o'clock .	B. ,,	426
801.	Bread and Milk for Breakfast .	B. ,,	427
802.	There's Snow on the Fields .	B. ,,	427
803.	Dead in the Cold, a song-singing Thrush .	B. ,,	427
804.	I dug and dug amongst the Snow .	B. ,,	427
805.	A City Plum is not a Plum .	B. ,,	427
806.	Your Brother has a Falcon .	B. ,,	427
807.	Hear what the mournful Linnets say .	B. ,,	427
808.	A Baby's Cradle with no Baby in it .	B. ,,	427
809.	Hop-o'-my-thumb and Little Jack Horner .	B. ,,	428
810.	Hope is like a Harebell trembling from its Birth .	B. ,,	428
811.	O Wind, why do you never rest .	B. ,,	428
812.	Crying, my little One, footsore and weary .	B. ,,	428
813.	Growing in the Vale .	B. ,,	428
814.	A Linnet in a gilded Cage .	B. ,,	428
815.	Wrens and Robins in the Hedge .	B. ,,	428
816.	My Baby has a mottled Fist .	B. ,,	428
817.	Why did Baby die .	B. ,,	428
818.	If all were Rain and never Sun .	B. ,,	429

No.	Title.	Year.	Page.
	SING-SONG—A NURSERY RHYME-BOOK, *continued*—		
819.	O Wind, where have you been	B. 1873	429
820.	Brownie, Brownie, let down your Milk	B. 1894	429
821.	On the grassy Banks	B. 1873	429
822.	Rushes in a watery Place	B. ,,	429
823.	Minnie and Mattie	B. ,,	429
824.	Heartsease in my Garden-bed	B. ,,	430
825.	If I were a Queen	B. ,,	430
826.	What are heavy? Sea-sand and Sorrow	B. ,,	430
827.	Stroke a Flint, and there is nothing to admire	B. 1894	430
828.	There is but one May in the Year	B. 1873	430
829.	The Summer Nights are short	B. ,,	430
830.	The Days are clear	B. ,,	430
831.	Twist me a Crown of Wind-flowers	B. ,,	430
832.	Brown and Furry	B. ,,	431
833.	A Toadstool comes up in a Night	B. ,,	431
834.	A Pocket-handkerchief to hem	B. ,,	431
835.	If a Pig wore a Wig	B. ,,	431
836.	Seldom 'Can't'	B. ,,	431
837.	1 and 1 are 2	B. ,,	431
838.	How many Seconds in a Minute?	B. ,,	431
839.	What will you give me for my Pound?	B. ,,	432
840.	January cold desolate	B. ,,	432
841.	What is pink? A Rose is pink	B. ,,	432
842.	Mother shake the Cherry-tree	B. ,,	432
843.	A Pin has a Head, but has no Hair	B. ,,	432
844.	Hopping Frog, hop here and be seen	B. ,,	433
845.	Where innocent bright-eyed Daisies are	B. ,,	433
846.	The City Mouse lives in a House	B. ,,	433
847.	What does the Donkey bray about?	B. ,,	433
848.	Three Plum Buns	B. ,,	433
849.	A Motherless soft Lambkin	B. ,,	433
850.	Dancing on the Hill-tops	B. ,,	434
851.	When Fishes set Umbrellas up	B. ,,	434
852.	The Peacock has a score of Eyes	B. ,,	434
853.	Pussy has a whiskered Face	B. ,,	434
854.	The Dog lies in his Kennel	B. ,,	434
855.	If Hope grew on a Bush	B. ,,	434
856.	I planted a Hand	R. ,,	434
857.	Under the Ivy Bush	B. ,,	434
858.	I am a King	B. 1894	434
859.	There is one that has a Head without an Eye	B. 1873	435
860.	If a Mouse could fly	B. ,,	435
861.	Sing me a Song	B. ,,	435
862.	The Lily has an air	B. ,,	435

No.	Title.	Year.	Page
	SING-SONG—A NURSERY RHYME-BOOK, *continued*—		
863.	Margaret has a Milking-pail	B. 1873	435
864.	In the Meadow—What in the Meadow?	B. ,,	435
865.	A frisky Lamb	B. ,,	435
866.	Mix a Pancake	B. ,,	436
867.	The Wind has such a rainy Sound	B. ,,	436
868.	Three little Children	B. ,,	436
869.	Fly away, fly away over the Sea	B. ,,	436
870.	Minnie bakes Oaten Cakes	B. ,,	436
871.	A White Hen Sitting	B. ,,	436
872.	Currants on a Bush	B. ,,	436
873.	Playing at Bob Cherry	B. 1894	436
874.	I have but one Rose in the World	B. 1873	437
875.	Rosy Maiden Winifred	B. ,,	437
876.	Blind from my Birth	B. 1894	437
877.	When the Cows come home the Milk is coming	B. 1873	437
878.	Roses blushing Red and White	B. ,,	437
879.	Ding a Ding	B. ,,	437
880.	A Ring upon her Finger	B. ,,	437
881.	Ferry me across the Water	B. ,,	438
882.	When a mounting Skylark sings	B. ,,	438
883.	Who has seen the Wind?	B. ,,	438
884.	The Horses of the Sea	B. ,,	438
885.	O Sailor, come Ashore	B. ,,	438
886.	A Diamond or a Coal?	B. ,,	438
887.	An Emerald is as green as Grass	B. ,,	438
888.	Boats sail on the Rivers	B. ,,	439
889.	The Lily has a smooth Stalk	B. ,,	439
890.	Hurt no living Thing	B. ,,	439
891.	I caught a little Lady-bird	B. 1873-94	439
892.	All the Bells were ringing	B. 1873	439
893.	Wee wee Husband	B. ,,	439
894.	I have a little Husband	B. ,,	439
895.	The dear Old Woman in the Lane	B. 1873-94	440
896.	Swift and Sure the Swallow	B. 1873	440
897.	I dreamt I caught a little Owl	B. ,,	440
898.	What does the Bee do?	B. ,,	440
899.	I have a Poll Parrot	B. 1873-94	440
900.	A House of Cards	B. 1873	440
901.	The Rose with such a bonny Blush	B. ,,	440
902.	The Rose that blushes Rosy Red	B. ,,	440
903.	Oh fair to See	B. ,,	440
904.	Clever little Willie Wee	B. 1873-94	441
905.	The Peach-tree on the Southern Wall	B. ,,	441
906.	A Rose has Thorns as well as Honey	B. 1873	441

No.	Title.	Year.	Page.
	SING-SONG—A NURSERY RHYME-BOOK, *continued*—		
907.	Is the Moon tired? She looks so pale	B. 1873	441
908.	If Stars dropped out of Heaven	B. ,,	441
909.	Good-bye in Fear, good-bye in Sorrow	B. ,,	441
910.	If the Sun could tell us half	B. ,,	442
911.	If the Moon came from Heaven	B. ,,	442
912.	O Lady Moon, your Horns point toward the East	B. ,,	442
913.	What do the Stars do	B. ,,	442
914.	Motherless Baby and Babyless Mother	B. ,,	442
915.	Crimson Curtains round my Mother's Bed	B. ,,	442
916.	Baby lies so fast asleep	B. ,,	442
917.	I know a Baby, such a Baby	B. ,,	442
918.	Lullaby, oh lullaby!	B. ,,	442
919.	Lie a-bed	B. ,,	443
	(*Close of Sing-song*)		
920.	An Alphabet	C. 1875	443
921.	Hadrian's Death-song Translated	. 1876	444
922.	My Mouse	. 1877	444
923.	A Poor Old Dog	C. 1879	444
924.	To William Bell Scott	. 1882	444
925.	Counterblast on Penny Trumpet	. ,,	444
926.	Mole and Earthworm	B. 1886	445
927.	To Mary Rossetti	C. 1887	445
928.	What will it be?	B. 1893	445
929.	Speechless	B. ,,	445
930.	Pleading	B. ,,	445
931.	A Sorrowful Sigh of a Prisoner	B. ,,	446
932.	Scarlet	B. ,,	446
933.	Homewards	B. ,,	446

ITALIAN POEMS

934.	Versi (Figlia, la Madre disse)	. 1849	446
935.	L'Incognita	C. 1850	446
936.	Nigella	C. ,,	447
937.	Chiesa e Signore	C. 1860	447

IL ROSSEGGIAR DELL' ORIENTE

938.	Amor Dormente?	. 1862	447
939.	Amor si sveglia?	. 1863	447
940.	Si rimanda la Tocca-caldaja	C. 1864	448
941.	Blumine risponde	. 1867	448
942.	Lassù fia caro il rivederci	. ,,	448
943.	Non son io la Rosa ma vi stetti appresso	. ,,	448

No.	Title.	Year.	Page
	IL ROSSEGGIAR DELL' ORIENTE, *continued*—		
944.	Lassuso il caro Fiore	1867	449
945.	Sapessi pure	,,	449
946.	Iddio c' illumini	,,	449
947.	Amicizia	,,	450
948.	Luscious and Sorrowful (Uccello delle rose e del dolore)	,,	450
949.	O Forza irresistibile Dell' umile Preghiera	,,	450
950.	Finestra mia orientale	,,	451
951.	Eppure allora venivi	1868	451
952.	Per Preferenza	,,	451
953.	Oggi	,,	452
954.	Ti do l' addio	,,	452
955.	Ripetizione	,,	452
956.	Amico e più che Amico Mio	,,	452
957.	Nostre voluntà quieti Virtù di Carità	,,	452
958.	Se Così Fosse	,,	453
	(*Close of Il Rosseggiar dell' Oriente*)		
959.	L' Uommibatto	1869	453
960.	Cor Mio (Cor mio, cor mio)	C. 1870	453
961.	Adriano	1876	453
	NINNA-NANNA		
962.	Angeli al Capo, al Piede	1878	453
963.	Amami, t' Amo	,,	453
964.	E Babbo e Mamma ha il nostro Figliolino	,,	454
965.	S' addormentò la nostra Figliolina	,,	454
966.	Cuccurucù, cuccurucù	,,	454
967.	Ohibò Piccina	,,	454
968.	Otto ore suonano	,,	454
969.	Nel Verno accanto al Fuoco	,,	454
970.	Gran Freddo è infuori, e dentro è Freddo un poco	,,	454
971.	Scavai la Neve, sì che scavai	,,	455
972.	Sì che il Fratello s' ha un Falconcello	,,	455
973.	Udite, si dolgono mesti Fringuelli	,,	455
974.	Ahi Culla vuota ed ahi Sepolcro pieno	,,	455
975.	Lugubre e vagabondo in Terra e in Mare	,,	455
976.	Aura dolcissima, ma donde siete?	,,	455
977.	Foss' io Regina	,,	455
978.	Pesano Rena e Pena	,,	455
979.	Basta una Notte a maturare il Fungo	,,	456
980.	Porco la Zucca fitta in Parrucca	,,	456
981.	Salta, Ranocchio, e mostrati	,,	456
982.	Spunta la Margherita	,,	456
983.	Agnellina Orfanellina	,,	456

CONTENTS xxxvii

No.	Title.	Year.	Page.
	NINNA-NANNA, *continued*—		
984.	Amico Pesce, piover vorrà	1878	456
985.	Sposa velata	,,	456
986.	Cavalli marittimi	,,	457
987.	O Marinaro, che mi apporti tu?	,,	457
988.	Arrossisce la Rosa, e perchè mai?	,,	457
989.	La Rosa china il Volto rosseggiato	,,	457
990.	O Ciliegia infiorita	,,	457
991.	In Tema e in Pena addio	,,	457
992.	D' un Sonno profondissimo	,,	457
993.	Ninna-nanna, Ninna-nanna	,,	457
994.	Capo che chinasi	,,	458
	(*Close of Ninna-nanna*)		
995.	Sognando	C. 1890	458
	NOTES BY W. M. ROSSETTI		459
	LIST OF FIRST LINES		495

SUPPLEMENT TO LIST OF CONTENTS

In the List of Contents the poems have been numbered, so as to facilitate reference to the present Table.

The under-mentioned poems were printed (not published) in the *Verses* (1847):—

Nos. 17, 20, 23 to 26, 28, 29, 30, 32 to 40, 42 to 47, 49 to 53, 57, 60, 64.

The under-mentioned were first published since Christina Rossetti's death, December 1894 :—

Nos. 4, 18, 19, 21, 22, 31, 41, 55, 56, 58, 59, 61, 62, 65, 67 to 73, 76, 77, 78, 172, 175, 176, 177, 179 to 186, 189, 259, 261, 263, 264, 265, 267, 269 to 272, 278, 313, 314, 347, 348, 401, 402, 403, 406, 407, 413, 414, 500, 521, 523, 524, 526, 527, 528, 532, 533, 539, 540, 543 to 547, 549 to 554, 556 to 565, 568 to 576, 579, 580, 581, 586, 587, 588, 590, 591, 592, 594 to 601, 607, 610, 613, 614, 616, 626, 628, 634, 641, 643, 644, 645, 649, 650, 655, 657, 659, 668, 669, 672, 673, 676, 685, 689, 695 to 699, 702, 710, 711, 716 to 726, 731, 767, 776, 778 to 782, 785, 786, 788, 789, 791, 793, 922, 925, 937 to 995.

The under-mentioned are now for the first time published :—

Nos. 27, 423, 604, 784, 787, 819, 826, 857, 872, 875, 926.

All other poems, not above enumerated, were issued during the authoress's lifetime, whether in volumes or otherwise—very generally in volumes.

APPENDIX

A.—CONTENTS OF THE COLLECTED EDITION ISSUED BY CHRISTINA ROSSETTI

THE FIRST SERIES

Goblin Market.
The Prince's Progress.
Maiden-Song.
Dream Land.
At Home.
The Poor Ghost.
Grown and Flown.
A Farm Walk.
A Portrait.
By the Sea.
Gone for ever.
Love from the North.
Maggie a Lady.
From Sunset to Star Rise.
Spring Quiet.
Winter Rain.
Vanity of Vanities.
Days of Vanity.
The Ghost's Petition.
Once for all.
Enrica, 1865.
A Chill.
Somewhere or Other.
Noble Sisters.
Jessie Cameron.
Spring.
Summer.
Autumn.
Winter: My Secret.
Autumn Violets.
A Dirge.
A Bird's-eye View.
Fata Morgana.
Memory.
'They desire a Better Country.'
Child's Talk in April.
A Green Cornfield.
The Lambs of Grasmere, 1860.
A Birthday.
A Bride Song.
Confluents.
Remember.
After Death.
The Lowest Room.
Dream-Love.
An End.
Dead Hope.
Twice.
My Dream.
Songs in a Cornfield.
On the Wing.
L. E. L.
Song.
The Hour and the Ghost.
Shall I forget.
Life and Death.
A Summer Wish.
A Year's Windfalls.
An Apple-Gathering.
Song.
Maude Clare.
Echo.
Another Spring.
Bird or Beast.

Eve.
A Daughter of Eve.
A Peal of Bells.
The Bourne.
Song.
Venus's Looking-Glass.
Love Lies Bleeding.
Bird Raptures.
The Queen of Hearts.
'No, thank you, John.'
Beauty is Vain.
May.
A Pause of Thought.
Twilight Calm.
Wife to Husband.
Three Seasons.
Mirage.
A Royal Princess.
My Friend.
Shut Out.
Sound Sleep.
Song.
Song.
Dead before Death.
Twilight Night.
Bitter for Sweet.
What would I give?
The First Spring Day.
A Bird Song.
A Smile and a Sigh.
One Day.
Rest.
The Convent Threshold.
Amor Mundi.
Up-Hill.
'The Iniquity of the Fathers upon the Children.'
In the Round Tower at Jhansi.
'Thy Brother's Blood crieth.'
'To-day for Me.'
A Christmas Carol.
'The Love of Christ which passeth Knowledge.'
'A Bruised Reed shall He not break.'
Long Barren.
Despised and Rejected.
A Better Resurrection.
If Only.
Advent.
The Three Enemies.
Consider.

Dost Thou not care?
Weary in Well-doing.
One Certainty.
By the Waters of Babylon.
Christian and Jew.
Good Friday.
Sweet Death.
Symbols.
'Consider the Lilies of the Field.'
The World.
A Testimony.
Paradise.
Sleep at Sea.
Mother Country.
'I will lift up mine Eyes unto the Hills.'
'The Master is come, and calleth for Thee.'
Who shall deliver me?
'When my Heart is vexed, I will complain.'
After Communion.
Martyrs' Song.
After this the Judgment.
Saints and Angels.
A Rose Plant in Jericho.
From House to Home.
Old and New Year Ditties.
Amen.
The Lowest Place.

THE SECOND SERIES

The Key-Note.
The Months: A Pageant.
Pastime.
'Italia, io ti saluto!'
Mirrors of Life and Death.
Birchington Churchyard.
A Ballad of Boding.
Yet a little while.
He and She.
Monna Innominata.
'Luscious and Sorrowful.'
One Sea-side Grave.
De Profundis.
Tempus Fugit.
Golden Glories.
Johnny.
Brother Bruin.
'Hollow-sounding and Mysterious.'

A Helpmeet for him.
Maiden May.
Till To-morrow.
Death-Watches.
Touching 'Never.'
Brandons both.
A Life's Parallels.
At Last.
Golden Silences.
In the Willow Shade.
Fluttered Wings.
A Fisher-Wife.
What's in a Name?
Mariana.
Memento Mori.
'One Foot on Sea, and one on Shore.'
A Song of Flight.
Buds and Babies.
A Wintry Sonnet.
Boy Johnny.
Freaks of Fashion.
An October Garden.
'Summer is ended.'
Passing and Glassing.
'I will arise.'
Resurgam.
A Prodigal Son.
Sœur Louise de la Miséricorde.
To-day's Burden.
An 'immurata' Sister.
'There is a budding Morrow in Midnight.'
'If thou sayest, Behold, we knew it not.'
The Thread of Life.
An Old-World Thicket.
Exultate Deo.
'All Thy Works praise Thee, O Lord.'
Later Life.
'For Thine own Sake, O my God.'
Until the Day Break.
A Hope Carol.
'Of him that was ready to perish.'
Christmas Carols.
A Candlemas Dialogue.
'Behold the Man!'
The Descent from the Cross.
Mary Magdalene and the other Mary.
'It is Finished.'
An Easter Carol.
'Behold a shaking.'
All Saints.
'Take care of Him.'
Patience of Hope.
A Martyr.
Why?
'Love is strong as Death.'

B.—POEMS BY CHRISTINA ROSSETTI, EXTANT IN MS. (A FEW IN PRINT ALSO), BUT NOT USED IN THE PRESENT EDITION, NOR IN THE NEW POEMS PRINTED IN 1896.

	Date.
1. Heaven	1842
2. Corydon's Lament and Resolution	1843
3. Rosalind	,,
4. The Water-spirit's Song (an extract from this appears in Mr. Mackenzie Bell's book)	1844
5. Pitia a Damone	,,
6. The Faithless Shepherdess	,,
7. Ariadne to Theseus	,,
8. A Hymn for Christmas Day	,,
9. Love and Death	,,
10. Despair	,,
11. Easter Morning	,,
12. Song (The faith of years is broken)	,,

		Date
13. A Tirsi	.	1845
14. The Last Words of St. Telemachus	.	,,
15. Lord Thomas and Fair Margaret	.	,,
16. Charade [on the word 'Sonnet']	.	,,
17. Hope in Grief	.	,,
18. The Rose	.	1846
19. On Lady Isabella	.	,,
20. Divine and Human Pleading	.	,,
21. The Ruined Cross	.	,,
22. Amore e Dispetto	.	,,
23. Sappho	.	,,
24. Song (I saw her, she was lovely)	.	,,
25. The Last Words of Sir Eustace Grey	.	,,
26. Eva	.	,,
27. Young men aye were fickle found	.	1847
28. A Counsel	.	,,
29. One of the Dead	.	,,
30. The Trees' Counselling	.	,,
31. O Death, where is thy Sting	.	1847 or 1848
32. Peter the Hermit's Benediction	.	,,
33. Undine	.	1848
34. Floral Teaching	.	,,
35. Death	.	,,
36. Nydia	.	,,
37. Ellen Middleton	.	,,
38. St. Andrew's Church	.	,,
39. Grown Cold	.	,,
40. Zara (The pale sad face of her I wronged)	.	,,
41. Sleep, sleep	.	,,
42. What Sappho would have said, had her leap cured instead of killing her	.	,,
43. Ten Bouts-rimés Sonnets	.	1848-49

They begin with the following lines:—(1) Listen, and I will tell you of a face; (2) Strange voices sing among the planets which; (3) From early dawn until the flush of noon; (4) Surely there is an aching void within; (5) The spring is come again, not as at first; (6) You who look on past ages as a glass; (7) Who shall my wandering thoughts steady and fix; (8) Along the highroad the way is too long; (9) O thou who tell'st me that all hope is over; (10) O glorious sea that in each climbing wave.

44. Sonnet (Some say that love and joy are one, and so)	.	1849
45. The Last Complaint	.	,,
46. Have you Forgotten?	.	,,
47. A Year Afterwards	.	,,
48. A Dream (Oh for my love, my only love)	.	1851
49. Song (I have loved you for long long years, Ellen)	.	1852
50. Let them rejoice in their Beds	.	1853
51. Like as we are (MS. incomplete)	.	,,
52. All night I dream you love me well	.	,,
53. Epitaph	.	,,

APPENDIX xliii

		Date.
54. Our Heaven	. . . .	1854
55. Guesses	. . . .	,,
56. Zara (I dreamed that loving me he would love on) . . .		1855
57. An Answer (MS. incomplete)		1856
58. The Massacre of Perugia (MS. incomplete) . . .		1859
59. Verses on a Picnic near Sunderland . . .		,,
60. Verses to W. B. Scott (dos-à-dos)		1866

C.—SOME LEADING THEMES, OR KEY-NOTES OF FEELING, IN THE POEMS OF CHRISTINA ROSSETTI

1. *Personal Experiences and Emotions.*—From House to Home—A Pageant (p. 54)—Monna Innominata—An Old-World Thicket (p. 65)—Later Life, Nos. 4, 12, 17, 21, 22, 27—Lines to my Grandfather—Wishes—I do set my Bow in the Cloud—Death is swallowed up in Victory—Two Pursuits—Afterward he repented, and went—Can I know it? Nay—Doeth well, . . . doeth better—Balm in Gilead—Thou knewest, thou oughtest therefore—Bury Hope out of sight—A Churchyard Song of Patient Hope—Old and New Year Ditties—A Better Resurrection—The Heart knoweth its own Bitterness (when all the over-work of life)—Our mothers, lovely women pitiful—For Henrietta Polydore—Ash-Wednesday (Jesus, do I love Thee?)—The offering of the New Law—For a Mercy received—Come unto Me—Who shall deliver me?—A Rose Plant in Jericho—Weigh all my Faults and Follies righteously—Lord, grant me grace to love Thee in my pain—Lord, make me one with thine own faithful ones—Three Stages—Looking Forward—Shut out—Downcast - Introspective—Memory—L. E. L.—Twilight Night—What would I give—A Sketch—Shall I forget?—En Route—Italia io ti Saluto—An Immurata Sister—By Way of Remembrance—Cor Mio (Still sometimes in my secret heart of hearts) Meeting (I said good-bye in hope)—They desire a Better Country (I would not if I could undo my past)—Confluents—Valentines to my Mother—Parted—The Key-note—Yet a Little While (I dreamed and did not seek : to-day I seek)—One Seaside Grave—My Mouse—Il Rosseggiar dell' Oriente.

2. *Death.*—Later Life, Nos. 26, 27—The Dead Bride—Night and Death—Song (The stream moaneth as it floweth)—Death is swallowed up in Victory—Sweet Death—Laughing Life cries at the Feast—Sooner or later, yet at last—God is our Hope and Strength—Song (When I am dead, my dearest)—Dream Land—After Death—Rest—Looking Forward—Life Hidden—Remember—Sound Sleep—Two Thoughts of Death—A Pause—Long looked for—The Last Look—A Peal of Bells—My Friend—At Home—Yet a Little While—Better so—Life and Death—Songs in a Cornfield (p. 370)—An Immurata Sister—Of my Life—Days of Vanity—Mirrors of Life and Death.

3. *The Aspiration for Rest.*—The Lotus-eaters—Sonnet from the Psalms—There remaineth therefore a Rest (In the grave will be no space)—There remaineth therefore a Rest for the People of God (Rest remains when all is done)—A Burden—In Patience—Weary in Well-doing—All Saints, Martyrs—Love loveth thee and Wisdom loveth thee—Three Stages, No. 3—Dream Land—Rest—Sound Sleep—From the Antique (The wind shall lull us yet)—Yet a Little While—To-day's Burden—Sleeping at Last—What will it be?

4. *Vanity of Vanities.*—The Lowest Room (p. 19)—One Certainty—A Testimony—Vanity of Vanities (Of all the downfalls in the world)—Sleep at Sea—Mother Country—Saints and Angels—If thou sayest, Behold we knew it not, No. 3—A Vain Shadow—Vanity of Vanities (Ah! woe is me for pleasure that is vain)—Maiden May—Sœur Louise de la Miséricorde—Il Rosseggiar dell' Oriente, No. 20.

5. *Love of Animals.*—Goblin Market (p. 2)—From House to Home (p. 21)—A Pageant (pp. 48 to 50)—An Old-World Thicket—All Thy Works praise Thee, O Lord (p. 71)—Later Life, No. 20—These all wait upon Thee—Twilight Calm—To what purpose is this Waste?—My Dream (Hear now a curious dream I dreamed last night)—The Lambs of Grasmere—A Chill—Summer (Winter is cold-hearted)—Bird or Beast—Eve—A Green Cornfield—Bird Raptures—Valentines to my Mother, 1885—Mirrors of Life and Death—Freaks of Fashion—A Frog's Fate—Brother Bruin—Child's Talk in April—Winter (Sweet blackbird is silenced with chaffinch and thrush)—Minnie and Mattie—Hopping Frog, hop here and be seen—When the Cows come home the milk is coming—Hurt no Living Thing—A poor old Dog—Mole and Earthworm.

6. *Winter.*—Later Life, No. 19—Bitter for Sweet—Seasons (In Springtime when the leaves are young)—Seasons (Crocuses and snowdrops wither)—Winter Rain—Seasons (Oh the cheerful budding-time)—A Year's Windfalls—What's in a name?—There is a budding morrow in Midnight—Winter (Sweet blackbird, etc.).

7. *The Loveliness of the Rose.*—Three Nuns (p. 15)—Gone for ever—The Solitary Rose—As the Apple-tree among the Trees of the Wood—A Rose Plant in Jericho—Have Patience—Queen Rose—Three Moments—A Year's Windfalls—Maiden May—Brandons both—An October Garden—Summer is Ended—To my Fior-di-Lisa—Hope is like a Harebell trembling from its Birth—The Lily has a smooth Stalk.

MEMOIR

GABRIELE ROSSETTI and his wife Frances Mary Lavinia (Polidori), marrying in April 1826, had four children. They were: Maria Francesca, born 17 February 1827; Gabriel Charles Dante (better known as Dante Gabriel), 12 May 1828; William Michael, 25 September 1829; and Christina Georgina, 5 December 1830. These were all born at No. 38 Charlotte Street, Portland Place, London. Christina, like the other children, was baptized in the Church of England. Her two godmothers were Lady Dudley Stuart, originally the Princess Christine Bonaparte, a daughter of Lucian, and of course niece of the great Napoleon—Rossetti being well known to several members of this world-famous family; and Miss Georgina Macgregor, a daughter of Sir Patrick Macgregor, and pupil of Mrs. Rossetti, who had before marriage been a governess in that house.

In my Memoir of Dante Gabriel Rossetti, published along with his *Family Letters* in 1895, I have given various particulars about our father Gabriele Rossetti, and a few about our mother. I shall not repeat them here, beyond what is necessary for my immediate purpose. Gabriele Rossetti was a native of Vasto in the Abruzzi, kingdom of Naples, born February 1783. His origin was quite undistinguished, his father being a blacksmith and locksmith, and his maternal grandfather a shoemaker; he had however, I believe, some hereditary connection with a family of more position, named Della Guardia, and either in the Rossetti or in the Della Guardia line of a previous period there had been some sort of local literary note. Gabriele Rossetti showed an early aptitude for drawing, and also for verse. He went towards 1803 to Naples, and held for a short time the official post of librettist to the Operatic Theatre of San Carlo, and for a much longer term that of custodian of Ancient Bronzes in the Naples Museum. He published in Naples some of his poetical compositions, but was more especially known and admired as an improvisatore. In 1820 he adhered to the movement, started by a military uprising, for obtaining a Constitution for the kingdom of Naples. The Bourbon king, Ferdinand I., granted and swore to the Constitution; and then rapidly revoked it, and treated its promoters as criminals. In the summer of 1821 Rossetti had to escape from Naples in disguise; sojourned for a while in Malta; and early in 1824 came over to London. He married the second daughter of Gaetano Polidori; he being at the time forty-three years of age, and she much younger, barely twenty-six. Polidori had, in his youth, been secretary to the celebrated dramatic poet Alfieri; he was a teacher of Italian in London, and author of many books, and had been the father of Dr. John Polidori, who became Byron's travelling physician in 1816, made some name as author of *The Vampyre*, and committed suicide in 1821.

In London Gabriele Rossetti (having no private means of subsistence whatever, and his wife nothing in hand, and only a modest contingent expectation) followed the same career as his father-in-law—that of teaching Italian. He was appointed Professor of Italian in King's College, London, in 1831; but this added little to his occupations, and next to nothing to his income. He published several books, both verse and prose. The verse procured him very considerable celebrity in Italy as a patriotic poet; the prose—largely concerned with the interpretation of Dante and other mediæval writers as being members of a secret school of daring speculators in politics and religion—was prohibited in Italy (and so indeed was the verse), but made a good deal of stir in England, earning some few partizans here and there, and a fair number of adversaries. Rossetti did not naturalize himself as an Englishman, but remained an Italian, and a highly patriotic Italian; neither did he protestantize, though in open and frequently published opposition to the papal system and pretensions.

Such was the household into which Christina Rossetti was born; a household of narrow means, according to the English standard of income and living (I suppose the years were very few in which Rossetti made, from all sources, more than an annual £300, and it must generally have been less); of no display and no inclination for display; of careful but not stingy economy—the father being highly inexpensive in all personal habits, and the mother an assiduous housewife from day to day and from year to year; of infallibly upright dealing and no indebtedness; of substantial but not self-indulgent comfort; of steady continuous occupation; of a high standard of right; of serious thinking and many intellectual interests—few of any other sort. These brief words of attestation are no more than my due to my parents; to point out the defects of my father, or to discover some in my mother, is not incumbent upon me, nor indeed is there anything of this kind which needs to be stated as relevant to the home-life of Christina Rossetti. I should add that Mrs. Rossetti (who was of wholly English extraction on her mother's side, as of wholly Italian extraction on her father's) was born and bred in London, and was of a decidedly English rather than Italian type of person and character; her education was good, her mind fully formed. The mutual affection and esteem of husband and wife were solid and unvarying; there was little dissent between them— except indeed an abstract dissent on subjects of religion—and quarrelling and nagging were unknown. Rossetti was mainly a free-thinker, although much in sympathy with the moral and spiritual teachings of the Gospel; his wife was a devout but not a sanctimonious member of the Church of England—the dominant tone of which was, towards the date of Christina's birth, the 'evangelical,' the 'high church' being as yet dormant.

Christina, as being the youngest of the four children, could not fail to be influenced to some extent, in her earliest years, by the qualities of her sister and brothers, as well as of her parents. Maria was mentally a precocious child, learning very early and easily all such matters as reading, writing, speaking two languages, etc.; indeed she was from first to last much the best of the four at all matters of acquired knowledge of that sort. She was of an upright and affectionate, but naturally a rather jealous, disposition, and of enthusiastic temperament; plunging with great ardour, before reaching the age of twelve or eleven, into such themes as the career of Napoleon, the Iliad, Grecian mythology, etc. From her earliest years she was devout; and, after being confirmed (towards 1840), she made religion her paramount concern, attending little in comparison to anything else. The character of Gabriel is perhaps pretty well understood by readers at the present day. In childhood as in manhood he was ardent, impulsive, dominant, generous, good-natured; not unfrequently passionate; determined to be a painter; eagerly susceptible to anything of a poetic, imaginative, or fanciful kind, but not to what partook of abstract or scientific knowledge. Of myself I will say nothing, except that I was a somewhat demure little boy, not quarrelsome and not teazing, and, as nearest to Christina in age, was regarded by her as a kind of ally against the thews, sinews, and dictation (such as they were), of our two very juvenile seniors.

The earliest years of a child's life are doubtless of great consequence in forming lines of character which afterwards deepen; but those very earliest years do not remain clear to the consciousness of the adult. Let us then, ignoring those first years, imagine Christina Rossetti at the age of five years completed, or about as far back as she would plainly remember in after life, and define a little of what she saw around her. It is the beginning of the year 1836, in which the family moved from No. 38 Charlotte Street to No. 50, a rather larger house, but still a small one. The father is now no less than fifty-three years old, the mother thirty-six.

The Rossetti household was thoroughly unconventional, living plainly and comfortably within their own walls, and being very little visible to outsiders. No Rossetti, and also no Polidori, had any idea of 'keeping in the fashion'; one or other of them (but this does not rightly apply to my mother) would have been found in 1860 dressing in very much the same mode as in 1835. Hence a kind of family tradition, which to some extent—though it was but a very minor extent in comparison—clung to Christina in her adult years. Our father was either occupied out-of-doors teaching, or was indoors writing about Dante, Freemasonry, and other light topics.

He was kind in his family, open-hearted, very animated in mind and manner, and on the whole cheerful, in spite of the bitterness of exile and the wrestle with fortune. The mother went out into society hardly at all, being wholly devoted to her domestic duties, with husband and four young children. The education of her two daughters was, from first to last, entirely her work—allowing for some trifles, such as singing and dancing lessons, and these had no appreciable sequel. There was nothing of the ascetic about her, nor yet any disregard for the social proprieties, as ordinarily accepted and applied : but an extreme indifference to 'showing off,' or putting herself forward in any way whatever, and a perfect willingness to forego all sorts of diversions and social distractions ; her duties, her requisite occupations, and the cultivation of her mind by miscellaneous readings in three languages, sufficed her. The children were constantly with their parents ; there was no separate nursery, and no rigid line drawn between the big ones and the little ones. Of English society there was extremely little—barely one or two families that we saw something of at moderate intervals ; but of Italian society—in the sense of Italians who hunted up and haunted our father as an old acquaintance or a celebrity—the stream was constant and copious. Singular personages these Italians (with occasionally some foreigner of a different nationality) were, in many instances ; almost all of them eager after something—few or none eager after those things which occupy the thoughts of the average Englishman—to increase his income, to rise a grade higher in social position, to set his children going in one of the approved grooves, to relax over the sporting columns of a newspaper. There were exiles, patriots, politicians, literary men, musicians, and some of inferior standing; fleshy good-natured Neapolitans, keen Tuscans, emphatic Romans. As we children were habituated from our earliest years to speaking Italian with our father, we were able to follow all or most of the speech of these 'natives' ; and a conspirator or a semi-brigand might present himself, and open out on his topics of predilection, without our being told to leave the room. All this even apart from our chiefly Italian blood—made us, no doubt, not a little different from British children in habit of thought and standard of association ; and, when Dante and Christina Rossetti proved, as poetic writers, somewhat devious from the British tradition and the insular mind, we may say, if not 'so much the better,' at any rate, 'no wonder.'

Apart from her sister and brothers, Christina had no relatives of nearly her own age. She received plenty of affection from her maternal grandparents and maiden aunts. Most of this branch of the family lived in those years in the country—at Holmer Green, near Little Missenden, Buckinghamshire. Through staying there from time to time Christina came to know something, and to love much, of rural appearances—gardens, poultry, ponds, frogs, etc. ; but this came to an end in 1839, when the Polidoris removed back into London, and from that time onward her experiences of anything countrified were decidedly sparse and scanty. Our father never took his family out of town for annual jaunts, as for instance to the seaside; there was little money to spend on any such relaxations, and not much disposition to be on the move. Later on (as may readily be guessed) Christina visited several of the ordinary seaside or other resorts: Brighton, Hastings, Clifton, Cheltenham, Sevenoaks, Torquay, etc.; she was a little in Scotland, never in Ireland. In childhood she was of a lively, and a somewhat capricious or even fractious, temper; but she was warm-natured, engaging, and a general favourite, considerably prettier than her elder sister Maria. She was by far the least bookish of the family—liking a few things heartily, such as *The Arabian Nights* and the lyric dramas of Metastasio, but generally not applying herself with assiduity to either her books or her studies. She 'picked up' things rather than acquired them.

I will give here three small anecdotes of Christina's childhood. They may be 'puerile' or 'silly,' yet are characteristic in their way, and have a kind of bearing upon her faculty as a writer. It appears to me that at the dates of the first two incidents my own age was still under seven, so Christina's was under six: in the third instance she may have been between seven and eight.

1. One day Mrs. Cipriani Potter (the wife of the Principal of the Royal Academy of Music, who was my godfather) called upon my mother. Christina was in the room, and our household tabby cat, who, being of mature age, wore that aspect of self-collected gravity with which we are all familiar. Christina made the remark, 'The cat looks very sedate,' and I can still remember the glance of amused surprise with which Mrs. Potter greeted the use, by such infantine lips, of such a 'dictionary-word,' so appositely introduced. 2. It appears to me that the very first verses composed and spoken by Christina (she was too young to *write* them) were these—they do not profess to be rhyme, but are metre, and correct metre:—

> Cecilia never went to school
> Without her gladiator.

There was no reason for coupling 'gladiator' with 'Cecilia.' The Christian name had been found, I fancy, in a book which we then often skimmed, named *The Looking-Glass for the Mind*, and something or other about gladiators had recently been heard by Christina, and the word (if nothing else) had hit her fancy. She understood this much—that a 'gladiator' would be a man capable of showing some fight for 'Cecilia' upon an emergency. Unmeaning as the lines and the association are, they are not without hinting at a certain oddity or whimsicality of combination which (mingled indeed with qualities of a very different kind) can be not unfrequently traced in the verse of her mature years. 3. Possibly the earliest thing which Christina wrote (or rather, I think, got some one to write from her dictation) was the beginning of a tale called perhaps *The Dervise*, on the model (more or less, *i.e.* very little) of *The Arabian Nights*. The dervise, I think, went down into a cavern, where he was to meet with some adventures not much less surprising than those of Aladdin. In the thick of the plot it occurred to Christina that she had not yet given her dervise a name, so she interjected a sentence, 'The Dervise's name was.Hassan,' and continued his perilous performances. This outraged the literary sense of Gabriel and the rest of us. I doubt whether, after *The Dervise*, Christina wrote anything else prior to 1840, the date of *Retribution*, which I have briefly mentioned in my Memoir of Dante Rossetti. This also must have been an oriental—I suppose a crusading—prose tale, as one incident was 'Sir Guy finding the letter of Ali.'

I do not seem to know of any other writing by my sister until we come to the date, 27 April 1842, of her first written verses, 'To my Mother.' These were soon privately printed by our grandfather Polidori. They open —in the spirit of filial love which was hers through life—her career as a poetess. From that point onward the present volume furnishes ample material for judging what she was like in heart, mind, feeling, aspiration, faculty, and executive gift; and I may leave that matter to speak for itself.

Christina was, I think, a tolerably healthy girl in mere childhood; but this state of things soon came to an end. She was not fully fifteen when her constitution became obviously delicate. She always received excellent medical advice, and was treated at different times for a variety of maladies. There was angina pectoris (actual or supposed), of which, after some long while, she seemed cured; then cough, with symptoms which were accounted ominous of decline or consumption, lasting on towards 1867; then exophthalmic bronchocele (or Dr. Graves's disease), which began in 1871, and was truly most formidable and prostrating, and which, after destroying for a while all her good looks, left her with permanent cardiac troubles, and an aspect, not indeed anything like so bad as it had been in the thick of the disease, but still sensibly altered. And yet she survived every single member of the Rossetti and Polidori families, myself and my children alone excepted. All these maladies were apart from her last and mortal illness, of which I must say a few words in its place. I have naturally much more reluctance than inclination to dwell upon any of these physical ills; but any one who did not understand that Christina was an almost constant and often a sadly-smitten invalid, seeing at times the countenance of Death very close to her own, would form an extremely incorrect notion of her corporal, and thus in some sense of her spiritual, condition. She was compelled, even if not naturally disposed, to regard this world as a 'valley of the shadow of death,' and to make near acquaintance with promises, and also with threatenings, applicable to a different world. As an invalid she had courage, patience, and even cheerfulness. I have heard her dwell upon the satisfaction—such as it is— of being ill, and interdicted from active exertion and the following-out of one's fancies. Perhaps the least unhealthy years of her womanhood were towards 1861, and again from 1867 to 1870—age thirty, going on to thirty-nine.

The fortunes of the Rossetti family, always modest enough, were at a low ebb from 1842 to 1854. Ill-health and partial blindness overtook our father, leading to the diminution, and ultimately the loss, of professional employment. The sustenance of the household devolved to some extent upon our mother, who went out teaching. Maria was a governess—at first a resident governess, but afterwards attending to pupils from her home. Dante Gabriel, until 1848, could earn nothing, and for some ensuing years very little, and the expenses of starting him in his pictorial vocation were not inconsiderable. For myself, I became an extra clerk in the Excise (or Inland Revenue) Office from 1845, earning a very moderate stipend, which gradually increased; and from 1850 I got some amount of paid literary employment as well. Christina, though she had no propensity to educational or other drudgery, was always most willing to do what might offer. In 1851-52 she assisted our mother in a small day-school at No. 38 Arlington Street, Mornington Crescent. This was far from prosperous, and in 1853 they two, along with our father, moved off to Frome-Selwood, Somerset, in hopes that another day-school might work better. This also proved a comparative failure; and early in 1854 I found myself sufficiently floated to allow of our all living again together in London—all, that is, except Dante Gabriel, who by this time had separate chambers of his own. We reunited in Upper Albany Street—the house now called No. 166 Albany Street; and from this time forward Christina simply lived at home —no longer under the necessity of teaching the small daughters of the neighbouring hairdresser or the neighbouring pork-butcher their p's and q's, but anxious to secure any literary pickings which might offer, and producing poems which the world has not as yet been willing to let die. Her earnings were decidedly meagre. I suppose that from 1854 to 1862 she seldom made £10 in a year; from 1862 to 1890 there might be (taking one year with another) an average of perhaps £40 per annum—less rather than more. By 1890 her poetic reputation was fully settled, and her profits were substantial, without being at all large. Of private income she had, so far as I remember, absolutely none up to 1867, and for many years after that a mere pittance. But, of course, she lived in comfort and security as a member of the family along with other members.

The family had scarcely got reunited in Albany Street when Gabriele Rossetti died, 26 April 1854.

I must now go back a little in date, and give some slight account of an 'affair of the heart' which brightened and darkened the life of Christina Rossetti.[1] There were two such incidents, at an interval of years. The

[1] Readers of her poems had not failed to see, and to say, that some such affair or affairs must have given rise to several of the compositions: but nothing distinct had been

first began in 1848, before she was aged eighteen, and ended in 1850, or possibly late in 1849. The second must have commenced[1] towards the close of 1862; except as a matter of feeling, it terminated towards the opening of 1867.

James Collinson was a painter, who fell in love with Christina soon after being introduced to her. He was chiefly a domestic painter, and had been enrolled in the 'Præraphaelite Brotherhood,' formed towards September 1848. He had originally been a member of the Church of England, and a devout one; but, before making acquaintance with Christina, he had been converted to Roman Catholicism. On explaining his feelings, he was informed that this difference in church-faith formed an obstacle not to be got over. From this fact it might appear that Christina—who already belonged to what was then called the Puseyite or Tractarian party in the English Church, or (as we should now say) the High Church party or Anglo-Catholics—was decidedly hostile to Roman Catholicism. I do not, however, think she was that. I consider that she held then—as she certainly did in later years—that the Roman Catholics are authentic members of the one veritable Church of Christ, but in some matters erroneous; she was, for instance, firmly opposed to anything savouring of Mariolatry. I do not see that her religious tenets were such as to make marriage with a Roman Catholic, in itself, distasteful to her, or contrary to her sense of duty: she may rather perhaps have been influenced by the consideration that, in the event of giving birth to children, she would be at odds with her husband as to the faith in which these should be brought up, with consequences which might expose their souls to peril and scathe. Anyhow she declined Collinson's offer, although, on general grounds, very well disposed towards him. Collinson then seems to have supposed that, after all, his religious convictions were not incompatible with membership in the English Church: he reverted to it, proposed to Christina again, and was accepted. But after a moderate while he found once more that his conscience pricked him, and he must at all hazards be a Roman Catholic. Such he re-became, and Christina (whose force of will, especially where any point of duty seemed to be concerned, was in full proportion to the family motto, *Frangas non flectas*) cancelled the engagement. I will not harshly condemn James Collinson for these successive tergiversations: he was a right-meaning man, of timorous conscience. But he had none the less struck a staggering blow at Christina Rossetti's peace of mind on the very threshold of womanly life, and a blow from which she did not fully recover for years. He died in 1881.

printed on the subject, prior to a note which I inserted in the volume *New Poems*, 1896. In that note I indicated the main facts very briefly, not giving names. It appears to me that there is now no serious reason for withholding the names. I therefore state them, along with the other particulars.

[1] See the series of Italian compositions, *Il Rosseggiar dell' Oriente*.

I must next deal with a personage of higher type, Charles Bagot Cayley, a man of letters and an author, but less author than scholar. Christina may first have known him as far back as 1847 or so, and again in 1854: but the two did not meet much until some such date as 1860. Towards 1847 he had been a pupil of my father for Italian; and he became an excellent Italian scholar (indeed a remarkable linguist generally), and produced a most able translation of Dante's *Comedia* in the original metre. He was a singularly unworldly person, which was no doubt in my sister's eyes a merit, and not a blemish. His precise religious opinions are not clear to me: he had been brought up in the Church of England. I suppose that, like so many other men of inquiring mind, he regarded all religions as much the same thing—a mixture of feeling with thought, and also with assumption and legend, not with verification. He may have considered Christianity the best of all religions, but not as being on a different plane from others, absolute truth as contrasted with fallacy. In course of time he proposed to Christina. She loved him deeply and permanently, but, on his declaring himself, she must no doubt have probed his faith, and found it either strictly wrong or wofully defective. So she declined his suit, but without ceasing to see and to cherish him as a friend. Knowing the state of her heart when the offer was made, I urged her to marry, and offered that they should both, if money difficulties stood in the way, share my home. But she had made up her mind on grounds which she recognized as higher than any considerations of either feeling or expediency, and she remained immovable. Years passed: she became an elderly and an old woman, and she loved the scholarly recluse to the last day of his life, 5 December 1883, and, to the last day of her own, his memory.

It may be added that Christina was extremely reticent in all matters in which her affections were deeply engaged. Of these two cases I knew a good deal directly, and could indirectly judge of much more; but it would have been both indelicate and futile to press her with inquiries, and of several details in the second case—though important to a close understanding of it—I never was cognizant.

As Mr. Cayley was so important a personage in the hushed life-drama of Christina Rossetti, I will here insert a portion of the obituary notice of him which I wrote, and which was printed in *The Athenæum:*—'Mr. Charles Bagot Cayley, B.A., of Trinity College, Cambridge, died suddenly, and apparently without any serious forewarning, of heart disease, in the night of the 4th-5th December, in his lodging at South Crescent, Bedford Square: he was found dead in the morning, having expired, it would seem, in perfect calm during sleep. This gentleman was the son of a Russia merchant, and younger brother of the celebrated mathematician, the Sadlerian Professor at Cambridge. He was born on 9 July 1823, and had therefore completed his sixtieth year. Several of his early years were passed in

Russia. . . . He published, many years ago, a volume of original poems named *Psyche's Interludes*. Some of the same compositions, with others added, re-appeared lately in a privately printed volume. Mr. Cayley was for many years past an active and valued member of the Philological Society. . . . A more complete specimen than Mr. Charles Cayley of the abstracted scholar in appearance and manner—the scholar who constantly lives an inward and unmaterial life, faintly perceptive of external facts and appearances—could hardly be conceived. He united great sweetness to great simplicity of character, and was not less polite than unworldly. In a small circle of intimates his death leaves a mournful blank: they " will not look upon his like again."'

Apart from these two matters, the life of Christina Rossetti presents hardly any incident. Her life had two motive powers,—religion and affection: hardly a third. And even the religion was far more a thing of the heart than of the mind: she clung to and loved the Christian creed because she loved Jesus Christ. 'Christ is God' was her one dominant idea. Faith with her was faith pure and absolute: an entire acceptance of a thing revealed—not a quest for any confirmation or demonstrative proof. There were few things she more disliked than an 'Evidences of Christianity': I dare say she never read one, but she must have glanced at one or other sufficiently to know that she disliked it. To learn that something in the Christian faith was credible *because it was reasonable*, or because it rested upon some historic evidence of fact, went against her. Her attitude of mind was: 'I believe because I am told to believe, and I know that the authority which tells me to believe is the only real authority extant, God.' To press her—'How do you know that it is God?' would have been no use; the ultimate response could only have come to this— 'My faith is faith; it is not evolved out of argumentation, nor does it seek the aid of that.' If she did not admit of discussion of her own belief, neither did she indulge in any discussion of the belief of others: no one knows this better than myself, with whom the field for debate, had she been minded to it, would have been a very large one. In fact, though enormously strict with herself in matters of religious faith and dogma, she was not intolerant of difference of opinion in others: she met on terms of close or amicable good-will many persons whom she knew to be decided disbelievers, not to speak of earnest and devout Dissenters. The Christian believer has before him two things: one, the promise of ecstatic bliss; the other, the decree of excessive misery. Some believers, perceiving themselves to be undoubted Christians in faith, become serenely or perhaps exuberantly happy in their inner selves: it may be said that Maria Rossetti was of these, for (at any rate in her later years) she felt the firmest confidence of salvation. Not so Christina, who always distrusted herself, and her relation to that standard of Christian duty which she constantly acknowledged and professed. In this regard her tone of mind was mainly despondent: it was painfully despondent in the last few months of her life, but as to that the physical minor reasons may have been as truly operative as the spiritual major reason. All her life long she felt—or rather she exaggerated—her deficiencies or backslidings: she did not face religion with that courageous yet modest front with which a virtuous woman, who knows something of the world, faces life. Passages can no doubt be found in her writings in which she is more hopeful than abased; in which her ardent aspirations towards heaven so identify her with its bliss that she seems to be almost there, or on the very threshold. These passages are of course perfectly genuine; but they are coupled with an awful sense of unworthiness, shadowed by an awful uncertainty. I will not dwell upon slighter matters—those which constituted her a 'devotee' in the ordinary sense—her perpetual church-going and communions, her prayers and fasts, her submission to clerical direction, her oblations, her practice of confession. It should be said that, while she had an intense reverence for the priestly function, she cared next to nothing about hierarchical distinctions: anything which assimilated the clerical order to a 'learned profession' forming part of the British constitution left her indifferent, or rather inimical.

I have often thought that Christina's proper place was in the Roman Catholic Church, yet I never traced any inclination in her to join it, nor did she ever manifest any wish to enter upon the conventual life—I think she held herself unworthy of attempting it. Her satisfaction in remaining a member of the English Church may have been due partly to her deep affection for her mother, who, though gradually conforming to the external practices of the High Church section, was far indeed from wishing to Romanize.

I have said that, along with religion, affection was the motive power of Christina's life. For all her kith and kin, but for her mother far beyond all the rest, her love was as deep as it was often silent. She was not demonstrative, though of a fondling habit as regards her mother. To the latter it may truly be said that her whole life was devoted: they were seldom severed, even for a few days together. When at last, in 1886, death divided them, she tended her two aged aunts with like assiduity, although it was impossible that her outflow of love towards either of them should have had any similar force and glow. Maria she was truly fond of, and she regarded her latterly as almost a saint; of Dante Gabriel she was, so far as natural predilection goes, still fonder—and I might say the same of myself. It will easily be understood that, much as she saw of *him* after they were both grown up, she saw far more of me, for until 1876 (and allowing for the short interval in 1853-54) she and I were always residing together.

Like her mother, Christina went very little into society; none the less she knew and appreciated several leading personages, whom I will name in the order of date (approximately) when she made acquaintance with them: all the members of the Præraphaelite Brotherhood, Madox Brown with his family,[1] Coventry Patmore, Professor Masson, Burne-Jones, William Morris, Ruskin (I question whether she saw him more than once, Dodgson, Dr. Garnett, Robert Browning (but, unfortunately, not Mrs. Browning), Swinburne, Jean Ingelow, Gosse, Watts-Dunton, Shields, Hall Caine. Many others could be named—Dr. Adolf Heimann, Canon Burrows, W. Bell Scott, James Hannay, J. R. Clayton, William Allingham, Dr. John Epps, Mrs. Bodichon, John L. Tupper, the Howitts, John Brett, Thomas and John Seddon, Henrietta Rintoul, Arthur Hughes, Adelaide Procter, Alexander Macmillan (her publisher, with whom she always had very amicable relations), William Ralston, Stillman, Anne Gilchrist, Dora Greenwell, Miss Alice Boyd, Mrs. Cameron, the Rev. Orby Shipley, Dr. Littledale, James Smetham, Hueffer, the Rev. Alfred Gurney, Dr. Hake, Prebendary Glendinning Nash (her clergyman in late years), Lady Mount-Temple, William Sharp, Professor Dunstan, Lisa Wilson, Miss Ellen Proctor, Mackenzie Bell. From a perusal of this list the reader will correctly infer that after the death of our father we saw little—next to nothing—of Italian society. There was, however, our cousin Teodorico Pietrocola-Rossetti, a leader in an Italian Evangelical movement, for whom and his Scottish wife Christina felt a sincere attachment. The physician whom my sister consulted was for many years Sir William Jenner there were also Dr. Hare, Dr. Crellin, Dr. Wilson Fox, Dr. Stewart, and others; and at the very last Dr. Abbott Anderson.

In company she was quiet, and reserved rather than otherwise, but made every now and then some remark which arrested attention. She was as a fact extremely shy. Most people probably perceived as much but she preserved a calm and collected demeanour, which may perhaps have imposed upon some of the unwary, and induced them to fancy her distant rather than backward. Upon her reputation as a poetess she never presumed, nor did she ever volunteer an allusion to any of her performances: in a roomful of mediocrities she consented to seem the most mediocre as the most modest of all.

In a life marked by so few external incidents, such matters as the deaths of relatives and friends count for much: I will mention the leading occurrences of this kind, along with some changes of residence, and the like—all in a very summary form. 1853, death of the Polidoris, grandmother and grandfather. 1854 (as already specified), death of our father Gabriele Rossetti. Later in the same year Christina wished to join her aunt Eliza Polidori in going out as a nurse to Scutari, in connection with the Crimean War, under the scheme planned out by Miss Nightingale but she was pronounced to be below the stipulated age, so this did not take effect. 1861, Christina's first foreign trip, with our mother and

---

[1] To avoid tediousness, I do not mention the family in the several instances; but may be taken that very generally, when a married person is mentioned, the family also was known to Christina.

self, to Paris, Rouen, Normandy (especially Coutances), and Jersey. 62, death of Lizzie Rossetti, the wife of Dante Gabriel. After this loss nte proposed that the family, amalgamating with him, should seek a w residence. There would have been our mother, all her children, and r somewhat invalided eldest aunt, Margaret Polidori, who as yet cupied separate apartments in my house in Albany Street: she would ve continued separate to a like degree. Dante wished also that Mr. gernon Swinburne should be in the house—for, as he truly said, he mself required some amount of intellectual incitement and diversion yond what the family could minister to him. To this proposal Christina, ;h the rest of us, assented; but it was soon set aside, as Dante came to refer a different arrangement. 1865, Christina's second and last foreign :p, in the same company as before, to North Italy (Como, Pavia, Brescia, rona, Milan, etc.), going out by the St. Gothard route (no tunnel was .n in existence), and returning by the Splügen route, Schaffhausen, Stras- urg, etc. 1867, death of Margaret Polidori, a very diligent religionist and church-goer; and removal of Christina, with our mother, Maria, and yself, to No. 56 Euston Square (now called 5 Endsleigh Gardens), a much more commodious house than any we had previously occupied. ''3, in view of my impending marriage to Lucy, daughter of the painter ord Madox Brown, Maria resolved to carry at once into execution a ;' at she had long entertained, that of entering the Anglican Sisterhood of All Saints. 1874, my marriage: my mother and Christina continued reside with us, but they not unfrequently spent a week or two with my other's two sisters, Charlotte and Eliza Polidori, who (after my wedding and their consequent removal from 56 Euston Square) had taken a house, Bloomsbury Square. Oliver Madox Brown, who was godson to Maria y son of Ford Madox Brown), died in November; and in the same .' Christina's cousin, still under thirty, Henrietta Polydore. 1876, considerations led to the dividing of our household: my wife and children, with myself, remaining in Endsleigh Gardens, while my mother and Christina moved off at Michaelmas to No. 30 Torrington Square. Hardly were they settled there when the illness from which Maria had been suffering for many weeks took a fatal turn, and she died in November. 1882, death of Dante Gabriel at Birchington-on-Sea, 9 April, after several weeks' affectionate nursing by our mother and Christina. 1883, death of our infant son Michael. As his end approached, Christina implored me to allow her to baptize him; to this I raised no objection, and she performed the rite unwitnessed, and I doubt whether any act of her life gave her more heartfelt satisfaction. 1885, death of our uncle, Henry Polidori, a Roman Catholic. 1886, 8 April, death of our mother, a loss to Christina which I forbear from dwelling upon. 1889, death of Franz Hueffer, the man of letters and musical expert and critic, husband of my wife's half-sister. 1890, death of Charlotte Polidori, aged eighty-seven, after some years of confinement to her bed, a most amiable good woman, less out-of-the-world than other Polidoris, but not less religious ; also death of our friend ever since 1847, William Bell Scott, a man whom Christina viewed with great predilection. When in 1892 his *Autobiographical Notes* were published, containing (as I informed her) several unkind and not too accurate passages about Dante Rossetti, she refused to look at the book, swayed, I think, as much by respect for Scott's memory as for her brother's. 1893, death of Eliza Polidori, aged eighty-three, after an illness still longer than Charlotte's, and more wearing to herself, and to Christina as her constant attendant ; also death of Ford Madox Brown. With the decease of Eliza Polidori, her last relative of the elder generation, the income of Christina (which had been tolerable enough since 1886) increased, and henceforward she had more than what sufficed for her very moderate requirements. At all periods of her life she had been 'a cheerful giver,' as far as her means allowed. Until a late date these means allowed but little : when they allowed ten-fold, she gave (I dare say) twenty-fold. 1894, April, death of my beloved wife. This is a long mortuary catalogue ; but many other deaths took place afflicting to Christina, few more so than those of her early and unfailing friends—Dr. Adolf Heimann, who had been Professor of German at University College, London ; and Canon Burrows of Rochester, who had for many years been the Incumbent of the church—Christ Church, Albany Street—which she frequented from about 1843 to 1867 or later.

The Canon died at an advanced age in a year—perhaps 1890—when Christina's own health and energies were little fitted to bear any strain. She was invited to write a biography of him, and would have felt much pleasure in doing so, but she found it imperative to decline. Another project which miscarried, at a slightly later date, was the proposal made by our admirable painter, George F. Watts, the recorder of so many faces of pre-eminent men and women, that Christina should sit to him for her portrait. She was worthy to do so, and, spite of her life-long shrinking from any sort of notoriety, was anything but indifferent to the distinction thus offered her ; but here again considerations of health and rapidly-ebbing life interposed an insuperable barrier. If any one thinks that Christina Rossetti was not the only loser by the failure of this project, I share his opinion.

It does not seem necessary, in this brief Memoir, to dwell upon any of the other incidents of her life—all in themselves insignificant. It was a life which did not consist of incidents : in few things, external ; in all its deeper currents, internal.

I am now approaching the end. To a chronic affection of the heart, with a recurrent sense of suffocation (but this had not of late seemed so formidable as at some earlier periods), were added towards the close of 1891 uneasy but not exactly painful sensations, which required to be explained.

Medical advice being taken, the explanation came: the case was one of cancer—a word which had always been pronounced in the family with a certain shrinking. Christina took the announcement most bravely. In May 1892 an operation of a very severe kind was performed by the distinguished surgeon Mr. Lawson—skilfully and successfully performed. After rallying from the shock to the system, Christina went on in comparative ease for some months, although it was too clearly foreseen that the malady would return. It did so towards the autumn of 1893: no further operation was then practicable, and only palliatives could be applied. Dropsy of the left arm and hand complicated her other illness. In August 1894 she took finally to her bed, in a calm and resigned mood, but, as the time advanced, with troublous agitation, both of the spirit and of the bodily frame. Not that she was ever abashed by pain, or craven-hearted—far indeed from that; but the terrors of her religion compassed her about, to the overclouding of its radiances. At the close of a week of collapse and semi-consciousness, she died without a struggle, in the act of inarticulate prayer, on the early morning of 29 December 1894—her attached nurse alone being present at the moment.

She was buried in Highgate Cemetery, in the same grave to which had been successively consigned her father, her sister-in-law Lizzie, and her mother. A reredos-painting, as a memorial of her, has been set up by subscription in Christ Church, Woburn Square. The design of it was supplied by an old acquaintance of hers, Sir Edward Burne-Jones; the actual painting is by Mr. T. M. Rooke. It is a very appropriate and fine design,—Christ uttering the words of consecration of the eucharistic elements, and the four Evangelists as recorders of the event.

Christina Rossetti was of an ordinary female middle height—slim in youth, but, in middle and advanced age, often rather over-plump; this had been the tendency of both her parents. Some people thought her extremely like her mother; I myself never saw this strongly—the mother's features were the more regular of the two, but not perhaps the more agreeable in combination. My sister's complexion was dark and uniform—yet much less dark than Maria's—and after early youth her cheeks were colourless. Her hair was a dark brown, with a good deal of gloss; not remarkably plenteous in youth, and only a little altered by age—to the last it was essentially brown, not grey. The same had been the case with her mother. Her eyes were originally a blueish-grey (portraits show this); but in adult years they might rather be called a greyish hazel, or a richly hazelled grey, and towards the close they may have told out to most persons as being a warm brown, of dark tint. They were always of full size; and, after the attack of exophthalmic bronchocele which began in 1871, they were over-prominent—even somewhat distressingly so at times, but by no means always. The forehead was ample, the lips not noticeably full, with a firm and also a sensitive expression, the chin rather prolonged and pointed in girlhood, but this was little or not at all observable later on; the facial contour shapely. Her nose was not far from being straight, but taking a slight outward curve towards the tip. Her hands were delicate; and her figure might be called good, without being remarkably fine. She had a good speaking and reading voice—singing she never attempted, apart from the ordinary congregational singing in church. Indeed, I believe that her speaking voice, though not nearly so rich and impressive as Maria's, was considered in youth uncommonly fine in tone and modulation; in her later years there was a certain degree of strain and fatigue in it, but, to many persons who only knew her in those years, this may hardly have been apparent. Her utterance was clear; her delivery—as indeed her whole aspect and demeanour—marked unmistakably by sincerity, consideration for others, and a modest but not the less definite self-regard. I recollect having once told her jocularly (she was perhaps barely seventeen at the time) that 'she would soon become so polite it would be impossible to live with her.' She was one of the last persons with whom any one would feel inspirited to take a liberty, though one might, without any sort of remonstrance, treat her as the least important of womankind.

A question has sometimes been raised as to the amount of good looks with which Christina Rossetti should be credited. She was certainly not what one understands by 'a beauty'; the term handsome did not apply to her, nor yet the term pretty. Neither was she 'a fine woman.' She has sometimes been called 'lovely' in youth; and this is true, if a refined and correct mould of face, along with elevated and deep expression, is loveliness. She was assuredly much nearer to being beautiful than ugly; and this, in my opinion, remained true of her throughout her life, for in advanced years her expression naturally deepened, although the traces left upon her by disease, as well as by time, marred her comeliness. However, there are several portraits of her which can be appealed to to settle the question of her good looks; and, as I can speak of the matter with knowledge, I will give a list of them—they are in my own possession, unless otherwise notified.

1. The earliest portrait is a full-face taken by Filippo Pistrucci (the brother of the celebrated medallist), towards 1837. The best version of this water-colour, which has an agreeable childish look, belongs to my daughter, Signora Agresti, of Rome. It was reproduced in Mr. Mackenzie Bell's book; the colour has now faded considerably. W. Bell Scott made an etching of it, and I possess another water-colour nearly similar—perhaps a preliminary study for the head. The hair is of a rather bright warm tint.

2. Pistrucci again tried his hand at Christina's face, towards 1843, water-colour, but made a woful failure; the mouth especially being misdrawn, with a conceited smirking expression. This head is so bad that, but for its being mounted from of old in the same frame with the heads of

the other three children, I should prefer to destroy it, or at any rate hide it away. It shows that by this date Christina's hair was no longer bright, but decidedly brown.

3. Towards 1846, or possibly 1845, Dante Gabriel made a careful pencil-drawing of the head, profile. It is a good likeness, rather (I think) below the level of Christina's attractiveness at that time. It is also a good drawing, but of course does not display the finer qualities of Dante's art, which developed at a later date. This drawing is reproduced in the volume named *Gabriele Rossetti*, brought out by me in 1901.

4. There is a pretty little pencil-drawing by him, of Christina seated in an easy-chair, in a semi-dozing pose. Her general air is well realized, without any great definition of the face. This I take to be as late as 1847.

5. As a frontispiece to her privately printed volume, *Verses*, of 1847, Dante drew, probably in the same year, a careful profile in pencil. It shows Christina with curls (so does No. 2) and with some thinness of contour. It is certainly like her, but not in the most attractive way.

6. In 1848 Dante painted an oil-head of Christina: it appears to be the first coloured work that he completed. It is a true likeness, and shows a face so well-moulded and agreeable as to be, in a fair sense, beautiful. This head is reproduced in the *Family Letters and Memoir* of my brother which I published in 1895; some defect in the surface of the pigment or the canvas interferes with the success of the reproduction.

7. About contemporary with this—for I know not which was the earlier—comes the pencil-head by Dante Gabriel, purchased by Mr. Sydney Morse soon after Christina's death. This also is a most truthful likeness, and a highly pleasing one—rather more matter-of-fact in expression than the preceding. It appears in Mr. Bell's book and elsewhere.

8. The little pencil-head by Dante Gabriel, published with Christina's tale *Maude* in 1897, seems also to appertain to 1848. It is a nice but slight sketch, with some archness of expression—a quality in which the poetess was by no means deficient. The original now belongs to Mr. Coulson Kernahan.

9. The head of Mary, in the oil-picture of *The Girlhood of Mary Virgin* painted by my brother in 1848-49, was studied from Christina, and is a real if not a literal portrait of her, allowing for changed colour in the hair. The picture (now belonging to Lady Jekyll) has been reproduced in various forms.

10. The profile in pencil, by my brother, which appears in the *New Poems*, 1896, exquisitely sweet in contour and expression, may have been done in 1849; as I have said elsewhere, it has something of the air of a study preliminary to No. 13, but not in the same pose.

11. The small oil-portrait by James Collinson, given in Mr. Bell's book. This is a true likeness of Christina: a true but also an ordinary one, done

by an artist whose eye for beauty was not keen, and whose style was stinted. Its date is 1849. In 1901 it figured in the Great Exhibition in Glasgow.

12. Towards the same time my brother did a small pencil half-figure of Christina, in profile. It is not important, but defines her general look well enough.

13. The picture by Dante Rossetti, *Ecce Ancilla Domini* (or *The Annunciation*), in the National British Gallery, 1849-50. The head of the Virgin was studied from Christina; it was however altered from time to time, and more than one person sat for it. I consider that it presents some substantial resemblance to Christina, and that the expression of *her* face more than any other is realized in it; a portrait it is not, and does not affect to be. When first exhibited, 1850, the likeness was more decided than it is now.

14. As shown in the book of Dante Rossetti's *Family Letters*, he drew a reminiscent caricature of Christina in August 1852; she is presented as listening in rapt attention to some verses improvised by a friend. The chief point observable in this caricature is that it gives the 'chin rather [or a good deal] prolonged and pointed,' on which I have before remarked.

15. The engaging pencil-drawing by Dante Rossetti reproduced in Mr. Bell's book—Christina seated and reading—October 1852; this affords an extremely good idea of the composed, orderly look of Christina in day-by-day life; modestly self-withdrawn, as incapable of parade in mental gifts as in toilet—but not incapable of making those gifts apparent when the occasion arose.

16. My brother's pen-and-ink design *Hesterna Rosa* (the property of Mr. F. G. Stephens), represents, with a motto from Sir Henry Taylor's *Philip van Artevelde*, two women in a tent with their paramours, who are playing at dice. One of the women, struck with a pang of remorse at the thought of her lapse from virtue, shades her face with her hand. I think it clear that this face is drawn from Christina, whom it resembles well; it is not from Miss Siddal, and at that date there was no other female head that he habitually drew.

17. In June 1853, when my sister was settled in Frome with our parents, I did a pencil sketch of her, the face being in rather full shadow. It has no pretensions as a work of art, but is not deficient in resemblance. There is also, from my hand, a profile outline, which may be of about the same date, but I think rather later; it preserves something, not only of her features, but of the placid, yet by no means unemotional, sweetness of her look.

18. In and about 1855 a friend, Miss (Henrietta) Rintoul, daughter of the then editor of *The Spectator*, took up photography as a diversion, and she made some photographs of Christina, which seem to be the earliest sun-pictures ever taken of her. Two of these photographs remain. In

both Christina is seated in a little balcony abutting on the leads of the house; alone in one instance—in the other along with myself. Both of these are very good likenesses of my sister; unfortunately, they have faded to a great extent.

19. Two photographs on glass were taken of Christina, along with Maria, in April 1855—three-quarter lengths. They are nearly, but not quite, identical, and both give her face with an air of brightness and animation, and of earnestness as well.

20. A photograph on glass, showing Christina along with our mother and Maria. I think the date may be 1856. This is the only portrait of Christina in which the hair is arranged (as customary in those years) over the ears, and with a plait coming circlet-wise across the head. It is an excellent likeness, attesting, by the irrefutable evidence of the sun, that she was not very far from being beautiful. This photograph is reproduced in the volume *Gabriele Rossetti*.

21. 1857 was the date of the publication of Tennyson's *Poems*, illustrated by Millais, Dante Rossetti, and others. On p. 119 is Rossetti's design of King Arthur in Avalon, 'watched by weeping queens.' The first face here (from the spectator's left) is taken from Christina, but is less like her on the engraved page than in the original drawing; she must also have sat for the profile to the extreme right, which is a very faithful likeness. Millais's design (p. 274) of the young lady (*Locksley Hall*) caught in possession of a love-letter is also not unlike Christina; I will not say, however, that it was done from her, for I cannot remember that, nor do I think it quite probable.

22. Three carte-de-visite photographs, taken (if I remember rightly) soon before Christina started on her Norman trip of 1861. These, again, are extremely good, rendering very well the subdued dignity and elegant (though not fashionable) quietude of her aspect. Two of the figures are standing—the third is seated, bonneted.

23. Towards 1862, soon after the publication of *Goblin Market*, and some laudatory critiques consequent thereon, Dante Gabriel noticed in *The Times* the critical phrase, 'Miss Rossetti can point to work which could not easily be mended.' By a wilful perversion of its obvious meaning, he knocked off a caricature (pen-and-ink) in which Christina, in a highly 'rampageous' mood, was kicking and pounding away with a hammer at the household clock, glass, and crockery; some bank-notes are in the fire. The caricature amused Christina, who preserved it; since it came into my possession I gave it to Signora Agresti. This is not much more like the poetess in visage than in action, but one can see whom it is meant for.

24. In the autumn of 1863 the Rev. Mr. Dodgson (of *Alice in Wonderland*) attended more than once in my brother's house, 16 Cheyne Walk, and took in the garden photographs of the members of the family

whom he found at hand. One (reproduced in Mr. Bell's book) represents my mother and Christina, half-figures; highly successful, and showing the contour of my sister's face to great advantage. There are also three family-groups, two of them comprising four figures, and the other five. The last is spoiled by splashes. In each of these Christina is capitally characterized; one is a standing figure, giving an intellectual profile, and one a seated figure, with a cheerful and somewhat bantering air.

25. In May 1865 my brother made a very careful pencil-profile of Christina, on a fairly large (not life-size) scale. It is in every respect a highly impressive drawing. It suffers from having been begun at first on too small a piece of paper; the penciling has got rubbed, more especially on the hair, and the joining of the added paper is disagreeably apparent. This formed a frontispiece for the volume compiled by me, *Præraphaelite Diaries and Letters*.

26. The best known of all the portraits of Christina is the drawing in coloured chalks, life-size, which Dante Rossetti executed in September 1866; it forms the frontispiece to Mr. Bell's book. This is a beautiful drawing, showing a face very chaste in outline, and distinguished in expression; it would be hard for any likeness to be more exact. I have seen it stated somewhere (and I believe *àpropos* of this very drawing) that one cannot trust Rossetti's likenesses, as he always idealized. Few statements could be more untruthful. Certainly he succeeded—and he succeeded—at bringing out the beauty and the fine expression of a face, rather than its more commonplace and mediocre aspect; but his likenesses are, with casual exceptions, very strict transcripts of the fact. Any one who supposes, for instance, that Mrs. William Morris (whom my brother so constantly drew and painted from 1857 onwards) was not precisely like what he represented her, makes a very great mistake.

27. In the same year, 1866, Christina was a visitor at Penkill Castle, Ayrshire, the seat of Miss (Alice) Boyd. Mr. W. Bell Scott was there at the same time; and, in one of his mural paintings in the Castle, he represented her as a personage (? Minerva) in the Court of Venus, from the poem by James I. of Scotland, *The King's Quair*. I saw this painting many years ago, and I believe that the likeness of Christina is fairly characteristic. It has been reproduced by Scott in an etching and otherwise, but not so as to be recognizable.

28. At some date, which I suppose to be towards 1868, she sat for three photographs, all produced perhaps at one sitting. The best is a carte-de-visite, seated full-length, a profile, in which the face has a very thoughtful and expressive look. It is not a flattering likeness, but truly a valuable one. Another seated half-figure, much larger, has that rather set and blank air which comes over the face of a person expecting to be photographed. The third, only head and shoulders, is the reverse of attractive, but the resemblance is there.

29. The tinted-chalk head of Christina, along with our mother, now in the National Portrait Gallery, was drawn by Dante Rossetti at Hunter's Forestal, Herne Bay, as he was recovering from an illness in the autumn of 1877. This profile is markedly like a certain aspect of Christina's face which was not exactly unwonted, but still was exceptional; there is a rather inscrutable sphinx-like look about it. Whenever I set eyes upon it, the lines from her poem, *From House to Home*, come into my mind—

> Therefore in patience I possess my soul;
> Yea therefore as a flint I set my face.

30. Just about the same date my brother did two other tinted-chalk heads of Christina. In one the head is erect, full-face; in the other, three-quarters view, it is slightly drooped; in each of them she wears the cap which she had assumed before 1877, and which continued to the last to be her habitual wear. The latter drawing has been reproduced ere now; not, I think, the former, but it was shown in the Wolverhampton Art Exhibition of 1902. Both these are fine works of art, and speaking likenesses; the erect head partakes, in a minor degree, of the expression which I have noted under No. 29. Anything more close than the drooped head to the features and the sentiment of my sister's face in her advanced years (she was aged forty-six at the time) cannot well be imagined.

31. It was, I believe, in this same year, 1877, that two photographs of Christina were taken by the skilled hands of Messrs. Elliott and Fry; these are the only photographs of her which seem to retain currency at the present day. It was no fault of Messrs. Elliott and Fry that neither portrait does her justice. They are both seated three-quarter figures, one of them in full face; this the sitter was accustomed to call 'the idiot,' and indeed it is sufficiently vacant-looking. The other is in profile, reading with lowered eyelids; it counts as the less unsatisfactory of the two. In both instances the eyeballs (from the cause to which I have already referred) are rather unpleasantly prominent.

I fully think that after this date Christina never sat for her likeness, whether to the sun or to an artist. It is a pity, for seventeen further years elapsed before her death; and there were periods when her face certainly told to better advantage than in the photographs No. 31. I have had in my hands three or four other slight sketches of her by my brother, which I have given away here and there—all of them belonging to the days of her youth or early maturity. Two of them are in the Public Library of Des Moines, in the State of Iowa (United States).

I have thus specified, under 31 numbers, 45 portraits of Christina Rossetti, from the age of six years to that of forty-six. Those which I have numbered 6, 7, 10, 20, 22, 24, 25, 26, and 30, would afford to any one who sees them a very exact knowledge of what she was like from the age of seventeen onwards ; and most of the others supplement them to some good purpose.

As yet I have said very little as to my sister's character, except that she was religious and affectionate in an eminent degree. It is time to proceed to some further detail.

In innate character she was vivacious, and open to pleasurable impressions ; and, during her girlhood, one might readily have supposed that she would develop into a woman of expansive heart, fond of society and diversions, and taking a part in them of more than average brilliancy. What came to pass was of course quite the contrary. In this result ill-health and an early blight to the affections told for much ; for much also an exceeding sensitiveness of conscience, acted upon by the strictest conceptions in religion. Of society (as one uses that term to mean fashionable or quasi-fashionable society) she saw nothing ; of amusements practically nothing. She was, I suppose, barely eighteen when she determined never again to enter a theatre, dramatic or operatic ; not perhaps that she considered plays and operas to be in themselves iniquitous, but rather that the moral tone of vocalists, actors, and actresses is understood to be lax, and it behoves a Christian not to contribute to the encouragement of lax moralists. In all such matters Christina was an Anglo-Catholic, and, among Anglo-Catholics, a Puritan ; and yet she looked without hardness of heart upon any individual who might have lapsed from virtue. As well as theatres, she gave up at an early age the game of chess, of which she was rather fond, and this simply because she thought it made her too eager for a win. Cards however she never relinquished, finding no sort of harm in them ; and, up to the death of our mother, or probably even later, she would take a hand at whist, cribbage, or bézique, playing for no stakes whatever.

She had a very strong sense of duty and the most rigid regard for truth, in which indeed she resembled all the members of her maternal stock. That she was affectionate in her family I have already said, and she had, besides, a rather unusual feeling of deference for 'the head of the family,' whoever he might be—my father, Dante Gabriel, and finally myself. This might be accounted rather Italian than English. With several people she was extremely friendly, and no one felt more strongly than she the Christian obligation of being at charity with all men. This she found in the long-run a pleasant duty ; but it had not been exactly in her nature from the first, as she was certainly born with a marked antipathy to anything which savoured of vulgarity or 'bumptiousness,' and with an instinctive disposition to 'hold her head high,' though not to assert herself in express terms. In Christina's character there was great dignity tempered—or rather indeed reinforced—by modesty ; and to this her bearing corresponded faithfully. I have already referred to her having been, and this from an early age, rather punctiliously polite ; and it may be that some persons who knew her

intellectual and literary standing in the eye of the world fancied that there
was something of affectation or even of sarcasm in this, which, however,
was not so. Her speech was often sprightly, or to some extent witty, as
well as still oftener simple, earnest, and grave—never abstract or argu-
mentative. She was replete with the spirit of self-postponement, which
passed into self-sacrifice whenever that quality was in demand. Such a
spirit is, in fact, the spirit of chivalry, and *noblesse oblige* might have been
her motto. Though shy, and even somewhat nervous, she was of unshaken
firmness, making up her mind pretty easily in any crisis of her life, and
abiding immovable. The narrow path was the only one for her, and a lion
in the same path made no difference. With firmness, she knew fortitude
also. A small point she was the first to concede ; but, as soon as a jot of
duty seemed involved in it, tenacity was in the very essence of her being.
A marked trait in her character was gratitude, a quality which she in-
herited from both her parents. For the slightest attention or service she
felt obliged ; and for anything of a serious kind, deeply and permanently
indebted. Although naturally of a rather indolent turn, disinclined to stick
to an occupation, and often better pleased to be doing nothing than anything, she acquired habits of much assiduity, and neglected no household
or other requirement which she perceived to have a claim upon her ; and
she was at once frugal and liberal. On self-indulgent luxuries, whether of
the table or the toilet or aught else, she spent practically nothing at any
period of life.

No precept of the Christian religion was more indelibly impressed upon
her mind and her sympathies than 'Judge not, that ye be not judged.'
She never—not even in thought, so far as thought was under her control—
imputed a bad motive to any one ; and to hear her talking scandal, or in-
dulging in ill-natured gossip, would have been equally impossible as to see
her putting on a pair of knickerbockers, or (as in Dante Gabriel's caricature
afore-mentioned) smashing the furniture. None the less she had a large fund
of discernment, and speedily fathomed defects in her acquaintances which
she never announced. Another text which she constantly bore in mind is
that one is not to do 'anything whereby thy brother stumbleth or is offended
or is made weak.' I have often thought that this trammelled her to some
extent in writing, for she was wont to construe the biblical precepts in a
very literal manner ; and that she would in some instances have expressed
herself with more latitude of thought and word, and to a more valuable
effect, but for the fear of saying something which would somehow turn to
the detriment of some timorous or dim-minded reader. She certainly felt
that to write anything for publication is to incur a great spiritual responsi-
bility.

This introduces us to what I regard as the one serious flaw in a
beautiful and admirable character—she was by far over-scrupulous. Scrupulosity may be a virtue : over-scrupulosity is at any rate a semi-virtue, but

it has, to my thinking, the full practical bearings of a defect. It is more befitting for a nunnery than for London streets. It weakens the mind, straitens the temperament and character, chills the impulse and the influence. Over-scrupulosity made Christina Rossetti shut up her mind to almost all things save the Bible, and the admonitions and ministrations of priests. To ponder for herself whether a thing was true or not ceased to be a part of her intellect. The only question was whether or not it conformed to the Bible, as viewed by Anglo-Catholicism. Her temperament and character, naturally warm and free, became 'a fountain sealed.' Not but that affection continued to flow in abundant measure, and the clear line of duty told out all the more apparent from receiving no side-lights. Impulse and *élan* were checked, both in act and in writing, but the most extreme spontaneity in poetic performance always remained. The influence of her work became intense for devout minds of a certain type, and for lovers of poetry in its pure essence; but for a great mass of readers, who might otherwise have been attracted and secured, the material proffered was too uniform and too restricted, and was too seldom concerned with breathing and diurnal actualities—never with rising currents of thought.

I must however guard myself here against being supposed to say, what a great number of critics and readers or half-readers have said before me, that Christina's poetry is 'morbid.' Morbid things are to be found in it—where are they not to be found? and the fact that her feelings and perceptions were coloured by an infirm physical condition has been already stated, and was inevitable. But I cannot acknowledge that, for a person who entertained the belief which Christina really and deeply did entertain —the professed belief of all Christians—there is anything morbid in saying that this present life is far from satisfactory, that death is the avenue to a different life, which will be of eternal duration and may be made of ineffable bliss, and that therefore death is a transition to be rather wished for than shunned. No one would regard as morbid a person who, during this mundane life, should elect to pass from a condition of serious distress into one of extreme and lasting happiness, at the cost of a few minutes of physical pain; and this is a contrast infinitely smaller than that between life on earth and the promised life in heaven. As Christina's faith in these things was of iron solidity, so was her attitude of mind, consequent upon her faith, logical and sound; and to speak of morbidity in relation to it seems a decided misapplication of the term. It is open to any of us not to believe in her premisses, and thus to dissent from her conclusion, but the real morbidity would be to reject her conclusion while we admit her premisses.

I have said elsewhere, but may as well repeat it here, that her habits of composition were entirely of the casual and spontaneous kind, from her earliest to her latest years. If something came into her head which she found suggestive of verse, she put it into verse. It came to her (I take it) very easily, without her meditating a possible subject, and without her making any great difference in the first from the latest form of the verses which embodied it; but *some* difference, with a view to right and fine detail of execution, she did of course make when needful. If the thing did not present itself before her, as something craving a vesture of verse at her hands, she did not write at all. What she wrote was pretty well known in the family as soon as her impeccably neat manuscript of it appeared in one of her little notebooks; but she did not show it about as an achievement, and still less had she, in the course of her work, invited any hint, counsel, or co-operation.

It may be asked—Did Christina Rossetti consider herself truly a poetess, and a good one? Truly a poetess, most decidedly yes; and, within the range of her subject and thought, and the limits of her executive endeavour, a good one. This did not make her in the least conceited or arrogant as regards herself, nor captious as to the work of others; but it did render her very resolute in setting a line of demarcation between a person who is a poet and another person who is a versifier. Pleadings *in misericordiam* were of no use with her, and she never could see any good reason why one who is not a poet should write in metre.

Christina was well versed in Italian and French; of German she knew some moderate amount; of Latin a mere smattering; Greek not at all. At no period of her life was she a great devourer of books, but the number of them which she had read in the course of her sixty-four years was necessarily considerable. Of science and philosophy she knew nothing, and to history she had no marked inclination; much more bias towards biography. Theology she studied, I think, very little indeed: there was the Bible, of which her knowledge was truly minute and ready, supplemented by the *Confessions* of Augustine and the *Imitation of Christ*. She also knew and liked *Pilgrim's Progress*. I question whether, apart from this one book of Augustine, she ever read any 'Father,' Latin or Greek, or desired to read him. To novel-reading she had no narrow-minded objection. Scott she certainly liked, and in early youth Dickens and Bulwer: Thackeray may have appeared to her too worldly and 'knowing,' but she understood his merits. She never, I think, looked into a book which was known or reputed to be 'improper,' and her acquaintance with French novels must have been extremely limited. Any such author as Rabelais would have been beyond measure repulsive to her—indeed, heartily despised as well as loathed; and Boccaccio, wherever he assimilates to a Rabelaisian side of things, would have shared the same fate. But it is certain to me that she never opened the pages of either. In poetry she was (need I say it?) capable of appreciating whatever is really good; and yet her affections, if not her perceptions, in poetry, were severely restricted. The one poet whom she really gloried in was Dante: next to him perhaps Homer, so far as she could estimate him in one or two English translations.

Tasso entranced her in girlhood, and perhaps retained a firm hold on her afterwards. Among very great authors, none (making allowance for Dante) seemed to appeal to her more than Plato: she read his *Dialogues* over and over again, with ever renewed or augmented zest. For Shakespear her intellectual reverence was of course very deep, but how far she delighted in him may be a different question. In tragedy, in feeling, in insight, in splendour of poetic expression, she must have known him supreme; but all the comic or 'Worldly Wiseman' side of Shakespear—except some bits of simple 'fun,' such as Dogberry and Verges—was certain to be distasteful to her. Humour, in its inner essence, she could enter into; but for any rollicking or cynical or unctuous aspect of humour she had no sort of relish. Sir Toby Belch and Falconbridge would simply repel her, and even Falstaff would find little indulgence and elicit only watery smiles. I say all this not as embodying any express remarks of hers, but because I understand her general habit of mind. Another great thing which she disliked was Milton's *Paradise Lost:* the only poems of his which she seems to me to have seriously loved were the sonnets. Among modern English poets, I should say that Shelley, or perhaps Coleridge, stood highest in her esteem; certainly not Wordsworth, whom she read scantily. As to Shelley, she can have known little beyond his lyrics; most of the long poems, as being 'impious,' remained unscanned. Tennyson she heartily enjoyed and admired, and Mrs. Browning; and Browning she honoured, without eager sympathy. The poems of William Morris were mostly unread by her—not unvalued. Of Swinburne she knew *Atalanta in Calydon*, and some few other things, including (I suppose) *Erechtheus;* and she regarded *Atalanta* as—what it is—a stupendous masterpiece. For one work by a poetess junior to herself she entertained an exceptional admiration—the tragic drama, *The Sentence* (relating to Caligula), by Augusta Webster. It would be possible to extend these remarks much, but here I may pause.

Christina had no politics; unless it be the rule 'Honesty is the best policy,' acting upon a constitution of mind much more conservative than inclined to change. In childhood she had, of course, through the influence and associations of her father, been nurtured in an atmosphere of bold political advance, tending to the revolutionary: this may have lingered with her as a kind of antidotal savour against conservatism, but hardly as a practical counterbalance. I do not think, however, that she ever viewed an Austrian—the bugbear of our early Italian environments—as quite on the same footing as men of other races. The two nations that she really liked, apart from those of the United Kingdom, were the Italians and the French. At the time of the great American war of secession, she was (like myself) a steady adversary of the slave-holders. As in politics, so in the fine arts of form—painting and sculpture—she had little fundamental opinion of her own, and no connoisseurship. She naturally adhered to what was high and noble in the arts, and would not have supposed that something inane and bad was good; but she neither possessed nor affected anything approaching to critical judgment in these matters. To music she was not insensitive; but she was ignorant, and it formed no part of her concern.

As to Christina Rossetti's poetry, I feel that it is my part rather to keep silence than to speak, especially when, as in the present instance, her poems are presented to the public, to be judged of as the public wills. I will however say thus much—that, fully conscious as I am of their limitations, I consider that on some grounds it is hardly possible to over-praise them. Her prose writings partake of the same qualities to a certain extent—of course a minor extent.

As I have given in my Preface a list of the volumes which have hitherto constituted her poems, I think it as well to add here a list of the prose volumes; and with that I terminate my summary account of a soul as pure, duteous, concentrated, loving, and devoted, as ever uttered itself in either prose or verse.

WILLIAM M. ROSSETTI.

LIST OF PROSE WORKS

1. Commonplace, and other Short Stories, 1870.
2. Annus Domini, a Prayer for each Day of the Year, 1874.
3. Speaking Likenesses, 1874.
4. Seek and Find, 1879.
5. Called to be Saints, 1881.
6. Letter and Spirit, 1883.
7. Time Flies, 1885.
8. The Face of the Deep, a Devotional Commentary on the Apocalypse, 1892.
9. Maude, 1897.

DEDICATORY SONNET

SONNETS are full of love, and this my tome
   Has many sonnets: so here now shall be
   One sonnet more, a love sonnet, from me
To her whose heart is my heart's quiet home,
   To my first Love, my Mother, on whose knee
I learnt love-lore that is not troublesome;
   Whose service is my special dignity,
And she my lodestar while I go and come.
And so because you love me, and because
   I love you, Mother, I have woven a wreath
     Of rhymes wherewith to crown your honoured name:
     In you not fourscore years can dim the flame
Of love, whose blessed glow transcends the laws
   Of time and change and mortal life and death.

Towards 1881.

THE LONGER POEMS

GOBLIN MARKET

Morning and evening
Maids heard the goblins cry:
'Come buy our orchard fruits,
Come buy, come buy:
Apples and quinces,
Lemons and oranges,
Plump unpecked cherries,
Melons and raspberries,
Bloom-down-cheeked peaches,
Swart-headed mulberries,
Wild free-born cranberries,
Crab-apples, dewberries,
Pine-apples, blackberries,
Apricots, strawberries;—
All ripe together
In summer weather,—
Morns that pass by,
Fair eves that fly;
Come buy, come buy:
Our grapes fresh from the vine,
Pomegranates full and fine,
Dates and sharp bullaces,
Rare pears and greengages,
Damsons and bilberries,
Taste them and try:
Currants and gooseberries,
Bright-fire-like barberries,
Figs to fill your mouth,
Citrons from the South,
Sweet to tongue and sound to eye;
Come buy, come buy.'

Evening by evening
Among the brookside rushes,
Laura bowed her head to hear,
Lizzie veiled her blushes:
Crouching close together
In the cooling weather,
With clasping arms and cautioning
    lips,
With tingling cheeks and finger tips.
'Lie close,' Laura said,
Pricking up her golden head:
'We must not look at goblin men,
We must not buy their fruits:
Who knows upon what soil they fed
Their hungry thirsty roots?'
'Come buy,' call the goblins
Hobbling down the glen.
'Oh,' cried Lizzie, 'Laura, Laura,
You should not peep at goblin men.'
Lizzie covered up her eyes,
Covered close lest they should look;
Laura reared her glossy head,
And whispered like the restless brook:
'Look, Lizzie, look, Lizzie,
Down the glen tramp little men.
One hauls a basket,
One bears a plate,
One lugs a golden dish
Of many pounds' weight.
How fair the vine must grow
Whose grapes are so luscious;
How warm the wind must blow
Through those fruit bushes.'

'No,' said Lizzie: 'No, no, no;
Their offers should not charm us,
Their evil gifts would harm us.'
She thrust a dimpled finger
In each ear, shut eyes and ran:
Curious Laura chose to linger
Wondering at each merchant man.
One had a cat's face,
One whisked a tail,
One tramped at a rat's pace,
One crawled like a snail,
One like a wombat prowled obtuse and furry,
One like a ratel tumbled hurry skurry.
She heard a voice like voice of doves
Cooing all together:
They sounded kind and full of loves
In the pleasant weather.

Laura stretched her gleaming neck
Like a rush-imbedded swan,
Like a lily from the beck,
Like a moonlit poplar branch,
Like a vessel at the launch
When its last restraint is gone.

Backwards up the mossy glen
Turned and trooped the goblin men,
With their shrill repeated cry,
'Come buy, come buy.'
When they reached where Laura was
They stood stock still upon the moss,
Leering at each other,
Brother with queer brother;
Signalling each other,
Brother with sly brother.
One set his basket down,
One reared his plate;
One began to weave a crown
Of tendrils, leaves, and rough nuts brown
(Men sell not such in any town);
One heaved the golden weight
Of dish and fruit to offer her:

'Come buy, come buy,' was still their cry.
Laura stared but did not stir,
Longed but had no money.
The whisk-tailed merchant bade her taste
In tones as smooth as honey,
The cat-faced purr'd,
The rat-paced spoke a word
Of welcome, and the snail-paced even was heard;
One parrot-voiced and jolly
Cried 'Pretty Goblin' still for 'Pretty Polly';
One whistled like a bird.

But sweet-tooth Laura spoke in haste:
'Good Folk, I have no coin;
To take were to purloin:
I have no copper in my purse,
I have no silver either,
And all my gold is on the furze
That shakes in windy weather
Above the rusty heather.'
'You have much gold upon your head,'
They answered all together:
'Buy from us with a golden curl.'
She clipped a precious golden lock,
She dropped a tear more rare than pearl,
Then sucked their fruit globes fair or red.
Sweeter than honey from the rock,
Stronger than man-rejoicing wine,
Clearer than water flowed that juice;
She never tasted such before,
How should it cloy with leng use?
She sucked and sucked and s the more
Fruits which that unknown or bore;

She sucked until her lips were sore ;
Then flung the emptied rinds away
But gathered up one kernel stone,
And knew not was it night or day
As she turned home alone.

Lizzie met her at the gate
Full of wise upbraidings :
' Dear, you should not stay so late,
Twilight is not good for maidens ;
Should not loiter in the glen
In the haunts of goblin men.
Do you not remember Jeanie,
How she met them in the moonlight,
Took their gifts both choice and many,
Ate their fruits and wore their flowers
Plucked from bowers
Where summer ripens at all hours ?
But ever in the noonlight
She pined and pined away ;
Sought them by night and day,
Found them no more, but dwindled and grew grey ;
Then fell with the first snow,
While to this day no grass will grow
Where she lies low :
I planted daisies there a year ago
That never blow.
You should not loiter so.'
' Nay, hush,' said Laura :
' Nay, hush, my sister :
I ate and ate my fill,
Yet my mouth waters still :
To-morrow night I will
Buy more ;' and kissed her.
' Have done with sorrow ;
I'll bring you plums to-morrow
Fresh on their mother twigs,
Cherries worth getting ;
You cannot think what figs
My teeth have met in,
What melons icy-cold

Piled on a dish of gold
Too huge for me to hold,
What peaches with a velvet nap,
Pellucid grapes without one seed :
Odorous indeed must be the mead
Whereon they grow, and pure the wave they drink
With lilies at the brink,
And sugar-sweet their sap.'

Golden head by golden head,
Like two pigeons in one nest
Folded in each other's wings,
They lay down in their curtained bed :
Like two blossoms on one stem,
Like two flakes of new-fall'n snow,
Like two wands of ivory
Tipped with gold for awful kings.
Moon and stars gazed in at them,
Wind sang to them lullaby,
Lumbering owls forebore to fly,
Not a bat flapped to and fro
Round their nest :
Cheek to cheek and breast to breast
Locked together in one nest.

Early in the morning
When the first cock crowed his warning,
Neat like bees, as sweet and busy,
Laura rose with Lizzie :
Fetched in honey, milked the cows,
Aired and set to rights the house,
Kneaded cakes of whitest wheat,
Cakes for dainty mouths to eat,
Next churned butter, whipped up cream,
Fed their poultry, sat and sewed ;
Talked as modest maidens should :
Lizzie with an open heart,
Laura in an absent dream,
One content, one sick in part ;

One warbling for the mere bright
   day's delight,
One longing for the night.

At length slow evening came:
They went with pitchers to the
   reedy brook;
Lizzie most placid in her look,
Laura most like a leaping flame.
They drew the gurgling water from
   its deep.
Lizzie plucked purple and rich
   golden flags,
Then turning homeward said: 'The
   sunset flushes
Those furthest loftiest crags;
Come, Laura, not another maiden
   lags.
No wilful squirrel wags,
The beasts and birds are fast asleep.'
But Laura loitered still among the
   rushes,
And said the bank was steep.

And said the hour was early still,
The dew not fall'n, the wind not
   chill;
Listening ever, but not catching
The customary cry,
'Come buy, come buy,'
With its iterated jingle
Of sugar-baited words:
Not for all her watching
Once discerning even one goblin
Racing, whisking, tumbling, hob-
   bling—
Let alone the herds
That used to tramp along the glen,
In groups or single,
Of brisk fruit-merchant men.

Till Lizzie urged, 'O Laura, come;
I hear the fruit-call, but I dare not
   look:
You should not loiter longer at this
   brook:
Come with me home.
The stars rise, the moon bends her
   arc,
Each glow-worm winks her spark,
Let us get home before the night
   grows dark:
For clouds may gather
Though this is summer weather,
Put out the lights and drench us
   through;
Then if we lost our way what should
   we do?'

Laura turned cold as stone
To find her sister heard that cry
   alone,
That goblin cry,
'Come buy our fruits, come buy.'
Must she then buy no more such
   dainty fruit?
Must she no more such succous
   pasture find,
Gone deaf and blind?
Her tree of life drooped from the
   root:
She said not one word in her heart's
   sore ache:
But peering thro' the dimness,
   nought discerning,
Trudged home, her pitcher dripping
   all the way;
So crept to bed, and lay
Silent till Lizzie slept;
Then sat up in a passionate yearning,
And gnashed her teeth for balked
   desire, and wept
As if her heart would break.

Day after day, night after nigh.
Laura kept watch in vain
In sullen silence of exceeding

She never caught again the goblin
  cry,
'Come buy, come buy;'—
She never spied the goblin men
Hawking their fruits along the glen:
But when the noon waxed bright
Her hair grew thin and grey;
She dwindled, as the fair full moon
  doth turn
To swift decay and burn
Her fire away.

One day remembering her kernel-
  stone
She set it by a wall that faced the
  south;
Dewed it with tears, hoped for a
  root,
Watched for a waxing shoot,
But there came none.
It never saw the sun,
It never felt the trickling moisture
  run:
While with sunk eyes and faded
  mouth
She dreamed of melons, as a
  traveller sees
False waves in desert drouth
With shade of leaf-crowned trees,
And burns the thirstier in the sand-
  ful breeze.

She no more swept the house,
Tended the fowls or cows,
Fetched honey, kneaded cakes of
  wheat,
Brought water from the brook:
But sat down listless in the chimney-
  nook
And would not eat.

Tender Lizzie could not bear
To watch her sister's cankerous care,
Yet not to share.

She night and morning
Caught the goblins' cry:
'Come buy our orchard fruits,
Come buy, come buy:'—
Beside the brook, along the glen,
She heard the tramp of goblin men,
The voice and stir
Poor Laura could not hear;
Longed to buy fruit to comfort her,
But feared to pay too dear.
She thought of Jeanie in her grave,
Who should have been a bride;
But who for joys brides hope to have
Fell sick and died
In her gay prime,
In earliest winter time,
With the first glazing rime,
With the first snow-fall of crisp
  winter time.

Till Laura dwindling
Seemed knocking at Death's door.
Then Lizzie weighed no more
Better and worse;
But put a silver penny in her purse,
Kissed Laura, crossed the heath
  with clumps of furze
At twilight, halted by the brook:
And for the first time in her life
Began to listen and look.

Laughed every goblin
When they spied her peeping:
Came towards her hobbling,
Flying, running, leaping,
Puffing and blowing,
Chuckling, clapping, crowing,
Clucking and gobbling,
Mopping and mowing,
Full of airs and graces,
Pulling wry faces,
Demure grimaces,
Cat-like and rat-like,
Ratel- and wombat-like,

Snail-paced in a hurry,
Parrot-voiced and whistler,
Helter skelter, hurry skurry,
Chattering like magpies,
Fluttering like pigeons,
Gliding like fishes,—
Hugged her and kissed her:
Squeezed and caressed her:
Stretched up their dishes,
Panniers, and plates:
'Look at our apples
Russet and dun,
Bob at our cherries,
Bite at our peaches,
Citrons and dates,
Grapes for the asking,
Pears red with basking
Out in the sun,
Plums on their twigs;
Pluck them and suck them,—
Pomegranates, figs.'

'Good folk,' said Lizzie,
Mindful of Jeanie:
'Give me much and many:'
Held out her apron,
Tossed them her penny.
'Nay, take a seat with us,
Honour and eat with us,'
They answered grinning:
'Our feast is but beginning.
Night yet is early,
Warm and dew-pearly,
Wakeful and starry:
Such fruits as these
No man can carry;
Half their bloom would fly,
Half their dew would dry,
Half their flavour would pass by.
Sit down and feast with us,
Be welcome guest with us,
Cheer you and rest with us.'—
'Thank you,' said Lizzie: 'But one
  waits

At home alone for me:
So without further parleying,
If you will not sell me any
Of your fruits though much and many,
Give me back my silver penny
I tossed you for a fee.'—
They began to scratch their pates,
No longer wagging, purring,
But visibly demurring,
Grunting and snarling.
One called her proud,
Cross-grained, uncivil;
Their tones waxed loud,
Their looks were evil.
Lashing their tails
They trod and hustled her,
Elbowed and jostled her,
Clawed with their nails,
Barking, mewing, hissing, mocking,
Tore her gown and soiled her
  stocking,
Twitched her hair out by the roots,
Stamped upon her tender feet,
Held her hands and squeezed their
  fruits
Against her mouth to make her eat.

White and golden Lizzie stood,
Like a lily in a flood,—
Like a rock of blue-veined stone
Lashed by tides obstreperously,—
Like a beacon left alone
In a hoary roaring sea,
Sending up a golden fire,—
Like a fruit-crowned orange-tree
White with blossoms honey-sweet
Sore beset by wasp and bee,—
Like a royal virgin town
Topped with gilded dome and sp
Close beleaguered by a fleet
Mad to tug her standard down.

One may lead a horse to water,
Twenty cannot make him drink.

Though the goblins cuffed and caught her,
Coaxed and fought her,
Bullied and besought her,
Scratched her, pinched her black as ink,
Kicked and knocked her,
Mauled and mocked her,
Lizzie uttered not a word;
Would not open lip from lip
Lest they should cram a mouthful in:
But laughed in heart to feel the drip
Of juice that syruped all her face,
And lodged in dimples of her chin,
And streaked her neck which quaked like curd.
At last the evil people,
Worn out by her resistance,
Flung back her penny, kicked their fruit
Along whichever road they took,
Not leaving root or stone or shoot;
Some writhed into the ground,
Some dived into the brook
With ring and ripple,
Some scudded on the gale without a sound,
Some vanished in the distance.

In a smart, ache, tingle,
Lizzie went her way;
Knew not was it night or day;
Sprang up the bank, tore thro' the furze,
Threaded copse and dingle,
And heard her penny jingle
Bouncing in her purse,—
Its bounce was music to her ear.
She ran and ran
As if she feared some goblin man
Dogged her with gibe or curse
Or something worse:
But not one goblin skurried after,
Nor was she pricked by fear;

The kind heart made her windy-paced
That urged her home quite out of breath with haste
And inward laughter.

She cried, 'Laura,' up the garden,
'Did you miss me?
Come and kiss me.
Never mind my bruises,
Hug me, kiss me, suck my juices
Squeezed from goblin fruits for you,
Goblin pulp and goblin dew.
Eat me, drink me, love me;
Laura, make much of me;
For your sake I have braved the glen
And had to do with goblin merchant men.'

Laura started from her chair,
Flung her arms up in the air,
Clutched her hair:
'Lizzie, Lizzie, have you tasted
For my sake the fruit forbidden?
Must your light like mine be hidden,
Your young life like mine be wasted,
Undone in mine undoing,
And ruined in my ruin,
Thirsty, cankered, goblin-ridden?'—
She clung about her sister,
Kissed and kissed and kissed her:
Tears once again
Refreshed her shrunken eyes,
Dropping like rain
After long sultry drouth;
Shaking with aguish fear, and pain,
She kissed and kissed her with a hungry mouth.

Her lips began to scorch,
That juice was wormwood to her tongue,
She loathed the feast:
Writhing as one possessed she leaped and sung,
Rent all her robe, and wrung

Her hands in lamentable haste,
And beat her breast.
Her locks streamed like the torch
Borne by a racer at full speed,
Or like the mane of horses in their flight,
Or like an eagle when she stems the light
Straight toward the sun,
Or like a caged thing freed,
Or like a flying flag when armies run.

Swift fire spread through her veins, knocked at her heart,
Met the fire smouldering there
And overbore its lesser flame;
She gorged on bitterness without a name:
Ah fool, to choose such part
Of soul-consuming care!
Sense failed in the mortal strife:
Like the watch-tower of a town
Which an earthquake shatters down,
Like a lightning-stricken mast,
Like a wind-uprooted tree
Spun about,
Like a foam-topped waterspout
Cast down headlong in the sea,
She fell at last;
Pleasure past and anguish past,
Is it death or is it life?

Life out of death.
That night long Lizzie watched by her,
Counted her pulse's flagging stir,
Felt for her breath,
Held water to her lips, and cooled her face
With tears and fanning leaves.
But when the first birds chirped about their eaves,
And early reapers plodded to the place
Of golden sheaves,
And dew-wet grass
Bowed in the morning winds so brisk to pass,
And new buds with new day
Opened of cup-like lilies on the stream,
Laura awoke as from a dream,
Laughed in the innocent old way,
Hugged Lizzie but not twice or thrice;
Her gleaming locks showed not one thread of grey,
Her breath was sweet as May,
And light danced in her eyes.

Days, weeks, months, years
Afterwards, when both were wives
With children of their own;
Their mother-hearts beset with fears,
Their lives bound up in tender lives;
Laura would call the little ones
And tell them of her early prime,
Those pleasant days long gone
Of not-returning time:
Would talk about the haunted glen,
The wicked quaint fruit-merchant men,
Their fruits like honey to the throat
But poison in the blood
(Men sell not such in any town):
Would tell them how her sister stood
In deadly peril to do her good,
And win the fiery antidote:
Then joining hands to little hands
Would bid them cling together,—
'For there is no friend like a sister
In calm or stormy weather;
To cheer one on the tedious way,
To fetch one if one goes astray,
To lift one if one totters down,
To strengthen whilst one stands.'

27 April 1859.

REPINING

SHE sat alway through the long day
Spinning the weary thread away;
And ever said in undertone,
'Come, that I be no more alone.'

From early dawn to set of sun
Working, her task was still undone;
And the long thread seemed to in-
 crease
Even while she spun and did not
 cease.
She heard the gentle turtle-dove
Tell to its mate a tale of love;
She saw the glancing swallows fly,
Ever a social company;
She knew each bird upon its nest
Had cheering songs to bring it rest;
None lived alone save only she:—
The wheel went round more wearily;
She wept and said in undertone,
'Come, that I be no more alone.'

Day followed day and still she sighed
For love, and was not satisfied;
Until one night, when the moonlight
Turned all the trees to silver-white,
She heard, what ne'er she heard be-
 fore,
A steady hand undo the door.
The nightingale since set of sun
Her throbbing music had not done,
And she had listened silently;
But now the wind had changed, and
 she
Heard the sweet song no more, but
 heard
Beside her bed a whispered word:
'Damsel, rise up; be not afraid;
For I am come at last,' it said.

She trembled, though the voice was
 mild;
She trembled like a frightened
 child;—
Till she looked up, and then she saw
The unknown speaker without awe.
He seemed a fair young man, his eyes
Beaming with serious charities;
His cheek was white but hardly
 pale;
And a dim glory like a veil
Hovered about his head, and shone
Through the whole room till night
 was gone.

So her fear fled; and then she said,
Leaning upon her quiet bed:
'Now thou art come, I prythee stay,
That I may see thee in the day,
And learn to know thy voice, and
 hear
It evermore calling me near.'

He answered, 'Rise and follow me.'
But she looked upwards wonderingly:
'And whither wouldst thou go,
 friend? stay
Until the dawning of the day.'
But he said: 'The wind ceaseth,
 Maid;
Of chill nor damp be thou afraid.'

She bound her hair up from the
 floor,
And passed in silence from the door.

So they went forth together, he
Helping her forward tenderly.
The hedges bowed beneath his
 hand;
Forth from the streams came the
 dry land
As they passed over; evermore
The pallid moonbeams shone before;
And the wind hushed, and nothing
 stirred;

Not even a solitary bird,
Scared by their footsteps, fluttered by
Where aspen-trees stood steadily.

As they went on, at length a sound
Came trembling on the air around;
The undistinguishable hum
Of life, voices that go and come
Of busy men, and the child's sweet
High laugh, and noise of trampling
    feet.

Then he said, 'Wilt thou go and
    see?'
And she made answer joyfully:
'The noise of life, of human life,
Of dear communion without strife,
Of converse held 'twixt friend and
    friend;
Is it not here our path shall end?'
He led her on a little way
Until they reached a hillock: 'Stay.'

It was a village in a plain.
High mountains screened it from the
    rain
And stormy wind; and nigh at hand
A bubbling streamlet flowed o'er
    sand
Pebbly and fine, and sent life up
Green succous stalk and flower-cup.

Gradually, day's harbinger,
A chilly wind began to stir.
It seemed a gentle powerless breeze
That scarcely rustled through the
    trees;
And yet it touched the mountain's
    head
And the paths man might never
    tread.
But hearken: in the quiet weather
Do all the streams flow down to-
    gether?—

No, 'tis a sound more terrible
Than though a thousand rivers fell.
The everlasting ice and snow
Were loosened then, but not to flow;—
With a loud crash like solid thunder
The avalanche came, burying under
The village; turning life and breath
And rest and joy and plans to
    death.

'Oh let us fly, for pity fly!
Let us go hence, friend, thou and I.
There must be many regions yet
Where these things make not
    desolate.'

He looked upon her seriously;
Then said: 'Arise and follow me.'
The path that lay before them was
Nigh covered over with long grass;
And many slimy things and slow
Trailed on between the roots below.
The moon looked dimmer than
    before;
And shadowy cloudlets floating o'er
Its face sometimes quite hid its light,
And filled the skies with deeper night.

At last, as they went on, the noise
Was heard of the sea's mighty voice;
And soon the ocean could be seen
In its long restlessness serene.
Upon its breast a vessel rode
That drowsily appeared to nod
As the great billows rose and fell,
And swelled to sink, and sank to
    swell.

Meanwhile the strong wind had
    come forth
From the chill regions of the North,
The mighty wind invisible.
And the low waves began to swell;
And the sky darkened overhead;

And the moon once looked forth,
    then fled
Behind dark clouds; while here and
    there
The lightning shone out in the air,
And the approaching thunder rolled
With angry pealings manifold.
How many vows were made, and
    prayers
That in safe times were cold and
    scarce!
Still all availed not; and at length
The waves arose in all their strength,
And fought against the ship, and
    filled
The ship.   Then were the clouds
    unsealed,
And the rain hurried forth, and beat
On every side and over it.

Some clung together, and some kept
A long stern silence, and some wept.
Many half crazed looked on in
    wonder
As the strong timbers rent asunder;
Friends forgot friends, foes fled to
    foes ;—
And still the water rose and rose.

'Ah woe is me! Whom I have seen
Are now as though they had not been.
In the earth there is room for birth,
And there are graves enough in
    earth ;
Why should the cold sea, tempest-
    torn,
Bury those whom it hath not borne?'

        ered not, and they went on.
        y of the heavens was gone;
        m gleamed not nor any star ;
        ds were rustling near and far,
        n the trees the dry leaves fell
        sad sound unspeakable.

The air was cold; till from the South
A gust blew hot, like sudden drouth,
Into their faces; and a light,
Glowing and red, shone through the
    night.

A mighty city full of flame
And death and sounds without a
    name.
Amid the black and blinding smoke,
The people, as one man, awoke.
Oh happy they who yesterday
On the long journey went away!
Whose pallid lips, smiling and chill,
While the flames scorch them smile
    on still ;
Who murmur not, who tremble not
When the bier crackles fiery hot ;
Who dying said in love's increase,
' Lord, let thy servant part in peace.'

Those in the town could see and hear
A shaded river flowing near ;
The broad deep bed could hardly
    hold
Its plenteous waters calm and cold.
Was flame-wrapt all the city wall,
The city gates were flame-wrapt all.

What was man's strength, what
    puissance then ?
Women were mighty as strong men.
Some knelt in prayer, believing still,
Resigned into a righteous will,
Bowing beneath the chastening rod,
Lost to the world, but found of
    God.
Some prayed for friend, for child,
    for wife ;
Some prayed for faith; some prayed
    for life ;
While some, proud even in death,
    hope gone,
Steadfast and still, stood looking on.

'Death—death—oh let us fly from
   death!
Where'er we go it followeth;
All these are dead; and we alone
Remain to weep for what is gone.
What is this thing? thus hurriedly
To pass into eternity;
To leave the earth so full of mirth;
To lose the profit of our birth;
To die and be no more; to cease,
Having numbness that is not peace.
Let us go hence; and, even if thus
Death everywhere must go with us,
Let us not see the change, but see
Those who have been or still shall be.'

He sighed, and they went on together.
Beneath their feet did the grass
   wither;
Across the heaven high overhead
Dark misty clouds floated and fled;
And in their bosom was the thunder,
And angry lightnings flashed out
   under,
Forked and red and menacing;
Far off the wind was muttering;
It seemed to tell, not understood,
Strange secrets to the listening
   wood.

Upon its wings it bore the scent
Of blood of a great armament:
Then saw they how on either side
Fields were down-trodden far and
   wide.
That morning at the break of day
Two nations had gone forth to slay.

As a man soweth so he reaps.
The field was full of bleeding heaps;
Ghastly corpses of men and horses
That met death at a thousand sources;
Cold limbs and putrefying flesh;
Long love-locks clotted to a mesh
That stifled: stiffened mouths be-
   neath
Staring eyes that had looked on death.

But these were dead: these felt no
   more
The anguish of the wounds they bore.
Behold, they shall not sigh again,
Nor justly fear, nor hope in vain.
'What if none wept above them?—is
The sleeper less at rest for this?
Is not the young child's slumber sweet
When no man watcheth over it?

These had deep calm; but all around
There was a deadly smothered soun
The choking cry of agony
From wounded men who could not
   die;
Who watched the black wing of the
   raven
Rise like a cloud 'twixt them and
   heaven,
And in the distance flying fast
Beheld the eagle come at last.

She knelt down in her agony.
'O Lord, it is enough,' said she:
'My heart's prayer putteth me to
   shame;
Let me return to whence I came.
Thou who for love's sake didst re-
   prove,
Forgive me for the sake of love.'
December 1847.

THREE NUNS

I

Sospira questo core,
E non so dir perchè.

SHADOW, shadow on the wall,
   Spread thy shelter over me;

Wrap me with a heavy pall,
  With the dark that none may see:
Fold thyself around me, come;
Shut out all the troublesome
Noise of life; I would be dumb.

Shadow, thou hast reached my feet;
  Rise and cover up my head;
Be my stainless winding-sheet,
  Buried before I am dead.
Lay thy cool upon my breast:
Once I thought that joy was best,
Now I only care for rest.

By the grating of my cell
  Sings a solitary bird;
Sweeter than the vesper bell,
  Sweetest song was ever heard.[1]
Sing upon thy living tree;
Happy echoes answer thee;
Happy songster, sing to me.

When my yellow hair was curled,
  Though men saw and called me fair,
I was weary in the world
  Full of vanity and care.
Gold was left behind, curls shorn,
When I came here; that same morn
Made a bride no gems adorn.

Here wrapt in my spotless veil,
  Curtained from intruding eyes,
I whom prayers and fasts turn pale
  Wait the flush of Paradise.
But the vigil is so long
My heart sickens:—sing thy song,
  e bird that canst do no wrong.

  on, making me forget
  esent sorrow and past sin.

      "Sweetest eyes were ever seen."
                E. B. BROWNING.

Sing a little longer yet:
  Soon the matins will begin;
And I must turn back again
To that aching, worse than pain,—
I must bear and not complain.

Sing; that in thy song I may
  Dream myself once more a child
In the green woods far away,
  Plucking clematis and wild
Hyacinths, till pleasure grew
Tired, yet so was pleasure too,
Resting with no work to do.

In the thickest of the wood
  I remember long ago
How a stately oaktree stood
  With a sluggish pool below
Almost shadowed out of sight;
On the waters dark as night
Water-lilies lay like light.

There, while yet a child, I thought
  I could live as in a dream;
Secret, neither found not sought;
  Till the lilies on the stream,
Pure as virgin purity,
Would seem scarce too pure for me:—
Ah but that can never be!

II

    Sospirerà d' amore,
    Ma non lo dice a me.

I loved him; yes, where was the sin?
  I loved him with my heart and soul;
    But I pressed forward to no goal,
There was no prize I strove to win.
Show me my sin that I may see:
Throw the first stone, thou Pharisee.

I loved him, but I never sought
  That he should know that I was fair.

I prayed for him; was my sin
    prayer?
I sacrificed, he never bought;
He nothing gave, he nothing took;
We never bartered look for look.

My voice rose in the sacred choir,
    The choir of nuns: do you condemn
    Even if when kneeling among
        them
Faith, zeal, and love, kindled a fire,
And I prayed for his happiness
Who knew not? was my error this?

I only prayed that in the end
    His trust and hope may not be
        vain;
    I prayed not we may meet again:
I would not let our names ascend,
No not to Heaven, in the same
        breath;
Nor will I join the two in death.

Oh sweet is death, for I am weak
    And weary, and it giveth rest.
The crucifix lies on my breast,
And all night long it seems to speak
Of rest; I hear it through my sleep,
And the great comfort makes me
    weep.

Oh sweet is death that bindeth up
    The broken and the bleeding
        heart.
    The draught chilled, but a cordial
        part
Lurked at the bottom of the cup;
And for my patience will my Lord
Give an exceeding great reward.

Yea the reward is almost won,
    A crown of glory and a palm.

Soon I shall sing the unknown
    psalm;
Soon gaze on light, not on the sun;
And soon with surer faith shall pray
For him, and cease not night nor
    day.

My life is breaking like a cloud—
    God judgeth not as man doth
        judge—
    Nay, bear with me: you need not
        grudge
This peace; the vows that I have
    vowed
Have all been kept: Eternal Strength
Holds me, though mine own fails at
    length.

Bury me in the Convent-ground
    Among the flowers that are so
        sweet;
    And lay a green turf at my feet,
Where thick trees cast a gloom
    around;
At my head let a cross be, white
Through the long blackness of the
    night.

Now kneel and pray beside my bed
    That I may sleep being free from
        pain;
    And pray that I may wake again
After His likeness who hath said
(Faithful is He who promiseth)
We shall be satisfied therewith.

III

Rispondimi, cor mio,
    Perchè sospiri tu?
Risponde: Voglio Dio,
    Sospiro per Gesù.

My heart is as a freeborn bird
    Caged in my cruel breast,

That flutters, flutters evermore,
  Nor sings nor is at rest,
But beats against the prison bars,
  As knowing its own nest
Far off beyond the clouded west.

My soul is as a hidden fount
  Shut in by clammy clay
That struggles with an upward moan,
  Striving to force its way
Up through the turf, over the grass,
  Up up into the day
Where twilight no more turneth grey.

Oh for the grapes of the True Vine
  Growing in Paradise,
Whose tendrils join the Tree of Life
  To that which maketh wise—
Growing beside the Living Well
  Whose sweetest waters rise
Where tears are wiped from tearful
    eyes!

Oh for the waters of that Well
  Round which the Angels stand—
Oh for the Shadow of the Rock
  On my heart's weary land—
Oh for the Voice to guide me when
  I turn to either hand,
Guiding me till I reach heaven's
    strand!

Thou world from which I am come
    out,
  Keep all thy gems and gold;
Keep thy delights and precious
    things,
  Thou that art waxing old.
My heart shall beat with a new life
  When thine is dead and cold;
When thou dost fear I shall be bold.

When Earth shall pass away with all
  Her pride and pomp of sin,

The City builded without hands
  Shall safely shut me in.
All the rest is but vanity
  Which others strive to win:
Where their hopes end my joys
    begin.

I will not look upon a rose
  Though it is fair to see:
The flowers planted in Paradise
  Are budding now for me:
Red roses like love visible
  Are blowing on their tree,
Or white like virgin purity.

I will not look unto the sun
  Which setteth night by night:
In the untrodden courts of heaven
  My crown shall be more bright.
Lo in the New Jerusalem
  Founded and built aright
My very feet shall tread on light.

With foolish riches of this world
  I have bought treasure where
Nought perisheth: for this white
    veil
  I gave my golden hair;
I gave the beauty of my face
  For vigils, fasts, and prayer;
I gave all for this cross I bear.

My heart trembled when first I took
  The vows which must be kept.
At first it was a weariness
  To watch when once I slept:
The path was rough and sharp with
    thorns;
  My feet bled as I stept;
The cross was heavy and I wept.

While still the names rang in mine
    ears
  Of daughter, sister, wife,

The outside world still looked so
    fair
  To my weak eyes, and rife
With beauty, my heart almost failed;
  Then in the desperate strife
I prayed, as one who prays for life,—

Until I grew to love what once
  Had been so burdensome.
So now, when I am faint because
  Hope deferred seems to numb
My heart, I yet can plead, and say,
  Although my lips are dumb—
The Spirit and the Bride say, Come.
12 *February* 1849 to 10 *May* 1850.

THE LOWEST ROOM

LIKE flowers sequestered from the
    sun
  And wind of summer, day by day
I dwindled paler, whilst my hair
  Showed the first tinge of grey.

'Oh what is life, that we should
    live?
  Or what is death, that we must
    die?
A bursting bubble is our life:
  I also, what am I?'

'What is your grief? now tell me,
    sweet,
  That I may grieve,' my sister
    said;
And stayed a white embroidering
    hand
  And raised a golden head:

Her tresses showed a richer mass,
  Her eyes looked softer than my
    own;
Her figure had a statelier height,
  Her voice a tenderer tone.

'Some must be second and not first;
  All cannot be the first of all:
Is not this too but vanity?
  I stumble like to fall.

'So yesterday I read the acts
  Of Hector and each clangorous
    king
With wrathful great Æacides:—
  Old Homer leaves a sting.'

The comely face looked up again,
  The deft hand lingered on the
    thread.
'Sweet, tell me what is Homer's
    sting,
  Old Homer's sting,' she said.

'He stirs my sluggish pulse like
    wine,
  He melts me like the wind of spice,
Strong as strong Ajax' red right
    hand,
  And grand like Juno's eyes.

'I cannot melt the sons of men,
  I cannot fire and tempest-toss:—
Besides, those days were golden days,
  Whilst these are days of dross.'

She laughed a feminine low laugh,
  Yet did not stay her dexterous
    hand:
'Now tell me of those days,' she
    said,
  'When time ran golden sand.'

'Then men were men of might and
    right,
  Sheer might, at least, and weighty
    swords:
Then men in open blood and fire
  Bore witness to their words—

'Crest-rearing kings with whistling
　　spears;
But if these shivered in the shock
They wrenched up hundred-rooted
　　trees,
　　Or hurled the effacing rock.

'Then hand to hand, then foot to
　　foot,
　　Stern to the death-grip grappling
　　　then,
Who ever thought of gunpowder
　　Amongst these men of men?

'They knew whose hand struck home
　　the death,
They knew who broke but would
　　not bend,
Could venerate an equal foe
　　And scorn a laggard friend.

'Calm in the utmost stress of doom,
　　Devout toward adverse powers
　　　above,
They hated with intenser hate
　　And loved with fuller love.

'Then heavenly beauty could allay
　　As heavenly beauty stirred the
　　　strife:
By them a slave was worshipped
　　more
　　Than is by us a wife.'

She laughed again, my sister laughed;
　　Made answer o'er the laboured
　　　cloth,
'I rather would be one of us
　　Than wife, or slave, or both.'

'Oh better then be slave or wife
　　Than fritter now blank life away:
Then night had holiness of night,
　　And day was sacred day.

'The princess laboured at her loom,
　　Mistress and handmaiden alike;
Beneath their needles grew the field
　　With warriors armed to strike.

'Or, look again, dim Dian's face
　　Gleamed perfect through the at-
　　　tendant night;
Were such not better than those
　　holes
　　Amid that waste of white?

'A shame it is, our aimless life;
　　I rather from my heart would feed
From silver dish in gilded stall
　　With wheat and wine the steed,

'The faithful steed that bore my lord
　　In safety through the hostile land,
The faithful steed that arched his
　　neck
　　To fondle with my hand.'

Her needle erred; a moment's pause,
　　A moment's patience, all was well.
Then she: 'But just suppose the
　　horse,
　　Suppose the rider fell?

'Then captive in an alien house,
　　Hungering on exile's bitter
　　　bread,—
They happy, they who won the lot
　　Of sacrifice,' she said.

Speaking she faltered, while her look
　　Showed forth her passion like a
　　　glass;
With hand suspended, kindling eye,
　　Flushed cheek, how fair she
　　　was!

'Ah well, be those the days of dross;
　　This, if you will, the age of gold:

Yet had those days a spark of warmth,
  While these are somewhat cold—

'Are somewhat mean and cold and slow,
  Are stunted from heroic growth:
We gain but little when we prove
  The worthlessness of both.'

'But life is in our hands,' she said:
  'In our own hands for gain or loss:
Shall not the Sevenfold Sacred Fire
  Suffice to purge our dross?

'Too short a century of dreams,
  One day of work sufficient length;
Why should not you, why should not I,
  Attain heroic strength?

'Our life is given us as a blank;
  Ourselves must make it blest or curst:
Who dooms me I shall only be
  The second, not the first?

'Learn from old Homer, if you will,
  Such wisdom as his books have said:
In one the acts of Ajax shine,
  In one of Diomed.

'Honoured all heroes whose high deeds
  Through life, through death, enlarge their span;
Only Achilles in his rage
  And sloth is less than man.'

'Achilles only less than man?
  He less than man who, half a god,
Discomfited all Greece with rest,
  Cowed Ilion with a nod?

'He offered vengeance, lifelong grief
  To one dear ghost, uncounted price:
Beasts, Trojans, adverse gods, himself,
  Heaped up the sacrifice.

'Self-immolated to his friend,
  Shrined in world's wonder, Homer's page,
Is this the man, the less than men
  Of this degenerate age?'

'Gross from his acorns, tusky boar
  Does memorable acts like his;
So for her snared offended young
  Bleeds the swart lioness.'

But here she paused; our eyes had met,
  And I was whitening with the jeer;
She rose; 'I went too far,' she said;
  Spoke low; 'Forgive me, dear.

'To me our days seem pleasant days,
  Our home a haven of pure content;
Forgive me if I said too much,
  So much more than I meant.

'Homer, though greater than his gods,
  With rough-hewn virtues was sufficed
And rough-hewn men: but what are such
  To us who learn of Christ?'

The much-moved pathos of
  Her almost tearful eyes,
Grown pale, confessed the of love
  Which only made he

For mild she was, of few soft
    words,
Most gentle, easy to be led,
Content to listen when I spoke
    And reverence what I said ;

I elder sister by six years ;
    Not half so glad, or wise, or
        good :
Her words rebuked my secret self
    And shamed me where I stood.

She never guessed her words re-
    proved
A silent envy nursed within,
A selfish, souring discontent,
    Pride-born, the devil's sin.

I smiled, half bitter, half in jest :
    'The wisest man of all the wise
Left for his summary of life
    "Vanity of vanities."

'Beneath the sun there's nothing
    new :
Men flow, men ebb, mankind
    flows on :
If I am wearied of my life,
    Why so was Solomon.

'Vanity of vanities he preached
    Of all he found, of all he sought :
Vanities of vanities, the gist
    Of all the words he taught.

'This in the wisdom of the world,
    In Homer's page, in all, we find :
As the sea is not filled, so yearns
    Man's universal mind.

'This Homer felt, who gave his men
    With glory but a transient state :
His very Jove could not reverse
    Irrevocable fate.

'Uncertain all their lot save this—
    Who wins must lose, who lives
        must die :
All trodden out into the dark
    Alike, all vanity.'

She scarcely answered when I paused
    But rather to herself said : 'One
Is here,' low-voiced and loving, 'yea,
    Greater than Solomon.'

So both were silent, she and I :
    She laid her work aside, and went
Into the garden-walks, like Spring,
    All gracious with content ;

A little graver than her wont,
    Because her words had fretted me ;
Not warbling quite her merriest tune
    Bird-like from tree to tree.

I chose a book to read and dream :
    Yet half the while with furtive eyes
Marked how she made her choice of
    flowers
    Intuitively wise,

And ranged them with instinctive
    taste
Which all my books had failed to
    teach ;
Fresh rose herself, and daintier
    Than blossom of the peach.

By birthright higher than myself,
    Though nestling of the self-same
        nest :
No fault of hers, no fault of mine,
    But stubborn to digest.

I watched her, till my book unmarked
    Slid noiseless to the velvet floor ;
Till all the opulent summer-world
    Looked poorer than before.

Just then her busy fingers ceased,
  Her fluttered colour went and
    came:
I knew whose step was on the walk,
  Whose voice would name her
    name.

   *   *   *   *   *

Well, twenty years have passed since
    then:
  My sister now, a stately wife
Still fair, looks back in peace and sees
    The longer half of life—

The longer half of prosperous life,
  With little grief, or fear, or fret:
She, loved and loving long ago,
  Is loved and loving yet.

A husband honourable, brave,
  Is her main wealth in all the world:
And next to him one like herself,
  One daughter golden-curled;

Fair image of her own fair youth,
  As beautiful and as serene,
With almost such another love
  As her own love has been.

Yet, though of world-wide charity,
  And in her home most tender
    dove,
Her treasure and her heart are stored
  In the home-land of love:

She thrives, God's blessed husbandry;
  Most like a vine which full of
    fruit
Doth cling and lean and climb
    toward heaven
  While earth still binds its root.

I sit and watch my sister's face:
  How little altered since the hours
When she, a kind light-hearted girl,
  Gathered her garden flowers,

Her song just mellowed by regret
  For having teased me with her
    talk;
Then all-forgetful as she heard
  One step upon the walk.

While I? I sat alone and watched;
  My lot in life, to live alone
In mine own world of interests,
  Much felt but little shown.

Not to be first: how hard to learn
  That lifelong lesson of the past;
Line graven on line and stroke on
    stroke,
  But, thank God, learned at
    last.

So now in patience I possess
  My soul year after tedious year,
Content to take the lowest place,
  The place assigned me here.

Yet sometimes, when I feel my
    strength
  Most weak, and life most burden-
    some,
I lift mine eyes up to the hills
  From whence my help shall
    come:

Yea, sometimes still I lift my heart
  To the Archangelic trumpet-burst,
When all deep secrets shall be shown,
  And many last be first.

30 *September* 1856.

FROM HOUSE TO HOME

THE first was like a dream through
  summer heat,
  The second like a tedious numbing
    swoon

While the half-frozen pulses lagged
    to beat
  Beneath a winter moon.

'But,' says my friend, 'what was
    this thing and where?'
  It was a pleasure-place within my
    soul;
An earthly paradise supremely fair
  That lured me from the goal.

The first part was a tissue of hugged
    lies;
  The second was its ruin fraught
    with pain:
Why raise the fair delusion to the
    skies
  But to be dashed again?

My castle stood of white transparent
    glass
  Glittering and frail with many a
    fretted spire,
But when the summer sunset came
    to pass
  It kindled into fire.

My pleasaunce was an undulating
    green,
  Stately with trees whose shadows
    slept below,
With glimpses of smooth garden-
    beds between
  Like flame or sky or snow.

Swift squirrels on the pastures took
    their ease,
  With leaping lambs safe from the
    unfeared knife;
All singing-birds rejoicing in those
    trees
  Fulfilled their careless life.

Woodpigeons cooed there, stock-
    doves nestled there;
My trees were full of songs and
    flowers and fruit;
Their branches spread a city to the
    air
  And mice lodged in their root.

My heath lay farther off, where
    lizards lived
  In strange metallic mail, just spied
    and gone;
Like darted lightnings here and there
    perceived
  But nowhere dwelt upon.

Frogs and fat toads were there to
    hop or plod
  And propagate in peace, an un-
    couth crew,
Where velvet-headed rushes rustling
    nod
  And spill the morning dew.

All caterpillars throve beneath my
    rule,
  With snails and slugs in corners
    out of sight;
I never marred the curious sudden
    stool
  That perfects in a night.

Safe in his excavated gallery
  The burrowing mole groped on
    from year to year;
No harmless hedgehog curled be-
    cause of me
  His prickly back for fear.

Oft-times one like an angel walked
    with me,
  With spirit-discerning eyes like
    flames of fire
But deep as the unfathomed endless
    sea,
  Fulfilling my desire:

And sometimes like a snowdrift he was fair,
  And sometimes like a sunset glorious red,
And sometimes he had wings to scale the air
  With aureole round his head.

We sang our songs together by the way,
  Calls and recalls and echoes of delight;
So communed we together all the day,
  And so in dreams by night.

I have no words to tell what way we walked,
  What unforgotten path now closed and sealed:
I have no words to tell all things we talked,
  All things that he revealed:

This only can I tell: that hour by hour
  I waxed more feastful, lifted up and glad;
I felt no thorn-prick when I plucked a flower,
  Felt not my friend was sad.

'To-morrow,' once I said to him with smiles.
  'To-night,' he answered gravely; and was dumb,
But pointed out the stones that numbered miles
  And miles and miles to come.

'Not so,' I said: 'to-morrow shall be sweet:
  To-night is not so sweet as coming days.'

Then first I saw that he had turned his feet,
  Had turned from me his face:
Running and flying miles and miles he went,
  But once looked back to beckon with his hand,
And cry: 'Come home, O love, from banishment:
  Come to the distant land.'

That night destroyed me like an avalanche;
  One night turned all my summer back to snow:
Next morning not a bird upon my branch,
  Not a lamb woke below,—

No bird, no lamb, no living breathing thing;
  No squirrel scampered on my breezy lawn,
No mouse lodged by his hoard: all joys took wing
  And fled before that dawn.

Azure and sun were starved from heaven above,
  No dew had fallen, but biting frost lay hoar:
O love, I knew that I should meet my love,
  Should find my love no more.

'My love no more,' I muttered, stunned with pain:
  I shed no tear, I wrung no passionate hand,
Till something whispered: 'You shall meet again,
  Meet in a distant land.'

Then with a cry like famine I arose,
  I lit my candle, searched from
    room to room,
Searched up and down; a war of
    winds that froze
Swept through the blank of gloom.

I searched day after day, night after
    night;
  Scant change there came to me
    of night or day:
'No more,' I wailed, 'no more:'
    and trimmed my light,
And gnashed but did not pray,

Until my heart broke and my spirit
    broke:
  Upon the frost-bound floor I
    stumbled, fell,
And moaned: 'It is enough: with-
    hold the stroke.
Farewell, O love, farewell.'

Then life swooned from me. And
    I heard the song
  Of spheres and spirits rejoicing
    over me:
One cried: 'Our sister, she hath
    suffered long.'—
One answered: 'Make her see.'

One cried: 'Oh blessèd she who
    no more pain,
  Who no more disappointment
    shall receive.'—
One answered: 'Not so: she must
    live again;
Strengthen thou her to live.'

So while I lay entranced a curtain
    seemed
  To shrivel with crackling from
    before my face:

Across mine eyes a waxing radiance
    beamed
And showed a certain place.

I saw a vision of a woman, where
  Night and new morning strive for
    domination;
Incomparably pale, and almost fair,
  And sad beyond expression.

Her eyes were like some fire-
    enshrining gem,
  Were stately like the stars, and
    yet were tender;
Her figure charmed me like a windy
    stem
  Quivering and drooped and
    slender.

I stood upon the outer barren ground,
  She stood on inner ground that
    budded flowers;
While circling in their never-slacken-
    ing round
Danced by the mystic hours.

But every flower was lifted on a thorn,
  And every thorn shot upright from
    its sands
To gall her feet; hoarse laughter
    pealed in scorn
With cruel clapping hands.

She bled and wept, yet did not
    shrink; her strength
  Was strung up until daybreak of
    delight:
She measured measureless sorrow
    toward its length,
  And breadth, and depth, and
    height.

Then marked I how a chain sustained
    her form,

A chain of living links not made nor riven:
It stretched sheer up through lightning, wind, and storm,
And anchored fast in heaven.

One cried: 'How long? yet founded on the Rock
She shall do battle, suffer, and attain.'—
One answered: 'Faith quakes in the tempest shock—
Strengthen her soul again.'

I saw a cup sent down and come to her
Brimfull of loathing and of bitterness:
She drank with livid lips that seemed to stir
The depth, not make it less.

But as she drank I spied a hand distil
New wine and virgin honey; making it
First bitter-sweet, then sweet indeed, until
She tasted only sweet.

Her lips and cheeks waxed rosy-fresh and young;
Drinking she sang 'My soul shall nothing want;'
And drank anew: while soft a song was sung,
A mystical slow chant.

One cried: 'The wounds are faithful of a friend:
The wilderness shall blossom as a rose.'—
One answered: 'Rend the veil, declare the end,
Strengthen her ere she goes.'

Then earth and heaven were rolled up like a scroll;
Time and space, change and death, had passed away;
Weight, number, measure, each had reached its whole:
The day had come, that day.

Multitudes—multitudes—stood up in bliss,
Made equal to the angels, glorious, fair;
With harps, palms, wedding-garments, kiss of peace,
And crowned and haloed hair.

They sang a song, a new song in the height,
Harping with harps to Him who is strong and true:
They drank new wine, their eyes saw with new light,
Lo all things were made new.

Tier beyond tier they rose and rose and rose,
So high that it was dreadful, flames with flames:
No man could number them, no tongue disclose
Their secret sacred names.

As though one pulse stirred all, one rush of blood
Fed all, one breath swept through them myriad-voiced,
They struck their harps, cast down their crowns, they stood
And worshipped and rejoiced.

Each face looked one way like a moon new-lit,
Each face looked one way towards its Sun of Love;

Drank love and bathed in love and
    mirrored it
  And knew no end thereof.
Glory touched glory on each blessèd
    head,
  Hands locked dear hands never
    to sunder more :
These were the new-begotten from
    the dead
  Whom the great birthday bore.

Heart answered heart, soul answered
    soul at rest,
  Double against each other, filled,
    sufficed :
All loving, loved of all; but loving best
  And best beloved of Christ.

I saw that one who lost her love in
    pain,
  Who trod on thorns, who drank
    the loathsome cup ;
The lost in night, in day was found
    again ;
  The fallen was lifted up.

They stood together in the blessèd
    noon,
  They sang together through the
    length of days ;
Each loving face bent Sunwards like
    a moon
  New-lit with love and praise.

Therefore, O friend, I would not if
    I might
  Rebuild my house of lies, wherein
    I joyed
One time to dwell: my soul shall
    walk in white,
  Cast down but not destroyed.

Therefore in patience I possess my
    soul ;

Yea, therefore as a flint I set my
    face,
To pluck down, to build up again
    the whole—
  But in a distant place.

These thorns are sharp, yet I can
    tread on them ;
  This cup is loathsome, yet He
    makes it sweet :
My face is steadfast toward Jeru-
    salem,
  My heart remembers it.

I lift the hanging hands, the feeble
    knees—
  I, precious more than seven times
    molten gold—
Until the day when from His
    storehouses
  God shall bring new and old ;

Beauty for ashes, oil of joy for grief,
  Garment of praise for spirit of
    heaviness :
Although to-day I fade as doth a leaf,
  I languish and grow less.

Although to-day He prunes my twigs
    with pain,
  Yet doth His blood nourish and
    warm my root :
To-morrow I shall put forth buds
    again
  And clothe myself with fruit.

Although to-day I walk in tedious
    ways,
  To-day His staff is turned into a
    rod,
Yet will I wait for Him the appointed
    days
  And stay upon my God.
19 *November* 1858.

THE PRINCE'S PROGRESS

TILL all sweet gums and juices flow,
Till the blossom of blossoms blow,
The long hours go and come and go;
   The bride she sleepeth, waketh, sleepeth,
Waiting for one whose coming is slow:—
   Hark! the bride weepeth.

'How long shall I wait, come heat come rime?'—
'Till the strong Prince comes, who must come in time'
(Her women say): 'there's a mountain to climb,
   A river to ford. Sleep, dream and sleep;
Sleep' (they say): 'we've muffled the chime;
   Better dream than weep.'

In his world-end palace the strong Prince sat,
Taking his ease on cushion and mat;
Close at hand lay his staff and his hat
   'When wilt thou start? the bride waits, O youth.'—
'Now the moon's at full; I tarried for that;
   Now I start in truth.

'But tell me first, true voice of my doom,
Of my veiled bride in her maiden bloom;
Keeps she watch through glare and through gloom,
   Watch for me asleep and awake?'—
'Spell-bound she watches in one white room,
   And is patient for thy sake.

'By her head lilies and rosebuds grow;
The lilies droop, will the rosebuds blow?
The silver slim lilies hang the head low;
   Their stream is scanty, their sunshine rare:
Let the sun blaze out, and let the stream flow,
   They will blossom and wax fair.

'Red and white poppies grow at her feet.
The blood-red wait for sweet summer heat,
Wrapped in bud-coats, hairy and neat;
   But the white buds swell, one day they will burst,
Will open their death cups drowsy and sweet:—
   Which will open the first?'

Then a hundred sad voices lifted a wail,
And a hundred glad voices piped on the gale:
'Time is short, life is short,' they took up the tale:
   'Life is sweet, love is sweet, use to-day while you may;
Love is sweet, and to-morrow may fail;
   Love is sweet, use to-day.'

While the song swept by, beseeching and meek,
Up rose the Prince with a flush on his cheek,
Up he rose to stir and to seek,
   Going forth in the joy of his strength;

trong of limb if of purpose weak,
　　Starting at length.

'orth he set in the breezy morn,
.cross green fields of nodding corn,
.s goodly a Prince as ever was born,
　Carolling with the carolling lark;—
.ure his bride will be won and worn
　　Ere fall of the dark.

io light his step, so merry his smile,
\ milkmaid loitered beside a stile,
;et down her pail and rested awhile,
　A wave-haired milkmaid, rosy and
　　white ;
The Prince, who had journeyed at
　　least a mile,
　Grew athirst at the sight.

'Will you give me a morning
　　draught?'—
'You're kindly welcome,' she said,
　and laughed.
He lifted the pail, new milk he
　quaffed ;
　Then wiping his curly black beard
　　like silk :
'Whitest cow that ever was calved
　Surely gave you this milk.'

Was it milk now, or was it cream ?
Was she a maid, or an evil dream ?
Her eyes began to glitter and gleam ;
　He would have gone, but he stayed
　　instead ;
Green they gleamed as he looked in
　them :
　'Give me my fee,' she said.—

'I will give you a jewel of gold.'—
'Not so; gold is heavy and cold.'—
'I will give you a velvet fold
　Of foreign work your beauty to
　　deck.'—

'Better I like my kerchief rolled
　Light and white round my
　　neck.'—

'Nay,' cried he, 'but fix your own
　fee.'—
She laughed, 'You may give the full
　moon to me,
Or else sit under this apple-tree
　Here for one idle day by my side ;
After that I'll let you go free,
　And the world is wide.'

Loth to stay, yet to leave her slack,
He half turned away, then he quite
　turned back :
For courtesy's sake he could not
　lack
　To redeem his own royal pledge ;
Ahead too the windy heaven lowered
　black
　With a fire-cloven edge.

So he stretched his length in the
　apple-tree shade,
Lay and laughed and talked to the
　maid,
Who twisted her hair in a cunning
　braid
　And writhed it in shining serpent-
　　coils,
And held him a day and a night fast
　laid
　In her subtle toils.

At the death of night and the birth
　of day,
When the owl left off his sober play,
And the bat hung himself out of the
　way,
　Woke the song of mavis and
　　merle,
And heaven put off its hodden grey
　For mother-o'-pearl.

Peeped up daisies here and there,
Here, there, and everywhere;
Rose a hopeful lark in the air,
 Spreading out towards the sun his
  breast;
While the moon set solemn and fair
 Away in the West.

'Up, up, up,' called the watchman
  lark,
In his clear réveillée; 'Hearken, oh
  hark!
Press to the high goal, fly to the mark.
 Up, O sluggard, new morn is born;
If still asleep when the night falls
  dark,
 Thou must wait a second morn.'

'Up, up, up,' sad glad voices swelled;
'So the tree falls and lies as it's felled.
Be thy bands loosed, O sleeper, long
  held
 In sweet sleep whose end is not
  sweet.
Be the slackness girt and the softness
  quelled
 And the slowness fleet.'

Off he set. The grass grew rare,
A blight lurked in the darkening air,
The very moss grew hueless and
  spare,
 The last daisy stood all astunt;
Behind his back the soil lay bare,
 But barer in front.

A land of chasm and rent, a land
Of rugged blackness on either hand:
If water trickled its track was tanned
 With an edge of rust to the chink;
If one stamped on stone or on sand
 It returned a clink.

A lifeless land, a loveless land,
Without fair or nest on either hand:

Only scorpions jerked in the sand,
 Black as black iron, or dusty pale;
From point to point sheer rock was
  manned
 By scorpions, in mail.

A land of neither life nor death,
Where no man buildeth or fashioneth,
Where none draws living or dying
  breath;
 No man cometh or goeth there,
No man doeth, seeketh, saith,
 In the stagnant air.

Some old volcanic upset must
Have rent the crust and blackened
  the crust,
Wrenched and ribbed it beneath its
  dust,
 Above earth's molten centre at
  seethe,
Heaved and heaped it by huge up-
  thrust
 Of fire beneath.

Untrodden before, untrodden since:
Tedious land for a social Prince;
Halting, he scanned the outs and ins,
 Endless, labyrinthine, grim,
Of the solitude that made him wince
 Laying wait for him.

By bulging rock and gaping cleft,
Even of half mere daylight reft,
Rueful he peered to right and left,
 Muttering in his altered mood:
'The fate is hard that weaves my
  weft,
 Though my lot be good.'

Dim the changes of day to night,
Of night scarce dark to day no
  bright.

Till his road wound towards the right,
Still he went, and still he went,
Till one night he spied a light,
    In his discontent.

But it flashed from a yawn-mouthed cave,
Like a red-hot eye from a grave.
No man stood there of whom to crave
Rest for wayfarer plodding by:
Though the tenant were churl or knave
    The Prince might try.

On he passed and tarried not,
Groping his way from spot to spot,
Towards where the cavern flare glowed hot:
An old, old mortal, cramped and double,
Was peering into a seething-pot,
    In a world of trouble.

The veriest atomy he looked,
With grimy fingers clutching and crooked,
Tight skin, a nose all bony and hooked,
And a shaking, sharp, suspicious way;
Blinking, his eyes had scarcely brooked
    The light of day.

Stared the Prince, for the sight was new;
Stared, but asked without more ado;
'May a weary traveller lodge with you,
Old father, here in your lair?
In your country the inns seem few,
    And scanty the fare.'

The head turned not to hear him speak;
The old voice whistled as through a leak
(Out it came in a quavering squeak):
'Work for wage is a bargain fit:
If there's aught of mine that you seek
    You must work for it.

' Buried alive from light and air
This year is the hundredth year,
I feed my fire with a sleepless care,
    Watching my potion wane or wax:
Elixir of Life is simmering there,
    And but one thing lacks.

' If you're fain to lodge here with me,
Take that pair of bellows you see—
Too heavy for my old hands they be—
    Take the bellows and puff and puff:
When the steam curls rosy and free
    The broth's boiled enough.

'Then take your choice of all I have;
I will give you life if you crave.
Already I'm mildewed for the grave,
    So first myself I must drink my fill:
But all the rest may be yours, to save
    Whomever you will.'

'Done,' quoth the Prince, and the bargain stood.
First he piled on resinous wood,
Next plied the bellows in hopeful mood;
    Thinking, 'My love and I will live.
If I tarry, why life is good,
    And she may forgive.'

The pot began to bubble and boil;
The old man cast in essence and oil,
He stirred all up with a triple coil
   Of gold and silver and iron wire,
Dredged in a pinch of virgin soil,
   And fed the fire.

But still the steam curled watery white;
Night turned to day and day to night;
One thing lacked, by his feeble sight
   Unseen, unguessed by his feeble mind:
Life might miss him, but Death the blight
   Was sure to find.

So when the hundredth year was full
The thread was cut and finished the school.
Death snapped the old worn-out tool,
   Snapped him short while he stood and stirred
(Though stiff he stood as a stiff-necked mule)
   With never a word.

Thus at length the old crab was nipped.
The dead hand slipped, the dead finger dipped
In the broth as the dead man slipped:—
   That same instant, a rosy red
Flushed the steam, and quivered and clipped
   Round the dead old head.

The last ingredient was supplied
(Unless the dead man mistook or lied).
Up started the Prince, he cast aside
   The bellows plied through the tedious trial,
Made sure that his host had died
   And filled a phial.

'One night's rest,' thought 1 Prince: 'This done,
Forth I speed with the rising sun
With the morrow I rise and run,
   Come what will of wind or weather.
This draught of life, when my bri is won,
   We'll drink together.'

Thus the dead man stayed in 1 grave,
Self-chosen, the dead man in 1 cave;
There he stayed, were he fool knave,
   Or honest seeker who had n found:
While the Prince outside was prom to crave
   Sleep on the ground.

'If she watches, go bid her sleep;
Bid her sleep, for the road is steep
He can sleep who holdeth her chea
   Sleep and wake and sleep again
Let him sow, one day he shall reap
   Let him sow the grain.

'When there blows a sweet gard rose,
Let it bloom and wither if no m knows:
But if one knows when the swe thing blows,
   Knows, and lets it open and dro
If but a nettle his garden grows
   He hath earned the crop.'

Through his sleep the summor rang,
Into his ears it sobbed and it sang

Slow he woke with a drowsy pang,
    Shook himself without much
        debate,
Turned where he saw green branches
        hang,
    Started though late.

For the black land was travelled o'er.
He should see the grim land no more.
A flowering country stretched before
    His face when the lovely day
        came back:
He hugged the phial of Life he bore,
    And resumed his track.

By willow courses he took his path,
Spied what a nest the kingfisher
        hath,
Marked the fields green to after-
        math,
    Marked where the red-brown
        field-mouse ran,
Loitered a while for a deep stream
        bath,
    Yawned for a fellow-man.

Up on the hills not a soul in view,
In the vale not many nor few;
Leaves, still leaves and nothing new.
    It's oh for a second maiden, at
        least,
To bear the flagon, and taste it too,
    And flavour the feast.

Lagging he moved, and apt to
        swerve;
Lazy of limb, but quick of nerve.
length the water-bed took a curve,
The deep river swept its bankside
        bare;
ters streamed from the hill-
        reserve—
    Waters here, waters there.

High above and deep below,
Bursting, bubbling, swelling the flow,
Like hill torrents after the snow,—
    Bubbling, gurgling, in whirling
        strife,
Swaying, sweeping to and fro,—
    He must swim for his life.

Which way?—which way?—his
        eyes grew dim
With the dizzying whirl—which way
        to swim?
The thunderous downshoot deafened
        him;
    Half he choked in the lashing
        spray:
Life is sweet, and the grave is
        grim—
    Which way?—which way?

A flash of light, a shout from the
        strand:
'This way—this way; here lies the
        land!'
His phial clutched in one drowning
        hand;
    He catches—misses—catches a
        rope;
His feet slip on the slipping sand:
    Is there life?—is there hope?

Just saved, without pulse or breath—
Scarcely saved from the gulp of
        death;
Laid where a willow shadoweth—
    Laid where a swelling turf is
        smooth.
(O Bride! but the Bridegroom
        lingereth
    For all thy sweet youth.)

Kind hands do and undo,
Kind voices whisper and coo:

'I will chafe his hands'—'And I'
  —'And you
  Raise his head, put his hair aside.'
(If many laugh, one well may rue:
  Sleep on, thou Bride.)

So the Prince was tended with care:
One wrung foul ooze from his
  clustered hair;
Two chafed his hands, and did not
  spare;
But one propped his head that
  drooped awry:
Till his eyes oped, and at unaware
  They met eye to eye.

Oh a moon face in a shadowy place,
And a light touch and a winsome
  grace,
And a thrilling tender voice which
  says:
'Safe from waters that seek the
  sea—
Cold waters by rugged ways—
  Safe with me.'

While overhead bird whistles to bird,
And round about plays a gamesome
  herd:
'Safe with us'—some take up the
  word—
'Safe with us, dear lord and
  friend:
All the sweeter if long deferred
  Is rest in the end.'

Had he stayed to weigh and to scan,
He had been more or less than a
  man:
He did what a young man can,
  Spoke of toil and an arduous
  way—
Toil to-morrow, while golden ran
  The sands of to-day.

Slip past, slip fast,
Uncounted hours from first to last,
Many hours till the last is past,
  Many hours dwindling to one—
One hour whose die is cast,
  One last hour gone.

Come, gone—gone for ever—
Gone as an unreturning river—
Gone as to death the merriest liver—
  Gone as the year at the dying
  fall—
To-morrow, to-day, yesterday,
  never—
  Gone once for all.

Came at length the starting-day,
With last words, and last last words
  to say,
With bodiless cries from far away—
  Chiding wailing voices that rang
Like a trumpet-call to the tug and
  fray;
  And thus they sang:

'Is there life?—the lamp burns
  low;
Is there hope?—the coming is
  slow:
The promise promised so long ago,
  The long promise, has not been
  kept.
Does she live?—does she die?—she
  slumbers so
  Who so oft has wept.

'Does she live!—does she die?—she
  languisheth
As a lily drooping to death,
As a drought-worn bird with failing
  breath,
  As a lovely vine without a stay,
As a tree whereof the owner saith,
  "Hew it down to-day."'

Stung by that word, the Prince was fain
To start on his tedious road again.
He crossed the stream where a ford was plain,
   He clomb the opposite bank though steep,
And swore to himself to strain and attain
   Ere he tasted sleep.

Huge before him a mountain frowned
With foot of rock on the valley ground,
And head with snows incessant crowned,
   And a cloud mantle about its strength,
And a path which the wild goat hath not found
   In its breadth and length.

But he was strong to do and dare:
If a host had withstood him there,
He had braved a host with little care
   In his lusty youth and his pride,
Tough to grapple though weak to snare.
   He comes, O Bride.

Up he went where the goat scarce clings,
Up where the eagle folds her wings,
Past the green line of living things,
   Where the sun cannot warm the cold,—
Up he went as a flame enrings
   Where there seems no hold.

Up a fissure barren and black,
Till the eagles tired upon his track,
And the clouds were left behind his back,
   Up till the utmost peak was past:

Then he gasped for breath and his strength fell slack—
   He paused at last.

Before his face a valley spread
Where fatness laughed, wine, oil, and bread,
Where all fruit-trees their sweetness shed,
   Where all birds made love to their kind,
Where jewels twinkled, and gold lay red
   And not hard to find.

Midway down the mountain side
(On its green slope the path was wide)
Stood a house for a royal bride,
   Built all of changing opal stone,
The royal palace, till now descried
   In his dreams alone.

Less bold than in days of yore,
Doubting now though never before,
Doubting he goes and lags the more:
   Is the time late? does the day grow dim?
Rose, will she open the crimson core
   Of her heart to him?

Above his head a tangle glows
Of wine-red roses, blushes, snows,
Closed buds and buds that unclose,
   Leaves, and moss, and prickles too;
His hand shook as he plucked a rose,
   And the rose dropped dew.

Take heart of grace! the potion of Life
May go far to woo him a wife:
If she frown, yet a lover's strife
   Lightly raised can be laid again:

A hasty word is never the knife
    To cut love in twain.

Far away stretched the royal land,
Fed by dew, by a spice-wind fanned.
Light labour more, and his foot
    would stand
    On the threshold, all labour done ;
Easy pleasure laid at his hand,
    And the dear Bride won.

His slackening steps pause at the
    gate—
Does she wake or sleep?—the time
    is late—
Does she sleep now, or watch and
    wait?
    She has watched, she has waited
    long,
Watching athwart the golden grate
    With a patient song.

Fling the golden portals wide,
The Bridegroom comes to his
    promised Bride :
Draw the gold-stiff curtains aside,
    Let them look on each other's
    face,
She in her meekness, he in his
    pride—
    Day wears apace.

Day is over, the day that wore.
What is this that comes through the
    door,
The face covered, the feet before?
    This that coming takes his breath ;
This Bride not seen, to be seen no
    more
    Save of Bridegroom Death?

Veiled figures carrying her
Sweep by yet make no stir ;
There is a smell of spice and myrrh,

A bride-chant burdened with one
    name ;
The bride-song rises steadier
    Than the torches' flame :—

' Too late for love, too late for joy,
    Too late, too late !
You loitered on the road too long,
    You trifled at the gate :
The enchanted dove upon her branch
    Died without a mate ;
The enchanted princess in her tower
    Slept, died, behind the grate ;
Her heart was starving all this while
    You made it wait.

' Ten years ago, five years ago,
    One year ago,
Even then you had arrived in time,
    Though somewhat slow ;
Then you had known her living face
    Which now you cannot know :
The frozen fountain would have
    leaped,
    The buds gone on to blow,
The warm south wind would have
    awaked
    To melt the snow.

' Is she fair now as she lies ?
    Once she was fair ;
Meet queen for any kingly king,
    With gold-dust on her hair.
Now these are poppies in her locks,
    White poppies she must wear ;
Must wear a veil to shroud her face
    And the want graven there :
Or is the hunger fed at length,
    Cast off the care ?

' We never saw her with a smile
    Or with a frown ;
Her bed seemed never soft to her,
    Though tossed of down ;

She little heeded what she wore,
   Kirtle, or wreath, or gown;
We think her white brows often
    ached
   Beneath her crown,
Till silvery hairs showed in her locks
   That used to be so brown.

'We never heard her speak in haste;
   Her tones were sweet,
And modulated just so much
   As it was meet:
Her heart sat silent through the noise
   And concourse of the street.
There was no hurry in her hands,
   No hurry in her feet;
There was no bliss drew nigh to her,
   That she might run to greet.

'You should have wept her yesterday,
   Wasting upon her bed:
But wherefore should you weep to-day
   That she is dead?
Lo we who love weep not to-day,
   But crown her royal head.
Let be these poppies that we strew,
   Your roses are too red:
Let be these poppies, not for you
   Cut down and spread.'
    11 *October* 1861 to *March* 1865.

A ROYAL PRINCESS

'I a Princess king-descended, deckt
   with jewels, gilded, drest,
Would rather be a peasant with her
   baby at her breast,
For all I shine so like the sun, and
   am purple like the west.

Two and two my guards behind, two
   and two before,
Two and two on either hand, they
   guard me evermore;

Me, poor dove that must not coo—
   eagle that must not soar.

All my fountains cast up perfumes,
   all my gardens grow
Scented woods and foreign spices,
   with all flowers in blow
That are costly, out of season as the
   seasons go.

All my walls are lost in mirrors,
   whereupon I trace
Self to right hand, self to left hand,
   self in every place,
Self-same solitary figure, self-same
   seeking face.

Then I have an ivory chair high to
   sit upon,
Almost like my father's chair which
   is an ivory throne;
There I sit uplift and upright, there
   I sit alone.

Alone by day, alone by night, alone
   days without end;
My father and my mother give me
   treasures, search and spend—
O my father! O my mother! have
   you ne'er a friend?

As I am a lofty princess, so my
   father is
A lofty king, accomplished in all
   kingly subtilties,
Holding in his strong right hand
   world-kingdoms' balances.

He has quarrelled with his neighbours, he has scourged his foes;
Vassal counts and princes follow
   where his pennon goes,
Long-descended valiant lords whom
   the vulture knows,

On whose track the vulture swoops,
    when they ride in state
To break the strength of armies and
    topple down the great :
Each of these my courteous servant,
    none of these my mate.

My father counting up his strength
    sets down with equal pen
So many head of cattle, head of
    horses, head of men ;
These for slaughter, these for labour,
    with the how and when.

Some to work on roads, canals ; some
    to man his ships ;
Some to smart in mines beneath
    sharp overseers' whips ;
Some to trap fur-beasts in lands
    where utmost winter nips.

Once it came into my heart, and
    whelmed me like a flood,
That these too are men and women,
    human flesh and blood ;
Men with hearts and men with souls,
    though trodden down like mud.

Our feasting was not glad that night,
    our music was not gay :
On my mother's graceful head I
    marked a thread of grey,
My father frowning at the fare
    seemed every dish to weigh.

I sat beside them sole princess in my
    exalted place,
My ladies and my gentlemen stood
    by me on the dais :
A mirror showed me I look old and
    haggard in the face ;

It showed me that my ladies all are
    fair to gaze upon,
Plump, plenteous-haired, to every
    one love's secret lore is known,
They laugh by day, they sleep by
    night ; ah me, what is a throne ?

The singing men and women sang
    that night as usual,
The dancers danced in pairs and sets,
    but music had a fall,
A melancholy windy fall as at a
    funeral.

Amid the toss of torches to my
    chamber back we swept ;
My ladies loosed my golden chain ;
    meantime I could have wept
To think of some in galling chains
    whether they waked or slept.

I took my bath of scented milk,
    delicately waited on :
They burned sweet things for my
    delight, cedar and cinnamon,
They lit my shaded silver lamp, and
    left me there alone.

A day went by, a week went by. One
    day I heard it said :
' Men are clamouring, women,
    children, clamouring to be fed ;
Men like famished dogs are howling
    in the streets for bread.'

So two whispered by my door, not
    thinking I could hear,
Vulgar naked truth, ungarnished for
    a royal ear ;
Fit for cooping in the background,
    not to stalk so near.

But I strained my utmost sense to
    catch this truth, and mark :
' There are families out grazing, like
    cattle in the park.'

'A pair of peasants must be saved,
  even if we build an ark.'

A merry jest, a merry laugh: each
  strolled upon his way;
One was my page, a lad I reared and
  bore with day by day;
One was my youngest maid, as sweet
  and white as cream in May.

Other footsteps followed softly with
  a weightier tramp;
Voices said: 'Picked soldiers have
  been summoned from the camp,
To quell these base-born ruffians who
  make free to howl and stamp.'

'Howl and stamp?' one answered:
  'They made free to hurl a stone
At the minister's state coach, well
  aimed and stoutly thrown.'
'There's work then for the soldiers, for
  this rank crop must be mown.'

'One I saw, a poor old fool with
  ashes on his head,
Whimpering because a girl had
  snatched his crust of bread:
Then he dropped; when some one
  raised him, it turned out he was
  dead.'

'After us the deluge,' was retorted
  with a laugh:
'If bread's the staff of life they must
  walk without a staff.'
'While I've a loaf they're welcome
  to my blessing and the chaff.'

These passed. 'The king': stand
  up. Said my father with a
  smile:
'Daughter mine, your mother comes
  to sit with you awhile;

She's sad to-day, and who but you
  her sadness can beguile?'

He too left me. Shall I touch my
  harp now while I wait,—
(I hear them doubling guard below
  before our palace gate)—
Or shall I work the last gold stitch
  into my veil of state;

Or shall my woman stand and read
  some unimpassioned scene,—
There's music of a lulling sort in
  words that pause between;
Or shall she merely fan me while I
  wait here for the queen?

Again I caught my father's voice in
  sharp word of command:
'Charge' a clash of steel: 'Charge
  again, the rebels stand.
Smite and spare not, hand to hand;
  smite and spare not, hand to
  hand.'

There swelled a tumult at the gate,
  high voices waxing higher;
A flash of red reflected light lit the
  cathedral spire;
I heard a cry for faggots, then I
  heard a yell for fire.

'Sit and roast there with your meat,
  sit and bake there with your
  bread,
You who sat to see us starve,' one
  shrieking woman said:
'Sit on your throne and roast with
  your crown upon your head.'

Nay, this thing will I do, while my
  mother tarrieth,
I will take my fine spun gold, but
  not to sew therewith,

I will take my gold and gems, and
  rainbow fan and wreath;

With a ransom in my lap, a king's
  ransom in my hand,
I will go down to this people, will
  stand face to face, will stand
Where they curse king, queen, and
  princess of this cursed land.

They shall take all to buy them
  bread, take all I have to give;
I, if I perish, perish; they to-day
  shall eat and live;
I, if I perish, perish—that's the
  goal I half conceive:

Once to speak before the world, rend
  bare my heart, and show
The lesson I have learned, which is
  death, is life, to know.
I, if I perish, perish: in the name
  of God I go.

22 *October* 1861.

MAIDEN-SONG

LONG ago and long ago
  And long ago still,
There dwelt three merry maidens
  Upon a distant hill.
One was tall Meggan,
  And one was dainty May,
But one was fair Margaret,
  More fair than I can say,
Long ago and long ago.

When Meggan pluckt the thorny
  rose,
  And when May pulled the brier,
Half the birds would swoop to see,
  Half the beasts drew nigher,
Half the fishes of the streams
  Would dart up to admire.
But, when Margaret pluckt a flag-
  flower
  Or poppy hot aflame,
All the beasts and all the birds
  And all the fishes came
To her hand more soft than snow.

Strawberry leaves and May-dew
  In brisk morning air,
Strawberry leaves and May-dew
  Make maidens fair.
'I go for strawberry leaves,'
  Meggan said one day:
'Fair Margaret can bide at home,
  But you come with me, May:
Up the hill and down the hill,
  Along the winding way
You and I are used to go.'

So these two fair sisters
  Went with innocent will
Up the hill and down again,
  And round the homestead hill:
While the fairest sat at home,
  Margaret like a queen,
Like a blush-rose, like the moon
  In her heavenly sheen,
Fragrant-breathed as milky cow
  Or field of blossoming bean,
Graceful as an ivy bough
  Born to cling and lean;
Thus she sat to sing and sew.

When she raised her lustrous eyes
  A beast peeped at the door;
When she downward cast her eyes
  A fish gasped on the floor;
When she turned away her eyes
  A bird perched on the sill,
Warbling out its heart of love,
  Warbling warbling still,
With pathetic pleadings low.

Light-foot May with Meggan
  Sought the choicest spot,
Clothed with thyme-alternate grass:
  Then, while day waxed hot,
Sat at ease to play and rest,
  A gracious rest and play;
The loveliest maidens near or far,
  When Margaret was away,
Who sat at home to sing and sew.

Sun-glow flushed their comely cheeks,
  Wind-play tossed their hair,
Creeping things among the grass
  Stroked them here and there;
Meggan piped a merry note,
  A fitful wayward lay
While shrill as bird on topmost twig
  Piped merry May;
Honey-smooth the double flow.

Sped a herdsman from the vale,
  Mounting like a flame;
All on fire to hear and see,
  With floating locks he came.
Looked neither north nor south,
  Neither east nor west,
But sat him down at Meggan's feet
  As love-bird on his nest,
And wooed her with a silent awe,
  With trouble not expressed;
She sang the tears into his eyes,
  The heart out of his breast:
So he loved her, listening so.

She sang the heart out of his breast,
  The words out of his tongue;
Hand and foot and pulse he paused
  Till her song was sung.
Then he spoke up from his place
  Simple words and true:
'Scanty goods have I to give,
  Scanty skill to woo;

But I have a will to work,
  And a heart for you:
Bid me stay or bid me go.'

Then Meggan mused within herself:
  'Better be first with him
Than dwell where fairer Margaret sits,
  Who shines my brightness dim,
For ever second where she sits,
  However fair I be:
I will be lady of his love,
  And he shall worship me;
I will be lady of his herds
  And stoop to his degree,
At home where kids and fatlings grow.'

Sped a shepherd from the height
  Headlong down to look,
(White lambs followed, lured by love
  Of their shepherd's crook):
He turned neither east nor west,
  Neither north nor south,
But knelt right down to May, for love
  Of her sweet-singing mouth;
Forgot his flocks, his panting flocks
  In parching hill-side drouth;
Forgot himself for weal or woe.

Trilled her song and swelled her song
  With maiden coy caprice
In a labyrinth of throbs,
  Pauses, cadences;
Clear-noted as a dropping brook,
  Soft-noted like the bees,
Wild-noted as the shivering wind
  Forlorn through forest-trees:
Love-noted like the wood-pigeon
  Who hides herself for love,
Yet cannot keep her secret safe,
  But coos and coos thereof:
Thus the notes rang loud or low.

He hung breathless on her breath;
  Speechless, who listened well;
Could not speak or think or wish
  Till silence broke the spell.
Then he spoke, and spread his
    hands,
  Pointing here and there:
'See my sheep and see the lambs,
  Twin lambs which they bare.
All myself I offer you,
  All my flocks and care,
Your sweet song hath moved me so.'

In her fluttered heart young May
  Mused a dubious while:
'If he loves me as he says'—
  Her lips curved with a smile:
'Where Margaret shines like the
    sun
  I shine but like a moon;
If sister Meggan makes her choice
  I can make mine as soon;
At cockcrow we were sister-maids,
  We may be brides at noon.'
Said Meggan 'Yes'; May said not
  'No.'

Fair Margaret stayed alone at home;
  Awhile she sang her song,
Awhile sat silent, then she thought
  'My sisters loiter long.'
That sultry noon had waned away,
  Shadows had waxen great:
'Surely,' she thought within herself,
  'My sisters loiter late.'
She rose, and peered out at the
    door,
  With patient heart to wait,
And heard a distant nightingale
  Complaining of its mate;
Then down the garden slope she
    walked,
  Down to the garden gate,
Leaned on the rail and waited so.

The slope was lightened by her eyes
  Like summer lightning fair,
Like rising of the haloed moon
  Lightened her glimmering hair,
While her face lightened like the sun
  Whose dawn is rosy white.
Thus crowned with maiden majesty
  She peered into the night,
Looked up the hill and down the hill,
  To left hand and to right,
Flashing like fire-flies to and fro.

Waiting thus in weariness
  She marked the nightingale
Telling, if any one would heed,
  Its old complaining tale.
Then lifted she her voice and sang,
  Answering the bird:
Then lifted she her voice and sang;
  Such notes were never heard
From any bird when Spring's in
    blow.

The king of all that country,
  Coursing far, coursing near,
Curbed his amber-bitted steed,
  Coursed amain to hear;
All his princes in his train,
  Squire and knight and peer,
With his crown upon his head,
  His sceptre in his hand,
Down he fell at Margaret's knees
  Lord king of all that land,
To her highness bending low.

Every beast and bird and fish
  Came mustering to the sound,
Every man and every maid
  From miles of country round:
Meggan on her herdsman's arm,
  With her shepherd May,
Flocks and herds trooped at their
    heels
  Along the hill-side way;

No foot too feeble for the ascent,
  Not any head too grey ;
Some were swift and none were slow.

So Margaret sang her sisters home
  In their marriage mirth ;
Sang free birds out of the sky,
  Beasts along the earth,
Sang up fishes of the deep—
  All breathing things that move—
Sang from far and sang from near
  To her lovely love ;
Sang together friend and foe ;

Sang a golden-bearded king
  Straightway to her feet,
Sang him silent where he knelt
  In eager anguish sweet.
But when the clear voice died away,
  When longest echoes died,
He stood up like a royal man
  And claimed her for his bride.
So three maids were wooed and won
  In a brief May-tide,
Long ago and long ago.
  6 *July* 1863.

'THE INIQUITY OF THE
FATHERS UPON THE
CHILDREN'

OH the rose of keenest thorn !
One hidden summer morn
Under the rose I was born.

I do not guess his name
Who wrought my Mother's shame,
And gave me life forlorn ;
But my Mother, Mother, Mother,
I know her from all other.
My Mother pale and mild,
Fair as ever was seen,

She was but scarce sixteen,
Little more than a child,
When I was born
To work her scorn.
With secret bitter throes,
In a passion of secret woes,
She bore me under the rose.

One who my Mother nursed
Took me from the first :—
'O nurse, let me look upon
This babe that costs so dear ;
To-morrow she will be gone :
Other mothers may keep
Their babes awake and asleep,
But I must not keep her here.'—
Whether I know or guess,
I know this not the less.

So I was sent away
That none might spy the truth :
And my childhood waxed to youth
And I left off childish play.
I never cared to play
With the village boys and girls ;
And I think they thought me proud,
I found so little to say
And kept so from the crowd :
But I had the longest curls
And I had the largest eyes,
And my teeth were small like pearls.
The girls might flout and scout me,
But the boys would hang about me,
In sheepish mooning wise.

Our one-street village stood
A long mile from the town,
A mile of windy down
And bleak one-sided wood,
With not a single house.
Our town itself was small,
With just the common shops,
And throve in its small way.
Our neighbouring gentry reared

The good old-fashioned crops,
And made old-fashioned boasts
Of what John Bull would do
If Frenchman Frog appeared,
And drank old-fashioned toasts,
And made old-fashioned bows
To my Lady at the Hall.

My Lady at the Hall
Is grander than they all :
Hers is the oldest name
In all the neighbourhood ;
But the race must die with her
Though she's a lofty dame,
For she's unmarried still.
Poor people say she's good,
And has an open hand
As any in the land,
And she's the comforter
Of many sick and sad ;
My nurse once said to me
That everything she had
Came of my Lady's bounty :
' Though she's greatest in the county
She's humble to the poor,—
No beggar seeks her door
But finds help presently.
I pray both night and day
For her, and you must pray :
But she'll never feel distress
If needy folk can bless.'

I was a little maid
When here we came to live
From somewhere by the sea.
Men spoke a foreign tongue
There where we used to be
When I was merry and young,
Too young to feel afraid ;
The fisher folk would give
A kind strange word to me,
There by the foreign sea :
I don't know where it was,
But I remember still

Our cottage on a hill,
And fields of flowering grass
On that fair foreign shore.

I liked my old home best,
But this was pleasant too :
So here we made our nest
And here I grew.
And now and then my Lady
In riding past our door
Would nod to Nurse and speak,
Or stoop and pat my cheek ;
And I was always ready
To hold the field-gate wide
For my Lady to go through ;
My Lady in her veil
So seldom put aside,
My Lady grave and pale.

I often sat to wonder
Who might my parents be,
For I knew of something under
My simple-seeming state.
Nurse never talked to me
Of mother or of father,
But watched me early and late
With kind suspicious cares :
Or not suspicious, rather
Anxious, as if she knew
Some secret I might gather
And smart for unawares.
Thus I grew.

But Nurse waxed old and grey,
Bent and weak with years.
There came a certain day
That she lay upon her bed,
Shaking her palsied head,
With words she gasped to say
Which had to stay unsaid.
Then with a jerking hand
Held out so piteously
She gave a ring to me
Of gold wrought curiously,—

A ring which she had worn
Since the day that I was born,
She once had said to me.
I slipped it on my finger;
Her eyes were keen to linger
On my hand that slipped it on;
Then she sighed one rattling sigh
And stared on with sightless eye:—
The one who loved me was gone.

How long I stayed alone
With the corpse I never knew,
For I fainted dead as stone.
When I came to life once more
I was down upon the floor,
With neighbours making ado
To bring me back to life.
I heard the sexton's wife
Say: 'Up, my lad, and run
To tell it at the Hall;
She was my Lady's nurse,
And done can't be undone:
I'll watch by this poor lamb.
I guess my Lady's purse
Is always open to such:
I'd run up on my crutch
A cripple as I am,'
(For cramps had vexed her much)
'Rather than this dear heart
Lack one to take her part.'

For days day after day
On my weary bed I lay
Wishing the time would pass;
Oh so wishing that I was
Likely to pass away:
For the one friend whom I knew
Was dead, I knew no other,
Neither father nor mother;
And I, what should I do?

One day the sexton's wife
Said: 'Rouse yourself, my dear:
My Lady has driven down

From the Hall into the town,
And we think she's coming here.
Cheer up, for life is life.'

But I would not look or speak,
Would not cheer up at all.
My tears were like to fall;
So I turned round to the wall
And hid my hollow cheek,
Making as if I slept,
As silent as a stone,
And no one knew I wept.
What was my Lady to me,
The grand lady from the Hall?
She might come, or stay away,
I was sick at heart that day:
The whole world seemed to be
Nothing, just nothing to me,
For aught that I could see.

Yet I listened where I lay.
A bustle came below,
A clear voice said: 'I know:
I will see her first alone,
It may be less of a shock
If she's so weak to-day.'—
A light hand turned the lock,
A light step crossed the floor,
One sat beside my bed:
But never a word she said.

For me, my shyness grew
Each moment more and more:
So I said never a word,
And neither looked nor stirred;
I think she must have heard
My heart go pit-a-pat:
Thus I lay, my Lady sat,
More than a mortal hour—
(I counted one and two
By the house-clock while I lay):
I seemed to have no power
To think of a thing to say,

Or do what I ought to do,
Or rouse myself to a choice.

At last she said: 'Margaret,
Won't you even look at me?'
A something in her voice
Forced my tears to fall at last,
Forced sobs from me thick and fast;
Something not of the past,
Yet stirring memory;
A something new, and yet
Not new, too sweet to last,
Which I never can forget.

I turned and stared at her:
Her cheek showed hollow-pale;
Her hair like mine was fair,
A wonderful fall of hair
That screened her like a veil;
But her height was statelier,
Her eyes had depth more deep:
I think they must have had
Always a something sad,
Unless they were asleep.

While I stared, my Lady took
My hand in her spare hand
Jewelled and soft and grand,
And looked with a long long look
Of hunger in my face;
As if she tried to trace
Features she ought to know,
And half hoped, half feared, to find.
Whatever was in her mind,
She heaved a sigh at last,
And began to talk to me.

'Your nurse was my dear nurse,
And her nursling's dear,' said she:
'No one told me a word
Of her getting worse and worse,
Till her poor life was past'
(Here my Lady's tears dropped fast).
'I might have been with her,
I might have promised and heard,
But she had no comforter.
She might have told me much
Which now I shall never know,
Never never shall know.'
She sat by me sobbing so,
And seemed so woe-begone,
That I laid one hand upon
Hers with a timid touch,
Scarce thinking what I did,
Not knowing what to say:
That moment her face was hid
In the pillow close by mine,
Her arm was flung over me,
She hugged me, sobbing so
As if her heart would break,
And kissed me where I lay.

After this she often came
To bring me fruit or wine
Or sometimes hothouse flowers;
And at nights I lay awake
Often and often thinking
What to do for her sake.
Wet or dry it was the same:
She would come in at all hours,
Set me eating and drinking
And say I must grow strong;
At last the day seemed long,
And home seemed scarcely home,
If she did not come.

Well, I grew strong again:
In time of primroses,
I went to pluck them in the lane;
In time of nestling birds,
I heard them chirping round the house;
And all the herds
Were out at grass when I grew strong,
And days were waxen long,
And there was work for bees
Among the May-bush boughs,
And I had shot up tall,
And life felt after all

Pleasant, and not so long,
When I grew strong.

I was going to the Hall
To be my Lady's maid:
'Her little friend,' she said to me,
'Almost her child,'
She said and smiled,
Sighing painfully;
Blushing, with a second flush
As if she blushed to blush.

Friend, servant, child: just this
My standing at the Hall;
The other servants call me 'Miss,'
My Lady calls me 'Margaret,'
With her clear voice musical.
She never chides when I forget
This or that; she never chides.
Except when people come to stay
(And that's not often) at the Hall,
I sit with her all day
And ride out when she rides.
She sings to me and makes me sing;
Sometimes I read to her,
Sometime we merely sit and talk.
She noticed once my ring
And made me tell its history;
That evening in our garden walk
She said she should infer
The ring had been my father's first,
Then my mother's, given for me
To the nurse who nursed
My mother in her misery,
That so quite certainly
Some one might know me, who . . .
Then she was silent, and I too.

I hate when people come:
The women speak and stare
And mean to be so civil.
This one will stroke my hair,
That one will pat my cheek
And praise my Lady's kindness,
Expecting me to speak;

I like the proud ones best
Who sit as struck with blindness,
As if I wasn't there.
But if any gentleman
Is staying at the Hall
(Though few come prying here),
My Lady seems to fear
Some downright dreadful evil,
And makes me keep my room
As closely as she can:
So I hate when people come,
It is so troublesome.
In spite of all her care,
Sometimes to keep alive
I sometimes do contrive
To get out in the grounds
For a whiff of wholesome air,
Under the rose you know:
It's charming to break bounds,
Stolen waters are sweet,
And what's the good of feet
If for days they mustn't go?
Give me a longer tether,
Or I may break from it.

Now I have eyes and ears,
And just some little wit.
'Almost my Lady's child;'
I recollect she smiled,
Sighed and blushed together.
Then her story of the ring
Sounds not improbable;
She told it me so well
It seemed the actual thing.—
Oh keep your counsel close:
But I guess under the rose,
In long past summer weather
When the world was blossoming
And the rose upon its thorn—
I guess not who he was
Flawed honour like a glass,
And made my life forlorn;
But my Mother, Mother, Mother,
Oh I know her from all other.

My Lady, you might trust
Your daughter with your fame.
Trust me, I would not shame
Our honourable name,
For I have noble blood
Though I was bred in dust
And brought up in the mud.
I will not press my claim,
Just leave me where you will:
But you might trust your daughter,
For blood is thicker than water
And you're my mother still.

So my Lady holds her own
With condescending grace,
And fills her lofty place
With an untroubled face
As a queen may fill a throne.
While I could hint a tale—
(But then I am her child)—
Would make her quail;
Would set her in the dust,
Lorn with no comforter,
Her glorious hair defiled
And ashes on her cheek:
The decent world would thrust
Its finger out at her,
Not much displeased I think
To make a nine days' stir;
The decent world would sink
Its voice to speak of her.

Now this is what I mean
To do, no more, no less:
Never to speak, or show
Bare sign of what I know.
Let the blot pass unseen;
Yea, let her never guess
I hold the tangled clue
She huddles out of view.
Friend, servant, almost child—
So be it and nothing more
On this side of the grave.

Mother, in Paradise
You'll see with clearer eyes;
Perhaps in this world even
When you are like to die
And face to face with Heaven
You'll drop for once the lie:
But you must drop the mask, not I.

My Lady promises
Two hundred pounds with me
Whenever I may wed
A man she can approve:
And since besides her bounty
I'm fairest in the county
(For so I've heard it said,
Though I don't vouch for this),
Her promised pounds may move
Some honest man to see
My virtues and my beauties;
Perhaps the rising grazier,
Or temperance publican,
May claim my wifely duties.
Meanwhile I wait their leisure
And grace-bestowing pleasure,
I wait the happy man;
But if I hold my head
And pitch my expectations
Just higher than their level,
They must fall back on patience.
I may not mean to wed,
Yet I'll be civil.

Now sometimes in a dream
My heart goes out of me
To build and scheme,
Till I sob after things that seem
So pleasant in a dream:
A home such as I see
My blessed neighbours live in
With father and with mother,
All proud of one another,
Named by one common name
From baby in the bud
To full-blown workman Father;

It's little short of Heaven.
I'd give my gentle blood
To wash my special shame
And drown my private grudge.
I'd toil and moil much rather,
The dingiest cottage drudge
Whose mother need not blush,
Than live here like a lady
And see my Mother flush
And hear her voice unsteady
Sometimes, yet never dare
Ask to share her care.

Of course the servants sneer
Behind my back at me;
Of course the village girls,
Who envy me my curls
And gowns and idleness,
Take comfort in a jeer;
Of course the ladies guess
Just so much of my history
As points the emphatic stress
With which they laud my Lady.
The gentlemen who catch
A casual glimpse of me
And turn again to see,
Their valets on the watch
To speak a word with me,
All know and sting me wild;
Till I am almost ready
To wish that I were dead—
No faces more to see,
No more words to be said,
My Mother safe at last
Disburdened of her child,
And the past past.

'All equal before God'—
Our Rector has it so,
And sundry sleepers nod.
It may be so; I know
All are not equal here,
And when the sleepers wake
They make a difference.

'All equal in the grave'—
That shows an obvious sense:
Yet something which I crave
Not death itself brings near;
How should death half atone
For all my past, or make
The name I bear my own?

I love my dear old Nurse
Who loved me without gains;
I love my mistress even,
Friend, Mother, what you will.
But I could almost curse
My Father for his pains;
And sometimes at my prayer
Kneeling in sight of Heaven
I almost curse him still:
Why did he set his snare
To catch at unaware
My Mother's foolish youth,—
Load me with shame that's hers,
And her with something worse,
A lifelong lie for truth?

I think my mind is fixed
On one point and made up:
To accept my lot unmixed;
Never to drug the cup
But drink it by myself.
I'll not be wooed for pelf;
I'll not blot out my shame
With any man's good name;
But nameless as I stand,
My hand is my own hand,
And nameless as I came
I go to the dark land.

'All equal in the grave'—
I bide my time till then:
'All equal before God'—
To-day I feel His rod,
To-morrow He may save.
                Amen.

March 1865.

THE MONTHS:

A PAGEANT.

PERSONIFICATIONS.

Boys. *Girls.*
JANUARY. FEBRUARY.
MARCH. APRIL.
JULY. MAY.
AUGUST. JUNE.
OCTOBER. SEPTEMBER.
DECEMBER. NOVEMBER.

ROBIN REDBREASTS; LAMBS AND SHEEP;
NIGHTINGALE AND NESTLINGS.

Various Flowers, Fruits, etc.

Scene: A COTTAGE WITH ITS GROUNDS.

[A room in a large comfortable cottage; a fire burning on the hearth; a table on which the breakfast things have been left standing. January discovered seated by the fire.]

JANUARY.

COLD the day and cold the drifted snow,
Dim the day until the cold dark night.
     [Stirs the fire.
Crackle, sparkle, faggot; embers glow:
Some one may be plodding through the snow
Longing for a light,
For the light that you and I can show.
If no one else should come,
Here Robin Redbreast's welcome to a crumb,
And never troublesome:
Robin, why don't you come and fetch your crumb?

Here's butter for my hunch of bread,
 And sugar for your crumb;
Here's room upon the hearthrug,
 If you'll only come.

In your scarlet waistcoat,
 With your keen bright eye,
Where are you loitering?
 Wings were made to fly!

Make haste to breakfast,
 Come and fetch your crumb,
For I'm as glad to see you
 As you are glad to come.

[Two Robin Redbreasts are seen tapping with their beaks at the lattice, which January opens. The birds flutter in, hop about the floor, and peck up the crumbs and sugar thrown to them. They have scarcely finished their meal when a knock is heard at the door. January hangs a guard in front of the fire, and opens to February, who appears with a bunch of snowdrops in her hand.]

Good-morrow, sister.

FEBRUARY.

   Brother, joy to you!
I've brought some snowdrops; only just a few,
But quite enough to prove the world awake,
Cheerful and hopeful in the frosty dew
And for the pale sun's sake.

[She hands a few of her snowdrops to January, who retires into the background. While February stands arranging the remaining snowdrops in a glass of water on the window-sill, a soft butting and bleating are heard outside. She opens the door, and sees one foremost lamb, with other sheep and lambs bleating and crowding towards her.]

O you, you little wonder, come—come in,
You wonderful, you woolly soft white lamb:

You panting mother ewe, come too,
And lead that tottering twin
Safe in:
Bring all your bleating kith and kin,
Except the horny ram.

[February opens a second door in the background, and the little flock files through into a warm and sheltered compartment out of sight.]

The lambkin tottering in its walk
 With just a fleece to wear;
The snowdrop drooping on its stalk
 So slender,—
Snowdrop and lamb, a pretty pair,
Braving the cold for our delight,
 Both white,
 Both tender.

[A rattling of doors and windows; branches seen without, tossing violently to and fro.]

How the doors rattle, and the branches
 sway!
Here's brother March comes whirling
 on his way
With winds that eddy and sing:—

[She turns the handle of the door, which bursts open, and discloses March hastening up, both hands full of violets and anemones.]

Come, show me what you bring;
For I have said my say, fulfilled my
 day,
And must away.

MARCH

[Stopping short on the threshold.]

I blow an arouse
 Through the world's wide house
To quicken the torpid earth:
 Grappling I fling
 Each feeble thing,
But bring strong life to the birth.

I wrestle and frown,
 And topple down;
I wrench, I rend, I uproot;
 Yet the violet
 Is born where I set
The sole of my flying foot,

[Hands violets and anemones to February, who retires into the background.]

And in my wake
 Frail wind-flowers quake,
And the catkins promise fruit.
 I drive ocean ashore
 With rush and roar,
And he cannot say me nay:
 My harpstrings all
 Are the forests tall,
Making music when I play.
 And as others perforce,
 So I on my course
Run and needs must run,
 With sap on the mount
 And buds past count
And rivers and clouds and sun,
 With seasons and breath
 And time and death
And all that has yet begun.

[Before March has done speaking, a voice is heard approaching accompanied by a twittering of birds. April comes along singing, and stands outside and out of sight to finish her song.]

APRIL

[Outside.]

Pretty little three
Sparrows in a tree,
 Light upon the wing;
 Though you cannot sing
 You can chirp of Spring:
Chirp of Spring to me,
Sparrows, from your tree.

Never mind the showers,
Chirp about the flowers
　While you build a nest:
　Straws from east and west,
　Feathers from your breast,
Make the snuggest bowers
In a world of flowers.

You must dart away
From the chosen spray,
　You intrusive third
　Extra little bird;
　Join the unwedded herd!
These have done with play,
And must work to-day.

[Appearing at the open door.]

Good-morrow and good-bye: if others fly,
Of all the flying months you're the most flying.

MARCH.

You're hope and sweetness, April.

APRIL.

　　　　Birth means dying,
As wings and wind mean flying;
So you and I and all things fly or die;
And sometimes I sit sighing to think of dying.
But meanwhile I've a rainbow in my showers,
And a lapful of flowers,
And these dear nestlings aged three hours;
And here's their mother sitting;
Their father's merely flitting
To find their breakfast somewhere in my bowers.

[As she speaks April shows March her apron full of flowers and nest full of birds. March wanders away into the grounds. April, without entering the cottage, hangs over the hungry nestlings watching them.]

What beaks you have, you funny things,
　What voices shrill and weak;
Who'd think that anything that sings
　Could sing through such a beak?
Yet you'll be nightingales one day,
　And charm the country side,
When I'm away and far away
　And May is queen and bride.

[May arrives unperceived by April, and gives her a kiss. April starts and looks round.]

Ah May, good-morrow, May, and so good-bye.

MAY.

That's just your way, sweet April, smile and sigh:
Your sorrow's half in fun,
Begun and done
And turned to joy while twenty seconds run.
I've gathered flowers all as I came along,
At every step a flower
Fed by your last bright shower,—

[She divides an armful of all sorts of flowers with April, who strolls away through the garden.]

And gathering flowers I listened to the song
Of every bird in bower.

The world and I are far too full of bliss

To think or plan or toil or care ;
   The sun is waxing strong,
   The days are waxing long,
      And all that is
         Is fair.

Here are my buds of lily and of rose,
   And here's my namesake blossom may ;
   And from a watery spot
   See here forget-me-not,
      With all that blows
         To-day.

Hark to my linnets from the hedges green,
   Blackbird and lark and thrush and dove,
   And every nightingale
   And cuckoo tells its tale,
      And all they mean
         Is love.

[June appears at the further end of the garden, coming slowly towards May, who, seeing her, exclaims]

Surely you're come too early, sister June.

JUNE.

Indeed I feel as if I came too soon
To round your young May moon
And set the world a-gasping at my noon.
Yet come I must. So here are strawberries
Sun-flushed and sweet, as many as you please ;
And here are full-blown roses by the score,
More roses, and yet more.

[May, eating strawberries, withdraws among the flower beds.]

The sun does all my long day's work for me,
   Raises and ripens everything ;
   I need but sit beneath a leafy tree
      And watch and sing.

[Seats herself in the shadow of a laburnum.]

Or if I'm lulled by note of bird and bee,
   Or lulled by noontide's silence deep,
   I need but nestle down beneath my tree
      And drop asleep.

[June falls asleep ; and is not awakened by the voice of July, who behind the scenes is heard half singing, half calling.]

JULY

[Behind the scenes.]

Blue flags, yellow flags, flags all freckled,
Which will you take ? yellow, blue, speckled !
Take which you will, speckled, blue, yellow,
Each in its way has not a fellow.

[Enter July, a basket of many-coloured irises slung upon his shoulders, a bunch of ripe grass in one hand, and a plate piled full of peaches balanced upon the other. He steals up to June, and tickles her with the grass. She wakes.]

JUNE.

What, here already ?

JULY.

      Nay, my tryst is kept ;
The longest day slipped by you while you slept.
I've brought you one curved pyramid of bloom,
        [Hands her the plate.]

Not flowers but peaches, gathered
    where the bees,
As downy, bask and boom
In sunshine and in gloom of trees.
But get you in, a storm is at my
    heels;
The whirlwind whistles and wheels,
Lightning flashes and thunder peals,
Flying and following hard upon my
    heels.

[June takes shelter in a thickly-woven arbour.]

The roar of a storm sweeps up
    From the east to the lurid west,
The darkening sky, like a cup,
    Is filled with rain to the brink;
The sky is purple and fire,
    Blackness and noise and unrest;
The earth, parched with desire,
    Opens her mouth to drink.

Send forth thy thunder and fire,
    Turn over thy brimming cup,
O sky, appease the desire
    Of earth in her parched unrest;
Pour out drink to her thirst,
    Her famishing life lift up;
Make thyself fair as at first,
    With a rainbow for thy crest.

Have done with thunder and fire,
    O sky with the rainbow crest;
O earth, have done with desire,
    Drink, and drink deep, and rest.

[Enter August, carrying a sheaf made up of different kinds of grain.]

Hail, brother August, flushed and
    warm
And scatheless from my storm.
Your hands are full of corn, I see,
As full as hands can be:

And earth and air both smell as
    sweet as balm
In their recovered calm,
And that they owe to me.

[July retires into a shrubbery.]

AUGUST.

Wheat sways heavy, oats are airy,
    Barley bows a graceful head,
Short and small shoots up canary,
    Each of these is some one's bread:
Bread for man or bread for beast,
    Or at very least
    A bird's savoury feast.

Men are brethren of each other,
    One in flesh and one in food;
And a sort of foster-brother
    Is the litter or the brood
Of that folk in fur or feather
    Who, with men together,
    Breast the wind and weather.

[August descries September toiling across the lawn.]

My harvest home is ended; and I spy
September drawing nigh
With the first thought of Autumn in
    her eye,
And the first sigh
Of Autumn wind among her locks
    that fly.

[September arrives, carrying upon her head a basket heaped high with fruit.]

SEPTEMBER.

Unload me, brother. I have brought
    a few
Plums and these pears for you,
A dozen kinds of apples, one or two
Melons, some figs all bursting
    through

Their skins, and pearled with dew
These damsons violet-blue.

[While September is speaking, August lifts the basket to the ground, selects various fruits, and withdraws slowly along the gravel walk, eating a pear as he goes.]

My song is half a sigh
Because my green leaves die;
Sweet are my fruits, but all my
leaves are dying;
And well may Autumn sigh,
And well may I
Who watch the sere leaves flying.

My leaves that fade and fall,
I note you one and all;
I call you, and the Autumn wind is
calling,
Lamenting for your fall,
And for the pall
You spread on earth in falling.

And here's a song of flowers to suit
such hours:
A song of the last lilies, the last
flowers,
Amid my withering bowers.

In the sunny garden bed
Lilies look so pale,
Lilies droop the head
In the shady grassy vale;
If all alike they pine
In shade and in shine,
If everywhere they grieve,
Where will lilies live?

[October enters briskly, some leafy twigs bearing different sorts of nuts in one hand, and a long ripe hop-bine trailing after him from the other. A dahlia is stuck in his buttonhole.]

OCTOBER.

Nay, cheer up sister. Life is not
quite over,
Even if the year has done with corn
and clover,
With flowers and leaves; besides, in
fact it's true,
Some leaves remain and some flowers
too
For me and you.
Now see my crops:

[Offering his produce to September.]

I've brought you nuts and hops;
And when the leaf drops, why, the
walnut drops.

[October wreathes the hop-bine about September's neck, and gives her the nut twigs. They enter the cottage together, but without shutting the door. She steps into the background: he advances to the hearth, removes the guard, stirs up the smouldering fire, and arranges several chestnuts ready to roast.]

Crack your first nut and light your
first fire,
Roast your first chestnut crisp on
the bar;
Make the logs sparkle, stir the blaze
higher,
Logs are cheery as sun or as star,
Logs we can find wherever we are.

Spring one soft day will open the
leaves,
Spring one bright day will lure
back the flowers;
Never fancy my whistling wind
grieves,
Never fancy I've tears in my
showers:
Dance, nights and days! and
dance on, my hours!

[Sees November approaching.]

Here comes my youngest sister, looking dim
And grim,
With dismal ways.
What cheer, November?

NOVEMBER

[Entering and shutting the door.]

Nought have I to bring,
Tramping a-chill and shivering,
Except these pine-cones for a blaze,—
Except a fog which follows,
And stuffs up all the hollows,—
Except a hoar frost here and there,—
Except some shooting stars
Which dart their luminous cars
Trackless and noiseless through the keen night air.

[October, shrugging his shoulders, withdraws into the background, while November throws her pine-cones on the fire, and sits down listlessly.]

The earth lies fast asleep, grown tired
  Of all that's high or deep;
There's nought desired and nought required
  Save a sleep.
I rock the cradle of the earth,
  I lull her with a sigh;
And know that she will wake to mirth
  By and by.

[Through the window December is seen running and leaping in the direction of the door. He knocks.]

Ah, here's my youngest brother come at last:

[Calls out without rising.]

Come in, December.

[He opens the door and enters, loaded with evergreens in berry, etc.]

Come, and shut the door,
For now it's snowing fast;
It snows, and will snow more and more;
Don't let it drift in on the floor.
But you, you're all aglow; how can you be
Rosy and warm and smiling in the cold?

DECEMBER.

Nay, no closed doors for me,
But open doors and open hearts and glee
To welcome young and old.

  Dimmest and brightest month am I;
My short days end, my lengthening days begin;
What matters more or less sun in the sky,
  When all is sun within?

[He begins making a wreath as he sings.]

  Ivy and privet dark as night,
I weave with hips and haws a cheerful show,
And holly for a beauty and delight,
  And milky mistletoe.

While high above them all I set
Yew twigs and Christmas roses pure and pale;
Then Spring her snowdrop and her violet
  May keep, so sweet and frail;

May keep each merry singing bird,
Of all her happy birds that singing build:

For I've a carol which some shep-
    herds heard
Once in a wintry field.

[While December concludes his song all the other Months troop in from the garden, or advance out of the background. The Twelve join hands in a circle, and begin dancing round to a stately measure as the Curtain falls.]

Summer 1879.

A BALLAD OF BODING

THERE are sleeping dreams and
    waking dreams;
What seems is not always as it seems.

I looked out of my window in the
    sweet new morning,
And there I saw three barges of
    manifold adorning
Went sailing toward the East:
The first had sails like fire,
The next like glittering wire,
But sackcloth were the sails of the
    least;
And all the crews made music, and
    two had spread a feast.

The first choir breathed in flutes,
And fingered soft guitars;
The second won from lutes
Harmonious chords and jars,
With drums for stormy bars:
But the third was all of harpers and
    scarlet trumpeters;
Notes of triumph, then
An alarm again,
As for onset, as for victory, rallies,
    stirs,
Peace at last and glory to the van-
    quishers.

The first barge showed for figure-
    head a Love with wings;
The second showed for figurehead a
    Worm with stings;
The third, a Lily tangled to a Rose
    which clings.
The first bore for freight gold and
    spice and down;
The second bore a sword, a sceptre,
    and a crown;
The third, a heap of earth gone to
    dust and brown.
Winged Love meseemed like Folly
    in the face;
Stinged Worm meseemed loathly in
    his place;
Lily and Rose were flowers of grace.

Merry went the revel of the fire-
    sailed crew,
Singing, feasting, dancing to and fro:
Pleasures ever changing, ever grace-
    ful, ever new;
Sighs, but scarce of woe;
All the sighing
Wooed such sweet replying;
All the sighing, sweet and low,
Used to come and go
For more pleasure, merely so.
Yet at intervals some one grew
    tired
Of everything desired,
And sank, I knew not whither, in
    sorry plight,
Out of sight.

The second crew seemed ever
Wider-visioned, graver,
More distinct of purpose, more sus-
    tained of will;
With heads erect and proud,
And voices sometimes loud;
With endless tacking, counter-tack-
    ing,

All things grasping, all things
    lacking,
It would seem;
Ever shifting helm, or sail, or shroud,
Drifting on as in a dream.
Hoarding to their utmost bent,
Feasting to their fill,
Yet gnawed by discontent,
Envy, hatred, malice, on their road
    they went.
Their freight was not a treasure,
Their music not a pleasure;
The sword flashed, cleaving through
    their bands,
Sceptre and crown changed hands.

The third crew as they went
Seemed mostly different;
They toiled in rowing, for to them
    the wind was contrary,
As all the world might see.
They laboured at the oar,
While on their heads they bore
The fiery stress of sunshine more
    and more.
They laboured at the oar hand-
    sore,
Till rain went splashing,
And spray went dashing,
Down on them, and up on them,
    more and more.
Their sails were patched and rent,
Their masts were bent,
In peril of their lives they worked
    and went.
For them no feast was spread,
No soft luxurious bed
Scented and white,
No crown or sceptre hung in sight;
In weariness and painfulness,
In thirst and sore distress,
They rowed and steered from left
    to right
With all their might.

Their trumpeters and harpers round
    about
Incessantly played out,
And sometimes they made answer
    with a shout;
But oftener they groaned or wept,
And seldom paused to eat, and
    seldom slept.
I wept for pity watching them, but
    more
I wept heart-sore
Once and again to see
Some weary man plunge overboard,
    and swim
To Love or Worm ship floating
    buoyantly:
And there all welcomed him.

The ships steered each apart and
    seemed to scorn each other,
Yet all the crews were inter-
    changeable;
Now one man, now another,—
Like bloodless spectres some, some
    flushed by health,—
Changed openly, or changed by
    stealth,
Scaling a slippery side, and scaled
    it well.
The most left Love ship, hauling
    wealth
Up Worm ship's side;
While some few hollow-eyed
Left either for the sack-sailed boat;
But this, though not remote,
Was worst to mount, and whoso left
    it once
Scarce ever came again,
But seemed to loathe his erst
    companions,
And wish and work them bane.

Then I knew (I know not how) there
    lurked quicksands full of dread,

A BALLAD OF BODING

Rocks and reefs and whirlpools in
    the water bed,
Whence a waterspout
Instantaneously leaped out,
Roaring as it reared its head.
Soon I spied a something dim
Many-handed, grim,
That went flitting to and fro the first
    and second ship;
It puffed their sails full out
With puffs of smoky breath
From a smouldering lip,
And cleared the waterspout
Which reeled roaring round about
Threatening death.
With a horny hand it steered,
And a horn appeared
On its sneering head upreared
Haughty and high
Against the blackening lowering sky.
With a hoof it swayed the waves;
They opened here and there,
Till I spied deep open graves
Full of skeletons
That were men and women once
Foul or fair;
Full of things that creep
And fester in the deep
And never breathe the clean life-
    nurturing air.

The third bark held aloof
From the Monster with the hoof,
Despite his urgent beck,
And fraught with guile
Abominable his smile;
Till I saw him take a flying leap on
    to that deck.
Then full of awe,
With these same eyes I saw
His head incredible retract its horn
Rounding like babe's new born,
While silvery phosphorescence played
About his dis-horned head.

The sneer smoothed from his lip,
He beamed blandly on the ship;
All winds sank to a moan,
All waves to a monotone
(For all these seemed his realm),
While he laid a strong caressing
    hand upon the helm.

Then a cry well nigh of despair
Shrieked to heaven, a clamour of
    desperate prayer.
The harpers harped no more,
While the trumpeters sounded sore,
An alarm to wake the dead from
    their bed:
To the rescue, to the rescue, now
    or never,
To the rescue, O ye living, O ye dead,
Or no more help or hope for ever!—
The planks strained as though they
    must part asunder,
The masts bent as though they must
    dip under,
And the winds and the waves at length
Girt up their strength,
And the depths were laid bare,
And heaven flashed fire and volleyed
    thunder
Through the rain-choked air,
And sea and sky seemed to kiss
In the horror and the hiss
Of the whole world shuddering every-
    where.

Lo! a Flyer swooping down
With wings to span the globe,
And splendour for his robe
And splendour for his crown.
He lighted on the helm with a foot
    of fire,
And spun the Monster overboard:
And that monstrous thing abhorred,
Gnashing with balked desire,
Wriggled like a worm infirm

Up the Worm
Of the loathly figurehead.
There he crouched and gnashed;
And his head re-horned, and gashed
From the other's grapple, dripped
    bloody red.

I saw that thing accurst
Wreak his worst
On the first and second crew:
Some with baited hook
He angled for and took,
Some dragged overboard in a net
    he threw;
Some he did to death
With hoof or horn or blasting breath.

I heard a voice of wailing
Where the ships went sailing,
A sorrowful voice prevailing
Above the sound of the sea,
Above the singers' voices,
And musical merry noises;
All songs had turned to sighing,
The light was failing,
The day was dying—
Ah me
That such a sorrow should be!

There was sorrow on the sea and
    sorrow on the land
When Love ship went down by the
    bottomless quicksand
To its grave in the bitter wave.
There was sorrow on the sea and
    sorrow on the land
When Worm ship went to pieces on
    the rock-bound strand,
And the bitter wave was its grave.
But land and sea waxed hoary
In whiteness of a glory
Never told in story
Nor seen by mortal eye,
When the third ship crossed the bar
Where whirls and breakers are,
And steered into the splendours of
    the sky;
That third bark and that least
Which had never seemed to feast,
Yet kept high festival above sun and
    moon and star.

Before 1882.

MONNA INNOMINATA

A SONNET OF SONNETS

BEATRICE, immortalized by 'altissimo poeta . . . cotanto amante'; Laura, celebrated by a great though an inferior bard, —have alike paid the exceptional penalty of exceptional honour, and have come down to us resplendent with charms, but (at least, to my apprehension) scant of attractiveness. These heroines of world-wide fame were preceded by a bevy of unnamed ladies, 'donne innominate,' sung by a school of less conspicuous poets; and in that land and that period which gave simultaneous birth to Catholics, to Albigenses, and to Troubadours, one can imagine many a lady as sharing her lover's poetic aptitude, while the barrier between them might be one held sacred by both, yet not such as to render mutual love incompatible with mutual honour.

Had such a lady spoken for herself, the portrait left us might have appeared more tender, if less dignified, than any drawn even by a devoted friend. Or had the Great Poetess of our own day and nation only been unhappy instead of happy, her circumstances would have invited her to bequeath to us, in lieu of the 'Portuguese Sonnets,' an inimitable 'donna innominata' drawn not from fancy but from feeling, and worthy to occupy a niche beside Beatrice and Laura.

I

'Lo dì che han detto a' dolci amici addio.'
                        DANTE.
'Amor, con quanto sforzo oggi mi vinci!'
                       PETRARCA.

COME back, who wait and
    watch for you:—

Or come not yet, for it is over then,
And long it is before you come
    again,
So far between my pleasures are and
    few.
While, when you come not, what I
    do I do
    Thinking 'Now when he comes,'
      my sweetest 'when':
    For one man is my world of all
      the men
This wide world holds; O love, my
    world is you.
Howbeit, to meet you grows almost
    a pang
    Because the pang of parting
      comes so soon;
My hope hangs waning, waxing,
    like a moon
    Between the heavenly days on
      which we meet:
Ah me, but where are now the songs
    I sang
    When life was sweet because you
      called them sweet?

2

'Era già l'ora che volge il desio.'—DANTE.
'Ricorro al tempo ch' io vi vidi prima.'
                        PETRARCA.

I wish I could remember that first day,
    First hour, first moment of your
      meeting me,
    If bright or dim the season, it
      might be
Summer or Winter for aught I can
    say;
So unrecorded did it slip away,
    So blind was I to see and to fore-
      see,
    So dull to mark the budding of
      my tree
That would not blossom yet for
    many a May.

If only I could recollect it, such
    A day of days! I let it come
      and go
    As traceless as a thaw of bygone
      snow;
It seemed to mean so little, meant
    so much;
If only now I could recall that touch,
    First touch of hand in hand—Did
      one but know!

3

'O ombre vane, fuor che ne l'aspetto!'
                           DANTE.
'Immaginata guida la conduce.'
                        PETRARCA.

I dream of you, to wake: would that
    I might
    Dream of you and not wake but
      slumber on;
Nor find with dreams the dear
    companion gone,
As, Summer ended, Summer birds
    take flight.
In happy dreams I hold you full in
    sight,
    I blush again who waking look
      so wan;
    Brighter than sunniest day that
      ever shone,
In happy dreams your smile makes
    day of night.
Thus only in a dream we are at one,
    Thus only in a dream we give
      and take
    The faith that maketh rich who
      take or give;
    If thus to sleep is sweeter than to
      wake,
      To die were surely sweeter
        than to live,
Though there be nothing new be-
    neath the sun.

4

'Poca favilla gran fiamma seconda.'
                DANTE.
'Ogni altra cosa, ogni pensier va fore,
E sol ivi con voi rimansi amore.'
                PETRARCA.

I loved you first: but afterwards your love,
    Outsoaring mine, sang such a loftier song
As drowned the friendly cooings of my dove.
    Which owes the other most? My love was long,
And yours one moment seemed to wax more strong;
I loved and guessed at you, you construed me
And loved me for what might or might not be—
    Nay, weights and measures do us both a wrong.
For verily love knows not 'mine' or 'thine';
    With separate 'I' and 'thou' free love has done,
        For one is both and both are one in love:
Rich love knows nought of 'thine that is not mine;'
    Both have the strength and both the length thereof,
    Both of us, of the love which makes us one.

5

'Amor che a nullo amato amar perdona.'
                DANTE.
'Amor m'addusse in sì gioiosa spene.'
                PETRARCA.

O my heart's heart, and you who are to me
    More than myself myself, God be with you,
Keep you in strong obedience leal and true
To Him whose noble service setteth free;
Give you all good we see or can foresee,
    Make your joys many and your sorrows few,
    Bless you in what you bear and what you do,
Yea, perfect you as He would have you be.
So much for you; but what for me, dear friend?
    To love you without stint and all I can,
To-day, to-morrow, world without an end;
To love you much and yet to love you more,
    As Jordan at his flood sweeps either shore;
    Since woman is the helpmeet made for man.

6

'Or puoi la quantitate
Comprender de l'amor che a te mi scalda.'
                DANTE.
'Non vo' che da tal nodo amor mi sciogli.'
                PETRARCA.

Trust me, I have not earned your dear rebuke,—
    I love, as you would have me, God the most;
    Would lose not Him, but you, must one be lost,
Nor with Lot's wife cast back a faithless look,
Unready to forego what I forsook;
    This say I, having counted up the cost,
    This, though I be the feeblest of God's host,

The sorriest sheep Christ shepherds
    with His crook.
Yet while I love my God the most,
    I deem
  That I can never love you over-
      much ;
    I love Him more, so let me love
        you too ;
  Yea, as I apprehend it, love is such
I cannot love you if I love not Him,
    I cannot love Him if I love not
        you.

7

'Qui primavera sempre ed ogni frutto.'
                               DANTE.
'Ragionando con meco ed io con lui.'
                            PETRARCA.

'Love me, for I love you' — and
    answer me,
  'Love me, for I love you': so
      shall we stand
  As happy equals in the flowering
      land
Of love, that knows not a dividing
    sea.
Love builds the house on rock and
    not on sand,
  Love laughs what while the winds
      rave desperately ;
And who hath found love's citadel
    unmanned?
  And who hath held in bonds love's
      liberty?—
My heart's a coward though my
    words are brave—
  We meet so seldom, yet we surely
      part
  So often ; there's a problem for
      your art !
  Still I find comfort in his Book
      who saith,
Though jealousy be cruel as the
    grave,

And death be strong, yet love
    is strong as death.

8

'Come dicesse a Dio, D'altro non calme.'
                               DANTE.
'Spero trovar pietà non che perdono.'
                            PETRARCA.

'I, if I perish, perish'—Esther spake:
    And bride of life or death she made
        her fair
    In all the lustre of her perfumed
        hair
And smiles that kindle longing but
    to slake.
She put on pomp of loveliness, to
    take
    Her husband through his eyes at
        unaware ;
    She spread abroad her beauty for
        a snare,
Harmless as doves and subtle as a
    snake.
She trapped him with one mesh of
    silken hair,
    She vanquished him by wisdom of
        her wit,
    And built her people's house
        that it should stand :—
    If I might take my life so in my
        hand,
And for my love to Love put up my
    prayer,
    And for love's sake by Love be
        granted it !

9

'O dignitosa coscienza e netta !'—DANTE.
'Spirto più acceso di virtuti ardenti.'
                            PETRARCA.

Thinking of you, and all that was,
    and all
  That might have been and now
      can never be,

I feel your honoured excellence, and see
Myself unworthy of the happier call:
For woe is me who walk so apt to fall,
  So apt to shrink afraid, so apt to flee,
  Apt to lie down and die (ah woe is me!)
Faithless and hopeless turning to the wall.
And yet not hopeless quite nor faithless quite,
Because not loveless; love may toil all night,
  But take at morning; wrestle till the break
  Of day, but then wield power with God and man :—
So take I heart of grace as best I can,
Ready to spend and be spent for your sake.

10

  'Con miglior corso e con migliore stella.'
                                  DANTE.
  'La vita fugge e non s'arresta un' ora.'
                                PETRARCA.

Time flies, hope flags, life plies a wearied wing;
  Death following hard on life gains ground apace;
  Faith runs with each and rears an eager face,
Outruns the rest, makes light of everything,
Spurns earth, and still finds breath to pray and sing;
  While love ahead of all uplifts his praise,
  Still asks for grace and still gives thanks for grace,
Content with all day brings and night will bring.
Life wanes; and when love folds his wings above
Tired hope, and less we feel his conscious pulse,
  Let us go fall asleep, dear friend, in peace:
  A little while, and age and sorrow cease;
  A little while, and life reborn annuls
Loss and decay and death, and all is love.

11

  'Vien dietro a me e lascia dir le genti.'
                                  DANTE.
  'Contando i casi della vita nostra.'
                                PETRARCA.

Many in aftertimes will say of you
  'He loved her'—while of me what will they say?
  Not that I loved you more than just in play,
For fashion's sake as idle women do.
Even let them prate; who know not what we knew
  Of love and parting in exceeding pain,
  Of parting hopeless here to meet again,
Hopeless on earth, and heaven is out of view.
But by my heart of love laid bare to you,
  My love that you can make not void nor vain,
Love that foregoes you but to claim anew
Beyond this passage of the gate of death,
  I charge you at the Judgment make it plain
My love of you was life and not a breath.

MONNA INNOMINATA 63

12

'Amor che ne la mente mi ragiona.'
　　　　　　　　　　　DANTE.
'Amor vien nel bel viso di costei.'
　　　　　　　　　　　PETRARCA.

If there be any one can take my place
　And make you happy whom I
　　grieve to grieve,
　Think not that I can grudge it,
　　but believe
I do commend you to that nobler
　　grace,
That readier wit than mine, that
　　sweeter face;
　Yea, since your riches make me
　　rich, conceive
　I too am crowned, while bridal
　　crowns I weave,
And thread the bridal dance with
　　jocund pace.
For if I did not love you, it might be
That I should grudge you some
　　one dear delight;
　But since the heart is yours
　　that was mine own,
　Your pleasure is my pleasure,
　　right my right,
Your honourable freedom makes me
　　free,
　And you companioned I am not
　　alone.

13

'E drizzeremo gli occhi al Primo Amore.'
　　　　　　　　　　　DANTE.
'Ma trovo peso non da le mie braccia.'
　　　　　　　　　　　PETRARCA.

If I could trust mine own self with
　　your fate,
　Shall I not rather trust it in God's
　　hand?
　Without Whose Will one lily doth
　　not stand,
Nor sparrow fall at his appointed
　　date;
　Who numbereth the innumerable
　　sand,
　Who weighs the wind and water
　　with a weight,
To Whom the world is neither small
　　nor great,
　Whose knowledge foreknew every
　　plan we planned.
Searching my heart for all that
　　touches you,
　I find there only love and love's
　　goodwill
Helpless to help and impotent to
　　do,
　Of understanding dull, of sight most
　　dim;
And therefore I commend you back
　　to Him
　Whose love your love's capacity
　　can fill.

14

'E la Sua Volontade è nostra pace.'
　　　　　　　　　　　DANTE.
'Sol con questi pensier, con altre chiome.'
　　　　　　　　　　　PETRARCA.

Youth gone, and beauty gone if ever
　　there
　Dwelt beauty in so poor a face as
　　this;
　Youth gone and beauty, what
　　remains of bliss?
I will not bind fresh roses in my hair,
　To shame a cheek at best but little
　　fair,—
　Leave youth his roses, who can
　　bear a thorn,—
I will not seek for blossoms anywhere,
　Except such common flowers as
　　blow with corn.
Youth gone and beauty gone, what
　　doth remain?

The longing of a heart pent up forlorn,
  A silent heart whose silence loves and longs;
  The silence of a heart which sang its songs
While youth and beauty made a summer morn,
Silence of love that cannot sing again.

Before 1882.

AN OLD-WORLD THICKET

'Una selva oscura.'—DANTE.

AWAKE or sleeping (for I know not which)
  I was or was not mazed within a wood
  Where every mother-bird brought up her brood
Safe in some leafy niche
Of oak or ash, of cypress or of beech,

Of silvery aspen trembling delicately,
  Of plane or warmer-tinted sycomore,
  Of elm that dies in secret from the core,
Of ivy weak and free,
Of pines, of all green lofty things that be.

Such birds they seemed as challenged each desire;
  Like spots of azure heaven upon the wing,
  Like downy emeralds that alight and sing,
Like actual coals on fire,
Like anything they seemed, and everything.

Such mirth they made, such warblings and such chat,
  With tongue of music in a well-tuned beak,
  They seemed to speak more wisdom than we speak,
To make our music flat
And all our subtlest reasonings wild or weak.

Their meat was nought but flowers like butterflies,
  With berries coral-coloured or like gold;
  Their drink was only dew, which blossoms hold
Deep where the honey lies;
Their wings and tails were lit by sparkling eyes.

The shade wherein they revelled was a shade
  That danced and twinkled to the unseen sun;
  Branches and leaves cast shadows one by one,
And all their shadows swayed
In breaths of air that rustled and that played.

A sound of waters neither rose nor sank,
  And spread a sense of freshness through the air;
  It seemed not here or there, but everywhere,
As if the whole earth drank,
Root fathom-deep and strawberry on its bank.

But I who saw such things as I have said
  Was overdone with utter weariness;

And walked in care, as one whom
    fears oppress,
    Because above his head
Death hangs, or damage, or the
    dearth of bread.

Each sore defeat of my defeated life
    Faced and outfaced me in that
    bitter hour;
    And turned to yearning palsy all
    my power,
    And all my peace to strife,
Self stabbing self with keen lack-pity
    knife.

Sweetness of beauty moved me to
    despair,
    Stung me to anger by its mere
    content,
    Made me all lonely on that way
    I went,
    Piled care upon my care,
Brimmed full my cup, and stripped
    me empty and bare:

For all that was but showed what
    all was not,
    But gave clear proof of what
    might never be;
    Making more destitute my poverty,
    And yet more blank my lot,
And me much sadder by its jubilee.

Therefore I sat me down: for where-
    fore walk?
    And closed mine eyes: for where-
    fore see or hear?
    Alas, I had no shutter to mine ear,
    And could not shun the talk
Of all rejoicing creatures far or
    near.

Without my will I hearkened and I
    heard
    (Asleep or waking, for I know not
    which),

Till note by note the music
    changed its pitch;
    Bird ceased to answer bird,
And every wind sighed softly if it
    stirred.

The drip of widening waters seemed
    to weep,
    All fountains sobbed and gurgled
    as they sprang,
    Somewhere a cataract cried out in
    its leap
    Sheer down a headlong steep;
High over all cloud-thunders gave
    a clang.

Such universal sound of lamentation
    I heard and felt, fain not to feel
    or hear;
    Nought else there seemed but
    anguish far and near;
    Nought else but all creation
Moaning and groaning wrung by
    pain or fear,

Shuddering in the misery of its
    doom:
    My heart then rose a rebel against
    light,
    Scouring all earth and heaven
    and depth and height,
    Ingathering wrath and gloom,
Ingathering wrath to wrath and
    night to night.

Ah me, the bitterness of such revolt,
    All impotent, all hateful, and all
    hate,
That kicks and breaks itself against
    the bolt
    Of an imprisoning fate,
    And vainly shakes, and cannot
    shake the gate.

Agony to agony, deep called to
  deep,
 Out of the deep I called of my
  desire;
 My strength was weakness and
  my heart was fire;
 Mine eyes, that would not weep
Or sleep, scaled height and depth,
  and could not sleep;

The eyes, I mean, of my rebellious
  soul,
 For still my bodily eyes were
  closed and dark:
 A random thing I seemed without
  a mark,
  Racing without a goal,
 Adrift upon life's sea without an
  ark.

More leaden than the actual self of
  lead
 Outer and inner darkness weighed
  on me.
 The tide of anger ebbed. Then
  fierce and free
  Surged full above my head
 The moaning tide of helpless
  misery.

Why should I breathe, whose breath
  was but a sigh?
 Why should I live, who drew such
  painful breath?
Oh weary work, the unanswerable
  why!—
  Yet I, why should I die,
 Who had no hope in life, no hope
  in death?

Grasses and mosses and the fallen
  leaf
 Make peaceful bed for an in-
  definite term;

But underneath the grass there
  gnaws a worm—
 Haply, there gnaws a grief—
Both, haply always; not, as now, so
  brief.

The pleasure I remember, it is past
 The pain I feel is passing passing
  by;
 Thus all the world is passing, and
  thus I:
  All things that cannot last
 Have grown familiar, and are born
  to die.

And being familiar, have so long been
  borne
 That habit trains us not to break
  but bend:
 Mourning grows natural to us who
  mourn
  In foresight of an end,
 But that which ends not who shall
  brave or mend?

Surely the ripe fruits tremble on
  their bough,
 They cling and linger trembling
  till they drop:
 I, trembling, cling to dying life; for
  how
  Face the perpetual Now?
 Birthless and deathless, void of
  start or stop,

Void of repentance, void of hope and
  fear,
 Of possibility, alternative,
 Of all that ever made us bear to
  live
  From night to morning here,
 Of promise even which has no
  gift to give.

The wood, and every creature of the
        wood,
    Seemed mourning with me in an
        undertone ;
    Soft scattered chirpings and a
        windy moan,
        Trees rustling, where they stood
And shivered, showed compassion
        for my mood.

Rage to despair ; and now despair
        had turned
    Back to self-pity and mere weari-
        ness,
With yearnings like a smouldering
        fire that burned,
        And might grow more or less,
And might die out or wax to white
        excess.

Without, within me, music seemed
        to be ;
    Something not music, yet most
        musical,
    Silence and sound in heavenly
        harmony ;
        At length a pattering fall
    Of feet, a bell, and bleatings, broke
        through all.

Then I looked up. The wood lay
        in a glow
    From golden sunset and from
        ruddy sky ;
    The sun had stooped to earth
        though once so high ;
        Had stooped to earth, in slow
Warm dying loveliness brought near
        and low.

Each water drop made answer to
        the light,
    Lit up a spark and showed the
        sun his face ;
    Soft purple shadows paved the
        grassy space
        And crept from height to height,
    From height to loftier height crept
        up apace.

While opposite the sun a gazing
        moon
    Put on his glory for her coronet,
    Kindling her luminous coldness to
        its noon,
        As his great splendour set ;
    One only star made up her train
        as yet.

Each twig was tipped with gold, each
        leaf was edged
    And veined with gold from the
        gold-flooded west ;
    Each mother-bird, and mate-bird,
        and unfledged
        Nestling, and curious nest,
    Displayed a gilded moss or beak
        or breast.

And filing peacefully between the
        trees,
    Having the moon behind them,
        and the sun
    Full in their meek mild faces, walked
        at ease
        A homeward flock, at peace
    With one another and with every
        one.

A patriarchal ram with tinkling bell
    Led all his kin ; sometimes one
        browsing sheep
    Hung back a moment, or one
        lamb would leap
        And frolic in a dell ;
    Yet still they kept together, journey-
        ing well,

And bleating, one or other, many or few,
  Journeying together toward the sunlit west;
Mild face by face, and woolly breast by breast,
  Patient, sun-brightened too,
Still journeying toward the sunset and their rest.

Before 1882.

ALL THY WORKS PRAISE THEE, O LORD

A PROCESSIONAL OF CREATION

ALL

I ALL-CREATION sing my song of praise
To God Who made me and vouchsafes my days,
And sends me forth by multitudinous ways.

SERAPH

I, like my Brethren, burn eternally
With love of Him Who is Love, and loveth me;
The Holy, Holy, Holy Unity.

CHERUB

I, with my Brethren, gaze eternally
On Him Who is Wisdom, and Who knoweth me;
The Holy, Holy, Holy Trinity.

ALL ANGELS

We rule, we serve, we work, we store His treasure,
Whose vessels are we brimmed with strength and pleasure;
Our joys fulfil, yea, overfill our measure.

HEAVENS

We float before the Presence Infinite,
We cluster round the Throne in our delight,
Revolving and rejoicing in God's sight.

FIRMAMENT

I, blue and beautiful, and framed of air,
At sunrise and at sunset grow most fair;
His glory by my glories I declare.

POWERS

We Powers are powers because He makes us strong;
Wherefore we roll all rolling orbs along,
We move all moving things, and sing our song.

SUN

I blaze to Him in mine engarlanding
Of rays, I flame His whole burnt-offering,
While as a bridegroom I rejoice and sing.

MOON

I follow, and am fair, and do His Will;
Through all my changes I am faithful still,
Full-orbed or strait His mandate to fulfil.

STARS

We Star-hosts numerous, innumerous,
Throng space with energy untumultuous,
And work His Will Whose eye beholdeth us.

Galaxies and Nebulæ

No thing is far or near; and therefore we
Float neither far nor near; but where we be
Weave dances round the Throne perpetually.

Comets and Meteors

Our lights dart here and there, whirl to and fro,
We flash and vanish, we die down and glow;
All doing His Will Who bids us do it so.

Showers

We give ourselves; and be we great or small,
Thus are we made like Him Who giveth all,
Like Him Whose gracious pleasure bids us fall.

Dews

We give ourselves in silent secret ways,
Spending and spent in silence full of grace;
And thus are made like God, and show His praise.

Winds

We sift the air and winnow all the earth;
And God Who poised our weights and weighs our worth
Accepts the worship of our solemn mirth.

Fire

My power and strength are His Who fashioned me,
Ordained me image of His Jealousy,
Forged me His weapon fierce exceedingly.

Heat

I glow unto His glory, and do good:
I glow, and bring to life both bud and brood;
I glow, and ripen harvest-crops for food.

Winter and Summer

Our wealth and joys and beauties celebrate
His wealth of beauty Who sustains our state,
Before Whose changelessness we alternate.

Spring and Autumn

I hope,—
    And I remember,—
        We give place
Either to other with contented grace,
Acceptable and lovely all our days.

Frost

I make the unstable stable, binding fast
The world of waters prone to ripple past:
Thus praise I God, Whose mercies I forecast.

Cold

I rouse and goad the slothful apt to nod,
I stir and urge the laggards with my rod:
My praise is not of men, yet I praise God.

Snow

My whiteness shadoweth Him Who is most fair,

All spotless: yea, my whiteness which
    I wear
Exalts His Purity beyond compare.

VAPOURS

We darken sun and moon, and blot
    the day,
The good Will of our Maker to obey:
Till to the glory of God we pass
    away.

NIGHT

Moon and all stars I don for diadem
To make me fair: I cast myself and
    them
Before His feet Who knows us gem
    from gem.

DAY

I shout before Him in my plenitude
Of light and warmth, of hope and
    wealth and food;
Ascribing all good to the Only Good.

LIGHT AND DARKNESS

I am God's dwelling-place,—
                And also I
Make His pavilion,—
                Lo, we bide and fly
Exulting in the Will of God Most
    High.

LIGHTNING AND THUNDER

We indivisible flash forth His Fame,
We thunder forth the glory of His
    Name,
In harmony of resonance and flame.

CLOUDS

Sweet is our store, exhaled from sea
    or river:
We wear a rainbow, praising God
    the Giver
Because His mercy is for ever and
    ever.

EARTH

I rest in Him rejoicing: resting so
And so rejoicing, in that I am low:
Yet known of Him, and following on
    to know.

MOUNTAINS

Our heights which laud Him, sink
    abased before
Him higher than the highest ever-
    more:
God higher than the highest we
    adore.

HILLS

We green-tops praise Him, and we
    fruitful heads,
Whereon the sunshine and the dew
    He sheds:
We green-tops praise Him, rising
    from our beds.

GREEN THINGS

We all green things, we blossoms
    bright or dim,
Trees, bushes, brushwood, corn and
    grasses slim,
We lift our many-favoured lauds to
    Him.

ROSE—LILY—VIOLET

I praise Him on my thorn which I
    adorn,—
And I, amid my world of thistle and
    thorn,—
And I, within my veil where I am born.

APPLE—CITRON—POMEGRANATE

We Apple-blossom, Citron, Pome-
    granate,
We clothed of God without our toil
    and fret,
We offer fatness where His Throne
    is set.

Vine—Cedar—Palm

I proffer Him my sweetness, who am sweet,—
I bow my strength in fragrance at His feet,—
I wave myself before His Judgment seat.

Medicinal Herbs

I bring refreshment,—
　　I bring ease and calm,—
I lavish strength and healing,—
　　I am balm,—
We work His pitiful Will and chant our psalm.

A Spring

Clear my pure fountain, clear and pure my rill,
My fountain and mine outflow deep and still;
I set His semblance forth and do His Will.

Sea

To-day I praise God with a sparkling face,
My thousand thousand waves all uttering praise:
To-morrow I commit me to His Grace.

Floods

We spring and swell meandering to and fro,
From height to depth, from depth to depth we flow,
We fertilize the world, and praise Him so.

Whales and Sea Mammals

We Whales and Monsters gambol in His sight,
Rejoicing every day and every night,
Safe in the tender keeping of His Might.

Fishes

Our fashions and our colours and our speeds
Set forth His praise Who framed us and Who feeds,
Who knows our number and regards our needs.

Birds

Winged Angels of this visible world, we fly
To sing God's praises in the lofty sky;
We scale the height to praise our Lord most High.

Eagle and Dove

I the sun-gazing Eagle,—
　　I the Dove
With plumes of softness and a note of love,—
We praise by divers gifts One God above.

Beasts and Cattle

We forest Beasts,—
　　We Beasts of hill or cave,—
We border-loving Creatures of the wave,—
We praise our King with voices deep and grave.

Small Animals

God forms us weak and small, but pours out all
We need, and notes us while we stand or fall:
Wherefore we praise Him, weak and safe and small.

LAMB

I praise my loving Lord, Who maketh me
His type by harmless sweet simplicity:
Yet He the Lamb of lambs incomparably.

LION

I praise the Lion of the Royal Race,
Strongest in fight and swiftest in the chase:
With all my might I leap and lavish praise.

ALL MEN

All creatures sing around us, and we sing:
We bring our own selves as our offering,
Our very selves we render to our King.

ISRAEL

Flock of our Shepherd's pasture and His fold,
Purchased and well-beloved from days of old,
We tell His praise which still remains untold.

PRIESTS

We free-will Shepherds tend His sheep and feed;
We follow Him while caring for their need;
We follow praising Him, and them we lead.

SERVANTS OF GOD

We love God, for He loves us; we are free
In serving Him, who serve Him willingly:
As kings we reign, and praise His Majesty.

HOLY AND HUMBLE PERSONS

All humble souls He calls and sanctifies;
All holy souls He calls to make them wise;
Accepting all, His free-will sacrifice.

BABES

He maketh me,—
    And me,—
        And me,—
            To be
His blessed little ones around His knee,
Who praise Him by mere love confidingly.

WOMEN

God makes our service love, and makes our wage
Love: so we wend on patient pilgrimage,
Extolling Him by love from age to age.

MEN

God gives us power to rule: He gives us power
To rule ourselves, and prune the exuberant flower
Of youth, and worship Him hour after hour.

SPIRITS AND SOULS—

Lo in the hidden world we chant our chant
To Him Who fills us that we nothing want,
To Him Whose bounty leaves our craving scant.

OF BABES—

With milky mouths we praise God, from the breast

Called home betimes to rest the perfect rest,
By love and joy fulfilling His behest.

OF WOMEN—

We praise His Will which made us what He would,
His Will which fashioned us and called us good,
His Will our plenary beatitude.

OF MEN

We praise His Will Who bore with us so long,
Who out of weakness wrought us swift and strong,
Champions of right and putters-down of wrong.

ALL

Let everything that hath or hath not breath,
Let days and endless days, let life and death,
Praise God, praise God, praise God, His creature saith.

Before 1882.

LATER LIFE: A DOUBLE SONNET OF SONNETS

1

BEFORE the mountains were brought forth, before
Earth and the world were made, then God was God:
And God will still be God when flames shall roar
Round earth and heaven dissolving at His nod:
And this God is our God, even while His rod
Of righteous wrath falls on us smiting sore:
And this God is our God for evermore,
Through life, through death, while clod returns to clod.
For though He slay us we will trust in Him;
We will flock home to Him by divers ways:
Yea, though He slay us we will vaunt His praise,
Serving and loving with the Cherubim,
Watching and loving with the Seraphim,
Our very selves His praise through endless days.

2

Rend hearts and rend not garments for our sins;
Gird sackcloth not on body but on soul;
Grovel in dust with faces toward the goal
Nor won nor neared: he only laughs who wins.
Not neared the goal, the race too late begins;
All left undone, we have yet to do the whole;
The sun is hurrying west and toward the pole
Where darkness waits for earth with all her kins.
Let us to-day while it is called to-day
Set out, if utmost speed may yet avail—
The shadows lengthen and the light grows pale:
For who through darkness and the shadow of death,

Darkness that may be felt, shall find
  a way,
  Blind - eyed, deaf - eared, and
    choked with failing breath?

3

Thou Who didst make and knowest
    whereof we are made,
  Oh bear in mind our dust and
    nothingness,
  Our wordless tearless numbness
    of distress:
Bear Thou in mind the burden Thou
    hast laid
Upon us, and our feebleness unstayed
  Except Thou stay us: for the
    long long race
  Which stretches far and far before
    our face
Thou knowest, — remember Thou
    whereof we are made.
If making makes us Thine then
    Thine we are,
  And if redemption we are twice
    Thine own:
If once Thou didst come down from
    heaven afar
To seek us and to find us, how not
    save?
  Comfort us, save us, leave us not
    alone,
Thou who didst die our death and
    fill our grave.

4

So tired am I, so weary of to-day,
  So unrefreshed from foregone
    weariness,
  So overburdened by foreseen
    distress,
So lagging and so stumbling on my
    way,
I scarce can rouse myself to watch
    or pray,

To hope, or aim, or toil for more
    or less,—
  Ah always less and less, even
    while I press
Forward and toil and aim as best I
    may.
Half-starved of soul and heartsick
    utterly,
  Yet lift I up my heart and soul
    and eyes
  (Which fail in looking upward)
    toward the prize:
Me, Lord, Thou seest though I see
    not Thee;
  Me now, as once the Thief in
    Paradise,
Even me, O Lord my Lord, remember me.

5

Lord, Thou Thyself art Love and
    only Thou;
  Yet I who am not love would fain
    love Thee;
  But Thou alone being Love canst
    furnish me
With that same love my heart is
    craving now.
Allow my plea! for if Thou disallow,
  No second fountain can I find
    but Thee;
  No second hope or help is left to
    me,
No second anything, but only Thou.
O Love, accept, according my request;
  O Love, exhaust, fulfilling my
    desire:
  Uphold me with the strength that
    cannot tire,
Nerve me to labour till Thou bid me
    rest,
  Kindle my fire from Thine unkindled fire,

And charm the willing heart from
   out my breast.

6

We lack, yet cannot fix upon the lack:
   Not this, nor that ; yet somewhat,
      certainly.
   We see the things we do not yearn
      to see
Around us : and what see we glancing
      back ?
Lost hopes that leave our hearts upon
      the rack,
   Hopes that were never ours yet
      seemed to be,
   For which we steered on life's salt
      stormy sea
Braving the sunstroke and the frozen
      pack.
If thus to look behind is all in vain,
   And all in vain to look to left or
      right,
Why face we not our future once
      again,
Launching with hardier hearts across
      the main,
   Straining dim eyes to catch the
      invisible sight,
   And strong to bear ourselves in
      patient pain ?

7

To love and to remember ; that is
      good :
   To love and to forget ; that is
      not well :
   To lapse from love to hatred ;
      that is hell
And death and torment, rightly
      understood.
Soul dazed by love and sorrow,
      cheer thy mood ;
   More blest art thou than mortal
      tongue can tell :

Ring not thy funeral but thy
      marriage bell,
And salt with hope thy life's insipid
      food.
Love is the goal, love is the way we
      wend,
   Love is our parallel unending line
      Whose only perfect Parallel is
      Christ,
Beginning not begun, End without
      end :
   For He Who hath the Heart
      of God sufficed
   Can satisfy all hearts,—yea, thine
      and mine.

8

We feel and see with different hearts
      and eyes :—
   Ah Christ, if all our hearts could
      meet in Thee,
   How well it were for them and
      well for me,
Our hearts Thy dear accepted sacri-
      fice.
Thou, only Life of hearts and Light
      of eyes,
   Our life, our light, if once we turn
      to Thee,
   So be it, O Lord, to them and so
      to me ;
Be all alike Thine own dear sacrifice.
Thou Who by death hast ransomed
      us from death,
   Thyself God's sole well-pleasing
      Sacrifice,
      Thine only sacred Self I plead
      with Thee :
      Make Thou it well for them
      and well for me
That Thou hast given us souls and
      wills and breath,
   And hearts to love Thee, and to
      see Thine eyes.

9

Star Sirius and the Pole Star dwell afar
  Beyond the drawings each of other's strength.
  One blazes through the brief bright summer's length
Lavishing life-heat from a flaming car;
  While one unchangeable upon a throne
Broods o'er the frozen heart of earth alone,
Content to reign the bright particular star
  Of some who wander or of some who groan.
They own no drawings each of other's strength,
  Nor vibrate in a visible sympathy,
  Nor veer along their courses each toward each:
Yet are their orbits pitched in harmony
Of one dear heaven, across whose depth and length
  Mayhap they talk together without speech.

10

Tread softly! all the earth is holy ground.
  It may be, could we look with seeing eyes,
  This spot we stand on is a Paradise
Where dead have come to life and lost been found,
Where Faith has triumphed, Martyrdom been crowned,
  Where fools have foiled the wisdom of the wise;
From this same spot the dust of saints may rise,
And the King's prisoners come to light unbound.
O earth, earth, earth, hear thou thy Maker's Word:
  'Thy dead thou shalt give up, nor hide thy slain.'
Some who went weeping forth shall come again
  Rejoicing from the east or from the west,
As doves fly to their windows, love's own bird
  Contented and desirous to the nest.[1]

11

Lifelong our stumbles, lifelong our regret,
  Lifelong our efforts failing and renewed,
  While lifelong is our witness, 'God is good,'
Who bore with us till now, bears with us yet,
Who still remembers and will not forget,
  Who gives us light and warmth and daily food;
And gracious promises half understood,
And glories half unveiled, whereon to set
Our heart of hearts and eyes of our desire;
  Uplifting us to longing and to love,
Luring us upward from this world of mire,

---

[1] 'Quali colombe dal disio chiamate
Con l'ali aperte e ferme al dolce nido
Volan per l'aer dal voler portate.'
DANTE.

Urging us to press on and mount above
Ourselves and all we have had experience of,
Mounting to Him in love's perpetual fire.

12

A dream there is wherein we are fain to scream,
While struggling with ourselves we cannot speak:
And much of all our waking life, as weak
And misconceived, eludes us like the dream.
For half life's seemings are not what they seem,
And vain the laughs we laugh, the shrieks we shriek;
Yea, all is vain that mars the settled meek
Contented quiet of our daily theme.
When I was young I deemed that sweets are sweet:
But now I deem some searching bitters are
Sweeter than sweets, and more refreshing far,
And to be relished more, and more desired,
And more to be pursued on eager feet,
On feet untired, and still on feet though tired.

13

Shame is a shadow cast by sin: yet shame
Itself may be a glory and a grace,
Refashioning the sin-disfashioned face;
A nobler bruit than hollow-sounded fame,
A new-lit lustre on a tarnished name,
One virtue pent within an evil place,
Strength for the fight, and swiftness for the race,
A stinging salve, a life-requickening flame.
A salve so searching we may scarcely live,
A flame so fierce it seems that we must die,
An actual cautery thrust into the heart:
Nevertheless, men die not of such smart;
And shame gives back what nothing else can give,
Man to himself,—then sets him up on high.

14

When Adam and when Eve left Paradise,
Did they love on and cling together still,
Forgiving one another all that ill
The twain had wrought on such a different wise?
She propped upon his strength, and he in guise
Of lover though of lord, girt to fulfil
Their term of life and die when God should will;
Lie down and sleep, and having slept arise.
Boast not against us, O our enemy!
To-day we fall, but we shall rise again;
We grope to-day, to-morrow we shall see:
What is to-day that we should fear to-day?

 A morrow cometh which shall sweep
  away
 Thee and thy realm of change and
  death and pain.

15

Let woman fear to teach and bear to
 learn,
 Remembering the first woman's
  first mistake.
 Eve had for pupil the inquiring
  snake,
Whose doubts she answered on a
 great concern ;
But he the tables so contrived to turn,
 It next was his to give and hers
  to take ;
 Till man deemed poison sweet for
  her sweet sake,
And fired a train by which the world
 must burn.
Did Adam love his Eve from first to
 last ?
 I think so ; as we love who works
  us ill,
 And wounds us to the quick, yet
  loves us still.
Love pardons the unpardonable past :
Love in a dominant embrace holds
 fast
 His frailer self, and saves without
  her will.

16

Our teachers teach that one and one
 make two :
 Later, Love rules that one and
  one make one :
 Abstruse the problems ! neither
  need we shun,
But skilfully to each should yield its
 due.
The narrower total seems to suit the
 few,
The wider total suits the common
 run ;
 Each obvious in its sphere like
  moon or sun ;
 Both provable by me, and both by
  you.
Befogged and witless, in a wordy maze
 A groping stroll perhaps may do
  us good ;
 If cloyed we are with much we
  have understood,
If tired of half our dusty world and
 ways,
 If sick of fasting, and if sick of
  food ;—
And how about these long still-
 lengthening days ?

17

Something this foggy day, a some-
 thing which
 Is neither of this fog nor of to-day,
 Has set me dreaming of the winds
  that play
Past certain cliffs, along one certain
 beach,
 And turn the topmost edge of
  waves to spray :
 Ah pleasant pebbly strand so far
  away,
So out of reach while quite within
 my reach,
 As out of reach as India or Cathay !
I am sick of where I am and where
 I am not,
 I am sick of foresight and of
  memory,
 I am sick of all I have and all I see,
 I am sick of self, and there is
  nothing new ;
Oh weary impatient patience of my
 lot !—
 Thus with myself : how fares it,
  Friends, with you ?

18

So late in Autumn half the world's
    asleep,
    And half the wakeful world looks
        pinched and pale;
For dampness now, not freshness,
    rides the gale;
And cold and colourless comes
    ashore the deep
    With tides that bluster or with
        tides that creep;
    Now veiled uncouthness wears an
        uncouth veil
Of fog, not sultry haze; and blight
    and bale
Have done their worst, and leaves
    rot on the heap.
So late in Autumn one forgets the
    Spring,
    Forgets the Summer with its
        opulence,
The callow birds that long have found
    a wing,
    The swallows that more lately gat
        them hence:
Will anything like Spring, will any-
    thing
    Like Summer, rouse one day the
        slumbering sense?

19

Here now is Winter. Winter, after all,
    Is not so drear as was my boding
        dream
    While Autumn gleamed its latest
        watery gleam
On sapless leafage too inert to fall.
Still leaves and berries clothe my
    garden wall
    Where ivy thrives on scantiest
        sunny beam;
    Still here a bud and there a
        blossom seem
Hopeful, and robin still is musical.

Leaves, flowers, and fruit, and one
    delightful song,
    Remain; these days are short, but
        now the nights,
    Intense and long, hang out their
        utmost lights;
Such starry nights are long, yet not
    too long;
Frost nips the weak, while strengthen-
    ing still the strong
    Against that day when Spring sets
        all to rights.

20

A hundred thousand birds salute the
    day:—
    One solitary bird salutes the night:
Its mellow grieving wiles our grief
    away,
    And tunes our weary watches to
        delight;
It seems to sing the thoughts we
    cannot say,
    To know and sing them, and to
        set them right;
Until we feel once more that May is
    May,
    And hope some buds may bloom
        without a blight.
This solitary bird outweighs, outvies,
    The hundred thousand merry-
        making birds;
Whose innocent warblings yet might
    make us wise,
    Would we but follow when they bid
        us rise,
    Would we but set their notes of
        praise to words
And launch our hearts up with them
    to the skies.

21

A host of things I take on trust: I take
    The nightingales on trust, for few
        and far

Between those actual summer moments are
When I have heard what melody they make.
So chanced it once at Como on the Lake:
But all things, then, waxed musical; each star
   Sang on its course, each breeze sang on its car,
All harmonies sang to senses wide awake.
All things in tune, myself not out of tune,
   Those nightingales were nightingales indeed:
   Yet truly an owl had satisfied my need,
And wrought a rapture underneath that moon,
   Or simple sparrow chirping from a reed;
For June that night glowed like a doubled June.

22

The mountains in their overwhelming might
   Moved me to sadness when I saw them first,
And afterwards they moved me to delight;
   Struck harmonies from silent chords which burst
   Out into song, a song by memory nursed;
For ever unrenewed by touch or sight
Sleeps the keen magic of each day or night,
   In pleasure and in wonder then immersed.
All Switzerland behind us on the ascent,
All Italy before us, we plunged down
   St. Gothard, garden of forget-me-not:
   Yet why should such a flower choose such a spot?
Could we forget that way which once we went
   Though not one flower had bloomed to weave its crown?

23

Beyond the seas we know stretch seas unknown,
   Blue and bright-coloured for our dim and green;
   Beyond the lands we see stretch lands unseen
With many-tinted tangle overgrown;
And icebound seas there are like seas of stone,
   Serenely stormless as death lies serene;
   And lifeless tracts of sand, which intervene
Betwixt the lands where living flowers are blown.
This dead and living world befits our case
   Who live and die: we live in wearied hope,
We die in hope not dead; we run a race
To-day, and find no present halting-place;
   All things we see lie far within our scope,
And still we peer beyond with craving face.

24

The wise do send their hearts before them to
   Dear blessed Heaven, despite the veil between;

The foolish nurse their hearts
    within the screen
Of this familiar world, where all we do
Or have is old, for there is nothing
    new:
    Yet elder far that world we have
        not seen;
God's Presence antedates what
    else hath been:
Many the foolish seem, the wise
    seem few.
Oh foolishest fond folly of a heart
    Divided, neither here nor there at
        rest!
        That hankers after Heaven, but
            clings to earth;
        That neither here nor there
            knows thorough mirth,
Half-choosing, wholly missing, the
        good part :⊢
    Oh fool among the foolish, in thy
        quest!

25

When we consider what this life we
    lead
    Is not, and is: how full of toil
        and pain,
    How blank of rest and of sub-
        stantial gain,
Beset by hunger earth can never feed,
And propping half our hearts upon
    a reed;
    We cease to mourn lost treasures,
        mourned in vain,
    Lost treasures we are fain and yet
        not fain
To fetch back for a solace of our need.
For who that feel this burden and
    this strain,
    This wide vacuity of hope and
        heart,
Would bring their cherished well-
    beloved again:

To bleed with them and wince
    beneath the smart,
To have with stinted bliss such lavish
    bane,
To hold in lieu of all so poor a
    part?

26

This Life is full of numbness and of
    balk,
    Of haltingness and baffled short-
        coming,
    Of promise unfulfilled, of every-
        thing
That is puffed vanity and empty talk:
    Its very bud hangs cankered on the
        stalk,
    Its very song-bird trails a broken
        wing,
    Its very Spring is not indeed like
        Spring,
But sighs like Autumn round an
    aimless walk.
This Life we live is dead for all its
    breath;
    Death's self it is, set off on
        pilgrimage,
    Travelling with tottering steps the
        first short stage:
        The second stage is one mere
            desert dust
    Where Death sits veiled amid
        creation's rust :—
Unveil thy face, O Death, who art
    not Death.

27

I have dreamed of Death :—what
    will it be to die
    Not in a dream, but in the literal
        truth,
    With all Death's adjuncts ghastly
        and uncouth,
The pang that is the last and the
    last sigh?

Too dulled, it may be, for a last
    good-bye,
Too comfortless for any one to
    soothe,
A helpless charmless spectacle of
    ruth
Through long last hours, so long
    while yet they fly.
So long to those who hopeless in
    their fear
Watch the slow breath and look
    for what they dread :
While I supine with ears that cease
    to hear,
    With eyes that glaze, with heart-
        pulse running down
    (Alas! no saint rejoicing on her bed),
    May miss the goal at last, may
        miss a crown.

28

In life our absent friend is far away :
    But death may bring our friend
        exceeding near,
Show him familiar faces long s
    dear
And lead him back in reach of word
    we say.
He only cannot utter yea or nay
    In any voice accustomed to ou
        ear ;
    He only cannot make his fac
        appear
And turn the sun back on ou
    shadowed day.
The dead may be around us, dea
    and dead ;
    The unforgotten dearest dead ma
        be
    Watching us with unslumbering
        eyes and heart,
Brimful of words which cannot ye
    be said,
    Brimful of knowledge they ma
        not impart,
    Brimful of love for you and love
        for me.

Before 1882.

JUVENILIA

TO MY MOTHER
ON THE ANNIVERSARY OF HER BIRTH
(Presented with a Nosegay)

To-day's your natal day ;
    Sweet flowers I bring :
Mother, accept I pray
    My offering.

And may you happy live,
    And long us bless ;
Receiving as you give
    Great happiness.

27 *April* 1842.

THE CHINAMAN

'Centre of Earth!' a Chinama
    he said,
And bent over a map his pig-tail
    head,—
That map in which, portrayed
    colours bright,
China, all dazzling, burst upon t
    sight ;
'Centre of Earth!' repeatedly
    cries,
'Land of the brave, the beautif
    the wise!'

Thus he exclaimed; when lo his
    words arrested
Showed what sharp agony his head
    had tested.
He feels a tug—another, and
    another—
And quick exclaims, 'Hallo! what's
    now the bother?'
But soon, alas, perceives. And, 'Why,
    false night,
Why not from men shut out the
    hateful sight?
The faithless English have cut off
    my tail,
And left me my sad fortunes to
    bewail.
Now in the streets I can no more
    appear,
For all the other men a pig-tail wear.'
He said, and furious cast into the fire
His tail: those flames became its
    funeral-pyre.

1842.

HYMN

To the God who reigns on high,
    To the Eternal Majesty,
To the Blessed Trinity,
    Glory on earth be given,
In the sea and in the sky,
    And in the highest heaven.

2 *July* 1843.

LOVE AND HOPE

Love for ever dwells in
    heaven,—
    Hope entereth not there.
To despairing man Love's
    given,—
    Hope dwells not with despair.
Love reigneth high, and reigneth low,
    and reigneth everywhere.

In the inmost heart Love
    dwelleth,—
    It may not quenchèd be;
E'en when the life-blood welleth,
    Its fond effects we see
In the name that leaves the lips the
    last — fades last from
    memory.

And when we shall awaken,
    Ascending to the sky,
Though Hope shall have
    forsaken,
    Sweet Love shall never die:
For perfect Love and perfect bliss
    shall be our lot on high.

9 *October* 1843.

ON ALBINA

The roses lingered in her cheeks
    When fair Albina fainted;
O gentle reader, could it be
    That fair Albina painted?

June 1844.

FORGET ME NOT

'Forget me not, forget me not!'
    The maiden once did say,
When to some far-off battlefield
    Her lover sped away.

'Forget me not, forget me not!'
    Says now the chamber-maid,
When the traveller on his journey
    No more will be delayed.

19 *August* 1844.

CHARITY

I PRAISED the myrtle and the rose,
  At sunrise in their beauty lying:
I passed them at the short day's close,
      And both were dying.

The summer sun his rays was throwing
  Brightly: yet ere I sought my rest
His last cold ray, more deeply glowing,
      Died in the west.

After this bleak world's stormy weather,
  All, all, save Love alone, shall die;
For Faith and Hope shall merge together
      In Charity.

20 *September* 1844.

EARTH AND HEAVEN

WATER calmly flowing,
Sunlight deeply glowing,
Swans some river riding
That is gently gliding
By the fresh green rushes,
The sweet rose that blushes,
Hyacinths whose dower
Is both scent and flower,
Skylark's soaring motion,
Sunrise from the ocean,
Jewels that lie sparkling
'Neath the waters darkling,
Seaweed, coral, amber,
Flowers that climb and clamber
Or more lowly flourish
There the earth may nourish:
All these are beautiful,
Of beauty earth is full:
Say, to our promised heaven
Can greater charms be given?
Yes, for aye in heaven doth dwell,
Glowing, indestructible,
What here below finds tainted birth
In the corrupted sons of earth:
For, filling there and satisfying
Man's soul unchanging and undying,
Earth's fleeting joys and beauties far above,
      In heaven is Love.

28 *December* 1844.

LOVE EPHEMERAL

LOVE is sweet, and so are flowers
Blooming in bright summer bowers;
So are waters, clear and pure,
In some hidden fountain's store;
So is the soft southern breeze
Sighing low among the trees;
So is the bright queen of heaven
Reigning in the quiet even.
Yet the pallid moon may breed
Madness in man's feeble seed;
And the wind's soft influence
Often breathes the pestilence;
And the waves may sullied be
As they hurry to the sea;
Flowers soon must fade away:
Love endures but for a day.

25 *February* 1845.

BURIAL ANTHEM

FLESH of our flesh, bone of our bone—
For thou and we in Christ are one—
Thy soul unto its rest hath flown,

And thou hast left us all alone
   Our weary race to run
In doubt and want and sin and
    pain,
Whilst thou wilt never sin again.
For us remaineth heaviness;
Thou never more shalt feel distress,—
   For thou hast found repose
Beside the bright eternal river,
That clear and pure flows on for ever
   And sings as on it flows.
And it is better far for thee
   To reach at once thy rest
Than share with us earth's misery,
   Or tainted joy at best.
Brother, we will not mourn for thee,
   Although our hearts be weary
Of struggling with our enemy
   When all around is dreary:
But we will pray that still we may
Press onward in the narrow way,
With a calm thankful resignation,
And joy in this our desolation;
And we will hope at length to be
With our Great Head—and, friend,
   with thee—
     Beside that river blest.
3 *March* 1845.

LINES TO MY GRANDFATHER

Dear Grandpapa,—To be obedient,
   I'll try and write a letter;
Which (as I hope you'll deem expedient)
   Must serve for lack of better.

My Muse of late was not prolific;—
   And sometimes I must feel
To make a verse a task terrific
   Rather of woe than weal.

As I have met with no adventure
   Of wonder and refulgence,
I must write plain things at a
    venture,
   And trust to your indulgence.

The apple-tree is showing
   Its blossom of bright red,
With a soft colour glowing
   Upon its leafy bed.

The pear-tree's pure white blossom
   Like stainless snow is seen;
And all earth's genial bosom
   Is clothed with varied green.

The fragrant may is blooming,
   The yellow cowslip blows;
Among its leaves entombing
   Peeps forth the pale primrose.

The king-cup flowers and daisies
   Are opening hard by;
And many another raises
   Its head, to please and die.

I love the gay wild flowers
   Waving in fresh Spring air:—
Give me uncultured bowers
   Before the bright parterre.

And now my letter is concluded;
   To do well I have striven;
And, though news is well-nigh excluded,
   I hope to be forgiven.

With love to all the beautiful
   And those who cannot slaughter,
I sign myself—Your dutiful
   Affectionate grand-daughter.
1 *May* 1845.

SUMMER

Hark to the song of greeting!
    The tall trees
Murmur their welcome in the southern breeze;
Amid the thickest foliage many a bird
Sits singing, their shrill matins scarcely heard
    One by one, but all together
    Welcoming the sunny weather;
    In every bower hums a bee
    Fluttering melodiously;
Murmurs joy in every brook,
Rippling with a pleasant look :
What greet they with their guileless bliss?
    What welcome with a song like this?

See in the south a radiant form,
    Her fair head crowned with roses;
    From her bright footpath flies the storm;
    Upon her breast reposes
Many an unconfinèd tress,
Golden, glossy, motionless.
Face and form are love and light,
Soft ineffably, yet bright.
All her path is strewn with flowers;
Round her float the laughing Hours;
Heaven and Earth make joyful din,
Welcoming sweet Summer in.

And now she alights on the earth
    To play with her children the flowers;
She touches the stems, and the buds have birth,
    And gently she trains them in bowers.
And the bees and the birds are glad,
    And the wind catches warmth from her breath,
And around her is nothing sad
    Nor any traces of death.
See now she lays her down
With roses for her crown,
With jessamine and myrtle
Forming her fragrant kirtle.
Conquered by softest slumbers,
No more the hours she numbers—
    The hours that intervene
    Ere she may wing her flight
    Far from this smiling scene
    With all her love and light,
And leave the flowers and the summer bowers
To wither in autumn and winter hours.

And must they wither then?
    Their life and their perfume
    Sinking so soon again
    Into their earthy tomb.
Let us bind her as she lies
Ere the fleeting moment flies,
Hand and foot and arm and bosom,
With a chain of bud and blossom;
Twine red roses round her hands;
Round her feet twine myrtle bands.
Heap up flowers, higher, higher,—
Tulips like a glowing fire,
Clematis of milky whiteness,
Sweet geraniums' varied brightness,
Honeysuckle, commeline,
Roses, myrtles, jessamine;
Heap them higher, bloom on bloom,
Bury her as in a tomb.

But alas they are withered all,
    And how can dead flowers bind her?
She pushes away her pall,

And she leaves the dead behind
   her:
And she flies across the seas,
   To gladden for a time
The blossoms and the bees
   Of some far-distant clime.
4 *December* 1845.

SERENADE

COME, wander forth with me: the
   orange flowers
Breathe faintest perfume from the
   summer bowers.
Come, wander forth with me: the
   moon on high
Shines proudly in a flood of brilliancy;
   Around her car each burning star
Gleams like a beacon from afar.
   The night wind scarce disturbs
     the sea
As it sighs forth so languidly,
Laden with sweetness like a bee;
And all is still, below, above,
Save murmurs of the turtle-dove
That murmurs ever of its love.
For now 'tis the hour, the balmy
   hour,
When the strains of love have
   chiefly power;
When the maid looks forth from
   her latticed bower,
With a gentle yielding smile,
Donning her mantle all the while.
Now the moon beams down on
   high
From her halo brilliantly,
By the dark clouds unencumbered
That once o'er her pale face
   slumbered:
Far from her mild rays flutters
   Folly,
For on them floats calm Melan-
   choly;—

A passionless sadness without
   dread,
Like the thought of those we love,
   long dead;
Full of hope and chastened joy,
Heavenly, without earth's alloy.
Listen, dearest: all is quiet—
Slumbering the world's toil and
   riot;
And all is fair in earth and sky and
   sea.
   Come, wander forth with me.
4 *December* 1845.

THE END OF TIME

THOU who art dreary
   With a cureless woe,
Thou who art weary
   Of all things below,
Thou who art weeping
   By the loved sick bed,
Thou who art keeping
   Watches o'er the dead,—
Hope, hope! old Time flies fast
   upon his way,
And soon will cease the night, and
   soon will dawn the day.

The rose blooms brightly,
   But it fades ere night;
And youth flies lightly,
   Yet how sure its flight!
And still the river
   Merges in the sea;
And Death reigns ever
   Whilst old Time shall be;—
Yet hope! old Time flies fast upon
   his way,
And soon will cease the night, and
   soon will dawn the day.

All we most cherish
   In this world below,

What though it perish?
It has aye been so.
So through all ages
It has ever been,
To fools and sages,
Noble men and mean:—
Yet hope, still hope! for Time
  flies on his way,
And soon will end the night, and
  soon will dawn the day.

All of each nation
Shall that morning see
With exultation
Or with misery:
From watery slumbers,
From the opening sod,
Shall rise up numbers
To be judged by God.
Then hope and fear, for Time
  speeds on his way,
And soon must end the night, and
  soon must dawn the day.

9 *December* 1845.

COUPLET

'COME cheer up, my lads, 'tis to
  glory we steer'—
As the soldier remarked whose post
  lay in the rear.

Circa 1845.

AMORE E DOVERE

CHIAMI il mio core
  Crudele, altero:
No non è vero,
  Crudel non è:
T' amo, t' amai—
E tu lo sai—
Men del dovere,
  Ma più di me.

O ruscelletto,
  Dì al Dio d' Amore
Che questo petto,
  Che questo core,
A lui ricetto
  Più non darà.
L' alme tradisce
  Senza rimorso;
Non compatisce,
  Non dà soccorso,
E si nudrisce
  Di crudeltà.—

T' intendo, ti lagni,
Mio povero core;
T' intendo, l' Amore
Si lagna di me.
Deh placati alfine!
Mi pungon le spine
Che vengon da te.

1845 *to* 1847.

MOTHER AND CHILD

'WHAT art thou thinking of,' said
  the mother,
  'What art thou thinking of, my
    child?'
'I was thinking of heaven,' he
  answered her,
  And looked up in her face and
    smiled.

'And what didst thou think of
  heaven?' she said;
  'Tell me, my little one.'
'Oh I thought that there the flowers
  never fade,
  That there never sets the sun.'

'And wouldst thou love to go thither,
  my child,
  Thither wouldst thou love to go,

And leave the pretty flowers that
    wither,
And the sun that sets below?'

'Oh I would be glad to go there,
    mother,
To go and live there now;
And I would pray for thy coming,
    mother;—
My mother, wouldst not thou?'
10 *January* 1846.

MARY MAGDALENE

SHE came in deep repentance,
    And knelt down at His feet
Who can change the sorrow into joy,
    The bitter into sweet.

She had cast away her jewels
    And her rich attire,
And her breast was filled with a holy
    shame,
    And her heart with a holy fire.

Her tears were more precious
    Than her precious pearls—
Her tears that fell upon His feet
    As she wiped them with her curls.

Her youth and her beauty
    Were budding to their prime;
But she wept for the great trans-
    gression,
    The sin of other time.

Trembling betwixt hope and fear,
    She sought the King of Heaven,
Forsook the evil of her ways,
    Loved much, and was forgiven.
8 *February* 1846.

ON THE DEATH OF A CAT

A FRIEND OF MINE AGED TEN
    YEARS AND A HALF

WHO shall tell the lady's grief
When her Cat was past relief?
Who shall number the hot tears
Shed o'er her, belov'd for years?
Who shall say the dark dismay
Which her dying caused that day?

Come, ye Muses, one and all,
Come obedient to my call;
Come and mourn with tuneful breath
Each one for a separate death;
And, while you in numbers sigh,
I will sing her elegy.

Of a noble race she came,
And Grimalkin was her name.
Young and old full many a mouse
Felt the prowess of her house;
Weak and strong full many a rat
Cowered beneath her crushing pat;
And the birds around the place
Shrank from her too close embrace.
But one night, reft of her strength,
She lay down and died at length:
Lay a kitten by her side
In whose life the mother died.
Spare her line and lineage,
Guard her kitten's tender age,
And that kitten's name as wide
Shall be known as hers that died.
And whoever passes by
The poor grave where Puss doth
    lie,
Softly, softly let him tread,
Nor disturb her narrow bed.
14 *March* 1846.

TO ELIZABETH READ

WITH SOME POSTAGE-STAMPS FOR A COLLECTION

Sweetest Elizabeth, accept, I pray,
   These lowly stamps I send in homage true :
One hundred humble servants in their way
   Are not to be despised, though poor to view.
Their livery of red and black—nor gay
Nor sober all—is typical of you,
In whom are gravity and gladness mixt :
Thought here, smiles there—perfection lies betwixt.

17 *March* 1846.

LOVE ATTACKED

Love is more sweet than flowers,
   But sooner dying ;
Warmer than sunny hours,
   But faster flying ;

Softer than music whispers,
   Springing with day,
To murmur till the vespers,
   Then die away ;

More kind than friendship's greeting,
   But as untrue ;
Brighter than hope, but fleeting
   More swiftly too.

Like breath of summer breezes
   Gently it sighs,
But soon alas one ceases,
   The other dies :

And like an inundation
   It leaves behind
An utter desolation
   Of heart and mind.

Who then would court Love's presence,
   If here below
It can but be the essence
   Of restless woe?

Returned or unrequited,
   'Tis still the same ;
The flame was never lighted,
   Or sinks the flame.

Yet all, both fools and sages,
   Have felt its power,
In distant lands and ages,—
   Here, at this hour.

Then what from fear and weeping
   Shall give me rest?
Oh tell me, ye who sleeping
   At length are blest !

In answer to my crying,
   Sounds like incense
Rose from the earth, replying,
   ' Indifference.'

21 *April* 1846.

LOVE DEFENDED

Who extols a wilderness ?
Who hath praised indifference ?
Foolish one, thy words are sweet,
   But devoid of sense.

As the man who ne'er hath seen,
Or as he who cannot hear,
Is the heart that hath no part
   In Love's hope and fear.

True, the blind do not perceive
The unsightly things around ;
True, the deaf man trembleth not
   At an awful sound.

But the face of heaven and earth,
And the murmur of the main,
Surely are a recompense
   For a little pain.

So, though Love may not be free
Always from a taint of grief,
If its sting is very sharp,
   Great is its relief.
23 *April* 1846.

THE MARTYR

   SEE, the sun hath risen—
   Lead her from the prison ;
She is young and tender,—lead her
     tenderly :
   May no fear subdue her,
   Lest the saints be fewer—
Lest her place in heaven be lost
     eternally.

   Forth she came, not trem-
     bling,
   No nor yet dissembling
An o'erwhelming terror weighing her
     down, down ;
   Little, little heeding
   Earth, but inly pleading
For the strength to triumph and to
     win a crown.

   All her might was rallied
   To her heart ; not pallid
Was her cheek, but glowing with a
     glorious red ;
   Glorious red and saintly,
   Never paling faintly,
But still flushing, kindling still, with-
     out thought of dread.

   On she went, on faster,
   Trusting in her Master,
Feeling that His eye watched o'er
     her lovingly ;
   He would prove and try her,
   But would not deny her
When her soul had past, for His
     sake, patiently.

   'Christ,' she said, 'receive
     me,—
   Let no terrors grieve me,—
Take my soul and guard it with Thy
     heavenly cares :
   Take my soul and guard it,—
   Take it and reward it
With the love Thou bearest for the
     love it bears.'

   Quickened with a fire
   Of sublime desire,
She looked up to heaven, and she
     cried aloud :
   'Death, I do entreat thee,
   Come ! I go to meet thee ;
Wrap me in the whiteness of a virgin
     shroud.'

   On she went, hope-laden—
   Happy, happy maiden !
Never more to tremble, and to weep
     no more :
   All her sins forgiven,
   Straight the path to heaven,
Through the glowing fire, lay her
     feet before.

   On she went, on quickly,
   And her breath came thickly,
With the longing to see God coming
     pantingly :
   Now the fire is kindled,
   And her flesh has dwindled
Unto dust ;—her soul is mounting up
     on high :

Higher, higher mounting,
　　The swift moments counting,—
Fear is left beneath her, and the
　　chastening rod:
　　Tears no more shall blind
　　　her;
　　Trouble lies behind her;
Satisfied with hopeful rest, and replete
　　with God.

24 *May* 1846.

THE DYING MAN TO HIS BETROTHED

ONE word—'tis all I ask of thee;
　　One word—and that is little now
That I have learned thy wrong of me;
　　And thou too art unfaithful—thou!
O thou sweet poison, sweetest death,
O honey between serpent's teeth,
Breathe on me with thy scorching
　　breath!

The last poor hope is fleeting now,
　　And with it life is ebbing fast;
I gaze upon thy cold white brow,
　　And loathe and love thee to the
　　　last.
And still thou keepest silence,—still
Thou look'st on me: for good or ill
Speak out, that I may know thy will.

Thou weepest, woman, and art pale:
　　Weep not, for thou shalt soon be
　　　free;
My life is ending like a tale
　　That was but never more shall be.
O blessed moments, ye fleet fast,
And soon the latest shall be past,
And she will be content at last.

Nay, tremble not, I have not curst
　　Thy house or mine, or thee or me.
The moment that I saw thee first,
　　The moment that I first loved
　　　thee,—
Curse *them?*—Alas I can but bless
In this mine hour of heaviness:—
Nay, sob not so in thy distress.

I have been harsh, thou say'st of me;—
　　God knows my heart was never so;
It never could be so to thee.
And now it is too late—I know
Thy grief—forgive me, love, 'tis o'er;
For I shall never trouble more
Thy life that was so calm before.

I pardon thee; mayst thou be blest!
　　Say, wilt thou sometimes think of
　　　me?
Oh may I, from my happy rest,
　　Still look with love on thine and
　　　thee,—
And may I pray for thee alway,
And for thy love still may I pray,
Waiting the everlasting day!

Stoop over me;—ah this is death!
　　I scarce can see thee at my side:
Stoop lower; let me feel thy breath,
　　O thou, mine own, my promised
　　　bride!
Pardon me, love;—I pardon thee:
And may our pardon sealèd be
Throughout the long eternity.

The pains of death my senses cover
　　Oh for His sake who died for men,
Be thou more true to this thy lover
　　Than thou hast been to me:
　　　Amen.
And, if he chide thee wrongfully,
One little moment think on me,
And thou wilt bear it patiently.

And now, O God, I turn to Thee:
  Thou only, Father, canst not fail:
Lord, Thou hast tried and broken me,
  And yet Thy mercy shall prevail.
Saviour, through Thee I am forgiven;—
Do Thou receive my soul, bloodshriven,
O Christ, who art the Gate of Heaven!

14 *July* 1846.

LISETTA ALL' AMANTE

Perdona al primo eccesso
D' un tenero dolore;
A te promisi il core,
  E vo' serbarlo a te.
Ma dimmi e mi consola:
M' ami tu ancor, cor mio?
Se a te fedel son io,
  Sarai fedele a me?

Chè se nell' alma ingrata
Pensi ad abbandonarmi,
Anch' io saprò scordarmi
  D' un amator crudel.
Ma crederlo non voglio,
Ma non lo vo' pensare;
Chè nol potrei lasciare,
  Chè gli sarei fedel.

Folkestone, 11 *August* 1846.

THE DEAD BRIDE

There she lay so still and pale,
  With her bridal robes around her:
Joy is fleeting, life is frail,
  Death had found her.

Gone for ever: gone away
  From the love and light of earth;
Gone for ever: who shall say
  Where her second birth?

Had her life been good and kind?
  Had her heart been meek and pure?
Was she of a lowly mind,
  Ready to endure?

Did she still console the sad,
  Soothe the widow's anguish wild,
Make the poor and needy glad,
  Tend the orphan child?

Who shall say what hope and fear
  Crowded in her short life's span?
If the love of God was dear,
  Or the love of man?

Happy bride if single-hearted
  Her first love to God was given;
If from this world she departed
  But to dwell in heaven;

If her faith on heaven was fixed
  And her hope; if charity
Filled her full of light unmixed
  With earth's vanity.

But alas, if tainted pleasure
  Won her heart and held it here,
Where is now her failing treasure,
  All her gladness where? . . .

Hush, too curious questioner;
  Hush, and think thine own sins o'er.
Little canst thou learn from her;
  For we know no more

Than that there she lies all pale
    With her bridal robes around her:
Joy is fleeting—life is frail—
    Death hath found her.
Folkestone, 10 *September* 1846.

WILL THESE HANDS NE'ER BE CLEAN?

AND who is this lies prostrate at thy feet?
And is he dead, thou man of wrath and pride?
    Yes, now thy vengeance is complete,
    Thy hate is satisfied.
What had he done to merit this of thee?
Who gave thee power to take away his life?
O deeply-rooted direful enmity
    That ended in long strife!
See where he grasped thy mantle as he fell,
Staining it with his blood; how terrible
Must be the payment due for this in hell!

And dost thou think to go and see no more
Thy bleeding victim, now the struggle's o'er?
    To find out peace in other lands,
    And wash the red mark from thy hands?
It shall not be; for everywhere
He shall be with thee; and the air
Shall smell of blood, and on the wind
    His groans pursue thee close behind.
When waking he shall stand before thee;
And when at length sleep shall come o'er thee,
Powerless to move, alive to dream,
So dreadful shall thy visions seem
That thou shalt own them even to be
More hateful than reality.
What time thou stoopest down to drink
Of limpid waters, thou shalt think
It is thy foe's blood bubbles up
From the polluted fountain's cup,
That stains thy lip, that cries to heaven
    For vengeance—and it shall be given.

And when thy friends shall question thee,
    'Why art thou changed so heavily?'
Trembling and fearful shalt thou say
    'I am not changed,' and turn away:
For such an outcast thou shalt be
Thou wilt not dare ask sympathy.

And so thy life will pass, and day by day
The current of existence flow away;
And, though to thee earth shall be hell and breath
Vengeance, yet thou shalt tremble more at death.
And one by one thy friends will learn to fear thee,
And thou shalt live without a hope to cheer thee;
Lonely amid a thousand, chained though free,
The curse of memory shall cling to thee:

Ages may pass away, worlds rise
  and set—
    But thou shalt not forget.
Folkestone, 16 *September* 1846.

GONE FOR EVER

O HAPPY rosebud blooming
  Upon thy parent tree,
Nay, thou art too presuming;
For soon the earth entombing
  Thy faded charms shall be,
And the chill damp consuming.

O happy skylark springing
  Up to the broad blue sky,
Too fearless in thy winging,
Too gladsome in thy singing,
  Thou also soon shalt lie
Where no sweet notes are ringing.

And through life's shine and shower
  We shall have joy and pain:
But in the summer bower
And at the morning hour
  We still shall look in vain
For the same bird and flower.
14 *October* 1846.

PRESENT AND FUTURE

WHAT is life that we should love it,
  Cherishing it evermore,
Never prizing aught above it,
  Ever loth to give it o'er?
Is it goodness? is it gladness?
Nay, 'tis more of sin and sadness;
  Nay, of weariness 'tis more.

Earthly joys are very fleeting,
  Earthly sorrows very long;
Parting ever follows meeting,
  Night succeeds to evensong.

Storms may darken in the morning
And eclipse the sun's bright dawning,
  And the chilly gloom prolong.

But, though clouds may screen and
  hide it,
  The sun shines for evermore.
Then bear grief in hope: abide it,
  Knowing that it must give o'er:
And the darkness shall flee from us,
And the sun beam down upon us
  Ever glowing more and more.
5 *November* 1846.

THE TIME OF WAITING

LIFE is fleeting, joy is fleeting,
Coldness follows love and greeting,
Parting still succeeds to meeting.

If I say 'Rejoice to-day,'
Sorrow meets me in the way:
I cannot my will obey.

If I say 'My grief shall cease;
Now then I will live in peace':
My cares instantly increase.

When I look up to the sky,
Thinking to see light on high,
Clouds my searching glance defy.

When I look upon the earth
For the flowers that should have
  birth,
I find dreariness and dearth.

And the winds sigh on for ever,
Murmurs still the flowing river,
On the graves the sunbeams quiver.

And destruction waxeth bold,
And the earth is growing old,
And I tremble in the cold.

And my weariness increases
To an ache that never ceases
And a pain that ne'er decreases.

And the times are turbulent,
And the Holy Church is rent,
And who tremble or repent?

And loud cries do ever rise
To the portals of the skies
From our earthly miseries;

From love slighted, not requited;
From high hope that should have
    lighted
All our path up, now benighted;

From the woes of humankind;
From the darkness of the mind;
From all anguish undefined;

From the heart that's crushed and
    sinking;
From the brain grown blank with
    thinking;
From the spirit sorrow drinking.

All cry out with pleading strong:
'Vengeance, Lord! how long, how
    long
Shall we suffer this great wrong?'

And the pleading and the cry
Of earth's sons are heard on high,
And are noted verily.

When this world shall be no more,
The oppressors shall endure
The great vengeance which is sure.

And the sinful shall remain
To an endless death and pain;
But the good shall live again,—

Never more to be oppressed;
Balm shall heal the bleeding breast,
And the weary be at rest.

All shall vanish of dejection,
Grief and fear and imperfection,
In that glorious resurrection.

Heed not then a night of sorrow,
If the dawning of the morrow
From past grief fresh beams shall
    borrow.

Thankful for whate'er is given,
Strive we, as we ne'er have striven,
For love's sake to be forgiven.

Then, the dark clouds opening,
Even to us the sun shall bring
Gladness, and sweet flowers shall
    spring.

For Christ's guiding love alway,
For the everlasting day,
For meek patience, let us pray.
    16 *November* 1846.

TASSO AND LEONORA

A GLORIOUS vision hovers o'er his
    soul,
  Gilding the prison and the weary
    bed,—
  Though hard the pillow placed
    beneath his head,
Though brackish be the water in the
    bowl
Beside him; he can see the planets
    roll
  In glowing adoration, without
    dread;
  Knowing how, by unerring wisdom
    led,
They struggle not against the strong
    control.

When suddenly a star shoots from
    the skies,
  Than all the other stars more
    purely bright,
Replete with heavenly loves and
    harmonies.
  He starts :—what meets his full
    awakening sight?
Lo! Leonora, with large humid eyes,
  Gazing upon him in the misty light.
    19 *December* 1846.

LOVE

LOVE is all happiness, love is all
    beauty,
Love is the crown of flaxen heads
    and hoary;
Love is the only everlasting duty;
And love is chronicled in endless
    story,
And kindles endless glory.
    24 *February* 1847.

THE SOLITARY ROSE

O HAPPY rose, red rose, that bloom-
    est lonely
  Where there are none to gather
    while they love thee;
That art perfumed by thine own
    fragrance only,
  Resting like incense round thee
    and above thee;—
Thou bearest nought save some pure
    stream that flows,
    O happy rose.

What though for thee no nightin-
    gales are singing?
  They chant one eve, but hush them
    in the morning.
Near thee no little moths and bees
    are winging

To steal thy honey when the day
    is dawning;—
Thou keep'st thy sweetness till the
    twilight's close,
    O happy rose.

Then rest in peace, thou lone and
    lovely flower;
  Yea be thou glad, knowing that
    none are near thee,
To mar thy beauty in a wanton hour,
  And scatter all thy leaves nor deign
    to wear thee.
Securely in thy solitude repose,
    O happy rose.
    15 *March* 1847.

THE SONG OF THE STAR

I AM a Star dwelling on high
In the azure of the vaulted sky.
I shine on the land and I shine on
    the sea,
And the little breezes talk to me.
The waves rise towards me everyone,
And forget the brightness of the sun;
The growing grass springs up to-
    wards me,
And forgets the day's fertility.
My face is light, and my beam is life,
And my passionless being hath no
    strife.
In me no love is turned to hate,
No fullness is made desolate;
Here is no hope, no fear, no grief,
Here is no pain and no relief;
Nor birth nor death hath part in me,
But a profound tranquillity.
The blossoms that bloomed yesterday
Unaltered shall bloom on to-day,
And on the morrow shall not fade.
Within the everlasting shade
The fountain gushing up for ever
Flows on to the eternal river,

That, running by a reedy shore,
Bubbles, bubbles evermore.
The happy birds sing in the trees
To the music of the southern breeze;
And they fear no lack of food,
Chirping in the underwood;
For ripe seeds and berried bushes
Serve the finches and the thrushes,
And all feathered fowls that dwell
In that shade majestical.
Beyond all clouds and all mistiness
I float in the strength of my loveliness.
And I move round the sun with a measured motion
In the blue expanse of the skyey ocean;
And I hear the song of the angel throng
In a river of ecstasy flow along,
Without a pausing, without a hushing,
Like an everlasting fountain's gushing
That of its own will bubbles up
From a white untainted cup.
Countless planets float round me,
Differing all in majesty;
Smaller some, and some more great,
Amethystine, roseate,
Golden, silvery, glowing blue,
Hueless, and of every hue.
Each and all, both great and small,
With a cadence musical,
Shoot out rays of glowing praise
Never ending, but always
Hymning the Creator's might
Who hath filled them full of light;
Pealing through eternity,
Filling out immensity;
Sun and moon and stars together
In heights where is no cloudy weather;
Where is nor storm nor mist nor rain,
Where night goeth not to come again.
On and on and on for ever,
Never ceasing, sinking never,
Voiceless adorations rise
To the heaven above the skies.
We all chant with a holy harmony,
No discord marreth our melody;
Here are no strifes nor envyings,
But each with love joyously sings,
For ever and ever floating free
In the azure light of infinity.

19 March 1847.

RESURRECTION EVE

He resteth: weep not;
The living sleep not
With so much calm.
  He hears no chiding
  And no deriding,
  Hath joy for sorrow,
  For night hath morrow,
For wounds hath balm,
For life's strange riot
Hath death and quiet.
Who would recall him
  Of those that love him?
No fears appall him,
No ills befall him;
  There's nought above him
Save turf and flowers
  And pleasant grass.
Pass the swift hours,
  How swiftly pass!
The hours of slumber
He doth not number;
Grey hours of morning
Ere the day's dawning;
  Brightened by gleams
  Of the sunbeams,—
  By the foreseeing
  Of resurrection,
  Of glorious being,
  Of full perfection,

Of sins forgiven
  Before the face
    Of men and spirits;
Of God in heaven,
  The resting-place
    That he inherits.

8 April 1847.

THE DEAD CITY

Once I rambled in a wood
With a careless hardihood,
  Heeding not the tangled way;
  Labyrinths around me lay,
But for them I never stood.

On, still on, I wandered on,
And the sun above me shone;
  And the birds around me winging
  With their everlasting singing
Made me feel not quite alone.

In the branches of the trees
Murmured like the hum of bees
  The low sound of happy breezes,
  Whose sweet voice that never ceases
Lulls the heart to perfect ease.

Streamlets bubbled all around
On the green and fertile ground,
  Through the rushes and the grass,
  Like a sheet of liquid glass,
With a soft and trickling sound.

And I went, I went on faster,
Contemplating no disaster;
  And I plucked ripe blackberries,
  But the birds with envious eyes
Came and stole them from their master.

For the birds here were all tame;
Some with bodies like a flame;
  Some that glanced the branches through,
  Pure and colourless as dew;
Fearlessly to me they came.

Before me no mortal stood
In the mazes of that wood;
  Before me the birds had never
  Seen a man, but dwelt for ever
In a happy solitude:

Happy solitude, and blest
With beatitude of rest;
  Where the woods are ever vernal,
  And the life and joy eternal,
Without death's or sorrow's test.

O most blessed solitude!
O most full beatitude!
  Where are quiet without strife
  And imperishable life,
Nothing marred and all things good.

And the bright sun, life-begetting,
Never rising, never setting,
  Shining warmly overhead,
  Nor too pallid nor too red,
Lulled me to a sweet forgetting—

Sweet forgetting of the time;
And I listened for no chime
  Which might warn me to be gone;
  But I wandered on, still on,
'Neath the boughs of oak and lime.

Know I not how long I strayed
In the pleasant leafy shade;
  But the trees had gradually
  Grown more rare, the air more free,
The sun hotter overhead.

Soon the birds no more were seen
Glancing through the living green,
  And a blight had passed upon
  All the trees, and the pale sun
Shone with a strange lurid sheen.

Then a darkness spread around:
I saw nought; I heard no sound:
  Solid darkness overhead,
  With a trembling cautious tread
Passed I o'er the unseen ground.

But at length a pallid light
Broke upon my searching sight;
  A pale solitary ray
  Like a star at dawn of day
Ere the sun is hot and bright.

Towards its faintly glimmering beam
I went on as in a dream—
  A strange dream of hope and fear—
  And I saw, as I drew near,
'Twas in truth no planet's gleam;

But a lamp above a gate
Shone in solitary state,
  O'er a desert drear and cold,
  O'er a heap of ruins old,
O'er a scene most desolate.

By that gate I entered lone
A fair city of white stone;
  And a lovely light to see
  Dawned, and spread most gradually,
Till the air grew warm and shone.

Through the splendid streets I strayed
In that radiance without shade;
  Yet I heard no human sound;
  All was still and silent round
As a city of the dead.

All the doors were open wide;
Lattices on every side
  In the wind swung to and fro—
  Wind that whispered very low,
'Go and see the end of pride.'

With a fixed determination
Entered I each habitation;
  But they all were tenantless.
  All was utter loneliness,
All was deathless desolation.

In the noiseless market-place
Was no careworn busy face;
  There were none to buy or sell,
  None to listen or to tell,
In this silent emptiness.

Through the city on I went
Full of awe and wonderment.
  Still the light around me shone,
  And I wandered on, still on,
In my great astonishment.

Till at length I reached a place
Where amid an ample space
  Rose a palace for a king;
  Golden was the turreting,
And of solid gold the base.

The great porch was ivory,
And the steps were ebony;
  Diamond and chrysoprase
  Set the pillars in a blaze,
Capitalled with jewelry.

None was there to bar my way,
And the breezes seemed to say,
  'Touch not these, but pass them by,
  Pressing onwards'; therefore I
Entered in and made no stay.

All around was desolate.
I went on; a silent state
 Reigned in each deserted room,
 And I hastened through the gloom
Till I reached an outer gate.

Soon a shady avenue,
Blossom-perfumed, met my view;
 Here and there the sunbeams fell
 On pure founts whose sudden swell
Up from marble basons flew.

Every tree was fresh and green;
Not a withered leaf was seen
 Through the veil of flowers and fruit;
 Strong and sapful were the root,
The top boughs, and all between.

Vines were climbing everywhere
Full of purple grapes and fair;
 And far off I saw the corn
 With its heavy head down borne
By the odour-laden air.

Who shall strip the bending vine?
Who shall tread the press for wine?
 Who shall bring the harvest in
 When the pallid ears begin
In the sun to glow and shine?

On I went alone, alone,
Till I saw a tent that shone
 With each bright and lustrous hue;
 It was trimmed with jewels too,
And with flowers; not one was gone.

Then the breezes whispered me:
'Enter in, and look, and see
 How for luxury and pride
 A great multitude have died.'
And I entered tremblingly.

Lo a splendid banquet laid
In the cool and pleasant shade.
 Mighty tables everything
 Of sweet Nature's furnishing
That was rich and rare displayed;

And each strange and luscious cate
Practised art makes delicate;
 With a thousand fair devices
 Full of odours and of spices;
And a warm voluptuous state.

All the vessels were of gold,
Set with gems of worth untold.
 In the midst a fountain rose
 Of pure milk, whose rippling flows
In a silver bason rolled.

In green emerald baskets were
Sun-red apples, streaked and fair;
 Here the nectarine and peach
 And ripe plum lay, and on each
The bloom rested everywhere.

Grapes were hanging overhead,
Purple, pale, and ruby-red;
 And in panniers all around
 Yellow melons shone, fresh found,
With the dew upon them spread.

And the apricot and pear
And the pulpy fig were there,
 Cherries and dark mulberries,
 Bunchy currants, strawberries,
And the lemon wan and fair:

And unnumbered others too,
Fruits of every size and hue,
 Juicy in their ripe perfection,
 Cool beneath the cool reflection
Of the curtains' skyey blue.

All the floor was strewn with flowers
Fresh from sunshine and from
    showers,
  Roses, lilies, jessamine;
  And the ivy ran between,
Like a thought in happy hours.

And this feast too lacked no guest
With its warm delicious rest;
  With its couches softly sinking,
  And its glow not made for thinking,
But for careless joy at best.

Many banqueters were there,
Wrinkled age, the young, the fair;
  In the splendid revelry
  Flushing cheek and kindling eye
Told of gladness without care.

Yet no laughter rang around,
Yet they uttered forth no sound;
  With the smile upon his face
  Each sat moveless in his place,
Silently, as if spellbound.

The low whispering voice was gone,
And I felt awed and alone.
  In my great astonishment
  To the feasters up I went—
Lo they all were turned to stone!

Yea they all were statue-cold,
Men and women, young and old;
  With the life-like look and smile
  And the flush; and all the while
The hard fingers kept their hold.

Here a little child was sitting
With a merry glance, befitting
  Happy age and heedless heart;
  There a young man sat apart,
With a forward look unweeting.

Nigh them was a maiden fair,
And the ringlets of her hair
  Round her slender fingers twined;
  And she blushed as she reclined,
Knowing that her love was there.

Here a dead man sat to sup,
In his hand a drinking-cup;
  Wine-cup of the heavy gold,
  Human hand stony and cold,
And no life-breath struggling up.

There a mother lay and smiled
Down upon her infant child;
  Happy child and happy mother,
  Laughing back to one another
With a gladness undefiled.

Here an old man slept, worn out
With the revelry and rout;
  Here a strong man sat and gazed
  On a girl whose eyes upraised
No more wandered roundabout.

And none broke the stillness—none;
I was the sole living one.
  And methought that silently
  Many seemed to look on me
With strange steadfast eyes that
    shone.

Full of fear I would have fled;
Full of fear I bent my head,
  Shutting out each stony guest—
  When I looked again, the feast
And the tent had vanished.

Yes, once more I stood alone
Where the happy sunlight shone,
  And a gentle wind was sighing,
  And the little birds were flying,
And the dreariness was gone.

All these things that I have said
Awed me and made me afraid.
  What was I that I should see
  So much hidden mystery?
And I straightway knelt and prayed.
9 April 1847.

THE ROSE

O ROSE, thou flower of flowers, thou
    fragrant wonder,
Who shall describe thee in thy
    ruddy prime,
Thy perfect fullness in the summer-
    time,
When the pale leaves blushingly
    part asunder
And show the warm red heart lies
    glowing under?
Thou shouldst bloom surely in
    some sunny clime,
Untouched by blights and chilly
    winter's rime,
Where lightnings never flash nor
    peals the thunder.
And yet in happier spheres they
    cannot need thee
So much as we do with our weight
    of woe;
Perhaps they would not tend, perhaps
    not heed thee,
  And thou wouldst lonely and
    neglected grow:
And He who is all wise, He hath
    decreed thee
  To gladden earth and cheer all
    hearts below.
17 April 1847.

SPRING QUIET

GONE were but the Winter,
  Come were but the Spring,
I would go to a covert
  Where the birds sing;

Where, in the whitethorn
  Singeth a thrush,
And a robin sings
  In the holly-bush.

Full of fresh scents
  Are the budding boughs
Arching high over
  A cool green house;

Full of sweet scents,
  And whispering air
Which sayeth softly:
  'We spread no snare;

'Here dwell in safety,
  Here dwell alone,
With a clear stream,
  And a mossy stone.

'Here the sun shineth
  Most shadily;
Here is heard an echo
  Of the far sea,
    Though far off it be.'
Towards May 1847.

I HAVE FOUGHT A GOOD FIGHT

'WHO art thou that comest with a
    steadfast face
Through the hushed arena to the
    burying-place?'
'I am one whose footprints marked
    upon the sand
Cry in blood for vengeance on a
    guilty land.'

'How are these thy garments white
    as whitest snow
Though thy blood hath touched them
    in its overflow?'

'My blood cannot stain them, nor
   my tears make white;
One than I more mighty, He hath
   made them bright.'

'Say, do thy wounds pain thee open
   every one,
Wounds that now are glowing clearer
   than the sun?'
'Nay, they are my gladness un-
   alloyed by grief;
Like a desert-fountain, or a long
   relief.

'When the lion had thee in his
   deadly clasp,
Was there then no terror in thy
   stifled gasp?'
'Though I felt the crushing, and
   the grinding teeth,
He was with me ever, He who
   comforteth.'

'Didst thou hear the shouting, as
   of a great flood,
Crying out for vengeance, crying out
   for blood?'
'I heard it in silence, and was not
   afraid,
While for the mad people silently I
   prayed.'

'Did their hate not move thee? art
   thou heedless then
Of the fear of children and the curse
   of men?'
'God looked down upon me from
   the heaven above,
And I did not tremble, happy in
   His love.'

July 1847.

WISHES

OH would that I were very far away
   Among the lanes, with hedges all
      around,
   Happily listening to the dreamy
      sound
Of distant sheep-bells, smelling the
   new hay
And all the wild flowers scattered
   in my way:
   Or would that I were lying on
      some mound
   Where shade and butterflies and
      thyme abound,
Beneath the trees, upon a sunny day:
Or would I strolled beside the mighty
   sea—
   The sea before, and the tall cliffs
      behind;
While winds from the warm south
   might tell to me
   How health and joy for all men
      are designed:—
But, be I where I may, would I had
   thee,
   And heard thy gentle voice, my
      Mother kind.

22 *July* 1847.

THE DREAM

REST, rest; the troubled breast
Panteth evermore for rest:—
Be it sleep or be it death,
Rest is all it coveteth.

Tell me, dost thou remember the
   old time
We sat together by that sunny
   stream,
And dreamed our happiness was
   too sublime
Only to be a dream?

Gazing, till steadfast gazing made us
    blind,
  We watched the fishes leaping
    at their play;
Thinking our love too tender and
    too kind
    Ever to pass away.

And some of all our thoughts were
    true at least
  What time we thought together
    by that stream;
Thy happiness has evermore in-
    creased,—
    My love was not a dream.

And, now that thou art gone, I often
    sit
  On its green margin, for thou
    once wert there;
And see the clouds that, floating
    over it,
    Darken the quiet air.

Yes oftentimes I sit beside it now,
  Hearkening the wavelets ripple
    o'er the sands;
Until again I hear thy whispered vow
    And feel thy pressing hands.

Then the bright sun seems to stand
    still in heaven,
  The stream sings gladly as it
    onward flows,
The rushes grow more green, the
    grass more even,
    Blossoms the budding rose.

I say: 'It is a joy-dream; I will
    take it;
  He is not gone—he will return
    to me.'
What found'st thou in my heart that
    thou shouldst break it?—
    How have I injured thee?

Oh I am weary of life's passing show,
  Its pageant and its pain.
I would I could lie down lone in my
    woe,
    Ne'er to rise up again;
I would I could lie down where none
    might know;
    For truly love is vain.

Truly love's vain; but oh how vainer
    still
  Is that which is not love, but
    seems!
Concealed indifference, a covered ill,
    A very dream of dreams.
1847.

ELEANOR

CHERRY-RED her mouth was,
    Morning-blue her eye,
Lady-slim her little waist
    Rounded prettily;
And her sweet smile of gladness
    Made every heart rejoice:
But sweeter even than her smile
    The tones were of her voice.

Sometimes she spoke, sometimes she
    sang;
  And evermore the sound
Floated, a dreamy melody,
    Upon the air around;
'As though a wind were singing
    Far up beside the sun,
Till sound and warmth and glory
    Were blended all in one.

Her hair was long and golden,
    And clustered unconfined
Over a forehead high and white
    That spoke a noble mind.
Her little hand, her little foot,
    Were ready evermore
To hurry forth to meet a friend;
    She smiling at the door.

But if she sang or if she spoke,
   'Twas music soft and grand,
As though a distant singing sea
   Broke on a tuneful strand;
As though a blessed Angel
   Were singing a glad song,
Halfway between the earth and heaven
   Joyfully borne along.
   30 *July* 1847.

ISIDORA

LOVE, whom I have loved too well,
   Turn thy face away from me;
For I heed nor heaven nor hell
   While mine eyes can look on thee.
Do not answer, do not speak,
For thy voice can make me weak.

I must choose 'twixt God and man,
   And I dare not hesitate:
Oh how little is life's span,
   And Eternity how great!
Go out from me; for I fear
Mine own strength while thou art here.

Husband, leave me; but know this:
   I would gladly give my soul
So that thine might dwell in bliss
   Free from the accurst control,
So that thou mightest go hence
In a hopeful penitence.

Yea from hell I would look up,
   And behold thee in thy place,
Drinking of the living cup,
   With the joy-look on thy face,
And the light that shines alone
From the glory of the Throne.

But how could my endless loss
   Be thine everlasting gain?
Shall thy palm grow from my cross?
   Shall thine ease be in my pain?

Yea thine own soul witnesseth
Thy life is not in my death.

It were vain that I should die—
   That we thus should perish both;
Thou wouldst gain no peace thereby;
   And in truth I should be loth
By the loss of my salvation
To increase thy condemnation.

Little infant, his and mine,
   Would that I were as thou art;
Nothing breaks that sleep of thine,
   And ah nothing breaks thy heart;
And thou knowest naught of strife,
The heart's death for the soul's life.

None misdoubt thee, none misdeem
   Of thy wishes and thy will.
All thy thoughts are what they seem,
   Very pure and very still;
And thou fearest not the voice
That once made thy heart rejoice.

Oh how calm thou art, my child!
   I could almost envy thee.
Thou has neither wept nor smiled,
   Thou that sleepest quietly.
Would I also were at rest
With the one that I love best.

Husband, go. I dare not hearken
   To thy words or look upon
Those despairing eyes that darken
   Down on me—But he is gone!
Nay, come back, and be my fate
As thou wilt!—It is too late.

I have conquered; it is done,
   Yea the death-struggle is o'er,
And the hopeless quiet won:—
   I shall see his face no more:—
And mine eyes are waxing dim
Now they cannot look on him.

And my heart-pulses are growing
   Very weak, and through my whole
Life-blood a slow chill is going :—
   Blessed Saviour, take my soul
To Thy Paradise and care :—
Paradise, will he be there?
   9 *August* 1847.

ZARA

Now the pain beginneth and the
   word is spoken ;—
   Hark unto the tolling of the church-
     yard chime!—
Once my heart was gladsome, now
   my heart is broken,—
   Once my love was noble, now it
     is a crime.

But the fear is over; yea what now
   shall pain me?
   Arm thee in thy sorrow, O most
     desolate!
Weariness and weakness, these shall
   now sustain me,—
   Pride and bitter grieving, burning
     love and hate.

Yea the fear is over, the strong fear
   and trembling ;
   I can doubt no longer, he is gone
     indeed.
Rend thy hair, lost woman, weep
   without dissembling ;
   The heart torn forth from it, shall
     the breast not bleed?

Happy she who looketh on his
   beauty's glory!
   Happy she who listeneth to his
     gentle word!
Yet, O happy maiden, sorrow lies
   before thee ;
   Greeting hath been given, parting
     must be heard.

He shall leave thee also, he who now
   hath left me,
   With a weary spirit and an aching
     heart ;
Thou shalt be bereaved by him who
   hath bereft me ;
   Thou hast sucked the honey,—
     feel the stinging's smart.

Let the cold gaze on him, let the
   heartless hear him,
   For he shall not hurt them, they
     are safe in sooth :
But let loving women shun that man
   and fear him,
   Full of cruel kindness and devoid
     of ruth.

When ye call upon him, hope for no
   replying ;
   When ye gaze upon him, think
     not he will look ;
Hope not for his pity when your
   heart is sighing ;
   Such another, waiting, weeping,
     he forsook.

Hath the heaven no thunder where-
   with to denounce him?
   Hath the heaven no lightning
     wherewith to chastise?
O my heart and spirit, O my soul,
   renounce him
   Who hath called for vengeance
     from the distant skies :

Vengeance which pursues thee,
   vengeance which shall find thee,
   Crushing thy false spirit, scathing
     thy fair limb :—
O ye thunders, deafen, O ye light-
   nings, blind me ;
   Winds and storms from heaven,
     strike me but spare him!

I forgive thee, dearest, cruel, I for-
    give thee ;—
  May thy cup of sorrow be poured
    out for me ;
Though the dregs be bitter, yet they
    shall not grieve me,
  Knowing that I drink them, O my
    love, for thee.
      1847.

THE NOVICE

I LOVE one and he loveth me :
Who sayeth this ? who deemeth this?
And is this thought a cause of bliss,
  Or source of misery?

The loved may die, or he may
    change :
And if he die thou art bereft ;
Or if he alter nought is left
  Save life that seemeth strange.

A weary life, a hopeless life,
Full of all ill and fear-oppressed ;
A weary life that looks for rest
  Alone after death's strife.

And love's joy hath no quiet even ;
It evermore is variable.
Its gladness is like war in hell
  More than repose in heaven.

Yea it is as a poison-cup
That holds one quick fire-draught
    within ;
For when the life seems to begin
  The slow death looketh up.

Then bring me to a solitude
Where love may neither come nor go ;
Where very peaceful waters flow,
  And roots are found for food ;

Where the wild honey-bee booms by,
And trees and bushes freely give
Ripe fruit and nuts : there I would
    live,
  And there I fain would die.

There autumn leaves may make my
    grave,
And little birds sing over it ;
And there cool twilight winds may
    flit
  And shadowy branches wave.
      4 *September* 1847.

IMMALEE

I GATHER thyme upon the sunny
    hills,
  And its pure fragrance ever glad-
    dens me,
  And in my mind having tran-
    quillity
I smile to see how my green basket
    fills.
And by clear streams I gather
    daffodils ;
  And in dim woods find out the
    cherry-tree,
  And take its fruit and the wild
    strawberry
And nuts and honey ; and live free
    from ills.
I dwell on the green earth, 'neath
    the blue sky,
  Birds are my friends, and leaves
    my rustling roof :
The deer are not afraid of me, and I
  Hear the wild goat, and hail its
    hastening hoof ;
The squirrels sit perked as I pass
    them by,
  And even the watchful hare stands
    not aloof.
      21 *September* 1847.

HEART'S CHILL BETWEEN

I DID not chide him, though I knew
    That he was false to me.
Chide the exhaling of the dew,
    The ebbing of the sea,
The fading of a rosy hue—
    But not inconstancy.

Why strive for love when love is o'er—
    Why bind a restive heart?
He never knew the pain I bore
    In saying—'We must part,
Let us be friends and nothing more':
    Oh woman's shallow art!

But it is over, it is done:
    I hardly heed it now:
So many weary years have run
    Since then I think not how
Things might have been—but greet each one
    With an unruffled brow.

What time I am where others be
    My heart seems very calm—
Stone-calm: but, if all go from me,
    There comes a vague alarm,
A shrinking in the memory
    From some forgotten harm.

And often through the long long night,
    Waking when none are near,
I feel my heart beat fast with fright,
    Yet know not what I fear:
Oh how I long to see the light,
    And the sweet birds to hear!

To have the sun upon my face,
    To look up through the trees,
To walk forth in the open space
    And listen to the breeze,—
And not to dream the burial-place
    Is clogging my weak knees.

Sometimes I can nor weep nor pray,
    But am half stupefied;
And then all those who see me say
    Mine eyes are opened wide
And that my wits seem gone astray:—
    Ah would that I had died!

Would I could die and be at peace—
    Or living could forget!
My grief nor grows nor doth decrease,
    But ever is. And yet
Methinks now that all this shall cease
    Before the sun shall set.

22 September 1847.

LADY ISABELLA

Heart warm as summer, fresh as spring,
Gracious as autumn's harvesting,
Pure as the winter's snows; as white
A hand as lilies in sunlight;
Eyes glorious as a midnight star;
Hair shining as the chestnuts are;
A step firm and majestical;
A voice singing and musical;
A soft expression, kind address;
Tears for another's heaviness;
Bright looks; an action full of grace;
A perfect form, a perfect face;
All these become a woman well,
And these had Lady Isabel.

27 September 1847.

NIGHT AND DEATH

Now the sunlit hours are o'er,
Rise up from thy shadowy shore,
Happy Night, whom Chaos bore.

Better is the peaceful treasure
Of thy musings without measure
Than the day's unquiet pleasure.

Bring the holy moon ; so pale
She herself seems but a veil
For the sun, where no clouds sail.

Bring the stars, thy progeny ;
Each a little lamp on high
To light up an azure sky.

Sounds incomprehensible
In the shining planets dwell
Of thy sister Queen to tell.

Of that sister Nature saith
She hath power o'er life and breath ;
And her name is written Death.

She is fairer far than thou ;
Grief her head can never bow,
Joy is stamped upon her brow.

She is full of gentleness,
And of faith and hope ; distress
Finds in her forgetfulness.

In her arms who lieth down
Never more is seen to frown,
Though he wore a thorny crown.

Whoso sigheth in unrest,
If his head lean on her breast,
Witnesseth she is the best.

All the riches of the earth,
Weighed by her, are nothing worth :
She is the eternal birth.

In her treasure-house are found
Stored abundantly around
Almsdeeds done without a sound ;

Long forbearance ; patient will ;
Fortitude in midst of ill ;
Hope, when even fear grew still ;

Kindness given again for hate ;
Hearts resigned though desolate ;
Meekness, which is truly great ;

Bitter tears of penitence ;
Changeless love's omnipotence :—
And nought lacketh recompense

In her house no tainted thing
Winneth any entering ;
There the poor have comforting.

There they wait a little time
Till the Angel-uttered chime
Sound the eternal matin-prime.

Then, upraised in joyfulness,
They shall know her, and confess
She is blessed and doth bless.

When earth's fleeting day is flown,
All created things shall own,
Death is Life, and Death alone.
28 *September* 1847.

DEATH'S CHILL BETWEEN

CHIDE not : let me breathe a little,
  For I shall not mourn him long ;
Though the life-cord was so brittle,
  The love-cord was very strong.
I would wake a little space
Till I find a sleeping-place.

You can go,—I shall not weep ;
  You can go unto your rest.
My heart-ache is all too deep,
  And too sore my throbbing breast.
Can sobs be, or angry tears,
Where are neither hopes nor fears ?

Though with you I am alone
 And must be so everywhere,
I will make no useless moan,—
 None shall say, 'She could not
  bear.'
While life lasts I will be strong,—
But I shall not struggle long.

Listen, listen!—Everywhere
 A low voice is calling me,
And a step is on the stair,
 And one comes you do not see.
Listen, listen!—Evermore
A dim hand knocks at the door.

Hear me! He is come again,
 My own dearest is come back.
Bring him in from the cold rain;
 Bring wine, and let nothing lack.
Thou and I will rest together,
Love, until the sunny weather.

I will shelter thee from harm,
 Hide thee from all heaviness.
Come to me, and keep thee warm
 By my side in quietness.
I will lull thee to thy sleep
With sweet songs: we will not weep.

Who hath talked of weeping?—Yet
 There is something at my heart
Gnawing, I would fain forget,
 And an aching and a smart.—
Ah, my mother, 'tis in vain,
For he is not come again.

29 *September* 1847.

THE LOTUS-EATERS

ULYSSES TO PENELOPE

IN a far distant land they dwell,
 Incomprehensible,
Who love the shadow more than
  light,
More than the sun the moon,
Cool evening more than noon,
Pale silver more than gold that
  glitters bright.
A dark cloud overhangs their
  land
 Like a mighty hand,
Never moving from above it;
A cool shade and moist and
  dim,
With a twilight purple rim,
 And they love it.
And sometimes it giveth rain,
 But soon it ceaseth as before,
And earth drieth up again,—
 Then the dews rise more and
  more,
Till it filleth, dropping o'er;
But no forked lightnings flit,
And no thunders roll in it.
Through the land a river flows,
With a sleepy sound it goes:
 Such a drowsy noise, in sooth,
 Those who will not listen
  hear not:
 But, if one is wakeful, fear
  not—
It shall lull him to repose,
 Bringing back the dreams of
  youth.
Hemlock groweth, poppy bloweth,
 In the fields where no man
  moweth:
And the vine is full of wine
And are full of milk the kine,
And the hares are all secure,
And the birds are wild no more,
And the forest-trees wax old,
And winds stir, or hot or cold,—
And yet no man taketh care,
All things resting everywhere.

7 *October* 1847.

SONNET

FROM THE PSALMS

ALL through the livelong night I lay
    awake,
  Watering my couch with tears of
    heaviness.
  None stood beside me in my sore
    distress :—
Then cried I to my heart: If thou
    wilt, break,
But be thou still; no moaning will
    I make,
  Nor ask man's help, nor kneel
    that he may bless.
So I kept silence in my haughti-
    ness,
Till lo the fire was kindled, and I
    spake—
Saying: Oh that I had wings like
    to a dove,
  Then would I flee away and be at
    rest :
I would not pray for friends or hope
    or love,
  But still the weary throbbing of
    my breast :
And, gazing on the changeless
    heavens above,
  Witness that such a quietness is
    best.

7 November 1847.

SONG

THE stream moaneth as it floweth,
The wind sigheth as it bloweth,
Leaves are falling, Autumn goeth,
  Winter cometh back again;
And the air is very chilly,
And the country rough and hilly,
  And I shiver in the rain.
Who will help me? who will love me?
Heaven sets forth no light above me:
Ancient memories reprove me,
Long-forgotten feelings move me,
  I am full of heaviness.
Earth is cold, too cold the sea:
Whither shall I turn and flee?
Is there any hope for me?
Any ease for my heart-aching,
Any sleep that hath no waking,
Any night without day-breaking,
  Any rest from weariness?

Hark the wind is answering:
  Hark the running stream replieth:
  There is rest for him that dieth :
  In the grave whoever lieth
Nevermore hath sorrowing.
Holy slumber, holy quiet,
Close the eyes and still the riot:
And the brain forgets its thought,
  And the heart forgets its beating.
  Earth and earthly things are
    fleeting;
There is what all men have sought—
Long unchangeable repose,
Lulling us from many woes.

7 November 1847.

THE WORLD'S HARMONIES

OH listen, listen, for the Earth
  Hath silent melody :
Green grasses are her lively chords,
  And blossoms : and each tree,
Chestnut and oak and sycamore,
  Makes solemn harmony.

Oh listen, listen, for the Sea
  Is calling unto us :
Her notes are the broad liquid
    waves
  Mighty and glorious.
Lo the first man and the last man
  Hath heard, shall hearken thus.

The Sun on which men cannot look,
  Its splendour is so strong,
Which wakeneth life and giveth life,
  Rolling in light along,
From day-dawn to dim eventide
  Sings the eternal song.

And the Moon taketh up the hymn,
  And the Stars answer all:
And all the Clouds and all the Winds
  And all the Dews that fall
And Frost and fertilizing Rain
  Are mutely musical.

Fishes and Beasts and feathered Fowl
  Swell the eternal chaunt,
That riseth through the lower air,
  Over the rainbow slant,
Up through the unseen palace-gates,
  Fearlessly jubilant.

Before the everlasting Throne
  It is acceptable:
It hath no pause or faltering:
  The Angels know it well:
Yea in the highest heaven of heavens
  Its sound is audible.

Yet than the voice of the whole World
  There is a sweeter voice,
That maketh all the Cherubim
  And Seraphim rejoice:
That all the blessed Spirits hail
  With undivided choice:

That crieth at the golden door
  And gaineth entrance in:
That the palm-branch and radiant crown
  And glorious throne may win:—
The lowly prayer of a Poor Man
  Who turneth from his sin.
    20 *November* 1847.

THE LAST ANSWER

(*Written to Bouts-rimés.*)

She turned round to me with her steadfast eyes.
  'I tell you I have looked upon the dead;
  Have kissed the brow and the cold lips,' she said;
'Have called upon the sleeper to arise.
He loved me, yet he stirred not: on this wise,
  Not bowing in weak agony my head,
  But all too sure of what life is, to dread,
Learned I that love and hope are fallacies.'
She gazed quite calmly on me: and I felt
  Awed and astonished and almost afraid:
    For what was I to have admonished her?
Then, being full of doubt and fear, I knelt,
  And tears came to my eyes even as I prayed:
    But she meanwhile only grew statelier.
    2 *December* 1847.

DEVOTIONAL POEMS

I DO SET MY BOW IN THE CLOUD

The roses bloom too late for me:
The violets I shall not see:
Even the snowdrops will not come
Till I have passed from home to home:
From home on earth to home in heaven,
Here penitent and there forgiven.

Mourn not, my Father, that I seek
One who is strong when I am weak.
Through the dark passage, verily,
His rod and staff shall comfort me:
He shall support me in the strife
Of death that dieth into life:
He shall support me, He receive
My soul when I begin to live,
And more than I can ask for give.

He from the heaven-gates built above
Hath looked on me in perfect love.
From the heaven-walls to me He calls
To come and dwell within those walls:
With Cherubim and Seraphim
And Angels: yea, beholding Him.

His care for me is more than mine,
Father; His love is more than thine.
Sickness and death I have from thee,
From Him have immortality.
He giveth gladness where He will,
Yet chasteneth His beloved still.

Then tell me: is it not enough
To feel that, when the path is rough
And the sky dark and the rain cold,
His promise standeth as of old?

When heaven and earth have past away
Only His righteous word shall stay,
And we shall know His will is best.
Behold: He is a haven-rest,
A sheltering-rock, a hiding-place,
For runners steadfast in the race;
Who, toiling for a little space,
Had light through faith when sight grew dim,
And offered all their world to Him.

December 1847.

DEATH IS SWALLOWED UP IN VICTORY

'Tell me: doth it not grieve thee to lie here,
And see the cornfields waving not for thee,
Just in the waking summer of the year?'
'I fade from earth, and lo along with me
The season that I love will fade away:
How should I look for autumn longingly?'
'Yet autumn beareth fruit whilst day by day
The leaves grow browner with a mellow hue,
Declining to a beautiful decay.'
'Decay is death, with which I have to do,
And see it near: behold, it is more good
Than length of days and length of sorrow too.'

'But thy heart hath not dwelt in
  solitude ;
Many have loved and love thee :
  dost not heed
Free love, for which in vain have
  others sued ? '
    'I thirst for love, love is mine
      only need,
    Love such as none hath borne me
      nor can bear,
    True love that prompteth thought
      and word and deed.'
'Here it is not : why seek it otherwhere ?
Nay, bow thy head, and own that
  on this earth
Are many goodly things and sweet
  and fair.'
    'There are tears in man's laughter :
      in his mirth
    There is a fearful forward look ; and lo
    An infant's cry gives token of its
      birth.'
'I mark the ocean of Time ebb and
  flow :
He who hath care one day and is
  perplext
To-morrow may have joy in place of
  woe.'
    'Evil becomes good : and to this
      annext
    Good becomes evil : speak of it no
      more :
    My heart is wearied and my spirit
      vext.'
'Is there no place it grieves thee to
  give o'er ?
Is there no home thou lov'st, and
  so wouldst fain
Tarry a little longer at the door ? '
    I must go hence and not return
      again :
    But the friends whom I have shall
      come to me,
    And dwell together with me safe
      from pain.'
'Where is that mansion mortals
  cannot see ?
Behold, the tombs are full of
  worms : shalt thou
Rise thence and soar up skywards
  gloriously ? '
    'Even as the planets shine we
      know not how,
    We shall be raised then, changed
      yet still the same—
    Being made like Christ, yea being
      as He is now.'
'Thither thou go'st whence no man
  ever came :
Death's voyagers return not, and
  in death
There is no room for speech or sign
  or fame.'
    'There is room for repose that
      comforteth ;
    There weariness is not : and there
      content
    Broodeth for ever, and hope
      hovereth.'
'When the stars fall and when the
  graves are rent,
Shalt thou have safety ? shalt thou
  look for life
When the great light of the broad
  sun is spent ? '
    'These elements shall consum-
      mate their strife,
    This heaven and earth shall shrivel
      like a scroll,
    And then be re-created, beauty-
      rife.'
'Who shall abide it when from pole
  to pole
The world's foundations shall be
  overthrown ?
Who shall abide to scan the perfect
  whole ? '

'He who hath strength given to
    him, not his own :
He who hath faith in that which is
    not seen,
    And patient hope : who trusts in
        Love alone.'
'Yet thou—the death-struggle must
    intervene
    Ere thou win rest : think better
        of it : think
Of all that is and shall be and hath
    been.'
    'The cup my Father giveth me to
        drink,
Shall I not take it meekly? though
    my heart
    Tremble a moment, it shall never
        shrink.'
'Satan will wrestle with thee when
    thou art
    In the last agony; and Death
        will bring
Sins to remembrance ere thy spirit
    part.'
    'In that great hour of unknown
        suffering
God shall be with me, and His arm
    made bare
    Shall fight for me : yea, under-
        neath His wing
I shall lie safe at rest and freed
    from care.'
        20 *February* 1848.

SYMBOLS

I WATCHED a rosebud very long
    Brought on by dew and sun and
        shower,
    Waiting to see the perfect flower :
Then, when I thought it should be
    strong,
    It opened at the matin hour
And fell at evensong.

I watched a nest from day to day,
    A green nest full of pleasant shade,
    Wherein three speckled eggs were
        laid :
But when they should have hatched
    in May,
    The two old birds had grown
        afraid
Or tired, and flew away.

Then in my wrath I broke the bough
    That I had tended so with care,
    Hoping its scent should fill the air;
I crushed the eggs, not heeding how
    Their ancient promise had been
        fair :
I would have vengeance now.

But the dead branch spoke from the
    sod,
    And the eggs answered me again :
    Because we failed dost thou com-
        plain ?
Is thy wrath just ? And what if God,
    Who waiteth for thy fruits in vain,
Should also take the rod ?
        7 *January* 1849.

SWEET DEATH

THE sweetest blossoms die.
    And so it was that, going day by
        day
    Unto the Church to praise and
        pray,
And crossing the green churchyard
    thoughtfully,
    I saw how on the graves the
        flowers
    Shed their fresh leaves in showers,
And how their perfume rose up to
    the sky
Before it passed away.

The youngest blossoms die.
  They die and fall and nourish the rich earth
  From which they lately had their birth;
Sweet life, but sweeter death that passeth by
  And is as though it had not been:—
All colours turn to green;
The bright hues vanish, and the odours fly,
The grass hath lasting worth.

And youth and beauty die.
  So be it, O my God, Thou God of Truth:
  Better than beauty and than youth
  Are Saints and Angels, a glad company;
  And Thou, O Lord, our Rest and Ease,
  Art better far than these.
Why should we shrink from our full harvest? why
  Prefer to glean with Ruth?
  9 February 1849.

A CHRISTMAS CAROL

THANK God, thank God, we do believe:
Thank God that this is Christmas Eve.
Even as we kneel upon this day,
Even so, the ancient legends say,
Nearly two thousand years ago
The stalled ox knelt, and even so
The ass knelt full of praise, which they
Could not express, while we can pray.
Thank God, thank God, for Christ was born
Ages ago, as on this morn.

In the snow-season undefiled
God came to earth a little child:
He put His ancient glory by
To live for us and then to die.

How shall we thank God? How shall we
Thank Him and praise Him worthily?
What will He have who loved us thus?
What presents will He take from us?
Will He take gold, or precious heap
Of gems? or shall we rather steep
The air with incense, or bring myrrh?
What man will be our messenger
To go to Him and ask His will?
Which having learned, we will fulfil
Though He choose all we most prefer:—
What man will be our messenger?

Thank God, thank God, the Man is found,
Sure-footed, knowing well the ground.
He knows the road, for this the way
He travelled once, as on this day.
He is our Messenger beside,
He is our door and path and Guide:
He also is our Offering:
He is the gift that we must bring.
Let us kneel down with one accord
And render thanks unto the Lord:
For unto us a Child is born
Upon this happy Christmas morn;
For unto us a Son is given,
Firstborn of God and Heir of Heaven.
7 March 1849.

FOR ADVENT

SWEET sweet sound of distant waters, falling
  On a parched and thirsty plain:

Sweet sweet song of soaring skylark,
 calling
On the sun to shine again:
Perfume of the rose, only the fresher
 For past fertilizing rain:
Pearls amid the sea, a hidden treasure
 For some daring hand to gain:—
Better, dearer than all these
 Is the earth beneath the trees:
Of a much more priceless worth
 Is the old brown common earth.

Little snow-white lamb, piteously
 bleating
For thy mother far away:
Saddest sweetest nightingale, re-
 treating
With thy sorrow from the day:
Weary fawn whom night has over-
 taken,
From the herd gone quite astray:
Dove whose nest was rifled and for-
 saken
In the budding month of May:—
Roost upon the leafy trees,
Lie on earth and take your
 ease:
Death is better far than birth:
You shall turn again to earth.

Listen to the never-pausing murmur
 Of the waves that fret the shore:
See the ancient pine that stands the
 firmer
For the storm-shock that it bore:
And the moon her silver chalice
 filling
With light from the great sun's
 store:
And the stars which deck our
 temple's ceiling
As the flowers deck its floor:
Look and hearken while you may,
For these things shall pass away:

All these things shall fail and
 cease:
Let us wait the end in peace.

Let us wait the end in peace, for truly
 That shall cease which was before:
Let us see our lamps are lighted, duly
 Fed with oil nor wanting more:
Let us pray while yet the Lord will
 hear us,
 For the time is almost o'er:
Yea, the end of all is very near us:
 Yea, the Judge is at the door.
Let us pray now, while we may:
 It will be too late to pray
When the quick and dead shall all
 Rise at the last trumpet-call.

12 *March* 1849.

TWO PURSUITS

A VOICE said, 'Follow, follow': and
 I rose
And followed far into the dreamy
 night,
Turning my back upon the
 pleasant light.
It led me where the bluest water
 flows,
And would not let me drink: where
 the corn grows
I dared not pause, but went un-
 cheered by sight
Or touch: until at length in evil
 plight
It left me, wearied out with many
 woes.
Some time I sat as one bereft of
 sense:
But soon another voice from very
 far
 Called, 'Follow, follow': and
 I rose again.

Now on my night has dawned a
    blessed star:
    Kind steady hands my sinking
      steps sustain,
And will not leave me till I shall go
    hence.
12 *April* 1849.

ONE CERTAINTY

VANITY of vanities, the Preacher
    saith,
    All things are vanity. The eye
      and ear
Cannot be filled with what they
    see and hear.
Like early dew, or like the sudden
    breath
Of wind, or like the grass that
    withereth,
    Is man, tossed to and fro by hope
      and fear:
    So little joy hath he, so little
      cheer,
Till all things end in the long dust
    of death.
To-day is still the same as yesterday,
    To-morrow also even as one of
      them;
      And there is nothing new under
        the sun:
      Until the ancient race of Time
        be run,
    The old thorns shall grow out of
      the old stem,
And morning shall be cold and
    twilight grey.
2 *June* 1849.

A TESTIMONY

I SAID of laughter: it is vain.
    Of mirth I said: what profits it?
Therefore I found a book, and writ
Therein how ease and also pain,
How health and sickness, every one
Is vanity beneath the sun.

Man walks in a vain shadow; he
    Disquieteth himself in vain.
    The things that were shall be
      again;
The rivers do not fill the sea,
But turn back to their secret source;
The winds too turn upon their course.

Our treasures moth and rust corrupt,
    Or thieves break through and steal,
      or they
    Make themselves wings and fly
      away.
One man made merry as he supped,
Nor guessed how when that night
    grew dim
His soul would be required of him.

We build our houses on the sand
    Comely withoutside and within;
    But when the winds and rains begin
To beat on them, they cannot stand:
They perish, quickly overthrown,
Loose from the very basement stone.

All things are vanity, I said:
    Yea vanity of vanities.
    The rich man dies; and the poor
      dies:
The worm feeds sweetly on the dead.
Whate'er thou lackest, keep this
    trust:
All in the end shall have but dust:

The one inheritance, which best
    And worst alike shall find and
      share:
    The wicked cease from troubling
      there,

And there the weary be at rest;
There all the wisdom of the wise
Is vanity of vanities.

Man flourishes as a green leaf,
  And as a leaf doth pass away;
  Or as a shade that cannot stay
And leaves no track, his course is
  brief:
Yet man doth hope and fear and plan
Till he is dead:—oh foolish man!

Our eyes cannot be satisfied
  With seeing, nor our ears be filled
  With hearing: yet we plant and
    build
And buy and make our borders wide;
We gather wealth, we gather care,
But know not who shall be our heir.

Why should we hasten to arise
  So early, and so late take rest?
  Our labour is not good; our best
Hopes fade; our heart is stayed on
  lies.
Verily, we sow wind; and we
Shall reap the whirlwind, verily.

He who hath little shall not lack;
  He who hath plenty shall decay:
  Our fathers went; we pass away;
Our children follow on our track:
So generations fail, and so
They are renewed and come and go.

The earth is fattened with our dead;
  She swallows more and doth not
    cease:
  Therefore her wine and oil increase
And her sheaves are not numberèd;
Therefore her plants are green, and
  all
Her pleasant trees lusty and tall.

Therefore the maidens cease to sing,
  And the young men are very sad;
  Therefore the sowing is not glad,
And mournful is the harvesting.
Of high and low, of great and
  small,
Vanity is the lot of all.

A King dwelt in Jerusalem;
  He was the wisest man on earth;
  He had all riches from his birth,
And pleasures till he tired of them:
Then, having tested all things, he
Witnessed that all are vanity.

31 *August* 1849.

SONGS FOR STRANGERS AND PILGRIMS

(*From a March* 1850 *to before* 1893.)

'Her Seed; It shall bruise thy head.'

ASTONISHED Heaven looked on when
  man was made,
  When fallen man reproved seemed
    half forgiven;
Surely that oracle of hope, first said.
Astonished Heaven.

Even so while one by one lost
  souls are shriven,
A mighty multitude of quickened
  dead;
  Christ's love outnumbering ten
    times sevenfold seven.

Even so while man still tosses high
  his head,
  While still the All-Holy Spirit's
    strife is striven;—
Till one last trump shake earth, and
  undismayed
Astonished Heaven.

Before 1887.

Judge nothing before the time.

LOVE understands the mystery, whereof
We can but spell a surface history:
Love knows, remembers: let us trust in Love:
Love understands the mystery.

Love weighs the event, the long pre-history,
Measures the depth beneath, the height above,
The mystery, with the ante-mystery.

To love and to be grieved befits a dove
Silently telling her bead-history:
Trust all to Love, be patient and approve:
Love understands the mystery.
Before 1886.

HOW great is little man!
Sun, moon, and stars respond to him,
Shine or grow dim
Harmonious with his span.

How little is great man!
More changeable than changeful moon,
Nor half in tune
With Heaven's harmonious plan.

Ah rich man! ah poor man!
Make ready for the testing day
When wastes away
What bears not fire or fan.

Thou heir of all things, man,
Pursue the saints by heavenward track:
They looked not back;
Run thou, as erst they ran.

Little and great is man:
Great if he will, or if he will
A pigmy still;
For what he will he can.
Before 1893.

MAN'S life is but a working day
Whose tasks are set aright:
A time to work, a time to pray,
And then a quiet night.
And then, please God, a quiet night
Where palms are green and robes are white;
A long-drawn breath, a balm for sorrow,
And all things lovely on the morrow.
19 *March* 1864.

IF not with hope of life,
Begin with fear of death:
Strive the tremendous life-long strife
Breath after breath.

Bleed on beneath the rod;
Weep on until thou see;
Turn fear and hope to love of God
Who loveth thee.

Turn all to love, poor soul;
Be love thy watch and ward;
Be love thy starting-point, thy goal,
And thy reward.
Before 1893.

The day is at hand.

WATCH yet a while,
Weep till that day shall dawn when thou shalt smile:
Watch till the day
When all save only Love shall pass away.

Then Love rejoicing shall forget to weep,
Shall hope or fear no more, or watch or sleep,
But only love and stint not, deep beyond deep.
Now we sow love in tears, but then shall reap.
Have patience as True Love's own flock of sheep:
Have patience with His Love
Who served for us, Who reigns for us above.
Before 1886.

Endure hardness.

A COLD wind stirs the blackthorn
  To burgeon and to blow,
Besprinkling half-green hedges
  With flakes and sprays of snow.

Thro' coldness and thro' keenness,
  Dear hearts, take comfort so:
Somewhere or other doubtless
  These make the blackthorn blow.
Before 1886.

'Whither the Tribes go up, even the Tribes of the Lord.'

LIGHT is our sorrow for it ends to-morrow,
  Light is our death which cannot hold us fast;
So brief a sorrow can be scarcely sorrow,
  Or death be death so quickly past.

One night, no more, of pain that turns to pleasure,
  One night, no more, of weeping weeping sore;
And then the heaped-up measure beyond measure,
  In quietness for evermore.

Our face is set like flint against our trouble,
  Yet many things there are which comfort us;
This bubble is a rainbow-coloured bubble,
  This bubble-life tumultuous.

Our sails are set to cross the tossing river,
  Our face is set to reach Jerusalem;
We toil awhile, but then we rest for ever,
  Sing with all Saints and rest with them.
Before 1882.

WHERE never tempest heaveth,
Nor sorrow grieveth,
Nor death bereaveth,
Nor hope deceiveth,
    Sleep.

Where never shame bewaileth,
Nor serpent traileth,
Nor death prevaileth,
Nor harvest faileth,
    Reap.
Before 1893.

MARVEL of marvels, if I myself shall behold
With mine own eyes my King in His city of gold;
Where the least of lambs is spotless white in the fold,
Where the least and last of saints in spotless white is stoled,
Where the dimmest head beyond a moon is aureoled.
O saints, my beloved, now mouldering to mould in the mould,
Shall I see you lift your heads, see your cerements unrolled,

See with these very eyes? who now in darkness and cold
Tremble for the midnight cry, the rapture, the tale untold,
'The Bridegroom cometh, cometh, His Bride to enfold.'

Cold it is, my beloved, since your funeral bell was tolled:
Cold it is, O my King, how cold alone on the wold.
Before 1893.

What is that to thee? follow thou Me.

LIE still, my restive heart, lie still:
God's Word to thee saith, 'Wait and bear.'
The good which He appoints is good,
The good which He denies were ill:
Yea, subtle comfort is thy care,
Thy hurt a help not understood.

'Friend, go up higher,' to one: to one,
'Friend, enter thou My joy,' He saith:
To one, 'Be faithful unto death.'
For some a wilderness doth flower,
Or day's work in one hour is done:—
'But thou, couldst thou not watch one hour?'

Lord, I had chosen another lot,
But then I had not chosen well;
Thy choice and only Thine is good:
No different lot, search heaven or hell,
Had blessed me, fully understood;
None other, which Thou orderest not.
Before 1886.

'Worship God.'

LORD, if Thy word had been 'Worship Me not,
For I than thou am holier: draw not near':
We had besieged Thy Face with prayer and tear
And manifold abasement in our lot,
Our crooked ground, our thorned and thistled plot;
Envious of flawless Angels in their sphere,
Envious of brutes, and envious of the mere
Unliving and undying unbegot.
But now Thou hast said, 'Worship Me, and give
Thy heart to Me, My child'; now therefore we
Think twice before we stoop to worship Thee:
We proffer half a heart while life is strong
And strung with hope; so sweet it is to live!
Wilt Thou not wait? Yea, Thou hast waited long.
Before 1893.

'Afterward he repented, and went.'

LORD, when my heart was whole I kept it back
And grudged to give it Thee.
Now then that it is broken, must I lack
Thy kind word 'Give it Me'?
Silence would be but just, and Thou art just.
Yet since I lie here shattered in the dust,
With still an eye to lift to Thee,
A broken heart to give,
I think that Thou wilt bid me live,
And answer 'Give it Me.'
Before 1886.

Are they not all Ministering Spirits?

LORD, whomsoever Thou shalt send to me,
    Let that same be
    Mine Angel predilect:
Veiled or unveiled, benignant or austere,
Aloof or near;
    Thine, therefore mine, elect.

So may my soul nurse patience day by day,
Watch on and pray
    Obedient and at peace;
Living a lonely life in hope, in faith;
Loving till death,
    When life, not love, shall cease.

. . . Lo, thou mine Angel with transfigured face
Brimful of grace,
    Brimful of love for me!
Did I misdoubt thee all that weary while,
Thee with a smile
    For me as I for thee?

Before 1893.

OUR life is long. Not so, wise Angels say
Who watch us waste it, trembling while they weigh
Against eternity one squandered day.

Our life is long. Not so, the Saints protest,
Filled full of consolation and of rest:
'Short ill, long good, one long unending best.'

Our life is long. Christ's word sounds different:

'Night cometh: no more work when day is spent.'
Repent and work to-day, work and repent.

Lord, make us like Thy Host who day nor night
Rest not from adoration, their delight,
Crying 'Holy, Holy, Holy,' in the height.

Lord, make us like Thy Saints who wait and long
Contented: bound in hope and freed from wrong,
They speed (may be) their vigil with a song.

Lord, make us like Thyself; for thirty-three
Slow years of toil seemed not too long to Thee,
That where Thou art there Thy Beloved might be.

Before 1886.

LORD, what have I to offer? sickening fear
    And a heart-breaking loss.
Are these the cross Thou givest me? then dear
    I will account this cross.

If this is all I have, accept even this
    Poor priceless offering,
A quaking heart with all that therein is,
    O Thou my thorn-crowned King.

Accept the whole, my God, accept my heart
    And its own love within:

Wilt Thou accept us and not sift
    apart?
  —Only sift out my sin.
Before 1886.

  JOY is but sorrow,
    While we know
  It ends to-morrow:—
    Even so!
  Joy with lifted veil
  Shows a face as pale
As the fair changing moon so fair
    and frail.

  Pain is but pleasure,
    If we know
  It heaps up treasure:—
    Even so!
  Turn, transfigured Pain,
  Sweetheart, turn again,
For fair thou art as moonrise after
    rain.
Before 1886.

'CAN I know it?'—'Nay.'—
'Shall I know it?'—'Yea,
When all mists have cleared away
For ever and aye.'—

'Why not then to-day?'—
'Who hath said thee nay?
Lift a hopeful heart and pray
In a humble way.'—

'Other hearts are gay.'—
'Ask not joy to-day:
Toil to-day along thy way
Keeping grudge at bay.'—

'On a past May-day
Flowers pranked all the way;
Nightingales sang out their say
On a night of May.'—

'Dost thou covet May
On an Autumn day?
Foolish memory saith its say
Of sweets past away.'—

'Gone the bloom of May,
Autumn beareth bay:
Flowerless wreath for head grown
    grey
Seemly were to-day.'—

'Dost thou covet bay?
Ask it not to-day:
Rather for a palm-branch pray;
None will say thee nay.'
  Before 1893.

When my heart is vexed I will complain.

'THE fields are white to harvest,
    look and see,
Are white abundantly.
The full-orbed harvest moon shines
    clear,
The harvest time draws near,
Be of good cheer.'

'Ah woe is me!
I have no heart for harvest time,
Grown sick with hope deferred from
    chime to chime.'

'But Christ can give thee heart Who
    loveth thee:
Can set thee in the eternal ecstasy
Of His great jubilee:
Can give thee dancing heart and
    shining face,
And lips filled full of grace,
And pleasures as the rivers and the
    sea.
Who knocketh at His door
He welcomes evermore:
Kneel down before

That ever-open door
(The time is short) and smite
Thy breast, and pray with all thy
    might.'

'What shall I say?'
                'Nay, pray.
Tho' one but say "Thy Will be done,"
He hath not lost his day
At set of sun.'
    Before 1886.

'Praying always.'

AFTER midnight, in the dark
    The clock strikes one,
        New day has begun.
Look up and hark!
With singing heart forestall the
    carolling lark.

After mid-day, in the light
    The clock strikes one,
        Day-fall has begun.
Cast up, set right
The day's account against the on-
    coming night.

After noon and night, one day
    For ever one
        Ends not, once begun.
Whither away,
O brothers and O sisters? Pause
    and pray.
    Before 1886.

'As thy days, so shall thy strength be.'

DAY that hath no tinge of night,
    Night that hath no tinge of day,
These at last will come to sight
        Not to fade away.

This is twilight that we know,
    Scarcely night and scarcely day;
This hath been from long ago
        Shed around man's way:

Step by step to utter night,
    Step by step to perfect day,
To the Left Hand or the Right
        Leading all away.

This is twilight: be it so;
    Suited to our strength our day:
Let us follow on to know,
        Patient by the way.
    Before 1893.

A HEAVY heart, if ever heart was
    heavy,
    I offer Thee this heavy heart of
        me.
Are such as this the hearts Thou art
    fain to levy
    To do and dare for Thee, to
        bleed for Thee?
    Ah blessed heaviness if such they
        be!

Time was I bloomed with blossom
    and stood leafy,
    How long before the fruit if fruit
        there be:
Lord, if by bearing fruit my heart
    grows heavy,
    Leafless and bloomless yet accept
        of me
    The stripped fruit-bearing heart I
        offer Thee.

Lifted to Thee my heart weighs not
    so heavy,
    It leaps and lightens lifted up to
        Thee;
It sings, it hopes to sing amid the
    bevy

Of thousand thousand choirs that
    sing, and see
Thy Face, me loving, for Thou
    lovest me.
Before 1886.

IF love is not worth loving, then
    life is not worth living,
    Nor aught is worth remembering
    but well forgot ;
For store is not worth storing and
    gifts are not worth giving,
    If love is not ;

And idly cold is death-cold, and
    life-heat idly hot,
And vain is any offering and vainer
    our receiving,
    And vanity of vanities is all our
    lot.

Better than life's heaving heart is
    death's heart unheaving,
    Better than the opening leaves
    are the leaves that rot,
For there is nothing left worth
    achieving or retrieving,
    If love is not.
Before 1886.

WHAT is it Jesus saith unto the
    soul ?
    ' Take up the Cross, and come
    and follow Me.'
One word He saith to all men :
    none may be
Without a cross yet hope to touch
    the goal.
Then heave it bravely up, and brace
    thy whole
    Body to bear ; it will not weigh
    on thee
Past strength ; or if it crush thee
    to thy knee

Take heart of grace, for grace shall
    be thy dole.
Give thanks to-day, and let to-morrow
    take
    Heed to itself ; to-day imports
    thee more.
    To-morrow may not dawn like
    yesterday :
    Until that unknown morrow go
    thy way,
Suffer and work and strive for Jesus'
    sake :—
    Who tells thee what to-morrow
    keeps in store ?
2 *March* 1850 *to before* 1886.

THEY lie at rest, our blessed dead ;
The dews drop cool above their
    head,
They knew not when fleet summer
    fled.

Together all, yet each alone ;
Each laid at rest beneath his own
Smooth turf or white allotted stone.

When shall our slumber sink so
    deep,
And eyes that wept and eyes that
    weep
Weep not in the sufficient sleep ?

God be with you, our great and
    small,
Our loves, our best beloved of all,
Our own beyond the salt sea-wall.
    Before 1886.

' Ye that fear Him, both small and great.'

GREAT or small below,
    Great or small above ;
Be we Thine, whom Thou dost know
    And love :

First or last on earth,
    First or last in Heaven;
Only weighted with Thy worth,
    And shriven.

Wise or ignorant,
    Strong or weak; Amen;
Sifted now, cast down, in want :—
    But then?

Then,—when sun nor moon,
    Time nor death, finds place,
Seeing in the eternal noon
    Thy Face:

Then,—when tears and sighing,
    Changes, sorrows, cease;
Living by Thy Life undying
    In peace:

Then,—when all creation
    Keeps its jubilee,
Crowned amid Thy holy nation;
Crowned, discrowned, in adoration
    Of Thee.
Before 1882.

Called to be Saints.

THE lowest place. Ah, Lord, how steep and high
    That lowest place whereon a saint shall sit!
Which of us halting, trembling, pressing nigh,
    Shall quite attain to it?

Yet, Lord, Thou pressest nigh to hail and grace
    Some happy soul, it may be still unfit
For Right Hand or for Left Hand, but whose place
    Waits there prepared for it.
Before 1886.

THE sinner's own fault? So it was.
    If every own fault found us out,
    Dogged us and hedged us round about,
What comfort should we take because
    Not half our due we thus wrung out?

Clearly his own fault. Yet I think
    My fault in part, who did not pray
    But lagged and would not lead the way.
I, haply, proved his missing link.
    God help us both to mend and pray.
Before 1886.

WHO cares for earthly bread tho' white?
    Nay, heavenly sheaf of harvest corn!
Who cares for earthly crown to-night?
    Nay, heavenly crown to-morrow morn!
I will not wander left or right,
    The straightest road is shortest too;
And since we hold all hope in view
And triumph where is no more pain,
    To-night I bid good night to you
And bid you meet me there again.
Before 1886.

LAUGHING Life cries at the feast,—
    Craving Death cries at the door,—
'Fish or fowl or fatted beast?'
    'Come with me, thy feast is o'er.'—
'Wreathe the violets.'—'Watch them fade.'—
'I am sunshine.'—' I am shade :
I am the sun-burying west.'—
'I am pleasure.'—' I am rest :
Come with me, for I am best.'
Before 1886.

The end is not yet.

HOME by different ways. Yet all
  Homeward bound thro' prayer
    and praise,
Young with old, and great with
    small,
  Home by different ways.

  Many nights and many days
Wind must bluster, rain must fall,
    Quake the quicksand, shift the
      haze.

Life hath called and death will call
  Saints who praying kneel at gaze,
Ford the flood or leap the wall,
  Home by different ways.
Before 1886.

WHO would wish back the Saints
    upon our rough
  Wearisome road?
    Wish back a breathless soul
      Just at the goal?
My soul, praise God
For all dear souls which have enough.

I would not fetch one back to hope
    with me
  A hope deferred,
    To taste a cup that slips
      From thirsting lips:
Hath he not heard
And seen what was to hear and see?

How could I stand to answer the
    rebuke
  If one should say:
    'O friend of little faith,
    Good was my death,
    And good my day
Of rest, and good the sleep I took'?
13 *December* 1861.

'That which hath been is named already,
    and it is known that it is Man.'
'EYE hath not seen':—yet man
    hath known and weighed
A hundred thousand marvels that
    have been:
What is it which (the Word of Truth
    hath said)
  Eye hath not seen?

'Ear hath not heard':—yet harpings
    of delight,
Trumpets of triumph, song and
    spoken word,
Man knows them all: what lovelier,
    loftier might
  Hath ear not heard?

'Nor heart conceived':—yet man
    hath now desired
Beyond all reach, beyond his hope
    believed,
Loved beyond death: what fire shall
    yet be fired
  No heart conceived?

'Deep calls to deep':—man's depth
    would be despair
But for God's deeper depth: we
    sow to reap.
Have patience, wait, betake ourselves
    to prayer:
  Deep answereth deep.
Before 1886

OF each sad word which is more
    sorrowful,
  'Sorrow' or 'Disappointment'?
    I have heard
Subtle inflections, baffling subtlest
    rule,
  Of each sad word.

Sorrow can mourn: and lo a
    mourning bird
Sings sweetly to sweet echoes of its
    dule,
    While silent disappointment
    broods unstirred.

Yet both nurse hope, where Penitence
    keeps school
Who makes fools wise and saints
    of them that erred:
Wise men shape stepping stone, or
    curb, or tool,
Of each sad word.
Before 1886.

I see that all things come to an end.

I

No more! while sun and planets fly,
    And wind and storm and seasons
    four,
And while we live and while we
    die,—
    No more.

Nevertheless old ocean's roar,
    And wide earth's multitudinous cry,
    And echo's pent reverberant store,

Shall hush to silence by and by:
    Ah rosy world gone cold and
    hoar!
Man opes no more a mortal eye,
    No more.
Before 1886.

But Thy Commandment is exceeding broad.

II

Once again to wake, nor wish to
    sleep;
    Once again to feel, nor feel a pain!

Rouse thy soul to watch and pray
    and weep
Once again.

Hope afresh, for hope shall not
    be vain:
Start afresh along the exceeding
    steep
    Road to glory, long and rough
    and plain.

Sow and reap: for while these
    moments creep,
Time and earth and life are on
    the wane:
Now, in tears; to-morrow, laugh
    and reap
Once again.
Before 1886.

Sursum Corda.

'Lift up your hearts.' 'We lift
    them up.' Ah me!
I cannot, Lord, lift up my heart to
    Thee:
Stoop, lift it up, that where Thou art
    I too may be.

'Give Me thy heart.' I would not
    say Thee nay,
But have no power to keep or give
    away
My heart: stoop, Lord, and take it
    to Thyself to-day.

Stoop, Lord, as once before, now
    once anew;
Stoop, Lord, and hearken, hearken,
    Lord, and do,
And take my will, and take my heart,
    and take me too.
Before 1886.

O YE, who are not dead and fit
Like blasted tree beside the pit
But for the axe that levels it,

Living show life of love, whereof
The force wields earth and heaven
    above :
Who knows not love begetteth love ?

Love poises earth in space, Love rolls
Wide worlds rejoicing on their poles,
And girds them round with aureoles.

Love lights the sun, Love thro' the
    dark
Lights the moon's evanescent arc,
Lights up the star, lights up the spark.

O ye who taste that love is sweet,
Set waymarks for all doubtful feet
That stumble on in search of it.

Sing notes of love : that some who
    hear
Far off inert may lend an ear,
Rise up and wonder and draw near.

Lead life of love : that others who
Behold your life may kindle too
With love, and cast their lot with you.
Before 1886.

WHERE shall I find a white rose
    blowing ?—
  Out in the garden where all sweets
    be.—
But out in my garden the snow was
    snowing
  And never a white rose opened for
    me.
Nought but snow and a wind were
    blowing
        And snowing.

Where shall I find a blush rose
    blushing ?—
  On the garden wall or the garden
    bed.—
But out in my garden the rain was
    rushing
  And never a blush rose raised its
    head.
Nothing glowing, flushing or blush-
    ing :
        Rain rushing.

Where shall I find a red rose bud-
    ding ?—
  Out in the garden where all things
    grow.—
But out in my garden a flood was
    flooding
  And never a red rose began to
    blow.
Out in a flooding what should be
    budding ?
        All flooding !

Now is winter and now is sorrow,
  No roses but only thorns to-
    day :
Thorns will put on roses to-morrow,
  Winter and sorrow scudding away.
No more winter and no more sorrow
        To-morrow.
Circa 1884.

Redeeming the Time.

A LIFE of hope deferred too often is
A life of wasted opportunities ;
A life of perished hope too often is
A life of all-lost opportunities :
Yet hope is but the flower and not
    the root,
And hope is still the flower and not
    the fruit ;—

Arise and sow and weed: a day
    shall come
When also thou shalt keep thy
    harvest home.
Before 1886.

Now they desire a Better Country.

LOVE said nay, while Hope kept
    saying
    All his sweetest say,
Hope so keen to start a-maying !—
    Love said nay.

Love was bent to watch and pray ;
Long the watching, long the praying ;
    Hope grew drowsy, pale and grey.

Hope in dreams set off a-straying,
    All his dream-world flushed by
        May ;
While unslumbering, praying, weigh-
    ing,
    Love said nay.
Before 1886.

A CASTLE-BUILDER'S WORLD

The line of Confusion, and the stones of emptiness.

UNRIPE harvest there hath none to
    reap it
    From the misty gusty place,
Unripe vineyard there hath none to
    keep it
    In unprofitable space.
Living men and women are not found
    there,
    Only masks in flocks and shoals ;
Flesh-and-bloodless hazy masks
    surround there
    Ever wavering orbs and poles ;
Flesh-and-bloodless vapid masks
    abound there,
    Shades of bodies without souls.
Before 1886.

These all wait upon Thee.

INNOCENT eyes not ours
    Are made to look on flowers,
Eyes of small birds and insects
    small :
Morn after summer morn
    The sweet rose on her thorn
Opens her bosom to them all.
    The least and last of things
    That soar on quivering wings,
Or crawl among the grass blades
    out of sight,
Have just as clear a right
To their appointed portion of delight
    As Queens or Kings.
22 January 1853.

'Doeth well . . . doeth better.'

MY love whose heart is tender said
    to me,
    'A moon lacks light except her
        sun befriend her.
Let us keep tryst in heaven, dear
    Friend,' said she,
My love whose heart is tender.

From such a loftiness no words
    could bend her :
Yet still she spoke of 'us' and spoke
    as 'we,'
Her hope substantial, while my
    hope grew slender.

Now keeps she tryst beyond earth's
    utmost sea,
    Wholly at rest, tho' storms should
        toss and rend her ;
And still she keeps my heart and
    keeps its key,
    My love whose heart is tender.
Before 1886.

OUR heaven must be within our-
    selves,
  Our home and heaven the work
    of faith
All thro' this race of life which shelves
          Downward to death.

So faith shall build the boundary
    wall,
  And hope shall plant the secret
    bower,
That both may show magnifical
          With gem and flower.

While over all a dome must spread,
  And love shall be that dome
    above ;
And deep foundations must be laid,
          And these are love.
    Before 1886.

            Vanity of Vanities.

OF all the downfalls in the world,
  The flutter of an Autumn leaf
  Grows grievous by suggesting
    grief :
Who thought, when Spring was first
    unfurled,
Of this ? The wide world lay em-
    pearled ;
Who thought of frost that nips the
    world ?
          Sigh on, my ditty.

There lurk a hundred subtle stings
  To prick us in our daily walk :
An apple cankered on its stalk,
A robin snared for all his wings,
A voice that sang but never sings ;
Tea, sight or sound or silence stings.
          Kind Lord, show pity.
    5 August 1858.

THE hills are tipped with sunshine,
    while I walk
  In shadows dim and cold :
The unawakened rose sleeps on her
    stalk
  In a bud's fold,
  Until the sun flood all the world
    with gold.

The hills are crowned with glory,
    and the glow
  Flows widening down apace :
Unto the sunny hill-tops I, set low,
  Lift a tired face,—
  Ah happy rose, content to wait
    for grace !

How tired a face, how tired a brain,
    how tired
  A heart I lift, who long
For something never felt but still
    desired ;
  Sunshine and song,
Song where the choirs of sunny
    heaven stand choired.
    Before 1893.

SCARCE tolerable life, which all life
    long
  Is dominated by one dread of
    death ;
Is such life, life ? if so who
    pondereth
  May call salt sweetness or call dis-
    cord song.
Ah me, this solitude where swarms
    a throng !
  Life slowly grows and dwindles
    breath by breath :
  Death slowly grows on us ; no
    word it saith,
  Its cords all lengthened and its
    pillars strong.

Life dies apace, a life that but de-
    ceives:
  Death reigns as tho' it lived, and
    yet is dead:
Where is the life that dies not but
    that lives?
The sweet long life, immortal, ever
    young,
True life that wooes us with a silver
    tongue
  Of hope, much said and much
    more left unsaid.
Circa 1884.

ALL heaven is blazing yet
  With the meridian sun:
Make haste, unshadowing sun, make
    haste to set;
  O lifeless life, have done.
I choose what once I chose;
  What once I willed, I will:
Only the heart its own bereavement
    knows;
  O clamorous heart, lie still.

That which I chose, I choose;
  That which I willed, I will;
That which I once refused, I still
    refuse:
  O hope deferred, be still.
That which I chose and choose
  And will is Jesus' Will:
He hath not lost his life who seems
    to lose:
  O hope deferred, hope still.
Before 1886.

Balm in Gilead.

HEARTSEASE I found, where Love-
    lies-bleeding
  Empurpled all the ground:
Whatever flowers I missed unheeding,
    Heartsease I found.

Yet still my garden mound
Stood sore in need of watering, weed-
    ing,
  And binding growths unbound.

Ah when shades fell, to light succeed-
    ing,
  I scarcely dared look round:
'Love-lies-bleeding' was all my
    pleading;
  Heartsease I found.
Before 1886.

'In the day of his Espousals.'

THAT Song of Songs which is
    Solomon's
  Sinks and rises, and loves and
    longs,
Thro' temperate zones and torrid
    zones,
  That Song of Songs.

Fair its floating moon with her
    prongs:
Love is laid for its paving stones:
  Right it sings without thought of
    wrongs.

Doves it hath with music of moans,
  Queens in throngs and damsels
    in throngs,
High tones and mysterious under-
    tones,
  That Song of Songs.
Before 1886.

'She came from the uttermost part of the earth.'

'THE half was not told me,' said
    Sheba's Queen,
  Weighing that wealth of wisdom
    and of gold:

'Thy fame falls short of this that I
    have seen:
The half was not told.

'Happy thy servants who stand
    to behold,
Stand to drink in thy gracious
    speech and mien;
Happy, thrice happy, the flock of
    thy fold.

'As the darkened moon while a
    shadow between
Her face and her kindling sun is
    rolled,
I depart; but my heart keeps
    memory green:
The half was not told.'
Before 1886.

'ALLELUIA! or Alas! my heart is
    crying:
So yours is sighing;
Or replying with content undying,
    Alleluia!

'Alas' grieves overmuch for pain
    that is ending,
Hurt that is mending,
Life descending soon to be ascend-
    ing.—
        Alleluia!
Before 1893.

THE Passion Flower hath sprung
    up tall,
Hath east and west its arms
    outspread;
The heliotrope shoots up its head
To clear the shadow of the wall:
Down looks the Passion Flower,
    The heliotrope looks upward still,
        Hour by hour
    On the heavenward hill.

The Passion Flower blooms red or
    white,
A shadowed white, a cloudless
    red;
Caressingly it droops its head,
Its leaves, its tendrils, from the
    light:
Because that lowlier flower
    Looks up, but mounts not half so
        high,
        Hour by hour
    Tending toward the sky.
Before 1893.

God's Acre.

HAIL, garden of confident hope!
    Where sweet seeds are quickening
        in darkness and cold;
    For how sweet and how young
        will they be
    When they pierce thro' the mould.
Balm, myrtle, and heliotrope
    There watch and there wait out
        of sight for their Sun:
    While the Sun, which they see
        not, doth see
    Each and all one by one.
Before 1893.

The Flowers appear on the Earth.

YOUNG girls wear flowers,
    Young brides a flowery wreath,
But next we plant them
    In garden plots of death.
Whose lot is best—
The maiden's curtained rest,
    Or bride's whose hoped-for sweet
    May yet outstrip her feet?
Ah what are such as these
To death's sufficing ease?
He sleeps indeed who sleeps in
    peace
    Where night and morning meet.

Dear are the blossoms
  For bride's or maiden's head,
But dearer planted
  Around our blessed dead.
Those mind us of decay
And joys that fade away;
  These preach to us perfection,
  Long love and resurrection.
We make our graveyards fair,
For spirit-like birds of air,
For Angels may be finding there
  Lost Eden's own delection.
    26 March 1855.

    'Thou knewest . . . thou oughtest
        therefore.'

BEHOLD in heaven a floating dazzling cloud,
  So dazzling that I could but cry Alas!
Alas, because I felt how low I was;
Alas, within my spirit if not aloud,
Foreviewing my last breathless bed and shroud:
  Thus pondering, I glanced downward on the grass;
And the grass bowed when airs of heaven would pass,
Lifting itself again when it had bowed.
That grass spake comfort; weak it was and low,
  Yet strong enough and high enough to bend
  In homage at a message from the sky:
  As the grass did and prospered, so will I;
Tho' knowing little, doing what I know,
  And strong in patient weakness till the end.
    Before 1893.

Go in Peace.

CAN peach renew lost bloom,
Or violet lost perfume,
Or sullied snow turn white as overnight?
Man cannot compass it, yet never fear:
The leper Naaman
Shows what God will and can.
God Who worked there is working here;
Wherefore let shame, not gloom, betinge thy brow.
God Who worked then is working now.
    Before 1893.

Half dead.

O CHRIST the Life, look on me where I lie
  Ready to die:
O Good Samaritan, nay, pass not by.

O Christ, my Life, pour in Thine oil and wine
  To keep me Thine;
Me ever Thine, and Thee for ever mine.

Watch by Thy saints and sinners, watch by all
  Thy great and small:
Once Thou didst call us all,—O Lord, recall.

Think how Thy saints love sinners, how they pray
  And hope alway,
And thereby grow more like Thee day by day.

O Saint of saints, if those with
    prayer and vow
        Succour us now. . . .
It was not they died for us, it was
        Thou.
Before 1893.

'One of the Soldiers with a Spear pierced
        His Side.'

AH Lord, we all have pierced Thee:
    wilt Thou be
Wroth with us all to slay us all?
Nay, Lord, be this thing far from
    Thee and me;
By whom should we arise, for we
    are small,
By whom if not by Thee?

Lord, if of us who pierced Thee
    Thou spare one,
Spare yet one more to love Thy
    Face,
And yet another of poor souls undone,
    Another, and another—God of
        grace,
Let mercy overrun.
Before 1893.

WHERE love is, there comes sorrow
To-day or else to-morrow:
    Endure the mood,
Love only means our good.

Where love is, there comes pleasure
With or withouten measure,
    Early or late
Cheering the sorriest state.

Where love is, all perfection
Is stored for heart's delection;
    For where love is
Dwells every sort of bliss.

Who would not choose a sorrow
Love's self will cheer to-morrow?
    One day of sorrow,
Then such a long to-morrow!
Before 1886.

BURY Hope out of sight,
    No book for it and no bell;
It never could bear the light
    Even while growing and well:
Think if now it could bear
The light on its face of care
And grey scattered hair.

No grave for Hope in the earth,
    But deep in that silent soul
Which rang no bell for its birth
    And rings no funeral toll.
Cover its once bright head;
Nor odours nor tears be shed:
It lived once, it is dead.

Brief was the day of its power,
    The day of its grace how brief:
As the fading of a flower,
    As the falling of a leaf,
So brief its day and its hour;
No bud more and no bower
Or hint of a flower.

Shall many wail it? not so:
    Shall one bewail it? not one:
Thus it hath been from long ago,
    Thus it shall be beneath the
        sun.
O fleet sun, make haste to flee;
O rivers, fill up the sea;
O Death, set the dying free.

The sun nor loiters nor speeds,
    The rivers run as they ran,
Thro' clouds or thro' windy reeds
    All run as when all began.

Only Death turns at our cries :—
Lo the Hope we buried with sighs
Alive in Death's eyes!
Before 1886.

A Churchyard Song of Patient Hope.

ALL tears done away with the bitter
    unquiet sea,
  Death done away from among
    the living at last,
Man shall say of sorrow -- Love
    grant it to thee and me !—
  At last, 'It is past.'

Shall I say of pain 'It is past,' nor
    say it with thee,
  Thou heart of my heart, thou soul
    of my soul, my Friend ?
Shalt thou say of pain 'It is past,'
    nor say it with me
  Beloved to the end ?
Before 1893.

ONE woe is past. Come what come
    will,
  Thus much is ended and made
    fast :
Two woes may overhang us still ;
  One woe is past.

    As flowers when winter puffs its
      last
Wake in the vale, trail up the hill,
  Nor wait for skies to overcast ;

So meek souls rally from the chill
  Of pain and fear and poisonous
    blast,
To lift their heads: come good, come
    ill,
  One woe is past.
Before 1893.

Take no thought for the morrow.

WHO knows ? God knows : and
    what He knows
  Is well and best.
The darkness hideth not from Him,
    but glows
Clear as the morning or the evening
    rose
  Of east or west.

Wherefore man's strength is to sit
    still :
  Not wasting care
To antedate to-morrow's good or
    ill ;
Yet watching meekly, watching with
    good will,
  Watching to prayer.

Some rising or some setting ray
  From east or west,
If not to-day, why then another
    day
Will light each dove upon the home-
    ward way
  Safe to her nest.
Before 1893.

Consider the Lilies of the field.

SOLOMON most glorious in array
    Put not on his glories without
      care :—
Clothe us as Thy lilies of a day,
    As the lilies Thou accountest fair
      Lilies of Thy making,
      Of Thy love partaking,
    Filling with free fragrance earth
      and air :
    Thou Who gatherest lilies, gather
      us and wear.
Before 1893.

'Son, remember.'

I LAID beside thy gate am Lazarus;
  See me or see me not, I still am
    there,
  Hungry and thirsty, sore and sick
    and bare,
Dog-comforted and crumbs-solici-
    tous:
While thou in all thy ways art
    sumptuous,
  Daintily clothed, with dainties for
    thy fare:
Thus a world's wonder thou art
    quit of care,
And, be I seen or not seen, I am thus.
One day a worm for thee, a worm
    for me:
  With my worm angel songs and
    trumpet-burst
    And plenitude an end of all
      desire:
But what for thee, alas! but what
    for thee?
  Fire and an unextinguishable
    thirst,
  Thirst in an unextinguishable
    fire.

Before 1893.

Heaviness may endure for a night, but
  Joy cometh in the morning.

NO thing is great on this side of the
    grave,
  Nor any thing of any stable worth:
  Whatso is born from earth returns
    to earth:
No thing we grasp proves half the
    thing we crave:
The tidal wave shrinks to the ebbing
    wave:
  Laughter is folly, madness lurks
    in mirth:
Mankind sets off a-dying from the
    birth:
Life is a losing game, with what to
    save?
Thus I sat mourning like a mournful
    owl,
  And like a doleful dragon made ado,
    Companion of all monsters of
    the dark:
When lo the light cast off its nightly
    cowl,
    And up to heaven flashed a
      carolling lark,
  And all creation sang its hymn
    anew.

While all creation sang its hymn anew
  What could I do but sing a stave
    in tune?
  Spectral on high hung pale the
    vanishing moon
Where a last gleam of stars hung
    paling too.
Lark's lay—a cockcrow—with a
    scattered few
  Soft early chirpings—with a tender
    croon
  Of doves—a hundred thousand
    calls, and soon
A hundred thousand answers sweet
    and true.
These set me singing too at un-
    awares:
  One note for all delights and
    charities,
    One note for hope reviving with
      the light,
  One note for every lovely thing
    that is;
Till while I sang my heart shook off
    its cares
    And revelled in the land of no
      more night.

Before 1886.

The Will of the Lord be done.

O LORD, fulfil Thy Will,
Be the days few or many, good or ill:
Prolong them, to suffice
For offering up ourselves Thy sacrifice;
Shorten them if Thou wilt,
To make in righteousness an end of guilt.
Yea, they will not be long
To souls who learn to sing a patient song;
Yea, short they will not be
To souls on tiptoe to flee home to Thee.
O Lord, fulfil Thy Will:
Make Thy Will ours, and keep us patient still,
Be the days few or many, good or ill.
Before 1893.

Lay up for yourselves treasures in Heaven.

TREASURE plies a feather,
   Pleasure spreadeth wings,
Taking flight together,—
   Ah my cherished things!

Fly away, poor pleasure,
   That art so brief a thing:
Fly away, poor treasure,
   That hast so swift a wing.

Pleasure, to be pleasure,
   Must come without a wing:
Treasure, to be treasure,
   Must be a stable thing.

Treasure without feather,
   Pleasure without wings,
Elsewhere dwell together
   And are heavenly things.
Before 1886.

Whom the Lord loveth He chasteneth.

'ONE sorrow more? I thought the tale complete.'—
He bore amiss who grudges what he bore:
Stretch out thy hands and urge thy feet to meet
One sorrow more.

Yea, make thy count for two or three or four:
The kind Physician will not slack to treat
His patient while there's rankling in the sore.

Bear up in anguish, ease will yet be sweet;
Bear up all day, for night has rest in store:
Christ bears thy burden with thee, rise and greet
One sorrow more.
Before 1886.

'Then shall ye shout.'

IT seems an easy thing
Mayhap one day to sing;
Yet the next day
We cannot sing or say.

Keep silence with good heart,
While silence fits our part:
Another day
We shall both sing and say.

Keep silence, counting time
To strike in at the chime:
Prepare to sound,—
Our part is coming round.

Can we not sing or say?
　In silence let us pray,
　And meditate
Our love-song while we wait.
Before 1886.

EVERYTHING that is born must die;
　Everything that can sigh may sing;
Rocks in equal balance, low or high,
　Everything.

Honeycomb is weighed against a sting;
Hope and fear take turns to touch the sky;
Height and depth respond alternating.

O my soul, spread wings of love to fly,
　Wings of dove that soars on home-bound wing:
Love trusts Love, till Love shall justify
　Everything.
Before 1886.

LORD, grant us calm, if calm can set forth Thee;
　Or tempest, if a tempest set Thee forth;
Wind from the east or west or south or north,
Or congelation of a silent sea,
With stillness of each tremulous aspen tree.

Still let fruit fall, or hang upon the tree;
　Still let the east and west, the south and north,
Curb in their winds, or plough a thundering sea;
　Still let the earth abide to set Thee forth,
Or vanish like a smoke to set forth Thee.
Before 1893.

Changing Chimes.

IT was not warning that our fathers lacked,
　It is not warning that we lack to-day.
The Voice that cried still cries:
　'Rise up and act:
Watch alway,—watch and pray,
　—watch alway,—
　　　　　　　All men.'

Alas, if aught was lacked goodwill was lacked;
　Alas, goodwill is what we lack to-day.
O gracious Voice, grant grace that all may act,
Watch and act,—watch and pray,
　—watch alway.—
　　　　　　　Amen.
Before 1893.

Thy Servant will go and fight with this Philistine.

SORROW of saints is sorrow of a day,
　Gladness of saints is gladness evermore:
Send on thy hope, send on thy will before,
To chant God's praise along the narrow way.
Stir up His praises if the flesh would sway,

Exalt His praises if the world
   press sore,
Peal out His praises if black
   Satan roar
A hundred thousand lies to say
   them nay,
Devil and Death and Hades, three-
   fold cord
Not quickly broken, front thee to
   thy face;
Front thou them with a face of
   tenfold flint:
Shout for the battle, David!
   never stint
Body or breath or blood, but,
   proof in grace,
Die for thy Lord, as once for thee
   thy Lord.
Before 1893.

THRO' burden and heat of the day
   How weary the hands and the
      feet
That labour with scarcely a stay,
   Thro' burden and heat!

Tired toiler whose sleep shall be
   sweet,
Kneel down, it will rest thee to pray:
Then forward, for daylight is fleet.

Cool shadows show lengthening and
   grey,
Cool twilight will soon be com-
   plete;
What matters this wearisome way
   Thro' burden and heat?
Before 1886.

'Then I commended Mirth.'
'A MERRY heart is a continual
   feast.'
Then take we life and all things
   in good part:
To fast grows festive while we keep
   at least
A merry heart.

Well pleased with nature and well
   pleased with art;
A merry heart makes cheer for man
   and beast,
And fancies music in a creaking
   cart.

Some day, a restful heart whose toils
   have ceased,
A heavenly heart gone home from
   earthly mart:
To-day, blow wind from west or
   wind from east,
A merry heart.
Before 1886.

SORROW hath a double voice,
   Sharp to-day but sweet to-morrow:
Wait in patience, hope, rejoice,
   Tried friends of sorrow.

Pleasure hath a double taste,
   Sweet to-day but sharp to-morrow:
Friends of pleasure, rise in haste,
   Make friends with sorrow.

Pleasure set aside to-day
   Comes again to rule to-morrow;
Welcomed sorrow will not stay,
   Farewell to sorrow!
Before 1886.

SHADOWS to-day, while shadows
   show God's Will,
Light were not good except He
   sent us light,
Shadows to-day, because this day
   is night

Whose marvels and whose mysteries
    fulfil
Their course and deep in darkness
    serve Him still.
  Thou dim aurora, on the extremest
    height
  Of airy summits wax not over-
    bright ;
Refrain thy rose, refrain thy daffo-
    dil.
Until God's Word go forth to kindle
    thee
  And garland thee and bid thee
    stoop to us,
    Blush in the heavenly choirs
      and glance not down :
  To-day we race in darkness for
    a crown,
In darkness for beatitude to be,
  In darkness for the city luminous.
Before 1893.

Truly the Light is sweet.

LIGHT colourless doth colour all
    things else :
Where light dwells pleasure dwells
And peace excels.
  Then rise and shine,
  Thou shadowed soul of mine,
  And let a cheerful rainbow make
    thee fine.

Light, fountain of all beauty and
    delight,
Leads day forth from the night,
Turns blackness white.
  Light waits for thee
  Where all have eyes to see :
  Oh well is thee, and happy shalt
    thou be.
Before 1893.

Are ye not much better than they?

THE twig sprouteth,
The moth outeth,
The plant springeth,
The bird singeth :
Tho' little we sing to-day
Yet are we better than they ;
Tho' growing with scarce a showing,
Yet, please God, we are growing.

The twig teacheth,
The moth preacheth,
The plant vaunteth,
The bird chanteth,
God's mercy overflowing,
Merciful past man's knowing.
Please God to keep us growing
Till the awful day of mowing.
Before 1893.

Yea, the sparrow hath found her an house.

WISEST of sparrows that sparrow
    which sitteth alone
  Perched on the housetop, its own
    upper chamber, for nest ;
Wisest of swallows that swallow
    which timely has flown
  Over the turbulent sea to the land
    of its rest :
    Wisest of sparrows and swallows,
      if I were as wise !

Wisest of spirits that spirit which
    dwelleth apart
  Hid in the Presence of God for a
    chapel and nest,
Sending a wish and a will and a
    passionate heart
  Over the eddy of life to that
    Presence in rest :
    Seated alone and in peace till
      God bids it arise.
Before 1893.

I am small and of no reputation.

THE least, if so I am ;
  If so, less than the least,
May I reach heaven to glorify the Lamb
  And sit down at the Feast.

I fear and I am small,
  Whence am I of good cheer ;
For I, who hear Thy call, have heard Thee call
  To Thee the small who fear.
Before 1893.

O CHRIST my God Who seest the unseen,
  O Christ my God Who knowest the unknown,
Thy mighty Blood was poured forth to atone
  For every sin that can be or hath been.

O Thou Who seest what I cannot see,
  Thou Who didst love us all so long ago,
  O Thou Who knowest what I must not know,
Remember all my hope, remember me.
Before 1886.

YEA, if Thou wilt, Thou canst put up Thy sword ;
  But what if Thou shouldst sheathe it to the hilt
Within the heart that sues to Thee, O Lord ?
  Yea, if Thou wilt.

For if Thou wilt Thou canst purge out the guilt
  Of all, of any, even the most abhorred :
Thou canst pluck down, rebuild, build up the unbuilt.

Who wanders canst Thou gather by love's cord ?
  Who sinks, uplift from the undersucking silt
To set him on Thy rock within Thy ward ?
  Yea, if Thou wilt.
Before 1886.

SWEETNESS of rest when Thou sheddest rest,
  Sweetness of patience till then ;
Only the Will of our God is best
  For all the millions of men.

For all the millions on earth to-day,
  On earth and under the earth ;
Waiting for earth to vanish away,
  Waiting to come to the birth.
Before 1893.

O FOOLISH Soul ! to make thy count
  For languid falls and much forgiven,
When like a flame thou mightest mount
  To storm and carry heaven.

A life so faint,—is this to live ?
  A goal so mean,—is this a goal ?
Christ love thee, remedy, forgive,
  Save thee, O foolish Soul.
Before 1893.

BEFORE the beginning Thou hast foreknown the end,
  Before the birthday the death-bed was seen of Thee:
Cleanse what I cannot cleanse, mend what I cannot mend,
  O Lord All-Merciful, be merciful to me.

While the end is drawing near I know not mine end;
  Birth I recall not, my death I cannot foresee:
O God, arise to defend, arise to befriend,
  O Lord All-Merciful, be merciful to me.

Before 1893.

THE goal in sight! Look up and sing,
  Set faces full against the light,
Welcome with rapturous welcoming
  The goal in sight.

Let be the left, let be the right:
Straight forward make your footsteps ring
  A loud alarum thro' the night.

Death hunts you, yea, but reft of sting;
  Your bed is green, your shroud is white:
Hail Life and Death and all that bring
  The goal in sight.

Before 1886.

LOOKING back along life's trodden way,
  Gleams and greenness linger on the track;

Distance melts and mellows all to-day,
  Looking back.

Rose and purple and a silvery grey,
  Is that cloud the cloud we called so black?
Evening harmonizes all to-day,
  Looking back.

Foolish feet so prone to halt or stray,
  Foolish heart so restive on the rack!
Yesterday we sighed, but not to-day,
  Looking back.

Before 1886.

THE WATCHERS

SHE fell asleep among the flowers
In the sober autumn hours.

Three there are about her bed,
At her side and feet and head.

At her head standeth the Cross
For which all else she counted loss:

Still and steadfast at her feet
Doth her Guardian Angel sit:

Prayers of truest love abide
Wrapping her on every side.

The holy Cross standeth alone,
Beneath the white moon, whitest stone.

Evil spirits come not near
Its shadow, shielding from all fear:

Once she bore it in her breast,
Now it certifies her rest.

Humble violets grow around
Its base, sweetening the grassy
    ground,

Leaf-hidden : so she hid from praise
Of men her pious holy ways.

Higher about it, twining close,
Clingeth a crimson thorny rose :

So from her heart's good seed of love
Thorns sprang below, flowers spring
    above.

Though yet his vigil doth not cease,
Her Angel sits in perfect peace,

With white folded wings : for she
He watches now is pure as he.

He watches with his loving eyes
For the day when she shall rise :

When full of glory and of grace
She shall behold him face to face.

Though she is safe for ever, yet
Human love doth not forget :

But prays that in her deep
Grave she may sleep a blessed sleep,

Till when time and the world are
    past
She may find mercy at the last.

So these three do hedge her in
From sorrow, as death does from sin.

So freed from earthly taint and pain
May they all meet in heaven.
    Amen.
      25 *May* 1850.

THE THREE ENEMIES

THE FLESH

'SWEET, thou art pale.'
              'More pale to see,
Christ hung upon the cruel tree
And bore His Father's wrath for me.'

'Sweet, thou art sad.'
              'Beneath a rod
More heavy, Christ for my sake trod
The winepress of the wrath of God.'

'Sweet, thou art weary.'
              'Not so Christ ;
Whose mighty love of me sufficed
For Strength, Salvation, Eucharist.'

'Sweet, thou art footsore.'
              'If I bleed,
His feet have bled ; yea in my need
His Heart once bled for mine indeed.'

THE WORLD

'Sweet, thou art young.'
              'So He was young
Who for my sake in silence hung
Upon the Cross with Passion wrung.'

'Look, thou art fair.'
              'He was more fair
Than men, Who deigned for me to
    wear
A visage marred beyond compare.'

'And thou hast riches.'
              'Daily bread :
All else is His : Who, living, dead,
For me lacked where to lay His
    Head.'

'And life is sweet.'
              'It was not so
To Him, Whose Cup did overflow
With mine unutterable woe.'

THE DEVIL

'Thou drinkest deep.'
        'When Christ would sup
He drained the dregs from out my
    cup:
So how should I be lifted up?'

'Thou shalt win Glory.'
            'In the skies,
Lord Jesus, cover up mine eyes
Lest they should look on vanities.'

'Thou shalt have Knowledge.'
            'Helpless dust!
In thee, O Lord, I put my trust:
Answer Thou for me, Wise and Just.'

'And Might.'—
      'Get thee behind me. Lord,
Who hast redeemed and not abhorred
My soul, oh keep it by Thy Word.'
15 *June* 1851.

BEHOLD, I STAND AT THE DOOR AND KNOCK

WHO standeth at the gate?—A
    woman old,
  A widow from the husband of her
    love.
'O lady, stay, this wind is piercing
    cold,
  Oh look at the keen frosty moon
    above;
I have no home, am hungry, feeble,
    poor.'—
  'I'm really very sorry, but I can
    Do nothing for you; there's the
    clergyman,'
The lady said, and shivering closed
    the door.

Who standeth at the gate?—Way-
    worn and pale
  A grey-haired man asks charity
    again.
'Kind lady, I have journeyed far,
    and fail
  Through weariness; for I have
    begged in vain
Some shelter, and can find no
    lodging-place.'—
  She answered: 'There's the work-
    house very near;
  Go, for they'll certainly receive
    you there'—
Then shut the door against his
    pleading face.

Who standeth at the gate?—A
    stunted child,
  Her sunk eyes sharpened with
    precocious care.
'O lady, save me from a home
    defiled,
  From shameful sights and sounds
    that taint the air:
Take pity on me, teach me some-
    thing good.'—
  'For shame, why don't you work
    instead of cry?
  I keep no young impostors here,
    not I.'
She slammed the door, indignant
    where she stood.

Who standeth at the gate, and will
    be heard?
  Arise, O woman, from thy comforts
    now:
Go forth again to speak the careless
    word,
  The cruel word unjust, with
    hardened brow.
But who is this, that standeth not to
    pray

As once, but terrible to judge thy sin?
This whom thou wouldst not succour nor take in
Nor teach but leave to perish by the way.
'Thou didst it not unto the least of these,
And in them hast not done it unto Me.
Thou wast as a princess rich and at ease—
Now sit in dust and howl for poverty.
Three times I stood beseeching at thy gate,
Three times I came to bless thy soul and save:
But now I come to judge for what I gave,
And now at length thy sorrow is too late.'
1 December 1851.

ADVENT

'COME,' Thou dost say to Angels,
To blessed Spirits, 'Come':
'Come,' to the lambs of Thine own flock,
Thy little ones, 'Come home.'

'Come,' from the many-mansioned house
The gracious word is sent;
'Come,' from the ivory palaces
Unto the Penitent.

O Lord, restore us deaf and blind,
Unclose our lips though dumb:
Then say to us, 'I come with speed,'
And we will answer, 'Come.'
12 December 1851.

ALL SAINTS

THEY have brought gold and spices to my King,
Incense and precious stuffs and ivory:
O holy Mother mine, what can I bring
That so my Lord may deign to look on me?
They sing a sweeter song than I can sing,
All crowned and glorified exceedingly:
I, bound on earth, weep for my trespassing,—
They sing the song of love in heaven, set free.
Then answered me my Mother, and her voice
Spake to my heart, yea answered in my heart:
'Sing, saith He to the heavens, to earth, Rejoice:
Thou also lift thy heart to Him above:
He seeks not thine, but thee such as thou art,
For lo His banner over thee is Love.'
20 January 1852.

EYE HATH NOT SEEN

OUR feet shall tread upon the stars
Less bright than we.
The everlasting shore shall bound
A fairer sea
Than that which cold
Now glitters in the sun like gold.

Oh good, oh blest! but who shall say
How fair, how fair,

Is the light-region where no cloud
  Darkens the air,
    Where weary eyes
Rest on the green of Paradise?

There cometh not the wind nor rain
  Nor sun nor snow:
    The Trees of Knowledge and of Life
Bud there and blow,
  Their leaves and fruit
Fed from an undecaying root.

There Angels flying to and fro
  Are not more white
Than Penitents some while ago,
    Now Saints in light:
Once soiled and sad—
Cleansed now and crowned, fulfilled and glad.

Now yearning through the perfect rest
  Perhaps they gaze
Earthwards upon their best-beloved
    In all earth's ways:
Longing, but not
With pain, as used to be their lot.

The hush of that beatitude
  Is ages long,
Sufficing Virgins, Prophets, Saints,
  Till the new song
Shall be sent up
From lips which drained the bitter cup.

If but the thought of Paradise
  Gives joy on earth,
What shall it be to enter there
  Through second birth?
To find once more
Our dearest treasure gone before?

To find the Shepherd of the sheep,
  The Lamb once slain,
Who leads His own by living streams—
  Never again
To thirst, or need
Aught in green pastures where they feed.

But from the altar comes a cry
  Awful and strong
From martyred Saints: 'How long,' they say,
  'O Lord, how long,
Holy and True,
Shall vengeance for our blood be due?'

Then the Lord gives them robes of white,
  And bids them stay
In patience till the time be full
  For the last day—
The day of dread
When the last sentence shall be said;

When heaven and earth shall flee away,
  And the great deep
Shall render up her dead, and earth
  Her sons that sleep,
And day of grace
Be hid for ever from Thy face.

Oh hide us, till Thy wrath be past,
  Our grief, our shame,
With Peter and with Magdalene,
  And him whose name
No record tells
Who by Thy promise with Thee dwells.

1 *May* 1852.

A BRUISED REED SHALL HE NOT BREAK

I WILL accept thy will to do and be,
  Thy hatred and intolerance of sin,
Thy will at least to love, that burns within
  And thirsteth after Me :
So will I render fruitful, blessing still,
  The germs and small beginnings in thy heart,
Because thy will cleaves to the better part.—
    Alas, I cannot will.

Dost not thou will, poor soul? Yet I receive
  The inner unseen longings of the soul,
I guide them turning towards Me :
  I control
    And charm hearts till they grieve :
If thou desire, it yet shall come to pass,
  Though thou but wish indeed to choose My love ;
For I have power in earth and heaven above.—
    I cannot wish, alas !

What, neither choose nor wish to choose ? and yet
  I still must strive to win thee and constrain :
For thee I hung upon the cross in pain,
  How then can I forget ?
If thou as yet dost neither love nor hate
  Nor choose nor wish,—resign thyself, be still,
Till I infuse love, hatred, longing, will.—
    I do not deprecate.

13 June 1852.

ST. ELIZABETH OF HUNGARY

WHEN if ever life is sweet,
  Save in heart in all a child,
  A fair virgin undefiled,
Knelt she at her Saviour's feet :
While she laid her royal crown,
  Thinking it too mean a thing
  For a solemn offering,
Careless on the cushions down.

Fair she was as any rose,
  But more pale than lilies white :
Her eyes full of deep repose
  Seemed to see beyond our sight.
Hush, she is a holy thing :
  Hush, her soul is in her eyes,
  Seeking far in Paradise
For her Light, her Love, her King.

16 June 1852.

MOONSHINE

FAIR the sun riseth,
  Bright as bright can be,
Fair the sun shineth
  On a fair fair sea.

'Across the water
Wilt thou come with me,
Miles and long miles, love,
Over the salt sea ?'

'If thou wilt hold me
Truly by the hand,
I will go with thee
Over sea and sand.

'If thou wilt hold me
That I shall not fall,
I will go with thee,
Love, in spite of all.'

Fair the moon riseth
On her heavenly way,
   Making the waters
   Fairer than by day.

A little vessel
Rocks upon the sea,
   Where stands a maiden
   Fair as fair can be.

Her smile rejoices
Though her mouth is mute:
   She treads the vessel
   With her little foot.

Truly he holds her
Faithful to his pledge,
   Guiding the vessel
   From the water's edge.

Fair the moon saileth
   With her pale fair light,
Fair the girl gazeth
   Out into the night.

Saith she, 'Like silver
Shines thy hair, not gold':
   Saith she, 'I shiver
   In thy steady hold.

'Love,' she saith weeping,
'Loose thy hold awhile;
   My heart is freezing
   In thy freezing smile.'

The moon is hidden
By a silver cloud,
   Fair as a halo
   Or a maiden's shroud.

No more beseeching,
Ever on they go:
   The vessel rocketh
   Softly to and fro:

And still he holds her
That she shall not fall,
   Till pale mists whiten
   Dimly over all.

Onward and onward,
Far across the sea:
   Onward and onward,
   Pale as pale can be:

Onward and onward,
Ever hand in hand,
   From sun and moonlight
   To another land.

16 June 1852.

I LOOK FOR THE LORD

OUR wealth has wasted all away,
   Our pleasures have found wings;
The night is long until the day;
   Lord, give us better things—
A ray of light in thirsty night
   And secret water-springs.

Our love is dead, or sleeps, or else
   Is hidden from our eyes:
Our silent love, while no man tells
   Or if it lives or dies.
Oh give us love, O Lord, above
   In changeless Paradise.

Our house is left us desolate,
   Even as Thy word hath said.
Before our face the way is great;
   Around us are the dead.
Oh guide us, save us from the grave,
   As Thou Thy saints hast led.

Lead us where pleasures evermore
   And wealth indeed are placed,

And home on an eternal shore,
And love that cannot waste:
Where joy Thou art unto the heart,
And sweetness to the taste.

28 *September* 1852.

THE HEART KNOWETH ITS OWN BITTERNESS

WEEP yet awhile,—
Weep till that day shall dawn
  when thou shalt smile:
Watch till the day
When all save only love shall pass
  away.

Weep, sick and lonely,
Bow thy heart to tears,
For none shall guess the secret
  Of thy griefs and fears.
Weep, till the day dawn,
  Refreshing dew:
  Weep till the spring:
  For genial showers
  Bring up the flowers,
  And thou shalt sing
In summertime of blossoming.

Heart-sick and silent,
  Weep and watch in pain.
  Weep for hope perished,
  Not to live again:
Weep for love's hope and fear
  And passion vain.
  Watch till the day
When all save only love shall pass
  away.

Then love rejoicing
Shall forget to weep:
Shall hope or fear no more.
  Or watch, or sleep,

But only love and cease not,
  Deep beyond deep.
Now we sow love in tears,
  But then shall reap.
Have patience as the Lord's own
  flock of sheep:
Have patience with His love
Who died below, who lives for thee
  above.

23 *December* 1852.

WHITSUN EVE

THE white dove cooeth in her downy
  nest,
Keeping her young ones warm be-
  neath her breast:
The white moon saileth through the
  cool clear sky,
Screened by a tender mist in passing
  by:
The white rose buds, with thorns
  upon its stem,
All the more precious and more dear
  for them:
The stream shines silver in the tufted
  grass,
The white clouds scarcely dim it as
  they pass;
Deep in the valleys lily cups are
  white,
They send up incense all the holy
  night.
Our souls are white, made clean in
  Blood once shed:
White blessèd Angels watch around
  our bed:—
O spotless Lamb of God, still keep
  us so,
Thou who wert born for us in time
  of snow.

18 *May* 1853.

THERE REMAINETH THEREFORE A REST FOR THE PEOPLE OF GOD

I

'Ye have forgotten the exhortation.'

COME, blessed sleep, most full, most perfect, come :
  Come, sleep, if so I may forget the whole ;
  Forget my body and forget my soul,
Forget how long life is and troublesome.
Come, happy sleep, to soothe my heart or numb,
  Arrest my weary spirit or control :
  Till light be dark to me from pole to pole,
And winds and echoes and low songs be dumb.
Come, sleep, and lap me into perfect calm,
  Lap me from all the world and weariness :
Come, secret sleep, with thine unuttered psalm,
  Safe sheltering in a hidden cool recess :
Come, heavy dreamless sleep, and close and press
Upon mine eyes thy fingers dropping balm.

II

'Which speaketh unto you as unto children.'

ART thou so weary then, poor thirsty soul ?
  Have patience, in due season thou shalt sleep.
Mount yet a little while, the path is steep :
Strain yet a little while to reach the goal :
Do battle with thyself, achieve, control :
  Till night come down with blessed slumber deep
  As love, and seal thine eyes no more to weep
Through long tired vigils while the planets roll.
Have patience, for thou too shalt sleep at length,
  Lapt in the pleasant shade of Paradise.
My Hands that bled for thee shall close thine eyes,
  My Heart that bled for thee shall be thy rest :
I will sustain with everlasting strength,
  And thou, with John, shalt lie upon My breast.

12 July 1853.

A HARVEST

O GATE of death, of the blessed night,
  That shall open not again
On this world of shame and sorrow,
  Where slow ages wax and wane,
Where are signs and seasons, days and nights,
  And mighty winds and rain.

Is the day wearing toward the west ?—
  Far off cool shadows pass,
A visible refreshment
  Across the sultry grass :
Far off low mists are mustering,
  A broken shifting mass.

Still in the deepest knowledge
Some depth is left unknown:
Still in the merriest music lurks
A plaintive undertone:
Still with the closest friend some throb
Of life is felt alone.

Time's summer breath is sweet, his sands
Ebb sparkling as they flow,
Yet some are sick that this should end
Which is from long ago:—
Are not the fields already white
To harvest in the glow?—

There shall come another harvest
Than was in days of yore:
The reapers shall be Angels,
Our God shall purge the floor:—
No more seed-time, no more harvest,
Then for evermore.

1 *August* 1853.

THE ELEVENTH HOUR

FAINT and worn and aged
One stands knocking at a gate;
Though no light shines in the casement,
Knocking though so late.
It has struck eleven
In the courts of heaven,
Yet he still doth knock and wait.

While no answer cometh
From the heavenly hill,
Blessed Angels wonder
At his earnest will.
Hope and fear but quicken
While the shadows thicken:
He is knocking, knocking still.

Grim the gate unopened
Stands with bar and lock:
Yet within the unseen Porter
Hearkens to the knock.—
Doing and undoing,
Faint and yet pursuing,
This man's feet are on the Rock.

With a cry unceasing
Knocketh, prayeth he:
'Lord have mercy on me
When I cry to Thee.'
With a knock unceasing
And a cry increasing:
'O my Lord, remember me.'

Still the Porter standeth,
Love-constrained He standeth near,
While the cry increaseth
Of that love and fear:
'Jesus, look upon me—
Christ, hast Thou foregone me?—
If I must, I perish here.'

Faint the knocking ceases,
Faint the cry and call:
Is he lost indeed for ever,
Shut without the wall?
Mighty Arms surround him,
Arms that sought and found him,
Held, withheld, and bore through all.

O celestial mansion,
Open wide the door:
Crown and robes of whiteness,
Stone inscribed before,
Flocking Angels bear them;
Stretch thy hand and wear them,
Sit thou down for evermore.

5 *September* 1853.

SLEEP AT SEA

SOUND the deep waters:—
Who shall sound that deep?—

Too short the plummet,
  And the watchmen sleep.
Some dream of effort
  Up a toilsome steep;
Some dream of pasture grounds
  For harmless sheep.

White shapes flit to and fro
  From mast to mast;
They feel the distant tempest
  That nears them fast:
Great rocks are straight ahead
  Great shoals not past;
They shout to one another
  Upon the blast.

Oh soft the streams drop music
  Between the hills,
And musical the birds' nests
  Beside those rills:
The nests are types of home
  Love-hidden from ills,
The nests are types of spirits
  Love-music fills.

So dream the sleepers,
  Each man in his place;
The lightning shows the smile
  Upon each face:
The ship is driving,—driving,—
  It drives apace:
And sleepers smile, and spirits
  Bewail their case.

The lightning glares and reddens
  Across the skies;
It seems but sunset
  To those sleeping eyes.
When did the sun go down
  On such a wise?
From such a sunset
  When shall day arise?

'Wake,' call the spirits:
  But to heedless ears:
They have forgotten sorrows
  And hopes and fears;
They have forgotten perils
  And smiles and tears;
Their dream has held them long,
  Long years and years.

'Wake,' call the spirits again:
  But it would take
A louder summons
  To bid them awake.
Some dream of pleasure
  For another's sake:
Some dream, forgetful
  Of a lifelong ache.

One by one slowly,
  Ah how sad and slow!
Wailing and praying
  The spirits rise and go:
Clear stainless spirits,
  White, as white as snow;
Pale spirits, wailing
  For an overthrow.

One by one flitting,
  Like a mournful bird
Whose song is tired at last
  For no mate heard.
The loving voice is silent,
  The useless word;
One by one flitting
  Sick with hope deferred.

Driving and driving,
  The ship drives amain:
While swift from mast to mast
  Shapes flit again,
Flit silent as the silence
  Where men lie slain;
Their shadow cast upon the sails
  Is like a stain.

No voice to call the sleepers,
  No hand to raise:
They sleep to death in dreaming
  Of length of days.
Vanity of vanities,
  The Preacher says:
Vanity is the end
  Of all their ways.

17 *October* 1853.

CONSIDER THE LILIES OF THE FIELD

FLOWERS preach to us if we will
    hear: —
The rose saith in the dewy morn:
' I am most fair ;
Yet all my loveliness is born
Upon a thorn.'
The poppy saith amid the corn:
' Let but my scarlet head appear
And I am held in scorn ;
Yet juice of subtle virtue lies
Within my cup of curious dyes.'
The lilies say : ' Behold how we
Preach without words of purity.'
The violets whisper from the shade
Which their own leaves have made :
' Men scent our fragrance on the
    air,
Yet take no heed
Of humble lessons we would read.'

But not alone the fairest flowers :
The merest grass
Along the roadside where we pass,
Lichen and moss and sturdy weed,
Tell of His love who sends the
    dew,
The rain and sunshine too,
To nourish one small seed.

21 *October* 1853.

WHO HAVE A FORM OF GODLINESS

WHEN I am sick and tired it is
    God's will :
Also God's will alone is sure and
    best :—
So in my weariness I find my
    rest,
And so in poverty I take my fill.
Therefore I see my good in midst
    of ill,
Therefore in loneliness I build my
    nest,
And through hot noon pant toward
    the shady west,
And hope in sickening disappoint-
    ment still.
So, when the times of restitution
    come,
  The sweet times of refreshing
      come at last,
    My God shall fill my longings
        to the brim :
    Therefore I wait and look and
        long for Him :
Not wearied though the work is
    wearisome,
  Nor fainting though the time be
      almost past.

18 *December* 1853.

SOME FEASTS AND FASTS

(*From* 1853 *to before* 1893.)

ADVENT SUNDAY

BEHOLD, the Bridegroom cometh :
    go ye out
With lighted lamps and garlands
    round about
To meet Him in a rapture with a
    shout.

It may be at the midnight, black as
    pitch,
Earth shall cast up her poor, cast
    up her rich.

It may be at the crowing of the
    cock
Earth shall upheave her depth,
    uproot her rock.

For lo, the Bridegroom fetcheth
    home the Bride:
His Hands are Hands she knows,
    she knows His Side.

Like pure Rebekah at the appointed
    place,
Veiled, she unveils her face to meet
    His Face.

Like great Queen Esther in her
    triumphing,
She triumphs in the Presence of her
    King.

His Eyes are as a Dove's, and she's
    Dove-eyed;
He knows His lovely mirror, sister,
    Bride.

He speaks with Dove-voice of ex-
    ceeding love,
And she with love-voice of an
    answering Dove

Behold, the Bridegroom cometh:
    go we out
With lamps ablaze and garlands
    round about
To meet Him in a rapture with a
    shout.
    Before 1886.

ADVENT.

EARTH grown old, yet still so green,
    Deep beneath her crust of
        cold
Nurses fire unfelt, unseen:
    Earth grown old.

    We who live are quickly
        told:
Millions more lie hid between
    Inner swathings of her fold.

When will fire break up her screen?
    When will life burst thro' her
        mould?
Earth, earth, earth, thy cold is keen,
    Earth grown old.
    Before 1886.

SOONER or later: yet at last
The Jordan must be past;

It may be he will overflow
His banks the day we go;

It may be that his cloven deep'
Will stand up on a heap.

Sooner or later: yet one day
We all must pass that way;

Each man, each woman, humbled,
    pale,
Pass veiled within the veil;

Child, parent, bride, companion,
Alone, alone, alone.

For none a ransom can be paid,
A suretyship be made:

I, bent by mine own burden, must
Enter my house of dust;

I, rated to the full amount,
Must render mine account.

When earth and sea shall empty all
Their graves of great and small;

When earth wrapt in a fiery flood
Shall no more hide her blood;

When mysteries shall be revealed;
All secrets be unsealed;

When things of night, when things
  of shame,
Shall find at last a name,

Pealed for a hissing and a curse
Throughout the universe:

Then Awful Judge, most Awful God,
Then cause to bud Thy rod,

To bloom with blossoms, and to give
Almonds; yea, bid us live.

I plead Thyself with Thee, I plead
Thee in our utter need:

Jesus, most Merciful of Men,
Show mercy on us then;

Lord God of Mercy and of men,
Show mercy on us then.
  Before 1882.

CHRISTMAS EVE

CHRISTMAS hath a darkness
  Brighter than the blazing noon,
Christmas hath a chillness
  Warmer than the heat of June,
Christmas hath a beauty
  Lovelier than the world can show:
For Christmas bringeth Jesus,
  Brought for us so low.

Earth, strike up your music,
  Birds that sing and bells that ring;
Heaven hath answering music
  For all Angels soon to sing:
Earth, put on your whitest
  Bridal robe of spotless snow:
For Christmas bringeth Jesus,
  Brought for us so low.
  Before 1886.

CHRISTMAS DAY

A BABY is a harmless thing
  And wins our hearts with one
    accord,
And Flower of Babies was their
    King,
  Jesus Christ our Lord:
Lily of lilies He
  Upon His Mother's knee;
Rose of roses, soon to be
Crowned with thorns on leafless
    tree.

A lamb is innocent and mild
  And merry on the soft green sod;
And Jesus Christ, the Undefiled,
  Is the Lamb of God:
Only spotless He
Upon his Mother's knee;
White and ruddy, soon to be
Sacrificed for you and me.

Nay, lamb is not so sweet a word,
  Nor lily half so pure a name;
Another name our hearts hath stirred,
  Kindling them to flame:
'Jesus' certainly
Is music and melody:
Heart with heart in harmony
Carol we and worship we.
  Before 1886.

CHRISTMASTIDE

LOVE came down at Christmas,
    Love all lovely, Love Divine;
Love was born at Christmas,
    Star and Angels gave the sign.

Worship we the Godhead,
    Love Incarnate, Love Divine;
Worship we our Jesus:
    But wherewith for sacred sign?

Love shall be our token,
    Love be yours and love be mine,
Love to God and all men,
    Love for plea and gift and sign.
Before 1886.

ST. JOHN, APOSTLE

EARTH cannot bar flame from ascending,
Hell cannot bind light from descending,
Death cannot finish life never ending.

Eagle and sun gaze at each other,
Eagle at sun, brother at Brother,
Loving in peace and joy one another.

O St. John, with chains for thy wages,
Strong thy rock where the storm-blast rages,
Rock of refuge, the Rock of Ages.

Rome hath passed with her awful voice,
Earth is passing with all her joys,
Heaven shall pass away with a noise.

So from us all follies that please us,
So from us all falsehoods that ease us,—
Only all saints abide with their Jesus.

Jesus, in love looking down hither,
Jesus, by love draw us up thither,
That we in Thee may abide together.
Before 1893.

'BELOVED, let us love one another,'
    says St. John,
Eagle of eagles calling from above:
Words of strong nourishment for life to feed upon,
    'Beloved, let us love.'

Voice of an eagle, yea, Voice of the Dove:
If we may love, winter is past and gone;
Publish we, praise we, for lo it is enough.

More sunny than sunshine that ever yet shone,
Sweetener of the bitter, smoother of the rough,
Highest lesson of all lessons for all to con,
    'Beloved, let us love.'
Before 1886.

HOLY INNOCENTS

THEY scarcely waked before they slept,
    They scarcely wept before they laughed;
They drank indeed death's bitter draught,
    But all its bitterest dregs were kept
And drained by Mothers while they wept.

From Heaven the speechless Infants
    speak:
  Weep not (they say), our Mothers
    dear,
  For swords nor sorrows come
    not here.
Now we are strong who were so
    weak,
And all is ours we could not seek.

We bloom among the blooming
    flowers,
  We sing among the singing
    birds;
  Wisdom we have who wanted
    words:
Here morning knows not evening
    hours,
All's rainbow here without the
    showers.

And softer than our Mother's breast,
  And closer than our Mother's
    arm,
  Is here the Love that keeps us
    warm
And broods above our happy nest.
Dear Mothers, come: for Heaven
    is best.

Before 1882.

UNSPOTTED lambs to follow the
    one Lamb,
  Unspotted doves to wait on the
    one Dove;
To whom Love saith, 'Be with Me
    where I am,'
And lo their answer unto Love is
    love.

For tho' I know not any note they
    know,
  Nor know one word of all their
    song above,

I know Love speaks to them, and
    even so
I know the answer unto Love is
    love.

Before 1893.

EPIPHANY

'LORD Babe, if Thou art He
  We sought for patiently,
Where is Thy court?
Hither may prophecy and star
    resort;
Men heed not their report.'—
  'Bow down and worship, righteous
    man:
  This Infant of a span
  Is He man sought for since the
    world began!'—
'Then, Lord, accept my gold, too
    base a thing
For Thee, of all kings King.'—

'Lord Babe, despite Thy youth
I hold Thee of a truth
Both Good and Great:
But wherefore dost Thou keep so
    mean a state,
Low-lying desolate?'—
  'Bow down and worship, righteous
    seer:
  The Lord our God is here
  Approachable, Who bids us all
    draw near.'—
'Wherefore to Thee I offer frank-
    incense,
Thou Sole Omnipotence.'—

'But I have only brought
Myrrh; no wise afterthought
Instructed me
To gather pearls or gems, or choice
    to see
Coral or ivory.'—

'Not least thine offering proves thee wise:
For myrrh means sacrifice,
And He that lives, this Same is He that dies.'—
'Then here is myrrh: alas, yea woe is me
That myrrh befitteth Thee.'—

Myrrh, frankincense, and gold:
And lo from wintry fold
Good-will doth bring
A Lamb, the innocent likeness of this King
Whom stars and seraphs sing:
And lo the bird of love, a Dove,
Flutters and coos above:
And Dove and Lamb and Babe agree in love:—
Come all mankind, come all creation hither,
Come, worship Christ together.
Before 1886.

EPIPHANYTIDE

TREMBLING before Thee we fall down to adore Thee,
Shamefaced and trembling we lift our eyes to Thee:
O First and with the last! annul our ruined past,
Rebuild us to Thy glory, set us free
From sin and from sorrow to fall down and worship Thee.

Full of pity view us, stretch Thy sceptre to us,
Bid us live that we may give ourselves to Thee:
O faithful Lord and true! stand up for us and do,
Make us lovely, make us new, set us free—
Heart and soul and spirit—to bring all and worship Thee.
Before 1893.

SEPTUAGESIMA
'So run that ye may obtain.'

ONE step more, and the race is ended;
One word more, and the lesson's done;
One toil more, and a long rest follows
At set of sun.

Who would fail, for one step withholden?
Who would fail, for one word unsaid?
Who would fail, for a pause too early?
Sound sleep the dead.

One step more, and the goal receives us;
One word more, and life's task is done;
One toil more, and the Cross is carried
And sets the sun.
Before 1886.

SEXAGESIMA
'Cursed is the ground for thy sake.'

YET earth was very good in days of old,
And earth is lovely still:
Still for the sacred flock she spreads the fold,
For Sion rears the hill.

Mother she is and cradle of our race,
A depth where treasures lie,
The broad foundation of a holy place,
Man's step to scale the sky.

She spreads the harvest-field which
    Angels reap,
And lo the crop is white;
She spreads God's Acre where the
    happy sleep
All night that is not night.

Earth may not pass till heaven shall
    pass away,
Nor heaven may be renewed
Except with earth: and once more
    in that day
Earth shall be very good.
Before 1893.

              •

THAT Eden of earth's sunrise cannot
    vie
With Paradise beyond her sunset sky
    Hidden on high.

Four rivers watered Eden in her
    bliss,
But Paradise hath One which perfect
    is
    In sweetnesses.

Eden had gold, but Paradise hath
    gold
Like unto glass of splendours manifold
    Tongue hath not told.

Eden had sun and moon to make
    her bright;
But Paradise hath God and Lamb
    for light,
And hath no night.

Unspotted innocence was Eden's
    best;
Great Paradise shows God's fulfilled
    behest,
    Triumph and rest.

Hail, Eve and Adam, source of death
    and shame!
New life has sprung from death, and
    Jesu's Name
    Clothes you with fame.

Hail Adam, and hail Eve! your
    children rise
And call you blessed, in their glad
    surmise
    Of Paradise
Before 1893.

QUINQUAGESIMA

LOVE is alone the worthy law of love:
    All other laws have presupposed
        a taint:
    Love is the law from kindled saint
        to saint,
From lamb to lamb, from dove to
    answering dove.
Love is the motive of all things that
    move
    Harmonious by free will without
        constraint:
    Love learns and teaches: love
        shall man acquaint
With all he lacks, which all his lack
    is love.
Because Love is the fountain, I
    discern
    The stream as love: for what but
        love should flow
        From fountain Love? not bitter
            from the sweet!
    I ignorant, have I laid claim to
        know?
        Oh teach me, Love, such knowledge as is meet
For one to know who is fain to love
    and learn.
Before 1893.

PITEOUS my rhyme is
What while I muse of love and pain,
Of love mis-spent, of love in vain,
Of love that is not loved again:
    And is this all then?
    As long as time is,
Love loveth. Time is but a span,
The dalliance space of dying man:
And is this all immortals can?
    The gain were small then.

    Love loves for ever,
And finds a sort of joy in pain,
And gives with nought to take again,
And loves too well to end in vain:
    Is the gain small then?
    Love laughs at 'never,'
Outlives our life, exceeds the span
Appointed to mere mortal man:
All which love is and does and can
    Is all in all then.
    Before 1886.

ASH WEDNESDAY

MY God, my God, have mercy on my sin,
For it is great; and if I should begin
To tell it all, the day would be too small
    To tell it in.

My God, Thou wilt have mercy on my sin
For Thy Love's sake: yea, if I should begin
To tell This all, the day would be too small
    To tell it in.
    Before 1886.

GOOD Lord, to-day
I scarce find breath to say:
Scourge, but receive me.
For stripes are hard to bear, but worse
Thy intolerable curse;
    So do not leave me.

Good Lord, lean down
In pity, tho' Thou frown;
    Smite, but retrieve me:
For so Thou hold me up to stand
And kiss Thy smiting hand,
    It less will grieve me.
    Before 1893.

LENT

IT is good to be last not first,
    Pending the present distress;
It is good to hunger and thirst,
    So it be for righteousness.
It is good to spend and be spent,
    It is good to watch and to pray:
Life and Death make a goodly Lent
    So it leads us to Easter Day.
    Before 1886.

EMBERTIDE

I SAW a Saint.—How canst thou tell that he
    Thou sawest was a Saint?—
I saw one like to Christ so luminously
By patient deeds of love, his mortal taint
Seemed made his groundwork for humility.

And when he marked me downcast utterly
    Where foul I sat and faint,
Then more than ever Christ-like kindled he;
    And welcomed me as I had been a saint,
Tenderly stooping low to comfort me.

Christ bade him, 'Do thou likewise.'
    Wherefore he
  Waxed zealous to acquaint
His soul with sin and sorrow, if so be
  He might retrieve some latent saint :—
'Lo, I, with the child God hath given to me!'

Before 1893.

MID-LENT

IS any grieved or tired? Yea, by God's Will :
  Surely God's Will alone is good and best :
  O weary man, in weariness take rest,
O hungry man, by hunger feast thy fill.
Discern thy good beneath a mask of ill,
  Or build of loneliness thy secret nest :
  At noon take heart, being mindful of the west ;
At night wake hope, for dawn advances still.
At night wake hope. Poor soul, in such sore need
  Of wakening and of girding up anew,
  Hast thou that hope which fainting doth pursue?
No saint but hath pursued and hath been faint ;
Bid love wake hope, for both thy steps shall speed,
  Still faint yet still pursuing, O thou saint.

Before 1886.

PASSIONTIDE

IT is the greatness of Thy love, dear Lord, that we would celebrate
  With sevenfold powers.
Our love at best is cold and poor, at best unseemly for Thy state,
  This best of ours.
Creatures that die, we yet are such as Thine own hands deigned to create :
  We frail as flowers,
We bitter bondslaves ransomed at a price incomparably great
  To grace Heaven's bowers.

Thou callest : 'Come at once'—and still Thou callest us : 'Come late, tho' late'—
  (The moments fly)—
'Come, every one that thirsteth, come — Come prove Me, knocking at My gate'—
  (Some souls draw nigh !)—
'Come thou who waiting seekest Me—Come thou for whom I seek and wait'—
  (Why will we die ?)—
'Come and repent : come and amend : come joy the joys unsatiate'—
  —(Christ passeth by . . .)—
Lord, pass not by—I come—and I—and I. Amen.

Before 1893.

PALM SUNDAY

'He treadeth the winepress of the fierceness and wrath of Almighty God.'

I LIFT mine eyes, and see
Thee, tender Lord, in pain upon the tree,
Athirst for my sake and athirst for me.

'Yea, look upon Me there,
Compassed with thorns and bleeding everywhere,
For thy sake bearing all, and glad to bear.'

I lift my heart to pray:
Thou Who didst love me all that darkened day,
Wilt Thou not love me to the end alway?

'Yea, thee My wandering sheep,
Yea, thee My scarlet sinner slow to weep,
Come to Me, I will love thee and will keep.'

Yet am I racked with fear:
Behold the unending outer darkness drear,
Behold the gulf unbridgeable and near!

'Nay, fix thy heart, thine eyes,
Thy hope upon My boundless sacrifice:
Will I lose lightly one so dear-bought prize?'

Ah Lord, it is not Thou,
Thou that wilt fail; yet woe is me, for how
Shall I endure who half am failing now?

'Nay, weld thy resolute will
To Mine: glance not aside for good or ill:
I love thee; trust Me still and love Me still.'

Yet Thou Thyself hast said,
When Thou shalt sift the living from the dead
Some must depart shamed and uncomforted.

'Judge not before that day:
Trust Me with all thy heart, even tho' I slay:
Trust Me in love, trust on, love on, and pray.'
Before 1893.

MONDAY IN HOLY WEEK

'The Voice of my Beloved.'

ONCE I ached for thy dear sake:
Wilt thou cause Me now to ache?
Once I bled for thee in pain:
Wilt thou rend My Heart again?
Crown of thorns and shameful tree,
Bitter death I bore for thee,
Bore My Cross to carry thee,
And wilt thou have nought of Me?
1853.

TUESDAY IN HOLY WEEK

By Thy long-drawn anguish to atone,
Jesus Christ, show mercy on Thine own:
Jesus Christ, show mercy and atone
Not for other sake except Thine own.

Thou Who thirsting on the Cross didst see
All mankind and all I love and me,
Still from Heaven look down in love and see
All mankind and all I love and me.
Before 1886.

WEDNESDAY IN HOLY WEEK

Man's life is death. Yet Christ endured to live,
Preaching and teaching, toiling to and fro,
Few men accepting what He yearned to give,
Few men with eyes to know
His Face, that Face of Love He stooped to show.

Man's death is life. For Christ endured to die
In slow unuttered weariness of pain,
A curse and an astonishment, passed by,
Pointed at, mocked again
By men for whom He shed His Blood—in vain?

Before 1886.

MAUNDY THURSDAY

'And the Vine said . . . Should I leave my wine which cheereth God and man, and go to be promoted over the trees?'

The great Vine left its glory to reign as Forest King.
'Nay,' quoth the lofty forest trees, 'we will not have this thing;
We will not have this supple one enring us with its ring.
Lo from immemorial time our might towers shadowing:
Not we were born to curve and droop, not we to climb and cling:
We buffet back the buffeting wind, tough to its buffeting:
We screen great beasts, the wild fowl build in our heads and sing,
Every bird of every feather from off our tops takes wing:
I a king, and thou a king, and what king shall be our king?'

Nevertheless the great Vine stooped to be the Forest King,
While the forest swayed and murmured like seas that are tempesting:
Stooped and drooped with thousand tendrils in thirsty languishing;
Bowed to earth and lay on earth for earth's replenishing;
Put off sweetness, tasted bitterness, endured time's fashioning;
Put off life and put on death:—and lo it was all to bring
All its fellows down to a death which hath lost the sting,
All its fellows up to a life in endless triumphing,—
I a king, and thou a king, and this King to be our King.

Before 1886.

GOOD FRIDAY MORNING

'Bearing His Cross.'

Up Thy Hill of Sorrows
Thou all alone,
Jesus, man's Redeemer,
Climbing to a Throne:
Thro' the world triumphant,
Thro' the Church in pain,
Which think to look upon Thee
No more again.

Upon my hill of sorrows
I, Lord, with Thee,
Cheered, upheld, yea carried
If a need should be:

Cheered, upheld, yea carried,
  Never left alone,
Carried in Thy heart of hearts
  To a throne.
Before 1893.

GOOD FRIDAY

LORD Jesus Christ, grown faint upon
    the Cross,
  A sorrow beyond sorrow in Thy
    look,
    The unutterable craving for my
      soul;
    Thy love of me sufficed
To load upon Thee and make good
    my loss
  In face of darkened heaven and
    earth that shook :—
    In face of earth and heaven,
      take Thou my whole
      Heart, O Lord Jesus Christ.
Before 1886.

GOOD FRIDAY EVENING

'Bring forth the Spear.'

No Cherub's heart or hand for us
    might ache,
  No Seraph's heart of fire had half
    sufficed :
Thine own were pierced and broken
    for our sake,
  O Jesus Christ.

Therefore we love Thee with our
    faint good-will,
  We crave to love Thee not as
    heretofore,
To love Thee much, to love Thee
    more, and still
    More and yet more.
Before 1893.

'A bundle of myrrh is my Well-beloved
  unto me.'

THY Cross cruciferous doth flower
    in all
  And every cross, dear Lord,
    assigned to us :
Ours lowly-statured crosses ; Thine
    how tall,
  Thy Cross cruciferous.

Thy Cross alone life-giving,
    glorious :
For love of Thine, souls love their
    own when small,
  Easy and light, or great and
    ponderous.

Since deep calls deep, Lord, hearken
    when we call ;
  When cross calls Cross racking
    and emulous :—
Remember us with him who shared
    Thy gall,
  Thy Cross cruciferous.
Before 1893.

EASTER EVEN

THE tempest over and gone, the
    calm begun,
  Lo, 'it is finished' and the Strong
    Man sleeps :
All stars keep vigil watching for the
    sun,
  The moon her vigil keeps.

A garden full of silence and of
    dew
  Beside a virgin cave and entrance
    stone :
Surely a garden full of Angels
    too,
  Wondering, on watch, alone.

They who cry 'Holy, Holy, Holy,'
  still
Veiling their faces round God's
  Throne above,
May well keep vigil on this heavenly
  hill
  And cry their cry of love,

Adoring God in His new mystery
  Of Love more deep than hell,
  more strong than death ;
Until the day break and the shadows
  flee,
  The Shaking and the Breath.
Before 1886.

(Our Church Palms are budding willow
  twigs.)

WHILE Christ lay dead the widowed
  world
  Wore willow green for hope un-
  done :
Till, when bright Easter dews im-
  pearled
  The chilly burial earth,
All north and south, all east and
  west,
  Flushed rosy in the arising sun ;
Hope laughed, and Faith resumed
  her rest,
  And Love remembered mirth.
Before 1893.

EASTER DAY

WORDS cannot utter
  Christ His returning :
Mankind, keep jubilee,
  Strip off your mourning,
  Crown you with garlands,
  Set your lamps burning.

Speech is left speechless ;
  Set you to singing,
Fling your hearts open wide,
  Set your bells ringing :
  Christ the Chief Reaper
  Comes, His sheaf bringing.

Earth wakes her song-birds,
  Puts on her flowers,
Leads out her lambkins,
  Builds up her bowers :
  This is man's spousal day,
  Christ's day and ours.
Before 1886.

EASTER MONDAY

OUT in the rain a world is growing
  green,
  On half the trees quick buds are
  seen
  Where glued-up buds have
  been.
Out in the rain God's Acre stretches
  green,
  Its harvest quick tho' still unseen :
  For there the Life hath been.

If Christ hath died His brethren
  well may die,
  Sing in the gate of death, lay by
  This life without a sigh :
For Christ hath died and good it is
  to die ;
  To sleep when so He lays us by,
  Then wake without a sigh.

Yea, Christ hath died, yea, Christ is
  risen again :
  Wherefore both life and death
  grow plain
  To us who wax and wane ;

For Christ Who rose shall die no
    more again :
  Amen : till He makes all things
    plain
  Let us wax on and wane.
Before 1886.

EASTER TUESDAY

'TOGETHER with my dead body
    shall they arise.'
  Shall my dead body arise ? then
    amen and yea
On track of a home beyond the
    uttermost skies
  Together with my dead body
    shall they.

We know the way : thank God Who
    hath showed us the way !
  Jesus Christ our Way to beautiful
    Paradise,
Jesus Christ the Same for ever, the
    Same to-day.

Five Virgins replenish with oil their
    lamps, being wise,
  Five Virgins awaiting the Bride-
    groom watch and pray :
And if I one day spring from my
    grave to the prize,
  Together with my dead body
    shall they.
Before 1893.

ROGATIONTIDE

WHO scatters tares shall reap no
    wheat,
But go hungry while others eat.

Who sows the wind shall not reap
    grain ;
The sown wind whirleth back again.

What God opens must open be,
Tho' man pile the sand of the sea.

What God shuts is opened no more,
Tho' man weary himself to find the
    door.
Before 1886.

ASCENSION EVE

O LORD Almighty Who hast formed
    us weak,
  With us whom Thou hast formed
    deal fatherly ;
Be found of us whom Thou hast
    deigned to seek,
  Be found that we the more may
    seek for Thee ;
Lord, speak and grant us ears to
    hear Thee speak ;
  Lord, come to us and grant us
    eyes to see ;
Lord, make us meek, for Thou
    Thyself art meek ;
  Lord, Thou art Love, fill us with
    charity.
O Thou the Life of living and of
    dead,
  Who givest more the more Thy-
    self hast given,
    Suffice us as Thy saints Thou
      hast sufficed ;
That beautified, replenished, com-
    forted,
  Still gazing off from earth and up
    at heaven,
    We may pursue Thy steps,
      Lord Jesus Christ.
Before 1893.

ASCENSION DAY

'A Cloud received Him out of their sight.'

WHEN Christ went up to Heaven the Apostles stayed
   Gazing at Heaven with souls and wills on fire,
Their hearts on flight along the track He made,
   Winged by desire.

Their silence spake: 'Lord, why not follow Thee?
   Home is not home without Thy Blessed Face,
Life is not life. Remember, Lord, and see,
   Look back, embrace.

'Earth is one desert waste of banishment,
   Life is one long-drawn anguish of decay.
Where Thou wert wont to go we also went:
   Why not to-day?'

Nevertheless a cloud cut off their gaze:
   They tarry to build up Jerusalem,
Watching for Him, while thro' the appointed days
   He watches them.

They do His Will, and doing it rejoice,
   Patiently glad to spend and to be spent:
Still He speaks to them, still they hear His Voice
   And are content.

For as a cloud received Him from their sight,
   So with a cloud will He return ere long:
Therefore they stand on guard by day, by night,
   Strenuous and strong.

They do, they dare, they beyond seven times seven
   Forgive, they cry God's mighty word aloud:
Yet sometimes haply lift tired eyes to Heaven—
   'Is that His cloud?'

Before 1886.

WHITSUN EVE

'As many as I love.'—Ah Lord, Who lovest all,
   If thus it is with Thee why sit remote above,
Beholding from afar, stumbling and marred and small,
   So many Thou dost love?

Whom sin and sorrow make their worn reluctant thrall;
   Who fain would flee away but lack the wings of dove;
Who long for love and rest; who look to Thee, and call
   To Thee for rest and love.

Before 1893.

WHITSUN DAY

'When the Day of Pentecost was fully come.'

AT sound as of rushing wind, and sight as of fire,
   Lo flesh and blood made spirit and fiery flame,

Ambassadors in Christ's and the
    Father's Name,
    To woo back a world's desire.

These men chose death for their life
    and shame for their boast,
For fear courage, for doubt in-
    tuition of faith,
Chose love that is strong as death
    and stronger than death
    In the power of the Holy Ghost.
Before 1886.

WHITSUN MONDAY

'A pure River of Water of Life.'

WE know not a voice of that River,
    If vocal or silent it be,
Where for ever and ever and ever
    It flows to no sea.

More deep than the seas is that River,
    More full than their manifold tides,
Where for ever and ever and ever
    It flows and abides.

Pure gold is the bed of that River
    (The gold of that land is the best),
Where for ever and ever and ever
    It flows on at rest.

Oh goodly the banks of that River,
    Oh goodly the fruits that they bear,
Where for ever and ever and ever
    It flows and is fair.

For lo on each bank of that River
    The Tree of Life life-giving grows,
Where for ever and ever and ever
    The Pure River flows.
Before 1893.

WHITSUN TUESDAY

LORD Jesus Christ, our Wisdom and
    our Rest,
Who wisely dost reveal and wisely
    hide,
Grant us such grace in wisdom to
    abide
According to Thy Will whose Will
    is best.
Contented with Thine uttermost be-
    hest,
Too sweet for envy and too high
    for pride;
All simple-souled, dove-hearted
    and dove-eyed,
Soft-voiced, and satisfied in humble
    nest.
Wondering at the bounty of Thy
    Love
Which gives us wings of silver
    and of gold;
Wings folded close, yet ready to
    unfold
When Thou shalt say, 'Winter
    is past and gone:'
When Thou shalt say, 'Spouse,
    sister, love and dove,
Come hither, sit with Me upon
    My Throne.'
Before 1886.

TRINITY SUNDAY

MY God, Thyself being Love Thy
    heart is love,
And love Thy Will and love Thy
    Word to us,
Whether Thou show us depths
    calamitous
Or heights and flights of rapturous
    peace above.

O Christ the Lamb, O Holy Ghost
    the Dove,
  Reveal the Almighty Father unto
    us;
  That we may tread Thy courts
    felicitous,
Loving Who loves us, for our God
    is Love.
Lo, if our God be Love thro' heaven's
    long day,
  Love is He thro' our mortal
    pilgrimage,
  Love was He thro' all aeons
    that are told.
We change, but Thou remainest;
    for Thine age
  Is, Was, and Is to come, nor
    new nor old;
We change, but Thou remainest;
    yea and yea!
    Before 1893.

CONVERSION OF ST. PAUL

O BLESSED Paul elect to grace,
  Arise and wash away thy sin,
Anoint thy head and wash thy face,
  Thy gracious course begin.
To start thee on thy outrunning race
Christ shows the splendour of His
    Face:
What will that Face of splendour be
When at the goal He welcomes thee?
    Before 1886.

IN weariness and painfulness St.
    Paul
  Served God and pleased Him:
    after-saints no less
Can wait on and can please Him,
    one and all
  In weariness and painfulness,
By faith and hope triumphant
    thro' distress:
Not with the rankling service of a
    thrall;
But even as loving children trust
    and bless,

Weep and rejoice, answering their
    Father's call,
  Work with tired hands, and for-
    ward upward press
On sore tired feet still rising when
    they fall,
  In weariness and painfulness.
    Before 1886.

VIGIL OF THE PRESENTATION

LONG and dark the nights, dim and
    short the days,
Mounting weary heights on our
    weary ways,
  Thee our God we praise.
Scaling heavenly heights by un-
    earthly ways,
Thee our God we praise all our
    nights and days,
  Thee our God we praise.
    Before 1893.

FEAST OF THE PRESENTATION

O FIRSTFRUITS of our grain,
Infant and Lamb appointed to be
    slain,
A Virgin and two doves were all
    Thy train,
With one old man for state,
When Thou didst enter first Thy
    Father's gate.

Since then Thy train hath been
Freeman and bondman, bishop, king
    and queen,

With flaming candles and with gar-
    lands green :
Oh happy all who wait
One day or thousand days around
    Thy gate !

And these have offered Thee,
Beside their hearts, great stores for
    charity,
Gold, frankincense, and myrrh ; if
    such may be
For savour or for state
Within the threshold of Thy golden
    gate.

Then snowdrops and my heart
I'll bring, to find those blacker than
    Thou art :
Yet, loving Lord, accept us in good
    part ;
And give me grace to wait,
A bruisèd reed bowed low before
    Thy gate.

Before 1882.

THE PURIFICATION OF ST. MARY THE VIRGIN

PURITY born of a Maid :
Was such a Virgin defiled ?
Nay, by no shade of a shade.
She offered her gift of pure love,
A dove with a fair fellow-dove.
She offered her Innocent Child
The Essence and Author of Love ;
The Lamb that indwelt by the
    Dove
Was spotless and holy and mild ;
More pure than all other,
More pure than His Mother,
Her God and Redeemer and Child.

Before 1886.

VIGIL OF THE ANNUNCIATION

ALL weareth, all wasteth,
All flitteth, all hasteth,
All of flesh and time :—
Sound, sweet heavenly chime,
Ring in the unutterable eternal
    prime.

Man hopeth, man feareth,
Man droopeth :—Christ cheereth,
Compassing release,
Comforting with peace,
Promising rest where strife and
    anguish cease.

Saints waking, saints sleeping,
Rest well in safe keeping ;
Well they rest to-day
While they watch and pray,—
But their to-morrow's rest what
    tongue shall say ?

Before 1893.

FEAST OF THE ANNUNCIATION

WHERETO shall we liken this Blessed
    Mary Virgin,
Fruitful shoot from Jesse's root
    graciously emerging ?
Lily we might call her, but Christ
    alone is white ;
Rose delicious, but that Jesus is the
    one Delight ;
Flower of women, but her Firstborn
    is mankind's one flower :
He the Sun lights up all moons thro'
    their radiant hour.
'Blessed among women, highly
    favoured,' thus
Glorious Gabriel hailed her, teaching
    words to us :

Whom devoutly copying we too cry
    'All hail!'
Echoing on the music of glorious
    Gabriel.
Before 1886.

HERSELF a rose, who bore the Rose,
    She bore the Rose and felt its
        thorn.
    All Loveliness new-born
Took on her bosom its repose,
    And slept and woke there night
        and morn.

Lily herself, she bore the one
    Fair Lily; sweeter, whiter, far
    Than she or others are:
The Sun of Righteousness her Son,
    She was His morning star.

She gracious, He essential Grace,
    He was the Fountain, she the rill:
    Her goodness to fulfil
And gladness, with proportioned pace
    He led her steps thro' good and
        ill.

Christ's mirror she of grace and love,
    Of beauty and of life and death:
    By hope and love and faith
Transfigured to His Likeness, 'Dove,
    Spouse, Sister, Mother,' Jesus
        saith.
Before 1882.

ST. MARK

ONCE like a broken bow Mark
    sprang aside;
Yet grace recalled him to a worthier
    course,
To feeble hands and knees increas-
    ing force,
    Till God was magnified.

And now a strong Evangelist, St.
    Mark
Hath for his sign a Lion in his
    strength;
And thro' the stormy water's breadth
    and length
    He helps to steer God's Ark.

Thus calls he sinners to be peni-
    tents,
He kindles penitents to high desire,
He mounts before them to the sphere
    of saints,
    And bids them come up higher.
Before 1882.

ST. BARNABAS

'Now when we had discovered Cyprus, we
left it on the left hand.'—*Acts* xxi. 3.
'We sailed under Cyprus, because the
winds were contrary.'—*Acts* xxvii. 4.

ST. BARNABAS, with John his sister's
    son,
    Set sail for Cyprus; leaving in
        their wake
That Chosen Vessel who for Jesus'
    sake
Proclaimed the Gentiles and the
    Jews at one.

Divided while united, each must run
    His mighty course not hell should
        overtake;
    And pressing toward the mark
        must own the ache
Of love, and sigh for heaven not yet
    begun.
For saints in life-long exile yearn to
    touch
    Warm human hands, and com-
        mune face to face;
        But these we know not ever
        met again:

Yet once St. Paul at distance over-
      much
   Just sighted Cyprus; and once
      more in vain
   Neared it and passed;—not there
      his landing-place.

Before 1882.

VIGIL OF ST. PETER

O JESU, gone so far apart
   Only my heart can follow Thee,
That look which pierced St. Peter's
      heart
      Turn now on me.

Thou who dost search me thro' and
      thro'
   And mark the crooked ways I
      went,
Look on me, Lord, and make me too
      Thy penitent.

Before 1893.

ST. PETER

'LAUNCH out into the deep,' Christ
      spake of old
   To Peter: and he launched into
      the deep;
   Strengthened should tempest wake
      which lay asleep,
Strengthened to suffer heat or suffer
      cold.
Thus, in Christ's Prescience: patient
      to behold
   A fall, a rise, a scaling Heaven's
      high steep;
   Prescience of Love, which deigned
      to overleap
The mire of human errors manifold.

Lord, Lover of Thy Peter, and of him
   Beloved with craving of a humbled
      heart
   Which eighteen hundred years
      have satisfied;
Hath he his throne among Thy
      Seraphim
   Who love? or sits he on a throne
      apart,
   Unique, near Thee, to love Thee
      human-eyed?

Before 1893.

ST. PETER once: 'Lord, dost Thou
      wash my feet?'—
   Much more I say: Lord, dost Thou
      stand and knock
   At my closed heart more rugged
      than a rock,
Bolted and barred, for Thy soft touch
      unmeet,
Nor garnished nor in any wise made
      sweet?
   Owls roost within and dancing
      satyrs mock.
   Lord, I have heard the crowing of
      the cock
And have not wept: ah, Lord, Thou
      knowest it.
Yet still I hear Thee knocking, still
      I hear:
'Open to Me, look on Me eye to
      eye,
   That I may wring thy heart and
      make it whole;
And teach thee love because I hold
      thee dear,
   And sup with thee in gladness
      soul with soul,
   And sup with thee in glory by
      and by.'

Before 1893.

I FOLLOWED Thee, my God, I
    followed Thee
  To see the end :
I turned back flying from Gethse-
    mane,
Turned back on flying steps to see
  Thy Face, my God, my Friend.

Even fleeing from Thee my heart
    clave to Thee :
  I turned perforce
Constrained, yea chained by love
    which maketh free ;
I turned perforce, and silently
  Followed along Thy course.

Lord, didst Thou know that I was
    following Thee ?
  I weak and small
Yet Thy true lover, mean tho' I must
    be,
Sinning and sorrowing—didst Thou
    see ?
  O Lord, Thou sawest all.

I thought I had been strong to die
    for Thee ;
  I disbelieved
Thy word of warning spoken
    patiently :
My heart cried, 'That be far from
    me,'
  Till Thy bruised heart I grieved.

Once I had urged : 'Lord, this be
    far from Thee' : —
  Rebel to light,
It needed first that Thou shouldst
    die for me
Or ever I could plumb and see
  Love's lovely depth and height.

Alas that I should trust myself, not
    Thee ;
  Not trust Thy word :
I faithless slumberer in Gethsemane,
Blinded and rash ; who instantly
  Put trust, but in a sword.

Ah Lord, if even at the last in Thee
    I had put faith,
I might even at the last have coun-
    selled me,
And not have heaped up cruelty
  To sting Thee in Thy death.

Alas for me, who bore to think on
    Thee
  And yet to lie !
While Thou, O Lord, didst bear to
    look on me
Goaded by fear to blasphemy,
  And break my heart and die.

No balm I find in Gilead, yet in Thee
    Nailed to Thy palm
I find a balm that wrings and com-
    forts me :
Balm wrung from Thee by agony,
  My balm, mine only balm.

Oh blessed John who standeth close
    to Thee,
  With Magdalene,
And Thine own Mother praying
    silently,
Yea, blessed above women she,
  Now blessed even as then.

And blessed the scorned thief who
    hangs by Thee,
  Whose thirsting mouth
Thirsts for Thee more than water,
    whose eyes see,
Whose lips confess in ecstasy
  Nor feel their parching drouth.

Like as the hart the water-brooks I
    Thee
  Desire, my hands
I stretch to Thee; O kind Lord,
    pity me:
Lord, I have wept, wept bitterly,
  I driest of dry lands.

Lord, I am standing far far off from
    Thee;
  Yet is my heart
Hanging with Thee upon the ac-
    cursed tree;
The nails, the thorns, pierce Thee
    and me:
  My God, I claim my part—

Scarce in Thy throne and kingdom;
    yet with Thee
  In shame, in loss,
In Thy forsaking, in Thine agony:
Love crucified, behold even me,
  Me also bear Thy cross.
Before 1882.

VIGIL OF ST. BARTHOLOMEW

LORD, to Thine own grant watchful
    hearts and eyes;
  Hearts strung to prayer, awake
    while eyelids sleep;
  Eyes patient till the end to watch
    and weep.
So will sleep nourish power to wake
    and rise
With Virgins who keep vigil and
    are wise,
  To sow among all sowers who
    shall reap,
  From out man's deep to call Thy
    vaster deep,
And tread the uphill track to
    Paradise.

Sweet souls! so patient that they
    make no moan,
  So calm on journey that they
    seem at rest,
  So rapt in prayer that half they
    dwell in heaven,
  Thankful for all withheld and
    all things given;
  So lit by love that Christ shines
    manifest
Transfiguring their aspects to His
    own.
Before 1893.

ST. BARTHOLOMEW

HE bore an agony whereof the
    name
  Hath turned his fellows pale:
But what if God should call us to
    the same,
  Should call, and we should fail?

Nor earth nor sea could swallow up
    our shame,
  Nor darkness draw a veil:
For he endured that agony whose
    name
  Hath made his fellows quail.
Before 1886.

ST. MICHAEL AND ALL ANGELS

'Ye that excel in strength.'

SERVICE and strength, God's Angels
    and Archangels;
  His Seraphs fires, and lamps His
    Cherubim:
Glory to God from highest and from
    lowest,
  Glory to God in everlasting hymn
    From all His creatures.

Princes that serve, and Powers that
    work His pleasure,
  Heights that soar to'ard Him,
    Depths that sink to'ard Him;
Flames fire out-flaming, chill beside
    His Essence;
  Insight all-probing, save where
    scant and dim
      To'ard its Creator.

Sacred and free exultant in God's
    pleasure,
  His Will their solace, thus they
    wait on Him;
And shout their shout of ecstasy
    eternal,
  And trim their splendours that
    they burn not dim
      To'ard their Creator.

Wherefore with Angels, wherefore
    with Archangels,
  With lofty Cherubs, loftier Sera-
    phim,
We laud and magnify our God
    Almighty,
  And veil our faces rendering love
    to Him
      With all His creatures.
  Before 1882.

VIGIL OF ALL SAINTS

Up, my drowsing eyes!
  Up, my sinking heart!
Up to Jesus Christ arise!
  Claim your part
In all raptures of the skies.

Yet a little while,
  Yet a little way,
Saints shall reap and rest and smile
  All the day.
Up! let's trudge another mile.
  Before 1886.

ALL SAINTS

As grains of sand, as stars, as drops
    of dew,
  Numbered and treasured by the
    Almighty Hand,
  The Saints triumphant throng
    that holy land
Where all things and Jerusalem are
    new.
We know not half they sing or half
    they do,
  But this we know, they rest and
    understand;
  While like a conflagration freshly
    fanned
Their love glows upward, outward,
    thro' and thro'.
Lo like a stream of incense
    launched on flame
  Fresh Saints stream up from
    death to life above,
  To shine among those others
    and rejoice:
What matters tribulation whence
    they came?
  All love and only love can find
    a voice
  Where God makes glad His
    Saints, for God is Love.
Before 1886.

ALL SAINTS: MARTYRS

Once slain for Him who first was
    slain for them,
  Now made alive in Him for ever-
    more,
  All luminous and lovely in their
    gore,
With no more buffeting winds or
    tides to stem,
The Martyrs look for New Jerusalem;

And cry 'How long?' remember-
  ing all they bore,
'How long?' with heart and eyes
  sent on before
Toward consummated throne and
  diadem.
'How long?' White robes are
  given to their desire;
'How long?' deep rest that is
  and is to be;
  With a great promise of the
    oncoming host,
Loves to their love and fires to flank
  their fire:
  So rest they, worshiping in-
    cessantly
    One God, the Father, Son, and
      Holy Ghost.
Before 1893.

'I gave a sweet smell.'

SAINTS are like roses when they
    flush rarest,
Saints are like lilies when they
    bloom fairest,
  Saints are like violets sweetest of
    their kind:
    Bear in mind
    This to-day. Then to-
      morrow:
All like roses rarer than the rarest,
All like lilies fairer than the fairest,
  All like violets sweeter than we
    know.
    Be it so.
    To-morrow blots out sorrow.
Before 1886.

HARK! the Alleluias of the great
    salvation,
  Still beginning, never ending,
    still begin,
The thunder of an endless adoration:

Open ye the gates, that the righteous
    nation
  Which have kept the truth may
    enter in.

Roll ye back, ye pearls, on your
    twelvefold station:
  No more deaths to die, no more
    fights to win!
Lift your heads, ye gates, that the
    righteous nation,
Led by the Great Captain of their
    sole salvation,
  Having kept the truth, may enter
    in.
Before 1893.

A SONG FOR THE LEAST OF ALL
SAINTS

LOVE is the key of life and death,
  Of hidden heavenly mystery:
Of all Christ is, of all He saith,
    Love is the key.

As three times to His Saint He saith,
  He saith to me, He saith to thee,
Breathing His Grace-conferring
    Breath:
    'Lovest thou Me?'

Ah, Lord, I have such feeble faith,
  Such feeble hope to comfort me:
But love it is, is strong as death,
    And I love Thee.
Before 1893.

SUNDAY BEFORE ADVENT

THE end of all things is at hand.
  We all
  Stand in the balance trembling
    as we stand;
Or if not trembling, tottering to a fall.
  The end of all things is at hand.

O hearts of men, covet the un-
    ending land !
O hearts of men, covet the musical,
    Sweet, never-ending waters of
    that strand !

While Earth shows poor, a slippery
    rolling ball,
    And Hell looms vast, a gulf un-
    plumbed, unspanned,
And Heaven flings wide its gates to
    great and small,
The end of all things is at hand.
Before 1893.

THERE REMAINETH THERE-
FORE A REST

IN the grave will be no space
    For the purple of the proud—
    They must mingle with the crowd :
    In the wrappings of a shroud
Jewels would be out of place.

There no laughter shall be heard,
    Nor the heavy sound of sighs :
    Sleep shall seal the aching eyes :
    All the ancient and the wise
There shall utter not a word.

Yet it may be we shall hear
    How the mounting skylark sings
    And the bell for matins rings ;
    Or perhaps the whisperings
Of white Angels sweet and clear.

What a calm when all is done,
    Wearing vigil, prayer, and fast !
    All fulfilled from first to last :
    All the length of time gone past
And eternity begun.

Fear and hope and chastening rod
    Urge us on the narrow way :
    Bear we still as best we may
    Heat and burden of the day,
Struggling, panting up to God.
17 *February* 1854.

PARADISE

ONCE in a dream I saw the flowers
    That bud and bloom in Paradise ;
    More fair they are than waking
        eyes
Have seen in all this world of ours.
And faint the perfume-bearing rose,
    And faint the lily on its stem,
And faint the perfect violet,
    Compared with them.

I heard the songs of Paradise :
    Each bird sat singing in his place ;
    A tender song so full of grace
It soared like incense to the skies.
Each bird sat singing to his mate
    Soft cooing notes among the trees :
The nightingale herself were cold
    To such as these.

I saw the fourfold River flow,
    And deep it was, with golden sand ;
    It flowed between a mossy land
With murmured music grave and low.
It hath refreshment for all thirst,
    For fainting spirits strength and
        rest ;
Earth holds not such a draught as
        this
    From east to west.

The Tree of Life stood budding
    there,
    Abundant with its twelvefold
        fruits ;
    Eternal sap sustains its roots,
Its shadowing branches fill the air.

Its leaves are healing for the world,
    Its fruit the hungry world can feed,
Sweeter than honey to the taste
    And balm indeed.

I saw the Gate called Beautiful;
    And looked, but scarce could look within;
I saw the golden streets begin,
And outskirts of the glassy pool.
Oh harps, oh crowns of plenteous stars,
    Oh green palm branches many-leaved—
Eye hath not seen, nor ear hath heard,
    Nor heart conceived.

I hope to see these things again,
    But not as once in dreams by night;
To see them with my very sight,
And touch and handle and attain:
To have all heaven beneath my feet
    For narrow way that once they trod;
To have my part with all the saints,
    And with my God.

28 February 1854.

YE HAVE FORGOTTEN THE EXHORTATION

ANGEL

Bury thy dead, dear friend,
    Between the night and day:
Where depths of summer shade are cool,
    And murmurs of a summer pool
    And windy murmurs stray:—

SOUL

Ah gone away,
    Ah dear and lost delight,
Gone from me and for ever out of sight!

ANGEL

Bury thy dead, dear love,
    And make his bed most fair above:
The latest buds shall still
Blow there, and the first violets too,
    And there a turtle-dove
    Shall brood and coo:—

SOUL

I cannot make the nest
So warm but he may find it chill
    In solitary rest.

ANGEL

Bury thy dead heart-deep:
Take patience till the sun be set:
There are no tears for him to weep,
    No doubts to haunt him yet:
Take comfort, he will not forget:—

SOUL

Then I will watch beside his sleep:
    Will watch alone,
    And make my moan
Because the harvest is so long to reap.

ANGEL

The fields are white to harvest, look and see,
    Are white abundantly.

The harvest-moon shines full
    and clear,
  The harvest-time is near,
  Be of good cheer :—

SOUL

  Ah woe is me!
  I have no heart for harvest-
    time,
Grown sick with hope deferred from
    chime to chime.

ANGEL

But One can give thee heart, thy
    Lord and his,
  Can raise both thee and
    him
  To shine with Seraphim,
And pasture where the eternal
    fountain is ;
  Can give thee of that tree
  Whose leaves are health for
    thee ;
  Can give thee robes made clean
    and white,
  And love, and all delight,
And beauty where the day turns not
    to night.
  Who knocketh at His door,
  And presseth in, goes out no
    more.
  Kneel as thou hast not knelt
    before—
  The time is short — and
    smite
Upon thy breast and pray with all
    thy might :—

SOUL

O Lord, my heart is broken for my
    sin :
  Yet hasten Thine own day
  And come away.

Is not time full ? Oh put the sickl[e]
    in,
  O Lord, begin !
10 *May* 1854.

THE WORLD

By day she woos me, soft, exceed[-]
    ing fair :
  But all night as the moon s[o]
    changeth she ;
  Loathsome and foul with hideou[s]
    leprosy,
And subtle serpents gliding in he[r]
    hair.
By day she woos me to the oute[r]
    air,
  Ripe fruits, sweet flowers, an[d]
    full satiety :
  But thro' the night a beast sh[e]
    grins at me,
A very monster void of love and
    prayer.
By day she stands a lie : by nigh[t]
    she stands
  In all the naked horror of th[e]
    truth,
With pushing horns and clawed a[nd]
    clutching hands.
Is this a friend indeed, that I sho[uld]
    sell
  My soul to her, give her my [life]
    and youth,
Till my feet, cloven too, take h[old]
    on hell ?
27 *June* 1854.

UNFORGOTTEN

O UNFORGOTTEN !
How long ago ? one spirit saith.
As long as life even unto death.
The passage of a poor frail bre[ath]

O unforgotten!
An unforgotten load of love,
A load of grief all griefs above,
A blank blank nest without its dove.

As long as time is:—
No longer? Time is but a span,
The dalliance-space of empty man:
And is this all immortals can?

Ever and ever,
Beyond all time, beyond all space:
Now shadows darkening heart and
  face;
Then glory in a glorious place.

Sad heart and spirit,
Bowed now, yea broken, for a while—
Lagging and toiling mile by mile,
Yet pressing toward the Eternal
  Smile.

O joy eternal!
O youth eternal without flaw!—
Thee not the blessed Angels saw,
Rapt in august adoring awe.

Not the dead have thee,
Not yet, O all-surpassing peace:
Not till this veiling world shall cease
And harvest yield its whole increase.

Not the dead know thee,
Not dead nor living nor unborn:
Who in the new-sown field at morn
Can measure out the harvest corn?—

Yet they shall know thee:
And we with them, and unborn men
With us, shall know and have thee
  when
The single grain shall wax to ten.
  1855.

ZION SAID

O SLAIN for love of me, canst Thou
  be cold,
 Be cold and far away in my
   distress?
Is Thy love also changed, growing
  less and less,
 That carried me through all the
   days of old?
O Slain for love of me, O Love
  untold,
 See how I flag and fail through
   weariness:
I flag, while sleepless foes dog
  me and press
On me: behold, O Lord, O Love,
  behold!
I am sick for home, the home of
  love indeed—
 I am sick for Love, that dearest
   name for Thee:
Thou who hast bled, see how my
  heart doth bleed:
Open thy bleeding Side and let me
  in:
Oh hide me in Thy Heart from
  doubt and sin,
 Oh take me to Thyself and comfort
   me.
 31 *December* 1855.

HYMN AFTER GABRIELE ROSSETTI

FIRST VERSION

T' amo e fra dolci affanni.

MY Lord, my love! in love's unrest
 How often have I said,
'Blessed that John who on Thy
  breast
  Reclined his head.'

Thy touch it was, Love's Pelican,
   Transformed him from above,
And made him amongst men the man
   To show forth holy love.

Yet shall I envy blessed John?
   Nay not so verily,
While Thou indwellest as Thine own
   Me, even me:
Upbuilding with Thy Manhood's
   worth
My frail humanity;
Yea Thy Divinehood pouring forth,
   In fullness filling me.

Me, Lord, Thy temple consecrate,
   Me unto Thee alone;
Within my heart set up Thy state
   And mount Thy throne:
The Seraphim in ecstasy
   Fall prone around Thy house,
For which of them hath tasted Thee,
   My Manna and my Spouse?

Now Thou dost wear me for a robe
   And sway and warm me through,
I scarce seem lesser than the globe,
   Thy temple too:
O God, who for Thy dwelling-place
   Dost take delight in me,
The ungirt immensity of space
   Hath not encompassed Thee.

SECOND VERSION

My Lord, my Love! in pleasant pain
   How often have I said,
'Blessed that John who on Thy breast
   Laid down his head.'
It was that contact all divine
   Transformed him from above,
And made him amongst men the man
   To show forth holy love.

Yet shall I envy blessed John?
   Nay not so verily,
Now that Thou, Lord, both Man and God,
   Dost dwell in me:
Upbuilding with Thy Manhood's might
   My frail humanity;
Yea, Thy Divinehood pouring forth,
   In fullness filling me.

Me, Lord, Thy temple consecrate,
   Even me to Thee alone;
Lord, reign upon my willing heart
   Which is Thy throne:
To Thee the Seraphim fall down
   Adoring round Thy house;
For which of them hath tasted Thee,
   My Manna and my Spouse?

Now that Thy life lives in my soul
   And sways and warms it through,
I scarce seem lesser than the world,
   Thy temple too.
O God, who dwellest in my heart,
   My God who fillest me,
The broad immensity itself
   Hath not encompassed Thee.

Circa 1855.

I WILL LIFT UP MINE EYES UNTO THE HILLS

I AM pale with sick desire,
   For my heart is far away
From this world's fitful fire
   And this world's waning day;
In a dream it overleaps
   A world of tedious ills
To where the sunshine sleeps
   On the everlasting hills.—

Say the Saints: 'There Angels ease us
  Glorified and white.'
They say: 'We rest in Jesus,
  Where is not day or night.'

My soul saith: I have sought
  For a home that is not gained,
I have spent yet nothing bought,
  Have laboured but not attained;
My pride strove to mount and grow,
  And hath but dwindled down;
My love sought love, and lo!
  Hath not attained its crown.—
Say the Saints: 'Fresh souls increase us,
  None languish or recede.'
They say: 'We love our Jesus,
  And He loves us indeed.'

I cannot rise above,
  I cannot rest beneath,
I cannot find out love,
  Or escape from death;
Dear hopes and joys gone by
  Still mock me with a name;
My best beloved die,
  And I cannot die with them.—
Say the Saints: 'No deaths decrease us
  Where our rest is glorious.'
They say: 'We live in Jesus
  Who once died for us.'

Oh my soul, she beats her wings
  And pants to fly away
Up to immortal things
  In the heavenly day:
Yet she flags and almost faints:
  Can such be meant for me?—
'Come and see,' say the Saints;
  Saith Jesus: 'Come and see.'

Say the Saints: 'His pleasures please us
  Before God and the Lamb.'
'Come and taste My sweets,' saith Jesus:
  'Be with Me where I am.'

1 *February* 1856.

HOW LONG?

My life is long—Not so the Angels say
Who watch me waste it, trembling whilst they weigh
Against eternity my lavished day.

My life is long—Not so the Saints in peace
Judge, filled with plenitude that cannot cease:
Oh life was short which bought such large increase!

My life is long—Christ's word is different:
The heat and burden of the day were spent
On Him,—to me refreshing times are sent.

Give me an Angel's heart, that day nor night
Rests not from adoration its delight,
Still crying 'Holy holy' in the height.

Give me the heart of Saints, who, laid at rest
In better Paradise than Abraham's breast,
In the everlasting Rock have made their nest.

Give me Thy heart, O Christ, who thirty-three
Slow years of sorrow countedst short for me,
That where Thou art there Thy beloved might be.
14 *April* 1856.

AMEN

It is over. What is over?
  Nay, now much is over truly!—
Harvest days we toiled to sow for;
  Now the sheaves are gathered newly,
  Now the wheat is garnered duly.

It is finished. What is finished?
  Much is finished known or unknown:
Lives are finished; time diminished;
  Was the fallow field left unsown?
  Will these buds be always unblown?

It suffices. What suffices?
  All suffices reckoned rightly:
Spring shall bloom where now the ice is,
  Roses make the bramble sightly,
  And the quickening sun shine brightly,
  And the latter wind blow lightly,
And my garden teem with spices.
20 *April* 1856.

A MARTYR

It is over the horrible pain,
  All is over the struggle and doubt:
She's asleep though her friends stand and weep,
  She's asleep while the multitudes shout:
Not to wake to her anguish again,
  Not to wake until death is cast out.

Stoop, look at the beautiful face,
  See the smile on the satisfied mouth,
The hands crost—she hath conquered not lost:
  She hath drunk who was fevered with drouth:
She shall sleep in her safe resting-place
  While the hawk spreads her wings toward the South.

She shall sleep while slow seasons are given,
  While daylight and darkness go round:
Her heart is at rest in its nest,
  Her body at rest in the ground:
She has travelled the long road to heaven,
  She sought it and now she has found.

Will you follow the track that she trod,
  Will you tread in her footsteps, my friend?
That pathway is rough, but enough
  Are the light and the balm that attend.
Do I tread in her steps, O my God,—
  Shall I joy with her joy in the end?
23 *April* 1856.

NOW THEY DESIRE

There is a sleep we have not slept,
  Safe in a bed unknown:
There hearts are staunched that long have wept
  Alone or bled alone:

Sweet sleep that dreams not, or
    whose dream
  Is foretaste of the truth:
Sweet sleep whose sweets are what
    they seem,
  Refreshing more than youth.

There is a sea whose waters clear
  Are never tempest-tost:
There is a home whose children dear
  Are saved, not one is lost:
There Cherubim and Seraphim
  And Angels dwell with Saints,
Whose lustre no more dwindleth dim,
  Whose ardour never faints.

There is a Love which fills desire
  And can our love requite:
Like fire it draws our lesser fire,
  Like greater light our light:
For it we agonize in strife,
  We yearn, we famish thus—
Lo in the far-off land of life
  Doth it not yearn for us?

O fair, O fair Jerusalem,
  How fair, how far away,
When shall we see thy Jasper-gem
  That gives thee light for day?
Thy sea of glass like fire, thy streets
  Of glass like virgin gold,
Thy royal Elders on their seats,
  Thy four Beasts manifold?

Fair City of delights, the Bride
  In raiment white and clean,
When shall we see thee loving-eyed,
  Sun-girdled, happy Queen?
Without a wrinkle or a spot,
  Blood-cleansed, blood-purchased
    once:
In how fair ground is fallen the lot
  Of all thy happy sons!

Dove's eyes beneath thy parted lock,
  A dove's soft voice is thine:
Thy nest is safe within the Rock,
  Safe in the very Vine:
Thy walls salvation buildeth them
  And all thy gates are praise,
O fair, O fair Jerusalem,
  In sevenfold day of days.

13 *August* 1856.

A CHRISTMAS CAROL

For my Godchildren.

THE Shepherds had an Angel,
  The Wise Men had a star,
But what have I, a little child,
  To guide me home from far,
Where glad stars sing together
  And singing angels are?—

Lord Jesus is my Guardian,
  So I can nothing lack:
The lambs lie in His bosom
  Along life's dangerous track:
The wilful lambs that go astray
  He bleeding fetches back.

Lord Jesus is my guiding star,
  My beacon-light in heaven:
He leads me step by step along
  The path of life uneven:
He, true light, leads me to that
    land
  Whose day shall be as seven.

Those Shepherds through the lonely
    night
  Sat watching by their sheep,
Until they saw the heavenly host
  Who neither tire nor sleep,
All singing 'Glory glory'
  In festival they keep.

Christ watches me, His little lamb,
    Cares for me day and night,
That I may be His own in heaven:
    So angels clad in white
Shall sing their 'Glory glory'
    For my sake in the height.

The Wise Men left their country
    To journey morn by morn,
With gold and frankincense and myrrh,
    Because the Lord was born:
God sent a star to guide them
    And sent a dream to warn.

My life is like their journey,
    Their star is like God's book;
I must be like those good Wise Men
    With heavenward heart and look:
But shall I give no gifts to God?—
    What precious gifts they took!

Lord, I will give my love to Thee,
    Than gold much costlier,
Sweeter to Thee than frankincense,
    More prized than choicest myrrh:
Lord, make me dearer day by day,
    Day by day holier;

Nearer and dearer day by day:
    Till I my voice unite,
And sing my 'Glory glory'
    With angels clad in white;
All 'Glory glory' given to Thee
    Through all the heavenly height.
6 October 1856.

NOT YOURS BUT YOU

'HE died for me: what can I offer Him?
    Toward Him swells incense of perpetual prayer:
His court wear crowns and aureoles round their hair:'
His ministers are subtle Cherubim;
Ring within ring, white intense Seraphim
    Leap like immortal lightnings through the air.
What shall I offer Him? defiled and bare,
My spirit broken and my brightness dim.'—
'Give Me thy youth.'—'I yield it to Thy rod,
    As Thou didst yield Thy prime of youth for me.'—
      'Give Me thy life.'—'I give it breath by breath;
    As Thou didst give Thy life so give I Thee.'—
'Give Me thy love.'—'So be it, my God, my God,
    As Thou hast loved me even to bitter death.'
27 October 1856.

AFTER THIS THE JUDGMENT

As eager homebound traveller to the goal,
    Or steadfast seeker on an unsearched main,
Or martyr panting for an aureole,
    My fellow-pilgrims pass me, and attain
That hidden mansion of perpetual peace
    Where keen desire and hope dwell free from pain.
That gate stands open of perennial ease;
    I view the glory till I partly long,
Yet lack the fire of love which quickens these.

O passing Angel, speed me with a song,
A melody of heaven to reach my heart
And rouse me to the race and make me strong;
Till in such music I take up my part
Swelling those Hallelujahs full of rest,
One, tenfold, hundredfold, with heavenly art,
Fulfilling north and south and east and west,
Thousand, ten thousandfold, innumerable,
All blent in one yet each one manifest;
Each one distinguished and beloved as well
As if no second voice in earth or heaven
Were lifted up the Love of God to tell.
Ah Love of God, which thine own Self hast given
To me most poor, and made me rich in love,
Love that dost pass the tenfold seven times seven,
Draw Thou mine eyes, draw Thou my heart above,
My treasure and my heart store Thou in Thee;
Brood over me with yearnings of a dove;
Be Husband, Brother, closest Friend to me;
Love me as very mother loves her son,
Her sucking firstborn fondled on her knee:
Yea, more than mother loves her little one;
For, earthly, even a mother may forget
And feel no pity for its piteous moan.
But thou, O Love of God, remember yet,
Through the dry desert, through the waterflood
(Life, death), until the Great White Throne is set.
If now I am sick in chewing the bitter cud
Of sweet past sin, though solaced by Thy grace
And ofttimes strengthened by Thy Flesh and Blood,
How shall I then stand up before Thy face
When from Thine eyes repentance shall be hid
And utmost Justice stand in Mercy's place?
When every sin I thought or spoke or did
Shall meet me at the inexorable bar,
And there be no man standing in the mid
To plead for me; while star fallen after star
With heaven and earth are like a ripened shock,
And all time's mighty works and wonders are
Consumed as in a moment; when no rock
Remains to fall on me, no tree to hide,
But I stand all creation's gazing-stock,
Exposed and comfortless on every side,
Placed trembling in the final balances
Whose poise this hour, this moment, must be tried.—

Ah Love of God, if greater love than
 this
 Hath no man, that a man die for
 his friend,
And if such love of love Thine own
 Love is,
 Plead with Thyself, with me,
 before the end ;
Redeem me from the irrevocable past;
 Pitch Thou Thy Presence round
 me to defend ;
Yea seek with piercèd feet, yea hold
 me fast
 With piercèd hands whose wounds
 were made by love.
Not what I am, remember what
 Thou wast
 When darkness hid from Thee
 Thy heavens above,
And sin Thy Father's Face, while
 Thou didst drink
 The bitter cup of death, didst
 taste thereof
For every man ; while Thou wast
 nigh to sink
 Beneath the intense intolerable
 rod,
Grown sick of love ; not what I am,
 but think
 Thy Life then ransomed mine,
 my God, my God !
 12 *December* 1856.

OLD AND NEW YEAR
DITTIES

1

New Year met me somewhat sad :
 Old Year leaves me tired,
Stripped of favourite things I had,
 Baulked of much desired :
Yet farther on my road to-day,
God willing, farther on my way.

New Year coming on apace,
 What have you to give me ?
Bring you scathe or bring you grace,
Face me with an honest face,
 You shall not deceive me :
Be it good or ill, be it what you will,
It needs shall help me on my road,
My rugged way to heaven, please
 God.
 13 *December* 1856.

2

Watch with me, men, women, and
 children dear,
You whom I love, for whom I hope
 and fear,
Watch with me this last vigil of the
 year.
Some hug their business, some their
 pleasure scheme ;
Some seize the vacant hour to sleep
 or dream ;
Heart locked in heart some kneel
 and watch apart.

Watch with me, blessed spirits, who
 delight
All through the holy night to walk
 in white,
Or take your ease after the long-
 drawn fight.
I know not if they watch with me :
 I know
They count this eve of resurrection
 slow,
And cry 'How long?' with urgent
 utterance strong.

Watch with me, Jesus, in my loneli-
 ness :
Though others say me nay, yet say
 Thou yes ;
Though others pass me by, stop
 Thou to bless.

Yea, Thou dost stop with me this
   vigil night;
To-night of pain, to-morrow of
   delight:
I, Love, am Thine; Thou, Lord my
   God, art mine.

31 December 1858.

3

Passing away, saith the World,
   passing away:
Chances, beauty, and youth, sapped
   day by day:
Thy life never continueth in one
   stay.
Is the eye waxen dim, is the dark
   hair changing to grey
That hath won neither laurel nor
   bay?
I shall clothe myself in Spring and
   bud in May:
Thou, root-stricken, shalt not rebuild
   thy decay
On my bosom for aye.
Then I answered: Yea.

Passing away, saith my Soul, passing
   away:
With its burden of fear and hope,
   of labour and play,
Hearken what the past doth witness
   and say:
Rust in thy gold, a moth is in thine
   array,
A canker is in thy bud, thy leaf
   must decay.
At midnight, at cockcrow, at morn-
   ing, one certain day
Lo the Bridegroom shall come and
   shall not delay;
Watch thou and pray.
Then I answered: Yea.

Passing away, saith my God, passing
   away:
Winter passeth after the long delay:
New grapes on the vine, new figs
   on the tender spray,
Turtle calleth turtle in Heaven's
   May.
Though I tarry, wait for Me, trust
   Me, watch and pray:
Arise, come away, night is past and
   lo it is day,
My love, My sister, My spouse, thou
   shalt hear Me say.
Then I answered: Yea.

31 December 1860.

A BETTER RESURRECTION

I HAVE no wit, no words, no tears;
   My heart within me like a stone
Is numbed too much for hopes or
   fears.
   Look right, look left, I dwell alone;
I lift mine eyes, but dimmed with
   grief
   No everlasting hills I see;
My life is in the falling leaf:
   O Jesus, quicken me.

My life is like a faded leaf,
   My harvest dwindled to a husk:
Truly my life is void and brief
   And tedious in the barren dusk;
My life is like a frozen thing,
   No bud nor greenness can I see;
Yet rise it shall—the sap of Spring;
   O Jesus, rise in me.

My life is like a broken bowl,
   A broken bowl that cannot hold
One drop of water for my soul
   Or cordial in the searching cold:

Cast in the fire the perished thing;
  Melt and remould it, till it be
A royal cup for Him, my King:
  O Jesus, drink of me.
30 *June* 1857.

THE HEART KNOWETH ITS OWN BITTERNESS

WHEN all the over-work of life
  Is finished once, and fast asleep
We swerve no more beneath the knife
  But taste that silence cool and deep;
Forgetful of the highways rough,
  Forgetful of the thorny scourge,
  Forgetful of the tossing surge,
Then shall we find it is enough?

How can we say 'enough' on earth—
  'Enough' with such a craving heart?
I have not found it since my birth,
  But still have bartered part for part.
I have not held and hugged the whole,
  But paid the old to gain the new:
  Much have I paid, yet much is due,
Till I am beggared sense and soul.

I used to labour, used to strive
  For pleasure with a restless will:
Now if I save my soul alive
  All else what matters, good or ill?
I used to dream alone, to plan
  Unspoken hopes and days to come:—
  Of all my past this is the sum—
I will not lean on child of man.

To give, to give, not to receive!
  I long to pour myself, my soul,
Not to keep back or count or leave,
  But king with king to give the whole.
I long for one to stir my deep—
  I have had enough of help and gift—
  I long for one to search and sift
Myself, to take myself and keep.

You scratch my surface with your pin,
  You stroke me smooth with hushing breath:—
Nay pierce, nay probe, nay dig within,
  Probe my quick core and sound my depth.
You call me with a puny call,
  You talk, you smile, you nothing do:
  How should I spend my heart on you,
My heart that so outweighs you all?

Your vessels are by much too strait:
  Were I to pour, you could not hold.—
Bear with me: I must bear to wait,
  A fountain sealed through heat and cold.
Bear with me days or months or years:
  Deep must call deep until the end
  When friend shall no more envy friend
Nor vex his friend at unawares.

Not in this world of hope deferred,
  This world of perishable stuff:—

Eye hath not seen nor ear hath heard
  Nor heart conceived that full
    'enough':
Here moans the separating sea,
  Here harvests fail, here breaks
    the heart:
  There God shall join and no
    man part,
I full of Christ and Christ of me.
27 August 1857.

DIVERS WORLDS. TIME AND ETERNITY

(*From 27 August 1857 to before 1893.*)

EARTH has clear call of daily bells,
  A chancel-vault of gloom and star,
  A rapture where the anthems are,
A thunder when the organ swells:
Alas, man's daily life—what else?—
Is out 'of tune with daily bells.

While Paradise accords the chimes
  Of Earth and Heaven, its patient
    pause
  Is rest fulfilling music's laws.
Saints sit and gaze, where oftentimes
Precursive flush of morning climbs
And air vibrates with coming chimes.
6 August 1858.

Escape to the Mountain.

I PEERED within, and saw a world
    of sin;
  Upward, and saw a world of
    righteousness;
Downward, and saw darkness and
    flame begin
  Which no man can express.

I girt me up, I gat me up to flee
  From face of darkness and devour-
    ing flame:
And fled I had, but guilt is load-
    ing me
  With dust of death and shame.

Yet still the light of righteousness
    beams pure,
  Beams to me from the world of
    far-off day:—
Lord, Who hast called them happy
    that endure,
  Lord, make me such as they.
Before 1893.

I LIFT mine eyes to see: earth
    vanisheth.
  I lift up wistful eyes and bend my
    knee:
Trembling, bowed down, and face to
    face with Death,
  I lift mine eyes to see.

  Lo what I see is Death that
    shadows me:
Yet whilst I, seeing, draw a shudder-
    ing breath,
  Death like a mist grows rare
    perceptibly.

Beyond the darkness light, beyond
    the scathe
  Healing, beyond the Cross a palm-
    branch tree,
Beyond Death Life, on evidence of
    faith:
  I lift mine eyes to see.
Before 1893.

Yet a little while.

HEAVEN is not far, tho' far the sky
  Overarching earth and main.
It takes not long to live and die,
  Die, revive, and rise again.

Not long: how long? Oh long re-
  echoing song!
O Lord, how long?
  Before 1893.

Behold, it was very good.

ALL things are fair, if we had eyes
    to see
  How first God made them goodly
    everywhere:
And goodly still in Paradise they
    be,—
  All things are fair.

O Lord, the solemn heavens Thy
    praise declare;
The multi-fashioned saints bring
    praise to Thee,
  As doves fly home and cast away
    their care.

As doves on divers branches of their
    tree,
  Perched high or low, sit all con-
    tented there,
Not mourning any more; in each
    degree
  All things are fair.
    Before 1893.

Whatsoever is right, that shall ye receive.

WHEN all the overwork of life
    Is finished once, and fallen asleep
We shrink no more beneath the knife,
    But having sown prepare to reap;
Delivered from the crossway rough,
    Delivered from the thorny scourge,
Delivered from the tossing surge,
Then shall we find—(please God!)
    —it is enough?

Not in this world of hope deferred,
    This world of perishable stuff;
Eye hath not seen, nor ear hath
    heard,
  Nor heart conceived that full
    'enough!';
Here moans the separating sea,
  Here harvests fail, here breaks the
    heart;
  There God shall join and no man
    part,
All one in Christ, so one—(please
    God!)—with me.
  27 *August* 1857.

THIS near-at-hand land breeds pain
    by measure:
That far-away land overflows with
    treasure
  Of heaped-up good pleasure.

Our land that we see is befouled by
    evil:
The land that we see not makes
    mirth and revel,
  Far from death and devil.

This land hath for music sobbing and
    sighing:
That land hath soft speech and sweet
    soft replying
  Of all loves undying.

This land hath for pastime errors and
    follies:
That land hath unending unflagging
    solace
  Of full-chanted 'Holies.'

'Up and away,' call the Angels to
    us;
'Come to our home where no foes
    pursue us,
  And no tears bedew us;

'Where that which riseth sets again
    never,
Where that which springeth flows in
    a river
        For ever and ever;

'Where harvest justifies labour of
    sowing,
Where that which budded comes to
    the blowing,
        Sweet beyond your knowing.

'Come and laugh with us, sing in
    our singing;
Come, yearn no more, but rest in
    your clinging.
        See what we are bringing;

'Crowns like our own crowns, robes
    for your wearing;
For love of you we kiss them in
    bearing,
        All good with you sharing:

'Over you gladdening, in you de-
    lighting;
Come from your famine, your failure,
    your fighting;
        Come to full wrong-righting.

'Come, where all balm is garnered
    to ease you;
Come, where all beauty is spread out
    to please you;
        Come, gaze upon Jesu.'
Before 1882.

'Was Thy Wrath against the Sea?'

THE sea laments with unappeasable
    Hankering wail of loss,
    Lifting its hands on high and
        passing by
    Out of the lovely light:
No foambow any more may crest
    that swell
Of clamorous waves which toss;
    Lifting its hands on high it
        passes by
    From light into the night.
Peace, peace, thou sea! God's wis-
    dom worketh well,
Assigns it crown or cross:
    Lift we all hands on high, and
        passing by
    Attest—God doeth right.
Before 1893.

And there was no more Sea.

VOICES from above and from be-
    neath,
Voices of creation near and far,
Voices out of life and out of death,
    Out of measureless space,
    Sun, moon, star,
        In oneness of contentment
            offering praise.

Heaven and earth and sea jubilant,
    Jubilant all things that dwell
        therein;
Filled to fullest overflow they chant,
    Still roll onward, swell,
    Still begin
        Never flagging praise intermin-
            able.

Thou who must fall silent in a while,
    Chant thy sweetest, gladdest, best,
        at once;
Sun thyself to-day, keep peace and
    smile;
    By love upward send
    Orisons,
        Accounting love thy lot and
            love thine end.
Before 1893.

ROSES on a brier,
  Pearls from out the bitter sea,
Such is earth's desire
  However pure it be.

Neither bud nor brier,
  Neither pearl nor brine for me:
Be stilled, my long desire;
  There shall be no more sea.

Be stilled, my passionate heart;
  Old earth shall end, new earth shall be:
Be still, and earn thy part
  Where shall be no more sea.

Before 1886.

WE are of those who tremble at Thy word;
  Who faltering walk in darkness toward our close
Of mortal life, by terrors curbed and spurred:
  We are of those.

  We journey to that land which no man knows
Who any more can make his voice be heard
  Above the clamour of our wants and woes.

Not ours the hearts Thy loftiest love hath stirred,
  Not such as we Thy lily and Thy rose;—
Yet, Hope of those who hope with hope deferred,
  We are of those.

Before 1893.

Awake thou that sleepest.

THE night is far spent, the day is at hand;
  Let us therefore cast off the works of darkness,
  And let us put on the armour of light.
Night for the dead in their stiffness and starkness!
  Day for the living who mount in their might
Out of their graves to the beautiful land.

Far, far away lies the beautiful land;
  Mount on wide wings of exceeding desire,
    Mount, look not back, mount to life and to light,
  Mount by the gleam of your lamps all on fire
    Up from the dead men and up from the night.
The night is far spent, the day is at hand.

Before 1893.

WE know not when, we know not where,
  We know not what that world will be;
But this we know—it will be fair
  To see.

With heart athirst and thirsty face
  We know and know not what shall be;
Christ Jesus bring us of His grace
  To see.

Christ Jesus bring us of His grace,
  Beyond all prayers our hope can
    pray,
One day to see Him face to Face,
  One day.
Before 1886.

I will lift up mine eyes unto the Hills.

WHEN sick of life and all the world—
How sick of all desire but Thee!—
I lift mine eyes up to the hills,
  Eyes of my heart that see,
I see beyond all death and ills
Refreshing green for heart and eyes,
The golden streets and gateways
    pearled,
  The trees of Paradise.

'There is a time for all things,'
    saith
The Word of Truth, Thyself the
    Word:
And many things Thou reasonest of:
  A time for hope deferred,
But time is now for grief and
    fears;
A time for life, but now is death;
Oh when shall be the time of love
  When Thou shalt wipe our tears?

Then the new Heavens and Earth
    shall be
Where righteousness shall dwell in-
    deed;
There shall be no more blight, nor
    need,
  Nor barrier of the sea;
No sun and moon alternating,
  For God shall be the Light thereof;
No sorrow more, no death, no sting,
  For God Who reigns is Love.
Before 1886.

Then whose shall those things be?

OH what is earth, that we should
    build
Our houses here, and seek concealed
Poor treasure, and add field to field,
And heap to heap and store to
    store,
Still grasping more and seeking
    more,
While step by step Death nears the
    door?
Before 1886.

His Banner over me was Love.

IN that world we weary to attain,
  Love's furled banner floats at large
    unfurled;
There is no more doubt and no more
    pain
  In that world.

There are gems and gold and
    inlets pearled;
There the verdure fadeth not again;
  There no clinging tendrils droop
    uncurled.

Here incessant tides stir up the main,
  Stormy miry depths aloft are
    hurled:
There is no more sea, or storm, or
    stain,
  In that world.
Before 1886.

BELOVED, yield thy time to God, for
    He
  Will make eternity thy recom-
    pense;
Give all thy substance for His Love,
    and be
  Beatified past earth's experience.

Serve Him in bonds, until He set
    thee free;
  Serve Him in dust, until He lift
    thee thence;
Till death be swallowed up in
    victory
  When the great trumpet sounds to
    bid thee hence.
Shall setting day win day that will
    not set?
  Poor price wert thou to spend thy-
    self for Christ,
  Had not His wealth thy poverty
    sufficed:
Yet since He makes His garden
    of thy clod,
Water thy lily, rose, or violet,
  And offer up thy sweetness unto
    God.
Before 1893.

TIME seems not short:
  If so I call to mind
    Its vast prerogative to loose or
      bind,
And bear and strike amort
    All humankind.

Time seems not long:
  If I peer out and see
    Sphere within sphere, time in
      eternity,
And hear the alternate song
    Cry endlessly.

Time greatly short,
  O time so briefly long,
    Yea, time sole battle-ground of
      right and wrong:
Art thou a time for sport
    And for a song?
Before 1893.

THE half moon shows a face of
    plaintive sweetness
  Ready and poised to wax or
    wane;
A fire of pale desire in incomplete-
    ness,
  Tending to pleasure or to pain:—
Lo while we gaze she rolleth on in
    fleetness
  To perfect loss or perfect gain.

Half bitterness we know, we know
    half sweetness;
  This world is all on wax, on
    wane:
When shall completeness round
    time's incompleteness,
  Fulfilling joy, fulfilling pain?
Lo, while we ask, life rolleth on in
    fleetness
  To finished loss or finished gain.
Before 1893.

As the Doves to their windows.'

THEY throng from the east and the
    west,
  The north and the south, with a
    song;
To golden abodes of their rest
    They throng.

Eternity stretches out long:
Time, brief at its worst or its best,
    Will quit them of ruin and wrong.

A rainbow aloft for their crest,
  A palm for their weakness made
    strong:
As doves breast all winds to their
    nest,
    They throng.
Before 1893.

OH knell of a passing time,
  Will it never cease to chime?
Oh stir of the tedious sea,
  Will it never cease to be?
Yea, when night and when day,
  Moon and sun, pass away.

Surely the sun burns low,
  The moon makes ready to go,
Broad ocean ripples to waste,
  Time is running in haste,
Night is numbered, and day
  Numbered to pass away.
Before 1893.

TIME passeth away with its pleasure
    and pain,
  Its garlands of cypress and bay,
With wealth and with want, with a
    balm and a bane,
  Time passeth away.

  Eternity cometh to stay,
Eternity stayeth to go not again;
  Eternity barring the way,

Arresting all courses of planet or
    main,
  Arresting who plan or who pray,
Arresting creation: while grand in
    its wane
  Time passeth away.
Before 1893.

The Earth shall tremble at the Look of Him.

TREMBLE, thou earth, at the Presence
    of the Lord
  Whose Will conceived thee and
    brought thee to the birth,
Always, everywhere, thy Lord to be
    adored:
  Tremble, thou earth.

Wilt thou laugh time away in
    music and mirth?
Time hath days of pestilence, hath
    days of a sword,
  Hath days of hunger and thirst in
    desolate dearth.

Till eternity wake up the multichord
  Thrilled harp of heaven, and
    breathe full its organ's girth
For joy of heaven and infinite
    reward,
  Tremble, thou earth.
Before 1893.

TIME lengthening, in the lengthening
    seemeth long:
  But ended Time will seem a little
    space,
A little while from morn to evensong,
  A little while that ran a rapid race;
A little while, when once Eternity
  Denies proportion to the other's
    pace.
Eternity to be and be and be,
  Ever beginning, never ending
    still,
Still undiminished far as thought can
    see;
  Farther than thought can see, by
    dint of will
Strung up and strained and shooting
    like a star
  Past utmost bound of everlasting
    hill:
Eternity unswaddled, without bar,
  Finishing sequence in its awful
    sum;
Eternity still rolling forth its car,
  Eternity still here and still to
    come.
Before 1893.

All flesh is Grass.

So brief a life, and then an endless life
  Or endless death;
So brief a life, then endless peace or strife:
  Whoso considereth
How man but like a flower
  Or shoot of grass
Blooms an hour,
  Well may sigh 'Alas!'

So brief a life and then an endless grief
  Or endless joy;
So brief a life, then ruin or relief:
  What solace, what annoy
Of Time needs dwelling on?
  It is, it was,
It is done,
  While we sigh 'Alas!'

Yet saints are singing in a happy hope
  Forecasting pleasure,
Bright eyes of faith enlarging all their scope;
  Saints love beyond Time's measure:
Where love is, there is bliss
  That will not pass;
Where love is,
  Dies away 'Alas!'

Before 1893.

HEAVEN'S chimes are slow, but sure to strike at last:
  Earth's sands are slow, but surely dropping thro':
  And much we have to suffer, much to do,
  Before the time be past.

Chimes that keep time are neither slow nor fast:
  Not many are the numbered sands nor few:
  A time to suffer, and a time to do,
  And then the time is past.

Before 1886.

There remaineth therefore a Rest to the People of God.

REST remains when all is done,
  Work and vigil, prayer and fast,
  All fulfilled from first to last,
  All the length of time gone past
And eternity begun.

Fear and hope and chastening rod
  Urge us on the narrow way:
  Bear we now as best we may
  Heat and burden of to-day,
Struggling, panting up to God.

Before 1886.

PARTING after parting,
  Sore loss and gnawing pain:
Meeting grows half a sorrow
  Because of parting again.
When shall the day break
  That these things shall not be?
When shall new earth be ours
  Without a sea,
And time that is not time
  But eternity?

To meet, worth living for;
  Worth dying for, to meet;
To meet, worth parting for,
  Bitter forgot in sweet:
To meet, worth parting before,
  Never to part more.

June 1858 *and June* 1864.

They put their trust in Thee, and were not
    confounded.

I.

TOGETHER once, but never more
  While Time and Death run out
    their runs :
Tho' sundered now as shore from
    shore,
  Together once.

Nor rising suns, nor setting suns,
Nor life renewed which springtide
    bore,
  Make one again Death's sundered
    ones.

Eternity holds rest in store,
  Holds hope of long reunions :
But holds it what they hungered for
  Together once?

II.

Whatso it be, howso it be, Amen.
  Blessed it is, believing, not to see.
Now God knows all that is ; and we
    shall, then,
  Whatso it be

  God's Will is best for man whose
    will is free.
God's Will is better to us, yea, than
    ten
  Desires whereof He holds and
    weighs the key.

Amid her household cares He guides
    the wren,
  He guards the shifty mouse from
    poverty ;
He knows all wants, allots each
    where and when,
  Whatso it be.
Before 1886.

SHORT is time, and only time is
    bleak ;
  Gauge the exceeding height thou
    hast to climb :
Long eternity is nigh to seek :
  Short is time.

Time is shortening with the wintry
    rime :
  Pray and watch and pray, girt up
    and meek ;
Praying, watching, praying, chime
    by chime.

Pray by silence if thou canst not
    speak :
  Time is shortening ; pray on till
    the prime :
Time is shortening ; soul, fulfil thy
    week :
  Short is time.
Before 1893.

For Each.

MY harvest is done, its promise is
    ended,
  Weak and watery sets the sun,
Day and night in one mist are
    blended,
  My harvest is done.

Long while running, how short
    when run,
Time to eternity has descended,
  Timeless eternity has begun.

Was it the narrow way that I
    wended ?
  Snares and pits was it mine to
    shun ?
The scythe has fallen, so long sus-
    pended,
  My harvest is done.
Before 1893.

For All.

Man's harvest is past, his summer
  is ended,
Hope and fear are finished at last,
Day hath descended, night hath
  ascended
  Man's harvest is past.

Time is fled that fleeted so fast:
All the unmended remains unmended,
  The perfect, perfect: all lots are
  cast.

Waiting till earth and ocean be
  rended,
  Waiting for call of the trumpet
  blast,
Each soul at goal of that way it
  wended,—
  Man's harvest is past.
Before 1893.

ADVENT

THIS Advent moon shines cold and
  clear,
  These Advent nights are long;
Our lamps have burned year after
  year
  And still their flame is strong.
'Watchman, what of the night?' we
  cry,
  Heart-sick with hope deferred:
'No speaking signs are in the sky,'
  Is still the watchman's word.

The Porter watches at the gate,
  The servants watch within;
The watch is long betimes and late,
  The prize is slow to win.
'Watchman, what of the night?'
  But still
  His answer sounds the same:

'No daybreak tops the utmost hill,
  Nor pale our lamps of flame.'

One to another hear them speak
  The patient virgins wise:
'Surely He is not far to seek'—
  'All night we watch and rise.'
'The days are evil looking back,
  The coming days are dim;
Yet count we not His promise slack,
  But watch and wait for Him.'

One with another, soul with soul,
  They kindle fire from fire:
'Friends watch us who have touched
  the goal.'
  'They urge us, come up higher.'
'With them shall rest our waysore
  feet,
  With them is built our home,
With Christ.'—'They sweet, but
  He most sweet,
  Sweeter than honeycomb.'

There no more parting, no more pain,
  The distant ones brought near,
The lost so long are found again,
  Long lost but longer dear:
Eye hath not seen, ear hath not
  heard,
  Nor heart conceived that rest,
With them our good things long
  deferred,
  With Jesus Christ our Best.

We weep because the night is long,
  We laugh for day shall rise,
We sing a slow contented song
  And knock at Paradise.
Weeping we hold Him fast Who
  wept
  For us, we hold Him fast;
And will not let Him go except
  He bless us first or last.

Weeping we hold Him fast to-night;
We will not let Him go
Till daybreak smite our wearied
   sight
And summer smite the snow:
Then figs shall bud, and dove with
   dove
Shall coo the livelong day;
Then He shall say, 'Arise, My love,
My fair one, come away.'
2 *May* 1858.

CHRISTIAN AND JEW

A DIALOGUE

'OH happy happy land!
Angels like rushes stand
   About the wells of light.'—
      'Alas, I have not eyes for this fair
         sight:
Hold fast my hand.'—

'As in a soft wind, they
Bend all one blessed way,
   Each bowed in his own glory,
      star with star.'—
         'I cannot see so far;
Here shadows are.'—

'White-winged the cherubim,
Yet whiter seraphim,
   Glow white with intense fire of
      love.'—
'Mine eyes are dim:
   I look in vain above,
And miss their hymn.'—

'Angels, Archangels cry
One to other ceaselessly
   (I hear them sing)
   One "Holy, Holy, Holy" to their
      King.'—
'I do not hear them, I.'

'Joy to thee, Paradise,
   Garden and goal and nest!
Made green for wearied eyes;
   Much softer than the breast
Of mother-dove clad in a rainbow's
   dyes.

'All precious souls are there
   Most safe, elect by grace,
All tears are wiped for ever from
   their face:
Untired in prayer
   They wait and praise
Hidden for a little space.

'Boughs of the Living Vine,
They spread in summer shine
   Green leaf with leaf:
Sap of the Royal Vine, it stirs like
   wine
   In all both less and chief.

'Sing to the Lord,
   All spirits of all flesh, sing;
For He hath not abhorred
   Our low estate nor scorned our
      offering:
Shout to our King.'—

'But Zion said:
   My Lord forgetteth me.
Lo she hath made her bed
   In dust; forsaken weepeth she
Where alien rivers swell the
   sea.

'She laid her body as the ground,
   Her tender body as the ground
      to those
Who passed; her harpstrings cannot
   sound
In a strange land; discrowned
   She sits, and drunk with woes.'—

'O drunken not with wine,
  Whose sins and sorrows have ful-
    filled the sum,—
  Be not afraid, arise, be no more
    dumb;
Arise, shine,
  For thy light is come.'—

'Can these bones live?'—
              'God knows:
  The prophet saw such clothed
    with flesh and skin;
  A wind blew on them, and life
    entered in;
They shook and rose.
  Hasten the time, O Lord, blot
    out their sin,
  Let life begin.'

9 *July* 1858.

A BURDEN

THEY lie at rest asleep and dead,
The dew is cool above their head,
They knew not when past summer
  fled—   *Amen.*

They lie at rest and quite forget
The hopes and fears that wring us
  yet:
Their eyes are set, their heart is
  set—   *Amen.*

They lie with us, yet gone away
Hear nothing that we sob or say
Beneath the thorn of wintry May—
            Miserere.

They lie asleep with us, and take
Sweet rest although our heart should
  ache,
Rest on although our heart should
  break—   *Miserere.*

Together all yet each alone,
Each laid at rest beneath his own
Smooth turf or white appointed
  stone—   *Amen.*

When shall our slumbers be so deep,
And bleeding heart and eyes that
  weep
Lie lapped in the sufficient sleep?—
            Miserere.

We dream of them, and who shall say
They never dream while far away
Of us between the night and day?—
            Sursum Corda.

Gone far away: or it may be
They lean toward us and hear and
  see,
Yea and remember more than we—
            Amen.

For wherefore should we think them
  far
Who know not where those spirits are
That shall be glorious as a star?—
            Hallelujah.

Where chill or change can never
  rise,
Deep in the depth of Paradise
They rest world-wearied heart and
  eyes—   *Jubilate.*

Safe as a hidden brooding dove,
With perfect peace within, above,
They love, and look for perfect
  love—   *Hallelujah.*

We hope and love with throbbing
  breast,
They hope and love and are at rest:
And yet we question which is best—
            Miserere.

Oh what is earth, that we should
 build
Our houses here, and seek concealed
Poor treasure, and add field to field

And heap to heap and store to store,
Still grasping more and seeking more
While Death stands knocking at the
 door?—   *Cui bono?*

But one will answer: Changed and
 pale
And sick at heart, I thirst, I fail
For love, I thirst without avail—
              Miserrima.

Sweet love, a fountain sealed to me:
Sweet love, the one sufficiency
For all the longings that can be—
              Amen.

Oh happy they alone whose lot
Is love! I search from spot to spot:
In life, in death, I find it not—
              Miserrima.

Not found in life: nay verily.
I too have sought: come sit with
 me,
And grief for grief shall answer
 thee—   *Miserrima.*

Sit with me where the sapless leaves
Are heaped and sere: to him who
 grieves
What cheer have last year's harvest-
 sheaves?—   *Cui bono?*

Not found in life, yet found in death.
Hush, throbbing heart and sobbing
 breath!
There is a nest of love beneath

The sod, a home prepared before:
Our brethren whom one mother bore
Live there, and toil and ache no
 more—   *Hallelujah.*

Our friends, our kinsfolk, great and
 small,
Our loved, our best beloved of all,
They watch across the parting wall

(Do they not watch?) and count the
 creep
Of time, and sound the shallowing
 deep,
Till we in port shall also sleep—
              Hallelujah, Amen.
16 *July* 1858.

ONLY BELIEVE

I STOOD by weeping
 Yet a sorrowful silence keeping
While an Angel smote my love
 As she lay sleeping.

'Is there a bed above
More fragrant than these violets
That are white like death?'

'White like a dove,
Flowers in the blessed islets
 Breathe sweeter breath
All fair morns and twilights.'

'Is the gold there
More golden than these tresses?'

'There heads are aureoled
 And crowned like gold
With light most rare.'

'Are the bowers of Heaven
 More choice than these?'

'To them are given
  All odorous shady trees.

Earth's bowers are wildernesses,
  Compared with the recesses
    Made soft there now
Nest-like twixt bough and bough.'

'Who shall live in such a nest?'

'Heart with heart at rest:
All they whose troubles cease
    In peace:
  Souls that wrestled
  Now are nestled
  There at ease,—
Throng from east and west,
  From north and south,
To plenty from the land of drouth.'
September 1858.

NEW JERUSALEM AND ITS CITIZENS

(*From September* 1858 *to before* 1893.)

The Holy City, New Jerusalem.

JERUSALEM is built of gold,
  Of crystal, pearl, and gem:
Oh fair thy lustres manifold,
  Thou fair Jerusalem!
Thy citizens who walk in white
Have nought to do with day or night,
And drink the river of delight.

Jerusalem makes melody
  For simple joy of heart;
An organ of full compass she,
  One-tuned thro' every part:
While not to day or night belong
Her matins and her evensong,
The one thanksgiving of her throng.

Jerusalem a garden is,
  A garden of delight;
Leaf, flower, and fruit, make fair her trees,
  Which see not day or night:
Beside her River clear and calm
The Tree of Life grows with the Palm,
For triumph and for food and balm.

Jerusalem, where song nor gem
  Nor fruit nor waters cease,
God bring us to Jerusalem,
  God bring us home in peace;
The strong who stand, the weak who fall,
The first and last, the great and small,
Home one by one, home one and all.
Before 1882.

WHEN wickedness is broken as a tree
  Paradise comes to light, ah holy land!
  Whence death has vanished like a shifting sand,
  And barrenness is banished with the sea.
Its bulwarks are salvation fully manned,
  All gems it hath for glad variety,
  And pearls for pureness radiant glimmeringly,
  And gold for grandeur where all good is grand.
An inner ring of saints meets linked above,
  And linked of angels is an outer ring;
    For voice of waters or for thunders' voice

Lo harps and songs wherewith
    all saints rejoice,
  And all the trembling there of
    any string
Is but a trembling of enraptured
    love.
Before 1893.

JERUSALEM of fire
  And gold and pearl and gem,
Saints flock to fill thy choir,
  Jerusalem.

  Lo, thrones thou hast for them ;
Desirous they desire
  Thy harp, thy diadem,

Thy bridal white attire,
  A palm-branch from thy stem :
Thy holiness their hire,
  Jerusalem.
Before 1893.

She shall be brought unto the King.

THE King's Daughter is all glorious
    within,
  Her clothing of wrought gold sets
    forth her bliss ;
Where the endless choruses of
    heaven begin
  The King's Daughter is ;

Perfect her notes in the perfect
    harmonies ;
With tears wiped away, no conscience
    of sin,
  Loss forgotten and sorrowful
    memories ;

Alight with Cherubin, afire with
    Seraphin,
  Lily for pureness, rose for charities,

With joy won and with joy evermore
    to win,
  The King's Daughter is.
Before 1893.

WHO is this that cometh up not
    alone
  From the fiery - flying - serpent
    wilderness,
Leaning upon her own Beloved
    One ?
  Who is this ?

Lo, the King of kings' daughter,
    a high princess,
Going home as bride to her Hus-
    band's Throne,
  Virgin queen in perfected loveli-
    ness.

Her eyes a dove's eyes and her
    voice a dove's moan,
  She shows like a full moon for
    heavenliness :
Eager saints and angels ask in
    heaven's zone,
  Who is this ?
Before 1886.

WHO sits with the King in His
    Throne ? Not a slave but a
    Bride,
  With this King of all Greatness
    and Grace Who reigns not
    alone :
His Glory her glory, where glorious
    she glows at His side
  Who sits with the King in His
    Throne.

She came from dim uttermost
    depths which no Angel hath
    known,

Leviathan's whirlpool and Dragon's
  dominion worldwide,
 From the frost or the fire to
  Paradisiacal zone.

Lo, she is fair as a dove, silvery,
  golden, dove-eyed:
 Lo, Dragon laments and Death
  laments, for their prey is
  flown:
She dwells in the Vision of Peace,
  and her peace shall abide
 Who sits with the King in His
  Throne.
Before 1893.

Antipas.

HIDDEN from the darkness of our
  mortal sight,
Hidden in the Paradise of lovely
  light,
Hidden in God's Presence, worshipped face to face,
Hidden in the sanctuary of Christ's
  embrace.
Up, O Wills! to track him home
  among the blest;
Up, O Hearts! to know him in the
  joy of rest;
Where no darkness more shall hide
  him from our sight,
Where we shall be love with love,
  and light with light,
Worshiping our God together face
  to face,
Wishless in the sanctuary of Christ's
  embrace.
Before 1893.

'Beautiful for situation.'

A LOVELY city in a lovely land,
 Whose citizens are lovely, and
  whose King
Is Very Love; to Whom all
  Angels sing;
To Whom all saints sing crowned,
  their sacred band
Saluting Love with palm-branch in
  their hand:
 Thither all doves on gold or silver
  wing
 Flock home thro' agate windows
  glistering
Set wide, and where pearl gates
  wide open stand.
A bower of roses is not half so sweet,
 A cave of diamonds doth not
  glitter so,
  Nor Lebanon is fruitful set
  thereby:
 And thither thou, beloved, and
  thither I
 May set our heart and set our
  face and go,
Faint yet pursuing, home on tireless
  feet.
Before 1893

LORD, by what inconceivable dim
  road
 Thou leadest man on footsore
  pilgrimage!
 Weariness is his rest from stage
  to stage,
 Brief halting-places are his sole
  abode.
Onward he fares thro' rivers overflowed,
 Thro' deserts where all doleful
  creatures rage;
 Onward from year to year, from
  age to age,
He groans and totters onward with
  his load.
Behold how inconceivable his way;
 How tenfold inconceivable the
  goal,

His goal of hope deferred, his
 promised peace:
Yea, but behold him sitting
 down at ease,
Refreshed in body and refreshed
 in soul,
At rest from labour on the Sabbath
 Day.
Before 1893.

*As cold waters to a thirsty soul, so is good
news from a far country.*

'GOLDEN-HAIRED, lily-white,
 Will you pluck me lilies?
Or will you show me where they
 grow,
 Show where the limpid rill is?
But is your hair of gold or light,
 And is your foot of flake or fire,
And have you wings rolled up from
 sight
 And songs to slake desire?'

'I pluck fresh flowers of Paradise,
 Lilies and roses red,
A bending sceptre for my hand,
 A crown to crown my head.
I sing my songs, I pluck my flowers
Sweet-scented from their fragrant
 trees;
I sing, we sing, amid the bowers,
 And gather palm-branches.'

'Is there a path to Heaven
 My stumbling foot may tread?
And will you show that way to go,
 That bower and blossom bed?'
'The path to Heaven is steep and
 straight
 And scorched, but ends in shade
 of trees,
Where yet a while we sing and wait
 And gather palm-branches.'
Before 1886.

CAST down but not destroyed,
 chastened not slain:
Thy Saints have lived that life,
 but how can I?
I, who thro' dread of death do
 daily die
By daily foretaste of an unfelt pain.
Lo I depart who shall not come
 again;
 Lo as a shadow I am flitting by;
 As a leaf trembling, as a wheel I
 fly,
While death flies faster and my flight
 is vain.
Chastened not slain, cast down but
 not destroyed:—
If thus Thy Saints have struggled
 home to peace,
 Why should not I take heart
 to be as they?
 They too pent passions in a
 house of clay,
 Fear and desire, and pangs and
 ecstasies;
Yea, thus they joyed who now are
 overjoyed.
Before 1893.

LIFT up thine eyes to seek the invisible:
 Stir up thy heart to choose the
 still unseen:
 Strain up thy hope in glad perpetual green
To scale the exceeding height where
 all saints dwell.
Saints, is it well with you?—Yea, it
 is well.—
 Where they have reaped, by faith
 kneel thou to glean:
 Because they stooped so low to
 reap, they lean
Now over golden harps unspeak-
 able.—

But thou purblind and deafened, knowest thou
  Those glorious beauties unexperienced
    By ear or eye or by heart hitherto?—
I know Whom I have trusted: wherefore now
  All amiable, accessible tho' fenced,
    Golden Jerusalem floats full in view.
Before 1893.

Love is strong as Death.

As flames that consume the mountains, as winds that coerce the sea,
  Thy men of renown show forth Thy might in the clutch of death:
Down they go into silence, yet the Trump of the Jubilee
  Swells not Thy praise as swells it the breathless pause of their breath.

What is the flame of their fire, if so I may catch the flame;
What the strength of their strength, if also I may wax strong?
The flaming fire of their strength is the love of Jesu's Name,
  In Whom their death is life, their silence utters a song.
Before 1893.

Let them rejoice in their beds.

CRIMSON as the rubies, crimson as the roses,
  Crimson as the sinking sun,
Singing on his crimsoned bed each saint reposes,
  Fought his fight, his battle won;
Till the rosy east the day of days discloses,
  All his work, save waiting, done.

Far above the stars, while underneath the daisies,
  Resting, for his race is run,
Unto Thee his heart each quiet saint upraises,
  God the Father, Spirit, Son;
Unto Thee his heart, unto Thee his praises,
  O Lord God, the Three in One.
Before 1893.

SLAIN in their high places: fallen on rest
  Where the eternal peace lights up their faces,
In God's sacred acre breast to breast:—
  Slain in their high places.

From all tribes, all families, all races,
Gathered home together; east or west
  Sending home its tale of gifts and graces.

Twine, oh twine, heaven's amaranth for their crest,
  Raise their praise while home their triumph paces;
Kings by their own King of kings confessed,
  Slain in their high places.
Before 1893.

'What hath God wrought!'

THE shout of a King is among them. One day may I be

Of that perfect communion of lovers
    contented and free
In the land that is very far off, and
    far off from the sea.

The shout of the King is among them.
    One King and one song,
One thunder of manifold voices
    harmonious and strong,
One King and one love, and one
    shout of one worshiping throng.
    Before 1893.

Before the Throne, and before the Lamb.

As the voice of many waters all
    saints sing as one,
As the voice of an unclouded
    thundering ;
Unswayed by the changing moon
    and unswayed by the sun,
As the voice of many waters all
    saints sing.

Circling round the rainbow of
    their perfect ring,
Twelve thousand times twelve
    thousand voices in unison
Swell the triumph, swell the praise
    of Christ the King.

Where raiment is white of blood-
    steeped linen slowly spun,
Where crowns are golden of
    Love's own largessing,
Where eternally the ecstasy is but
    begun,
As the voice of many waters all
    saints sing.
    Before 1893.

He shall go no more out.

ONCE within, within for evermore :
    There the long beatitudes begin :
Overflows the still unwasting store,
    Once within.

Left without are death and doubt
    and sin ;
All man wrestled with and all he bore,
    Man who saved his life, skin after
    skin.

Blow the trumpet-blast unheard
    before,
Shout the unheard-of shout for
    these who win,
These, who cast their crowns on
    Heaven's high floor
Once within.
    Before 1893.

YEA, blessed and holy is he that hath
    part in the First Resurrection !
We mark well his bulwarks, we set
    up his tokens, we gaze, even we,
On this lustre of God and of Christ,
    this creature of flawless per-
    fection :
Yea, blessed and holy is he.

But what ? an offscouring of earth,
    a wreck from the turbulent sea,
A bloodstone unflinchingly hewn for
    the Temple's eternal erection,
One scattered and peeled, one
    sifted and chastened and
    scourged and set free ?

Yea, this is that worshipful stone
    of the Wise Master Builder's
    election,
Yea, this is that King and that
    Priest where all Hallows bow
    down the knee,
Yea, this man set nigh to the Throne
    is Jonathan of David's delection,
Yea, blessed and holy is he.
    Before 1893.

THE joy of Saints, like incense turned to fire
  In golden censers, soars acceptable;
    And high their heavenly hallelujahs swell
Desirous still with still-fulfilled desire.
Sweet thrill the harpstrings of the heavenly choir,
  Most sweet their voice while love is all they tell;
    Where love is all in all, and all is well
Because their work is love and love their hire.
All robed in white and all with palm in hand,
  Crowns too they have of gold and thrones of gold;
    The street is golden which their feet have trod,
Or on a sea of glass and fire they stand:
  And none of them is young, and none is old,
    Except as perfect by the Will of God.

Before 1893.

WHAT are these lovely ones, yea, what are these?
  Lo these are they who for pure love of Christ
Stripped off the trammels of soft silken ease,
  Beggaring themselves betimes, to be sufficed
Throughout heaven's one eternal day of peace:
  By golden streets, thro' gates of pearl unpriced,
They entered on the joys that will not cease,
  And found again all firstfruits sacrificed.

And wherefore have you harps, and wherefore palms,
  And wherefore crowns, O ye who walk in white?
Because our happy hearts are chanting psalms,
  Endless Te Deum for the ended fight;
While thro' the everlasting lapse of calms
  We cast our crowns before the Lamb our Might.

Before 1893.

The General Assembly and Church of the Firstborn.

BRING me to see, Lord, bring me yet to see
  Those nations of Thy glory and Thy grace
Who splendid in Thy splendour worship Thee.
  Light in all eyes, content in every face,
Raptures and voices one while manifold,
  Love and are well-beloved the ransomed race:—
Great mitred priests, great kings in crowns of gold,
  Patriarchs who head the army of their sons,
Matrons and mothers by their own extolled,
  Wise and most harmless holy little ones,
Virgins who, making merry, lead the dance,
  Full-breathed victorious racers from all runs,
Home-comers out of every change and chance,
  Hermits restored to social neighbourhood,

Aspects which reproduce One
    Countenance,
Life-losers with their losses all
    made good,
All blessed hungry and athirst
    sufficed,
All who bore crosses round the
    Holy Rood,
Friends, brethren, sisters, of Lord
    Jesus Christ.
Before 1893.

Every one that is perfect shall be as his Master.

How can one man, how can all men,
    How can we be like St. Paul,
Like St. John, or like St. Peter,
    Like the least of all
Blessed Saints? for we are small.

Love can make us like St. Peter,
    Love can make us like St. Paul,
Love can make us like the blessed
    Bosom friend of all,
Great St. John, tho' we are small.

Love which clings and trusts and
    worships,
    Love which rises from a fall,
Love which, prompting glad obedi-
    ence,
    Labours most of all,
Love makes great the great and
    small.
Before 1886.

'As dying, and behold we live!'
    So live the Saints while time is
        flying;
Make all they make, give all they
        give,
    As dying;
Bear all they bear without reply-
    ing;
They grieve as tho' they did not
    grieve,
Uplifting praise with prayer and
    sighing.

Patient thro' life's long-drawn
    reprieve,
Aloof from strife, at peace from
    crying,
The morrow to its day they leave,
    As dying.
Before 1893.

So great a cloud of Witnesses.

I THINK of the saints I have known,
    and lift up mine eyes
To the far-away home of beautiful
    Paradise,
Where the song of saints gives voice
    to an undividing sea
On whose plain their feet stand firm
    while they keep their jubilee.
As the sound of waters their voice,
    as the sound of thunderings,
While they all at once rejoice, while
    all sing and while each one
    sings;
Where more saints flock in, and
    more, and yet more, and again
    yet more,
And not one turns back to depart
    thro' the open entrance-door.

O sights of our lovely earth, O
    sound of our earthly sea,
Speak to me of Paradise, of all
    blessed saints to me:
Or keep silence touching them, and
    speak to my heart alone
Of the Saint of saints, the King of
    kings, the Lamb on the Throne.
Before 1893.

OUR Mothers, lovely women pitiful;
  Our Sisters, gracious in their life
    and death;
  To us each unforgotten memory
    saith:
'Learn as we learned in life's
    sufficient school,
Work as we worked in patience of
    our rule,
  Walk as we walked, much less
    by sight than faith,
  Hope as we hoped, despite our
    slips and scathe,
Fearful in joy and confident in
    dule.'
I know not if they see us or can
    see;
  But if they see us in our painful
    day,
    How looking back to earth
      from Paradise
    Do tears not gather in those
      loving eyes?—
  Ah happy eyes! whose tears are
    wiped away
Whether or not you bear to look
    on me.

Before 1893.

SAFE where I cannot lie yet,
  Safe where I hope to lie too,
Safe from the fume and the fret;
  You, and you,
  Whom I never forget.

Safe from the frost and the snow,
  Safe from the storm and the
    sun,
Safe where the seeds wait to grow
  One by one
And to come back in blow.

Before 1893.

'Is it well with the child?'

LYING a-dying.
Have done with vain sighing:
Life not lost but treasured,
God Almighty pleasured,
God's daughter fetched and carried,
Christ's bride betrothed and married.
Our tender little dove
Meek-eyed and simple,
Our love goes home to Love:
There shall she walk in white,
Where God shall be the Light,
And God the Temple.

3 *November* 1865.

DEAR Angels and dear disembodied
    Saints
  Unseen around us, worshiping in
    rest,
May wonder that man's heart so
    often faints,
  And his steps lag along the
    heavenly quest,
What while his foolish fancy moulds
    and paints
  A fonder hope than all they
    prove for best;
A lying hope which undermines
    and taints
  His soul, as sin and sloth make
    manifest.
Sloth, and a lie, and sin: shall
    these suffice
  The unfathomable heart of craving
    man,
    That heart which being a deep
      calls to the deep?
  Behold how many like us rose
    and ran
    When Christ, Life-giver, roused
      them from their sleep
To rise and run and rest in Paradise!

Before 1893.

To every seed his own body.'

BONE to his bone, grain to his grain of dust:
A numberless reunion shall make whole
Each blessed body for its blessed soul,
Refashioning the aspects of the just.
Each saint who died must live afresh, and must
Ascend resplendent in the aureole
Of his own proper glory to his goal,
As seeds their proper bodies all upthrust.
Each with his own not with another's grace,
Each with his own not with another's heart,
Each with his own not with another's face,
Each dove-like soul mounts to his proper place :—
O faces unforgotten! if to part
Wrung sore, what will it be to re-embrace?
Before 1893.

What good shall my life do me?

HAVE dead men long to wait?—

There is a certain term
For their bodies to the worm
And their souls at heaven gate:
Dust to dust, clod to clod,
These precious things of God,
Trampled underfoot by man
And beast the appointed years.—

Their longest life was but a span
For change and smiles and tears:
Is it worth while to live,
Rejoice and grieve,
Hope, fear, and die?
Man with man, truth with lie,
The slow show dwindles by:
At last what shall we have
Besides a grave?—

Lies and shows no more,
No fear, no pain,
But after hope and sleep
Dear joys again.
Those who sowed shall reap:
Those who bore
The Cross shall wear the Crown;
Those who clomb the steep
There shall sit down.

The Shepherd of the sheep
Feeds His flock there;
In watered pastures fair
They rest and leap.
'Is it worth while to live?'
Be of good cheer:
Love casts out fear:
Rise up, achieve.
September 1858.

THE LOVE OF CHRIST WHICH PASSETH KNOWLEDGE

I BORE with thee long weary days and nights,
  Through many pangs of heart, through many tears;
I bore with thee, thy hardness, coldness, slights,
  For three-and-thirty years.

Who else had dared for thee what I have dared?
  I plunged the depth most deep from bliss above;

I not My flesh, I not My spirit
    spared:
  Give thou Me love for love.

For thee I thirsted in the daily
    drouth,
For thee I trembled in the nightly
    frost:
Much sweeter thou than honey to
    My mouth:
  Why wilt thou still be lost?

I bore thee on My shoulders and
    rejoiced:
  Men only marked upon My
    shoulders borne
The branding cross; and shouted
    hungry-voiced,
  Or wagged their heads in scorn.

Thee did nails grave upon My hands,
    thy name
  Did thorns for frontlets stamp
    between Mine eyes:
I, Holy One, put on thy guilt and
    shame;
  I, God, Priest, Sacrifice.

A thief upon My right hand and
    My left;
  Six hours alone, athirst, in misery:
At length in death one smote My
    heart and cleft
  A hiding-place for thee.

Nailed to the racking cross, than
    bed of down
  More dear, whereon to stretch
    Myself and sleep:
So did I win a kingdom,—Share
    My crown;
  A harvest,—Come and reap.

15 *October* 1858.

A SHADOW OF DOROTHEA

'GOLDEN-HAIRED, lily-white,
  Will you pluck me lilies?
Or will you show me where they
    grow,
  Show where the summer rill is?
But is your hair of gold or light,
And is your foot of flake or fire,
And have you wings rolled up from
    sight,
  And joy to slake desire?'

'I pluck young flowers of Paradise,
  Lilies and roses red:
    A sceptre for my hand,
  A crown to crown my golden head.
Love makes me wise:
    I sing, I stand,
I pluck palm-branches in the
    sheltered land.'

'Is there a path to heaven
  My heavy foot may tread?
And will you show that way to go,
  That rose and lily bed?
Which day of all these seven
  Will lighten my heart of lead,
Will purge mine eyes and make me
    wise,
    Alive or dead?'

'There is a heavenward stair—
Mount, strain upwards, strain and
    strain—
Each step will crumble to your foot
That never shall descend again.
There grows a tree from ancient
    root
With healing leaves and twelvefold
    fruit
  In musical heaven-air:
    Feast with me there.'

'I have a home on earth I cannot
   leave,
I have a friend on earth I cannot
   grieve :
Come down to me, I cannot mount
   to you.'
   ' Nay, choose between us both,
   Choose as you are lief or loth :
You cannot keep these things and
   have me too.'
   11 *November* 1858.

FOR HENRIETTA POLYDORE

ON the land and on the sea
Jesus keep both you and me :

Going out and coming in,
Christ keep us both from shame
   and sin :

In this world, in the world to come,
Keep us safe and lead us home :

To-day in toil, to-night in rest,
Be best beloved and love us best.
   16 *January* 1859.

ASH WEDNESDAY

JESUS, do I love Thee?
Thou art far above me,
Seated out of sight,
Hid in heavenly light
Of most highest height.
Martyred hosts implore Thee,
Seraphs fall before Thee,
Angels and Archangels,
Cherub throngs adore Thee.
Blessed she that bore Thee !
All the saints approve Thee,
All the virgins love Thee.

I show as a blot
Blood hath cleansèd not,
As a barren spot
In thy fruitful lot ;
I, fig-tree fruit-unbearing,
Thou, righteous Judge unsparing :
What canst Thou do more to me
That shall not more undo me ?
Thy Justice hath a sound,
'Why cumbereth it the ground ?'
Thy Love with stirrings stronger
Pleads, 'Give it one year longer.'
Thou giv'st me time : but who
Save Thou shall give me dew,
Shall feed my root with blood
And stir my sap for good ?—
Oh by Thy gifts that shame me
Give more lest they condemn me.
Good Lord, I ask much of Thee,
But most I ask to love Thee :
Kind Lord, be mindful of me,
Love me and make me love Thee.
   21 *March* 1859.

A CHRISTMAS CAROL

BEFORE the paling of the stars,
   Before the winter morn,
   Before the earliest cock-crow
Jesus Christ was born :
   Born in a stable
   Cradled in a manger,
In the world His hands had made
   Born a stranger.

Priest and King lay fast asleep
   In Jerusalem,
Young and old lay fast asleep
   In crowded Bethlehem :
Saint and Angel, ox and ass,
   Kept a watch together,
   Before the Christmas daybreak
   In the winter weather.

Jesus on his Mother's breast
  In the stable cold,
Spotless Lamb of God was He,
  Shepherd of the fold:
Let us kneel with Mary Maid,
  With Joseph bent and hoary,
With Saint and Angel, ox and ass,
  To hail the King of Glory.
26 *August* 1859.

CHRIST OUR ALL IN ALL

(*From* 26 *August* 1859 *to before* 1893.)

The ransomed of the Lord.

THY lovely saints do bring Thee love,
  Incense and joy and gold;
Fair star with star, fair dove with
      dove,
  Beloved by Thee of old.
I, Master, neither star nor dove,
  Have brought Thee sins and
      tears;
Yet I too bring a little love
  Amid my flaws and fears.
A trembling love that faints and
      fails
  Yet still is love of Thee,
A wondering love that hopes and
      hails
  Thy boundless Love of me;
Love kindling faith and pure desire,
  Love following on to bliss,
A spark, O Jesu, from Thy fire,
  A drop from Thine abyss.
Before 1893.

LORD, we are rivers running to Thy
      sea,
Our waves and ripples all derived
      from Thee:
A nothing we should have, a nothing
      be,
  Except for Thee.
Sweet are the waters of Thy shore-
      less sea,
Make sweet our waters that make
      haste to Thee;
Pour in Thy sweetness, that our-
      selves may be
  Sweetness to Thee.
Before 1893.

An exceeding bitter cry.

CONTEMPT and pangs and haunting
      fears—
  Too late for hope, too late for ease,
  Too late for rising from the
      dead;
  Too late, too late to bend my
      knees,
    Or bow my head,
  Or weep, or ask for tears.
Hark! . . . One I hear Who calls
      to me:
  'Give Me thy thorn and grief
      and scorn,
  Give Me thy ruin and regret.
  Press on thro' darkness toward
      the morn:
    One loves thee yet:
    Have I forgotten thee?'
Lord, Who art Thou? Lord, is it
      Thou
  My Lord and God Lord Jesus
      Christ?
  How said I that I sat alone
  And desolate and unsufficed?
    Surely a stone
  Would raise Thy praises now!
Before 1893.

O LORD, when Thou didst call me,
      didst Thou know
My heart disheartened thro' and
      thro',

Still hankering after Egypt full
  in view
Where cucumbers and melons grow?
      —'Yea, I knew.'—

But, Lord, when Thou didst choose
  me, didst Thou know
  How marred I was and withered
    too,
  Nor rose for sweetness nor for
    virtue rue,
Timid and rash, hasty and slow?
      —'Yea, I knew.'—

My Lord, when Thou didst love
  me, didst Thou know
  How weak my efforts were, how
    few,
  Tepid to love and impotent to
    do,
Envious to reap while slack to sow?
      —'Yea, I knew.'—

Good Lord, Who knowest what I
  cannot know,
  And dare not know, my false, my
    true,
  My new, my old; Good Lord,
    arise and do
If loving Thou hast known me so.
      —'Yea, I knew.'—
    Before 1893.

Thou, God, seest me.

AH me that I should be
Exposed and open evermore to
    Thee!—
  'Nay, shrink not from My light,
  And I will make thee glorious in
    My sight
  With the overcoming Shulamite.'—
Yea, Lord, Thou moulding me.

. . . Without a hiding-place
To hide me from the terrors of Thy
    Face.—
  'Thy hiding-place is here
  In Mine own heart, wherefore
    the Roman spear
  For thy sake I accounted dear.'—
My Jesus! King of Grace.

. . . Without a veil, to give
Whiteness before Thy Face that I
    might live.—
  'Am I too poor to dress
  Thee in My royal robe of
    righteousness?
  Challenge and prove My Love's
    excess.'—
Give, Lord, I will receive.

. . . Without a pool wherein
To wash my piteous self and make
    me clean.—
  'My Blood hath washed away
  Thy guilt, and still I wash thee
    day by day:
  Only take heed to trust and
    pray.'—
Lord, help me to begin.
    Before 1893.

LORD JESUS, who would think that
    I am Thine?
  Ah who would think,
  Who sees me ready to turn back or
    sink,
    That Thou art mine?

I cannot hold Thee fast tho' Thou
    art mine:
  Hold Thou me fast,
  So earth shall know at last and
    heaven at last
    That I am Thine.
    Before 1886.

The Name of Jesus.

Jesus, Lord God from all eternity,
  Whom love of us brought down
    to shame,
I plead Thy Life with Thee,
  I plead Thy Death, I plead Thy
    Name.

Jesus, Lord God of every living soul,
  Thy Love exceeds its uttered fame,
Thy Will can make us whole,
  I plead Thyself, I plead Thy Name.
Before 1886.

Lord God of Hosts, most Holy and
    most High,
  What made Thee tell Thy Name
    of Love to me?
What made Thee live our life?
    what made Thee die?
    'My love of thee.'

I pitched so low, Thou so exceeding
    high,
  What was it made Thee stoop to
    look at me
While flawless sons of God stood
    wondering by?
    'My love of thee.'

What is there which can lift me up
    on high
  That we may dwell together, Thou
    with me,
When sin and death and suffering
    are gone by?
    'My love of thee.'

O Lord, what is that best thing hid
    on high
  Which makes heaven heaven as
    Thou hast promised me,

Yea, makes it Christ to live and gain
    to die?
    'My love of thee.'
Before 1886.

'Lord, what have I that I may
    offer Thee?
Look, Lord, I pray Thee, and see.'—

'What is it thou hast got?
Nay, child, what is it thou hast not?
Thou hast all gifts that I have given
    to thee:
Offer them all to Me,
The great ones and the small;
I will accept them one and all.'—

'I have a will, good Lord, but it is
    marred;
A heart both crushed and hard:
Not such as these the gift
Clean-handed lovely saints uplift.'—

'Nay, child, but wilt thou judge for
    Me?
I crave not thine, but thee.'—

'Ah Lord Who lovest me!
Such as I have now give I Thee.'
Before 1886.

If I should say 'my heart is in my
    home,'
I turn away from that high halidom
  Where Jesus sits: for nowhere
    else
  But with its treasure dwells
  The heart: this Truth and this
    experience tells.

If I should say 'my heart is in a
    grave,'
I turn away from Jesus risen to save:

I slight that death He died for me ;
I too deny to see
His beauty and desirability.

O Lord, Whose Heart is deeper than
  my heart,
Draw mine to Thine to worship
  where Thou art ;
For Thine own glory join the twain
  Never to part again,
Nor to have lived nor to have
  died in vain.
Before 1886.

LEAF from leaf Christ knows ;
Himself the Lily and the Rose :

Sheep from sheep Christ tells ;
Himself the Shepherd, no one else :

Star and star He names,
Himself outblazing all their flames :

Dove by dove, He calls
To set each on the golden walls :

Drop by drop, He counts
The flood of ocean as it mounts :

Grain by grain, His hand
Numbers the innumerable sand.

Lord, I lift to Thee
In peace what is and what shall be :

Lord, in peace I trust
To Thee all spirits and all dust.
Before 1882.

LORD, carry me.—Nay, but I grant
  thee strength
To walk and work thy way to
  Heaven at length.—

Lord, why then am I weak ?—Because I give
Power to the weak, and bid the
  dying live.—

Lord, I am tired.—He hath not
  much desired
The goal who at the starting-point
  is tired.—

Lord, dost Thou know ?—I know
  what is in man ;
What the flesh can, and what the
  spirit can.—

Lord, dost Thou care ?—Yea, for
  thy gain or loss
So much I cared, it brought Me to
  the Cross.—

Lord, I believe ; help Thou mine
  unbelief.—
Good is the word ; but rise, for life
  is brief.

The follower is not greater than the
  Chief :
Follow thou Me along My way of
  grief.
Before 1893.

LORD, I am here.—But, child, I look
  for thee
Elsewhere and nearer Me.—
Lord, that way moans a wide in-
  satiate sea :
How can I come to Thee ?—
Set foot upon the water, test and see
  If thou canst come to Me.—
Couldst Thou not send a boat to
  carry me,
Or dolphin swimming free ?—

Nay, boat nor fish if thy will faileth
  thee:
    For My Will too is free. —
O Lord, I am afraid.—Take hold on
  Me:
    I am stronger than the sea.—
Save, Lord, I perish.—I have hold
  of thee,
    I made and rule the sea,
I bring thee to the haven where
  thou wouldst be.

Before 1893.

NEW creatures; the Creator still the
  Same
    For ever and for ever: therefore
      we
Win hope from God's unsearch-
  able decree,
    And glorify His still unchanging
      Name.
We too are still the same; and still
  our claim,
    Our trust, our stay, is Jesus, none
      but He:
He still the Same regards us, and
  still we
    Mount toward Him in old love's
      accustomed flame.
We know Thy wounded Hands: and
  Thou dost know
    Our praying hands, our hands
      that clasp and cling
To hold Thee fast and not to let Thee
  go.
All else be new then, Lord, as
  Thou hast said:
    Since it is Thou, we dare not be
      afraid,
Our King of old and still our Self-
  same King.

Before 1893.

King of kings and Lord of lords.
IS this that Name as ointment pourèd
  forth
For which the virgins love Thee—
  King of kings
And Lord of lords? All Seraphs
  clad in wings;
All Cherubs and all Wheels which
  south and north,
Which east and west turn not in
  going forth;
  All many-semblanced ordered
    Spirits, as rings
  Of rainbow in unwonted fashion-
    ings,
Might answer, Yes. But we from
  south and north,
From east and west, a feeble folk
  who came
By desert ways in quest of land
  unseen,
A promised land of pasture ever
  green
And ever springing ever singing
  wave,
Know best Thy Name of Jesus:
  Blessed Name,
Man's life and resurrection from
  the grave.

Before 1893.

THY Name, O Christ, as incense
  streaming forth
Sweetens our names before God's
  Holy Face;
Luring us from the south and from
  the north
Unto the sacred place.
In Thee God's promise is Amen and
  Yea.
  What art Thou to us? Prize of
    every lot,

Shepherd and Door, our Life and
    Truth and Way :—
Nay, Lord, what art Thou not?
Before 1893.

The Good Shepherd.

'O SHEPHERD with the bleeding
    Feet,
Good Shepherd with the pleading
    Voice,
What seekest Thou from hill to
    hill?
Sweet were the valley pastures, sweet
    The sound of flocks that bleat their
        joys,
    And eat and drink at will.
Is one worth seeking, when Thou
    hast of Thine
        Ninety and nine?'

'How should I stay my bleeding
    Feet,
How should I hush my pleading
    Voice?
I Who chose death and clomb
    a hill,
Accounting gall and wormwood
    sweet,
That hundredfold might bud My
    joys
For love's sake and good will.
I seek My one, for all there bide of
    Mine
        Ninety and nine.'
Before 1893.

'Rejoice with Me.

'LITTLE Lamb, who lost thee?'—
    'I myself, none other.'—
'Little Lamb, who found thee?'—
    'Jesus, Shepherd, Brother.
Ah, Lord, what I cost Thee!
    Canst Thou still desire?'—

'Still Mine arms surround thee,
    Still I lift thee higher,
    Draw thee nigher.'
Before 1893.

SHALL not the Judge of all the earth
    do right?
Yea, Lord, altho' Thou say me
    nay.
Shall not His Will be to me life and
    light?
Yea, Lord, altho' Thou slay.

Yet, Lord, remembering turn and sift
    and see,
Remember tho' Thou sift me thro',
Remember my desire, remember me,
    Remember, Lord, and do.
Before 1886.

ME and my gift: kind Lord, behold,
    Be not extreme to test or sift;
Thy Love can turn to fire and gold
    Me and my gift.

Myself and mine to Thee I lift:
Gather us to Thee from the cold
    Dead outer world where dead
    things drift.

If much were mine, then manifold
    Should be the offering of my thrift:
I am but poor, yet love makes bold
    Me and my gift.
Before 1893.

'He cannot deny Himself.'

LOVE still is Love, and doeth all
    things well,
Whether He show me heaven or hell,
    Or earth in her decay
    Passing away
    On a day.

Love still is Love, tho' He should
    say 'Depart,'
And break my incorrigible heart,
    And set me out of sight
    Widowed of light
    In the night.

Love still is Love, is Love, if He
    should say,
'Come,' on that uttermost dread
    day;
    'Come,' unto very me,
    'Come where I be,
    Come and see.'

Love still is Love, whatever comes
    to pass:
O Only Love, make me Thy glass,
    Thy pleasure to fulfil
    By loving still,
    Come what will.
Before 1893.

Slain from the foundation of the world.

SLAIN for man, slain for me, O
    Lamb of God, look down;
Loving to the end, look down,
    behold and see:
Turn Thine Eyes of pity, turn not
    on us Thy frown,
    O Lamb of God, slain for man,
    slain for me.

Mark the wrestling, mark the race
    for indeed a crown;
Mark our chariots how we drive
    them heavily;
Mark the foe upon our track blasting
    thundering down,
    O Lamb of God, slain for man,
    slain for me.

Set as a Cloudy Pillar against them
    Thy frown,
Thy Face of Light toward us
    gracious utterly;
Help granting, hope granting, until
    Thou grant a crown,
    O Lamb of God, slain for man,
    slain for me.
Before 1893.

LORD JESU, Thou art sweetness to
    my soul:
I to myself am bitterness:
Regard my fainting struggle toward
    the goal,
    Regard my manifold distress,
    O Sweet Jesu.

Thou art Thyself my goal, O Lord
    my King:
Stretch forth Thy hand to save
    my soul:
What matters more or less of
    journeying?
    While I touch Thee I touch my
    goal,
    O Sweet Jesu.
Before 1893.

'I, LORD, Thy foolish sinner low
    and small,
Lack all.
His heart too high was set
Who asked, What lack I yet?
Woe's me at my most woeful pass!
I, Lord, who scarcely dare adore,
Weep sore:
Steeped in this rotten world I fear
    to rot.
Alas what lack I not?
Alas alas for me! alas
More and yet more!'—

'Nay, stand up on thy feet, betaking
    thee
To Me.
Bring fear; but much more bring
Hope to thy patient King:
What, is My pleasure in thy death?
I loved that youth who little knew
The true
Width of his want, yet worshipped
    with goodwill:
So love I thee, and still
Prolong thy day of grace and breath.
Rise up and do.'—

'Lord, let me know mine end, and
    certify
When I
Shall die and have to stand
Helpless on Either Hand,
Cut off, cut off, my day of grace.'—
'Not so: for what is that to thee?
    I see
The measure and the number of thy
    day.
Keep patience, tho' I slay;
Keep patience till thou see My Face.
Follow thou Me.'
    Before 1893.

    'Because He first loved us.'

'I WAS hungry, and Thou feddest me;
    Yea, Thou gavest drink to slake
        my thirst:
O Lord, what love gift can I offer
    Thee
    Who hast loved me first?'—

'Feed My hungry brethren for My
    sake;
    Give them drink, for love of them
        and Me:
Love them as I loved thee, when
        Bread I brake
        In pure love of thee.'—

'Yea, Lord, I will serve them by
    Thy grace;
    Love Thee, seek Thee, in them;
        wait and pray:
Yet would I love Thyself, Lord,
    face to face,
    Heart to heart, one day.'—

'Let to-day fulfil its daily task,
    Fill thy heart and hand to them
        and Me:
To-morrow thou shalt ask, and shalt
    not ask
    Half I keep for thee.'
    Before 1893.

LORD, hast Thou so loved us, and
    will not we
    Love Thee with heart and mind
        and strength and soul,
    Desiring Thee beyond our glorious
        goal,
Beyond the heaven of heavens
    desiring Thee?
Each saint, all saints cry out: Yea
    me, yea me,
    Thou hast desired beyond an
        aureole,
    Beyond Thy many Crowns, beyond
        the whole
Ninety and nine unwandering family.
Souls in green pastures of the watered
    land,
Faint pilgrim souls wayfaring thro'
    the sand,
    Abide with Thee and in Thee are
        at rest:
    Yet evermore, kind Lord, renew
        Thy quest
After new wanderers; such as once
    Thy Hand
    Gathered, Thy Shoulders bore,
        Thy Heart caressed.
    Before 1893.

As the dove, which found no rest
   For the sole of her foot, flew back
To the ark her only nest
   And found safety there;
Because Noah put forth his hand,
   Drew her in from ruin and wrack,
And was more to her than the land
   And the air:

So my spirit, like that dove,
   Fleeth away to an ark
Where dwelleth a Heart of Love,
   A Hand pierced to save,
Tho' the sun and the moon should fail,
Tho' the stars drop into the dark,
And my body lay itself pale
   In a grave.
Before 1893.

Thou art Fairer than the children of men.

A ROSE, a lily, and the Face of Christ,
   Have all our hearts sufficed:
For He is Rose of Sharon nobly born,
   Our Rose without a thorn;
And He is Lily of the Valley, He
   Most sweet in purity.
But when we come to name Him as He is,
   Godhead, Perfection, Bliss,
All tongues fall silent, while pure hearts alone
   Complete their orison.
Before 1886.

'As the Apple Tree among the trees of the wood.'

As one red rose in a garden where all other roses are white
   Blossoms alone in its glory, crowned all alone
In a solitude of own sweetness and fragrance of own delight,
   With loveliness not another's and thorns its own;
As one ruddy sun amid million orbs comely and colourless,
   Among all others, above all others is known;
As it were alone in the garden, alone in the heavenly place,
   Chief and centre of all, in fellowship yet alone.
Before 1893.

NONE other Lamb, none other Name,
   None other Hope in heaven or earth or sea,
None other Hiding-place from guilt and shame,
     None beside Thee.

My faith burns low, my hope burns low,
   Only my heart's desire cries out in me
By the deep thunder of its want and woe,
     Cries out to Thee.

Lord, Thou art Life tho' I be dead,
   Love's Fire Thou art, however cold I be:
Nor heaven have I, nor place to lay my head,
     Nor home, but Thee.
Before 1893.

Thy Friend and thy Father's Friend forget not.

FRIENDS, I commend to you the narrow way:
   Not because I, please God, will walk therein,

But rather for the Love Feast of that day,
　The exceeding prize which whoso will may win.
Earth is half spent and rotting at the core,
　Here hollow death's heads mock us with a grin,
　Here heartiest laughter leaves us tired and sore.
Men heap up pleasures and enlarge desire,
　Outlive desire, and famished evermore
　Consume themselves within the undying fire.
Yet not for this God made us: not for this
　Christ sought us far and near to draw us nigher,
Sought us and found and paid our penalties.
　If one could answer 'Nay' to God's command,
Who shall say 'Nay' when Christ pleads all He is
　For us, and holds us with a wounded Hand?

26 August 1859.

Surely He hath borne our griefs.

CHRIST'S Heart was wrung for me, if mine is sore;
　And if my feet are weary, His have bled;
　He had no place wherein to lay His Head;
If I am burdened, He was burdened more.
The cup I drink He drank of long before;
　He felt the unuttered anguish which I dread;

He hungered Who the hungry thousands fed,
　And thirsted Who the world's refreshment bore.
If grief be such a looking-glass as shows
　Christ's Face and man's in some sort made alike,
　　Then grief is pleasure with a subtle taste:
　Wherefore should any fret or faint or haste?
Grief is not grievous to a soul that knows
　Christ comes,—and listens for that hour to strike.

Before 1886.

They toil not neither do they spin.

CLOTHER of the lily, Feeder of the sparrow,
Father of the fatherless, dear Lord,
Tho' Thou set me as a mark against Thine arrow,
　As a prey unto Thy sword,
As a ploughed-up field beneath Thy harrow,
　As a captive in Thy cord,
Let that cord be love; and some day make my narrow
　Hallowed bed according to Thy Word. Amen.

Before 1893.

DARKNESS and light are both alike to Thee:
Therefore to Thee I lift my darkened face;
Upward I look with eyes that fail to see,
Athirst for future light and present grace.

I trust the Hand of Love I scarcely
    trace.
With breath that fails I cry, Re-
    member me :
Add breath to breath so I may
    run my race
That where Thou art there may Thy
    servant be.
For Thou art gulf and fountain of
    my love,
  I unreturning torrent to Thy sea,
    Yea Thou the measureless
    ocean for my rill :
  Seeking I find, and finding
    seek Thee still :
And oh that I had wings as hath a
    dove,
  Then would I flee away to rest
    with Thee.
Before 1886.

'And now why tarriest thou?'

LORD, grant us grace to mount by
    steps of grace
  From grace to grace nearer, my
    God, to Thee ;
  Not tarrying for to-morrow,
    Lest we lie down in sorrow
And never see
Unveiled Thy Face.

Life is a vapour vanishing in haste ;
  Life is a day whose sun grows
    pale to set ;
  Life is a stint and sorrow,
    One day and not the morrow ;
Precious, while yet
It runs to waste.

Lord, strengthen us ; lest fainting
    by the way
  We come not to Thee, we who
    come from far ;

Lord, bring us to that morrow
  Which makes an end of sorrow,
Where all saints are
On holyday.

Where all the saints rest who have
    heard Thy call,
  Have risen and striven and now
    rejoice in rest :
  Call us too home from sorrow
    To rest in Thee to-morrow ;
In Thee our Best,
In Thee our All.
Before 1893.

HAVE I not striven, my God, and
    watched and prayed ?
  Have I not wrestled in mine
    agony ?
  Wherefore still turn Thy Face of
    Grace from me ?
Is Thine Arm shortened that Thou
    canst not aid ?
Thy silence breaks my heart : speak
    tho' to upbraid,
  For Thy rebuke yet bids us follow
    Thee.
I grope and grasp not ; gaze, but
    cannot see.
When out of sight and reach my
    bed is made,
And piteous men and women cease
    to blame,
  Whispering and wistful of my
    gain or loss ;
  Thou Who for my sake once
    didst feel the Cross,
  Lord, wilt Thou turn and look
    upon me then,
And in Thy Glory bring to nought
    my shame,
  Confessing me to angels and to
    men ?
30 *September* 1863.

God is our Hope and Strength.

TEMPEST and terror below; but Christ the Almighty above.
Tho' the depth of the deep overflow, tho' fire run along on the ground,
Tho' all billows and flames make a noise,— and where is an Ark for the dove?—
Tho' sorrows rejoice against joys, and death and destruction abound:
Yet Jesus abolisheth death, and Jesus Who loves us we love;
His dead are renewed with a breath, His lost are the sought and the found.
Thy wanderers call and recall, Thy dead men lift out of the ground;
O Jesus, Who lovest us all, stoop low from Thy Glory above:
Where sin hath abounded make grace to abound and to superabound,
Till we gaze on Thee face unto Face, and respond to Thee love unto Love.

Before 1893.

DAY and night the Accuser makes no pause,
Day and night protest the Righteous Laws,
Good and Evil witness to man's flaws;
Man the culprit, man's the ruined cause,
Man midway to death's devouring jaws
And the worm that gnaws.

Day and night our Jesus makes no pause,
Pleads His own fulfilment of all laws,
Veils with His Perfections mortal flaws,
Clears the culprit, pleads the desperate cause,
Plucks the dead from death's devouring jaws
And the worm that gnaws.

Before 1893.

O MINE enemy
Rejoice not over me!
  Jesus waiteth to be gracious:
    I will yet arise,
Mounting free and far,
Past sun and star,
  To a house prepared and spacious
    In the skies.

Lord, for Thine own sake
Kindle my heart and break;
  Make mine anguish efficacious
    Wedded to Thine own:
Be not Thy dear pain,
Thy Love, in vain,
  Thou Who waitest to be gracious
    On Thy Throne.

Before 1893.

LORD, dost Thou look on me, and will not I
  Launch out my heart to Heaven to look on Thee?
  Here if one loved me I should turn to see,
And often think on him and often sigh,
And by a tender friendship make reply
  To love gratuitous poured forth on me,
  And nurse a hope of happy days to be,

And mean 'until we meet' in each
  good-bye.
Lord, Thou dost look and love is in
  Thine Eyes,
  Thy heart is set upon me day
    and night,
  Thou stoopest low to set me
    far above:
O Lord, that I may love Thee make
  me wise;
  That I may see and love Thee
    grant me sight;
  And give me love that I may
    give Thee love.
Before 1893.

Peace I leave with you.

TUMULT and turmoil, trouble and
  toil,
  Yet peace withal in a painful
    heart;
Never a grudge and never a broil,
  And ever the better part.

O my King and my heart's own
  choice,
  Stretch Thy Hand to Thy flutter-
    ing dove;
Teach me, call to me with Thy
  Voice,
  Wrap me up in Thy Love.
Before 1893.

O CHRIST our All in each, our All
  in all!
  Others have this or that, a love,
    a friend,
  A trusted teacher, a long-worked-
    for end:
But what to me were Peter or were
  Paul
  Without Thee? fame or friend if
    such might be?

Thee wholly will I love, Thee
  wholly seek,
Follow Thy foot-track, hearken for
  Thy call.
  O Christ mine All in all, my
    flesh is weak,
  A trembling fawning tyrant unto
    me:
  Turn, look upon me, let me
    hear Thee speak:
  Tho' bitter billows of Thine
    utmost sea
Swathe me, and darkness build
  around its wall,
Yet will I rise, Thou lifting when I
  fall,
  And if Thou hold me fast, yet
    cleave to Thee.
Before 1886.

BECAUSE Thy Love hath sought
  me,
  All mine is Thine and Thine is
    mine:
Because Thy Blood hath bought
  me,
  I will not be mine own but Thine.

I lift my heart to Thy Heart,
  Thy Heart sole resting-place for
    mine:
Shall Thy Heart crave for my heart,
  And shall not mine crave back
    for Thine?
Before 1893.

THY fainting spouse, yet still Thy
  spouse;
  Thy trembling dove, yet still Thy
    dove;
Thine own by mutual vows,
  By mutual love.

Recall Thy vows, if not her vows;
  Recall Thy Love, if not her love:
For weak she is, Thy spouse,
  And tired, Thy dove.
Before 1893.

> *Like as the hart desireth the water brooks.*

My heart is yearning:
  Behold my yearning heart,
    And lean low to satisfy
    Its lonely beseeching cry,
  For Thou its fulness art.

Turn, as once turning
  Thou didst behold Thy Saint
    In deadly extremity;
    Didst look, and win back to Thee
  His will frighted and faint.

Kindle my burning
  From Thine unkindled Fire;
    Fill me with gifts and with grace
    That I may behold Thy Face,
  For Thee I desire.

My heart is yearning,
  Yearning and thrilling thro'
    For Thy Love mine own of old,
    For Thy Love unknown, untold,
  Ever old, ever new.
Before 1893.

> *That where I am, there ye may be also.*

How know I that it looms lovely
    that land I have never seen,
With morning-glories and heartsease
    and unexampled green,
With neither heat nor cold in the
    balm-redolent air?
Some of this, not all, I know;
  but this is so;
Christ is there.

How know I that blessedness befalls
    who dwell in Paradise,
The outwearied hearts refreshing,
    rekindling the worn-out eyes,
All souls singing, seeing, rejoicing
    everywhere?
  Nay, much more than this I
    know; for this is so;
Christ is there.

O Lord Christ, Whom having not
    seen I love and desire to love,
O Lord Christ, Who lookest on me
    uncomely yet still Thy dove,
Take me to Thee in Paradise, Thine
    own made fair;
  For whatever else I know, this
    thing is so;
  Thou art there.
Before 1893.

> *Judge not according to the appearance.*

Lord, purge our eyes to see
Within the seed a tree,
  Within the glowing egg a bird,
  Within the shroud a butterfly:
Till taught by such, we see
Beyond all creatures Thee,
  And hearken for Thy tender word,
  And hear it, 'Fear not: it is I.'
Before 1893.

My God, wilt Thou accept, and will not we
  Give aught to Thee?
The kept we lose, the offered we retain
  Or find again.

Yet if our gift were lost, we well
    might lose
  All for Thy use:
Well lost for Thee Whose love is
    all for us
  Gratuitous.
Before 1893.

A CHILL blank world. Yet over
    the utmost sea
The light of a coming dawn is
    rising to me,
  No more than a paler shade of
    darkness as yet;
While I lift my heart, O Lord, my
    heart unto Thee
  Who hast not forgotten me, yea,
    Who wilt not forget.
Forget not Thy sorrowful servant,
    O Lord my God,
Weak as I cry, faint as I cry under-
    neath Thy rod,
  Soon to lie dumb before Thee a
    body devoid of breath,
Dust to dust, ashes to ashes, a sod
    to the sod:
  Forget not my life, O my Lord,
    forget not my death.
Before 1893.

The Chiefest among ten thousand.

O JESU, better than Thy gifts
  Art Thou Thine only Self to us!
Palm branch its triumph, harp uplifts
  Its triumph-note melodious:
    But what are such to such as we?
O Jesu, better than Thy saints
  Art Thou Thine only Self to us!
The heart faints and the spirit faints
  For only Thee all-Glorious,
    For Thee, O only Lord, for
      Thee.
Before 1893.

EASTER EVEN

THERE is nothing more that they
    can do
  For all their rage and boast:
Caiaphas with his blaspheming
    crew,
  Herod with his host;
Pontius Pilate in his judgment hall
  Judging their Judge and his,
Or he who led them all and passed
    them all,
  Arch-Judas with his kiss.

The sepulchre made sure with
    ponderous stone,
  Seal that same stone, O priest:
It may be thou shalt block the
    Holy One
  From rising in the east.
Set a watch about the sepulchre
  To watch on pain of death:
They must hold fast the stone if
    One should stir
  And shake it from beneath.

God Almighty, He can break a seal,
  And roll away a stone:
Can grind the proud in dust who
    would not kneel,
  And crush the mighty one.

There is nothing more that they
    can do
  For all their passionate care,
Those who sit in dust, the blessed
    few,
  And weep and rend their hair.
Peter, Thomas, Mary Magdalen,
  The Virgin unreproved,
Joseph and Nicodemus foremost
    men,
  And John the well-beloved.

Bring your finest linen and your
    spice,
Swathe the sacred Dead,
Bind with careful hands and piteous
    eyes
The napkin round His head :

Lay Him in the garden-rock to rest :
Rest you the Sabbath length :
The Sun that went down crimson in
    the west
Shall rise renewed in strength.

God Almighty shall give joy for
    pain,
Shall comfort him who grieves :
Lo He with joy shall doubtless come
    again
And with Him bring His sheaves.
23 *March* 1861.

THE OFFERING OF THE
NEW LAW

ONCE I thought to sit so high
In the palace of the sky :
Now I thank God for His grace
If I may fill the lowest place.

Once I thought to scale so soon
Heights above the changing moon :
Now I thank God for delay :—
To-day : it yet is called to-day.

While I stumble, halt and blind,
Lo He waiteth to be kind :
Bless me soon or bless me slow—
Except He bless I let not go.

Once for earth I laid my plan,
Once I leaned on strength of man :
When my hope was swept aside
I stayed my broken heart on pride :

Broken reed hath pierced my hand,
Fell my house I built on sand,
Roofless, wounded, maimed by sin,
Fightings without and fears within.

Yet, His tree, He feeds my root :
Yet, His branch, He prunes for fruit :
Yet, His sheep, these eves and
    morns
He seeks for me among the thorns.

With Thine Image stamped of old,
Find Thy coin more choice than
    gold :
Known to Thee by name, recall
To Thee Thy homesick prodigal.

Sacrifice and offering
None there is that I can bring—
None save what is Thine alone :
I bring Thee, Lord, but of Thine
    own.

Broken Body, Blood outpoured,
These I bring, my God, my Lord ;
Wine of Life and Living Bread,
With these for me Thy board is
    spread.
23 *May* 1861.

BY THE WATERS OF
BABYLON

BY the waters of Babylon
    We sit down and weep,
Far from the pleasant land
    Where our fathers sleep :
Far from our Holy Place
    From which the Glory is gone :
We sit in dust and weep
    By the waters of Babylon.

By the waters of Babylon
    The willow-trees grow rank :

We hang our harps thereon
  Silent upon the bank.
Before us the days are dark,
  And dark the days that are gone:
We grope in the very dark
  By the waters of Babylon.

By the waters of Babylon
  We thirst for Jordan yet,
We pine for Jerusalem
  Whereon our hearts are set:
Our priests defiled and slain,
  Our princes ashamed and gone,
Oh how should we forget
  By the waters of Babylon?

By the waters of Babylon
  Though the wicked grind the just,
Our seed shall yet strike root
  And shall shoot up from the dust:
The captive shall lead captive,
  The slave rise up and begone,
And thou too shalt sit in dust,
  O daughter of Babylon.
1 December 1861.

WITHIN THE VEIL

SHE holds a lily in her hand,
Where long ranks of Angels stand:
A silver lily for her wand.

All her hair falls sweeping down,
Her hair that is a golden brown,
A crown beneath her golden crown.

Blooms a rose-bush at her knee,
Good to smell and good to see:
It bears a rose for her, for me:

Her rose a blossom richly grown,
My rose a bud not fully blown
But sure one day to be mine own.
13 December 1861.

GOOD FRIDAY

AM I a stone, and not a sheep,
  That I can stand, O Christ, beneath Thy cross,
  To number drop by drop Thy Blood's slow loss,
And yet not weep?

Not so those women loved
  Who with exceeding grief lamented Thee;
  Not so fallen Peter weeping bitterly;
Not so the thief was moved;

Not so the Sun and Moon
  Which hid their faces in a starless sky,
  A horror of great darkness at broad noon—
I, only I.

Yet give not o'er,
  But seek Thy sheep, true Shepherd of the flock;
  Greater than Moses, turn and look once more
And smite a rock.
20 April 1862.

OUT OF THE DEEP

HAVE mercy, Thou my God—mercy, my God!
  For I can hardly bear life day by day.
  Be I here or there, I fret myself away:
Lo for Thy staff I have but felt Thy rod
  Along this tedious desert-path long trod.

When will Thy judgment judge
   me, yea or nay?
I pray for grace: but then my
   sins unpray
My prayer: on holy ground I fool
   stand shod—
While still Thou haunt'st me, faint
   upon the cross,
  A sorrow beyond sorrow in Thy
    look,
    Unutterable craving for my
     soul.
  All-faithful Thou, Lord: I, not
    Thou, forsook
    Myself: I traitor slunk back
     from the goal:
Lord, I repent — help Thou my
   helpless loss.
17 December 1862.

FOR A MERCY RECEIVED

THANK God who spared me what
   I feared!
  Once more I gird myself to run.
  Thy promise stands, Thou Faith-
    ful One.
Horror of darkness disappeared
  At length: once more I see the
    sun,

And dare to wait in hope for Spring,
  To face and bear the Winter's
    cold:
The dead cocoon shall yet unfold
And give to light the living wing:
  There's hidden sap beneath the
    mould.

My God, how could my courage
   flag
  So long as Thou art still the
    same?

For what were labour, failure,
   shame,
Whilst Thy sure promise doth not
   lag,
And Thou dost shield me with
   Thy Name?

Yet am I weak, my faith is weak,
  My heart is weak that pleads with
    Thee:
O Thou that art not far to seek,
  Turn to me, hearken when I speak,
  Stretch forth Thy hand to succour
    me.

Through many perils have I past,
  Deaths, plagues, and wonders,
    have I seen:
Till now Thy hand hath held me
   fast:
Lord, help me, hold me, to the last:
  Still be what Thou hast always
    been.

Open Thy Heart of Love to me,
  Give me Thyself, keep nothing
    back,
Even as I give myself to Thee.
  Love paid by love doth nothing
    lack,
  And Love to pay love is not slack.

Love doth so grace and dignify
  That beggars sue as king with
    king
Before the Throne of Grace on high:
My God, be gracious to my cry:
  My God, accept what gift I
    bring:—

A heart that loves: though soiled
   and bruised,
  Yet chosen by Thee in time of
    yore.

Who ever came and was refused
By thee? Do, Lord, as Thou art used
  To do, and make me love Thee more.

13 *January* 1863.

MARTYRS' SONG

WE meet in joy, though we part in sorrow;
We part to-night, but we meet to-morrow.
Be it flood or blood the path that's trod,
All the same it leads home to God:
Be it furnace-fire voluminous,
One like God's Son will walk with us.

What are these that glow from afar,
These that lean over the golden bar,
Strong as the lion, pure as the dove,
With open arms and hearts of love?
They the blessed ones gone before,
They the blessed for evermore.
Out of great tribulation they went
Home to their home of Heaven-content;
Through flood or blood or furnace-fire,
To the rest that fulfils desire.

What are these that fly as a cloud,
With flashing heads and faces bowed,
In their mouths a victorious psalm,
In their hands a robe and a palm?
Welcoming angels these that shine,
Your own angel, and yours, and mine;
Who have hedged us both day and night
On the left hand and on the right,
Who have watched us both night and day
Because the devil keeps watch to slay.

Light above light, and Bliss beyond bliss,
Whom words cannot utter, lo Who is This?
As a King with many crowns He stands,
And our names are graven upon His hands:
As a Priest, with God-uplifted eyes,
He offers for us His Sacrifice;
As the Lamb of God for sinners slain,
That we too may live He lives again;
As our Champion behold Him stand,
Strong to save us, at God's Right Hand.

God the Father give us grace
To walk in the light of Jesus' Face:
God the Son give us a part
In the hiding-place of Jesus' Heart:
God the Spirit so hold us up
That we may drink of Jesus' cup.

Death is short, and life is long;
Satan is strong, but Christ more strong.
At His Word Who hath led us hither
The Red Sea must part hither and thither.
At His Word Who goes before us too
Jordan must cleave to let us through.

Yet one pang searching and sore,
And then Heaven for evermore:
Yet one moment awful and dark,

Then safety within the Veil and the
    Ark;
Yet one effort by Christ His grace,
Then Christ for ever face to face.

God the Father we will adore,
In Jesus' Name, now and evermore :
God the Son we will love and thank
In this flood and on the farther bank;
God the Holy Ghost we will praise,
In Jesus' Name through endless
    days :
God Almighty, God Three in One,
God Almighty, God alone.
    20 *March* 1863.

CONSIDER

CONSIDER
The lilies of the field whose bloom
        is brief :
    We are as they ;
    Like them we fade away
As doth a leaf.

    Consider
The sparrows of the air of small
        account ;
    Our God doth view
Whether they fall or mount,—
    He guards us too.

    Consider
The lilies that do neither spin nor toil,
    Yet are most fair : —
    What profits all this care
And all this coil?

    Consider
The birds that have no barn nor
        harvest-weeks ;
    God gives them food :—
Much more our Father seeks
    To do us good.
    7 *May* 1863.

THE LOWEST PLACE

GIVE me the lowest place ; not that
        I dare
    Ask for that lowest place, but
        Thou hast died
That I might live and share
    Thy glory by Thy side.

Give me the lowest place : or if for
        me
    That lowest place too high, make
        one more low
Where I may sit and see
    My God and love Thee so.
    25 *July* 1863.

COME UNTO ME

OH for the time gone by when
        thought of Christ
    Made His yoke easy and His
        burden light !
    When my heart stirred within me
        at the sight
Of altar spread for awful Eucharist :
When all my hopes His promises
        sufficed :
    When my soul watched for Him,
        by day, by night :
    When my lamp lightened and
        my robe was white,
And all seemed loss except the
        pearl unpriced.
Yet, since He calls me still with
        tender call,
    Since He remembers whom I
        half forgot,
    I even will run my race and bear
        my lot :
For Faith the walls of Jericho cast
        down,

And Hope to whoso runs holds
 forth a crown,
And Love is Christ, and Christ is
 all in all.
23 *February* 1864.

WHO SHALL DELIVER ME?

GOD strengthen me to bear myself;
That heaviest weight of all to bear,
Inalienable weight of care.

All others are outside myself;
I lock my door and bar them out,
The turmoil, tedium, gad-about.

I lock my door upon myself,
And bar them out; but who shall
 wall
Self from myself, most loathed of
 all?

If I could once lay down myself,
And start self-purged upon the race
That all must run! Death runs
 apace.

If I could set aside myself,
And start with lightened heart upon
The road by all men overgone!

God harden me against myself,
This coward with pathetic voice
Who craves for ease, and rest, and
 joys:

Myself, arch-traitor to myself;
My hollowest friend, my deadliest
 foe,
My clog whatever road I go.

Yet One there is can curb myself,
Can roll the strangling load from
 me,
Break off the yoke and set me free.
1 *March* 1864.

IN PATIENCE

I WILL not faint, but trust in God
 Who this my lot hath given:
He leads me by the thorny road
 Which is the road to heaven.
Though sad my day that lasts so long,
 At evening I shall have a song:
Though dim my day until the night,
 At evening-time there shall be light.

My life is but a working day
 Whose tasks are set aright:
A while to work, a while to pray,
 And then a quiet night.
And then, please God, a quiet night
Where Saints and Angels walk in
 white:
One dreamless sleep from work and
 sorrow,
But re-awakening on the morrow.
19 *March* 1864.

NONE WITH HIM

MY God, to live: how didst Thou
 bear to live,
 Preaching and teaching, toiling
 to and fro?
Few men accepting what Thou
 hadst to give,
 Few men prepared to know
Thy Face, to see the truth Thou
 cam'st to show.

My God, to die: how didst Thou
 bear to die
That long slow death in weariness
 of pain?
A curse and an astonishment, past
 by,
 Pointed at, mocked again,
By men for whom Thy blood was
 shed in vain.

Whilst I do hardly bear my easy
    life,
And hardly face my easy-coming
    death :
I turn to flee before the tug of
    strife ;
    And shrink with troubled breath
From sleep, that is not death,
    Thy Spirit saith.
14 *June* 1864.

BY THE WATERS OF BABYLON

B.C. 570

HERE, where I dwell, I waste to
    skin and bone ;
The curse is come upon me, and
    I waste
In penal torment powerless to
    atone.
The curse is come on me, which
    makes no haste
    And doth not tarry, crushing both
        the proud
Hard man and him the sinner
    double-faced.
Look not upon me, for my soul is
    bowed
Within me, as my body in this
    mire ;
My soul crawls dumb-struck, sore
    bestead and cowed.
As Sodom and Gomorrah scourged
    by fire,
As Jericho before God's trumpet-
    peal,
So we the elect ones perish in
    His ire.
Vainly we gird on sackcloth, vainly
    kneel
With famished faces toward Jeru-
    salem :

His heart is shut against us not
    to feel,
His ears against our cry He shutteth
    them,
His hand He shorteneth that He
    will not save,
His law is loud against us to
    condemn :
And we, as unclean bodies in the
    grave
Inheriting corruption and the dark,
Are outcast from His presence
    which we crave.
Our Mercy hath departed from His
    Ark,
Our Glory hath departed from
    His rest,
Our Shield hath left us naked as
    a mark
Unto all pitiless eyes made manifest.
Our very Father hath forsaken us,
Our God hath cast us from Him :
    we oppress'd
Unto our foes are even marvellous,
A hissing and a butt for pointing
    hands,
Whilst God Almighty hunts and
    grinds us thus ;
For He hath scattered us in alien
    lands,
Our priests, our princes, our
    anointed king,
And bound us hand and foot with
    brazen bands.
Here while I sit my painful heart
    takes wing
Home to the home-land I may see
    no more,
Where milk and honey flow,
    where waters spring
And fail not, where I dwelt in days
    of yore
Under my fig-tree and my fruitful
    vine,

There where my parents dwelt at
    ease before :
Now strangers press the olives that
    are mine,
    Reap all the corners of my harvest-
        field,
    And make their fat hearts wanton
        with my wine.
To them my trees, to them my
    gardens yield
    Their sweets and spices and their
        tender green,
    O'er them in noontide heat out-
        spread their shield.
Yet these are they whose fathers
    had not been
    Housed with my dogs, whom hip
        and thigh we smote
    And with their blood washed their
        pollutions clean,
Purging the land which spewed them
    from its throat ;
    Their daughters took we for a
        pleasant prey,
    Choice tender ones on whom the
        fathers doat.
Now they in turn have led our own
    away ;
    Our daughters and our sisters and
        our wives
    Sore weeping as they weep who
        curse the day,
To live, remote from help, dis-
    honoured lives,
    Soothing their drunken masters
        with a song,
    Or dancing in their golden tinkling
        gyves :
Accurst if they remember through
    the long
    Estrangement of their exile, twice
        accurst
    If they forget and join the ac-
        cursèd throng.

How doth my heart that is so wrung
    not burst
    When I remember that my way
        was plain,
    And that God's candle lit me at
        the first,
Whilst now I grope in darkness,
    grope in vain,
    Desiring but to find Him Who is
        lost,
    To find Him once again, but once
        again !
His wrath came on us to the utter-
    most,
    His covenanted and most righteous
        wrath :
    Yet this is He of Whom we made
        our boast,
Who lit the Fiery Pillar in our path,
    Who swept the Red Sea dry before
        our feet,
    Who in His jealousy smote kings,
        and hath
Sworn once to David : One shall fill
    thy seat
    Born of thy body, as the sun and
        moon
    Stablished for aye in sovereignty
        complete.
O Lord, remember David, and that
    soon.
    The Glory hath departed, Ichabod !
    Yet now, before our sun grow
        dark at noon,
Before we come to nought beneath
    Thy rod,
    Before we go down quick into the
        pit,
    Remember us for good, O God
        our God :—
Thy Name will I remember, praising
    it,
    Though Thou forget me, though
        Thou hide Thy face,

And blot me from the Book which
    Thou hast writ,
Thy Name will I remember in my
    praise
And call to mind Thy faithfulness
    of old,
Though as a weaver Thou cut off
    my days
And end me as a tale ends that
    is told.
29 June 1864.

DESPISED AND REJECTED

My sun has set, I dwell
In darkness as a dead man out of
    sight;
And none remains, not one, that I
    should tell
To him mine evil plight
This bitter night.
I will make fast my door
That hollow friends may trouble me
    no more.

'Friend, open to Me.'—'Who is
    this that calls?
Nay, I am deaf as are my walls:
Cease crying, for I will not hear
Thy cry of hope or fear.
Others were dear,
Others forsook me: what art thou
    indeed
That I should heed
Thy lamentable need?
Hungry should feed,
Or stranger lodge thee here?'

'Friend, My Feet bleed.
Open thy door to Me and comfort
    Me.'
'I will not open, trouble me no more.
Go on thy way footsore,
I will not rise and open unto thee.'

'Then is it nothing to thee? Open,
    see
Who stands to plead with thee.
Open, lest I should pass thee by,
    and thou
One day entreat my Face
And howl for grace,
And I be deaf as thou art now.
Open to Me.'

Then I cried out upon him: 'Cease,
Leave me in peace:
Fear not that I should crave
Aught thou mayst have.
Leave me in peace, yea trouble me
    no more,
Lest I arise and chase thee from my
    door.
What, shall I not be let
Alone, that thou dost vex me yet?'

But all night long that voice spake
    urgently,
'Open to Me.'
Still harping in mine ears:
'Rise, let Me in.'
Pleading with tears:
'Open to Me, that I may come to
    thee.'
While the dew dropped, while the
    dark hours were cold:
'My Feet bleed, see My Face,
See My Hands bleed that bring thee
    grace,
My Heart doth bleed for thee,—
Open to Me.'

So till the break of day:
Then died away
That voice, in silence as of sorrow;
Then footsteps echoing like a sigh
Passed me by,
Lingering footsteps slow to pass.

On the morrow
I saw upon the grass
Each footprint marked in blood, and
    on my door
The mark of blood for evermore.
   10 October 1864.

WEARY IN WELL-DOING

I WOULD have gone ; God bade me
    stay :
   I would have worked ; God bade
    me rest.
He broke my will from day to day ;
He read my yearnings unexprest,
   And said them nay.

Now I would stay ; God bids me go :
   Now I would rest ; God bids me
    work.
He breaks my heart tost to and fro ;
   My soul is wrung with doubts that
    lurk
   And vex it so.

I go, Lord, where Thou sendest
    me ;
   Day after day I plod and moil :
But, Christ my God, when will it be
   That I may let alone my toil
    And rest with Thee ?
   22 October 1864.

BIRDS OF PARADISE

GOLDEN-WINGED, silver-winged,
   Winged with flashing flame,
Such a flight of birds I saw,
   Birds without a name :
Singing songs in their own tongue—
   Song of songs—they came.

One to another calling,
   Each answering each,
One to another calling
   In their proper speech :
High above my head they wheeled,
   Far out of reach.

On wings of flame they went and
    came
   With a cadenced clang :
Their silver wings tinkled,
   Their golden wings rang ;
The wind it whistled through their
    wings
   Where in heaven they sang.

They flashed and they darted
   Awhile before mine eyes,
Mounting, mounting, mounting still,
   In haste to scale the skies,
Birds without a nest on earth,
   Birds of Paradise.

Where the moon riseth not
   Nor sun seeks the west,
There to sing their glory
   Which they sing at rest,
There to sing their love-song
   When they sing their best :—

Not in any garden
   That mortal foot hath trod,
Not in any flowering tree
   That springs from earthly sod,
But in the garden where they dwell,
   The Paradise of God.
   14 November 1864.

DOST THOU NOT CARE ?

'I LOVE and love not : Lord, it breaks
    my heart
   To love and not to love.
Thou veiled within Thy glory, gone
    apart
   Into Thy shrine which is above,

Dost Thou not love me, Lord, or care
    For this mine ill?'—
'I love thee here or there,
    I will accept thy broken heart—
        lie still.'

'Lord, it was well with me in time
    gone by
That cometh not again,
When I was fresh and cheerful, who
    but I?
I fresh, I cheerful: worn with pain
Now, out of sight and out of heart;
    O Lord, how long?'—
'I watch thee as thou art,
    I will accept thy fainting heart—
        be strong.'

'Lie still, be strong, to-day: but,
    Lord, to-morrow,
What of to-morrow, Lord?
Shall there be rest from toil, be truce
    from sorrow,
Be living green upon the sward,
Now but a barren grave to me,
    Be joy for sorrow?'—
'Did I not die for thee?
    Do I not live for thee? Leave
        Me to-morrow.'

24 December 1864.

I KNOW YOU NOT

O CHRIST, the Vine with living fruit,
    The twelvefold-fruited Tree of Life,
    The Balm in Gilead after strife,
    The Valley-lily and the Rose;
Stronger than Lebanon Thou Root;
Sweeter than clustered grapes Thou
        Vine;
O best, Thou Vineyard of red wine,
    Keeping Thy best wine till the
        close.

Pearl of great price Thyself alone,
    And ruddier than the ruby Thou;
Most precious lightening Jasper
        stone,
Head of the corner spurned before:
Fair gate of pearl, Thyself the Door;
Clear golden street, Thyself the Way;
    By Thee we journey toward Thee
        now,
Through Thee shall enter heaven one
        day.

I thirst for Thee, full fount and flood;
    My heart calls thine, as deep to
        deep:
        Dost Thou forget Thy sweat
            and pain,
    Thy provocation on the cross?
Heart-pierced for me, vouchsafe to
        keep
The purchase of Thy lavished Blood:
    The gain is Thine, Lord, if I gain;
    Or, if I lose, Thine own the
        loss.

At midnight, saith the Parable,
    A cry was made, the Bridegroom
        came;
    Those who were ready entered
        in:
The rest, shut out in death and
    shame,
    Strove all too late that feast to
        win,
    Their die was cast and fixed their
        lot;
A gulf divided heaven from hell;
    The Bridegroom said—I know you
        not.

But Who is this that shuts the door,
    And saith—I know you not—to
        them?
    I see the wounded hands and
        side,

The brow thorn-tortured long
    ago :
  Yea, This who grieved and bled
    and died,
This same is He who must con-
    demn ;
  He called, but they refused
    to know ;
So now He hears their cry no more.
Circa 1864.

IF ONLY

IF only I might love my God and
    die !—
  But now He bids me love Him and
    live on,
Now when the bloom of all my
    life is gone,
  The pleasant half of life has quite
    gone by.
My tree of hope is lopt that spread
    so high;
  And I forget how summer glowed
    and shone,
While autumn grips me with its
    fingers wan,
  And frets me with its fitful windy
    sigh.
When autumn passes then must
    winter numb,
  And winter may not pass a weary
    while.
  But when it passes spring shall
    flower again :
And in that spring who weepeth
    now shall smile—
  Yea, they shall wax who now
    are on the wane,
Yea, they shall sing for love when
    Christ shall come.
20 *February* 1865.

LONG BARREN

THOU who didst hang upon a barren
    tree,
My God, for me ;
  Though I till now be barren, now
    at length,
  Lord, give me strength
To bring forth fruit to Thee.

Thou who didst bear for me the
    crown of thorn,
Spitting and scorn ;
  Though I till now have put forth
    thorns, yet now
  Strengthen me Thou
That better fruit be borne.

Thou Rose of Sharon, Cedar of
    broad roots,
Vine of sweet fruits,
  Thou Lily of the vale with fade-
    less leaf,
  Of thousands Chief,
Feed Thou my feeble shoots.
21 *February* 1865.

YOUNG DEATH

LYING a-dying—
Such sweet things untasted,
Such rare beauties wasted :
Her hair a hidden treasure,
Her voice a lost pleasure :
Her soul made void of passion,
Her body going to nothing
Though long it took to fashion,
Soon to be a loathing.
Her road hath no turning.
Her light is burning burning
With last feeble flashes,
Dying from the birth :

Dust to dust, earth to earth,
  Ashes to ashes.

  .   .   .   .

Lo in the room, the upper,
She shall sit down to supper,
New-bathed from head to feet
  And on Christ gazing:
Her mouth kept clean and sweet
Shall laugh and sing, God praising.
Then shall be no more weeping
  Or fear or sorrow,
Or waking more or sleeping
  Or night or morrow,
Or cadence in the song
Of saints, or thirst or hunger:
The strong shall rise more strong,
  And the young younger.

  .   .   .   .

3 November 1865.

MOTHER COUNTRY

OH what is that country
  And where can it be,
Not mine own country,
  But dearer far to me?
Yet mine own country,
  If I one day may see
Its spices and cedars,
  Its gold and ivory.

As I lie dreaming,
  It rises, that land;
There rises before me
  Its green golden strand,
With the bowing cedars
  And the shining sand;
It sparkles and flashes
  Like a shaken brand.

Do angels lean nearer
  While I lie and long?
I see their soft plumage
  And catch their windy song,

Like the rise of a high tide
  Sweeping full and strong;
I mark the outskirts
  Of their reverend throng.

Oh what is a king here,
  Or what is a boor?
Here all starve together,
  All dwarfed and poor;
Here Death's hand knocketh
  At door after door,
He thins the dancers
  From the festal floor.

Oh what is a handmaid,
  Or what is a queen?
All must lie down together
  Where the turf is green,
The foulest face hidden,
  The fairest not seen;
Gone as if never
  They had breathed or been.

Gone from sweet sunshine
  Underneath the sod,
Turned from warm flesh and blood
  To senseless clod,
Gone as if never
  They had toiled or trod,
Gone out of sight of all
  Except our God.

Shut into silence
  From the accustomed song,
Shut into solitude
  From all earth's throng,
Run down though swift of foot,
  Thrust down though strong:
Life made an end of,
  Seemed it short or long.

Life made an end of,—
  Life but just begun;
Life finished yesterday,
  Its last sand run:

Life new-born with the morrow,
  Fresh as the sun:
While done is done for ever;
  Undone, undone.

And if that life is life,
  This is but a breath,
The passage of a dream
  And the shadow of death;
But a vain shadow
  If one considereth;
Vanity of vanities,
  As the Preacher saith.

7 February 1866.

AFTER COMMUNION

WHY should I call Thee Lord, Who art my God?
  Why should I call Thee Friend, Who art my Love?
    Or King, Who art my very Spouse above?
Or call Thy Sceptre on my heart Thy rod?
Lo now Thy banner over me is love,
All heaven flies open to me at Thy nod:
For Thou hast lit Thy flame in me a clod,
  Made me a nest for dwelling of Thy Dove.
    What wilt Thou call me in our home above,
Who now hast called me friend? how will it be
    When Thou for good wine settest forth the best?
Now Thou dost bid me come and sup with Thee,
    Now Thou dost make me lean upon Thy breast:
  How will it be with me in time of love?

23 February 1866.

A CHRISTMAS CAROL

IN the bleak mid-winter
  Frosty wind made moan,
Earth stood hard as iron,
  Water like a stone;
Snow had fallen, snow on snow,
  Snow on snow,
In the bleak mid-winter
  Long ago.

Our God, Heaven cannot hold Him
  Nor earth sustain;
Heaven and earth shall flee away
  When He comes to reign:
In the bleak mid-winter
  A stable-place sufficed
The Lord God Almighty
  Jesus Christ.

Enough for Him, whom cherubim
  Worship night and day,
A breastful of milk
  And a mangerful of hay;
Enough for Him, whom angels
  Fall down before,
The ox and ass and camel
  Which adore

Angels and archangels
  May have gathered there,
Cherubim and seraphim
  Thronged the air;
But only His mother
  In her maiden bliss
Worshipped the Beloved
  With a kiss.

What can I give Him,
  Poor as I am?
If I were a shepherd
  I would bring a lamb,

If I were a Wise Man
    I would do my part,—
Yet what I can I give Him,
    Give my heart.

Before 1872.

WRESTLING

ALAS my Lord,
How should I wrestle all the live-
    long night
With Thee my God, my strength
    and my delight?

How can it need
So agonized an effort and a strain
To make Thy face of mercy shine
    again?

How can it need
Such wringing out of breathless
    prayer to move
Thee to Thy wonted love, 'when
    Thou art Love?

Yet Abraham
So hung about Thine arm, out-
    stretcht and bared,
That for ten righteous Sodom had
    been spared.

Yet Jacob did
So hold Thee by the clenchèd hand
    of prayer
That he prevailed and Thou didst
    bless him there.

Elias prayed,
And sealed the founts of heaven:
    he prayed again,
And lo Thy blessing fell in showers
    of rain.

Gulpt by the fish
And by the pit, lost Jonah made
    his moan,
And Thou forgavest, waiting to
    atone.

All Nineveh
Fasting and girt in sackcloth raised
    a cry,
Which moved Thee ere the day of
    grace went by.

Thy Church prayed on
And on for blessed Peter in his
    strait,
Till opened of its own accord the
    gate.

Yea Thou my God
Hast prayed all night, and in the
    garden prayed,
Even while like melting wax Thy
    strength was made.

Alas for him
Who faints despite Thy pattern,
    King of Saints!
Alas alas for me the one that
    faints!

Lord, give us strength
To hold Thee fast until we hear
    Thy voice,
Which Thine own know who hearing
    it rejoice.

Lord, give us strength
To hold Thee fast until we see Thy
    Face,
Full fountain of all rapture and all
    grace.

But, when our strength
Shall be made darkness, and our
    bodies clay,
Hold Thou us fast and give us sleep
    till day.

Before 1875

THE MASTER IS COME, AND CALLETH FOR THEE

Who calleth?—Thy Father calleth,
    Run, O Daughter, to wait on
    Him:
He Who chasteneth but for a season
    Trims thy lamp that it burn not
    dim.

Who calleth?—Thy Master calleth,
    Sit, Disciple, and learn of Him:
He Who teacheth wisdom of Angels
    Makes thee wise as the Cherubim.

Who calleth?—Thy Monarch calleth,
    Rise, O Subject, and follow Him:
He is stronger than Death or Devil,
    Fear not thou if the foe be grim.

Who calleth?—Thy Lord God
    calleth,
    Fall, O Creature, adoring Him:
He is jealous, thy God Almighty,
    Count not dear to thee life or
    limb.

Who calleth?—Thy Bridegroom
    calleth,
    Soar, O Bride, with the Seraphim:
He Who loves thee as no man loveth
    Bids thee give up thy heart to
    Him.

Before 1876.

'WHEN MY HEART IS VEXED I WILL COMPLAIN'

'O Lord, how canst Thou say
    Thou lovest me—
Me whom thou settest in a barren
    land,
Hungry and thirsty on the burn-
    ing sand,
Hungry and thirsty where no waters
    be
Nor shadows of date-bearing tree:—
O Lord, how canst Thou say Thou
    lovest me?'

'I came from Edom by as parched
    a track,
    As rough a track beneath My
    bleeding feet.
I came from Edom seeking thee,
    and sweet
I counted bitterness; I turned not
    back
But counted life as death, and trod
    The winepress all alone: and I am
    God.'

'Yet, Lord, how canst Thou say
    Thou lovest me?
    For Thou art strong to comfort:
    and could I
    But comfort one I love who, like
    to die,
Lifts feeble hands and eyes that fail
    to see
In one last prayer for comfort—
    nay,
I could not stand aside or turn away.'

'Alas thou knowest that for thee I
    died,
    For thee I thirsted with the dying
    thirst;

I, blessèd, for thy sake was counted
    curst,
  In sight of men and angels crucified:
  All this and more I bore to prove
My love, and wilt thou yet mistrust
    My love?'

'Lord, I am fain to think Thou
    lovest me,
  For Thou art all in all and I am
    Thine;
  And lo Thy love is better than
    new wine,
  And I am sick of love in loving
    Thee.
But dost Thou love me? Speak
    and save,
For jealousy is cruel as the grave.'

'Nay, if thy love is not an empty
    breath,
  My love is as thine own—deep
    answers deep.
  Peace, peace: I give to My be-
    loved sleep—
Not death but sleep, for love is
    strong as death.
Take patience: sweet thy sleep
    shall be:
Yea thou shalt wake in Paradise
    with Me.'
  Before 1876.

SAINTS AND ANGELS

It's oh in Paradise that I fain would
    be,
  Away from earth and weariness
    and all beside:
Earth is too full of loss with its
    dividing sea,
  But Paradise upbuilds the bower
    for the bride.

Where flowers are yet in bud while
    the boughs are green,
  I would get quit of earth and get
    robed for heaven;
Putting on my raiment white within
    the screen,
  Putting on my crown of gold
    whose gems are seven.

Fair is the fourfold river that maketh
    no moan,
  Fair are the trees fruit-bearing
    of the wood,
Fair are the gold and bdellium and
    the onyx stone,
  And I know the gold of that
    land is good.

O my love, my dove, lift up your
    eyes
  Toward the eastern gate like an
    opening rose;
You and I who parted will meet in
    Paradise,
  Pass within and sing when the
    gates unclose.

This life is but the passage of a
    day,
  This life is but a pang and all is
    over,
But in the life to come which fades
    not away
  Every love shall abide and every
    lover.

He who wore out pleasure and
    mastered all lore,
  Solomon wrote 'Vanity of
    vanities':
Down to death, of all that went
    before
  In his mighty long life, the record
    is this.

With loves by the hundred, wealth
    beyond measure,
  Is this he who wrote 'Vanity of
    vanities'?
Yea, 'Vanity of vanities' he saith
    of pleasure,
  And of all he learned set his seal
    to this.

Yet we love and faint not, for our
    love is one,
  And we hope and flag not, for
    our hope is sure;
Although there be nothing new
    beneath the sun,
  And no help for life and for death
    no cure.

The road to death is life, the gate
    of life is death,
  We who wake shall sleep, we
    shall wax who wane;
Let us not vex our souls for stoppage
    of a breath,
  The fall of a river that turneth
    not again.

Be the road short, and be the gate
    near,—
  Shall a short road tire, a strait
    gate appall?
The loves that meet in Paradise
    shall cast out fear,
  And Paradise hath room for you
    and me and all.

Before 1876.

A ROSE PLANT IN JERICHO

AT morn I plucked a rose and gave
    it Thee,
  A rose of joy and happy love and
    peace,
A rose with scarce a thorn:
  But in the chillness of a second
    morn
My rose bush drooped, and all
    its gay increase
Was but one thorn that wounded
    me.

I plucked the thorn and offered it
    to Thee,
  And for my thorn Thou gavest
    love and peace,
    Not joy this mortal morn:
  If Thou hast given much
    treasure for a thorn,
Wilt Thou not give me for my
    rose increase
Of gladness, and all sweets to me?

My thorny rose, my love and pain,
    to Thee
  I offer; and I set my heart in
    peace,
    And rest upon my thorn:
  For verily I think to-morrow
    morn
Shall bring me Paradise, my
    gift's increase,
Yea, give Thy very Self to me.

Before 1876.

PATIENCE OF HOPE

THE flowers that bloom in sun and
    shade,
  And glitter in the dew—
    The flowers must fade.
The birds that build their nest and
    sing
  When lovely Spring is new
    Must soon take wing.

The sun that rises in his strength,
  To wake and warm the world,
    Must set at length.
The sea that overflows the shore
  With billows frothed and curled
    Must ebb once more.

All come and go, all wax and wane,
  O Lord, save only Thou,
    Who dost remain
The same to all eternity.
  All things which fail us now
    We trust to Thee.
Circa 1880.

I WILL ARISE

WEARY and weak,—accept my weariness;
  Weary and weak and downcast in my soul,
With hope growing less and less,
  And with the goal
Distant and dim,—accept my sore distress.
I thought to reach the goal so long ago,
  At outset of the race I dreamed of rest,
Not knowing what now I know
  Of breathless haste,
  Of long-drawn straining effort across the waste.
One only thing I knew, Thy love of me;
  One only thing I know, Thy sacred same
Love of me full and free,
  A craving flame
Of selfless love of me which burns in Thee.
How can I think of Thee, and yet grow chill?
Of Thee, and yet grow cold and nigh to death?
Re-energize my will,
  Rebuild my faith;
  I will arise and run, Thou giving me breath.
I will arise, repenting and in pain;
  I will arise, and smite upon my breast
And turn to Thee again;
  Thou choosest best;
Lead me along the road Thou makest plain.
Lead me a little way, and carry me
  A little way, and hearken to my sighs,
And store my tears with Thee,
  And deign replies
To feeble prayers;—O Lord, I will arise.
Before 1882.

A PRODIGAL SON

DOES that lamp still burn in my Father's house
  Which he kindled the night I went away?
I turned once beneath the cedar boughs,
  And marked it gleam with a golden ray;
  Did he think to light me home some day?

Hungry here with the crunching swine,
  Hungry harvest have I to reap;
In a dream I count my Father's kine,
  I hear the tinkling bells of his sheep,
  I watch his lambs that browse and leap.

There is plenty of bread at home,
  His servants have bread enough
    and to spare ;
The purple wine-fat froths with foam,
  Oil and spices make sweet the
    air,
  While I perish hungry and bare.

Rich and blessed those servants,
    rather
  Than I who see not my Father's
    face !
I will arise and go to my Father :—
  'Fallen from sonship, beggared
    of grace,
  Grant me, Father, a servant's
    place.'
Before 1882.

FOR THINE OWN SAKE, O MY GOD

WEARIED of sinning, wearied of
    repentance,
  Wearied of self, I turn, my God,
    to Thee ;
To Thee, my Judge, on Whose all-
    righteous sentence
  Hangs mine eternity :
I turn to Thee, I plead Thyself with
    Thee,—
  Be pitiful to me.

Wearied I loathe myself, I loathe my
    sinning,
  My stains, my festering sores, my
    misery :
Thou the Beginning, Thou ere my
    beginning
  Didst see and didst foresee
Me miserable, me sinful, ruined
    me,—
  I plead Thyself with Thee.

I plead Thyself with Thee Who art
    my maker,
  Regard Thy handiwork that cries
    to Thee ;
I plead Thyself with Thee Who wast
    partaker
  Of mine infirmity ;
Love made Thee what Thou art, the
    love of me,—
  I plead Thyself with Thee.
Before 1882.

UNTIL THE DAY BREAK

WHEN will the day bring its plea-
    sure ?
  When will the night bring its rest ?
Reaper and gleaner and thresher
  Peer toward the east and the
    west :—
  The Sower He knoweth, and He
    knoweth best.

Meteors flash forth and expire,
  Northern lights kindle and pale ;
These are the days of desire,
  Of eyes looking upward that fail ;
  Vanishing days as a finishing tale.

Bows down the crop in its glory,
  Tenfold, fiftyfold, hundredfold ;
The millet is ripened and hoary,
  The wheat ears are ripened to
    gold :—
  Why keep us waiting in dimness
    and cold ?

The Lord of the harvest, He knoweth
  Who knoweth the first and the last:
The Sower Who patiently soweth,
  He scanneth the present and past:
  He saith, 'What thou hast, what
    remaineth, hold fast.'

Yet, Lord, o'er Thy toil-wearied weepers
  The storm-clouds hang muttering and frown:
On threshers and gleaners and reapers,
  O Lord of the harvest, look down;
  Oh for the harvest, the shout, and the crown!

'Not so,' saith the Lord of the reapers,
  The Lord of the first and the last:
'O My toilers, My weary, My weepers,
  What ye have, what remaineth, hold fast.
  Hide in My heart till the vengeance be past.'
Before 1882.

'OF HIM THAT WAS READY TO PERISH'

LORD, I am waiting, weeping, watching for Thee:
  My youth and hope lie by me buried and dead,
  My wandering love hath not where to lay its head
  Except Thou say 'Come to Me.'

My noon is ended, abolished from life and light,
  My noon is ended, ended and done away,
  My sun went down in the hours that still were day,
  And my lingering day is night.

How long, O Lord, how long in my desperate pain
  Shall I weep and watch, shall I weep and long for Thee?
  Is Thy grace ended, Thy love cut off from me?
  How long shall I long in vain?

O God Who before the beginning hast seen the end,
  Who hast made me flesh and blood, not frost and not fire,
  Who hast filled me full of needs and love and desire
  And a heart that craves a friend,—

Who hast said 'Come to Me and I will give thee rest,'
  Who hast said 'Take on thee My yoke and learn of Me,'
  Who calledst a little child to come to Thee,
  And pillowedst John on Thy breast;

Who spak'st to women that followed Thee sorrowing,
  Bidding them weep for themselves and weep for their own;
  Who didst welcome the outlaw adoring Thee all alone,
  And plight Thy word as a King,—

By Thy love of these and of all that ever shall be,
  By Thy love of these and of all the born and unborn,
  Turn Thy gracious eyes on me and think no scorn
  Of me, not even of me.

Beside Thy Cross I hang on my cross in shame,
  My wounds, weakness, extremity cry to Thee:
  Bid me also to Paradise, also me,
  For the glory of Thy Name.
Before 1882.

BEHOLD THE MAN

SHALL Christ hang on the Cross, and we not look?
  Heaven, earth, and hell, stood gazing at the first,
  While Christ for long-cursed man was counted cursed;
Christ, God and Man, Whom God the Father strook
And shamed and sifted and one while forsook:—
  Cry shame upon our bodies we have nursed
  In sweets, our souls in pride, our spirits immersed
In wilfulness, our steps run all acrook.
Cry shame upon us! for He bore our shame
  In agony, and we look on at ease
  With neither hearts on flame nor cheeks on flame.
  What hast thou, what have I, to do with peace?
Not to send peace but send a sword He came,
  And fire and fasts and tearful night watches.

Before 1882.

THE DESCENT FROM THE CROSS

Is this the Face that thrills with awe
  Seraphs who veil their face above?
Is this the Face without a flaw,
  The Face that is the Face of Love?
Yea, this defaced, a lifeless clod,
  Hath all creation's love sufficed,
Hath satisfied the love of God,
  This Face the Face of Jesus Christ.

Before 1882.

IT IS FINISHED

DEAR Lord, let me recount to Thee
Some of the great things Thou hast done
  For me, even me
  Thy little one.

It was not I that cared for Thee,—
But Thou didst set Thy heart upon
  Me, even me
  Thy little one.

And therefore was it sweet to Thee
To leave Thy Majesty and Throne,
  And grow like me
  A Little One,

A swaddled Baby on the knee
Of a dear Mother of Thine own,
  Quite weak like me
  Thy little one.

Thou didst assume my misery,
And reap the harvest I had sown,
  Comforting me
  Thy little one.

Jerusalem and Galilee,—
Thy love embraced not those alone,
  But also me
  Thy little one.

Thy unblemished Body on the Tree
Was bared and broken to atone
  For me, for me
  Thy little one.

Thou lovedst me upon the Tree,—
Still me, hid by the ponderous stone,—
  Me always—me
  Thy little one.

And love of me arose with Thee
When death hell and lay overthrown:
    Thou lovedst me
    Thy little one.

And love of me went up with Thee
To sit upon Thy Father's Throne :
    Thou lovest me
    Thy little one.

Lord, as Thou me, so would I Thee
Love in pure love's communion,
    For Thou lov'st me
    Thy little one :

Which love of me bring back with
    Thee
To Judgment when the Trump is
    blown,
    Still loving me
    Thy little one.

Before 1882.

AN EASTER CAROL

SPRING bursts to-day,
For Christ is risen and all the earth's
    at play.

Flash forth, thou Sun,
The rain is over and gone, its work
    is done.

Winter is past,
Sweet Spring is come at last, is come
    at last.

Bud, Fig and Vine,
Bud, Olive, fat with fruit and oil and
    wine.

Break forth this morn
In roses, thou but yesterday a thorn.

Uplift thy head,
O pure white Lily through the
    Winter dead.

Beside your dams
Leap and rejoice, you merry-making
    Lambs.

All Herds and Flocks
Rejoice, all Beasts of thickets and
    of rocks.

Sing, Creatures, sing,
Angels and Men and Birds and
    everything.

All notes of Doves
Fill all our world : this is the time
    of loves.

Before 1882.

'BEHOLD A SHAKING'

I

MAN rising to the doom that shall
    not err,—
    Which hath most dread—the
        arouse of all or each ?
    All kindreds of all nations of all
        speech,
Or one by one of *him* and *him* and
    her ?
While dust reanimate begins to stir
    Here, there, beyond, beyond,
        reach beyond reach ;
    While every wave refashions on
        the beach
Alive or dead-in-life some seafarer.
Now meeting doth not join or
    parting part ;
    True meeting and true parting
        wait till then,
    When whoso meet are joined
        for evermore,

Face answering face and heart at
    rest in heart :—
        God bring us all rejoicing to
        the shore
        Of happy Heaven, His sheep
        home to the pen.

2

Blessed that flock safe penned in
    Paradise ;
Blessed this flock which tramps
    in weary ways.
All form one flock, God's flock ;
    all yield Him praise
By joy or pain, still tending toward
    the prize.
Joy speaks in praises there, and
    sings and flies
    Where no night is, exulting all
    its days ;
    Here, pain finds solace, for
    behold it prays ;
In both love lives the life that never
    dies.
Here life is the beginning of our death,
    And death the starting-point
    whence life ensues ;
    Surely our life is death, our
    death is life :
    Nor need we lay to heart our
    peace or strife,
But calm in faith and patience
    breathe the breath
    God gave, to take again when He
    shall choose.

Before 1882.

ALL SAINTS

THEY are flocking from the East
And the West,
They are flocking from the North
And the South,
Every moment setting forth
From realm of snake or lion,
Swamp or sand,
Ice or burning.
Greatest and least,
Palm in hand
And praise in mouth,
They are flocking up the path
    To their rest,
Up the path that hath
    No returning.
Up the steeps of Zion
They are mounting,
Coming, coming,
Throngs beyond man's counting ;
With a sound
Like innumerable bees
Swarming, humming,
Where flowering trees
Many-tinted,
Many-scented,
All alike abound
With honey,—
With a swell
Like a blast upswaying unrestrainable
From a shadowed dell
To the hill-tops sunny,—
With a thunder
Like the ocean when in strength
Breadth and length
It sets to shore.
More and more
Waves on waves redoubled pour
Leaping flashing to the shore ;
Unlike the under
Drain of ebb that loseth ground
For all its roar.

They are thronging
From the East and West,
From the North and South ;
Saints are thronging, loving, longing,

To their land
Of rest,
Palm in hand
And praise in mouth.
Before 1882.

'TAKE CARE OF HIM'

'THOU whom I love, for whom I died,
Lovest thou Me, My bride?'—
Low on my knees I love Thee, Lord,
Believed in and adored.

'That I love thee the proof is plain:
How dost thou love again?'—
In prayer, in toil, in earthly loss,
In a long-carried cross.

'Yea, thou dost love: yet one adept
Brings more for Me to accept.'—
I mould my will to match with Thine,
My wishes I resign.

'Thou givest much: then give the whole
For solace of My soul.'—
More would I give, if I could get:
But, Lord, what lack I yet?

'In Me thou lovest Me: I call
Thee to love Me in all.'—
Brim full my heart, dear Lord, that so
My love may overflow.

'Love me in sinners and in saints,
In each who needs or faints.'—
Lord, I will love Thee as I can
In every brother man.

'All sore, all crippled, all who ache,
Tend all for My dear sake.'—
All for Thy sake, Lord: I will see
In every sufferer Thee.

'So I at last, upon My Throne
Of glory, Judge alone,
So I at last will say to thee:
Thou diddest it to Me.'
Before 1882.

A MARTYR

THE VIGIL OF THE FEAST

INNER not outer, without gnash of teeth
Or weeping, save quiet sobs of some who pray
And feel the Everlasting Arms beneath,—
Blackness of darkness this, but not for aye;
Darkness that even in gathering fleeteth fast,
Blackness of blackest darkness close to day.
Lord Jesus, through Thy darkened pillar cast
Thy gracious eyes all-seeing cast on me
Until this tyranny be overpast.
Me, Lord, remember who remember Thee,
And cleave to Thee, and see Thee without sight,
And choose Thee still in dire extremity,
And in this darkness worship Thee my Light,
And Thee my Life adore in shadow of death,
Thee loved by day, and still beloved by night.

It is the Voice of my Beloved that
   saith :
    'I am the Way, the Truth, the
     Life, I go
   Whither that soul knows well that
    followeth.'
O Lord, I follow, little as I know ;
   At this eleventh hour I rise and
    take
   My life into my hand, and follow
    so,
With tears and heart-misgivings and
    heart-ache ;
   Thy feeblest follower, yet Thy
    follower
   Indomitable for Thine only sake.
To-night I gird my will afresh, and
    stir
   My strength, and brace my heart
    to do and dare,—
   Marvelling : Will to-morrow wake
    the whirr
Of the great rending wheel, or from
    his lair
   Startle the jubilant lion in his
    rage,
   Or clench the headsman's hand
    within my hair,
Or kindle fire to speed my pilgrimage,
   Chariot of fire and horses of sheer
    fire
   Whirling me home to heaven by
    one fierce stage ?—
Thy Will I will, I Thy desire desire ;
   Let not the waters close above
    my head,
   Uphold me that I sink not in this
    mire :
For flesh and blood are frail and
    sore afraid ;
   And young I am, unsatisfied and
    young,
   With memories, hopes, with crav-
    ings all unfed,

My song half sung, its sweetest notes
    unsung,
All plans cut short, all possibilities,
Because my cord of life is soon
    unstrung.
Was I a careless woman set at
    ease
That this so bitter cup is brimmed
    for me ?
Had mine own vintage settled on
    the lees ?
A word, a puff of smoke, would set
    me free ;
A word, a puff of smoke, over
    and gone : . . .
Howbeit, whom have I, Lord, in
    heaven but Thee ?
Yea, only Thee my choice is fixed
    upon
In heaven or earth, eternity or
    time :—
Lord, hold me fast, Lord, leave
    me not alone,
Thy silly heartless dove that sees
    the lime
Yet almost flutters to the tempting
    bough :
Cover me, hide me, pluck me from
    this crime.
A word, a puff of smoke, would save
    me now : . . .
But who, my God, would save me
    in the day
Of Thy fierce anger? only Saviour
    Thou.
Preoccupy my heart, and turn away
   And cover up mine eyes from
    frantic fear,
   And stop mine ears lest I be
    driven astray :
For one stands ever dinning in mine
    ear
How my grey Father withers in
    the blight

Of love for me, who cruel am and
    dear;
And how my Mother through this
    lingering night
    Until the day sits tearless in her
        woe,
    Loathing for love of me the happy
        light
Which brings to pass a concourse
    and a show
    To glut the hungry faces merci-
        less,
    The thousand faces swaying to
        and fro,
Feasting on me unveiled in helpless-
    ness,
    Alone,—yet not alone: Lord,
        stand by me
    As once by lonely Paul in his
        distress.
As blossoms to the sun I turn to
    Thee;
    Thy dove turns to her window,
        think no scorn;
    As one dove to an ark on shore-
        less sea,
To Thee I turn mine eyes, my heart
    forlorn.
    Put forth Thy scarred right Hand,
        kind Lord, take hold
    Of me Thine all-forsaken dove
        who mourn:
For Thou hast loved me since the
    days of old,
    And I love Thee Whom loving I
        will love
    Through life's short fever-fits of
        heat and cold;
Thy Name will I extol and sing
    thereof,
    Will flee for refuge to Thy Blessed
        Name.
    Lord, look upon me from Thy
        bliss above:

Look down on me, who shrink from
    all the shame
And pangs and desolation of my
    death,
Wrenched piecemeal or devoured
    or set on flame,
While all the world around me holds
    its breath
With eyes glued on me for a
    gazing-stock,
Pitiless eyes, while no man pitieth.
The floods are risen, I stagger in
    their shock,
My heart reels and is faint, I fail,
    I faint:
My God, set Thou me up upon
    the rock,
Thou Who didst long ago Thyself
    acquaint
With death, our death; Thou Who
    didst long ago
Pour forth Thy soul for sinner
    and for saint.
Bear me in mind, whom no one else
    will know;
Thou Whom Thy friends forsook,
    take Thou my part,
Of all forsaken in mine overthrow;
Carry me in Thy bosom, in Thy
    heart,
Carry me out of darkness into light,
To-morrow make me see Thee as
    Thou art.
Lover and friend Thou hidest from
    my sight.
Alas, alas, mine earthly love, alas,
For whom I thought to don the
    garments white
And white wreath of a bride, this
    rugged pass
Hath utterly divorced me from
    thy care.
Yea, I am to thee as a shattered
    glass

Worthless, with no more beauty lodging there,
Abhorred, lest I involve thee in my doom:
For sweet are sunshine and this upper air,
And life and youth are sweet, and give us room
For all most sweetest sweetnesses we taste:
Dear, what hast thou in common with a tomb?
I bow my head in silence, I make haste
Alone, I make haste out into the dark,
My life and youth and hope all run to waste.
Is this my body cold and stiff and stark,
Ashes made ashes, earth becoming earth,
Is this a prize for man to make his mark?
Am I that very I who laughed in mirth
A while ago, a little little while,
Yet all the while a-dying since my birth?
Now am I tired, too tired to strive or smile;
I sit alone, my mouth is in the dust:
Look Thou upon me, Lord, for I am vile.
In Thee is all my hope, is all my trust,
On Thee I centre all my self that dies,
And self that dies not with its mortal crust,
But sleeps and wakes, and in the end will rise
With hymns and hallelujahs on its lips,
Thee loving with the love that satisfies.
As once in Thine unutterable eclipse
The sun and moon grew dark for sympathy,
And earth cowered quaking underneath the drips
Of Thy slow Blood priceless exceedingly,
So now a little spare me, and show forth
Some pity, O my God, some pity of me.
If trouble comes not from the south or north,
But meted to us by Thy tender hand,
Let me not in Thine eyes be nothing worth:
Behold me where in agony I stand,
Behold me no man caring for my soul,
And take me to Thee in the far-off land,
Shorten the race and lift me to the goal.

Before 1882.

WHY?

'LORD, if I love Thee and Thou lovest me,
Why need I any more these toilsome days?
Why should I not run singing up Thy ways
Straight into heaven, to rest myself with Thee?
What need remains of death-pang yet to be,
If all my soul is quickened in Thy praise?
If all my heart loves Thee, what need the amaze,

Struggle and dimness of an
   agony?'—
'Bride whom I love, if thou too
   lovest Me,
   Thou needs must choose My Like-
      ness for thy dower:
      So wilt thou toil in patience, and
         abide
      Hungering and thirsting for that
         blessed hour
   When I My Likeness shall behold in
      thee,
      And thou therein shalt waken
         satisfied.'
Before 1882.

LOVE IS STRONG AS
DEATH

I HAVE not sought Thee, I have
   not found Thee,
   I have not thirsted for Thee:
And now cold billows of death sur-
   round me,
Buffeting billows of death astound
   me,—
   Wilt Thou look upon, wilt Thou
      see
   Thy perishing me?'

'Yea, I have sought thee, yea, I
   have found thee,
   Yea, I have thirsted for thee,
Yea, long ago with love's bands I
   bound thee:
Now the Everlasting Arms surround
   thee,—
   Through death's darkness I look
      and see
   And clasp thee to Me.'
Before 1882.

'IF THOU SAYEST, BEHOLD,
WE KNEW IT NOT.'—
PROVERBS xxiv. 11, 12.

1

I HAVE done I know not what,—
   what have I done?
My brother's blood, my brother's
   soul, doth cry:
And I find no defence, find no
   reply,
No courage more to run this race I run,
Not knowing what I have done, have
   left undone;
   Ah me, these awful unknown hours
      that fly,
   Fruitless it may be, fleeting fruit-
      less by,
Rank with death-savour underneath
   the sun!
For what avails it that I did not
   know
   The deed I did? what profits me
      the plea
That had I known I had not wronged
   him so?
   Lord Jesus Christ, my God,
      him pity Thou;
   Lord, if it may be, pity also me:
      In judgment pity, and in death,
         and now.

2

Thou Who hast borne all burdens,
   bear our load,
   Bear Thou our load whatever load
      it be;
   Our guilt, our shame, our helpless
      misery,
Bear Thou Who only canst, O God
   my God.
Seek us and find us, for we cannot
   Thee

Or seek or find or hold or cleave
    unto :
We cannot do or undo ; Lord,
    undo
    Our self-undoing, for Thine is the
        key
Of all we are not though we might
        have been.
    Dear Lord, if ever mercy moved
        Thy mind,
    If so be love of us can move
        Thee yet,
If still the nail-prints in Thy Hands
    are seen,
    Remember us,—yea how
        shouldst Thou forget ?
    Remember us for good, and seek,
        and find.

3

Each soul I might have succoured,
    may have slain,
All souls shall face me at the last
    Appeal,
    That great last moment poised for
        woe or weal,
    That final moment for man's bliss or
        bane.
Vanity of vanities, yea all is vain
    Which then will not avail or
        help or heal :
    Disfeatured faces, worn-out knees
        that kneel,
Will more avail than strength or
    beauty then.
Lord, by Thy Passion,—when Thy
    Face was marred
    In sight of earth and hell tumult-
        uous,
    And Thy heart failed in Thee
        like melting wax,
And Thy Blood dropped more
    precious than the nard,—

Lord, for Thy sake, not ours,
    supply our lacks,
For Thine own sake, not ours,
    Christ, pity us.
Before 1882.

THE THREAD OF LIFE

1

THE irresponsive silence of the land,
    The irresponsive sounding of the
        sea,
    Speak both one message of one
        sense to me :—
'Aloof, aloof, we stand aloof; so
    stand
Thou too aloof bound with the flaw-
    less band
    Of inner solitude ; we bind not
        thee ;
    But who from thy self-chain shall
        set thee free ?
What heart shall touch thy heart?
    what hand thy hand ? '—
And I am sometimes proud and
    sometimes meek,
    And sometimes I remember days
        of old
    When fellowship seemed not so far
        to seek
And all the world and I seemed
    much less cold,
    And at the rainbow's foot lay
        surely gold,
And hope felt strong and life itself
    not weak.

2

Thus am I mine own prison. Every-
    thing
Around me free and sunny and at
    ease :

Or if in shadow, in a shade of trees
Which the sun kisses, where the gay birds sing
And where all winds make various murmuring;
  Where bees are found, with honey for the bees;
  Where sounds are music, and where silences
Are music of an unlike fashioning.
Then gaze I at the merrymaking crew,
  And smile a moment and a moment sigh,
Thinking, Why can I not rejoice with you?
  But soon I put the foolish fancy by:
I am not what I have nor what I do;
  But what I was I am, I am even I.

3

Therefore myself is that one only thing
  I hold to use or waste, to keep or give;
My sole possession every day I live,
And still mine own despite Time's winnowing.
Ever mine own, while moons and seasons bring
  From crudeness ripeness mellow and sanative;
Ever mine own, till Death shall ply his sieve;
And still mine own, when saints break grave and sing.
And this myself as king unto my King

I give, to Him Who gave Himself for me;
Who gives Himself to me, and bids me sing
A sweet new song of His redeemed set free;
He bids me sing, O Death, where is thy sting?
And sing, O grave, where is thy victory?

Before 1882.

A SICK CHILD'S MEDITATION

PAIN and weariness, aching eyes and head,
  Pain and weariness all the day and night:
Yet the pillow's soft on my smooth soft bed,
  And fresh air blows in, and mother shades the light.

Thou, O Lord, in pain hadst no pillow soft,
  In Thy weary pain, in Thine agony:
But a cross of shame held Thee up aloft
  Where Thy very mother could do nought for Thee.

I would gaze on Thee, on Thy patient face;
  Make me like Thyself, patient, sweet, at peace;
Make my days all love, and my nights all praise,
  Till all days and nights and patient sufferings cease.

Circa 1885.

OUT OF THE DEEP HAVE I CALLED UNTO THEE, O LORD.

(From before 1886 to before 1893.)

ALONE Lord God, in Whom our trust and peace,
  Our love and our desire, glow bright with hope;
Lift us above this transitory scope
Of earth, these pleasures that begin and cease,
This moon which wanes, these seasons which decrease:
  We turn to Thee; as on an eastern slope
  Wheat feels the dawn beneath night's lingering cope,
Bending and stretching sunward ere it sees.
Alone Lord God, we see not yet we know;
  By love we dwell with patience and desire,
    And loving so and so desiring pray;
    Thy Will be done in earth as heaven to-day;
As yesterday it was, to-morrow so;
  Love offering love on love's self-feeding fire.

Before 1893.

SEVEN vials hold Thy wrath: but what can hold
  Thy mercy save Thine own Infinitude,
  Boundlessly overflowing with all good,
All lovingkindness, all delights untold?
Thy Love, of each created love the mould;
  Thyself, of all the empty plenitude;
  Heard of at Ephrata, found in the Wood,
For ever One, the Same, and Manifold.
Lord, give us grace to tremble with that dove
  Which Ark-bound winged its solitary way
  And overpast the Deluge in a day,
  Whom Noah's hand pulled in and comforted:
For we who much more hang upon Thy Love
  Behold its shadow in the deed he did.

Before 1893.

Where neither rust nor moth doth corrupt.

NERVE us with patience, Lord, to toil or rest,
  Toiling at rest on our allotted level;
  Unsnared, unscared by world or flesh or devil,
Fulfilling the good Will of Thy behest:
Not careful here to hoard, not here to revel;
But waiting for our treasure and our zest
Beyond the fading splendour of the west,
  Beyond this deathstruck life and deathlier evil.
Not with the sparrow building here a house:

But with the swallow tabernacling so
As still to poise alert to rise and go
On eager wings with wing-out-speeding wills
Beyond earth's gourds and past her almond boughs,
Past utmost bound of the everlasting hills.

Before 1893.

As the sparks fly upwards.

LORD, grant us wills to trust Thee with such aim
Of hope and passionate craving of desire
That we may mount aspiring, and aspire
Still while we mount; rejoicing in Thy Name,
Yesterday, this day, day by day the Same:
So sparks fly upward scaling heaven by fire,
Still mount and still attain not, yet draw nigher,
While they have being, to their fountain flame.
To saints who mount, the bottomless abyss
Is as mere nothing, they have set their face
Onward and upward toward that blessed place
Where man rejoices with his God, and soul
With soul, in the unutterable kiss
Of peace for every victor at the goal.

Before 1893.

LORD, make us all love all: that when we meet,
Even myriads of earth's myriads, at Thy Bar,
We may be glad as all true lovers are
Who having parted count reunion sweet.
Safe gathered home around Thy blessed Feet,
Come home by different roads from near or far,
Whether by whirlwind or by flaming car,
From pangs or sleep, safe folded round Thy seat.
Oh if our brother's blood cry out at us,
How shall we meet Thee Who hast loved us all,
Thee Whom we never loved, not loving him?
The unloving cannot chant with Seraphim,
Bear harp of gold or palm victorious,
Or face the Vision Beatifical.

Before 1893.

O LORD, I am ashamed to seek Thy Face
As tho' I loved Thee as Thy saints love Thee:
Yet turn from those Thy lovers, look on me,
Disgrace me not with uttermost disgrace;
But pour on me ungracious, pour Thy grace
To purge my heart and bid my will go free,
Till I too taste Thy hidden Sweetness, see

Thy hidden Beauty in the holy place.
O Thou Who callest sinners to repent,
  Call me Thy sinner unto penitence,
  For many sins grant me the greater love :
    Set me above the waterfloods, above
Devil and shifting world and fleshly sense,
Thy Mercy's all-amazing monument.

Before 1893.

IT is not death, O Christ, to die for Thee :
  Nor is that silence of a silent land
  Which speaks Thy praise so all may understand :
Darkness of death makes Thy dear lovers see
Thyself Who Wast and Art and Art to Be ;
  Thyself, more lovely than the lovely band
  Of saints who worship Thee on either hand,
Loving and loved thro' all eternity.
Death is not death, and therefore do I hope :
  Nor silence silence ; and I therefore sing
    A very humble hopeful quiet psalm,
Searching my heart-field for an offering ;
A handful of sun-courting heliotrope,
    Of myrrh a bundle, and a little balm.

Before 1893.

LORD, grant us eyes to see and ears to hear,
And souls to love and minds to understand,
And steadfast faces toward the Holy Land,
And confidence of hope, and filial fear,
And citizenship where Thy saints appear
Before Thee heart in heart and hand in hand,
And Alleluias where their chanting band
As waters and as thunders fill the sphere.
Lord, grant us what Thou wilt, and what Thou wilt
Deny, and fold us in Thy peaceful fold :
  Not as the world gives, give to us Thine own :
Inbuild us where Jerusalem is built
  With walls of jasper and with streets of gold,
    And Thou Thyself, Lord Christ, for Corner Stone.

Before 1893.

'Cried out with Tears.'

LORD, I believe, help Thou mine unbelief :
Lord, I repent, help mine impenitence :
Hide not Thy Face from me, nor spurn me hence,
Nor utterly despise me in my grief ;
Nor say me nay, who worship with the thief
Bemoaning my so long lost innocence :—

Ah me! my penitence a fresh offence,
Too tardy and too tepid and too brief.
Lord, must I perish, I who look to Thee?
  Look Thou upon me, bid me live, not die;
    Say 'Come,' say not 'Depart,' tho' Thou art just:
      Yea, Lord, be mindful how out of the dust
I look to Thee while Thou dost look on me,
  Thou Face to face with me and Eye to eye.

Before 1893.

O LORD, on Whom we gaze and dare not gaze,
  Increase our faith that gazing we may see,
    And seeing love, and loving worship Thee
Thro' all our days, our long and lengthening days.
O Lord, accessible to prayer and praise,
  Kind Lord, Companion of the two or three,
    Good Lord, be gracious to all men and me,
Lighten our darkness and amend our ways.
Call up our hearts to Thee, that where Thou art
  Our treasure and our heart may dwell at one:
    Then let the pallid moon pursue her sun,
So long as it shall please Thee, far apart,—
Yet art Thou with us, Thou to Whom we run,
We hand in hand with Thee and heart in heart.

Before 1893.

'I will come and heal him.'

O LORD God, hear the silence of each soul,
  Its cry unutterable of ruth and shame,
  Its voicelessness of self-contempt and blame:
Nor suffer harp and palm and aureole
Of multitudes who praise Thee at the goal
  To set aside Thy poor and blind and lame;
  Nor blazing Seraphs utterly to outflame
The spark that flies up from each earthly coal.
My price Thy priceless Blood; and therefore I
  Price of Thy priceless Blood am precious so
    That good things love me in their love of Thee:
    I comprehend not why Thou lovedst me
  With Thy so mighty Love; but this I know,
No man hath greater love than thus to die.

Before 1893.

AH Lord, Lord, if my heart were right with Thine
  As Thine with mine, then should I rest resigned
  Awaiting knowledge with a quiet mind

Because of heavenly wisdom's anodyne.
Then would Thy Love be more to me than wine,
    Then should I seek being sure at length to find,
    Then should I trust to Thee all humankind
Because Thy Love of them is more than mine.
Then should I stir up hope and comfort me
    Remembering Thy Cradle and Thy Cross;
    How Heaven to Thee without us had been loss,
    How Heaven with us is Thy one only Heaven,
Heaven shared with us thro' all eternity,
    With us long sought, long loved, and much forgiven.

Before 1893.

The gold of that land is good.

I LONG for joy, O Lord, I long for gold,
    I long for all Thou profferest to me,
I long for the unimagined manifold
    Abundance laid up in Thy treasury.
    I long for pearls, but not from mundane sea;
I long for palms, but not from earthly mould;
    Yet in all else I long for, long for Thee,
Thyself to hear and worship and behold.
For Thee, beyond the splendour of that day
    Where all is day and is not any night;
For Thee, beyond refreshment of that rest
    To which tired saints press on for its delight:—
Or if not thus for Thee, yet Thee I pray
    To make me long so till Thou make me blest.

Before 1893.

WEIGH all my faults and follies righteously,
    Omissions and commissions, sin on sin;
    Make deep the scale, O Lord, to weigh them in;
Yea, set the Accuser vulture-eyed to see
All loads ingathered which belong to me:
    That so in life the judgement may begin,
    And Angels learn how hard it is to win
One solitary sinful soul to Thee.
I have no merits for a counterpoise:
    Oh vanity my work and hastening day,
What can I answer to the accusing voice?
Lord, drop Thou in the counter-scale alone
    One Drop from Thine own Heart, and overweigh
My guilt, my folly, even my heart of stone.

Before 1886.

LORD, grant me grace to love Thee in my pain,
    Thro' all my disappointment love Thee still,

Thy love my strong foundation
    and my hill,
Tho' I be such as cometh not
    again,
A fading leaf, a spark upon the
    wane :
    So evermore do Thou Thy perfect
        Will,
    Beloved thro' all my good, thro'
        all mine ill,
Beloved tho' all my love beside be
    vain.
If thus I love Thee, how wilt Thou
    love me,
    Thou Who art greater than my
        heart ? (Amen !)
        Wilt Thou bestow a part, with-
        hold a part ?
The longing of my heart cries out
    to Thee,
    The hungering thirsting longing
        of my heart :
What I forewent wilt Thou not
    grant me then ?

Before 1886.

LORD, make me one with Thine own
    faithful ones,
    Thy Saints who love Thee and
    are loved by Thee ;
    Till the day break and till the
    shadows flee,
At one with them in alms and
    orisons ;
At one with him who toils and him
    who runs,
    And him who yearns for union
    yet to be ;
    At one with all who throng the
    crystal sea
And wait the setting of our moons
    and suns.
Ah my belovèd ones gone on before,

Who looked not back with hand
    upon the plough !
    If beautiful to me while still in
    sight,
    How beautiful must be your
    aspects now ;
    Your unknown, well-known
    aspects in that light
Which clouds shall never cloud for
    evermore.

Before 1893.

Light of Light.

O CHRIST our Light, Whom even
    in darkness we
    (So we look up) discern and gaze
    upon,
    O Christ, Thou loveliest Light
    that ever shone,
Thou Light of Light, Fount of all
    lights that be,
Grant us clear vision of Thy Light
    to see,
    Tho' other lights elude us, or
    be gone
Into the secret of oblivion,
Or gleam in places higher than
    man's degree.
Who looks on Thee looks full on his
    desire,
    Who looks on Thee looks full on
    Very Love :
        Looking, he answers well,
        'What lack I yet ?'
His heat and cold wait not on earthly
    fire,
    His wealth is not of earth to
    lose or get ;
Earth reels, but he has stored his
    store above.

Before 1893.

GIFTS AND GRACES

(From before 1886 to before 1893.)

LOVE loveth Thee, and wisdom
    loveth Thee ;
    The love that loveth Thee sits
        satisfied ;
    Wisdom that loveth Thee grows
        million-eyed,
Learning what was, and is, and is
    to be.
Wisdom and love are glad of all
    they see ;
    Their heart is deep, their hope is
        not denied ;
    They rock at rest on time's un-
        resting tide,
And wait to rest thro' long eternity.
Wisdom and love and rest, each
    holy soul
    Hath these to-day while day is
        only night :
    What shall souls have when
        morning brings to light
    Love, wisdom, rest, God's treasure
        stored above ?
Palm shall they have, and harp and
    aureole,
    Wisdom, rest, love—and lo ! the
        whole is love.

Before 1893.

LORD, give me love that I may love
    Thee much,
    Yea, give me love that I may love
        Thee more,
    And all for love may worship and
        adore
And touch Thee with love's conse-
    crated touch.
I halt to-day ; be love my cheerful
    crutch,
My feet to plod, some day my
    wings to soar :
Some day ; but, Lord, not any
    day before
Thou call me perfect, having made
    me such.
This is a day of love, a day of sorrow,
    Love tempering sorrow to a sort
        of bliss ;
    A day that shortens while we
        call it long :
A longer day of love will dawn to-
    morrow,
    A longer, brighter, lovelier day
        than this,
    Endless, all love, no sorrow,
        but a song.

Before 1893.

'As a king, . . . unto the King.'

LOVE doth so grace and dignify
    That beggars treat as king with
        king
Before the Throne of God most
    High :
Love recognizes love's own cry,
    And stoops to take love's offering.

A loving heart, tho' soiled and
    bruised ;
    A kindling heart, tho' cold before ;
Who ever came and was refused
By Love ? Do, Lord, as Thou art
    used
    To do, and make me love Thee
        more.

Before 1886.

O YE who love to-day,
Turn away
From Patience with her silver ray :

For Patience shows a twilight face,
   Like a half-lighted moon
When daylight dies apace.

But ye who love to-morrow,
Beg or borrow
To-day some bitterness of sorrow :
   For Patience shows a lustrous face,
     In depth of night her noon ;
Then to her sun gives place.
Before 1893*;*

   LIFE that was born to-day
   Must make no stay
     But tend to end
As blossom-bloom of May.
O Lord, confirm my root,
Train up my shoot,
     To live and give
Harvest of wholesome fruit.

Life that was born to die
Sets heart on high,
     And counts and mounts
Steep stages of the sky.
Two things, Lord, I desire
And I require ;
     Love's name, and flame
To wrap my soul in fire.

Life that was born to love
Sends heart above
     Both cloud and shroud,
And broods a peaceful dove.
Two things I ask of Thee ;
Deny not me ;
     Eyesight and light
Thy Blessed Face to see.
Before 1893.

    Perfect Love casteth out Fear.

LORD, give me blessed fear,
   And much more blessed love,
That fearing I may love Thee here
   And be Thy harmless dove :

Until Thou cast out fear,
   Until Thou perfect love,
Until Thou end mine exile here
   And fetch Thee home Thy dove.
Before 1893.

HOPE is the counterpoise of fear
While night enthralls us here.

Fear hath a startled eye that holds
   a tear :
Hope hath an upward glance, for
   dawn draws near
With sunshine and with cheer.
Fear gazing earthwards spies a bier ;
And sets herself to rear
A lamentable tomb where leaves
   drop sere,
Bleaching to congruous skeletons
   austere :
Hope chants a funeral hymn most
   sweet and clear,
And seems true chanticleer
Of resurrection and of all things
   dear
In the oncoming endless year.

Fear ballasts hope, hope buoys up
   fear,
And both befit us here.
   Before 1893.

   Subject to like Passions as we are.

WHOSO hath anguish is not dead in
   sin,
   Whoso hath pangs of utterless
     desire.
Like as in smouldering flax which
   harbours fire,—

Red heat of conflagration may begin,
Melt that hard heart, burn out the dross within,
  Permeate with glory the new man entire,
  Crown him with fire, mould for his hands a lyre
Of fiery strings to sound with those who win.
Anguish is anguish, yet potential bliss,
  Pangs of desire are birth-throes of delight ;
  Those citizens felt such who walk in white,
And meet, but no more sunder, with a kiss ;
Who fathom still-unfathomed mysteries,
  And love, adore, rejoice, with all their might.

Before 1893.

EXPERIENCE bows a sweet contented face,
  Still setting-to her seal that God is true :
  Beneath the sun, she knows, is nothing new ;
All things that go return with measured pace,
Winds, rivers, man's still recommencing race :—
  While Hope beyond earth's circle strains her view,
  Past sun and moon, and rain and rainbow too,
Enamoured of unseen eternal grace.
Experience saith, 'My God doth all things well' :
  And for the morrow taketh little care,
Such peace and patience garrison her soul :—
  While Hope, who never yet hath eyed the goal,
  With arms flung forth, and backward-floating hair,
Touches, embraces, hugs the invisible.

Before 1893.

Charity never faileth.

SUCH is Love, it comforts in extremity,
  Tho' a tempest rage around and rage above,
  Tempest beyond tempest, far as eye can see :
Such is Love

That it simply heeds its mourning inward Dove ;
  Dove which craves contented for a home to be
  Set amid the myrtles of an olive grove.

Dove-eyed Love contemplates the Twelve-fruited Tree,
  Marks the bowing palms which worship as they move ;
  Simply sayeth, simply prayeth, 'All for me !'
Such is Love

Before 1893.

The Greatest of these is Charity.

A MOON impoverished amid stars curtailed,
A sun of its exuberant lustre shorn,
A transient morning that is scarcely morn,
A lingering night in double dimness veiled.—

Our hands are slackened and our strength has failed :
  We born to darkness, wherefore were we born ?
  No ripening more for olive, grape, or corn :
Faith faints, hope faints, even love himself has paled.
Nay ! love lifts up a face like any rose
  Flushing and sweet above a thorny stem,
Softly protesting that the way he knows ;
  And as for faith and hope, will carry them
  Safe to the gate of New Jerusalem,
Where light shines full and where the palm-tree blows.

Before 1893.

ALL beneath the sun hasteth,
All that hath begun wasteth ;
Earth-notes change in tune
With the changeful moon,
Which waneth
While earth's chant complaineth.

Plumbs the deep, Fear descending ;
Scales the steep, Hope ascending ;
Faith betwixt the twain
Plies both goad and rein,
Half fearing,
All hopeful, day is nearing.

Before 1893.

IF thou be dead, forgive and thou shalt live ;
  If thou hast sinned, forgive and be forgiven ;
  God waiteth to be gracious and forgive,
  And open heaven.

Set not thy will to die and not to live ;
  Set not thy face as flint refusing heaven ;
Thou fool, set not thy heart on hell : forgive
  And be forgiven.

Before 1893.

Let Patience have her perfect work.

CAN man rejoice who lives in hourly fear ?
  Can man make haste who toils beneath a load ?
  Can man feel rest who has no fixed abode ?
All he lays hold of, or can see or hear,
  Is passing by, is prompt to disappear,
  Is doomed, foredoomed, continueth in no stay :
  This day he breathes in is his latter day,
This year of time is this world's latter year.
Thus in himself is he most miserable :
  Out of himself, Lord, lift him up to Thee,
  Out of himself and all these worlds that flee ;
  Hold him in patience underneath the rod,
Anchor his hope beyond life's ebb and swell,
  Perfect his patience in the love of God.

Before 1893.

PATIENCE must dwell with Love, for
    Love and Sorrow
Have pitched their tent together
    here:
Love all alone will build a house to-
    morrow,
    And Sorrow not be near.

To-day for Love's sake hope; still
    hope in Sorrow,
    Rest in her shade and hold her
    dear.
To-day she nurses thee; and lo
    to-morrow
    Love only will be near.

Before 1893.

Let everything that hath breath praise the Lord.

ALL that we see rejoices in the
    sunshine,
    All that we hear makes merry in
    the Spring:
God grant us such a mind to be
    glad after our kind,
    And to sing
    His praises evermore for every-
    thing.

Much that we see must vanish with
    the sunshine,
    Sweet Spring must fail, and fail
    the choir of Spring:
But Wisdom shall burn on when
    the lesser lights are gone,
    And shall sing
    God's praises evermore for every-
    thing.

Before 1893.

WHAT is the beginning? Love.
    What the course? Love still.
What the goal? The goal is Love
    on the happy hill.
Is there nothing then but Love,
    search we sky or earth?
There is nothing out of Love hath
    perpetual worth:
All things flag but only Love, all
    things fail or flee;
There is nothing left but Love
    worthy you and me.

Before 1893.

LORD, make me pure:
Only the pure shall see Thee as
    Thou art,
    And shall endure.
    Lord, bring me low;
For Thou wert lowly in Thy blessed
    heart:
    Lord, keep me so.

Before 1893.

LOVE, to be love, must walk Thy
    way
    And work Thy Will;
    Or if Thou say 'Lie still,'
Lie still and pray.

Love, Thine own Bride, with all
    her might
    Will follow Thee,
    And till the shadows flee
Keep Thee in sight.

Love will not mar her peaceful face
    With cares undue,
    Faithless and hopeless too
And out of place.

Love, knowing Thou much more
 art Love,
  Will sun her grief,
  And pluck her myrtle-leaf,
And be Thy dove.

Love here hath vast beatitude:
  What shall be hers
  Where there is no more curse,
But all is good?
  Before 1893.

LORD, I am feeble and of mean
    account:
Thou Who dost condescend as well
    as mount,
  Stoop Thou Thyself to me
  And grant me grace to hear and
    grace to see.

Lord, if Thou grant me grace to
    hear and see
Thy very Self Who stoopest thus
    to me,
  I make but slight account
  Of aught beside wherein to sink
    or mount
  Before 1893.

TUNE me, O Lord, into one harmony
  With Thee, one full responsive
    vibrant chord;
Unto Thy praise, all love and
    melody,
  Tune me, O Lord.

  Thus need I flee nor death nor
    fire nor sword:
  A little while these be, then cease
    to be;
  And sent by Thee not these
    should be abhorred.

Devil and world gird me with
    strength to flee,
  To flee the flesh, and arm me
    with Thy word:
As Thy Heart is to my heart, unto
    Thee
  Tune me, O Lord.
  Before 1893.

They shall be as white as snow.

WHITENESS most white. Ah to be
    clean again
  In mine own sight and God's
    most holy sight!
To reach thro' any flood or fire of
    pain
  Whiteness most white:

  To learn to hate the wrong and
    love the right
Even while I walk thro' shadows
    that are vain,
  Descending thro' vain shadows
    into night.

Lord, not to-day: yet some day
    bliss for bane
  Give me, for mortal frailty give
    me might,
Give innocence for guilt, and for
    my stain
  Whiteness most white.
  Before 1893.

THY lilies drink the dew,
  Thy lambs the rill, and I will
    drink them too;
For those in purity
And innocence are types, dear Lord,
    of Thee.
  The fragrant lily flower

Bows and fulfils Thy Will its lifelong
    hour ;
The lamb at rest and play
Fulfils Thy Will in gladness all the
    day ;
They leave to-morrow's cares
Until the morrow, what it brings it
    bears.
    And I, Lord, would be such ;
Not high or great or anxious over-
    much,
    But pure and temperate,
Earnest to do Thy Will betimes and
    late,
    Fragrant with love and praise
And innocence thro' all my appointed
    days ;
    Thy lily I would be,
Spotless and sweet, Thy lamb to
    follow Thee.

Before 1886.

When I was in trouble I called upon the Lord.

A BURDENED heart that bleeds and
    bears
    And hopes and waits in pain,
And faints beneath its fears and
    cares,
    Yet hopes again :

Wilt Thou accept the heart I bring,
    O gracious Lord and kind,
To ease it of a torturing sting,
    And staunch and bind ?

Alas, if Thou wilt none of this,
    None else have I to give :
Look Thou upon it as it is,
    Accept, relieve.

Or if Thou wilt not yet relieve,
    Be not extreme to sift ;
Accept a faltering will to give,
    Itself Thy gift.

Before 1886.

GRANT us such grace that we may
    work Thy Will
And speak Thy words and walk
    before Thy Face,
Profound and calm, like waters deep
    and still :
Grant us such grace.

Not hastening and not loitering
    in our pace
For gloomiest valley or for sultriest
    hill,
Content and fearless on our down-
    ward race.

As rivers seek a sea they cannot fill
    But are themselves filled full in
    its embrace,
Absorbed, at rest, each river and
    each rill :
Grant us such grace.

Before 1893.

Who hath despised the day of small things?

As violets so be I recluse and sweet,
    Cheerful as daisies unaccounted
    rare,
Still sunward-gazing from a lowly
    seat,
    Still sweetening wintry air.

While half-awakened Spring lags
    incomplete,
    While lofty forest trees tower
    bleak and bare,

Daisies and violets own remotest
  heat
And bloom and make them fair.
Before 1893.

'Do this, and he doeth it.'

CONTENT to come, content to go,
  Content to wrestle or to race,
Content to know or not to know,
  Each in his place ;

Lord, grant us grace to love Thee so
  That glad of heart and glad of face
At last we may sit, high or low,
  Each in his place ;

Where pleasures flow as rivers flow,
  And loss has left no barren trace,
And all that are are perfect so,
  Each in his place.
Before 1893.

'That no man take thy Crown.'

BE faithful unto death. Christ
    proffers thee
  Crown of a life that draws
    immortal breath :
To thee He saith, yea and He saith
    to me,
  'Be faithful unto death.'

To every living soul that same He
    saith,
  'Be faithful' : —whatsoever else we
    be,
Let us be faithful, challenging His
    faith.

Tho' trouble storm around us like
    the sea,
  Tho' hell surge up to scare us and
    to scathe.

Tho' heaven and earth betake them-
    selves to flee,
  'Be faithful unto death.'
Before 1893.

Ye are come unto Mount Sion.

FEAR, Faith, and Hope, have sent
    their hearts above :
  Prudence, Obedience, and Hu-
    mility,
  Climb at their call, all scaling
    heaven toward Love.
Fear hath least grace but great
    expediency ;
  Faith and Humility show grave
    and strong ;
  Prudence and Hope mount
    balanced equally.
Obedience marches marshalling
    their throng,
  Goes first, goes last, to left hand
    or to right ;
  And all the six uplift a pilgrim's
    song.
By day they rest not, nor they rest
    by night :
  While Love within them, with
    them, over them,
  Weans them and woos them from
    the dark to light.
Each plies for staff not reed with
    broken stem,
  But olive branch in pledge of
    patient peace ;
  Till Love being theirs in New
    Jerusalem
Transfigure them to Love, and so
    they cease.
  Love is the sole beatitude above :
  All other graces, to their vast
    increase
Of glory, look on Love and mirror
    Love.
Before 1893.

Sit down in the lowest room.

LORD, give me grace
To take the lowest place;
Nor even desire,
Unless it be Thy Will, to go up higher.
Except by grace,
I fail of lowest place;
Except desire
Sit low, it aims awry to go up higher.
Before 1893.

Lord, it is good for us to be here.

GRANT us, O Lord, that patience and that faith:
Faith's patience imperturbable in Thee,
Hope's patience till the long-drawn shadows flee,
Love's patience unresentful of all scathe.
Verily we need patience breath by breath;
Patience while Faith holds up her glass to see,
While Hope toils yoked in Fear's copartnery,
And Love goes softly on the way to death.
How gracious and how perfecting a grace
Must Patience be on which those others wait:
Faith with suspended rapture in her face,
Hope pale and careful hand in hand with Fear,
Love—ah good Love who would not antedate
God's Will, but saith, Good is it to be here.
Before 1893.

LORD, grant us grace to rest upon Thy word,
To rest in hope until we see Thy Face;
To rest thro' toil unruffled and un-stirred,
Lord, grant us grace.

This burden and this heat wear on apace:
Night comes, when sweeter than night's singing bird
Will swell the silence of our ended race.

Ah songs which flesh and blood have never heard
And cannot hear, songs of the silent place
Where rest remains! Lord, slake our hope deferred,
Lord, grant us grace!
Before 1893.

CHRISTMAS CAROLS

I

WHOSO hears a chiming for Christmas at the nighest
Hears a sound like Angels chanting in their glee,
Hears a sound like palm boughs waving in the highest,
Hears a sound like ripple of a crystal sea.

Sweeter than a prayer-bell for a saint in dying,
Sweeter than a death-bell for a saint at rest,
Music struck in Heaven with earth's faint replying,
'Life is good, and death is good, for Christ is Best.'

2

A holy heavenly chime
Rings fulness in of time,
And on His Mother's breast
Our Lord God ever-Blest
Is laid a Babe at rest.

Stoop, Spirits unused to stoop,
Swoop, Angels, flying swoop,
Adoring as you gaze,
Uplifting hymns of praise :—
'Grace to the Full of Grace!'

The cave is cold and strait
To hold the angelic state :
More strait it is, more cold,
To foster and infold
Its Maker one hour old.

Thrilled through with awestruck love,
Meek Angels poised above,
To see their God, look down :
'What, is there never a Crown
For Him in swaddled gown?

'How comes He soft and weak
With such a tender cheek,
With such a soft small hand?—
The very Hand which spann'd
Heaven when its girth was plann'd.

'How comes He with a voice
Which is but baby-noise?—
That Voice which spake with might
" Let there be light "—and light
Sprang out before our sight.

'What need hath He of flesh
Made flawless now afresh?
What need of human heart?—
Heart that must bleed and smart,
Choosing the better part.

'But see : His gracious smile
Dismisses us a while
To serve Him in His kin.
Haste we, make haste, begin
To fetch His brethren in.'

Like stars they flash and shoot,
The Shepherds they salute :
'Glory to God' they sing :
'Good news of peace we bring,
For Christ is born a King.'

3

Lo! newborn Jesus
  Soft and weak and small,
Wrapped in baby's bands
By His Mother's hands,
  Lord God of all.

Lord God of Mary,
  Whom His Lips caress
While He rocks to rest
On her milky breast
  In helplessness.

Lord God of shepherds
  Flocking through the cold,
Flocking through the dark
To the only Ark,
  The only Fold.

Lord God of all things
  Be they near or far,
Be they high or low ;
Lord of storm and snow,
  Angel and star.

Lord God of all men,—
　　　　My Lord and my God!
　　　Thou who lovest me,
　　　Keep me close to Thee
　　　　By staff and rod.

　　　Lo! newborn Jesus
　　　　Loving great and small,
　　　Love's free Sacrifice,
　　　Opening Arms and Eyes
　　　　To one and all.
Circa 1887.

A HOPE CAROL

A NIGHT was near, a day was near;
　Between a day and night
I heard sweet voices calling clear,
　Calling me:
I heard a whirr of wing on wing,
　But could not see the sight;
I long to see the birds that sing,
　I long to see.

Below the stars, beyond the moon,
　Between the night and day,
I heard a rising falling tune
　Calling me:
I long to see the pipes and strings
　Whereon such minstrels play;
I long to see each face that sings,
　I long to see.

To-day or may be not to-day,
　To-night or not to-night,
All voices that command or pray,
　Calling me,
Shall kindle in my soul such fire
　And in my eyes such light
That I shall see that heart's desire
　I long to see.
Before 1889.

CARDINAL NEWMAN

In the grave whither thou goest.

O WEARY Champion of the Cross, lie still:
　Sleep thou at length the all-embracing sleep:
　Long was thy sowing-day, rest now and reap:
Thy fast was long, feast now thy spirit's fill.
Yea take thy fill of love, because thy will
　Chose love not in the shallows but the deep:
　Thy tides were spring-tides, set against the neap
Of calmer souls: thy flood rebuked their rill.
Now night has come to thee—please God, of rest:
　So some time must it come to every man;
　　To first and last, where many last are first.
Now fixed and finished thine eternal plan,
　Thy best has done its best, thy worst its worst:
　　Thy best its best, please God, thy best its best.

16 *August* 1890.

YEA I HAVE A GOODLY HERITAGE

MY vineyard that is mine I have to keep,
　Pruning for fruit the pleasant twigs and leaves.

Tend thou thy cornfield: one day
   thou shalt reap
  In joy thy ripened sheaves.

Or, if thine be an orchard, graft and
   prop
  Food-bearing trees each watered
   in its place:
Or, if a garden, let it yield for crop
  Sweet herbs and herb of grace.—

But if my lot be sand where nothing
   grows?—
  Nay who hath said it? Tune a
   thankful psalm:
For, though thy desert bloom not as
   the rose,
  It yet can rear thy palm.

Circa 1890.

A CANDLEMAS DIALOGUE

'LOVE brought Me down: and can-
   not love make thee
Carol for joy to Me?
Hear cheerful robin carol from his
   tree,
Who owes not half to Me
  I won for thee.'

'Yea, Lord, I hear his carol's word-
   less voice;
And well may he rejoice
Who hath not heard of death's dis-
   cordant noise.
So might I too rejoice
With such a voice.'

'True, thou hast compassed death:
   but hast not thou
The tree of life's own bough?

Am I not Life and Resurrection
   now?
My Cross, balm-bearing bough
For such as thou.'

'Ah me, Thy Cross!——but that
   seems far away;
Thy Cradle-song to-day
I too would raise and worship Thee
   and pray:
Not empty, Lord, to-day
Send me away.'

'If thou wilt not go empty, spend
   thy store;
And I will give thee more,
Yea, make thee ten times richer than
   before.
Give more and give yet more
Out of thy store.'

'Because Thou givest me Thyself, I
   will
Thy blessed word fulfil,
Give with both hands, and hoard by
   giving still:
Thy pleasure to fulfil,
And work Thy Will.'

Before 1891.

MARY MAGDALENE AND THE OTHER MARY

A SONG FOR ALL MARIES

OUR Master lies asleep and is at
   rest:
  His Heart has ceased to bleed, His
    Eye to weep:
The sun ashamed has dropt down in
   the west:
  Our Master lies asleep.

Now we are they who weep, and
    trembling keep
Vigil, with wrung heart in a sighing
    breast,
    While slow time creeps, and slow
        the shadows creep.

Renew Thy youth, as eagle from the
    nest ;
    O Master, who hast sown, arise to
        reap :—
No cock-crow yet, no flush on
    eastern crest :
    Our Master lies asleep.

Before 1891.

A DEATH OF A FIRST-BORN

(14 *January* 1892.)

ONE young life lost, two happy
    young lives blighted,
    With earthward eyes we see :
With eyes uplifted, keener, farther-
    sighted,
    We look, O Lord, to Thee.

Grief hears a funeral knell : Hope
    hears the ringing
    Of birthday bells on high ;
Faith, Hope, and Love, make answer
    with soft singing,
    Half carol and half cry.

Stoop to console us, Christ, sole
    consolation,
    While dust returns to dust ;
Until that blessed day when all Thy
    nation
    Shall rise up of the Just.

January 1892.

FAINT YET PURSUING

1

BEYOND this shadow and this turbu-
    lent sea,
    Shadow of death and turbulent
        sea of death,
Lies all we long to have or long to
    be.
    Take heart, tired man, toil on
        with lessening breath,
Lay violent hands on heaven's high
    treasury,
    Be what you long to be through
        life-long scathe.
A little while Hope leans on
    Charity,
    A little while Charity heartens
        Faith :
A little while : and then what
    further while ?
    One while that ends not and that
        wearies not,
        For ever new whilst evermore
            the same.
    All things made new bear each
        a sweet new name ;
    Man's lot of death has turned to
        life his lot,
And tearful Charity to Love's own
    smile.

2

Press onward, quickened souls, who
    mounting move,
    Press onward, upward, fire with
        mounting fire ;
    Gathering volume of untold
        desire,

Press upward, homeward, dove with
    mounting dove.
Point me the excellent way that
    leads above;
  Woo me with sequent will, me
    too to aspire;
  With sequent heart to follow
    higher and higher,
To follow all who follow on to
    Love.
Up the high steep, across the golden
    sill,
  Up out of shadows into very
    light,
    Up out of dwindling life to life
    aglow,
  I watch you, my beloved, out of
    sight;—
Sight fails me, and my heart is
    watching still:
    My heart fails, yet I follow on
    to know.

Circa 1892.

THE WORLD.
SELF-DESTRUCTION

(*Before* 1893.)

A vain Shadow.

THE world,—what a world, ah
  me!
  Mouldy, worm-eaten, grey:
Vain as a leaf from a tree,
  As a fading day,
As veriest vanity,
  As the froth and the spray
Of the hollow-billowed sea,
  As what was and shall not be,
  As what is and passes away.

Lord, save us, we perish.

O LORD, seek us, O Lord, find us
  In Thy patient care;
Be Thy Love before, behind us,
  Round us, everywhere:
Lest the god of this world blind us,
  Lest he speak us fair,
Lest he forge a chain to bind us,
  Lest he bait a snare.
Turn not from us, call to mind us,
  Find, embrace us, bear;
Be Thy Love before, behind us,
  Round us, everywhere.

WHAT is this above thy head,
  O Man?—
The World, all overspread
  With pearls and golden rays
  And gems ablaze;
A sight which day and night
  Fills an eye's span.

What is this beneath thy feet,
  O Saint?—
The World, a nauseous sweet
  Puffed up and perishing;
  A hollow thing,
A lie, a vanity,
  Tinsel and paint.

What is she while time is
  time,
  O Man?—
In a perpetual prime
  Beauty and youth she hath;
And her footpath
Breeds flowers thro' dancing hours
  Since time began.

While time lengthens what is she,
  O Saint?—
Nought: yea, all men shall see
How she is nought at all,
When her death-pall
Of fire ends their desire
  And brands her taint.

Ah poor Man, befooled and slow
  And faint!
Ah poorest Man, if so
Thou turn thy back on bliss
And choose amiss!
For thou art choosing now:
  Sinner,—or Saint.

       Babylon the Great.

FOUL is she and ill-favoured, set askew:
  Gaze not upon her till thou dream her fair,
  Lest she should mesh thee in her wanton hair,
Adept in arts grown old yet ever new.
Her heart lusts not for love, but thro' and thro'
  For blood, as spotted panther lusts in lair;
  No wine is in her cup, but filth is there
Unutterable, with plagues hid out of view.
Gaze not upon her, for her dancing whirl
  Turns giddy the fixed gazer presently:
  Gaze not upon her, lest thou be as she
When, at the far end of her long desire,

Her scarlet vest and gold and gem and pearl
  And she amid her pomp are set on fire.

Standing afar off for the fear of her torment.

Is this the end? is there no end but this?
  Yea, none beside:
  No other end for pride
And foulness and besottedness.

Hath she no friend? hath she no clinging friend?
  Nay, none at all;
  Who stare upon her fall
Quake for themselves with hair on end.

Will she be done away? vanish away?
  Yea, like a dream;
  Yea, like the shades that seem
Somewhat, and lo are nought by day.

Alas for her amid man's helpless moan,
  Alas for her!
  She hath no comforter:
In solitude of fire she sits alone.

      O Lucifer, Son of the Morning!

O FALLEN star! a darkened light,
  A glory hurtled from its car,
Self-blasted from the holy height:
  O fallen star!

Fallen beyond earth's utmost bar,
Beyond return, beyond far sight
  Of outmost glimmering nebular.

Now blackness, which once walked
    in white;
Now death, whose life once glowed
    afar;
O son of dawn that loved the night,
    O fallen star!

Alas, alas! for the self-destroyed
    Vanish as images from a glass,
Sink down and die down by hope
    unbuoyed:—
    Alas, alas!

Who shall stay their ruinous mass?
Besotted, reckless, possessed, decoyed,
    They hurry to the dolorous pass.

Saints fall a-weeping who would
    have joyed,
    Sore they weep for a glory that was,
For a fulness emptied into the void,
    Alas, alas!

As froth on the face of the deep,
    As foam on the crest of the sea,
As dreams at the waking of sleep,
    As gourd of a day and a night,
As harvest that no man shall reap,
    As vintage that never shall be,
Is hope if it cling not aright,
    O my God, unto Thee.

Where their worm dieth not, and the fire is not quenched.

In tempest and storm, blackness of
    darkness for ever,
    A fire unextinguished, a worm's indestructible swarm;
Where no hope shall ever be more,
    and love shall be never,
    In tempest and storm;
Where the form of all things is
    fashionless, void of all form;
Where from death that severeth all,
    the soul cannot sever
    In tempest and storm.

Toll, bell, toll. For hope is flying
    Sighing from the earthbound soul:
Life is sighing, life is dying:
    Toll, bell, toll.

Gropes in its own grave the mole,
Wedding darkness, undescrying,
Tending to no different goal.

Self-slain soul, in vain thy sighing:
    Self-slain, who should make thee whole?
Vain the clamour of thy crying:
    Toll, bell, toll.

ALL THINGS

Jesus alone:—if thus it were to me;
    Yet thus it cannot be;
Lord, I have all things if I have but Thee.

Jesus and all:—precious His bounties are,
    Yet He more precious far;
Day's-eyes are many, one the Morning Star.

Jesus my all:—so let me rest in love,
    Thy peaceable poor dove,
Some time below till timeless time above.

Before 1893.

HEAVEN OVERARCHES

HEAVEN overarches earth and sea,
   Earth-sadness and sea-bitterness.
Heaven overarches you and me:
A little while and we shall be—
Please God—where there is no more sea
   Nor barren wilderness.
Heaven overarches you and me,
   And all earth's gardens and her graves.
Look up with me, until we see
The day break and the shadows flee.
What though to-night wrecks you and me
   If so to-morrow saves?

Circa 1893.

GENERAL POEMS

A PORTRAIT

1

SHE gave up beauty in her tender youth,
   Gave all her hope and joy and pleasant ways;
   She covered up her eyes lest they should gaze
On vanity, and chose the bitter truth.
Harsh towards herself, towards others full of ruth,
   Servant of servants, little known to praise,
   Long prayers and fasts trenched on her nights and days:
She schooled herself to sights and sounds uncouth
That with the poor and stricken she might make
   A home, until the least of all sufficed
Her wants; her own self learned she to forsake,
   Counting all earthly gain but hurt and loss.
So with calm will she chose and bore the cross
And hated all for love of Jesus Christ.

21 *November* 1850.

2

They knelt in silent anguish by her bed,
   And could not weep; but calmly there she lay.
   All pain had left her; and the sun's last ray
Shone through upon her, warming into red
The shady curtains. In her heart she said:
   'Heaven opens; I leave these and go away;

The Bridegroom calls,—shall the
  Bride seek to stay?'
Then low upon her breast she bowed
  her head.
O lily flower, O gem of priceless
    worth,
  O dove with patient voice and
    patient eyes,
O fruitful vine amid a land of
    dearth,
  O maid replete with loving
    purities,
Thou bowedst down thy head with
    friends on earth
  To raise it with the saints in
    Paradise.
24 *February* 1847.

THE WHOLE HEAD IS SICK AND THE WHOLE HEART FAINT.

WOE for the young who say that life
    is long,
  Who turn from the sun-rising to
    the West,
  Who feel no pleasure and can
    find no rest,
Who in the morning sigh for even-
    song.
Their hearts, weary because of this
    world's wrong,
  Yearn with a thousand longings
    unexprest;
  They have a wound no mortal
    ever drest,
An ill than all earth's remedies
    more strong.
For them the fount of gladness hath
    run dry,
  And in all Nature is no pleasant
    thing;
For them there is no glory in the
    sky,
  No sweetness in the breezes' mur-
    muring:
They say, 'The peace of heaven is
    placed too high,
  And this earth changeth and is
    perishing.'
6 *December* 1847.

VANITY OF VANITIES

AH woe is me for pleasure that is
    vain,
  Ah woe is me for glory that is
    past!
  Pleasure that bringeth sorrow at
    the last,
Glory that at the last bringeth no
    gain.
So saith the sinking heart; and so
    again
  It shall say till the mighty angel-
    blast
  Is blown, making the sun and
    moon aghast,
And showering down the stars like
    sudden rain.
And evermore men shall go fear-
    fully,
  Bending beneath their weight of
    heaviness;
And ancient men shall lie down
    wearily,
  And strong men shall rise up in
    weariness:
Yea even the young shall answer
    sighingly,
  Saying one to another 'How vain
    it is!'
1847.

THREE STAGES

1.—A PAUSE OF THOUGHT

I LOOKED for that which is not, nor can be,
   And hope deferred made my heart sick in truth:
   But years must pass before a hope of youth
Is resigned utterly.

I watched and waited with a steadfast will:
   And though the object seemed to flee away
   That I so longed for, ever day by day
I watched and waited still.

Sometimes I said: 'This thing shall be no more;
   My expectation wearies and shall cease;
   I will resign it now and be at peace':
Yet never gave it o'er.

Sometimes I said: 'It is an empty name
   I long for; to a name why should I give
   The peace of all the days I have to live?'—
Yet gave it all the same.

Alas thou foolish one! alike unfit
   For healthy joy and salutary pain:
   Thou knowest the chase useless, and again
Turnest to follow it.

14 February 1848.

2.—THE END OF THE FIRST PART

My happy happy dream is finished with,
   My dream in which alone I lived so long.
My heart slept — woe is me, it wakeneth;
   Was weak—I thought it strong.

Oh weary wakening from a life-true dream!
   Oh pleasant dream from which I wake in pain!
I rested all my trust on things that seem,
   And all my trust is vain.

I must pull down my palace that I built,
   Dig up the pleasure-gardens of my soul;
Must change my laughter to sad tears for guilt,
   My freedom to control.

Now all the cherished secrets of my heart,
   Now all my hidden hopes, are turned to sin.
Part of my life is dead, part sick, and part
   Is all on fire within.

The fruitless thought of what I might have been,
   Haunting me ever, will not let me rest.
A cold North wind has withered all my green,
   My sun is in the West.

But, where my palace stood, with the same stone
  I will uprear a shady hermitage:
And there my spirit shall keep house alone,
  Accomplishing its age.

There other garden-beds shall lie around,
  Full of sweet-briar and incense-bearing thyme:
There I will sit, and listen for the sound
  Of the last lingering chime.
18 *April* 1849.

3

I THOUGHT to deal the death-stroke at a blow:
  To give all, once for all, but never more:—
Then sit to hear the low waves fret the shore,
  Or watch the silent snow.

'Oh rest,' I thought, 'in silence and the dark:
  Oh rest, if nothing else, from head to feet:
Though I may see no more the poppied wheat,
  Or sunny soaring lark.

'These chimes are slow, but surely strike at last:
  This sand is slow, but surely droppeth through:
And much there is to suffer, much to do,
  Before the time be past.

'So will I labour, but will not rejoice:
Will do and bear, but will not hope again:

Gone dead alike to pulses of quick pain
  And pleasure's counterpoise.'

I said so in my heart: and so I thought
  My life would lapse, a tedious monotone:
I thought to shut myself and dwell alone
  Unseeking and unsought.

But first I tired, and then my care grew slack,
  Till my heart dreamed, and maybe wandered too:—
I felt the sunshine glow again, and knew
  The swallow on its track:

All birds awoke to building in the leaves,
  All buds awoke to fullness and sweet scent:
Ah too my heart woke unawares, intent
  On fruitful harvest-sheaves.

Full pulse of life, that I had deemed was dead;
  Full throb of youth, that I had deemed at rest.
Alas I cannot build myself a nest,
  I cannot crown my head

With royal purple blossoms for the feast,
  Nor flush with laughter, nor exult in song:—
These joys may drift, as time now drifts along;
  And cease, as once they ceased.

I may pursue, and yet may not attain,
Athirst and panting all the days I
    live:
Or seem to hold, yet nerve myself to
    give
    What once I gave, again.
25 *July* 1854.

LADY MONTREVOR

I DO not look for love that is a
    dream—
    I only seek for courage to be still;
To bear my grief with an unbend-
    ing will,
And when I am a-weary not to seem.
Let the round world roll on; let the
    sun beam;
    Let the wind blow, and let the
        rivers fill
The everlasting sea, and on the
    hill
The palms almost touch heaven, as
    children deem.
And, though young spring and
    summer pass away,
    And autumn and cold winter come
        again,
And though my soul, being tired
    of its pain,
Pass from the ancient earth, and
    though my clay
    Return to dust, my tongue shall
        not complain;—
No man shall mock me after this my
    day.
18 *February* 1848.

SONG

SHE sat and sang alway
    By the green margin of a stream,
Watching the fishes leap and play
    Beneath the glad sunbeam.

I sat and wept alway
    Beneath the moon's most shadowy
        beam,
Watching the blossoms of the May
    Weep leaves into the stream.

I wept for memory;
    She sang for hope that is so fair:
My tears were swallowed by the sea;
    Her songs died on the air.
26 *November* 1848.

BITTER FOR SWEET

SUMMER is gone with all its roses,
    Its sun and perfumes and sweet
        flowers,
    Its warm air and refreshing
        showers:
And even Autumn closes.

Yea, Autumn's chilly self is going,
    And Winter comes which is yet
        colder;
Each day the hoar-frost waxes
    bolder,
    And the last buds cease
        blowing.
1 *December* 1848.

SONG

WHEN I am dead, my dearest,
    Sing no sad songs for me;
Plant thou no roses at my head,
    Nor shady cypress tree:
Be the green grass above me
    With showers and dewdrops wet:
And if thou wilt, remember,
    And if thou wilt, forget.

I shall not see the shadows,
    I shall not feel the rain;
I shall not hear the nightingale
    Sing on as if in pain:

And dreaming through the twilight
    That doth not rise nor set,
Haply I may remember,
    And haply may forget.
12 *December* 1848.

ON KEATS

A GARDEN in a garden: a green spot
    Where all is green: most fitting
    slumber-place
    For the strong man grown weary
    of a race
Soon over. Unto him a goodly lot
Hath fallen in fertile ground; there
    thorns are not,
    But his own daisies; silence, full
    of grace,
    Surely hath shed a quiet on his
    face;
His earth is but sweet leaves that
    fall and rot.
What was his record of himself, ere
    he
    Went from us? 'Here lies one
    whose name was writ
    In water.' While the chilly
    shadows flit
    Of sweet St. Agnes' Eve, while
    basil springs—
    His name, in every humble heart
    that sings,
Shall be a fountain of love, verily.
18 *January* 1849 (Eve of St. Agnes).

HAVE PATIENCE

THE goblets all are broken,
    The pleasant wine is spilt,
    The songs cease. If thou wilt,
Listen, and hear truth spoken.
We take thought for the morrow,
    And know not we shall see it;
We look on death with sorrow,
    And cannot flee it.
Youth passes like the lightning,
    Not to return again,—
Just for a little bright'ning
    The confines of a plain,
Gilding the spires, and whit'ning
    The gravestones and the slain.
Youth passes like the odour
    From the white rose's cup
    When the hot sun drinks up
The dew that overflowed her:
Then life forsakes the petals
    That had been very fair;
    No beauty lingers there,
    And no bee settles.
But, when the rose is dead
    And the leaves fallen,
And when the earth has spread
    A snow-white pall on,
The thorn remains, once hidden
    By the green growth above it—
A darksome guest unbidden,
    With none to love it.
Manhood is turbulent,
    And old age tires;
That hath no still content,
    This no desires.
The present hath even less
    Joy than the past,
    And more cares fret it:—
Life is a weariness
    From first to last—
        Let us forget it:
Fill high and deep!—But how?
    The goblets all are broken.
Nay then, have patience now:
    For this is but a token
We soon shall have no need
    Of such to cheer us;
The palm-branches decreed
And crowns to be our meed
    Are very near us.
23 *January* 1849.

SONG

OH roses for the flush of youth,
    And laurel for the perfect prime ;
But pluck an ivy branch for me
    Grown old before my time.

Oh violets for the grave of youth,
    And bay for those dead in their prime ;
Give me the withered leaves I chose
    Before in the old time.
        6 February 1849.

AN END

LOVE, strong as Death, is dead.
Come, let us make his bed
Among the dying flowers :
A green turf at his head ;
And a stone at his feet,
Whereon we may sit
In the quiet evening hours.

He was born in the spring,
And died before the harvesting :
On the last warm summer day
He left us ; he would not stay
For autumn twilight cold and grey.
Sit we by his grave, and sing
He is gone away.

To few chords and sad and low
Sing we so :
Be our eyes fixed on the grass
Shadow-veiled as the years pass,
While we think of all that was
In the long ago.
    5 March 1849.

DREAM LAND

WHERE sunless rivers weep
Their waves into the deep,
She sleeps a charmèd sleep :
    Awake her not.
Led by a single star,
She came from very far
To seek where shadows are
    Her pleasant lot.

She left the rosy morn,
She left the fields of corn,
For twilight cold and lorn
    And water springs.
Through sleep, as through a veil,
She sees the sky look pale,
And hears the nightingale
    That sadly sings.

Rest, rest, a perfect rest
Shed over brow and breast ;
Her face is toward the west,
    The purple land.
She cannot see the grain
Ripening on hill and plain,
She cannot feel the rain
    Upon her hand.

Rest, rest, for evermore
Upon a mossy shore ;
Rest, rest at the heart's core
    Till time shall cease :
Sleep that no pain shall wake ;
Night that no morn shall break,
Till joy shall overtake
    Her perfect peace.
    April 1849.

AFTER DEATH

THE curtains were half drawn, the floor was swept
And strewn with rushes, rosemary and may
Lay thick upon the bed on which I lay,

Where through the lattice ivy-
    shadows crept.
He leaned above me, thinking that
    I slept
And could not hear him; but I
    heard him say,
    'Poor child, poor child': and as
    he turned away
Came a deep silence, and I knew he
    wept.
He did not touch the shroud, or
    raise the fold
That hid my face, or take my
    hand in his,
    Or ruffle the smooth pillows for
    my head:
He did not love me living; but
    once dead
He pitied me; and very sweet it
    is
To know he still is warm though I
    am cold.
    28 *April* 1849.

REST

O EARTH, lie heavily upon her eyes;
    Seal her sweet eyes weary of
    watching, Earth;
    Lie close around her; leave no
    room for mirth
With its harsh laughter, nor for
    sound of sighs.
She hath no questions, she hath no
    replies,
    Hushed in and curtained with a
    blessed dearth
    Of all that irked her from the
    hour of birth;
With stillness that is almost Paradise.
Darkness more clear than noonday
    holdeth her,
    Silence more musical than any
    song;

Even her very heart has ceased to
    stir:
Until the morning of Eternity
Her rest shall not begin nor end,
    but be;
    And when she wakes she will not
    think it long.
    15 *May* 1849.

LOOKING FORWARD

SLEEP, let me sleep, for I am sick
    of care;
    Sleep, let me sleep, for my pain
    wearies me.
Shut out the light; thicken the heavy
    air
With drowsy incense; let a distant
    stream
Of music lull me, languid as a dream,
    Soft as the whisper of a summer
    sea.

Pluck me no rose that groweth on a
    thorn,
    Nor myrtle white and cold as snow
    in June,
Fit for a virgin on her marriage
    morn:
But bring me poppies brimmed with
    sleepy death,
And ivy choking what it garlandeth,
    And primroses that open to the
    moon.

Listen, the music swells into a song,
    A simple song I loved in days of
    yore;
The echoes take it up and up along
The hills, and the wind blows it
    back again.—
Peace, peace, there is a memory in
    that strain
    Of happy days that shall return
    no more.

Oh peace! your music wakeneth
old thought,
  But not old hope that made my
life so sweet,
Only the longing that must end in
nought.
Have patience with me, friends, a
little while:
For soon, where you shall dance and
sing and smile,
  My quickened dust may blossom
at your feet.

Sweet thought that I may yet live
and grow green,
  That leaves may yet spring from
the withered root,
And buds and flowers and berries
half unseen.
Then, if you haply muse upon the
past,
Say this: Poor child, she has her
wish at last;
  Barren through life, but in death
bearing fruit.

8 June 1849.

LIFE HIDDEN

ROSES and lilies grow above the
place
  Where she sleeps the long sleep
that doth not dream.
If we could look upon her hidden face,
  Nor shadow would be there, nor
garish gleam
Of light; her life is lapsing like
a stream
That makes no noise but floweth on
apace
  Seawards, while many a shade
and shady beam
Vary the ripples in their gliding
chase.

She doth not see, but knows; she
doth not feel,
  And yet is sensible; she hears no
sound,
    Yet counts the flight of time
and doth not err.
Peace far and near, peace to
ourselves and her:
  Her body is at peace in holy
ground,
Her spirit is at peace where Angels
kneel.

23 July 1849.

REMEMBER

REMEMBER me when I am gone
away,
Gone far away into the silent land;
When you can no more hold me
by the hand,
Nor I half turn to go yet turning
stay.
Remember me when no more day
by day
You tell me of our future that you
plann'd:
Only remember me; you understand
It will be late to counsel then or
pray.
Yet if you should forget me for a
while
And afterwards remember, do not
grieve:
For if the darkness and corruption
leave
A vestige of the thoughts that
once I had,
Better by far you should forget and
smile
Than that you should remember
and be sad.

25 July 1849.

SOUND SLEEP

Some are laughing, some are weeping;
  She is sleeping, only sleeping.
Round her rest wild flowers are
  creeping;
There the wind is heaping, heaping
Sweetest sweets of Summer's keeping,
  By the corn-fields ripe for reaping.

There are lilies, and there blushes
  The deep rose, and there the
  thrushes
Sing till latest sunlight flushes
In the west; a fresh wind brushes
Through the leaves while evening
  hushes.

There by day the lark is singing
  And the grass and weeds are
  springing;
There by night the bat is winging;
There for ever winds are bringing
Far-off chimes of church-bells ringing.

Night and morning, noon and even,
  Their sound fills her dreams with
  Heaven:
The long strife at length is striven:
Till her grave-bands shall be riven,
Such is the good portion given
  To her soul at rest and shriven.
    13 *August* 1849.

QUEEN ROSE

The jessamine shows like a star;
  The lilies sway like sceptres slim;
Fair clematis from near and far
  Sets forth its wayward tangled
  whim;
Curved meadowsweet blooms rich
  and dim;—
But yet a rose is fairer far.

The jessamine is odorous; so
  Maid-lilies are, and clematis;
And where tall meadowsweet-flowers
  grow
A rare and subtle perfume is;—
What can there be more choice
  than these?—
A rose when it doth bud and blow.

Let others choose sweet jessamine,
  Or weave their lily-crown aright,
And let who love it pluck and twine
  Loose clematis, or draw delight
  From meadowsweets' cluster
  downy white—
The rose, the perfect rose, be mine.
    16 *August* 1849.

HOW ONE CHOSE

'Beyond the sea, in a green land
  Where only rivers are—
Beyond the clouds, in the clear sky
  Close by some quiet star—
Could you not fancy there might be
A home, Beloved, for you and me?'

'If there were such a home, my
    Friend,
  Truly prepared for us,
Full of palm-branches, or of crowns
  Sun-gemmed and glorious,
How should we reach it? Let us
  cease
From longing; let us be at peace.'

'The nightingale sang yestereve;
  A sweet song singeth she,
Most sad and without any hope,
  And full of memory;

But still methought it seemed to speak
To me of home, and bid me seek.'

'The nightingale ceased ere the morn:
 ' Her heart could not contain
The passion of her song, but burst
 With the long throbbing pain.
Now she hath rest which is the best,
And now I too would be at rest.'

'Last night I watched the mounting moon:
 Her glory was too pale
To shine through the black heavy clouds
 That wrapt her like a veil;
And yet with patience she passed through
The mists, and reached the depths of blue.'

'And when the road was travelled o'er
 And when the goal was won,
A little while and all her light
 Was swallowed by the sun:
The weary moon must seek again,—
Even so our search would be in vain.'

'Yet seek with me. And if our way
 Be long and troublesome,
And if our noon be hot until
 The chilly shadows come
Of evening,—till those shadows flee
In dawn, think, Love, it is with me.'

'Nay, seek alone: I am no mate
 For such as you, in truth:
My heart is old before its time;
 Yours yet is in its youth:
This home with pleasures girt about
Seek you, for I am wearied out.'
 6 *October* 1849.

SEEKING REST

My Mother said: 'The child is changed
 That used to be so still;
All the day long she sings and sings,
 And seems to think no ill;
She laughs as if some inward joy
 Her heart would overfill.'

My Sisters said: 'Now prythee tell
 Thy secret unto us:
Let us rejoice with thee; for all
 Is surely prosperous,
Thou art so merry: tell us, Sweet:
 We had not used thee thus.'

My Mother says: 'What ails the child
 Lately so blythe of cheer?
Art sick or sorry? Nay, it is
 The winter of the year;
Wait till the Springtime comes again,
 And the sweet flowers appear.'

My Sisters say: 'Come, sit with us,
 That we may weep with thee:
Show us thy grief that we may grieve:
 Yea haply, if we see
Thy sorrow, we may ease it; but
 Shall share it certainly.'

How should I share my pain, who kept
 My pleasure all my own?
My Spring will never come again:
 My pretty flowers have blown
For the last time; I can but sit
 And think and weep alone.
 10 *October* 1849.

ENDURANCE

Yes, I too could face death and
    never shrink.
  But it is harder to bear hated
    life;
  To strive with hands and knees
    weary of strife;
To drag the heavy chain whose
    every link
Galls to the bone; to stand upon
    the brink
Of the deep grave, nor drowse
    tho' it be rife
With sleep; to hold with steady
    hand the knife
Nor strike home:—this is courage,
    as I think.
Surely to suffer is more than to
    do.
  To do is quickly done: to suffer is
    Longer and fuller of heart-
    sicknesses.
  Each day's experience testifies of
    this.
Good deeds are many, but good
    lives are few:
  Thousands taste the full cup;
    who drains the lees?

Circa 1850.

WITHERING

Fade, tender lily,
  Fade, O crimson rose,
Fade every flower,
  Sweetest flower that blows.

Go, chilly autumn,
  Come, O winter cold;
Let the green stalks die away
  Into common mould.

Birth follows hard on death,
  Life on withering:
Hasten, we will come the sooner
  Back to pleasant spring.

Circa 1850.

TWILIGHT CALM

Oh pleasant eventide!
  Clouds on the western side
Grow grey and greyer, hiding the
    warm sun:
The bees and birds, their happy
    labours done,
  Seek their close nests and bide.

Screened in the leafy wood
  The stock-doves sit and brood:
The very squirrel leaps from bough
    to bough
But lazily; pauses; and settles now
  Where once he stored his food.

One by one the flowers close,
  Lily and dewy rose
Shutting their tender petals from the
    moon:
The grasshoppers are still; but not
    so soon
  Are still the noisy crows.

The dormouse squats and eats
  Choice little dainty bits
Beneath the spreading roots of a
    broad lime;
Nibbling his fill he stops from time
    to time
  And listens where he sits.

From far the lowings come
  Of cattle driven home:
From farther still the wind brings
    fitfully

The vast continual murmur of the
    sea,
  Now loud, now almost dumb.

  The gnats whirl in the air,
  The evening gnats; and there
The owl opes broad his eyes and
    wings to sail
For prey; the bat wakes; and the
    shell-less snail
  Comes forth, clammy and bare.

  Hark! that's the nightingale,
  Telling the self-same tale
Her song told when this ancient
    earth was young:
So echoes answered when her song
    was sung
  In the first wooded vale.

  We call it love and pain,
  The passion of her strain;
And yet we little understand or
    know:
Why should it not be rather joy that
    so
  Throbs in each throbbing vein?

  In separate herds the deer
  Lie; here the bucks, and here
The does, and by its mother sleeps
    the fawn:
Through all the hours of night until
    the dawn
  They sleep, forgetting fear.

  The hare sleeps where it lies,
  With wary half-closed eyes;
The cock has ceased to crow, the
    hen to cluck:
Only the fox is out, some heedless
    duck
  Or chicken to surprise.

  Remote, each single star
  Comes out, till there they are
All shining brightly. How the dews
    fall damp!
While close at hand the glow-worm
    lights her lamp,
  Or twinkles from afar.

  But evening now is done
  As much as if the sun
Day-giving had arisen in the East—
For night has come; and the great
    calm has ceased,
  The quiet sands have run.

7 February 1850.

TWO THOUGHTS OF DEATH

I

HER heart that loved me once is
    rottenness
  Now and corruption; and her
    life is dead
  That was to have been one with
    mine, she said.
The earth must lie with such a cruel
    stress
On eyes whereon the white lids
    used to press;
  Foul worms fill up her mouth so
    sweet and red;
  Foul worms are underneath her
    graceful head;
Yet these, being born of her from
    nothingness,
These worms are certainly flesh of
    her flesh.—
  How is it that the grass is rank
    and green
  And the dew-dropping rose is brave
    and fresh
Above what was so sweeter far than
    they?

Even as her beauty hath passed
    quite away,
Theirs too shall be as though it
    had not been.

2

So I said underneath the dusky
    trees:
But, because still I loved her
    memory,
I stooped to pluck a pale anemone,
And lo my hand lighted upon
    heartsease
Not fully blown: while with new
    life from these
Fluttered a starry moth that
    rapidly
Rose toward the sun: sunlighted
    flashed on me
Its wings that seemed to throb like
    heart-pulses.
Far far away it flew, far out of
    sight,—
From earth and flowers of earth
    it passed away
As though it flew straight up into
    the light.
Then my heart answered me:
    Thou fool, to say
That she is dead whose night is
    turned to day,
And no more shall her day turn
    back to night.
16 *March* 1850.

THREE MOMENTS

The Child said: 'Pretty bird,
Come back and play with me.'
The Bird said: 'It is in vain,
    For I am free.
I am free, I will not stay,
But will fly far away,
In the woods to sing and play,
    Far away, far away.'
The Child sought her Mother:
'I have lost my bird,' said she,
    Weeping bitterly.
But the Mother made her answer,
    Half sighing pityingly,
    Half smiling cheerily:
'Though thy bird come nevermore,
    Do not weep;
Find another playfellow,
    Child, and keep
Tears for future pain more deep.'

'Sweet rose, do not wither,'
    The Girl said.
But a blight had touched its heart
And it drooped its crimson head.
In the morning it had opened
    Full of life and bloom,
But the leaves fell one by one
    Till the twilight gloom.
One by one the leaves fell
By summer winds blown from their
    stem;
They fell upon the dewy earth
Which nourished once now tainted
    them.
    Again the young Girl wept
And sought her Mother's ear:
'My rose is dead so full of grace,
The very rose I meant to place
    In the wreath that I wear.'
'Nay, never weep for such as this,'
    The Mother answered her:
'But weave another crown, less fair
Perhaps, but fitter for thy hair.
And keep thy tears,' the Mother
    said,
    'For something heavier.'

The Woman knelt, but did not
    pray
Nor weep nor cry; she only said,

'Not this, not this!' and clasped
  her hands
Against her heart, and bowed her
  head,
While the great struggle shook the
  bed.
'Not this, not this!' tears did not
  fall;
'Not this!' it was all
She could say; no sobs would come;
The mortal grief was almost dumb.—
At length when it was over, when
She knew it was and would be so,
She cried: 'O Mother, where are
  they,
  The tears that used to flow
So easily? One single drop
Might save my reason now, or stop
My heart from breaking. Blessed
  tears
  Wasted in former years!'
Then the grave Mother made reply:
'O Daughter mine, be of good cheer,
Rejoicing thou canst shed no tear.
Thy pain is almost over now.
Once more thy heart shall throb
  with pain,
But then shall never throb again.
Oh happy thou who canst not weep,
  Oh happy thou!'

23 *March* 1850.

IS AND WAS

SHE was whiter than the ermine
  That half shadowed neck and
    hand,
And her tresses were more golden
  Than their golden band;
Snowy ostrich plumes she wore;
Yet I almost loved her more
In the simple time before.

Then she plucked the stately lilies,
Knowing not she was more fair,
And she listened to the skylark
  In the morning air.
Then, a kerchief all her crown,
She looked for the acorns brown,
Bent their bough, and shook them
  down.

Then she thought of Christmas holly
And of Maybloom in sweet May;
Then she loved to pick the cherries
  And to turn the hay.
She was humble then and meek,
And the blush upon her cheek
Told of much she could not speak.

Now she is a noble lady
With calm voice not over loud;
Very courteous in her action,
  Yet you think her proud;
Much too haughty to affect;
Too indifferent to direct
Or be angry or suspect;
Doing all from self-respect.

Spring 1850.

SONG

WE buried her among the flowers
  At falling of the leaf,
And choked back all our tears; her
  joy
  Could never be our grief.

She lies among the living flowers
  And grass, the only thing
That perishes;—or is it that
  Our Autumn was her Spring?

Doubtless, if we could see her face,
  The smile is settled there
Which almost broke our hearts when
  last
We knelt by her in prayer;

When, with tired eyes and failing
    breath
  And hands crossed on her breast,
Perhaps she saw her Guardian spread
  His wings above her rest.

So she sleeps hidden in the flowers;
  But yet a little while,
And we shall see her wake and rise,
  Fair, with the self-same smile.
14 *May* 1850.

ANNIE

ANNIE is fairer than her kith
  And kinder than her kin:
Her eyes are like the open heaven
  Holy and pure from sin:
Her heart is like an ordered house
  Good fairies harbour in:
Oh happy he who wins the love
  That I can never win!

Her sisters stand as hyacinths
  Around the perfect rose:
They bloom and open to the full,
  My bud will scarce unclose.
They are for every butterfly
  That comes and sips and goes:
My bud hides in the tender green
  Most sweet and hardly shows.

Oh cruel kindness in soft eyes
  That are no more than kind,
On which I gaze my heart away
  Till the tears make me blind!
How is it others find the way
  That I can never find
To make her laugh that sweetest
    laugh
  Which leaves all else behind?

Her hair is like the golden corn
  A low wind breathes upon:

Or like the golden harvest-moon
  When all the mists are gone:
Or like a stream with golden sands
  On which the sun has shone
Day after day in summertime
  Ere autumn leaves are wan.

I will not tell her that I love,
  Lest she should turn away
With sorrow in her tender heart
  Which now is light and gay.
I will not tell her that I love,
  Lest she should turn and say
That we must meet no more again
  For many a weary day.
26 *September* 1850.

A DIRGE

SHE was as sweet as violets in the
    Spring,
As fair as any rose in Summertime:
But frail are roses in their prime
And violets in their blossoming.
    Even so was she:
    And now she lies,
The earth upon her fast-closed
    eyes,
Dead in the darkness silently.

The sweet Spring violets never bud
    again,
The roses bloom and perish in a
    morn:
They see no second quickening lying
    lorn:
  Their beauty dies as though in
    vain.
    Must she die so
    For evermore,
  Cold as the sand upon the shore,
  As passionless for joy and woe?—

Nay she is worth much more than
　　flowers that fade,
And yet shall be made fair with
　　purple fruit :
　Branch of the Living Vine, whose
　　Root
From all eternity is laid.
　　Another Sun
　　Than this of ours
Has withered up indeed her
　　flowers
But ripened her grapes every one.
　　18 *January* 1851.

A SUMMER WISH

LIVE all thy sweet life through,
　Sweet Rose, dew-sprent,
Drop down thine evening dew,
To gather it anew
When day is bright :
　I fancy thou wast meant
Chiefly to give delight.

Sing in the silent sky,
　Glad soaring bird ;
Sing out thy notes on high
To sunbeam straying by
Or passing cloud ;
　Heedless if thou art heard,
Sing thy full song aloud.

Oh that it were with me
　As with the flower !
Blooming on its own tree
For butterfly and bee
Its summer morns :
　That I might bloom mine hour,
A rose in spite of thorns.

Oh that my work were done
　As birds' that soar
Rejoicing in the sun :

That when my time is run
And daylight too,
　I so might rest once more
Cool with refreshing dew.
　　21 *June* 1851.

SONG

IT is not for her even brow
　And shining yellow hair,
But it is for her tender eyes
　I think my love so fair :
Her tell-tale eyes that smile and
　weep
As frankly as they wake and sleep.

It is not for her rounded cheek
　I love and fain would win,
But it is for the blush that comes
　Straight from the heart within :
The honest blush of maiden shame
That blushes without thought of
　blame.

So in my dreams I never hear
　Her song, although she sings
As if a choir of spirits swept
　From earth with throbbing
　　wings :
I only hear the simple voice
Whose love makes many hearts
　rejoice.
　　1851.

A FAIR WORLD THOUGH
A FALLEN

YOU tell me that the world is fair,
　in spite
　Of the old Fall; and that I
　　should not turn
So to the grave, and let my spirit
　yearn

After the quiet of the long last
    night.
Have I then shut mine eyes against
    the light,
  Grief-deafened lest my spirit
    should discern?
  Yet how could I keep silence
    when I burn?
And who can give me comfort?—
    Hear the right.
Have patience with the weak and
    sick at heart:
  Bind up the wounded with a
    tender touch,
  Comfort the sad, tear-blinded
    as they go:—
For, though I failed to choose the
    better part,
  Were it a less unutterable woe
  If we should come to love this
    world too much?
30 *August* 1851.

BOOKS IN THE RUNNING BROOKS

'IT is enough, enough,' one said,
    At play among the flowers:
'I spy a rose upon the thorn,
    A rainbow in the showers;
I hear a merry chime of bells
    Ring out the passing hours.'
  Soft springs the fountain
    From the daisied ground,
  Softly falling on the moss
    Without a sound.

'It is enough,' she said, and fixed
    Calm eyes upon the sky:
'I watch a flitting tender cloud
    Just like a dove go by;
A lark is rising from the grass,
    A wren is building nigh.'
  Softly the fountain
    Threads its silver way,
  Screened by the scented bloom
    Of whitest May.

'Enough?' she whispered to her-
    self,
    As doubting: 'Is it so?
Enough to wear the roses fair,
    Oh sweetest flowers that blow?
Oh yes, it surely is enough—
    My happy home below!'
  A shadow stretcheth
    From the hither shore:
  The waters darken
    More and more and more.

'It is enough,' she says; but with
    A listless weary moan:
'Enough,' if mixing with her
    friends:
'Enough,' if left alone;
But to herself: 'Not yet enough
    This suffering, to atone?'
  The cold black waters
    Seem to stagnate there,
  Without a single wave
    Or breath of air.

And now she says: 'It is enough,'
    Half languid and half stirred:
'Enough,' to silence and to
    sound,
    Thorn, blossom, soaring bird:
'Enough,' she says; but with a
    lack
    Of something in the word.
  Defiled and turbid
    See the waters pass,
  Half light, half shadow,
    Struggling through the grass.

Ah will it ever dawn, that day
    When, calm for good or ill,

Her heart shall say: 'It is enough,
　For Thou art with me still;
It is enough, O Lord my God,
　Thine only blessed Will'?
　　Then shall the fountain sing
　　　And flow to rest,
　　　Clear as the sun-track
　　To the purple West.
26 *August* 1852.

THE SUMMER IS ENDED

WREATHE no more lilies in my hair,
　For I am dying, Sister sweet:
Or, if you will for the last time
　Indeed, why make me fair
　　Once for my winding-sheet.

Pluck no more roses for my breast,
　For I like them fade in my prime:
Or, if you will, why pluck them still,
　That they may share my rest
　　Once more for the last time.

Weep not for me when I am gone,
　Dear tender one, but hope and smile:
Or, if you cannot choose but weep,
　A little while weep on,
　　Only a little while.
11 *September* 1852.

AFTER ALL

'I THOUGHT your search was over.'
　　—'So I thought.'
　'But you are seeking still.'—'Yes, even so:
　Still seeking in mine own despite below
That which in heaven alone is found unsought:
Still spending for that thing which is not bought.'
　'Then chase no more this shifting empty show.'—
　'Amen: so bid a drowning man forego
The straw he clutches: will he so be taught?
You have a home where peace broods like a dove,
　Screened from the weary world's loud discontent:
You have home here: you wait for home above.
I must unlearn the pleasant ways I went:
Must learn another hope, another love,
　And sigh indeed for home in banishment.'
24 *October* 1852.

FROM THE ANTIQUE

THE wind shall lull us yet,
　The flowers shall spring above us:
And those who hate forget,
　And those forget who love us.

The pulse of hope shall cease,
　Of joy and of regretting:
We twain shall sleep in peace,
　Forgotten and forgetting.

For us no sun shall rise,
　Nor wind rejoice, nor river,
Where we with fast-closed eyes
　Shall sleep and sleep for ever.
10 *December* 1852.

TO WHAT PURPOSE IS THIS WASTE?

A WINDY shell singing upon the
    shore:
A lily budding in a desert place,
    Blooming alone
With no companion
To praise its perfect perfume and
    its grace:
A rose crimson and blushing at the
    core,
Hedged-in with thorns behind it and
    before:
A fountain in the grass,
    Whose shadowy waters pass
Only to nourish birds and furnish
    food
For squirrels of the wood:
An oak deep in the forest's heart,
    the house
Of black-eyed tiny mouse:
Its strong roots, fit for fuel, roofing
    in
The hoarded nuts, acorns, and
    grains of wheat—
Shutting them from the wind and
    scorching heat,
And sheltering them when the rains
    begin:

A precious pearl deep-buried in the
    sea
Where none save fishes be:
The fullest merriest note
For which the skylark strains his
    silver throat,
    Heard only in the sky
By other birds that fitfully
    Chase one another as they fly:
The ripest plum down-tumbled to
    the ground
By southern winds most musical of
    sound,
But by no thirsty traveller found:
Honey of wild bees in their ordered
    cells
Stored, not for human mouths to
    taste:—
I said smiling superior down: What
    waste
Of good, where no man dwells!

This I said on a pleasant day in June
Before the sun had set, though a
    white moon
Already flaked the quiet blue
    Which not a star looked through.
But still the air was warm, and
    drowsily
It blew into my face:
So, since that same day I had
    wandered deep
Into the country, I sought out a
    place
For rest beneath a tree,
And very soon forgot myself in sleep:
Not so mine own words had forgotten
    me.
Mine eyes were open to behold
    All hidden things,
And mine ears heard all secret
    whisperings:
So my proud tongue, that had
    been bold
To carp and to reprove,
Was silenced by the force of utter
    Love.

All voices of all things inanimate
Join with the song of Angels and
    the song
Of blessed spirits, chiming with
Their Hallelujahs. One wind wak-
    eneth
Across the sleeping sea, crisping
    along

The waves, and brushes through the
    great
Forests and tangled hedges, and
    calls out
    Of rivers a clear sound,
And makes the ripe corn rustle on
    the ground,
    And murmurs in a shell :
    Till all their voices swell
Above the clouds in one loud hymn
Joining the song of Seraphim,
Or like pure incense circle round
    about
The walls of heaven, or like a well-
    spring rise
    In shady Paradise.

    A lily blossoming unseen
    Holds honey in its silver cup
        Whereon a bee may sup,
Till being full she takes the rest
And stores it in her waxen nest :
While the fair blossom lifted up
On its one stately stem of green
Is type of her the Undefiled,
Arrayed in white, whose eyes are
    mild
As a white dove's, whose garment is
Blood-cleansed from all impurities
    And earthly taints,
Her robe the righteousness of
    Saints.

    And other eyes than ours
    Were made to look on flowers,
Eyes of small birds and insects
    small :
    The deep sun-blushing rose
    Round which the prickles close
Opens her bosom to them all.
    The tiniest living thing
    That soars on feathered wing,
Or crawls among the long grass out
    of sight,
    Has just as good a right
To its appointed portion of delight
    As any King.

Why should we grudge a hidden
    water-stream
To birds and squirrels while we have
    enough ?
As if a nightingale should cease to
    sing
Lest we should hear, or finch leafed
    out of sight
    Warbling its fill in summer light :
    As if sweet violets in the Spring
Should cease to blow, for fear our
    path should seem
    Less weary or less rough.

So every oak that stands a house
    For skilful mouse
And year by year renews its
    strength,
Shakes acorns from a hundred
    boughs
    Which shall be oaks at length.

Who hath weighed the waters and
    shall say
What is hidden in the depths from
    day ?
Pearls and precious stones and
    golden sands,
    Wondrous weeds and blossoms
        rare,
    Kept back from human hands,
    But good and fair,
A silent praise as pain is silent
    prayer.
A hymn and incense rising toward
    the skies,
    As our whole life should rise :
An offering without stint from earth
    below,
    Which Love accepteth so.

Thus is it with a warbling bird
With fruit bloom-ripe and full of
   seed,
With honey which the wild bees
   draw
From flowers, and store for future
   need
   By a perpetual law.
We want the faith that hath not
   seen
Indeed, but hath believed His
   truth
Who witnessed that His work was
   good :
So we pass cold to age from youth.
Alas for us, for we have heard
And known, but have not under-
   stood !

O earth, earth, earth, thou yet shalt
   bow
Who art so fair and lifted up,
Thou yet shalt drain the bitter cup.
Men's eyes that wait upon thee
   now,
All eyes shall see thee lost and
   mean,
Exposed and valued at thy worth,
While thou shalt stand ashamed
   and dumb.—
Ah when the Son of Man shall
   come,
Shall He find faith upon the earth?
22 *January* 1853.

NEXT OF KIN

THE shadows gather round me,
   while you are in the sun :
My day is almost ended, but yours
   is just begun :
The winds are singing to us both and
   the streams are singing still,

And they fill your heart with music,
   but mine they cannot fill.

Your home is built in sunlight,
   mine in another day :
Your home is close at hand, sweet
   friend, but mine is far away :
Your bark is in the haven where
   you fain would be :
I must launch out into the deep,
   across the unknown sea.

You, white as dove or lily or spirit
   of the light :
I, stained and cold and glad to hide
   in the cold dark night :
You, joy to many a loving heart and
   light to many eyes :
I, lonely in the knowledge earth is
   full of vanities.

Yet when your day is over, as mine
   is nearly done,
And when your race is finished,
   as mine is almost run,
You, like me, shall cross your hands
   and bow your graceful head :
Yea, we twain shall sleep together in
   an equal bed.
21 *February* 1853.

FOR ROSALINE'S ALBUM

Do you hear the low winds singing,
   And streams singing on their
      bed ?—
Very distant bells are ringing
   In a chapel for the dead :—
   Death-pale better than life-red.

Mother, come to me in rest,
   And bring little May to see.
Shall I bid no other guest ?

Seven slow nights have passed away
Over my forgotten clay:
   None must come save you and
     she.
February 1853.

WHAT?

STRENGTHENING as secret manna,
   Fostering as clouds above,
   Kind as a hovering dove,
   Full as a plenteous river,
Our glory and our banner
   For ever and for ever.

Dear as a dying cadence
Of music in the drowsy night:
   Fair as the flowers which maidens
   Pluck for an hour's delight,
   And then forget them quite.

Gay as a cowslip-meadow
   Fresh opening to the sun
   When new day is begun:
Soft as a sunny shadow
   When day is almost done.

Glorious as purple twilight,
   Pleasant as budding tree,
   Untouched as any islet
     Shrined in an unknown sea:
Sweet as a fragrant rose amid the
     dew:—
   As sweet, as fruitless too.

A bitter dream to wake from,
But oh how pleasant while we
     dream!
A poisoned fount to take from,
But oh how sweet the stream!
May 1853.

A PAUSE

THEY made the chamber sweet with
   flowers and leaves,
And the bed sweet with flowers on
   which I lay;
While my soul, love-bound, loitered
   on its way.
I did not hear the birds about the
   eaves,
Nor hear the reapers talk among
   the sheaves:
Only my soul kept watch from
   day to day,
My thirsty soul kept watch for one
   away:—
Perhaps he loves, I thought, remembers, grieves.
At length there came the step upon
   the stair,
Upon the lock the old familiar
   hand:
Then first my spirit seemed to scent
   the air
Of Paradise; then first the tardy
   sand
Of time ran golden; and I felt my
   hair
Put on a glory, and my soul
   expand.
10 June 1853.

THREE SEASONS

'A CUP for hope!' she said,
In springtime ere the bloom was old;
The crimson wine was poor and cold
By her mouth's richer red.

'A cup for love!' how low,
How soft the words; and all the while
Her blush was rippling with a smile
Like summer after snow.

'A cup for memory!'
Cold cup that one must drain alone :
While autumn winds are up and moan
  Across the barren sea.

Hope, memory, love :
Hope for fair morn, and love for day,
And memory for the evening grey
  And solitary dove.
18 *June* 1853.

HOLY INNOCENTS

SLEEP, little Baby, sleep ;
  The holy Angels love thee,
And guard thy bed, and keep
  A blessed watch above thee.
No spirit can come near
  Nor evil beast to harm thee :
Sleep, Sweet, devoid of fear
  Where nothing need alarm thee.

The Love which doth not sleep,
  The eternal Arms surround thee :
The Shepherd of the sheep
  In perfect love hath found thee.
Sleep through the holy night,
  Christ-kept from snare and sorrow,
Until thou wake to light
  And love and warmth to-morrow.
1 *July* 1853.

SEASONS

IN Springtime when the leaves are young,
Clear dewdrops gleam like jewels, hung
On boughs the fair birds roost among.

When Summer comes with sweet unrest,
Birds weary of their mother's breast,
And look abroad and leave the nest.

In Autumn ere the waters freeze,
The swallows fly across the seas :—
If we could fly away with these !

In Winter when the birds are gone,
The sun himself looks starved and wan,
And starved the snow he shines upon.
September 1853.

BURIED

THOU sleepest where the lilies fade,
  Thou dwellest where the lilies fade not :
Sweet, when thine earthly part decayed
  Thy heavenly part decayed not.

Thou dwellest where the roses blow,
  The crimson roses bud and blossom :
While on thine eyes is heaped the snow—
  The snow upon thy bosom.
1853.

A WISH

I WISH I were a little bird
  That out of sight doth soar ;
I wish I were a song once heard
  But often pondered o'er,
Or shadow of a lily stirred
  By wind upon the floor,
Or echo of a loving word
  Worth all that went before,
Or memory of a hope deferred
  That springs again no more.
1853.

TWO PARTED

'SING of a love lost and forgotten,
  Sing of a joy finished and o'er,

Sing of a heart core-cold and rotten,
  Sing of a hope springing no more.'
'Sigh for a heart aching and sore.'

'I was most true and my own love
  betrayed me,
I was most true and she would
  none of me.
Was it the cry of the world that
  dismayed thee?
Love, I had bearded the wide
  world for thee.'
'Hark to the sorrowful sound of
  the sea.'

'Still in my dreams she comes tender
  and gracious,
Still in my dreams love looks out
  of her eyes:
Oh that the love of a dream were
  veracious,
Or that thus dreaming I might
  not arise!'
'Oh for the silence that stilleth
  all sighs!'

1853.

AUTUMN

Care flieth,
Hope and Fear together:
  Love dieth
In the Autumn weather.

For a friend
Even Care is pleasant:
  When Fear doth end
Hope is no more present:
Autumn silences the turtle-dove:—
In blank Autumn who could speak
  of love?

1853.

SEASONS

Crocuses and snowdrops wither,
Violets, primroses together,
Fading with the fading Spring
Before a fuller blossoming.

O sweet Summer, pass not soon,
Stay awhile the harvest-moon:
O sweetest Summer, do not go,
For Autumn's next and next the
  snow.

When Autumn comes the days are
  drear,
It is the downfall of the year:
We heed the wind and falling leaf
More than the golden harvest-sheaf.

Dreary Winter come at last:
Come quickly, so be quickly past:
Dusk and sluggish Winter, wane
Till Spring and sunlight dawn again.

7 December 1853.

BALLAD

'Soft white lamb in the daisy
  meadow,
  Come hither and play with me,
For I am lonesome and I am tired
  Underneath the apple tree.'

'There's your husband if you are
  lonesome, lady,
  And your bed if you want for rest:
And your baby for a playfellow
  With a soft hand for your breast.'

'Fair white dove in the sunshine,
  Perched on the ashen bough,
Come and perch by me and coo to
  me
  While the buds are blowing now.'

'I must keep my nestlings warm,
　　lady,
　Underneath my downy breast:
There's your baby to coo and crow
　　to you
　While I brood upon my nest.'

'Faint white rose, come lie on my
　　heart,
　Come lie there with your thorn:
For I'll be dead at the vesper-bell
　And buried the morrow morn.'

'There's blood on your lily breast,
　　lady,
　Like roses when they blow,
And there's blood upon your little
　　hand
That should be white as snow:
I will stay amid my fellows
　Where the lilies grow.'

'But it's oh my own own little babe
　That I had you here to kiss,
And to comfort me in the strange
　　next world
Though I slighted you so in this.'

'You shall kiss both cheek and chin,
　　mother,
　And kiss me between the eyes,
Or ever the moon is on her way
　And the pleasant stars arise:
You shall kiss and kiss your fill,
　　mother,
　In the nest of Paradise.'

7 January 1854.

A SOUL

SHE stands as pale as Parian statues
　　stand;
　Like Cleopatra when she turned
　　at bay,
And felt her strength above the
　　Roman sway,
And felt the aspic writhing in her
　　hand.
Her face is steadfast toward the
　　shadowy land,
　For dim beyond it looms the land
　　of day:
　Her feet are steadfast, all the
　　arduous way
That foot-track doth not waver on
　　the sand.
She stands there like a beacon
　　through the night,
　A pale clear beacon where the
　　storm-drift is—
She stands alone, a wonder deathly-
　　white:
She stands there patient nerved with
　　inner might,
　Indomitable in her feebleness,
Her face and will athirst against the
　　light.

7 February 1854.

THE BOURNE

UNDERNEATH the growing grass,
　Underneath the living flowers,
　Deeper than the sound of showers:
There we shall not count the
　　hours
By the shadows as they pass.

Youth and health will be but vain,
　Beauty reckoned of no worth:
　There a very little girth
Can hold round what once the
　　earth
Seemed too narrow to contain.

17 February 1854.

DREAM-LOVE

YOUNG Love lies sleeping
  In May-time of the year,
Among the lilies,
  Lapped in the tender light:
White lambs come grazing,
  White doves come building there;
And round about him
  The May-bushes are white.

Soft moss the pillow
  For oh a softer cheek;
Broad leaves cast shadow
  Upon the heavy eyes:
There winds and waters
  Grow lulled and scarcely speak;
There twilight lingers
  The longest in the skies.

Young Love lies dreaming;
  But who shall tell the dream?
A perfect sunlight
  On rustling forest tips;
Or perfect moonlight
  Upon a rippling stream;
Or perfect silence,
  Or song of cherished lips.

Burn odours round him
  To fill the drowsy air;
Weave silent dances
  Around him to and fro;
For oh in waking
  The sights are not so fair,
And song and silence
  Are not like these below.

Young Love lies dreaming
  Till summer days are gone,—
Dreaming and drowsing
  Away to perfect sleep:
He sees the beauty
  Sun hath not looked upon,
And tastes the fountain
  Unutterably deep.

Him perfect music
  Doth hush unto his rest,
And through the pauses
  The perfect silence calms:
Oh poor the voices
  Of earth from east to west,
And poor earth's stillness
  Between her stately palms!

Young Love lies drowsing
  Away to poppied death;
Cool shadows deepen
  Across the sleeping face:
So fails the summer
  With warm delicious breath;
And what hath autumn
  To give us in its place?

Draw close the curtains
  Of branchèd evergreen;
Change cannot touch them
  With fading fingers sere:
Here the first violets
  Perhaps will bud unseen,
And a dove, may be,
  Return to nestle here.
19 *May* 1854.

FROM THE ANTIQUE

IT'S a weary life, it is, she said:—
  Doubly blank in a woman's lot:
I wish and I wish I were a man:
  Or, better than any being, were not:

Were nothing at all in all the world,
  Not a body and not a soul:
Not so much as a grain of dust
  Or drop of water from pole to pole.

Still the world would wag on the
    same,
  Still the seasons go and come :
Blossoms bloom as in days of old,
    Cherries ripen and wild bees hum.

None would miss me in all the
    world,
  How much less would care or
    weep :
I should be nothing, while all the rest
  Would wake and weary and fall
    asleep.
28 June 1854.

LONG LOOKED FOR

WHEN the eye hardly sees,
  And the pulse hardly stirs,
And the heart would scarcely quicken
  Though the voice were hers :
Then the longing wasting fever
  Will be almost past :
Sleep indeed come back again,
    And peace at last.

Not till then, dear friends,
Not till then, most like, most dear,
  The dove will fold its wings
    To settle here.
Then to all her coldness
  I also shall be cold ;
Then I also have forgotten
    Our happy love of old.

  Close mine eyes with care,
Cross my hands upon my breast,
  Let shadows and full silence
    Tell of rest :
For she yet may look upon me,
  Too proud to speak, but know
One heart less loves her in the world
  Than loved her long ago.

Strew flowers upon the bed
  And flowers upon the floor,
Let all be sweet and comely
  When she stands at the door :
Fair as a bridal chamber
  For her to come into,
When the sunny day is over
  At falling of the dew.

If she comes, watch her not,
  But careless turn aside :
She may weep if left alone
  With her beauty and her pride :
She may pluck a leaf perhaps
  Or a languid violet
When life and love are finished
  And even I forget.
12 August 1854.

LISTENING

SHE listened like a cushat dove
  That listens to its mate alone :
She listened like a cushat dove
  That loves but only one.

Not fair as men would reckon fair,
Nor noble as they count the line :
Only as graceful as a bough,
  And tendrils of the vine :
Only as noble as sweet Eve
  Your ancestress and mine.

And downcast were her dovelike eyes
And downcast was her tender cheek ;
Her pulses fluttered like a dove
  To hear him speak.
October 1854.

DEAD BEFORE DEATH

AH changed and cold, how changed
  and very cold,
  With stiffened smiling lips and
    cold calm eyes !

Changed, yet the same; much knowing, little wise,—
This was the promise of the days of old!
Grown hard and stubborn in the ancient mould,
Grown rigid in the sham of life-long lies:
We hoped for better things as years would rise,
But it is over as a tale once told.
All fallen the blossom that no fruitage bore,
All lost the present and the future time,
All lost, all lost, the lapse that went before:
So lost till death shut-to the opened door,
So lost from chime to everlasting chime,
So cold and lost for ever evermore.
2 *December* 1854.

ECHO

COME to me in the silence of the night;
Come in the speaking silence of a dream;
Come with soft rounded cheeks and eyes as bright
As sunlight on a stream;
Come back in tears,
O memory, hope, love of finished years.

O dream how sweet, too sweet, too bitter sweet,
Whose wakening should have been in Paradise,
Where souls brimfull of love abide and meet;
Where thirsting longing eyes
Watch the slow door
That opening, letting in, lets out no more.

Yet come to me in dreams, that I may live
My very life again though cold in death:
Come back to me in dreams, that I may give
Pulse for pulse, breath for breath:
Speak low, lean low,
As long ago, my love, how long ago.
18 *December* 1854.

THE FIRST SPRING DAY

I WONDER if the sap is stirring yet,
If wintry birds are dreaming of a mate,
If frozen snowdrops feel as yet the sun
And crocus fires are kindling one by one:
Sing, robin, sing;
I still am sore in doubt concerning Spring.

I wonder if the Springtide of this year
Will bring another Spring both lost and dear;
If heart and spirit will find out their Spring,
Or if the world alone will bud and sing:
Sing, hope, to me;
Sweet notes, my hope, soft notes for memory.

The sap will surely quicken soon or late,
The tardiest bird will twitter to a mate;

So Spring must dawn again with
  warmth and bloom,
Or in this world or in the world to
  come:
Sing, voice of Spring,
Till I too blossom and rejoice and
  sing.
  1 *March* 1855.

MY DREAM

HEAR now a curious dream I dreamed
  last night,
Each word whereof is weighed and
  sifted truth.

I stood beside Euphrates while it
  swelled
Like overflowing Jordan in its youth.
It waxed and coloured sensibly to
  sight;
Till out of myriad pregnant waves
  there welled
Young crocodiles, a gaunt blunt-
  featured crew,
Fresh-hatched perhaps and daubed
  with birthday dew.
The rest if I should tell, I fear my
  friend,
My closest friend, would deem the
  facts untrue;
And therefore it were wisely left
  untold;
Yet if you will, why, hear it to the
  end.

Each crocodile was girt with massive
  gold
And polished stones that with their
  wearers grew:
But one there was who waxed be-
  yond the rest,
Wore kinglier girdle and a kingly
  crown,
Whilst crowns and orbs and sceptres
  starred his breast.
All gleamed compact and green with
  scale on scale,
But special burnishment adorned his
  mail
And special terror weighed upon his
  frown;
His punier brethren quaked before
  his tail,
Broad as a rafter, potent as a flail.
So he grew lord and master of his
  kin:
But who shall tell the tale of all
  their woes?
An execrable appetite arose,
He battened on them, crunched, and
  sucked them in.
He knew no law, he feared no
  binding law,
But ground them with inexorable
  jaw.
The luscious fat distilled upon his
  chin,
Exuded from his nostrils and his
  eyes,
While still like hungry death he fed
  his maw;
Till, every minor crocodile being
  dead
And buried too, himself gorged to
  the full,
He slept with breath oppressed and
  unstrung claw.

Oh marvel passing strange which
  next I saw!
In sleep he dwindled to the common
  size,
And all the empire faded from his
  coat.
Then from far off a wingèd vessel
  came,
Swift as a swallow, subtle as a flame:

I know not what it bore of freight
 or host,
But white it was as an avenging
 ghost.
It levelled strong Euphrates in its
 course ;
Supreme yet weightless as an idle
 mote
It seemed to tame the waters without
 force
Till not a murmur swelled or billow
 beat.
Lo, as the purple shadow swept the
 sands,
The prudent crocodile rose on his
 feet,
And shed appropriate tears and
 wrung his hands.

What can it mean? you ask. I
 answer not
For meaning, but myself must echo,
 What ?
And tell it as I saw it on the spot.
9 *March* 1855.

THE LAST LOOK

HER face was like an opening rose,
 So bright to look upon :
But now it is like fallen snows,
 As cold, as dead, as wan.

Heaven lit with stars is more like
 her
 Than is this empty crust :
Deaf, dumb, and blind, it cannot stir,
 But crumbles back to dust.

No flower be taken from her bed
 For me, no lock be shorn :
I give her up, the early dead,
 The dead, the newly born.

If I remember her, no need
 Of formal tokens set ;
Of hollow token-lies indeed
 No need, if I forget.
23 *March* 1855.

I HAVE A MESSAGE UNTO THEE

(WRITTEN IN SICKNESS)

GREEN sprout the grasses,
Red blooms the mossy rose,
Blue nods the harebell
Where purple heather blows :
The water-lily, silver white,
 Is living fair as light :

Sweet jasmine-branches trail
A dusky starry veil :
Each goodly is to see,
Comely in its degree :
I only I, alas that this should be,
 Am ruinously pale.

New year renews the grasses,
The crimson rose renews,
Brings up the breezy bluebell,
Refreshes heath with dews :
Then water-lilies ever
Bud fresh upon the river :
Then jasmine lights its star
And spreads its arms afar :
I only in my spring
Can neither bud nor sing :
I find not honey but a sting
 Though fair the blossoms are.

For me no downy grasses,
For me no blossoms pluck :
But leave them for the breezes,
For honey-bees to suck,
For childish hands to pull
And pile their baskets full :

I will not have a crown
That soon must be laid down :
Trust me : I cannot care
A withering crown to wear,
I who may be immortally made fair
Where autumn turns not brown.

Spring, summer, autumn,
Winter, all will pass,
  With tender blossoms
And with fruitful grass.
  Sweet days of yore
Will pass to come no more,
  Sweet perfumes fly,
Buds languish and go by :
O bloom that cannot last,
O blossoms quite gone past,
I yet shall feast when you shall fast,
  And live when you shall die.

Your work-day fully ended,
Your pleasant task being done,
You shall finish with the stars,
  The moon and setting sun.
  You and these and time
Shall end with the last chime,—
For earthly solace given,
But needed not in heaven ;
Needed not perhaps
Through the eternal lapse.
Or else, all signs fulfilled,
What you foreshow may yield
Delights through heaven's own harvest field
With undecaying saps.

A blessing on the flowers
That God has made so good,
From crops of jealous gardens
To wildlings of a wood.
They show us symbols deep
Of how to sow and reap :
They teach us lessons plain
Of patient harvest-gain.

They still are telling of
  God's unimagined love :—
'Oh gift,' they say, 'all gifts above,
  Shall it be given in vain ?

' Better you had not seen us
  But shared the blind man's night,
Better you had not scented
  Our incense of delight,
Than only plucked to scorn
  The rosebud for its thorn :
Not so the instinctive thrush
  Hymns in a holly-bush.
Be wise betimes, and with the bee
  Suck sweets from prickly tree,
  To last when earth's are flown :
So God well pleased will own
Your work, and bless not time alone
  But ripe eternity.'
26 *March* 1855.

COBWEBS

IT is a land with neither night nor
    day,
  Nor heat nor cold, nor any wind
    nor rain,
  Nor hills nor valleys : but one
    even plain
Stretches through long unbroken
    miles away,
While through the sluggish air a
    twilight grey
  Broodeth : no moons or seasons
    wax and wane,
  No ebb and flow are there along
    the main,
No bud-time, no leaf-falling, there
    for aye :—
No ripple on the sea, no shifting
    sand,
  No beat of wings to stir the
    stagnant space :

No pulse of life through all the
    loveless land
And loveless sea ; no trace of days
    before,
  No guarded home, no toil-won
    resting-place,
No future hope, no fear for ever-
    more.
    October 1855.

MAY

I CANNOT tell you how it was ;
But this I know : it came to
    pass—
Upon a bright and breezy day
When May was young, ah pleasant
    May !
As yet the poppies were not born
Between the blades of tender corn ;
The last eggs had not hatched as
    yet,
Nor any bird forgone its mate.

I cannot tell you what it was ;
But this I know : it did but pass.
It passed away with sunny May,
With all sweet things it passed
    away,
And left me old, and cold, and grey.
    20 November 1855.

AN AFTER-THOUGHT

OH lost garden Paradise !—
  Were the roses redder there
  Than they blossom otherwhere ?
  Was the night's delicious shade
  More intensely star-inlaid ?
Who can tell what memories
Of lost beloved Paradise
Saddened Eve with sleepless eyes ?

Fair first mother lulled to rest
  In a choicer garden-nest,
Curtained with a softer shading
Than thy tenderest child is laid in,—
Was the sundawn brighter far
Than our daily sundawns are ?
Was that love, first love of all,
  Warmer, deeper, better worth,
  Than has warmed poor hearts of
    earth
Since the utter ruinous fall ?

Ah supremely happy once,
  Ah supremely broken-hearted
  When her tender feet departed
  From the accustomed paths of
    peace !
Catching Angel orisons
For the last last time of all,
  Shedding tears that would not
    cease
  For the bitter fall.

Yet the accustomed hand for leading,
  Yet the accustomed heart for
    love :
Sure she kept one part of Eden
  Angels could not strip her of.
Sure the fiery messenger
  Kindling for his outraged Lord,
  Willing with the perfect Will,
  Yet rejoiced the flaming sword,
    Chastening sore but sparing
      still,
Shut her treasure out with her.

What became of Paradise ?
  Did the cedars droop at all
  (Springtide hastening to the fall)
  Missing the beloved hand—
  Or did their green perfection
    stand
Unmoved beneath the perfect
    skies ?—

Paradise was rapt on high,
  It lies before the gate of
    Heaven:—
Eve now slumbers there forgiven,
  Slumbers Rachel comforted,
  Slumber all the blessed dead
Of days and months and years
    gone by,
A solemn swelling company.

They wait for us beneath the trees
Of Paradise, that lap of ease:
They wait for us, till God shall please.
Oh come the day of death, that day
Of rest which cannot pass away!
When the last work is wrought, the
    last
Pang of pain is felt and past,
And the blessed door made fast.

    18 *December* 1855.

TO THE END

THERE are lilies for her sisters—
  (Who so cold as they?)—
And heartsease for one I must not
    name
  When I am far away.
I shall pluck the lady lilies
  And fancy all the rest:
I shall pluck the bright-eyed hearts-
    ease
  For her sake I love the best:
As I wander on with weary feet
  Toward the twilight shadowy west.

O bird that flyest eastward
  Unto that sunny land,
Oh wilt thou light on lilies white
  Beside her whiter hand?
Soft summer wind that breathest
  Of perfumes and sweet spice,
Ah tell her what I dare not tell
  Of watchful waiting eyes,
Of love that yet may meet again
  In distant Paradise.

I go from earth to heaven
  A dim uncertain road,
A houseless pilgrim through the
    world
  Unto a sure abode:
While evermore an Angel
  Goes with me day and night,
A ministering spirit
  From the land of light,
My holy fellow-servant sent
  To guide my steps aright.

I wonder if the Angels
  Love with such love as ours,
If for each other's sake they pluck
  And keep eternal flowers.
Alone I am and weary,
  Alone yet not alone:
Her soul talks with me by the way
  From tedious stone to stone,
A blessed Angel treads with me
  The awful paths unknown.

When will the long road end in rest,
  The sick bird perch and brood?
When will my Guardian fold his
    wings
  At rest in the finished good?
Lulling, lulling me off to sleep:
  While Death's strong hand doth
    roll
My sins behind his back,
  And my life up like a scroll,
Till through sleep I hear kind Angels
  Rejoicing at the goal.

If her spirit went before me
  Up from night to day,
It would pass me like the lightning
  That kindles on its way.

I should feel it like the lightning
  Flashing fresh from heaven:
I should long for heaven sevenfold
    more,
  Yea and sevenfold seven:
Should pray as I have not prayed
    before,
  And strive as I have not striven.

She will learn new love in heaven,
  Who is so full of love;
She will learn new depths of tenderness
  Who is tender like a dove.
Her heart will no more sorrow,
  Her eyes will weep no more:
Yet it may be she will yearn
  And look back from far before:
Lingering on the golden threshold
  And leaning from the door.
18 *December* 1855.

MAY

'Sweet Life is dead.'—'Not so:
  I meet him day by day,
Where bluest fountains flow
And trees are white as snow,
  For it is time of May.
Even now from long ago
  He will not say me nay.
He is most fair to see:
And if I wander forth, I know
  He wanders forth with me.'

' But Life is dead to me:
    The worn-out year was failing,
    West winds took up a wailing
    To watch his funeral:
    Bare poplars shivered tall
  And lank vines stretched to see.
'Twixt him and me a wall
Was frozen of earth-like stone
    With brambles overgrown:
  Chill darkness wrapped him like a
      pall,
    And I am left alone.'

' How can you call him dead?
    He buds out everywhere:
    In every hedgerow rank,
    On every moss-grown bank,
  I find him here and there.
He crowns my willing head
  With May-flowers white and red,
He rears my tender heartsease-
    bed:
He makes my branch to bud and
    bear,
  And blossoms where I tread.
31 *December* 1855.

SHUT OUT

The door was shut. I looked between
  Its iron bars; and saw it lie,
  My garden, mine, beneath the sky,
Pied with all flowers bedewed and
    green.

From bough to bough the song-birds
    crossed,
  From flower to flower the moths
    and bees:
  With all its nests and stately trees
It had been mine, and it was lost.

A shadowless spirit kept the gate,
  Blank and unchanging like the
    grave.
  I, peering through, said; 'Let me
    have
Some buds to cheer my outcast
    state.'

He answered not. 'Or give me, then,
  But one small twig from shrub or tree ;
And bid my home remember me
Until I come to it again.'

The spirit was silent; but he took
  Mortar and stone to build a wall;
He left no loophole great or small
Through which my straining eyes might look.

So now I sit here quite alone,
  Blinded with tears; nor grieve for that,
For nought is left worth looking at
Since my delightful land is gone.

A violet bed is budding near,
  Wherein a lark has made her nest ;
  And good they are, but not the best ;
And dear they are, but not so dear.
20 *January* 1856.

BY THE WATER

THERE are rivers lapsing down
  Lily-laden to the sea :
Every lily is a boat
  For bees, one, two, or three :
I wish there were a fairy boat
  For you, my friend, and me.

And if there were a fairy boat
  And if the river bore us,
We should not care for all the past
  Nor all that lies before us,
Not for the hopes that buoyed us once,
  Not for the fears that tore us.

We would rock upon the river
  Scarcely floating by,
Rocking, rocking like the lilies,
  You, my friend, and I :
Rocking like the stately lilies
  Beneath the statelier sky.

But ah where is that river
  Whose hyacinth banks descend
Down to the sweeter lilies
  Till soft their shadows blend
Into a watery twilight ?—
  And ah where is my friend ?
7 *February* 1856.

A CHILLY NIGHT

I ROSE at the dead of night,
  And went to the lattice alone
To look for my Mother's ghost
  Where the ghostly moonlight shone.

My friends had failed one by one,
  Middle-aged, young, and old,
Till the ghosts were warmer to me
  Than my friends that had grown cold.

I looked and I saw the ghosts
  Dotting plain and mound :
They stood in the blank moonlight,
  But no shadow lay on the ground :
They spoke without a voice
  And they leaped without a sound.

I called : 'O my Mother dear,'—
  I sobbed : 'O my Mother kind,
Make a lonely bed for me
  And shelter it from the wind.

'Tell the others not to come
  To see me night or day :
But I need not tell my friends
  To be sure to keep away.'

My Mother raised her eyes,
  They were blank and could not
    see:
Yet they held me with their stare
  While they seemed to look at me.

She opened her mouth and spoke;
  I could not hear a word,
While my flesh crept on my bones
  And every hair was stirred.

She knew that I could not hear
  The message that she told
Whether I had long to wait
  Or soon should sleep in the mould:
I saw her toss her shadowless hair
  And wring her hands in the cold.

I strained to catch her words,
  And she strained to make me hear;
But never a sound of words
  Fell on my straining ear.

From midnight to the cockcrow
  I kept my watch in pain
While the subtle ghosts grew
    subtler
  In the sad night on the wane.

From midnight to the cockcrow
  I watched till all were gone,
Some to sleep in the shifting sea
  And some under turf and stone:
Living had failed and dead had failed,
  And I was indeed alone.
    11 *February* 1856.

LET PATIENCE HAVE HER PERFECT WORK

I SAW a bird alone,
  In its nest it sat alone,
For its mate was dead or flown
  Though it was early Spring.
Hard by were buds half-blown,
With cornfields freshly sown:
It could only perch and moan
  That used to sing:
Droop in sorrow left alone:
  A sad sad thing.

I saw a star alone,
  In blue heaven it hung alone,
A solitary throne
  In the waste of space:
Where no moon-glories are,
Where not a second star
Beams through night from near or far
  To that lone place.
Its beauties all unknown,
Its glories all alone,
  Sad in heaven's face.

Doth the bird desire a mate,
Pine for a second mate,
Whose first joy was so great
  With its own dove?
Doth the star supreme in night
Desire a second light
To make it seem less bright
In the shrine of heavenly height
  That is above?—

Ah better wait alone,
In nest or heaven alone,
Forsaken or unknown:
Till, time being past and gone,
Full eternity rolls on,
While patience reaps what it has sown
  In the harvest-land of love.
    12 *March* 1856.

IN THE LANE

WHEN my love came home to me,
  Pleasant summer bringing,
Every tree was out in leaf,
  Every bird was singing.

There I met her in the lane
  By those waters gleamy,
Met her toward the fall of day,
  Warm and dear and dreamy.
Did I loiter in the lane?
  None was there to see me.

Only roses in the hedge,
  Lilies on the river,
Saw our greeting fast and fond,
  Counted gift and giver,
Saw me take her to my home,
  Take her home for ever.

3 *May* 1856.

ACME

SLEEP, unforgotten sorrow, sleep awhile:
  Make even awhile as though I might forget;
  Let the wound staunch thy tedious fingers fret,
Till once again I look abroad and smile,
  Warmed in the sunlight: let no tears defile
This hour's content, no conscious thorns beset
  My path: O sorrow, slumber, slumber yet
A moment, rouse not yet the smouldering pile.
So shalt thou wake again with added strength,
  O unforgotten sorrow, stir again
The slackening fire, refine the lulling pain
  To quickened torture and a subtler edge.
The wrung cord snaps at last: beneath the wedge
The toughest oak groans long but rends at length.

9 *May* 1856.

A BED OF FORGET-ME-NOTS

IS Love so prone to change and rot
We are fain to rear Forget-me-not
By measure in a garden-plot?—

I love its growth at large and free
By untrod path and unlopped tree,
Or nodding by the unpruned hedge,
Or on the water's dangerous edge
Where flags and meadowsweet blow rank
With rushes on the quaking bank.

Love is not taught in learning's school,
Love is not parcelled out by rule:
Hath curb or call an answer got?—
So free must be Forget-me-not.
Give me the flame no dampness dulls,
The passion of the instinctive pulse,
Love steadfast as a fixèd star,
Tender as doves with nestlings are,
More large than time, more strong than death:
  This all creation travails of—
She groans not for a passing breath—
  This is Forget-me-not and Love.

17 *June* 1856.

LOOK ON THIS PICTURE AND ON THIS

I WISH we once were wedded,—
  then I must be true:
You should hold my will in yours to
  do or to undo:
But I hate myself now, Eva,
  when I look at you.

You have seen her hazel eyes, her
  warm dark skin,
Dark hair—but oh those hazel eyes
  a devil is dancing in :—
You, my saint, lead up to heaven,
  she lures down to sin.

She's so redundant, stately :—in
  truth now have you seen
Ever anywhere such beauty, such a
  stature, such a mien?
She may be queen of devils, but
  she's every inch a queen.

If you sing to me, I hear her subtler
  sweeter still
Whispering in each tender cadence
  strangely sweet to fill
All that lacks in music, all my soul
  and sense and will.

But you ask, 'Why struggle? I
  have given you up :
Take again your pledges, snap the
  cord and break the cup :
Feast you with your temptation,
  for I in heaven will sup.'

Can I bear to think upon you strong
  to break not bend,
Pale with inner intense passion,
  silent to the end,
Bear to leave you, bear to grieve
  you, O my dove, my friend?

Listening so, I hide mine eyes and
  fancy years to come :
You cherished in another home
  with no cares burdensome :
You straitened in a winding-sheet,
  pulseless, at peace, and dumb.

Open house and heart, barred to
  me alone the door :
Children bound to meet her,
  babies crow before :
Blessed wife and blessed mother
  whom I may see no more.

Or I fancy — In the grave her
  comely body lies :
She is 'tiring for the Bridegroom
  till the morning star shall rise,
Then to shine a glory in the nuptials
  of the skies.

No more yearning tenderness, no
  more pale regret :
She will not look for me when
  the marriage-guests are set,
She joys with joy eternal as we
  had never met.

I would that one of us were dead,
  were gone no more to meet,
Or she and I were dead together
  stretched here at your feet :
That she and I were strained together in one winding-sheet.

How have you the heart to face me
  with that passion in your stare
Deathly silent? Weep before me,
  rave at me in your despair :—
If you keep patience, wings will
  spring and a halo from your
  hair.

See now how proud you are, like
  us after all, no saint :
Not so upright but that you are
  bowed with the old bent :
White at white-heat, tainted with
  the devil's special taint.

Did I love you? Never from the
    first cold day to this :
You are not sufficient for my aim of
    life, my bliss :
You are not sufficient, but I found
    the one that is.

Then did I never love you ?—ah the
    sting struck home at last !
You are drooping, fainting, dying
    —the worst of death is past—
A light is on your face from the
    nearing heaven forecast.

Never ?—yes I loved you then : I
    loved, the word still charms :
For the first time, last time, lie
    here in my heart, my arms,
For the first last time, as if I
    shielded you from harms.

For after all I loved you, loved you
    then, I love you yet :
Listen, love, I love you : see, the
    seal of truth is set
On my face, in tears—you cannot
    see ? then feel them wet.

Pause at heaven's dear gate, look
    back, one moment back to
    grieve :
You go home through death to life :
    but I, I still must live :
On the threshold of heaven's love,
    O love, can you forgive ?—

Fully freely fondly, with heart-truth
    above an oath,
With eager utter pardon given un-
    asked and nothing loth,
Heaping coals of fire upon our
    heads, forgiving both.

One word more—not one ! One
    look more—too late, too late !
Lapped in love she sleeps who was
    lashed with scorn and hate :
Nestling in the lap of Love the dove
    has found a mate.

Night has come, the night of rest :
    day will come, that day :
To her glad dawn of glory kindled
    from the deathless ray :
To us a searching fire and strict
    balances to weigh.

The tearless tender eyes are closed,
    the tender lips are dumb—
I shall not see or hear them more
    until that day shall come :
Then they must speak ; what will
    they say ?—what then will be
    the sum ?—

Shall we stand upon the left, and
    she upon the right—
We smirched with endless death and
    shame, she glorified in white—
Will she sound our accusation in
    intolerable light ?

12 *July* 1856.

GONE BEFORE

SHE was most like a rose when it
    flushes rarest,
She was most like a lily when it
    blows fairest,
She was most like a violet sweetest
    on the bank :
Now she's only like the snow, cold
    and blank,
    After the sun sank.

She left us in the early days; she
    would not linger
For orange blossoms in her hair, or
    ring on finger:
    Did she deem windy grass more
        good than these?
Now the turf that's between us and
    the hedging trees
    Might as well be seas.

I had trained a branch she shelters
    not under,
I had reared a flower she snapped
    asunder:
    In the bush and on the stately
        bough
Birds sing; she who watched them
    track the plough
    Cannot hear them now.

Every bird has a nest hidden
    somewhere
For itself and its mate and joys
    that come there,—
    Though it soar to the clouds,
        finding there its rest:
You sang in the height, but no more
    with eager breast
    Stoop to your own nest.

If I could win you back from
    heaven-gate lofty,
Perhaps you would but grieve,
    returning softly:
Surely they would miss you in the
    blessed throng,
    Miss your sweet voice in their
        sweetest song,
    Reckon time too long.

Earth is not good enough for you,
    my sweet, my sweetest;
Life on earth seemed long to you,
    though to me fleetest;
I would not wish you back if a wish
    would do:
    Only, love, I long for heaven
        with you,
    Heart-pierced through and
        through.
12 *July* 1856.

THE HOUR AND THE GHOST

BRIDE

O LOVE, love, hold me fast,
He draws me away from thee;
I cannot stem the blast,
Nor the cold strong sea:
Far away a light shines
Beyond the hills and pines;
It is lit for me.

BRIDEGROOM

I have thee close, my dear,
No terror can come near;
Only far off the northern light shines
    clear.

GHOST

Come with me, fair and false,
To our home, come home.
It is my voice that calls:
Once thou wast not afraid
When I woo'd, and said,
'Come, our nest is newly made'—
Now cross the tossing foam.

BRIDE

Hold me one moment longer!
He taunts me with the past,
His clutch is waxing stronger;
Hold me fast, hold me fast.
He draws me from thy heart,
And I cannot withhold:
He bids my spirit depart

With him into the cold :—
Oh bitter vows of old!

BRIDEGROOM

Lean on me, hide thine eyes :
Only ourselves, earth and skies,
Are present here : be wise.

GHOST

Lean on me, come away,
I will guide and steady :
Come, for I will not stay :
Come, for house and bed are ready.
Ah sure bed and house,
For better and worse, for life and death,
Goal won with shortened breath !
Come, crown our vows.

BRIDE

One moment, one more word,
While my heart beats still,
While my breath is stirred
By my fainting will.
O friend, forsake me not,
Forget not as I forgot :
But keep thy heart for me,
Keep thy faith true and bright ;
Through the lone cold winter night
Perhaps I may come to thee.

BRIDEGROOM

Nay peace, my darling, peace :
Let these dreams and terrors cease :
Who spoke of death or change or aught but ease ?

GHOST

O fair frail sin,
O poor harvest gathered in !
Thou shalt visit him again
To watch his heart grow cold :
To know the gnawing pain
I knew of old ;
To see one much more fair
Fill up the vacant chair,
Fill his heart, his children bear ;
While thou and I together,
In the outcast weather,
Toss and howl and spin.

11 *September* 1856.

LIGHT LOVE

'OH sad thy lot before I came,
    But sadder when I go,—
My presence but a flash of flame,
    A transitory glow
Between two barren wastes like snow.
What wilt thou do when I am gone ?
    Where wilt thou rest, my dear ?
For cold thy bed to rest upon,
    And cold the falling year
Whose withered leaves are lost and sere.'

She hushed the baby at her breast :
    She rocked it on her knee :
'And I will rest my lonely rest,
    Warmed with the thought of thee,
Rest lulled to rest by memory.'
She hushed the baby with her kiss,
    She hushed it with her breast :
'Is death so sadder much than this ?
    Sure death that builds a nest
For those who elsewhere cannot rest.'

'Oh sad thy note, my mateless dove,
    With tender nestling cold :
But hast thou ne'er another love
    Left from the days of old
To build thy nest of silk and gold ?

To warm thy paleness to a blush
  When I am far away,—
To warm thy coldness to a flush
  And turn thee back to May,
And turn thy twilight back to day.'

She did not answer him a word,
  But leaned her face aside,
Sick with the pain of hope deferred
  And sore with wounded pride:
He knew his very soul had lied.
She strained his baby in her arms,
  His baby to her heart:
'Even let it go, the love that harms;
  We two will never part:
Mine own, his own, how dear thou art!'

'Now never tease me, tender-eyed,
  Sigh-voiced,' he said in scorn:
'For nigh at hand there blooms a bride,
  My bride before the morn:
Ripe-blooming she, as thou forlorn.
Ripe-blooming she, my rose, my peach:
  She wooes me day and night:
I watch her tremble in my reach:
  She reddens, my delight,
She ripens, reddens, in my sight.'

'And is she like a sunlit rose?
  Am I like withered leaves?
Haste where thy spicèd garden blows:
  But in bare autumn eves
Wilt thou have store of harvest-sheaves?
Thou leavest love, true love behind,
  To seek a love as true:
Go seek in haste,—but wilt thou find?
  Change new again for new,
Pluck up, enjoy, yea trample too.

'Alas for her, poor faded rose,
  Alas for her like me,
Cast down and trampled in the snows.'—
'Like thee? nay not like thee:
She leans, but from a guarded tree.
Farewell, and dream as long ago
  Before we ever met:
Farewell: my swift-paced horse seems slow.'—
She raised her eyes, not wet
But hard, to Heaven: 'Dost Thou forget?'
28 *October* 1856.

DOWNCAST

THESE roses are as perfect as of old,
  Those lilies wear their selfsame sunny white;
I, only I, am changed and sad and cold.
  The morning star still glorifies the night,
And musical that fountain in its swell
  Casts as of old its waters to the light.
Oh that I were a rose, so I might dwell
  Contented in a garden on my thorn,
Fulfilling mine appointed fragrance well;
  Or stainless lily in the summer morn—
Though no man pluck it, yet the honey-bee
  Knows it for sweetness in its bosom born.
Or that I were a star, from sea to sea

Guiding the seekers to their port
    of rest,
Guiding them till night's shuffling
    shadows flee;
Or that I were a spring to which,
    opprest
With desert drought, some wearied
    wayfarer
Comes from the barren regions of
    the West.
Then should I stand at peace, and
    should not err,
Or lighten and make beautiful
    the sky,
Or make more glad than frank-
    incense and myrrh.
But now it is not so: I, only I,
Am changed and sad and cold,
    while in my soul
The very fountain of delight is
    dry.
12 *December* 1856.

A TRIAD

THREE sang of love together: one
    with lips
Crimson, with cheeks and bosom
    in a glow,
Flushed to the yellow hair and
    finger-tips;
And one there sang who soft and
    smooth as snow
Bloomed like a tinted hyacinth at
    a show;
And one was blue with famine after
    love,
Who like a harpstring snapped
    rang harsh and low
The burden of what those were sing-
    ing of.
One shamed herself in love; one
    temperately
Grew gross in soulless love, a
    sluggish wife;
One famished died for love. Thus
    two of three
Took death for love and won him
    after strife;
One droned in sweetness like a
    fattened bee:
All on the threshold, yet all short
    of life.
18 *December* 1856.

LOVE FROM THE NORTH

I HAD a love in soft south land,
    Beloved through April far in May;
He waited on my lightest breath,
    And never dared to say me nay.

He saddened if my cheer was sad,
    But gay he grew if I was gay;
We never differed on a hair,
    My yes his yes, my nay his nay.

The wedding hour was come, the
    aisles
    Were flushed with sun and flowers
    that day;
I pacing balanced in my thoughts:
    'It's quite too late to think of
    nay.'—

My bridegroom answered in his
    turn,
    Myself had almost answered
    'yea:'
When through the flashing nave I
    heard
    A struggle and resounding 'nay.'

Bridemaids and bridegroom shrank
    in fear,
    But I stood high who stood at
    bay:

'And if I answer yea, fair Sir,
  What man art thou to bar with
    nay?'

He was a strong man from the north,
  Light-locked, with eyes of danger-
    ous grey:
'Put yea by for another time
  In which I will not say thee nay.'

He took me in his strong white arms,
  He bore me on his horse away
O'er crag, morass, and hairbreadth
    pass,
  But never asked me yea or nay.

He made me fast with book and
    bell,
  With links of love he makes me
    stay;
Till now I've neither heart nor power
  Nor will nor wish to say him nay.
19 December 1856.

IN AN ARTIST'S STUDIO

ONE face looks out from all his
    canvases,
  One selfsame figure sits or walks
    or leans:
  We found her hidden just behind
    those screens,
That mirror gave back all her love-
    liness.
A queen in opal or in ruby dress,
  A nameless girl in freshest
    summer-greens,
  A saint, an angel—every canvas
    means
The same one meaning, neither
    more nor less.
He feeds upon her face by day and
    night,
  And she with true kind eyes looks
    back on him,
Fair as the moon and joyful as the
    light:
  Not wan with waiting, not with
    sorrow dim;
Not as she is, but was when hope
    shone bright;
  Not as she is, but as she fills his
    dream.
24 December 1856.

FATA MORGANA

A BLUE-EYED phantom far before
  Is laughing, leaping toward the
    sun:
Like lead I chase it evermore,
  I pant and run.

It breaks the sunlight bound on
    bound:
  Goes singing as it leaps along
To sheep-bells with a dreamy sound
  A dreamy song.

I laugh, it is so brisk and gay;
  It is so far before, I weep:
I hope I shall lie down some day,
  Lie down and sleep.
18 April 1857.

ONE DAY

I WILL tell you when they met:
In the limpid days of Spring;
Elder boughs were budding yet,
Oaken boughs looked wintry still,
But primrose and veined violet
In the mossful turf were set,
While meeting birds made haste to
    sing
And build with right good will.

I will tell you when they parted;
When plenteous Autumn sheaves
    were brown
Then they parted heavy-hearted;
The full rejoicing sun looked down
As grand as in the days before;
Only they had lost a crown;
Only to them those days of yore
Could come back nevermore.

When shall they meet? I cannot
    tell,
Indeed, when they shall meet again,
Except some day in Paradise:
For this they wait, one waits in pain.
Beyond the sea of death Love lies
For ever, yesterday, to-day;
Angels shall ask them, 'Is it well?'
And they shall answer 'Yea.'
  6 *June* 1857.

INTROSPECTIVE

I WISH it were over the terrible pain,
Pang after pang again and again:
First the shattering ruining blow,
Then the probing steady and slow.

Did I wince? I did not faint:
My soul broke but was not bent:
Up I stand like a blasted tree
By the shore of the shivering sea.

On my boughs neither leaf nor fruit,
No sap in my uttermost root,
Brooding in an anguish dumb
On the short past and the long to-
    come.

Dumb I was when the ruin fell,
Dumb I remain and will never tell;
O my soul, I talk with thee,
But not another the sight must see.

I did not start when the torture
    stung,
I did not faint when the torture
    wrung:
Let it come tenfold if come it must,
But I will not groan when I bite
    the dust.
  30 *June* 1857.

A PEAL OF BELLS

STRIKE the bells wantonly,
    Tinkle tinkle well;
Bring me wine, bring me flowers,
    Ring the silver bell.
All my lamps burn scented oil,
    Hung on laden orange-trees,
Whose shadowed foliage is the foil
    To golden lamps and oranges.
Heap my golden plates with fruit,
    Golden fruit, fresh-plucked and
        ripe;
Strike the bells and breathe the
    pipe;
Shut out showers from summer
    hours—
Silence that complaining lute—
Shut out thinking, shut out pain,
From hours that cannot come again.

Strike the bells solemnly,
    Ding dong deep:
My friend is passing to his bed,
    Fast asleep;
There's plaited linen round his head,
    While foremost go his feet—
His feet that cannot carry him.
My feast's a show, my lights are
    dim;
    Be still, your music is not sweet,—
There is no music more for him.
    His lights are out, his feast is
        done:

His bowl that sparkled to the brim
Is drained, is broken, cannot hold;
My blood is chill, his blood is cold;
   His death is full, and mine begun.
7 July 1857.

IN THE ROUND TOWER AT JHANSI

8 JUNE 1857

A HUNDRED, a thousand to one; even so;
Not a hope in the world remained:
The swarming howling wretches below
   Gained and gained and gained.

Skene looked at his pale young wife.
'Is the time come?'—'The time is come.'
Young, strong, and so full of life,
   The agony struck them dumb.

Close his arm about her now,
   Close her cheek to his,
Close the pistol to her brow—
   God forgive them this!

'Will it hurt much?'—'No, mine own;
I wish I could bear the pang for both.'—
'I wish I could bear the pang alone:
   Courage, dear, I am not loth.'

Kiss and kiss: 'It is not pain
   Thus to kiss and die.
One kiss more.'—'And yet one again.'—
   'Good-bye.'—'Good-bye.'
September 1857.

DAY-DREAMS

GAZING through her chamber window
   Sits my soul's dear soul:
Looking northward, looking southward,
   Looking to the goal,
Looking back without control.

I have strewn thy path, beloved,
   With plumed meadowsweet,
Iris and pale perfumed lilies,
   Roses most complete:
Wherefore pause on listless feet?

But she sits and never answers,
   Gazing, gazing still
On swift fountain, shadowed valley,
   Cedared sunlit hill:
Who can guess or read her will?

Who can guess or read the spirit
   Shrined within her eyes,
Part a longing, part a languor,
   Part a mere surprise,
While slow mists do rise and rise?

Is it love she looks and longs for,
   Is it rest or peace,
Is it slumber self-forgetful
   In its utter ease,
Is it one or all of these?

So she sits and doth not answer
   With her dreaming eyes,
With her languid look delicious
   Almost paradise,
Less than happy, over-wise.

Answer me, O self-forgetful—
   Or of what beside?
Is it day-dream of a maiden,
   Vision of a bride,
Is it knowledge, love, or pride?

Cold she sits through all my kindling,
    Deaf to all I pray:
I have wasted might and wisdom,
    Wasted night and day:
Deaf she dreams to all I say.

Now if I could guess her secret,
    Were it worth the guess?—
Time is lessening, hope is lessening,
    Love grows less and less:
What care I for no or yes?

I will give her stately burial,
    Though, when she lies dead:
For dear memory of the past time,
    Of her royal head,
Of the much I strove and said.

I will give her stately burial,
    Stately willow-branches bent:
Have her carved in alabaster,
    As she dreamed and leant
While I wondered what she meant.
8 September 1857.

A NIGHTMARE

FRAGMENT

I HAVE a friend in ghostland—
Early found, ah me how early lost!—
Blood-red seaweeds drip along that
    coastland
    By the strong sea wrenched
        and tost.
. . . . .
If I wake he hunts me like a
    nightmare:
    I feel my hair stand up, my body
        creep:
Without light I see a blasting sight
    there,
    See a secret I must keep.
12 September 1857.

ANOTHER SPRING

IF I might see another Spring,
    I'd not plant summer flowers and
        wait:
I'd have my crocuses at once,
My leafless pink mezereons,
    My chill-veined snowdrops, choicer
        yet
    My white or azure violet,
Leaf-nested primrose; anything
    To blow at once, not late.

If I might see another Spring,
    I'd listen to the daylight birds
That build their nests and pair and
        sing,
Nor wait for mateless nightingale;
    I'd listen to the lusty herds,
    The ewes with lambs as white as
        snow,
I'd find out music in the hail
    And all the winds that blow.

If I might see another Spring—
    Oh stinging comment on my past
That all my past results in 'if'—
    If I might see another Spring
I'd laugh to-day, to-day is brief;
I would not wait for anything:
    I'd use to-day that cannot last,
    Be glad to-day and sing.
15 September 1857.

FOR ONE SAKE

ONE passed me like a flash of
    lightning by,
    To ring clear bells of heaven
        beyond the stars.
    Then said I: Wars and rumours
        of your wars

Are dull with din of what and where
    and why:
My heart is where these troubles
    draw not nigh:
  Let me alone till heaven shall
      burst its bars,
  Break up its fountains, roll its
      flashing cars
Earthwards with fire to test and
    purify.
Let me alone to-night, and one night
    more
  Of which I shall not count the
      eventide:
Its morrow will not be as days
    before.
Let me alone to dream, perhaps to
    weep:
  To dream of her the imperishable
      bride,
  Dream while I wake and dream on
      while I sleep.

25 *October* 1857.

MEMORY

I

I NURSED it in my bosom while it
    lived,
  I hid it in my heart when it was
      dead.
In joy I sat alone; even so I grieved
  Alone, and nothing said.

I shut the door to face the naked
    truth,
  I stood alone—I faced the truth
      alone,
Stripped bare of self-regard or forms
    or ruth
  Till first and last were shown.

I took the perfect balances and
    weighed;
  No shaking of my hand disturbed
      the poise;
Weighed, found it wanting: not a
    word I said,
  But silent made my choice.

None know the choice I made; I
    make it still.
  None know the choice I made
      and broke my heart,
Breaking mine idol: I have braced
    my will
  Once, chosen for once my part.

I broke it at a blow, I laid it cold,
  Crushed in my deep heart where
      it used to live.
My heart dies inch by inch; the
    time grows old,
  Grows old in which I grieve.

8 *November* 1857.

II

I have a room whereinto no one
    enters
  Save I myself alone:
  There sits a blessed memory on
      a throne,
There my life centres;

While winter comes and goes—oh
    tedious comer!—
  And while its nip-wind blows;
  While bloom the bloodless lily
      and warm rose
Of lavish summer.

If any should force entrance he
    might see there
  One buried yet not dead,
  Before whose face I no more bow
      my head
Or bend my knee there;

But often in my worn life's autumn weather
　I watch there with clear eyes,
And think how it will be in Paradise
When we're together.

　17 February 1865.

A BIRTHDAY

My heart is like a singing bird
　Whose nest is in a watered shoot:
My heart is like an apple-tree
　Whose boughs are bent with thickset fruit;
My heart is like a rainbow shell
　That paddles in a halcyon sea;
My heart is gladder than all these
　Because my love is come to me.

Raise me a dais of silk and down;
　Hang it with vair and purple dyes;
Carve it in doves and pomegranates,
　And peacocks with a hundred eyes;
Work it in gold and silver grapes,
　In leaves and silver fleurs-de-lys;
Because the birthday of my life
　Is come, my love is come to me.

　18 November 1857.

AN APPLE GATHERING

I plucked pink blossoms from mine apple-tree
　And wore them all that evening in my hair:
Then in due season when I went to see
　I found no apples there.

With dangling basket all along the grass
　As I had come I went the self-same track:
My neighbours mocked me while they saw me pass
　So empty-handed back.

Lilian and Lilias smiled in trudging by,
　Their heaped-up basket teazed me like a jeer;
Sweet-voiced they sang beneath the sunset sky,
　Their mother's home was near.

Plump Gertrude passed me with her basket full,
　A stronger hand than hers helped it along;
A voice talked with her through the shadows cool
　More sweet to me than song.

Ah Willie, Willie, was my love less worth
　Than apples with their green leaves piled above?
I counted rosiest apples on the earth
　Of far less worth than love.

So once it was with me you stooped to talk
　Laughing and listening in this very lane;
To think that by this way we used to walk
　We shall not walk again!

I let my neighbours pass me, ones and twos
　And groups; the latest said the night grew chill,

And hastened: but I loitered; while
  the dews
  Fell fast I loitered still.
23 *November* 1857.

WINTER: MY SECRET

I TELL my secret? No indeed, not I:
Perhaps some day, who knows?
But not to-day; it froze, and blows,
  and snows,
And you're too curious: fie!
You want to hear it? well:
Only, my secret's mine, and I won't
  tell.

Or, after all, perhaps there's none:
Suppose there is no secret after all,
But only just my fun.
To-day's a nipping day, a biting day;
In which one wants a shawl,
A veil, a cloak, and other wraps:
I cannot ope to every one who taps,
And let the draughts come whistling
  through my hall;
Come bounding and surrounding me,
Come buffeting, astounding me,
Nipping and clipping through my
  wraps and all.
I wear my mask for warmth: who
  ever shows
His nose to Russian snows
To be pecked at by every wind that
  blows?
You would not peck? I thank you
  for good will,
Believe, but leave that truth un-
  tested still.

Spring's an expansive time: yet I
  don't trust
March with its peck of dust,
Nor April with its rainbow-crowned
  brief showers,
Nor even May, whose flowers
One frost may wither through the
  sunless hours.

Perhaps some languid summer day,
  When drowsy birds sing less and
    less,
And golden fruit is ripening to
  excess,
If there's not too much sun nor too
  much cloud,
And the warm wind is neither still
  nor loud,
Perhaps my secret I may say,
Or you may guess.
23 *November* 1857.

MY FRIEND

Two days ago with dancing glancing
  hair,
  With living lips and eyes;
  Now pale, dumb, blind, she lies;
So pale, yet still so fair.

We have not left her yet, not yet
  alone;
  But soon must leave her where
  She will not miss our care,
Bone of our bone.

Weep not; O friends, we should
  not weep:
  Our friend of friends lies full of
    rest;
  No sorrow rankles in her breast,
Fallen fast asleep.

She sleeps below,
  She wakes and laughs above.
  To-day, as she walked, let us
    walk in love:
To-morrow follow so.
8 *December* 1857.

MAUDE CLARE

OUT of the church she followed them
  With a lofty step and mien :
His bride was like a village maid,
  Maude Clare was like a queen.

'Son Thomas,' his lady mother said,
  With smiles, almost with tears :
'May Nell and you but live as true
  As we have done for years ;

'Your father thirty years ago
  Had just your tale to tell ;
But he was not so pale as you,
  Nor I so pale as Nell.'

My lord was pale with inward strife,
  And Nell was pale with pride ;
My lord gazed long on pale Maude
    Clare
  Or ever he kissed the bride.

'Lo, I have brought my gift, my lord,
  Have brought my gift,' she said :
'To bless the hearth, to bless the
    board,
  To bless the marriage-bed.

'Here's my half of the golden chain
  You wore about your neck,
That day we waded ankle-deep
  For lilies in the beck.

'Here's my half of the faded leaves
  We plucked from budding bough,
With feet amongst the lily leaves,—
  The lilies are budding now.'

He strove to match her scorn with
    scorn,
  He faltered in his place :
'Lady,' he said,—'Maude Clare,' he
    said,—
  'Maude Clare' :—and hid his face.

She turned to Nell : 'My Lady Nell,
  I have a gift for you ;
Though, were it fruit, the bloom
    were gone,
  Or, were it flowers, the dew.

'Take my share of a fickle heart,
  Mine of a paltry love :
Take it or leave it as you will,
  I wash my hands thereof.'

'And what you leave,' said Nell,
  'I'll take,
And what you spurn I'll wear ;
For he's my lord for better and worse,
  And him I love, Maude Clare.

'Yea though you're taller by the
    head,
  More wise, and much more fair,
I'll love him till he loves me best—
  Me best of all, Maude Clare.'

Towards February 1858.

AUTUMN

I DWELL alone—I dwell alone,
    alone,
  Whilst full my river flows down
    to the sea,
Gilded with flashing boats
  That bring no friend to me :
O love-songs, gurgling from a
    hundred throats,
  O love-pangs, let me be.

Fair fall the freighted boats which
    gold and stone
  And spices bear to sea :
Slim gleaming maidens swell their
    mellow notes,
  Love-promising, entreating—
  Ah sweet but fleeting—

Beneath the shivering, snow-white
    sails.
Hush! the wind flags and fails—
Hush! they will lie becalmed in
    sight of strand—
Sight of my strand, where I do
    dwell alone;
Their songs wake singing echoes in
    my land—
They cannot hear me moan.

One latest, solitary swallow flies
    Across the sea, rough autumn-
        tempest-tost:
    Poor bird, shall it be lost?
Dropped down into this uncon-
    genial sea,
    With no kind eyes
    To watch it while it dies,
Unguessed, uncared for, free:
    Set free at last,
    The short pang past,
In sleep, in death, in dreamless sleep
    locked fast.

Mine avenue is all a growth of oaks,
    Some rent by thunder strokes,
    Some rustling leaves and acorns in
        the breeze;
    Fair fall my fertile trees,
    That rear their goodly heads, and
        live at ease.

A spider's web blocks all mine
    avenue;
    He catches down and foolish
        painted flies,
    That spider wary and wise.
Each morn it hangs a rainbow strung
    with dew
    Betwixt boughs green with sap,
    So fair, few creatures guess it is
        a trap:

I will not mar the web,
Though sad I am to see the small
    lives ebb.

It shakes—my trees shake—for a
    wind is roused
    In cavern where it housed:
    Each white and quivering sail
Of boats among the water-
    leaves
Hollows and strains in the full-
    throated gale:
    Each maiden sings again—
Each languid maiden, whom the
    calm
Had lulled to sleep with rest and
    spice and balm.
    Miles down my river to the sea
    They float and wane,
    Long miles away from me.

Perhaps they say: 'She
    grieves,
Uplifted like a beacon on her
    tower.'
    Perhaps they say: 'One
        hour
More, and we dance among the
    golden sheaves.'
Perhaps they say: 'One hour
    More, and we stand,
    Face to face, hand in
        hand;
Make haste, O slack gale, to the
    looked-for land!'

My trees are not in flower,
    I have no bower,
    And gusty creaks my tower,
And lonesome, very lonesome, is my
    strand.
14 *April* 1858.

UP-HILL

Does the road wind up-hill all the
    way?
  Yes, to the very end.
Will the day's journey take the whole
    long day?
  From morn to night, my friend.

But is there for the night a resting-
    place?
  A roof for when the slow dark
    hours begin.
May not the darkness hide it from
    my face?
  You cannot miss that inn.

Shall I meet other wayfarers at
    night?
  Those who have gone before.
Then must I knock, or call when
    just in sight?
  They will not keep you standing
    at that door.

Shall I find comfort, travel-sore and
    weak?
  Of labour you shall find the sum.
Will there be beds for me and all
    who seek?
  Yea, beds for all who come.
29 *June* 1858.

AT HOME

When I was dead, my spirit turned
    To seek the much-frequented
        house.
I passed the door, and saw my friends
    Feasting beneath green orange-
        boughs;
From hand to hand they pushed the
    wine,
They sucked the pulp of plum and
    peach;
They sang, they jested, and they
    laughed,
For each was loved of each.

I listened to their honest chat.
    Said one: 'To-morrow we shall be
Plod plod along the featureless sands,
    And coasting miles and miles of
        sea.'
Said one: 'Before the turn of tide
    We will achieve the eyrie-seat.'
Said one: 'To-morrow shall be like
    To-day, but much more sweet.'

'To-morrow,' said they, strong with
    hope,
    And dwelt upon the pleasant way:
'To-morrow,' cried they one and all,
    While no one spoke of yesterday.
Their life stood full at blessed noon;
    I, only I, had passed away:
'To-morrow and to-day,' they
        cried;
    I was of yesterday.

I shivered comfortless, but cast
    No chill across the tablecloth;
I all-forgotten shivered, sad
    To stay and yet to part how loth:
I passed from the familiar room,
    I who from love had passed away,
Like the remembrance of a guest
    That tarrieth but a day.
29 *June* 1858.

TO-DAY AND TO-MORROW

I

All the world is out in leaf,
  Half the world in flower,
Earth has waited weeks and weeks

For this special hour:
Faint the rainbow comes and goes
  On a sunny shower.

All the world is making love:
  Bird to bird in bushes,
Beast to beast in glades, and frog
  To frog among the rushes:
Wake, O south wind sweet with spice,
  Wake the rose to blushes.

Life breaks forth to right and left—
  Pipe wild-wood notes cheery.
Nevertheless there are the dead
  Fast asleep and weary—
To-day we live, to-day we love,
  Wake and listen, deary.

2

I wish I were dead, my foe,
  My friend, I wish I were dead,
With a stone at my tired feet
  And a stone at my tired head.

In the pleasant April days
  Half the world will stir and sing,
But half the world will slug and rot
  For all the sap of Spring.

29 June 1858.

THE CONVENT THRESHOLD

There's blood between us, love, my love,
There's father's blood, there's brother's blood;
And blood's a bar I cannot pass.
I choose the stairs that mount above,
Stair after golden sky-ward stair,
To city and to sea of glass.
My lily feet are soiled with mud,
With scarlet mud which tells a tale
Of hope that was, of guilt that was,
Of love that shall not yet avail;
Alas, my heart, if I could bare
My heart, this selfsame stain is there:
I seek the sea of glass and fire
To wash the spot, to burn the snare;
Lo, stairs are meant to lift us higher:
Mount with me, mount the kindled stair.

Your eyes look earthward, mine look up.
I see the far-off city grand,
Beyond the hills a watered land,
Beyond the gulf a gleaming strand
Of mansions where the righteous sup;
Who sleep at ease among their trees,
Or wake to sing a cadenced hymn
With Cherubim and Seraphim.
They bore the Cross, they drained the cup,
Racked, roasted, crushed, wrenched limb from limb,
They the offscouring of the world:
The heaven of starry heavens unfurled,
The sun before their face is dim.

You looking earthward, what see you?
Milk-white, wine-flushed among the vines,
Up and down leaping, to and fro,
Most glad, most full, made strong with wines,
Blooming as peaches pearled with dew,
Their golden windy hair afloat,
Love-music warbling in their throat,
Young men and women come and go.

You linger, yet the time is short :
Flee for your life, gird up your
    strength
To flee ; the shadows stretched at
    length
Show that day wanes, that night
    draws nigh ;
Flee to the mountain, tarry not.
Is this a time for smile and sigh,
For songs among the secret trees
Where sudden blue birds nest and
    sport ?
The time is short and yet you stay:
To-day, while it is called to-day,
Kneel, wrestle, knock, do violence,
    pray ;
To-day is short, to-morrow nigh :
Why will you die ? why will you
    die ?

You sinned with me a pleasant sin :
Repent with me, for I repent.
Woe's me the lore I must unlearn !
Woe's me that easy way we went,
So rugged when I would return !
How long until my sleep begin,
How long shall stretch these nights
    and days ?
Surely, clean Angels cry, she prays ;
She laves her soul with tedious
    tears :
How long must stretch these years
    and years ?

I turn from you my cheeks and
    eyes,
My hair which you shall see no
    more—
Alas for joy that went before,
For joy that dies, for love that dies!
Only my lips still turn to you,
My livid lips that cry, Repent !
O weary life, O weary Lent,
O weary time whose stars are few !

How should I rest in Paradise,
Or sit on steps of heaven alone ?
If Saints and Angels spoke of love,
Should I not answer from my throne,
Have pity upon me, ye my friends,
For I have heard the sound thereof.
Should I not turn with yearning eyes,
Turn earthwards with a pitiful pang ?
Oh save me from a pang in heaven !
By all the gifts we took and gave,
Repent, repent, and be forgiven.
This life is long, but yet it ends ;
Repent and purge your soul and
    save :
No gladder song the morning stars
Upon their birthday morning sang
Than Angels sing when one repents.

I tell you what I dreamed last
    night.
A spirit with transfigured face
Fire-footed clomb an infinite space.
I heard his hundred pinions clang,
Heaven-bells rejoicing rang and rang,
Heaven-air was thrilled with subtle
    scents,
Worlds spun upon their rushing cars:
He mounted shrieking 'Give me
    light !'
Still light was poured on him, more
    light ;
Angels, Archangels he outstripped,
Exultant in exceeding might,
And trod the skirts of Cherubim.
Still 'Give me light,' he shrieked ;
    and dipped
His thirsty face, and drank a sea,
Athirst with thirst it could not slake.
I saw him, drunk with knowledge,
    take
From aching brows the aureole
    crown—
His locks writhe like a cloven
    snake—

He left his throne to grovel down
And lick the dust of Seraphs' feet :
For what is knowledge duly weighed?
Knowledge is strong, but love is
    sweet ;
Yea all the progress he had made
Was but to learn that all is small
Save love, for love is all in all.

I tell you what I dreamed last
    night.
It was not dark, it was not light,
Cold dews had drenched my plen-
    teous hair
Through clay ; you came to seek me
    there,
And 'Do you dream of me ?' you
    said.
My heart was dust that used to leap
To you ; I answered half asleep :
'My pillow is damp, my sheets are
    red,
There's a leaden tester to my bed :
Find you a warmer playfellow,
A warmer pillow for your head,
A kinder love to love than mine.'
You wrung your hands : while I, like
    lead,
Crushed downwards through the
    sodden earth :
You smote your hands but not in
    mirth,
And reeled but were not drunk with
    wine.

For all night long I dreamed of
    you :
I woke and prayed against my will,
Then slept to dream of you again.
At length I rose and knelt and
    prayed.
I cannot write the words I said,
My words were slow, my tears were
    few ;
But through the dark my silence
    spoke
Like thunder. When this morning
    broke,
My face was pinched, my hair was
    grey,
And frozen blood was on the sill
Where stifling in my struggle I lay.

If now you saw me you would say :
Where is the face I used to love ?
And I would answer : Gone before ;
It tarries veiled in Paradise.
When once the morning star shall
    rise,
When earth with shadow flees away
And we stand safe within the door,
Then you shall lift the veil thereof.
Look up, rise up : for far above
Our palms are grown, our place is
    set ;
There we shall meet as once we met,
And love with old familiar love.
    9 *July* 1858.

YET A LITTLE WHILE

THESE days are long before I die :
    To sit alone upon a thorn
    Is what the nightingale forlorn
Does night by night continually :
    She swells her heart to ecstasy
    Until it bursts and she can die.

These days are long that wane and
    wax :
    Waxeth and wanes the ghostly
        moon,
    Achill and pale in cordial June :
What is it that she wandering lacks ?
    She seems as one that aches and
        aches,
    Most sick to wane, most sick to wax.

Of all the sad sights in the world
  The downfall of an Autumn leaf
  Is grievous and suggesteth grief :
Who thought when Spring was fresh
    unfurled
Of this ? when Spring-twigs gleamed
    impearled
Who thought of frost that nips the
    world ?

There are a hundred subtle stings
  To prick us in our daily walk :
  A young fruit cankered on its
    stalk,
A strong bird snared for all his
    wings,
A nest that sang but never sings :
Yea sight and sound and silence
    stings.

There is a lack in solitude,
  There is a load in throng of life :
  One with another genders strife,
To be alone yet is not good :
I know but of one neighbourhood
At peace and full—death's solitude.

Sleep soundly, dears, who lulled at
    last
  Forget the bird and all her pains,
  Forget the moon that waxes,
    wanes,
The leaf, the sting, the frostful blast :
Forget the troublous years that,
    past
In strife or ache, did end at last.

We have clear call of daily bells,
  A dimness where the anthems are,
  A chancel vault of sky and star,
A thunder if the organ swells :
Alas our daily life—what else ?—
Is not in tune with daily bells.

You have deep pause betwixt the
    chimes
  Of earth and heaven, a patient
    pause
  Yet glad with rest by certain laws :
You look and long : while oftentimes
Precursive flush of morning climbs,
And air vibrates with coming chimes.
6 *August* 1858.

FATHER AND LOVER

FATHER

IF underneath the water
  You comb your golden hair
With a golden comb, my daughter,
  Oh would that I were there !
If underneath the wave
You fill a slimy grave,
Would that I, who could not save,
  Might share.

LOVER

If my love Hero queens it
  In summer Fairyland,
    What would I be
    But the ring on her hand ?
    Her cheek when she leans it
    Would lean on me :—
    Or sweet, bitter-sweet,
    The flower that she wore
When we parted, to meet
  On the hither shore
Any more ? never more.
Circa 1858.

BY THE SEA

WHY does the sea moan evermore ?
  Shut out from heaven it makes its
    moan,
It frets against the boundary shore ;

All earth's full rivers cannot fill
The sea, that drinking thirsteth still.

Sheer miracles of loveliness
  Lie hid in its unlooked-on bed :
Anemones, salt, passionless,
Blow flower-like—just enough alive
To blow and multiply and thrive.

Shells quaint with curve or spot or spike,
  Encrusted live things argus-eyed,
All fair alike yet all unlike,
Are born without a pang, and die
Without a pang, and so pass by.
  11 *November* 1858.

WINTER RAIN

EVERY valley drinks,
  Every dell and hollow ;
Where the kind rain sinks and sinks,
  Green of Spring will follow.

Yet a lapse of weeks—
  Buds will burst their edges,
Strip their wool-coats, glue-coats, streaks,
  In the woods and hedges ;

Weave a bower of love
  For birds to meet each other,
Weave a canopy above
  Nest and egg and mother.

But for fattening rain
  We should have no flowers,
Never a bud or leaf again
  But for soaking showers ;

Never a mated bird
  In the rocking tree-tops,
Never indeed a flock or herd
  To graze upon the lea-crops.

Lambs so woolly white,
  Sheep the sun-bright leas on,
They could have no grass to bite
  But for rain in season.

We should find no moss
  In the shadiest places,
Find no waving meadow grass
  Pied with broad-eyed daisies :

But miles of barren sand,
  With never a son or daughter ;
Not a lily on the land,
  Or lily on the water.
  31 *January* 1859.

L. E. L.

'Whose heart was breaking for a little love.'

DOWNSTAIRS I laugh, I sport and jest with all ;
  But in my solitary room above
I turn my face in silence to the wall ;
  My heart is breaking for a little love.
    Though winter frosts are done,
    And birds pair every one,
And leaves peep out, for springtide is begun.

I feel no spring, while spring is well-nigh blown,
  I find no nest, while nests are in the grove :
Woe's me for mine own heart that dwells alone,
  My heart that breaketh for a little love.
    While golden in the sun
    Rivulets rise and run,
While lilies bud, for springtide is begun.

All love, are loved, save only I;
    their hearts
  Beat warm with love and joy,
    beat full thereof:
They cannot guess, who play the
    pleasant parts,
  My heart is breaking for a little
    love.
    While bee-hives wake and
      whirr,
    And rabbit thins his fur,
In living spring that sets the world
    astir.

I deck myself with silks and jewelry,
  I plume myself like any mated
    dove:
They praise my rustling show, and
    never see
  My heart is breaking for a little
    love.
    While sprouts green lavender
With rosemary and myrrh,
For in quick spring the sap is all
    astir.

Perhaps some saints in glory guess
    the truth,
  Perhaps some angels read it as
    they move,
And cry one to another full of ruth,
  ' Her heart is breaking for a little
    love.'
    Though other things have birth,
    And leap and sing for mirth,
When springtime wakes and clothes
    and feeds the earth.

Yet saith a saint, 'Take patience
    for thy scathe';
  Yet saith an angel: 'Wait, and
    thou shalt prove
True best is last, true life is born of
    death,

O thou, heart-broken for a little
    love.
  Then love shall fill thy girth,
  And love make fat thy dearth,
When new spring builds new heaven
    and clean new earth.'
15 *February* 1859.

SPRING

FROST-LOCKED all the winter,
Seeds, and roots, and stones of
    fruits,
What shall make their sap ascend
That they may put forth shoots?
Tips of tender green,
Leaf, or blade, or sheath;
Telling of the hidden life
That breaks forth underneath,
Life nursed in its grave by Death.

Blows the thaw-wind pleasantly,
Drips the soaking rain,
By fits looks down the waking sun:
Young grass springs on the plain;
Young leaves clothe early hedgerow
    trees;
Seeds, and roots, and stones of
    fruits,
Swoln with sap put forth their
    shoots;
Curled-headed ferns sprout in the
    lane;
Birds sing and pair again.

There is no time like Spring,
When life's alive in everything,
Before new nestlings sing,
Before cleft swallows speed their
    journey back
Along the trackless track—
God guides their wing,
He spreads their table that they
    nothing lack,—

Before the daisy grows a common
    flower,
Before the sun has power
To scorch the world up in his noon-
    tide hour.

There is no time like Spring,
Like Spring that passes by;
There is no life like Spring-life born
    to die,—
Piercing the sod,
Clothing the uncouth clod,
Hatched in the nest,
Fledged on the windy bough,
Strong on the wing:
There is no time like Spring that
    passes by,
Now newly born, and now
Hastening to die.
17 August 1859.

WHAT GOOD SHALL MY LIFE DO ME?

No hope in life: yet is there hope
In death, the threshold of man's
    scope.
Man yearneth (as the heliotrope

For ever seeks the sun) through
    light,
Through dark, for Love: all, read
    aright,
Is Love, for Love is infinite.

Shall not this infinite Love suffice
To feed thy dearth? Lift heart and
    eyes
Up to the hills, grow glad and wise.

The hills are glad because the sun
Kisses their round tops every one
Where silver fountains laugh and
    run:

Smooth pebbles shine beneath: be-
    side,
The grass, mere green, grows myriad-
    eyed
With pomp of blossoms veined or
    pied.

So every nest is glad whereon
The sun in tender strength has
    shone:
So every fruit he glows upon:

So every valley depth, whose herds
At pasture praise him without words:
So the winged ecstasies of birds.

If there be any such thing, what
Is there by sunlight betters not?
Nothing except dead things that
    rot.

Thou then who art not dead, and
    fit,
Like blasted tree beside the pit,
But for the axe that levels it,

Living show life of Love, whereof
The force wields earth and heaven
    above:
Who knows not Love begetteth
    Love?

Love in the gracious rain distils:
Love moves the subtle fountain-rills
To fertilize uplifted hills,

And seedful valleys fertilize:
Love stills the hungry lion's cries,
And the young raven satisfies:

Love hangs this earth in space:
    Love rolls
Fair worlds rejoicing on their poles.
And girds them round with aureoles.

Love lights the sun: Love through
    the dark
Lights the moon's evanescent arc:
Same Love lights up the glow-
    worm's spark:

Love rears the great: Love tends
    the small:
Breaks off the yoke, breaks down
    the wall:
Accepteth all, fulfilleth all.

O ye who taste that Love is sweet,
Set waymarks for the doubtful feet
That stumble on in search of it.

Sing hymns of Love, that those who
    hear
Far off in pain may lend an ear,
Rise up and wonder and draw near.

Lead lives of Love, that others who
Behold your lives may kindle too
With Love and cast their lots with
    you.
27 August 1859.

COUSIN KATE

I WAS a cottage-maiden
    Hardened by sun and air,
Contented with my cottage-mates,
    Not mindful I was fair.
Why did a great lord find me out
    And praise my flaxen hair?
Why did a great lord find me out
    To fill my heart with care?

He lured me to his palace-home—
    Woe's me for joy thereof—
To lead a shameless shameful life,
    His plaything and his love.

He wore me like a golden knot,
    He changed me like a glove:
So now I moan an unclean thing
    Who might have been a dove.

O Lady Kate, my Cousin Kate,
    You grew more fair than I:
He saw you at your father's gate,
    Chose you and cast me by.
He watched your steps along the lane,
    Your sport among the rye:
He lifted you from mean estate
    To sit with him on high.

Because you were so good and pure
    He bound you with his ring:
The neighbours call you good and
    pure,
    Call me an outcast thing.
Even so I sit and howl in dust,
    You sit in gold and sing:
Now which of us has tenderer heart?
    You had the stronger wing.

O Cousin Kate, my love was true,
    Your love was writ in sand:
If he had fooled not me but you,
    If you stood where I stand,
He had not won me with his love
    Nor bought me with his land:
I would have spit into his face
    And not have taken his hand.

Yet I've a gift you have not got
    And seem not like to get:
For all your clothes and wedding-
    ring
    I've little doubt you fret.
My fair-haired son, my shame, my
    pride,
    Cling closer, closer yet:
Your sire would give broad lands for
    one
    To wear his coronet.
18 November 1859.

SISTER MAUDE

Who told my mother of my shame,
   Who told my father of my dear?
Oh who but Maude, my sister Maude,
   Who lurked to spy and peer.

Cold he lies, as cold as stone,
   With his clotted curls about his face:
The comeliest corpse in all the world
   And worthy of a queen's embrace.

You might have spared his soul, sister,
   Have spared my soul, your own soul too:
Though I had not been born at all,
   He'd never have looked at you.

My father may sleep in Paradise,
   My mother at Heaven-gate:
But sister Maude shall get no sleep
   Either early or late.

My father may wear a golden gown,
   My mother a crown may win;
If my dear and I knocked at Heaven-gate
   Perhaps they'd let us in:
But sister Maude, O sister Maude,
   Bide *you* with death and sin.
      Circa 1860.

NOBLE SISTERS

'Now did you mark a falcon,
   Sister dear, sister dear,
Flying toward my window
   In the morning cool and clear?
With jingling bells about her neck,
   But what beneath her wing?
It may have been a ribbon,
   Or it may have been a ring.'—
'I marked a falcon swooping
   At the break of day:
And for your love, my sister dove,
   I 'frayed the thief away.'—

'Or did you spy a ruddy hound,
   Sister fair and tall,
Went snuffing round my garden bound,
   Or crouched by my bower wall?
With a silken leash about his neck;
   But in his mouth may be
A chain of gold and silver links,
   Or a letter writ to me.'—
'I heard a hound, highborn sister,
   Stood baying at the moon:
I rose and drove him from your wall
   Lest you should wake too soon.'—

'Or did you meet a pretty page
   Sat swinging on the gate?
Sat whistling whistling like a bird,
   Or may be slept too late:
With eaglets broidered on his cap,
   And eaglets on his glove.
If you had turned his pockets out,
   You had found some pledge of love.'—
'I met him at this daybreak,
   Scarce the east was red:
Lest the creaking gate should anger you
   I packed him home to bed.'—

'Oh patience, sister! Did you see
   A young man tall and strong,
Swift-footed to uphold the right
   And to uproot the wrong,

Come home across the desolate sea
  To woo me for his wife?
And in his heart my heart is locked,
  And in his life my life.'—
    'I met a nameless man, sister,
      Who loitered round our
        door:
      I said: Her husband loves
        her much
      And yet she loves him
        more.'—

'Fie, sister, fie, a wicked lie,
  A lie, a wicked lie!
I have none other love but him,
  Nor will have till I die.
And you have turned him from our
  door,
  And stabbed him with a lie:
I will go seek him thro' the world
  In sorrow till I die.'—
    'Go seek in sorrow, sister,
      And find in sorrow too:
    If thus you shame our father's
      name
      My curse go forth with
        you.'
Towards January 1860.

'NO, THANK YOU, JOHN'

I NEVER said I loved you, John;
  Why will you tease me day by
    day,
And wax a weariness to think upon
  With always 'do' and 'pray'?

You know I never loved you, John;
  No fault of mine made me your
    toast:
Why will you haunt me with a face
    as wan
  As shows an hour-old ghost?

I dare say Meg or Moll would take
  Pity upon you, if you'd ask:
And pray don't remain single for
    my sake
  Who can't perform that task.

I have no heart?—Perhaps I have
    not;
  But then you're mad to take
    offence
That I don't give you what I have
    not got:
  Use your own common sense.

Let bygones be bygones:
  Don't call me false, who owed
    not to be true:
I'd rather answer 'No' to fifty
    Johns
  Than answer 'Yes' to you.

Let's mar our pleasant days no
    more,
  Song-birds of passage, days of
    youth:
Catch at to-day, forget the days
    before;
  I'll wink at your untruth.

Let us strike hands as hearty
    friends;
  No more, no less; and friend-
    ship's good:
Only don't keep in view ulterior
    ends,
  And points not understood

In open treaty. Rise above
  Quibbles and shuffling off and
    on.
Here's friendship for you if you
    like: but love,—
  No, thank you, John.
27 March 1860.

MIRAGE

THE hope I dreamed of was a dream,
  Was but a dream; and now I wake,
Exceeding comfortless, and worn, and old,
  For a dream's sake.

I hang my harp upon a tree,
  A weeping willow in a lake;
I hang my silenced harp there, wrung and snapt
  For a dream's sake.

Lie still, lie still, my breaking heart;
  My silent heart, lie still and break:
Life, and the world, and mine own self, are changed
  For a dream's sake.
12 *June* 1860.

THE LAMBS OF GRASMERE, 1860

THE upland flocks grew starved and thinned:
  Their shepherds scarce could feed the lambs
Whose milkless mothers butted them,
  Or who were orphaned of their dams.
The lambs athirst for mother's milk
  Filled all the place with piteous sounds:
Their mothers' bones made white for miles
  The pastureless wet pasture grounds.

Day after day, night after night,
  From lamb to lamb the shepherds went,
With teapots for the bleating mouths,
  Instead of nature's nourishment.
The little shivering gaping things
  Soon knew the step that brought them aid,
And fondled the protecting hand,
  And rubbed it with a woolly head.

Then, as the days waxed on to weeks,
  It was a pretty sight to see
These lambs with frisky heads and tails
  Skipping and leaping on the lea,
Bleating in tender trustful tones,
  Resting on rocky crag or mound,
And following the beloved feet
  That once had sought for them and found.

These very shepherds of their flocks,
  These loving lambs so meek to please,
Are worthy of recording words
  And honour in their due degrées:
So I might live a hundred years,
  And roam from strand to foreign strand,
Yet not forget this flooded spring
  And scarce-saved lambs of Westmoreland.
24 *July* 1860.

PROMISES LIKE PIE-CRUST

PROMISE me no promises,
  So will I not promise you:
Keep we both our liberties,
  Never false and never true:
Let us hold the die uncast,
  Free to come as free to go:

For I cannot know your past,
  And of mine what can you know?
You, so warm, may once have been
  Warmer towards another one:
I, so cold, may once have seen
  Sunlight, once have felt the sun:
Who shall show us if it was
  Thus indeed in time of old?
Fades the image from the glass,
  And the fortune is not told.

If you promised, you might grieve
  For lost liberty again:
If I promised, I believe
  I should fret to break the chain.
Let us be the friends we were,
  Nothing more but nothing less:
Many thrive on frugal fare
  Who would perish of excess.
20 *April* 1861.

WIFE TO HUSBAND

PARDON the faults in me,
  For the love of years ago:
    Good-bye.
I must drift across the sea,
  I must sink into the snow,
    I must die.

You can bask in this sun,
  You can drink wine, and eat:
    Good-bye.
I must gird myself and run,
  Though with unready feet:
    I must die.

Blank sea to sail upon,
  Cold bed to sleep in:
    Good-bye.
While you clasp, I must be gone
  For all your weeping:
    I must die.

A kiss for one friend,
  And a word for two,—
    Good-bye:—
A lock that you must send,
  A kindness you must do:
    I must die.

Not a word for you,
  Not a lock or kiss,
    Good-bye.
We, one, must part in two;
  Verily death is this:
    I must die.
8 *June* 1861.

BETTER SO

FAST asleep, mine own familiar friend,
  Fast asleep at last:
  Though the pain was strong,
  Though the struggle long,
    It is past:
All thy pangs are at an end.

Whilst I weep, whilst death-bells toll,
  Thou art fast asleep,
With idle hands upon thy breast
    And heart at rest:
    Whilst I weep
Angels sing around thy singing soul.

I would not speak the word if I could raise
    My dead to life:
    I would not speak
If I could flush thy cheek
  And rouse thy pulses' strife
And send thy feet on the once-trodden ways.
13 *December* 1861.

OUR WIDOWED QUEEN

THE Husband of the widow care for her,
  The Father of the fatherless:
The faithful Friend, the abiding Comforter,
  Watch over her to bless.

Full twenty years of blameless married faith,
  Of love and honour questioned not,
Joys, griefs imparted: for the first time Death
  Sunders the common lot.

Christ help the desolate Queen upon her throne,
  Strengthen her hands, confirm her heart:
For she henceforth must bear a load alone
  Borne until now in part.

Christ help the desolate Woman in her home,
  Broken of heart, indeed bereft:
Shrinking from solitary days to come,
  Beggared though much is left.

Rise up, O Sons and Daughters of the Dead,
  Weep with your Mother where she weeps:
Yet not as sorrowing without hope be shed
  Your tears: he only sleeps.

Rise up, O Sons and Daughters of the realm,
  In pale reflected sorrow move:
Revere the widowed hand that holds the helm,
  Love her with double love.

In royal patience of her soul possest
  May she fulfil her length of days:
Then may her children rise and call her blest,
  Then may her Husband praise.

16 *December* 1861.

IN PROGRESS

TEN years ago it seemed impossible
  That she should ever grow so calm as this,
With self-remembrance in her warmest kiss
  And dim dried eyes like an exhausted well.
Slow-speaking when she has some fact to tell,
  Silent with long-unbroken silences,
  Centred in self yet not unpleased to please,
Gravèly monotonous like a passing bell.
Mindful of drudging daily common things,
  Patient at pastime, patient at her work,
    Wearied perhaps but strenuous certainly.
Sometimes I fancy we may one day see
  Her head shoot forth seven stars from where they lurk
And her eyes lightnings and her shoulders wings.

31 *March* 1862.

ON THE WING

ONCE in a dream (for once I dreamed of you)
  We stood together in an open field;

Above our heads two swift-winged
    pigeons wheeled,
Sporting at ease and courting full
    in view :—
When loftier still a broadening dark-
    ness flew,
  Down-swooping, and a ravenous
    hawk revealed;
  Too weak to fight, too fond to fly,
    they yield;
So farewell life and love and
    pleasures new.
Then as their plumes fell fluttering
    to the ground,
  Their snow-white plumage flecked
    with crimson drops,
    I wept, and thought I turned
    towards you to weep :
  But you were gone; while rust-
    ling hedgerow tops
Bent in a wind which bore to me a
    sound
    Of far-off piteous bleat of lambs
    and sheep.

17 December 1862.

SONG

Two doves upon the selfsame
    branch,
  Two lilies on a single stem,
Two butterflies upon one flower :—
  Oh happy they who look on them!

Who look upon them hand in
    hand
  Flushed in the rosy summer light;
Who look upon them hand in hand,
  And never give a thought to
    night.

Before 1863.

THE QUEEN OF HEARTS

How comes it, Flora, that, when-
    ever we
Play cards together, you invariably,
  However the pack parts,
  Still hold the Queen of Hearts?

I've scanned you with a scrutinizing
    gaze,
Resolved to fathom these your secret
    ways:
  But, sift them as I will,
  Your ways are secret still.

I cut and shuffle; shuffle, cut, again;
But all my cutting, shuffling, proves
    in vain :
  Vain hope, vain forethought too;
  That Queen still falls to you.

I dropped her once, prepense; but,
    ere the deal
Was dealt, your instinct seemed her
    loss to feel :
  'There should be one card
    more,'
  You said, and searched the
    floor.

I cheated once; I made a private
    notch
In Heart-Queen's back, and kept a
    lynx-eyed watch;
  Yet such another back
  Deceived me in the pack:

The Queen of Clubs assumed by
    arts unknown
An imitative dint that seemed my
    own;
  This notch, not of my doing,
  Misled me to my ruin.

It baffles me to puzzle out the clue,
Which must be skill, or craft, or
    luck in you:
    Unless, indeed, it be
    Natural affinity.
3 *January* 1863.

SEASONS

OH the cheerful Budding-time!
  When thorn-hedges turn to green,
When new leaves of elm and lime
  Cleave and shed their winter
    screen;
Tender lambs are born and baa,
  North wind finds no snow to bring,
Vigorous Nature laughs 'Ha ha!'
  In the miracle of Spring.

Oh the gorgeous Blossom-days!
  When broad flag-flowers drink
    and blow;
In and out in Summer-blaze
  Dragon-flies flash to and fro;
Ashen branches hang out keys;
  Oaks put forth the rosy shoot,
Wandering herds wax sleek at ease,
  Lovely blossoms end in fruit.

Oh the shouting Harvest-weeks!
  Mother Earth grown fat with
    sheaves;
Thrifty gleaner finds who seeks;
  Russet-golden pomp of leaves
Crowns the woods, to fall at length;
  Bracing winds are felt to stir,
Ocean gathers up her strength,
  Beasts renew their dwindled fur.

Oh the starving Winter lapse!
  Ice-bound, hunger-pinched, and
    dim;
Dormant roots recall their saps,

Empty nests show black and
    grim.
Short-lived sunshine gives no heat,
  Undue buds are nipped by frost,
Snow sets forth a winding-sheet,
  And all hope of life seems lost.
20 *January* 1863.

JUNE

COME, cuckoo, come:
  Come again, swift swallow:
Come and welcome! when you come
  Summer's sure to follow:
  June the month of months
  Flowers and fruitage brings too,
When green trees spread shadiest
    boughs,
  When each wild bird sings too.

May is scant and crude,
  Generous June is riper:
Birds fall silent in July,
  June has its woodland piper:
Rocks upon the maple-tops
  Homely-hearted linnet,
Full in hearing of his nest
  And the dear ones in it.

If the year would stand
  Still at June for ever,
With no further growth on land
  Nor further flow of river,
If all nights were shortest nights
And longest days were all the seven,
This might be a merrier world
  To my mind to live in.
5 *February* 1863.

A RING POSY

JESS and Jill are pretty girls,
  Plump and well to do,

In a cloud of windy curls:
  Yet I know who
Loves me more than curls or pearls.

I'm not pretty, not a bit—
  Thin and sallow-pale;
When I trudge along the street
  I don't need a veil:
Yet I have one fancy hit.

Jess and Jill can trill and sing
  With a flute-like voice,
Dance as light as bird on wing,
  Laugh for careless joys:
Yet it's I who wear the ring.

Jess and Jill will mate some day,
  Surely, surely:
Ripen on to June through May,
While the sun shines make their hay—
  Slacken steps demurely:
Yet even there I lead the way.
  20 *February* 1863.

HELEN GREY

BECAUSE one loves you, Helen Grey,
  Is that a reason you should pout,
  And like a March wind veer about,
And frown, and say your shrewish say?
Don't strain the cord until it snaps,
  Don't split the sound heart with your wedge,
  Don't cut your fingers with the edge
Of your keen wit; you may perhaps.

Because you're handsome, Helen Grey,
  Is that a reason to be proud?
Your eyes are bold, your laugh is loud,
Your steps go mincing on their way;
But so you miss that modest charm
  Which is the surest charm of all;
  Take heed, you yet may trip and fall,
And no man care to stretch his arm.

Stoop from your cold height, Helen Grey,
  Come down, and take a lowlier place,
  Come down, to fill it now with grace;
Come down you must perforce some day:
For years cannot be kept at bay,
  And fading years will make you old;
  Then in their turn will men seem cold,
When you yourself are nipped and grey.
  23 *February* 1863.

A YEAR'S WINDFALLS

ON the wind of January
  Down flits the snow,
Travelling from the frozen North
  As cold as it can blow.
Poor robin redbreast,
  Look where he comes;
Let him in to feel your fire,
  And toss him of your crumbs.

On the wind in February
  Snowflakes float still,
Half inclined to turn to rain,
  Nipping, dripping, chill.
Then the thaws swell the streams,
  And swollen rivers swell the sea:
If the winter ever ends,
  How pleasant it will be!

In the wind of windy March
  The catkins drop down,
Curly, caterpillar-like,
  Curious green and brown.
With concourse of nest-building birds
  And leaf-buds by the way,
We begin to think of flowers
  And life and nuts some day.

With the gusts of April
  Rich fruit-tree blossoms fall,
On the hedged-in orchard-green,
  From the southern wall.
Apple-trees and pear-trees
  Shed petals white or pink,
Plum-trees and peach-trees;
  While sharp showers sink and sink.

Little brings the May breeze
  Beside pure scent of flowers,
While all things wax and nothing wanes
  In lengthening daylight hours.
Across the hyacinth beds
  The wind lags warm and sweet,
Across the hawthorn tops,
  Across the blades of wheat.

In the wind of sunny June
  Thrives the red rose crop,
Every day fresh blossoms blow
  While the first leaves drop;
White rose and yellow rose
  And moss rose choice to find,
And the cottage cabbage-rose
  Not one whit behind.

On the blast of scorched July
  Drives the pelting hail
From thunderous lightning-clouds that blot
  Blue heaven grown lurid-pale.
Weedy waves are tossed ashore;
  Sea-things strange to sight
Gasp upon the barren shore
  And fade away in light.

In the parching August wind
  Corn-fields bow the head,
Sheltered in round valley depths,
  On low hills outspread.
Early leaves drop loitering down
  Weightless on the breeze,
First fruits of the year's decay
  From the withering trees.

In brisk wind of September
  The heavy-headed fruits
Shake upon their bending boughs
  And drop from the shoots;
Some glow golden in the sun,
  Some show green and streaked,
Some set forth a purple bloom,
  Some blush rosy-cheeked.

In strong blast of October
  At the equinox,
Stirred up in his hollow bed
  Broad ocean rocks;
Plunge the ships on his bosom,
  Leaps and plunges the foam,—
It's oh for mothers' sons at sea,
  That they were safe at home!

In slack wind of November
  The fog forms and shifts;
All the world comes out again
  When the fog lifts.
Loosened from their sapless twigs,
  Leaves drop with every gust;
Drifting, rustling, out of sight
  In the damp or dust.

Last of all, December,
  The year's sands nearly run,
Speeds on the shortest day,
  Curtails the sun;

With its bleak raw wind
    Lays the last leaves low,
Brings back the nightly frosts,
    Brings back the snow.
26 *February* 1863.

A BIRD'S-EYE VIEW

'CROAK, croak, croak,'
Thus the Raven spoke,
Perched on his crooked tree,
As hoarse as hoarse could be.
Shun him and fear him,
Lest the Bridegroom hear him ;
Scout him and rout-him
With his ominous eye about him.

Yet 'Croak, croak, croak,'
Still tolled from the oak,
From that fatal black bird,
Whether heard or unheard :
'O ship upon the high seas,
Freighted with lives and spices,
Sink, O ship,' croaked the Raven :
'Let the Bride mount to heaven.'

In a far foreign land
Upon the wave-edged sand,
Some friends gaze wistfully
Across the glittering sea.
'If we could clasp our sister,'
Three say, 'now we have missed her!'
'If we could kiss our daughter !'
Two sigh across the water.

Oh the ship sails fast
With silken flags at the mast,
And the home-wind blows soft.
But a Raven sits aloft,
Chuckling and choking,
Croaking, croaking, croaking.
Let the beacon-fire blaze higher ;
Bridegroom, watch ; the Bride draws
    nigher.

On a sloped sandy beach,
Which the spring-tide billows reach,
Stand a watchful throng
Who have hoped and waited long :
'Fie on this ship that tarries
With the priceless freight it carries !
The time seems long and longer :
O languid wind, wax stronger ;'—

Whilst the Raven perched at ease
Still croaks and does not cease,
One monotonous note
Tolled from his iron throat :
'No father, no mother,
But I have a sable brother :
He sees where ocean flows to,
And he knows what he knows too.'

A day and a night
They kept watch worn and white ;
A night and a day
For the swift ship on its way :
For the Bride and her maidens—
Clear chimes the bridal cadence—
For the tall ship that never
Hove in sight for ever.

On either shore, some
Stand in grief loud or dumb
As the dreadful dread
Grows certain though unsaid.
For laughter there is weeping,
And waking instead of sleeping,
And a desperate sorrow
Morrow after morrow.

Oh who knows the truth ?
How she perished in her youth,
And like a queen went down
Pale in her royal crown :
How she went up to glory
From the sea-foam chill and hoary,
From the sea-depth black and riven
To the calm that is in Heaven.

They went down, all the crew,
The silks and spices too,
The great ones and the small,
One and all, one and all.
Was it through stress of weather,
Quicksands, rocks, or all together?
Only the Raven knows this,
And he will not disclose this.—

After a day and a year
The bridal bell chimes clear;
After a year and a day
The Bridegroom is brave and gay.
Love is sound, faith is rotten:
The old Bride is forgotten:—
Two ominous Ravens only
Remember, black and lonely.

4 *March* 1863.

A DUMB FRIEND

I PLANTED a young tree when I was
  young:
But now the tree is grown and I
  am old:
There wintry robin shelters from the
  cold
  And tunes his silver tongue.

A green and living tree I planted it,
A glossy-foliaged tree of evergreen:
All through the noontide heat it
  spread a screen
  Whereunder I might sit.

But now I only watch it where it
  towers:
I, sitting at my window, watch it tost
By rattling gale or silvered by the
  frost;
  Or, when sweet summer
  flowers,

Wagging its round green head with
  stately grace
In tender winds that kiss it and go
  by.
It shows a green full age: and what
  show I?
  A faded wrinkled face.

So often have I watched it, till mine
  eyes
Have filled with tears and I have
  ceased to see,
That now it seems a very friend to
  me,
  In all my secrets wise.

A faithful pleasant friend, who year
  by year
Grew with my growth and strengthened with my strength,
But whose green lifetime shows a
  longer length:
  When I shall not sit here

It still will bud in spring, and shed
  rare leaves
In autumn, and in summer-heat give
  shade,
And warmth in winter: when my
  bed is made
  In shade the cypress weaves.

24 *March* 1863.

LIFE AND DEATH

LIFE is not sweet. One day it will
  be sweet
  To shut our eyes and die:
Nor feel the wild flowers blow, nor
  birds dart by
  With flitting butterfly,
Nor grass grow long above our
  heads and feet,

Nor hear the happy lark that soars
    sky-high,
Nor sigh that spring is fleet and
    summer fleet,
    Nor mark the waxing wheat,
Nor know who sits in our accustomed
    seat.

Life is not good. One day it will be
    good
    To die, then live again ;
To sleep meanwhile ; so, not to feel
    the wane
    Of shrunk leaves dropping in
        the wood,
Nor hear the foamy lashing of the
    main,
Nor mark the blackened bean-fields,
    nor, where stood
    Rich ranks of golden grain,
Only dead refuse stubble clothe the
    plain :
    Asleep from risk, asleep from
        pain.
24 *April* 1863.

TWILIGHT NIGHT

I

WE met hand to hand,
    We clasped hands close and fast,
As close as oak and ivy stand :
    But it is past ;
Come day, come night, day comes
    at last.

We loosed hand from hand,
    We parted face from face :
Each went his way to his own land
    At his own pace,
Each went to fill his separate
    place.

If we should meet one day,
    If both should not forget,
We shall clasp hands the accustomed
    way,
    As when we met,
So long ago, as I remember yet.
26 *August* 1864.

II

Where my heart is (wherever that
    may be)
    Might I but follow !
If you fly thither over heath and lea,
    O honey-seeking bee,
    O careless swallow,
Bid some for whom I watch keep
    watch for me.

Alas that we must dwell, my heart
    and I,
    So far asunder !
Hours wax to days, and days and
    days creep by ;
    I watch with wistful eye,
    I wait and wonder :
When will that day draw nigh—that
    hour draw nigh ?

Not yesterday, and not I think to-day ;
    Perhaps to-morrow.
Day after day 'To-morrow' thus I
    say :
    I watched so yesterday
    In hope and sorrow,
Again to-day I watch the accustomed
    way.
25 *June* 1863.

THE POOR GHOST

'OH whence do you come, my dear
    friend, to me,
With your golden hair all fallen
    below your knee,

And your face as white as snowdrops
    on the lea,
And your voice as hollow as the
    hollow sea?'

'From the other world I come back
    to you:
My locks are uncurled with dripping
    drenching dew.
You know the old, whilst I know the
    new:
But to-morrow you shall know this
    too.'

'Oh not to-morrow into the dark, I
    pray;
Oh not to-morrow, too soon to go
    away:
Here I feel warm and well-content
    and gay:
Give me another year, another day.'

'Am I so changed in a day and a
    night
That mine own only love shrinks
    from me with fright,
Is fain to turn away to left or right
And cover up his eyes from the
    sight?'

'Indeed I loved you, my chosen
    friend,
I loved you for life, but life has an
    end;
Through sickness I was ready to
    tend:
But death mars all, which we cannot
    mend.

'Indeed I loved you; I love you yet,
If you will stay where your bed is
    set,
Where I have planted a violet,
Which the wind waves, which the
    dew makes wet.'

'Life is gone, then love too is gone.
It was a reed that I leant upon:
Never doubt I will leave you alone
And not wake you rattling bone
    with bone.

'I go home alone to my bed,
Dug deep at the foot and deep at
    the head,
Roofed in with a load of lead,
Warm enough for the forgotten dead.

'But why did your tears soak through
    the clay,
And why did your sobs wake me
    where I lay?
I was away, far enough away:
Let me sleep now till the Judgment
    Day.'
25 July 1863.

MARGERY

WHAT shall we do with Margery?
    She lies and cries upon her bed,
    All lily-pale from foot to head:
    Her heart is sore as sore can be:
Poor guileless shamefaced Margery.

A foolish girl, to love a man
    And let him know she loved him
      so!
    She should have tried a different
      plan:
    Have loved, but not have let him
      know:
Then he perhaps had loved her so.

What can we do with Margery
    Who has no relish for her food?
    We'd take her with us to the sea—
    Across the sea—but where's the
      good?
She'd fret alike on land and sea.

Yes, what the neighbours say is true:
  Girls should not make themselves
    so cheap.
But now it's done what can we do?
  I hear her moaning in her sleep,
  Moaning and sobbing in her sleep.

I think—and I'm of flesh and
    blood—
  Were I that man for whom she
    cares,
  I would not cost her tears and
    prayers
To leave her just alone like mud,
  Fretting her simple heart with
    cares.

A year ago she was a child,
  Now she's a woman in her grief:
  The year's now at the falling leaf;
At budding of the leaves she smiled:
Poor foolish harmless foolish child.

It was her own fault? so it was.
  If every own fault found us out,
  Dogged us and snared us round-
    about,
What comfort should we take because
  Not half our due we thus wrung
    out?

At any rate the question stands:
  What now to do with Margery,
A weak poor creature on our hands?
  Something we must do: I'll not
    see
  Her blossom fade, sweet Margery.

Perhaps a change may after all
  Prove best for her: to leave
    behind
  These home-sights seen time out
    of mind;
To get beyond the narrow wall
Of home, and learn home is not all.

Perhaps this way she may forget,
  Not all at once, but in a while:
May come to wonder how she set
  Her heart on this slight thing,
    and smile
At her own folly, in a while.

Yet this I say and I maintain:
  Were I the man she's fretting for,
  I should my very self abhor
If I could leave her to her pain,
Uncomforted to tears and pain.

1 *October* 1863.

LAST NIGHT

WHERE were you last night? I
    watched at the gate;
  I went down early, I stayed down
    late.
    Were you snug at home, I
      should like to know,
  Or were you in the coppice wheed-
    ling Kate?

She's a fine girl, with a fine clear
    skin;
  Easy to woo, perhaps not hard to
    win.
    Speak up like a man and tell
      me the truth:
  I'm not one to grow downhearted
    and thin.

If you love her best, speak up
    like a man;
  It's not I will stand in the light
    of your plan:
    Some girls might cry and scold
      you a bit,
  And say they couldn't bear it; but
    I can.

Love was pleasant enough, and the days went fast;
Pleasant while it lasted, but it needn't last;
    Awhile on the wax, and awhile on the wane,
Now dropped away into the past.

Was it pleasant to you? To me it was:
Now clean gone as an image from glass,
    As a goodly rainbow that fades away,
As dew that steams upward from the grass;

As the first spring day or the last summer day,
As the sunset flush that leaves heaven grey,
    As a flame burnt out for lack of oil,
Which no pains relight or ever may.

Good luck to Kate and good luck to you:
I guess she'll be kind when you come to woo.
    I wish her a pretty face that will last,
I wish her a husband steady and true.

Hate you? not I, my very good friend;
All things begin and all have an end.
    But let broken be broken; I put no faith
In quacks who set up to patch and mend.

Just my love and one word to Kate—
Not to let time slip if she means to mate;
    For even such a thing has been known
As to miss the chance while we weigh and wait.

November 1863.

SOMEWHERE OR OTHER

SOMEWHERE or other there must surely be
    The face not seen, the voice not heard,
The heart that not yet—never yet—ah me!
    Made answer to my word.

Somewhere or other, may be near or far;
    Past land and sea, clean out of sight;
Beyond the wandering moon, beyond the star
    That tracks her night by night.

Somewhere or other, may be far or near;
    With just a wall, a hedge, between;
With just the last leaves of the dying year
    Fallen on a turf grown green.

Towards November 1863.

A CHILL

WHAT can lambkins do
All the keen night through?
Nestle by their woolly mother
The careful ewe.

What can nestlings do
In the nightly dew?
Sleep beneath their mother's wing
Till day breaks anew.

If in field or tree
There might only be
Such a warm soft sleeping-place
Found for me!
Towards December 1863.

SUMMER

WINTER is cold-hearted,
Spring is yea and nay,
Autumn is a weathercock
    Blown every way.
Summer days for me
When every leaf is on its tree;

When Robin's not a beggar,
And Jenny Wren's a bride,
And larks hang singing, singing, singing,
Over the wheat-fields wide,
And anchored lilies ride,
And the pendulum spider
Swings from side to side;

And blue-black beetles transact business,
And gnats fly in a host,
And furry caterpillars hasten
That no time be lost,
And moths grow fat and thrive,
And ladybirds arrive.

Before green apples blush,
Before green nuts embrown,
Why one day in the country
Is worth a month in town;
Is worth a day and a year
Of the dusty, musty, lag-last fashion
That days drone elsewhere.
15 January 1864.

BEAUTY IS VAIN

WHILE roses are so red,
While lilies are so white,
Shall a woman exalt her face
Because it gives delight?
She's not so sweet as a rose,
A lily's straighter than she,
And if she were as red or white
She'd be but one of three.

Whether she flush in love's summer
Or in its winter grow pale,
Whether she flaunt her beauty
Or hide it away in a veil,
Be she red or white
And stand she erect or bowed,
Time will win the race he runs with her,
And hide her away in a shroud.
20 January 1864.

WHAT WOULD I GIVE!

WHAT would I give for a heart of flesh to warm me through,
Instead of this heart of stone ice-cold whatever I do!
Hard and cold and small, of all hearts the worst of all.

What would I give for words, if only words would come!
But now in its misery my spirit has fallen dumb.
O merry friends, go your way, I have never a word to say.

What would I give for tears! not smiles but scalding tears,
To wash the black mark clean, and to thaw the frost of years,
To wash the stain ingrain, and to make me clean again.
28 January 1864.

THE GHOST'S PETITION

'THERE'S a footstep coming; look out and see.'—
　'The leaves are falling, the wind is calling;
No one cometh across the lea.'—

'There's a footstep coming; O sister, look.'—
　'The ripple flashes, the white foam dashes;
No one cometh across the brook.'—

'But he promised that he would come:
　To-night, to-morrow, in joy or sorrow,
He must keep his word, and must come home.

'For he promised that he would come:
　His word was given; from earth or heaven,
He must keep his word, and must come home.

'Go to sleep, my sweet sister Jane;
　You can slumber, who need not number
Hour after hour, in doubt and pain.

'I shall sit here awhile, and watch;
　Listening, hoping, for one hand groping
In deep shadow to find the latch.'

After the dark and before the light,
　One lay sleeping; and one sat weeping,
Who had watched and wept the weary night.

After the night and before the day,
　One lay sleeping; and one sat weeping—
Watching, weeping for one away.

There came a footstep climbing the stair;
　Some one standing out on the landing
Shook the door like a puff of air—

Shook the door and in he passed.
　Did he enter? In the room centre
Stood her husband: the door shut fast.

'O Robin, but you are cold—
　Chilled with the night-dew: so lily-white you
Look like a stray lamb from our fold.

'O Robin, but you are late:
　Come and sit near me—sit here and cheer me.'—
(Blue the flame burnt in the grate.)

'Lay not down your head on my breast:
　I cannot hold you, kind wife, nor fold you
In the shelter that you love best.

'Feel not after my clasping hand:
　I am but a shadow, come from the meadow
Where many lie, but no tree can stand.

'We are trees which have shed their leaves:
　Our heads lie low there, but no tears flow there;
Only I grieve for my wife who grieves.

'I could rest if you would not moan
  Hour after hour : I have no power
To shut my ears where I lie alone.

'I could rest if you would not cry ;
  But there's no sleeping while you
    sit weeping—
Watching, weeping so bitterly.'—

'Woe's me ! woe's me ! for this I
    have heard.
  Oh night of sorrow !—oh black
    to-morrow !
Is it thus that you keep your word ?

'O you who used so to shelter me
  Warm from the least wind—why,
    now the east wind
Is warmer than you, whom I quake
    to see.

'O my husband of flesh and blood,
  For whom my mother I left, and
    brother,
And all I had, accounting it good,

'What do you do there, underground,
  In the dark hollow ? I'm fain to
    follow.
What do you do there ?—what have
    you found ? '—

'What I do there I must not tell :
  But I have plenty ; kind wife,
    content ye :
It is well with us—it is well.

'Tender hand hath made our nest ;
  Our fear is ended, our hope is
    blended
With present pleasure, and we have
    rest.'

'Oh but Robin, I'm fain to come,
  If your present days are so
    pleasant,
For my days are so wearisome.

'Yet I'll dry my tears for your sake :
  Why should I tease you, who
    cannot please you
Any more with the pains I take ?'
7 April 1864.

HOPING AGAINST HOPE

IF he would come to-day, to-day,
    to-day,
  Oh what a day to-day would be !
But now he's away, miles and miles
    away
  From me across the sea.

O little bird, flying, flying, flying
  To your nest in the warm west,
Tell him as you pass that I am dying,
  As you pass home to your nest.

I have a sister, I have a brother,
  A faithful hound, a tame white
    dove ;
But I had another, once I had
    another,
  And I miss him, my love, my love !

In this weary world it is so cold, so
    cold,
  While I sit here all alone ;
I would not like to wait and to grow
    old,
  But just to be dead and gone.

Make me fair when I lie dead on
    my bed,
  Fair where I am lying :
Perhaps he may come and look upon
    me dead—
  He for whom I am dying.

Dig my grave for two, with a stone
    to show it,
  And on the stone write my
    name :

If he never comes, I shall never
    know it,
But sleep on all the same.
12 *April* 1864.

SUNSHINE

'THERE'S little sunshine in my heart,
    Slack to spring, lead to sink:
There's little sunshine in the world,
        I think.

'There's glow of sunshine in my
    heart
    (Cool wind, cool the glow):
There's flood of sunshine in the
    world,
        I know.'

Now if of these one spoke the truth,
    One spoke more or less:
But which was which I will not tell:
        You guess.
31 *May* 1864.

MEETING

IF we shall live, we live:
    If we shall die, we die:
If we live we shall meet again:
    But to-night, good-bye.
One word, let but one be heard—
    What, not one word?

If we sleep we shall wake again
    And see to-morrow's light:
If we wake, we shall meet again:
    But to-night, good-night.
Good-night, my lost and
    found—
    Still not a sound?

If we live, we must part:
If we die, we part in pain:
    If we die, we shall part
    Only to meet again.
By those tears on either cheek,
    To-morrow you will speak.

To meet, worth living for:
    Worth dying for, to meet.
To meet, worth parting for:
    Bitter forgot in sweet.
To meet, worth parting before.
    Never to part more.
11 *June* 1864.

TWICE

I TOOK my heart in my hand,
    (O my love, O my love),
I said: Let me fall or stand,
    Let me live or die,
But this once hear me speak—
    (O my love, O my love)—
Yet a woman's words are weak;
    You should speak, not I.

You took my heart in your hand
    With a friendly smile,
With a critical eye you scanned,
    Then set it down,
And said: It is still unripe,
    Better wait awhile;
Wait while the skylarks pipe,
    Till the corn grows brown.

As you set it down it broke—
    Broke, but I did not wince;
I smiled at the speech you spoke,
    At your judgment that I heard:
But I have not often smiled
    Since then, nor questioned since,
Nor cared for corn-flowers wild,
    Nor sung with the singing bird.

I take my heart in my hand,
  O my God, O my God,
My broken heart in my hand :
  Thou hast seen, judge Thou.
My hope was written on sand,
  O my God, O my God :
Now let Thy judgment stand—
  Yea, judge me now.

This contemned of a man,
  This marred one heedless day,
This heart take Thou to scan .
  Both within and without :
Refine with fire its gold,
  Purge Thou its dross away—
Yea hold it in Thy hold,
  Whence none can pluck it out.

I take my heart in my hand—
  I shall not die, but live—
Before Thy face I stand ;
  · I, for Thou callest such :
All that I have I bring,
  All that I am I give ;
Smile Thou and I shall sing,
  But shall not question much.
    June 1864.

A FARM WALK

THE year stood at its equinox
  And bluff the North was blowing,
A bleat of lambs came from the flocks,
  Green hardy things were growing :
I met a maid with shining locks
  Where milky kine were lowing.

She wore a kerchief on her neck,
  Her bare arm showed its dimple,
Her apron spread without a speck,
  Her air was frank and simple.

She milked into a wooden pail
  And sang a country ditty,
An innocent fond lovers' tale
  That was not wise nor witty,
Pathetically rustical,
  Too pointless for the city.

She kept in time without a beat
  As true as church-bell ringers,
Unless she tapped time with her feet,
  Or squeezed it with her fingers ;
Her clear unstudied notes were sweet
  As many a practised singer's.

I stood a minute out of sight,
  Stood silent for a minute,
To eye the pail, and creamy white
  The frothing milk within it ;

To eye the comely milking maid,
  Herself so fresh and creamy.
'Good day to you,' at last I said ;
  She turned her head to see me :
'Good day,' she said with lifted head ;
  Her eyes looked soft and dreamy.

And all the while she milked and milked
  The grave cow heavy-laden.
I've seen grand ladies plumed and silked,
  But not a sweeter maiden ;

But not a sweeter fresher maid
  Than this in homely cotton,
Whose pleasant face and silky braid
  I have not yet forgotten.

Seven springs have passed since then, as I
  Count with a sober sorrow ;

Seven springs have come and passed
  me by,
  And spring sets in to-morrow.

I've half a mind to shake myself
  Free just for once from London,
To set my work upon the shelf
  And leave it done or undone;

To run down by the early train,
  Whirl down with shriek and
    whistle,
And feel the bluff North blow again,
  And mark the sprouting thistle
Set up on waste patch of the lane
  Its green and tender bristle;

And spy the scarce-blown violet
    banks,
  Crisp primrose leaves and others,
And watch the lambs leap at their
    pranks
  And butt their patient mothers.—

Alas one point in all my plan
  My serious thoughts demur to:
Seven years have passed for maid
    and man,
  Seven years have passed for her
    too;

Perhaps my rose is overblown,
  Not rosy or too rosy;
Perhaps in farmhouse of her own
  Some husband keeps her cosy,
Where I should show a face un-
    known.—
  Good-bye, my wayside posy.
    11 *July* 1864.

UNDER WILLOWS

UNDER willows among the graves
  One was walking, ah welladay!
Where each willow her green boughs
    waves,
  Come April prime, come May.
Under willows among the graves
  She met her lost love, ah welladay!
Where in Autumn each wild wind
    raves
  And whirls sere leaves away.

He looked at her with a smile,
  She looked at him with a sigh,
Both paused to look awhile:
    Then he passed by,—
Passed by and whistled a tune:
She stood silent and still:
It was the sunniest day in June,
  Yet one felt a chill.

Under willows among the graves
I know a certain black black pool
Scarce wrinkled when Autumn raves.
    Under the turf is cool;
Under the water it must be cold:
Winter comes cold when Summer's
    past:
Though she live to be old, so old,
  She shall die at last.
    27 *July* 1864.

A SKETCH

THE blindest buzzard that I know
  Does not wear wings to spread
    and stir:
  Nor does my special mole wear
    fur,
And grub among the roots below:
He sports a tail indeed, but then
It's to a coat: he's man with men:
  His quill is cut to a pen.

In other points our friend's a mole,
  A buzzard, beyond scope of speech.
He sees not what's within his
    reach,

Misreads the part, ignores the whole;
Misreads the part, so reads in vain,
Ignores the whole though patent plain,—
    Misreads both parts again.

My blindest buzzard that I know,
    My special mole, when will you see?
Oh no, you must not look at me,
There's nothing hid for me to show.
I might show facts as plain as day:
But, since your eyes are blind, you'd say,
    'Where? What?' and turn away.
15 August 1864.

BIRD OR BEAST?

Did any bird come flying
    After Adam and Eve,
When the door was shut against them
    And they sat down to grieve?

I think not Eve's peacock
    Splendid to see,
And I think not Adam's eagle;
    But a dove may be.

Did any beast come pushing
    Through the thorny hedge
Into the thorny thistly world,
    Out from Eden's edge?

I think not a lion,
    Though his strength is such;
But an innocent loving lamb
    May have done as much.

If the dove preached from her bough,
    And the lamb from his sod,
The lamb and the dove
    Were preachers sent from God.
15 August 1864.

SONGS IN A CORNFIELD

A song in a cornfield
    Where corn begins to fall,
Where reapers are reaping,
    Reaping one, reaping all.
Sing pretty Lettice,
    Sing Rachel, sing May;
Only Marian cannot sing
    While her sweetheart's away.

Where is he gone to
    And why does he stay?
He came across the green sea
    But for a day,
Across the deep green sea
    To help with the hay.
His hair was curly yellow
    And his eyes were grey,
He laughed a merry laugh
    And said a sweet say.
Where is he gone to
    That he comes not home?
To-day or to-morrow
    He surely will come.
Let him haste to joy,
    Lest he lag for sorrow,
For one weeps to-day
    Who'll not weep to-morrow;
To-day she must weep
    For gnawing sorrow,
To-night she may sleep
    And not wake to-morrow.

May sang with Rachel
    In the waxing warm weather,
Lettice sang with them,
    They sang all together:—

'Take the wheat in your arm
    Whilst day is broad above,
Take the wheat to your bosom,
    But not a false false love.

Out in the fields
  Summer heat gloweth,
Out in the fields
  Summer wind bloweth,
Out in the fields
  Summer friend showeth,
Out in the fields
  Summer wheat groweth;
But in the winter,
  When summer heat is dead
And summer wind has veered
  And summer friend has fled,
Only summer wheat remaineth,
  White cakes and bread.
Take the wheat, clasp the wheat
  That's food for maid and dove;
Take the wheat to your bosom,
  But not a false false love.'

A silence of full noontide heat
  Grew on them at their toil:
The farmer's dog woke up from sleep,
  The green snake hid her coil
Where grass stood thickest; bird and beast
  Sought shadows as they could,
The reaping men and women paused
  And sat down where they stood;
They ate and drank and were refreshed,
  For rest from toil is good.

While the reapers took their ease,
  Their sickles lying by,
Rachel sang a second strain,
  And singing seemed to sigh:—

  'There goes the swallow—
  Could we but follow!
    Hasty swallow, stay,
    Point us out the way;
Look back, swallow, turn back, swallow, stop, swallow.

'There went the swallow—
Too late to follow:
  Lost our note of way,
  Lost our chance to-day;
Good-bye, swallow, sunny swallow, wise swallow.

'After the swallow
All sweet things follow:
  All things go their way,
  Only we must stay,
Must not follow; good-bye, swallow, good swallow.'

Then listless Marian raised her head
  Among the nodding sheaves;
Her voice was sweeter than that voice;
  She sang like one who grieves:
Her voice was sweeter than its wont
  Among the nodding sheaves;
All wondered while they heard her sing
  Like one who hopes and grieves:—

'Deeper than the hail can smite,
Deeper than the frost can bite,
Deep asleep through day and night,
  Our delight.

'Now thy sleep no pang can break,
No to-morrow bid thee wake,
Not our sobs who sit and ache
  For thy sake.

'Is it dark or light below?
Oh but is it cold like snow?
Dost thou feel the green things grow
  Fast or slow?

'Is it warm or cold beneath,
Oh but is it cold like death?
Cold like death, without a breath,
  Cold like death?'

If he comes to-day,
  He will find her weeping ;
If he comes to-morrow,
  He will find her sleeping ;
If he comes the next day,
  He'll not find her at all—
He may tear his curling hair,
  Beat his breast, and call.
26 *August* 1864.

IF I HAD WORDS

IF I had words, if I had words
  At least to vent my misery :—
But muter than the speechless herds
  I have no voice wherewith to cry.
I have no strength to lift my hands,
  I have no heart to lift mine eye,
My soul is bound with brazen bands,
  My soul is crushed and like to die.
My thoughts that wander here and there,
  That wander wander listlessly,
Bring nothing back to cheer my care,
  Nothing that I may live thereby.
My heart is broken in my breast,
  My breath is but a broken sigh—
Oh if there be a land of rest
  It is far off, it is not nigh.
If I had wings as hath a dove,
  If I had wings that I might fly,
I yet would seek the land of love
  Where fountains run which run not dry :
Though there be none that road to tell,
  And long that road is verily :
Then if I lived I should do well,
  And if I died I should but die.

If I had wings as hath a dove,
  I would not sift the what and why,
I would make haste to find out Love,
  If not to find at least to try.
I would make haste to Love, my rest—
  To Love, my truth that doth not lie :
Then if I lived it might be best,
  Or if I died I could but die.
3 *September* 1864.

JESSIE CAMERON

'JESSIE, Jessie Cameron,
  Hear me but this once,' quoth he.
'Good luck go with you, neighbour's son,
  But I'm no mate for you,' quoth she.
Day was verging toward the night
  There beside the moaning sea :
Dimness overtook the light
  There where the breakers be.
'O Jessie, Jessie Cameron,
  I have loved you long and true.'—
'Good luck go with you, neighbour's son,
  But I'm no mate for you.'

She was a careless fearless girl,
  And made her answer plain,
Outspoken she to earl or churl,
  Kindhearted in the main,
But somewhat heedless with her tongue
  And apt at causing pain ;
A mirthful maiden she and young,
  Most fair for bliss or bane.

'Oh long ago I told you so,
  I tell you so to-day:
Go you your way, and let me go
  Just my own free way.'

The sea swept in with moan and
   foam,
  Quickening the stretch of sand;
They stood almost in sight of home;
  He strove to take her hand.
'Oh can't you take your answer
   then,
  And won't you understand?
For me you're not the man of men,
  I've other plans are planned.
You're good for Madge, or good for
   Cis,
  Or good for Kate, may be:
But what's to me the good of this
  While you're not good for me?'

They stood together on the beach,
  They two alone,
And louder waxed his urgent speech,
  His patience almost gone:
'Oh, say but one kind word to me,
  Jessie, Jessie Cameron.'—
'I'd be too proud to beg,' quoth she,
  And pride was in her tone.
And pride was in her lifted head,
  And in her angry eye,
And in her foot, which might have
   fled
  But would not fly.

Some say that he had gipsy blood,
  That in his heart was guile:
Yet he had gone through fire and
   flood
  Only to win her smile.
Some say his grandam was a witch,
  A black witch from beyond the
   Nile,
Who kept an image in a niche
  And talked with it the while.

And by her hut far down the lane
  Some say they would not pass at
   night,
Lest they should hear an unked strain
  Or see an unked sight.

Alas for Jessie Cameron!—
  The sea crept moaning, moaning
   nigher;
She should have hastened to be-
   gone,—
  The sea swept higher, breaking
   by her:—
She should have hastened to her
   home
  While yet the west was flushed
   with fire,—
But now her feet are in the foam,
  The sea-foam sweeping higher.
O mother, linger at your door,
  And light your lamp to make it
   plain;
But Jessie she comes home no more.
  No more again.

They stood together on the strand,
  They only each by each;
Home, her home, was close at hand.
  Utterly out of reach.
Her mother in the chimney nook
  Heard a startled sea-gull screech,
But never turned her head to look
  Towards the darkening beach:
Neighbours here and neighbours
   there
  Heard one scream, as if a bird
Shrilly screaming cleft the air:—
  That was all they heard.

Jessie she comes home no more,
  Comes home never;
Her lover's step sounds at his door
  No more for ever.
And boats may search upon the sea
  And search along the river,

But none know where the bodies be ;
　Sea-winds that shiver,
Sea-birds that breast the blast,
　Sea-waves swelling,
Keep the secret first and last
　Of their dwelling.

Whether the tide so hemmed them
　　round
　With its pitiless flow
That when they would have gone
　　they found
　No way to go ;
Whether she scorned him to the last
　With words flung to and fro,
Or clung to him when hope was past,
　None will ever know :
Whether he helped or hindered her,
　Threw up his life or lost it well,
The troubled sea for all its stir
　Finds no voice to tell.

Only watchers by the dying
　Have thought they heard one pray
Wordless, urgent ; and replying
　One seem to say him nay :
And watchers by the dead have
　　heard
　A windy swell from miles away,
With sobs and screams, but not a
　　word
　Distinct for them to say :
And watchers out at sea have caught
　Glimpse of a pale gleam here or
　　there,
Come and gone as quick as thought,
　Which might be hand or hair.
　　October 1864.

GROWN AND FLOWN

I LOVED my love from green of
　　Spring
　Until sere Autumn's fall ;
But now that leaves are withering
　How should one love at all ?
　One heart's too small
For hunger, cold, love, everything.

I loved my love on sunny days
　Until late Summer's wane ;
But now that frost begins to glaze
　How should one love again ?
　Nay, love and pain
Walk wide apart in diverse ways.

I loved my love—alas to see
　That this should be, alas !
I thought that this could scarcely
　　be,
　Yet has it come to pass :
　Sweet sweet love was,
Now bitter bitter grown to me.
　　21 *December* 1864.

EVE

'WHILE I sit at the door,
Sick to gaze within,
Mine eye weepeth sore
For sorrow and sin :
As a tree my sin stands
To darken all lands ;
Death is the fruit it bore.

'How have Eden bowers grown
Without Adam to bend them ?
How have Eden flowers blown,
Squandering their sweet breath,
Without me to tend them ?
The Tree of Life was ours,
Tree twelvefold-fruited,
Most lofty tree that flowers,
Most deeply rooted :
I chose the Tree of Death.

'Hadst thou but said me nay,
　Adam my brother,
I might have pined away—
　I, but none other:
God might have let thee stay
　Safe in our garden,
By putting me away
　Beyond all pardon.

'I, Eve, sad mother
　Of all who must live,
I, not another,
　Plucked bitterest fruit to give
My friend, husband, lover.
　O wanton eyes, run over!
Who but I should grieve?
　Cain hath slain his brother:
Of all who must die mother,
　Miserable Eve!'

Thus she sat weeping,
　Thus Eve our mother,
Where one lay sleeping
　Slain by his brother.
Greatest and least
　Each piteous beast
To hear her voice
　Forgot his joys
And set aside his feast.

The mouse paused in his walk
　And dropped his wheaten stalk;
Grave cattle wagged their heads
　In rumination;
The eagle gave a cry
　From his cloud station:
Larks on thyme beds
　Forbore to mount or sing;
Bees drooped upon the wing;
　The raven perched on high
Forgot his ration;
　The conies in their rock,
A feeble nation,
　Quaked sympathetical;

The mocking-bird left off to mock:
　Huge camels knelt as if
In deprecation;
　The kind hart's tears were falling:
Chattered the wistful stork;
　Dove-voices with a dying fall
Cooed desolation,
　Answering grief by grief.

Only the serpent in the dust,
　Wriggling and crawling,
Grinned an evil grin and thrust
　His tongue out with its fork.
　　30 *January* 1865.

SHALL I FORGET?

SHALL I forget on this side of the
　　grave?
I promise nothing: you must wait
　　and see,
　　　Patient and brave.
(O my soul, watch with him, and he
　　with me.)

Shall I forget in peace of Paradise?
I promise nothing: follow, friend,
　　and see,
　　　Faithful and wise.
(O my soul, lead the way he walks
　　with me.)
　　21 *February* 1865.

AMOR MUNDI

'OH where are you going with your
　　love-locks flowing,
　On the west wind blowing along
　　this valley track?'
'The downhill path is easy, come
　　with me an it please ye,
　We shall escape the uphill by
　　never turning back.'

- So they two went together in glowing August weather,
    The honey-breathing heather lay to their left and right;
And dear she was to doat on, her swift feet seemed to float on
    The air like soft twin pigeons too sportive to alight.

'Oh what is that in heaven where grey cloud-flakes are seven,
    Where blackest clouds hang riven just at the rainy skirt?'
'Oh that's a meteor sent us, a message dumb, portentous,
    An undeciphered solemn signal of help or hurt.'

'Oh what is that glides quickly where velvet flowers grow thickly,
    Their scent comes rich and sickly?'
    'A scaled and hooded worm.'
'Oh what's that in the hollow, so pale I quake to follow?'
    'Oh that's a thin dead body which waits the eternal term.'

'Turn again, O my sweetest,—turn again, false and fleetest:
    This beaten way thou beatest, I fear, is hell's own track.'
'Nay, too steep for hill mounting; nay, too late for cost counting:
    This downhill path is easy, but there's no turning back.'
    21 *February* 1865.

FROM SUNSET TO RISE STAR

Go from me, summer friends, and tarry not:
    I am no summer friend, but wintry cold;
A silly sheep benighted from the fold,
A sluggard with a thorn-choked garden plot.
Take counsel, sever from my lot your lot,
    Dwell in your pleasant places, hoard your gold;
    Lest you with me should shiver on the wold,
Athirst and hungering on a barren spot.
For I have hedged me with a thorny hedge,
    I live alone, I look to die alone.
Yet sometimes when a wind sighs through the sedge
Ghosts of my buried years and friends come back,
    My heart goes sighing after swallows flown
On sometime summer's unreturning track.
    22 *February* 1865.

MAGGIE A LADY

You must not call me Maggie, you must not call me Dear,
    For I'm Lady of the Manor now stately to see;
And if there comes a babe, as there may some happy year,
    'Twill be little lord or lady at my knee.

Oh but what ails you, my sailor cousin Phil,
    That you shake and turn white like a cockcrow ghost?
You're as white as I turned once down by the mill,
    When one told me you and ship and crew were lost.

Philip my playfellow, when we were
    boy and girl
      (It was the Miller's Nancy told
      it to me),
Philip with the merry life in lip and
    curl,
    Philip my playfellow drowned in
    the sea!

I thought I should have fainted, but
    I did not faint;
    I stood stunned at the moment,
    scarcely sad,
Till I raised my wail of desolate
    complaint
    For you, my cousin, brother, all
    I had.

They said I looked so pale—some
    say so fair—
    My lord stopped in passing to
    soothe me back to life:
I know I missed a ringlet from my
    hair
    Next morning; and now I am
    his wife.

Look at my gown, Philip, and look
    at my ring—
    I'm all crimson and gold from
    top to toe:
All day long I sit in the sun and
    sing,
    Where in the sun red roses blush
    and blow.

And I'm the rose of roses, says my
    lord;
    And to him I'm more than the
    sun in the sky,
While I hold him fast with the
    golden cord
    Of a curl, with the eyelash of an
    eye.

His mother said fie, and his sisters
    cried shame,
    His highborn ladies cried shame
    from their place:
They said fie when they only heard
    my name,
    But fell silent when they saw my
    face.

Am I so fair, Philip? Philip, did
    you think
    I was so fair when we played boy
    and girl
Where blue forget-me-nots bloomed
    on the brink
    Of our stream which the mill-
    wheel sent awhirl?

If I was fair then, sure I'm fairer
    now,
    Sitting where a score of servants
    stand,
With a coronet on high days for my
    brow
    And almost a sceptre for my hand.

You're but a sailor, Philip, weather-
    beaten brown,
    A stranger on land and at home
    on the sea,
Coasting as best you may from town
    to town:
    Coasting along do you often think
    of me?

I'm a great lady in a sheltered
    bower,
    With hands grown white through
    having nought to do:
Yet sometimes I think of you hour
    after hour
    Till I nigh wish myself a child
    with you.

23 February 1865.

DEAD HOPE

Hope newborn one pleasant morn
  Died at even :
Hope dead lives nevermore,
  No not in heaven.

If his shroud were but a cloud
  To weep itself away—
Or were he buried underground
  To sprout some day !
But dead and gone is dead and gone,
  Vainly wept upon.

Nought we place above his face
  To mark the spot,
But it shows a barren place
  In our lot.

Hope has birth no more on earth
  Morn or even ;
Hope dead lives nevermore,
  No not in heaven.
15 March 1865.

EN ROUTE

Wherefore art thou strange, and
    not my mother?
Thou hast stolen my heart and
    broken it :
Would that I might call thy sons
    'My brother,'
  Call thy daughters 'Sister sweet' :
Lying in thy lap, not in another,
  Dying at thy feet.

  Farewell, land of love, Italy,
  Sister-land of Paradise :
With mine own feet I have trodden
    thee,
  Have seen with mine own eyes :
I remember, thou forgettest me,
  I remember thee.

Blessed be the land that warms my
    heart,
  And the kindly clime that cheers,
And the cordial faces clear from art,
  And the tongue sweet in mine ears:
Take my heart, its truest tenderest
    part,
  · Dear land, take my tears.
June 1865.

ENRICA, 1865

She came among us from the South,
  And made the North her home
    awhile ;
  Our dimness brightened in her
    smile,
Our tongue grew sweeter in her
    mouth.

We chilled beside her liberal glow,
  She dwarfed us by her ampler
    scale,
  Her full-blown blossom made us
    pale—
She Summer-like and we like snow.

We Englishwomen, trim, correct,
  All minted in the selfsame mould,
  Warm-hearted but of semblance
    cold,
All-courteous out of self-respect.

She, woman in her natural grace,
  Less trammelled she by lore of
    school,
  Courteous by nature not by rule,
Warm-hearted and of cordial face.

So for awhile she made her home
  Among us in the rigid North,
  She who from Italy came forth
And scaled the Alps and crossed the
    foam.

But, if she found us like our sea,
  Of aspect colourless and chill,
Rock-girt,—like it she found us still
  Deep at our deepest, strong and free.
1 *July* 1865.

HUSBAND AND WIFE

'OH kiss me once before I go,
  To make amends for sorrow:
Oh kiss me once before we part,
  For we mayn't meet to-morrow.

'And I was wrong to force your will,
  And wrong to mar your life:
But kiss me once before we part
  Because you are my wife.'

She turned her head and tossed her head,
  And puckered up her brow:
'I never kissed you yet,' said she,
  'And I'll not kiss you now.

'Though I'm your wife by might and right
  And forsworn marriage vow,
I never loved you yet,' said she,
  'And I don't love you now.'

So he went sailing on the sea,
  And she sat crossed and dumb,
While he went sailing on the sea
  Where the storm-winds come.

He'd been away a month and day
  Counting from morn to morn:
And many buds had turned to leaves,
  And many lambs been born;
And many buds had turned to flowers
  For Spring was in a glow,
When she was laid upon her bed
  As white and cold as snow.

'Oh let me kiss my baby once,
  Once before I die:
And bring it sometimes to my grave
  To teach it where I lie.

'And tell my husband, when he comes
  Safe back from sea,
To love the baby that I leave
  If ever he loved me:

'And tell him, not for might or right
  Or forsworn marriage vow,
But for the helpless baby's sake,
  I would have kissed him now.'
12 *July* 1865.

ITALIA, IO TI SALUTO

To come back from the sweet South, to the North
  Where I was born, bred, look to die;
Come back to do my day's work in its day,
  Play out my play—
Amen, amen, say I.

To see no more the country half my own,
  Nor hear the half familiar speech,
Amen, I say; I turn to that bleak North
  Whence I came forth—
The South lies out of reach.

But when our swallows fly back to
    the South,
  To the sweet South, to the sweet
    South,
The tears may come again into my
    eyes
    On the old wise,
And the sweet name to my mouth.
Towards July 1865.

WHAT TO DO?

O MY love and my own own deary!
What shall I do? my love is weary.
Sleep, O friend, on soft downy pillow,
Pass, O friend, as wind or as billow,
    And I'll wear the willow.

No stone at his head be set,
A swelling turf be his coverlet,
Bound round with a graveyard
    wattle,
Hedged round from the trampling
    cattle
    And the children's prattle.

I myself, instead of a stone,
Will sit by him to dwindle and
    moan:
Sit and weep with a bitter weeping,
Sit and weep where my love lies
    sleeping,
    While my life goes creeping.
4 August 1865.

A DAUGHTER OF EVE.

A FOOL I was to sleep at noon,
  And wake when night is chilly
Beneath the comfortless cold moon;
A fool to pluck my rose too soon,
  A fool to snap my lily.

My garden-plot I have not kept;
  Faded and all-forsaken,
I weep as I have never wept:
Oh it was summer when I slept,
  It's winter now I waken.

Talk what you please of future
    Spring
  And sun-warmed sweet to-
    morrow:—
Stripped bare of hope and every-
    thing,
No more to laugh, no more to
    sing,
  I sit alone with sorrow.
30 September 1865.

A DIRGE

WHY were you born when the snow
    was falling?
You should have come to the
    cuckoo's calling,
Or when grapes are green in the
    cluster,
Or at least when lithe swallows
    muster
  For their far off flying
  From summer dying.

Why did you die when the lambs
    were cropping?
You should have died at the apples'
    dropping,
When the grasshopper comes to
    trouble,
And the wheat-fields are sodden
    stubble,
  And all winds go sighing
  For sweet things dying.
21 November 1865.

AN 'IMMURATA' SISTER

LIFE flows down to death; we cannot bind
That current that it should not flee:
Life flows down to death, as rivers find
The inevitable sea.

Men work and think, but women feel;
And so (for I'm a woman, I)
And so I should be glad to die,
And cease from impotence of zeal,
And cease from hope, and cease from dread,
And cease from yearnings without gain,
And cease from all this world of pain,
And be at peace among the dead.

Hearts that die, by death renew their youth,
Lightened of this life that doubts and dies;
Silent and contented, while the Truth
Unveiled makes them wise.

Why should I seek and never find
That something which I have not had?
Fair and unutterably sad
The world hath sought time out of mind;
The world hath sought and I have sought,— .
Ah empty world and empty I!
For we have spent our strength for nought,
And soon it will be time to die.

Sparks fly upward toward the fount of fire,
Kindling, flashing, hovering :—
Kindle, flash, my soul; mount higher and higher,
Thou whole burnt-offering!
Circa 1865.

ONCE FOR ALL
(MARGARET)

I SAID: This is a beautiful fresh rose.
I said: I will delight me with its scent,
Will watch its lovely curve of languishment,
Will watch its leaves unclose, its heart unclose.
I said: Old earth has put away her snows,
All living things make merry to their bent,
A flower is come for every flower that went
In autumn, the sun glows, the south wind blows.
So walking in a garden of delight
I came upon one sheltered shadowed nook
Where broad leaf shadows veiled the day with night,
And there lay snow unmelted by the sun :—
I answered: Take who will the path I took,
Winter nips once for all; love is but one.
8 *January* 1866.

A SMILE AND A SIGH

A SMILE because the nights are short!
And every morning brings such pleasure

Of sweet love-making, harmless sport:
  Love that makes and finds its treasure;
  Love, treasure without measure.

A sigh because the days are long!
  Long long these days that pass in sighing,
A burden saddens every song.
  While time lags which should be flying,
  We live who would be dying.
February 1866.

IN A CERTAIN PLACE

I FOUND Love in a certain place
Asleep and cold — or cold and dead?—
All ivory-white upon his bed,
  All ivory-white his face.
  His hands were folded
On his quiet breast,
To his figure laid at rest
  Chilly bed was moulded.

His hair hung lax about his brow,
I had not seen his face before:
Or, if I saw it once, it wore
  Another aspect now.
  No trace of last night's sorrow,
  No shadow of to-morrow:
All at peace (thus all sorrows cease),
  All at peace.

  I wondered: Were his eyes
  Soft or falcon-clear?
  I wondered: As he lies
  Does he feel me near?
  In silence my heart spoke
  And wondered: If he woke
  And found me sitting nigh him
  And felt me sitting by him,
  If life flushed to his cheek,
  He living man with men,
  Then if I heard him speak
  Oh should I know him then?
6 *March* 1866.

CANNOT SWEETEN

'IF that's water you wash your hands in,
  Why is it black as ink is black?'
'Because my hands are foul with my folly:
  Oh the lost time that comes not back!'

'If that's water you bathe your feet in,
  Why is it red as wine is red?'
'Because my feet sought blood in their goings,
  Red, red is the track they tread.'

'Slew you mother or slew you father
  That your foulness passeth not by?'
'Not father, and oh not mother:
  I slew my love with an evil eye.'

'Slew you sister or slew you brother
  That in peace you have not a part?'
'Not brother and oh not sister:
  I slew my love with a hardened heart.

'He loved me because he loved me,
  Not for grace or beauty I had:
He loved me because he loved me:
  For his loving me I was glad.

'Yet I loved him not for his loving,
　While I played with his love and
　　truth,
Not loving him for his loving,
　Wasting his joy, wasting his
　　youth.

'I ate his life as a banquet,
　I drank his life as new wine,
　I fattened upon his leanness,
Mine to flourish and his to pine.

'So his life fled as running water,
　So it perished as water spilt :
If black my hands and my feet as
　　scarlet,
　Blacker, redder my heart of guilt.

'Cold as a stone, as hard, as heavy :
　All my sighs ease it no whit,
All my tears make it no cleaner,
　Dropping, dropping, dropping
　　on it.'
　　8 *March* 1866.

OF MY LIFE

I WEARY of my life
Through the long sultry day,
While happy creatures play
Their harmless lives away :—
　What is my life ?

I weary of my life
Through the slow tedious night,
While, earth and heaven's delight,
The moon walks forth in white :—
　What is my life ?

If I might, I would die :
My soul should flee away
To day that is not day
Where sweet souls sing and say -
　If I might die !

If I might, I would die :
My body out of sight,
All night that is not night
My soul should walk in white—
　If I might die !
15 *May* 1866.

SONG

OH what comes over the sea,
　Shoals and quicksands past :
And what comes home to me,
　Sailing slow, sailing fast ?

A wind comes over the sea
　With a moan in its blast ;
But nothing comes home to me,
　Sailing slow, sailing fast.

Let me be, let me be,
　For my lot is cast :
Land or sea all's one to me,
　And sail it slow or fast.
11 *June* 1866.

FROM METASTASIO

FIRST, last, and dearest,
　My love, mine own,
Thee best belovèd,
　Thee love alone,
Once and for ever
　So love I thee.

First as a suppliant
　Love makes his moan,
Then as a monarch
　Sets up his throne :
Once and for ever—
　So love I thee.
Circa 1868.

AUTUMN VIOLETS

KEEP love for youth, and violets for
    the spring :
  Or if these bloom when worn-out
    autumn grieves
  Let them lie hid in double shade
    of leaves,
Their own, and others' dropped
    down withering ;
For violets suit when home birds
    build and sing,
  Not when the outbound bird a
    passage cleaves ;
  Not with dry stubble of mown
    harvest sheaves,
But when the green world buds to
    blossoming.
Keep violets for the spring, and love
    for youth,
  Love that should dwell with
    beauty, mirth, and hope :
    Or if a later sadder love be
      born,
  Let this not look for grace beyond
    its scope,
But give itself, nor plead for answer-
    ing truth —
    A grateful Ruth tho' gleaning
      scanty corn.

Before 1869.

THEY DESIRE A BETTER COUNTRY *

I

I WOULD not if I could undo my
    past,
  Tho' for its sake my future is a
    blank ;
  My past for which I have myself
    to thank,
    For all its faults and follies first and
      last.
I would not cast anew the lot once
    cast,
  Or launch a second ship for one
    that sank,
  Or drug with sweets the bitterness
    I drank,
Or break by feasting my perpetual
    fast.
I would not if I could : for much
    more dear
  Is one remembrance than a hun-
    dred joys,
    More than a thousand hopes
      in jubilee ;
  Dearer the music of one tearful
    voice
    That unforgotten calls and calls
      to me,
' Follow me here, rise up, and follow
    here.'

II

What seekest thou, far in the un-
    known land ?
  In hope I follow joy gone on
    before ;
  In hope and fear persistent more
    and more,
As the dry desert lengthens out its
    sand.
Whilst day and night I carry in my
    hand
  The golden key to ope the golden
    door
  Of golden home ; yet mine eye
    weepeth sore,
For long the journey is that makes
    no stand.
And who is this that veiled doth
    walk with thee ?
  Lo this is Love that walketh at
    my right ;

One exile holds us both, and
  we are bound
To selfsame home-joys in the land
  of light.
Weeping thou walkest with him;
  weepeth he?—
  Some sobbing weep, some weep
    and make no sound.

III

A dimness of a glory glimmers here
  Thro' veils and distance from the
    space remote;
A faintest far vibration of a note
Reaches to us and seems to bring
  us near;
Causing our face to glow with braver
  cheer,
  Making the serried mist to stand
    afloat,
  Subduing languor with an anti-
    dote,
And strengthening love almost to
  cast out fear:
Till for one moment golden city walls
  Rise looming on us, golden walls
    of home,
Light of our eyes until the darkness
  falls;
  Then thro' the outer darkness
    burdensome
I hear again the tender voice that
  calls,
  'Follow me hither, follow, rise,
    and come.'

Before 1870.

BY WAY OF REMEMBRANCE

REMEMBER, if I claim too much of
  you,
  I claim it of my brother and my
    friend:
Have patience with me till the
  hidden end—
Bitter or sweet, in mercy shut from
  view.
Pay me my due; though I to pay
  your due
Am all too poor, and past what
  will can mend:
Thus of your bounty you must
  give and lend,
Still unrepaid by aught I look to
  do.
Still unrepaid by aught of mine on
  earth:
But overpaid, please God, when
  recompense
Beyond the mystic Jordan and new
  birth
Is dealt to virtue as to innocence.
When Angels singing praises in
  their mirth
Have borne you in their arms
  and fetched you hence.

Will you be there? my yearning
  heart has cried.
Ah me, my love, my love, shall I
  be there,
To sit down in your glory and to
  share
Your gladness, glowing as a virgin
  bride?
Or will another, dearer, fairer-eyed,
  Sit nigher to you in your jubilee,
And mindful one of other will you
  be
Borne higher and higher on joy's
  ebbless tide?
Yea, if I love I will not grudge you
  this:
I too shall float upon that heavenly
  sea
And sing my joyful praises with-
  out ache;

Your overflow of joy shall gladden me,
  My whole heart shall sing praises for your sake,
And find its own fulfilment in your bliss.

In Resurrection is it awfuller
  That rising of the All or of the Each—
Of all kins of all nations of all speech,
Or one by one of *him* and *him* and *her ?*
When dust reanimate begins to stir,
  Here, there, beyond, beyond, reach beyond reach ;
While every wave disgorges on its beach,
Alive or dead-in-life, some seafarer.
In Resurrection, on the day of days,
  That day of mourning throughout all the earth,
    In Resurrection may we meet again :
No more with stricken hearts to part in twain ;
As once in sorrow one, now one in mirth,
One in our resurrection-songs of praise.

I love you and you know it—this at least,
  This comfort is mine own in all my pain :
  You know it, and can never doubt again,
And love's mere self is a continual feast :
Not oath of mine nor blessing-word of priest
  Could make my love more certain or more plain.

Life as a rolling moon doth wax and wane—
O weary moon, still rounding, still decreased !
Life wanes : and when Love folds his wings above
  Tired joy, and less we feel his conscious pulse,
    Let us go fall asleep, dear Friend, in peace ;—
A little while, and age and sorrow cease ;
A little while, and love reborn annuls
Loss and decay and death—and all is love.

Towards October 1870.

AN ECHO FROM WILLOW-WOOD

O ye, all ye that walk in willow-wood.
              D. G. ROSSETTI.

Two gazed into a pool, he gazed and she,
  Not hand in hand, yet heart in heart, I think,
  Pale and reluctant on the water's brink,
As on the brink of parting which must be.
Each eyed the other's aspect, she and he,
  Each felt one hungering heart leap up and sink,
  Each tasted bitterness which both must drink,
There on the brink of life's dividing sea.
Lilies upon the surface, deep below
  Two wistful faces craving each for each,

Resolute and reluctant without
    speech :—
A sudden ripple made the faces flow,
    One moment joined, to vanish out
        of reach :
    So those hearts joined, and ah
        were parted so.
Circa 1870.

THE GERMAN-FRENCH CAMPAIGN

1870-1871

These two pieces, written during the suspense of a great nation's agony, aim at expressing human sympathy, not political bias.

I

THY BROTHER'S BLOOD CRIETH

ALL her corn-fields rippled in the
    sunshine,
    All her lovely vines, sweets-laden,
        bowed ;
Yet some weeks to harvest and to
    vintage :
When, as one man's hand, a cloud
Rose and spread, and, blackening,
    burst asunder
    In rain and fire and thunder.

Is there nought to reap in the day
    of harvest ?
    Hath the vine in her day no fruit
        to yield ?
Yea, men tread the press, but not
    for sweetness,
And they reap a red crop from
    the field.
Build barns, ye reapers, garner all
    aright,
    Though your souls be called
        to-night.

A cry of tears goes up from blacke[n]
    homesteads,
    A cry of blood goes up from re[ek]
        ing earth :
Tears and blood have a cry t[hat]
    pierces Heaven
    Through all its Hallelujah sw[eets]
        of mirth ;
God hears their cry, and though [He]
    tarry, yet
    He doth not forget.

Mournful Mother, prone in dust a[nd]
    weeping,
    Who shall comfort thee for th[ose]
        who are not ?
As thou didst, men do to thee ; an[d]
    heap the measure
    And heat the furnace sevenfol[d]
        hot :
As thou once, now these to thee—
    who pitieth thee
    From sea to sea ?

O thou King, terrible in strength,
    and building
    Thy strong future on thy past !
Though he drink the last, the King
    of Sheshach,
    Yet he shall drink at the last.
Art thou greater than great Babylon,
    Which lies overthrown ?

Take heed, ye unwise among the
    people ;
    O ye fools, when will ye under-
        stand ?—
He that planted the ear shall He
    not hear,
    Nor He smite who formed the
        hand ?
'Vengeance is Mine, is Mine,' thus
    saith the Lord :
    O Man, put up thy sword.

2

'TO-DAY FOR ME'

She sitteth still who used to
    dance,
She weepeth sore and more and
    more :—
Let us sit with thee weeping sore,
    O fair France.

She trembleth as the days advance
Who used to be so light of heart :—
We in thy trembling bear a part,
    Sister France.

Her eyes shine tearful as they
    glance :
'Who shall give back my slaughtered
    sons?
'Bind up,' she saith, 'my wounded
    ones.'—
    Alas, France!

She struggles in a deathly trance,
As in a dream her pulses stir,
She hears the nations calling her,
    'France, France, France!'

Thou people of the lifted lance,
Forbear her tears, forbear her
    blood;
Roll back, roll back, thy whelming
    flood,
    Back from France.

Eye not her loveliness askance,
Forge not for her a galling chain :
Leave her at peace to bloom again,
    Vine-clad France.

A time there is for change and
    chance,
A time for passing of the cup :

And One abides can yet bind up
    Broken France.

A time there is for change and
    chance :
Who next shall drink the trembling
    cup,
Wring out its dregs and suck them
    up
    After France?

Towards January 1871.

VENUS'S LOOKING-GLASS.

I marked where lovely Venus and
    her court
With song and dance and merry
    laugh went by ;
Weightless, their wingless feet
    seemed made to fly,
Bound from the ground, and in mid
    air to sport.
Left far behind I heard the dolphins
    snort,
Tracking their goddess with a
    wistful eye,
Around whose head white doves
    rose, wheeling high
Or low, and cooed after their tender
    sort.
All this I saw in Spring. Through
    summer heat
I saw the lovely Queen of Love
    no more.
But when flushed Autumn
    through the woodlands went
I spied sweet Venus walk amid the
    wheat :
Whom seeing, every harvester
    gave o'er
His toil, and laught and hoped
    and was content.

October 1872.

LOVE LIES BLEEDING

Love, that is dead and buried, yesterday
  Out of his grave rose up before my face;
  No recognition in his look, no trace
Of memory in his eyes dust-dimmed and grey;
  While I, remembering, found no word to say,
  But felt my quickened heart leap in its place;
  Caught afterglow thrown back from long-set days,
Caught echoes of all music past away.
Was this indeed to meet?—I mind me yet
  In youth we met when hope and love were quick,
    We parted with hope dead but love alive:
I mind me how we parted then heart-sick,
  Remembering, loving, hopeless, weak to strive:—
Was this to meet? Not so, we have not met.

Circa 1872.

DAYS OF VANITY

  A dream that waketh,
  Bubble that breaketh,
Song whose burden sigheth,
  A passing breath,
  Smoke that vanisheth,—
Such is life that dieth.

  A flower that fadeth,
  Fruit the tree sheddeth,
Trackless bird that flieth,
  Summer time brief,—
  Falling of the leaf,—
Such is life that dieth.

  A scent exhaling,
  Snow waters failing,
Morning dew that drieth,
  A windy blast,
  Lengthening shadows cast,
Such is life that dieth.

  A scanty measure,
  Rust-eaten treasure,
Spending that nought buyeth,
  Moth on the wing,
  Toil unprofiting,—
Such is life that dieth.

  Morrow by morrow
  Sorrow breeds sorrow,
For this my song sigheth;
  From day to night
  We lapse out of sight.—
Such is life that dieth.

Before 1873.

A BIRD SONG

It's a year almost that I have not seen her:
Oh last summer green things were greener,
Brambles fewer, the blue sky bluer!

It's surely summer, for there's a swallow:
Come one swallow, his mate will follow,
The bird-race quicken, and wheel and thicken.

Oh happy swallow whose mate will
  follow
O'er height, o'er hollow! I'd be a
  swallow,
To build this weather one nest
  together.
Before 1873.

COR MIO

STILL sometimes in my secret heart
  of hearts
  I say 'Cor mio' when I remember
    you,
  And thus I yield us both one
    tender due,
Welding one whole of two divided
  parts.
Ah Friend, too wise or unwise for
  such arts,
  Ah noble Friend, silent and strong
    and true,
  Would you have given me roses
    for the rue
For which I bartered roses in love's
  marts?
So late in autumn one forgets the
  spring,
  Forgets the summer with its
    opulence,
The callow birds that long have
  found a wing,
  The swallows that more lately got
    them hence:
Will anything like spring, will any-
  thing
  Like summer, rouse one day the
    slumbering sense?
Circa 1875.

MEETING

I SAID good-bye in hope;
  But, now we meet again,
I have no hope at all
  Of anything but pain,—
Our parting and our meeting
  Alike in vain.

Hope on through all your life
  Until the end, dear friend:
Live through your noble life
  Where joy and promise blend—
I too will live my life
  Until the end.

Long may your vine entwine,
Long may your fig-tree spread,
Their paradise of shade
Above your cherished head:
My shelter was a gourd,
  And it is dead.

Yet, when out of a grave
We are gathered home at last,
  Then may we own life spilt
No good worth holding fast:—
Death had its bitterness,
  But it is past.
Circa 1875.

A GREEN CORNFIELD

'And singing still dost soar and soaring
  ever singest.'

THE earth was green, the sky was
    blue:
  I saw and heard one sunny morn
A skylark hang between the two,
  A singing speck above the corn;

A stage below, in gay accord,
  White butterflies danced on the
    wing,
And still the singing skylark soared,
  And silent sank and soared to
    sing.

The cornfield stretched a tender green
  To right and left beside my walks;
I knew he had a nest unseen
  Somewhere among the million stalks.

And as I paused to hear his song
  While swift the sunny moments slid,
Perhaps his mate sat listening long,
  And listened longer than I did.
    Before 1876.

A BRIDE SONG

THROUGH the vales to my love!
To the happy small nest of home
Green from basement to roof;
Where the honey-bees come
To the window-sill flowers,
  And dive from above,
Safe from the spider that weaves
  Her warp and her woof
  In some outermost leaves.

Through the vales to my love!
  In sweet April hours
All rainbows and showers,
While dove answers dove,—
  In beautiful May,
When the orchards are tender
And frothing with flowers,—
  In opulent June
When the wheat stands up slender
By sweet-smelling hay,
And half the sun's splendour
Descends to the moon.

Through the vales to my love!
Where the turf is so soft to the feet
  And the thyme makes it sweet,
  And the stately foxglove
Hangs silent its exquisite bells;

And where water wells
The greenness grows greener,
And bulrushes stand
Round a lily to screen her.

Nevertheless, if this land,
Like a garden to smell and to sight,
Were turned to a desert of sand;
  Stripped bare of delight,
  All its best gone to worst,
  For my feet no repose,
No water to comfort my thirst,
And heaven like a furnace above.—
  The desert would be
As gushing of waters to me,
The wilderness be as a rose,
  If it led me to thee,
    O my love.
    Before 1876.

CONFLUENTS

As rivers seek the sea,
  Much more deep than they,
So my soul seeks thee
    Far away:
As running rivers moan
On their course alone,
    So I moan
    Left alone.

As the delicate rose
  To the sun's sweet strength
Doth herself unclose,
  Breadth and length;
So spreads my heart to thee
Unveiled utterly,
    I to thee
    Utterly.

As morning dew exhales
  Sunwards pure and free

So my spirit fails
  After thee.
As dew leaves not a trace
On the green earth's face;
  I, no trace
  On thy face.

Its goal the river knows,
  Dewdrops find a way,
Sunlight cheers the rose
  In her day:
Shall I, lone sorrow past,
Find thee at the last?
  Sorrow past,
  Thee at last?
Before 1876.

BIRD RAPTURES

THE sunrise wakes the lark to sing,
  The moonrise wakes the nightingale.
Come darkness, moonrise, everything
That is so silent, sweet, and pale,
Come, so ye wake the nightingale.

Make haste to mount, thou wistful moon,
  Make haste to wake the nightingale:
Let silence set the world in tune
To hearken to that wordless tale
Which warbles from the nightingale.

O herald skylark, stay thy flight
One moment, for a nightingale
Floods us with sorrow and delight.
  To-morrow thou shalt hoist the sail;
  Leave us to-night the nightingale.
Before 1876.

VALENTINES TO MY MOTHER

1876

FAIRER than younger beauties, more beloved
  Than many a wife,
By stress of Time's vicissitudes unmoved
  From settled calm of life;

Endearing rectitude to those who watch
  The verdict of your face,
Raising and making gracious those who catch
  A semblance of your grace:

With kindly lips of welcome, and with pleased
  Propitious eyes benign,
Accept a kiss of homage from your least
  Last Valentine.

1877

OWN Mother dear,
We all rejoicing here
Wait for each other,
Daughter for Mother,
Sister for Brother,
Till each dear face appear
Transfigured by Love's flame
  Yet still the same,—
  The same yet new,—
My face to you,
Your face to me,
Made lovelier by Love's flame
  But still the same;
  Most dear to see
In halo of Love's flame,
Because the same.
                C. G. for M. F. R.

1878

BLESSED Dear and Heart's Delight,
  Companion, Friend, and Mother mine,
  Round whom my fears and love entwine,—
  With whom I hope to stand and sing
  Where angels form the outer ring
Round singing Saints who, clad in white,
Know no more of day or night
  Or death or any changeful thing,
  Or anything that is not love,
Human love and Love Divine,—
  Bid me to that tryst above,
  Bless your Valentine.

1879

MOTHER mine,
  Whom every year
  Doth endear,—
Before sweet Spring
(That sweetest thing
Brimfull of bliss)
  Sets all the throng
    Of birds a-wooing,
    Billing and cooing,—
Your Valentine
  Sings you a song,
  Gives you a kiss.

1880

MORE shower than shine
  Brings sweet St. Valentine;
Warm shine, warm shower,
Bring up sweet flower on flower.
  Through shower and shine
Loves you your Valentine.
  Through shine, through shower,
Through summer's flush, through autumn's fading hour.

1881

Too cold almost for hope of Spring,
  Or firstfruits from the realm of flowers,
Your dauntless Valentine, I bring
  One sprig of love, and sing
  'Love has no Winter hours.'

If even in this world love is love
  (This wintry world which felt the Fall),
What must it be in heaven above
  Where love to great and small
  Is all in all?

1882

MY blessed Mother dozing in her chair
  On Christmas Day seemed an embodied Love,—
A comfortable Love with soft brown hair
  Softened and silvered to a tint of dove;
A better sort of Venus with an air
  Angelical from thoughts that dwell above;
A wiser Pallas in whose body fair
  Enshrined a blessed soul looks out thereof.
Winter brought holly then; now Spring has brought
  Paler and frailer snowdrops shivering;
And I have brought a simple humble thought—
  I her devoted duteous Valentine—
A lifelong thought which thrills this song I sing,
  A lifelong love to this dear Saint of mine.

1883

A world of change and loss, a world of death,
Of heart and eyes that fail, of labouring breath,
Of pains to bear and painful deeds to do :—
Nevertheless a world of life to come
And love ; where you're at home, while in our home
Your Valentine rejoices, having you.

1884

Another year of joy and grief,
Another year of hope and fear :
O Mother, is life long or brief?
We hasten while we linger here.

But, since we linger, love me still
And bless me still, O Mother mine,
While hand in hand we scale life's hill,
You guide, and I your Valentine.

1885

All the Robin Redbreasts
Have lived the winter through,
Jenny Wrens have pecked their fill
And found a work to do ;
Families of Sparrows
Have weathered wind and storm
With Rabbit on the stony hill
And Hare upon her form.

You and I, my Mother,
Have lived the winter through,
And still we play our daily parts
And still find work to do :
And still the cornfields flourish,
The olive and the vine,
And still you reign my Queen of Hearts
And I'm your Valentine.

1886

Winter's latest snowflake is the snowdrop flower,
Yellow crocus kindles the first flame of the Spring,
At that time appointed, at that day and hour,
When life reawakens and hope in everything.

Such a tender snowflake in the wintry weather,
Such a feeble flamelet for chilled St. Valentine,—
But blest be any weather which finds us still together,
My pleasure and my treasure, O blessed Mother mine.

MIRRORS OF LIFE AND DEATH

The mystery of Life, the mystery
Of Death, I see
Darkly as in a glass ;
Their shadows pass,
And talk with me.

As the flush of a Morning Sky,
As a Morning Sky colourless —
Each yields its measure of light
To a wet world or a dry ;
Each fares through day to night
With equal pace,
And then each one
Is done.

As the Sun with glory and grace
In his face,
Benignantly hot,
Graciously radiant and keen,
Ready to rise and to run,—
Not without spot,
Not even the Sun.

As the Moon
On the wax, on the wane,
With night for her noon;
Vanishing soon,
To appear again.

As Roses that droop
Half warm, half chill, in the languid
    May,
And breathe out a scent
Sweet and faint;
Till the wind gives one swoop
To scatter their beauty away.

As Lilies a multitude,
One dipping, one rising, one sinking,
On rippling waters, clear blue
And pure for their drinking;
One new dead, and one opened anew,
And all good.

As a cankered pale Flower,
With death for a dower,
Each hour of its life half dead;
With death for a crown
Weighing down
Its head.

As an Eagle, half strength and half
    grace,
Most potent to face
Unwinking the splendour of light;
Harrying the East and the West,
Soaring aloft from our sight;
Yet one day or one night dropped
    to rest
On the low common earth
Of his birth.

As a Dove,
Not alone,
In a world of her own
Full of fluttering soft noises
And tender sweet voices
Of love.

As a Mouse
Keeping house
In the fork of a tree,
With nuts in a crevice,
And an acorn or two;
What cares he
For blossoming boughs,
Or the song-singing bevies
Of birds in their glee,
Scarlet, or golden, or blue?

As a Mole grubbing underground:
When it comes to the light
It grubs its way back again,
Feeling no bias of fur
To hamper it in its stir,
Scant of pleasure and pain,
Sinking itself out of sight
Without sound.

As Waters that drop and drop,
Weariness without end,
That drop and never stop,
Wear that nothing can mend,
Till one day they drop—
Stop—
And there's an end,
And matters mend.

As Trees, beneath whose skin
We mark not the sap begin
To swell and rise,
Till the whole bursts out in green
We mark the falling leaves
When the wide world grieves
And sighs.

As a Forest on fire,
Where maddened creatures desire
Wet mud or wings
Beyond all those things
Which could assuage desire
On this side the flaming fire.

As Wind with a sob and sigh
To which there comes no reply

But a rustle and shiver
From rushes of the river;
As Wind with a desolate moan,
Moaning on alone.

As a Desert all sand,
Blank, neither water nor land
For solace or dwelling or culture,
Where the storms and the wild
    creatures howl;
Given over to lion and vulture,
To ostrich and jackal and owl:
Yet somewhere an oasis lies;
There waters arise
To nourish one seedling of balm
Perhaps, or one palm.

As the Sea,
Murmuring, shifting, swaying;
One time sunnily playing,
One time wrecking and slaying;
In whichever mood it be,
Worst or best,
Never at rest.

As still Waters and deep,
As shallow Waters that brawl,
As rapid Waters that leap
To their fall.

As Music, as Colour, as Shape,
Keys of rapture and pain
Turning in vain
In a lock which turns not again,
While breaths and moments escape.

As Spring, all bloom and desire;
As Summer, all gift and fire;
As Autumn, a dying glow;
As Winter, with nought to show:

Winter which lays its dead all out
    of sight,
All clothed in white,
All waiting for the long-awaited light.
Before 1878.

AN OCTOBER GARDEN

In my Autumn garden I was fain
    To mourn among my scattered
        roses;
    Alas for that last rosebud which
        uncloses
To Autumn's languid sun and rain
When all the world is on the wane!
    Which has not felt the sweet
        constraint of June,
    Nor heard the nightingale in tune.

Broad-faced asters by my garden
    walk,
    You are but coarse compared with
        roses:
    More choice, more dear that rose-
        bud which uncloses,
Faint-scented, pinched, upon its stalk,
That least and last which cold winds
    balk;
    A rose it is though least and last
        of all,
    A rose to me though at the fall.
Before 1878.

FREAKS OF FASHION

Such a hubbub in the nests,
    Such a bustle and squeak!
Nestlings, guiltless of a feather,
    Learning just to speak,
Ask—' And how about the fashions?'
    From a cavernous beak.

Perched on bushes, perched on
    hedges,
    Perched on firm hahas,
Perched on anything that holds them,
    Gay papas and grave mammas
Teach the knowledge-thirsty nest-
    lings:
    Hear the gay papas.

Robin says; 'A scarlet waistcoat
  Will be all the wear,
Snug, and also cheerful-looking
  For the frostiest air,
Comfortable for the chest too
  When one comes to plume and
    pair.'

'Neat grey hoods will be in vogue,'
  Quoth a Jackdaw; 'glossy grey,
Setting close, yet setting easy,
  Nothing fly-away;
Suited to our misty mornings,
  À la négligée.'

Flushing salmon, flushing sulphur,
  Haughty Cockatoos
Answer—'Hoods may do for mornings,
  But for evenings choose
High head-dresses, curved like crescents
  Such as well-bred persons use.'

'Top-knots, yes; yet more essential
  Still, a train or tail,'
Screamed the Peacock: 'gemmed and lustrous,
  Not too stiff, and not too frail;
Those are best which rearrange as
  Fans, and spread or trail.'

Spoke the Swan, entrenched behind
  An inimitable neck:
'After all, there's nothing sweeter
  For the lawn or lake
Than simple white, if fine and flaky
  And absolutely free from speck.'

'Yellow,' hinted a Canary,
  'Warmer, not less *distingué*.'
'Peach colour,' put in a Lory,
  'Cannot look *outré*.'
'All the colours are in fashion,
  And are right,' the Parrots say.

'Very well. But do contrast
  Tints harmonious,'
Piped a Blackbird, justly proud
  Of bill aurigerous;
'Half the world may learn a lesson
  As to that from us.'

Then a Stork took up the word:
  'Aim at height and *chic*:'
Not high heels, they're common; somehow,
  Stilted legs, not thick,
Nor yet thin;' he just glanced downward
  And snapped to his beak.

Here a rustling and a whirring,
  As of fans outspread,
Hinted that mammas felt anxious
  Lest the next thing said
Might prove less than quite judicious,
  Or even underbred.

So a mother Auk resumed
  The broken thread of speech:
'Let colours sort themselves, my dears,
  Yellow, or red, or peach;
The main points, as it seems to me,
  We mothers have to teach,

'Are form and texture, elegance,
  An air reserved, sublime;
The mode of wearing what we wear
  With due regard to month and clime.
But now, let's all compose ourselves,
  It's almost breakfast-time.'

A hubbub, a squeak, a bustle!
  Who cares to chatter or sing
With delightful breakfast coming?
  Yet they whisper under the wing:
'So we may wear whatever we like,
  Anything, everything!'

Circa 1878.

YET A LITTLE WHILE

DREAMED and did not seek: to-
    day I seek
  Who can no longer dream;
But now am all behindhand, waxen
    weak,
  And dazed amid so many things
    that gleam
  Yet are not what they seem.

I dreamed and did not work: to-day
    I work,
  Kept wide awake by care
And loss, and perils dimly guessed
    to lurk;
  I work and reap not, while my
    life goes bare
  And void in wintry air.

I hope indeed; but hope itself is fear
  Viewed on the sunny side;
I hope, and disregard the world
    that's here,
  The prizes drawn, the sweet things
    that betide;
  I hope, and I abide.
Before 1879.

PARTED

  HAD Fortune parted us,
    Fortune is blind;
  Had Anger parted us,
    Anger unkind—
  But since God parts us
    Let us part humbly,
  Bearing our burden
    Bravely and dumbly.

  And since there is but one
    Heaven, not another,
  Let us not close that door
    Against each other.

God's Love is higher than mine,
  Christ's tenfold proved,
Yet even I would die
  For thee, Beloved.
Circa 1880.

TO-DAY'S BURDEN

'ARISE, depart, for this is not your
    rest.'—
  Oh burden of all burdens, still to
    arise
  And still depart nor rest in any
    wise!
Rolling, still rolling thus from East
    to West,
  Earth journeys on her immemorial
    quest,
  Whom a moon chases in no
    different guise.
Thus stars pursue their courses,
    and thus flies
The sun, and thus all creatures
    manifest
Unrest the common heritage, the ban
  Flung broadcast to all humankind,
    on all
  Who live—for, living, all are
    bound to die.
That which is old, we know that it
    is man.
  These have no rest who sit and
    dream and sigh,
  Nor have those rest who wrestle
    and who fall.
Circa 1881.

THE KEY-NOTE

WHERE are the songs I used to
    know,
  Where are the notes I used to
    sing?

I have forgotten everything
I used to know so long ago;
Summer has followed after Spring;
  Now Autumn is so shrunk and sere
I scarcely think a sadder thing
  Can be the Winter of my year.

Yet Robin sings through Winter's
  rest,
  When bushes put their berries on;
  While they their ruddy jewels don,
He sings out of a ruddy breast;
The hips and haws and ruddy breast
  Make one spot warm where snow-
    flakes lie;
They break and cheer the unlovely
  rest
  Of Winter's pause—and why not
    I?
Before 1882.

HE AND SHE

'SHOULD one of us remember,
  And one of us forget,
I wish I knew what each will do,
  But who can tell as yet?'

'Should one of us remember,
  And one of us forget,
I promise you what I will do—
And I'm content to wait for you,
  And not be sure as yet.'
Before 1882.

'LUSCIOUS AND SORROW-
FUL'

BEAUTIFUL, tender, wasting away
  for sorrow;
Thus to-day; and how shall it be
  with thee to-morrow?
Beautiful, tender—what else?
  A hope tells.

Beautiful, tender, keeping the jubi-
In the land of home together, pa-
  death and sea;
No more change or death.
  more
    Salt sea-shore.
Before 1882.

DE PROFUNDIS

OH why is heaven built so far,
  Oh why is earth set so remote?
I cannot reach the nearest star
  That hangs afloat.

I would not care to reach the moon,
  One round monotonous of change;
Yet even she repeats her tune
  Beyond my range.

I never watch the scattered fire
  Of stars, or sun's far-trailing train.
But all my heart is one desire,
  And all in vain:

For I am bound with fleshly bands,
  Joy, beauty, lie beyond my scope:
I strain my heart, I stretch my hands,
  And catch at hope.
Before 1882.

TEMPUS FUGIT

LOVELY Spring,
A brief sweet thing,
Is swift on the wing;
Gracious Summer,
A slow sweet comer,
Hastens past;
Autumn while sweet
Is all incomplete
With a moaning blast.
Nothing can last,

Can be cleaved unto,
Can be dwelt upon.
It is hurried through,
It is come and gone,
Undone it cannot be done ;
It is ever to do,
Ever old, ever new,
Ever waxing old
And lapsing to Winter cold.
Before 1882.

GOLDEN GLORIES

THE buttercup is like a golden cup,
    The marigold is like a golden frill,
The daisy with a golden eye looks up,
    And golden spreads the flag beside the rill,
    And gay and golden nods the daffodil ;
The gorsey common swells a golden sea,
    The cowslip hangs a head of golden tips,
And golden drips the honey which the bee
    Sucks from sweet hearts of flowers and stores and sips.
Before 1882.

JOHNNY

FOUNDED ON AN ANECDOTE OF THE FIRST FRENCH REVOLUTION

JOHNNY had a golden head
    Like a golden mop in blow,
Right and left his curls would spread
    In a glory and a glow,
And they framed his honest face
Like stray sunbeams out of place.

Long and thick, they half could hide
    How threadbare his patched jacket hung ;
They used to be his Mother's pride ;
    She praised them with a tender tongue,
And stroked them with a loving finger
That smoothed and stroked and loved to linger.

On a doorstep Johnny sat,
    Up and down the street looked he ;
Johnny did not own a hat,
    Hot or cold tho' days might be ;
Johnny did not own a boot
To cover up his muddy foot.

Johnny's face was pale and thin,
    Pale with hunger and with crying ;
For his Mother lay within,
    Talked and tossed and seemed a-dying,
While Johnny racked his brains to think
How to get her help and drink,

Get her physic, get her tea,
    Get her bread and something nice ;
Not a penny piece had he,
    And scarce a shilling might suffice ;
No wonder that his soul was sad,
When not one penny piece he had.

As he sat there thinking, moping,
    Because his Mother's wants were many,
Wishing much but scarcely hoping
    To earn a shilling or a penny,
A friendly neighbour passed him by,
And questioned him, why did he cry.

Alas his trouble soon was told:
  He did not cry for cold or hunger,
Though he was hungry both and
    cold;
  He only felt more weak and
    younger,
Because he wished so to be old
And apt at earning pence or gold.

Kindly that neighbour was, but poor,
  Scant coin had he to give or
    lend;
And well he guessed there needed
    more
Than pence or shillings to befriend
The helpless woman in her strait,
So much loved, yet so desolate.

One way he saw, and only one:
  He would—he could—not give
    the advice,
And yet he must: the widow's son
  Had curls of gold would fetch their
    price;
Long curls which might be clipped,
    and sold
For silver, or perhaps for gold.

Our Johnny, when he understood
  Which shop it was that purchased
    hair,
Ran off as briskly as he could,
  And in a trice stood cropped and
    bare,
Too short of hair to fill a locket,
But jingling money in his pocket.

Precious money—tea and bread,
  Physic, ease, for Mother dear,
Better than a golden head:
  Yet our hero dropped one tear
When he spied himself close shorn,
Barer much than lamb new-born.

His Mother throve upon the mon
  Ate and revived and kissed
    son:
But oh when she perceived
    Johnny,
  And understood what he had d
All and only for her sake,
She sobbed as if her heart m
    break.

Before 1882.

'HOLLOW-SOUNDING AN
    MYSTERIOUS'

THERE'S no replying
To the Wind's sighing;
Telling, foretelling,
Dying, undying,
Dwindling and swelling,
Complaining, droning,
Whistling and moaning,
Ever beginning,
Ending, repeating,
Hinting and dinning,
Lagging and fleeting;—
We've no replying
Living or dying
To the Wind's sighing.

What are you telling,
Variable Wind-tone?
What would be teaching,
O sinking, swelling,
Desolate Wind-moan?
Ever for ever
Teaching and preaching,
Never, ah never
Making us wiser.
The earliest riser
Catches no meaning,
The last who hearkens
Garners no gleaning
Of wisdom's treasure,
While the world darkens.

       Living or dying,
       In pain, in pleasure,
       We've no replying
       To wordless, flying
       Wind's sighing.
Before 1882.

MAIDEN MAY

MAIDEN May sat in her bower,
In her blush rose bower in flower,
    Sweet of scent ;
Sat and dreamed away an hour,
    Half content, half uncontent.

Why should rose blossoms be born,
Tender blossoms, on a thorn,
    Though so sweet ?
Never a thorn besets the corn,
    Scentless, in its strength complete.

' Why are roses all so frail,
At the mercy of a gale,
    Of a breath ?
Yet so sweet and perfect pale,
    Still so sweet in life and death.'

Maiden May sat in her bower,
In her blush rose bower in flower,
    Where a linnet
Made one bristling branch the tower
    For her nest and young ones in it.

' Gay and clear the linnet trills ;
Yet the skylark, only, thrills
    Heaven and earth,
When he breasts the height, and fills
    Height and depth with song and
        mirth.

' Nightingales which yield to night
Solitary strange delight
    Reign alone :
But the lark for all his height
    Fills no solitary throne.

' While he sings, a hundred sing ;
Wing their flight, below his wing,
    Yet in flight ;
Each a lovely joyful thing
    To the measure of its delight.

' Why then should a lark be reckoned
One alone, without a second
    Near his throne ?
He in skyward flight unslackened,
    In his music, not alone.'

Maiden May sat in her bower ;
Her own face was like a flower
    Of the prime,
Half in sunshine, half in shower,
    In the year's most tender time.

Her own thoughts in silent song
Musically flowed along,
    Wise, unwise,
Wistful, wondering, weak or strong :
    As brook shallows sink or rise.

Other thoughts another day,
Maiden May, will surge and sway
    Round your heart ;
Wake, and plead, and turn at bay,
    Wisdom part, and folly part.

Time not far remote will borrow
Other joys, another sorrow,
    All for you ;
Not to-day, and yet to-morrow
    Reasoning false and reasoning
        true.

Wherefore greatest ?   Wherefore
        least ?
Hearts that starve and hearts that
        feast ?
    You and I ?
Stammering Oracles have ceased,
    And the whole earth stands at
        ' why ? '

Underneath all things that be
Lies an unsolved mystery;
   Over all
Spreads a veil impenetrably,
   Spreads a dense unlifted pall.

Mystery of mysteries;
This creation hears and sees
   High and low:
Vanity of vanities;
   This we test and *this* we know.

Maiden May, the days of flowering
Nurse you now in sweet embowering,
   Sunny days;
Bright with rainbows all the showering,
   Bright with blossoms all the ways.

Close the inlet of your bower,
Close it close with thorn and flower,
   Maiden May;
Lengthen out the shortening hour,—
   Morrows are not as to-day.

Stay to-day which wanes too soon,
Stay the sun and stay the moon,
   Stay your youth;
Bask you in the actual noon,
   Rest you in the present truth.

Let to-day suffice to-day:
For itself to-morrow may
   Fetch its loss,
Aim and stumble, say its say,
   Watch and pray and bear its cross.

Before 1882.

TILL TO-MORROW

LONG have I longed, till I am tired
   Of longing and desire;
Farewell my points in vain desired,
   My dying fire;
Farewell all things that die and tire.

Springtide and youth and useless pleasure
   And all my useless scheming,
My hopes of unattainable treasure,
   Dreams not worth dreaming,
Glow-worms that gleam but yield no warmth in gleaming,—

Farewell all shows that fade showing:
   My wish and joy stand over
Until to-morrow; Heaven is glowing
   Through cloudy cover;
Beyond all clouds loves me my Heavenly Lover.

Before 1882.

DEATH-WATCHES

THE Spring spreads one green lap of flowers
   Which Autumn buries at the fall.
No chilling showers of Autumn hours
   Can stay them or recall;
Winds sing a dirge, while earth lays out of sight
   Her garment of delight.

The cloven East brings forth the sun,
   The cloven West doth bury him
What time his gorgeous race is run,
   And all the world grows dim;
A funeral moon is lit in heaven's hollow,
   And pale the star-lights follow.

Before 1882.

TOUCHING 'NEVER'

BECAUSE you never yet have loved
  me, dear,
    Think you you never can nor
      ever will?
    Surely while life remains hope
      lingers still,
Hope the last blossom of life's dying
  year.
Because the season and mine age
  grow sere,
    Shall never Spring bring forth
      her daffodil,
    Shall never sweeter Summer feast
      her fill
Of roses with the nightingales they
  hear?
If you had loved me, I not loving
    you,
    If you had urged me with the
      tender plea
Of what our unknown years to come
  might do
(Eternal years, if Time should count
  too few),
  I would have owned the point
    you pressed on me
Was possible, or probable, or true.

Before 1882.

BRANDONS BOTH.

OH fair Milly Brandon, a young
  maid, a fair maid!
    All her curls are yellow and her
      eyes are blue,
    And her cheeks were rosy red till a
      secret care made
  Hollow whiteness of their bright-
    ness as a care will do.

Still she tends her flowers, but not
  as in the old days,
  Still she sings her songs, but not
    the songs of old:
If now it be high Summer her days
  seem brief and cold days,
  If now it be high Summer her
    nights are long and cold.

If you have a secret, keep it, pure
  maid Milly;
  Life is filled with troubles and the
    world with scorn;
And pity without love is at best
  times hard and chilly,
  Chilling sore and stinging sore a
    heart forlorn.

Walter Brandon, do you guess Milly
  Brandon's secret?
  Many things you know, but not
    everything,
With your locks like raven's plumage,
  and eyes like an egret,
  And a laugh that is music, and
    such a voice to sing.

Nelly Knollys, she is fair, but she is
  not fairer
  Than fairest Milly Brandon was
    before she turned so pale:
Oh but Nelly's dearer if she be not
  rarer,
  She need not keep a secret or
    blush behind a veil.

Beyond the first green hills, beyond
  the nearest valleys,
  Nelly dwells at home beneath her
    mother's eyes:
Her home is neat and homely, not
  a cot and not a palace,
  Just the home where love sets up
    his happiest memories.

Milly has no mother; and sad
   beyond another
Is she whose blessed mother is
   vanished out of call :
Truly comfort beyond comfort is
   stored up in a mother
Who bears with all, and hopes
   through all, and loves us all.

Where peacocks nod and flaunt up
   and down the terrace,
Furling and unfurling their scores
   of sightless eyes,
To and fro among the leaves and
   buds and flowers and berries
Maiden Milly strolls and pauses,
   smiles and sighs.

On the hedged-in terrace of her
   father's palace
She may stroll and muse alone,
   may smile or sigh alone,
Letting thoughts and eyes go wandering over hills and valleys
To-day her father's, and one day
   to be all her own.

If her thoughts go coursing down
   lowlands and up highlands,
It is because the startled game
   are leaping from their lair ;
If her thoughts dart homeward to
   the reedy river islands,
It is because the waterfowl rise
   startled here or there.

At length a footfall on the steps :
   she turns, composed and
   steady,
All the long-descended greatness
   of her father's house
Lifting up her head ; and there
   stands Walter keen and ready
For hunting or for hawking, a
   flush upon his brows.

'Good-morrow, fair cousin.' 'Good
   morrow, fairest cousin :
The sun has started on his course,
   and I must start to-day :
If you have done me one good turn
   you've done me many a dozen,
And I shall often think of you,
   think of you away.'

'Over hill and hollow what quarry
   will you follow,
Or what fish will you angle for
   beside the river's edge ?
There's cloud upon the hill-top and
   there's mist deep down the
   hollow,
And fog among the rushes and
   the rustling sedge.'

'I shall speed well enough be it
   hunting or hawking,
Or casting a bait toward the
   shyest daintiest fin.
But I kiss your hands, my cousin,
   I must not loiter talking,
For nothing comes of nothing,
   and I'm fain to seek and win.'

'Here's a thorny rose : will you
   wear it an hour,
Till the petals drop apart still
   fresh and pink and sweet ?
Till the petals drop from the drooping perished flower,
And only the graceless thorns are
   left of it.'

'Nay, I have another rose sprung
   in another garden,
Another rose which sweetens all
   the world for me.
Be you a tenderer mistress and be
   you a warier warden
Of your rose, as sweet as mine,
   and full as fair to see.'

'Nay, a bud once plucked there is
    no reviving,
  Nor is it worth your wearing now,
    nor worth indeed my own;
The dead to the dead, and the
    living to the living.
  It's time I go within, for it's time
    now you were gone.'

'Good-bye, Milly Brandon, I shall
    not forget you,
  Though it be good-bye between
    us for ever from to-day;
I could almost wish to-day that I
    had never met you,
  And I'm true to you in this one
    word that I say.'

'Good-bye, Walter. I can guess
    which thornless rose you covet;
  Long may it bloom and prolong
    its sunny morn:
Yet as for my one thorny rose, I do
    not cease to love it,
  And if it is no more a flower I
    love it as a thorn.'

Before 1882.

A LIFE'S PARALLELS

NEVER on this side of the grave
    again,
  On this side of the river,
On this side of the garner of the
    grain,
  Never.

Ever while time flows on and on and
    on,
  That narrow noiseless river,
Ever while corn bows heavy-headed,
    wan,
  Ever.

Never despairing, often fainting,
    rueing,
  But looking back, ah never!
Faint yet pursuing, faint yet still
    pursuing
  Ever.

Before 1882.

AT LAST

MANY have sung of love a root of
    bane:
  While to my mind a root of balm
    it is,
  For love at length breeds love;
    sufficient bliss
For life and death and rising up
    again.
Surely when light of Heaven makes
    all things plain,
  Love will grow plain with all its
    mysteries;
  Nor shall we need to fetch from
    over seas
Wisdom or wealth or pleasure safe
    from pain.
Love in our borders, love within our
    heart,
  Love all in all, we then shall bide
    at rest,
  Ended for ever life's unending
    quest,
  Ended for ever effort, change,
    and fear:
Love all in all;—no more that better
    part
  Purchased, but at the cost of
    all things here.

Before 1882.

GOLDEN SILENCES

There is silence that saith 'Ah me!'
There is silence that nothing saith;
  One the silence of life forlorn,
  One the silence of death;
One is, and the other shall be.

One we know and have known for
    long,
  One we know not, but we shall
    know,
  All we who have ever been
    born;
Even so, be it so,—
There is silence, despite a song.

Sowing day is a silent day,
  Resting night is a silent night;
  But whoso reaps the ripened
    corn
  Shall shout in his delight,
While silences vanish away.
  Before 1882.

IN THE WILLOW SHADE

I sat beneath a willow tree,
  Where water falls and calls;
While fancies upon fancies solaced
    me,
  Some true, and some were false.

Who set their heart upon a hope
  That never comes to pass
Droop in the end like fading helio-
    trope,
  The sun's wan looking-glass.

Who set their will upon a whim
  Clung to through good and ill
Are wrecked alike whether they sink
    or swim,
  Or hit or miss their will.

All things are vain that wax and
    wane,
  For which we waste our breath
Love only doth not wane and is
    vain,
  Love only outlives death.

A singing lark rose toward the
  Circling he sang amain;
He sang, a speck scarce visible
    high,
  And then he sank again.

A second like a sunlit spark
  Flashed singing up his track:
But never overtook that forem[ost]
    lark,
  And songless fluttered back.

A hovering melody of birds
  Haunted the air above;
They clearly sang contentment with-
    out words,
  And youth and joy and love.

O silvery weeping willow tree
  With all leaves shivering,
Have you no purpose but to shade
    me
  Beside this rippled spring?

On this first fleeting day of Spring,
  For Winter is gone by,
And every bird on every quivering
    wing
  Floats in a sunny sky;

On this first Summer-like soft day,
  While sunshine steeps the air,
And every cloud has gat itself
    away,
  And birds sing everywhere.

Have you no purpose in the world
  But thus to shadow me
With all your tender drooping twigs unfurled,
  O weeping willow tree?

With all your tremulous leaves outspread
  Betwixt me and the sun,
While here I loiter on a mossy bed
  With half my work undone;

My work undone, that should be done
  At once with all my might;
For after the long day and lingering sun
  Comes the unworking night.

This day is lapsing on its way,
  Is lapsing out of sight;
And after all the chances of the day
  Comes the resourceless night.

The weeping willow shook its head
  And stretched its shadow long;
The west grew crimson, the sun smouldered red,
  The birds forbore a song.

Slow wind sighed through the willow leaves,
  The ripple made a moan,
The world drooped murmuring like a thing that grieves;
  And then I felt alone.

I rose to go, and felt the chill,
  And shivered as I went;
Yet shivering wondered, and I wonder still,
  What more that willow meant;

That silvery weeping willow tree
  With all leaves shivering,
Which spent one long day overshadowing me
  Beside a spring in Spring.

Before 1882.

FLUTTERED WINGS

The splendour of the kindling day,
  The splendour of the setting sun,
These move my soul to wend its way,
  And have done
With all we grasp and toil amongst and say.

The paling roses of a cloud,
  The fading bow that arches space,
These woo my fancy toward my shroud;
  Toward the place
Of faces veiled, and heads discrowned and bowed.

The nation of the steadfast stars,
  The wandering star whose blaze is brief,
These make me beat against the bars
  Of my grief;
My tedious grief, twin to the life it mars.

O fretted heart tossed to and fro,
  So fain to flee, so fain to rest!
All glories that are high or low,
  East or west,
Grow dim to thee who art so fain to go.

Before 1882.

A FISHER-WIFE

THE soonest mended, nothing said;
  And help may rise from east or
    west,
But my two hands are lumps of
    lead,
  My heart sits leaden in my breast.

O north wind, swoop not from the
    north,
  O south wind, linger in the south,
Oh come not raving raging forth,
  To bring my heart into my mouth;

For I've a husband out at sea,
  Afloat on feeble planks of wood;
He does not know what fear may
    be;
  I would have told him if I could.

I would have locked him in my
    arms,
  I would have hid him in my
    heart;
For oh the waves are fraught with
    harms,
  And he and I so far apart!
Before 1882.

WHAT'S IN A NAME?

WHY has Spring one syllable less
Than any its fellow season?
There may be some other reason,
And I'm merely making a guess;
But surely it hoards such wealth
Of happiness, hope, and health,
Sunshine and musical sound,
It may spare a foot from its name,
Yet all the same
Superabound.

Soft-named Summer,
Most welcome comer,
Brings almost everything
Over which we dream or sing
Or sigh;
But then Summer wends its way
To-morrow,—to-day,—
Good-bye!

Autumn,—the slow name lingers,
While we likewise flag;
It silences many singers;
Its slow days drag,
Yet hasten at speed
To leave us in chilly need
For Winter to strip indeed.

In all-lack Winter,
Dull of sense and of sound,
We huddle and shiver
Beside our splinter
Of crackling pine,
Snow in sky and snow on ground.
Winter and cold
Can't last for ever!
To-day, to-morrow, the sun will shine
When we are old.
But some still are young,
Singing the song
Which others have sung,
Ringing the bells
Which others have rung,—
Even so!
We ourselves, who else?
We ourselves long
Long ago.
Before 1882.

MARIANA

NOT for me marring or making,
Not for me giving or taking;
  I love my Love and he loves not
    me,
  I love my Love and my heart is
    breaking.

Sweet is Spring in its lovely showing,
Sweet the violet veiled in blowing,
 Sweet it is to love and be loved;
Ah sweet knowledge beyond my
  knowing!

Who sighs for love sighs but for
  pleasure,
Who wastes for love hoards up a
  treasure;
 Sweet to be loved and take no
  count,
Sweet it is to love without measure.

Sweet my Love whom I loved to
  try for,
Sweet my Love whom I love and
  sigh for,
 Will you once love me and sigh
  for me,
You my Love whom I love and die
  for?

Before 1882.

MEMENTO MORI

Poor the pleasure
Doled out by measure,
Sweet though it be, while brief
As falling of the leaf;
Poor is pleasure
By weight and measure.

Sweet the sorrow
Which ends to-morrow;
Sharp though it be and sore,
It ends for evermore:
Zest of sorrow,
What ends to-morrow.

Before 1882.

ONE FOOT ON SEA, AND ONE ON SHORE

'Oh tell me once and tell me twice
 And tell me thrice to make it plain,
When we who part this weary day,
 When we who part shall meet
  again.'

'When windflowers blossom on the
  sea
 And fishes skim along the plain,
Then we who part this weary day,
 Then you and I shall meet again.'

'Yet tell me once before we part,
 Why need we part who part in
  pain?
If flowers must blossom on the sea,
 Why, we shall never meet again.

'My cheeks are paler than a rose,
 My tears are salter than the main,
My heart is like a lump of ice
 If we must never meet again.'

'Oh weep or laugh, but let me be,
 And live or die, for all's in vain;
For life's in vain since we must part,
 And parting must not meet again

'Till windflowers blossom on the sea
 And fishes skim along the plain;
Pale rose of roses, let me be,—
 Your breaking heart breaks mine
  again.'

Before 1882.

A SONG OF FLIGHT

While we slumber and sleep
The sun leaps up from the deep—
 Daylight born at the leap!—
Rapid, dominant, free,
Athirst to bathe in the uttermost sea.

While we linger at play—
If the year would stand at May!—
Winds are up and away
Over land, over sea,
To their goal wherever their goal
   may be.

It is time to arise,
To race for the promised prize,—
The Sun flies, the Wind flies—
We are strong, we are free,
And home lies beyond the stars and
   the sea.

Before 1882.

BUDS AND BABIES

A MILLION buds are born that never
      blow,
   That sweet with promise lift a
      pretty head
   To blush and wither on a barren
      bed
   And leave no fruit to show.

Sweet, unfulfilled.   Yet have I
      understood
   One joy, by their fragility made
      plain :
   Nothing was ever beautiful in vain,
      Or all in vain was good.

Before 1882.

BOY JOHNNY

' IF you'll busk you as a bride
   And make ready,
It's I will wed you with a ring,
   O fair lady.'

' Shall I busk me as a bride,
   I so bonny,
For you to wed me with a ring,
   O boy Johnny ? '

' When you've busked you as a bride
   And made ready,
Who else is there to marry you,
   O fair lady ? '

' I will find my lover out,
   I so bonny,
And you shall bear my wedding
      train,
   O boy Johnny.'

Before 1882.

SUMMER IS ENDED

To think that this meaningless thing
      was ever a rose,
   Scentless, colourless, *this!*
Will it ever be thus (who knows?)
   Thus with our bliss,
   If we wait till the close ?

Though we care not to wait for the
      end, there comes the end
   Sooner, later, at last,
   Which nothing can mar, nothing
      mend :
   An end locked fast,
   Bent we cannot re-bend.

Before 1882.

PASSING AND GLASSING

ALL things that pass
Are woman's looking-glass ;
They show her how her bloom must
   fade,
And she herself be laid
With withered roses in the shade ;

With withered roses and the fallen
    peach,
Unlovely, out of reach
    Of summer joy that was.

All things that pass
    Are woman's tiring-glass ;
The faded lavender is sweet,
Sweet the dead violet
Culled and laid by and cared for yet;
    The dried-up violets and dried
    lavender,
Still sweet, may comfort her,
    Nor need she cry Alas !

All things that pass
    Are wisdom's looking-glass ;
Being full of hope and fear, and still
Brimfull of good or ill,
According to our work and will ;
    For there is nothing new beneath
    the sun ;
Our doings have been done,
    And that which shall be was.
Before 1882.

SŒUR LOUISE DE LA MISÉRICORDE

(1674)

I HAVE desired, and I have been
    desired :
    But now the days are over of
    desire,
Now dust and dying embers mock
    my fire :
Where is the hire for which my life
    was hired ?
    Oh vanity of vanities, desire !

Longing and love, pangs of a
    perished pleasure,
    Longing and love, a disenkindled
    fire,
And memory a bottomless gulf
    of mire,
And love a fount of tears outrunning
    measure :
    Oh vanity of vanities, desire !

Now from my heart, love's deathbed,
    trickles, trickles,
    Drop by drop slowly, drop by
    drop of fire,
The dross of life, of love, of spent
    desire :
Alas my rose of life gone all to
    prickles !
    Oh vanity of vanities, desire !

Oh vanity of vanities, desire !
    Stunting my hope which might
    have strained up higher,
    Turning my garden-plot to barren
    mire ;
Oh death-struck love, oh disenkindled
    fire,
    Oh vanity of vanities, desire !
Before 1882.

PASTIME

A BOAT amid the ripples, drifting,
    rocking ;
Two idle people, without pause or
    aim ;
While in the ominous West there
    gathers darkness
    Flushed with flame.

A hay-cock in a hay-field, backing,
    lapping ;
Two drowsy people pillowed round-
    about ;
While in the ominous West across
    the darkness
    Flame leaps out.

Better a wrecked life than a life so
    aimless,
Better a wrecked life than a life so
    soft :
The ominous West glooms thunder-
    ing, with its fire
      Lit aloft.
Before 1882.

BIRCHINGTON CHURCH-YARD

A LOWLY hill which overlooks a flat,
    Half sea, half country side ;
    A flat-shored sea of low-voiced
      creeping tide
Over a chalky weedy mat.

A hill of hillocks, flowery and kept
    green
    Round Crosses raised for hope,
    With many-tinted sunsets where
      the slope
Faces the lingering western sheen.

A lowly hope, a height that is but
    low,
    While Time sets solemnly,
    While the tide rises of Eternity,
Silent and neither swift nor slow.
April 1882.

RESURGAM

FROM depth to height, from height
    to loftier height,
    The climber sets his foot and sets
      his face,
    Tracks lingering sunbeams to
      their halting-place,
And counts the last pulsations of the
    light.

Strenuous thro' day and unsurpris
    by night
— He runs a race with Time a:
    wins the race,
    Emptied and stripped of all s:
      only Grace,
Will, Love, a threefold panoply .
    might.
Darkness descends for light :e
    toiled to seek :
    He stumbles on the darkene
      mountain-head,
    Left breathless in the unbreat:
      able thin air,
    Made freeman of the living an:
      the dead :—
He wots not he has topped the to:
    most peak,
    But the returning sun will fi:_
      him there.
Before 1883.

MICHAEL F. M. ROSSETTI

Born 22 April 1881 ; Died 24 January
1883.

1

A HOLY Innocent gone home
Without so much as one sharp
    wounding word ;
A blessed Michael in heaven's lofty
    dome
    Without a sword.

2

Brief dawn and noon and setting
    time !
    Our rapid - rounding moon has
      fled ;
A black eclipse before the prime
    Has swallowed up that shining
      head.

Eternity holds up her looking-
    glass:—
  The eclipse of Time will
    pass,
And all that lovely light return to
    sight.

3

I watch the showers and think of
    flowers:
  Alas my flower that shows no fruit!
  My snowdrop plucked, my daisy
    shoot
    Plucked from the root.
Soon Spring will shower, the world
    will flower,
  A world of buds will promise fruit,
  Pear-trees will shoot and apples
    shoot
    Sound at the root.
Bud of an hour, far off you flower;
  My bud, far off you ripen fruit;
  My prettiest bud, my straightest
    shoot,
    Sweet at the root.

4

  The youngest bud of five,
  The least lamb of the fold,
Bud not to blossom, yet to thrive
    Away from cold:
  Lamb which we shall not see
  Leap at its pretty pranks,
Our lamb at rest and full of glee
    On heavenly banks.
January 1883.

A WINTRY SONNET

A ROBIN said: 'The Spring will
    never come,
And I shall never care to build
    again.'

A Rosebush said: 'These frosts are
    wearisome,
My sap will never stir for sun or
    rain.'
The half Moon said: 'These nights
    are fogged and slow,
I neither care to wax nor care to
    wane.'
The Ocean said: 'I thirst from
    long ago,
Because earth's rivers cannot fill
    the main.—'
When Springtime came, red Robin
    built a nest,
And trilled a lover's song in sheer
    delight.
Grey hoarfrost vanished, and the
    Rose with might
Clothed her in leaves and buds
    of crimson core.
The dim Moon brightened. Ocean
    sunned his crest,
Dimpled his blue, yet thirsted
    evermore.
Before 1884.

ONE SEA-SIDE GRAVE

UNMINDFUL of the roses,
  Unmindful of the thorn,
A reaper tired reposes
  Among his gathered corn:
So might I, till the morn!

Cold as the cold Decembers,
  Past as the days that set,
While only one remembers
  And all the rest forget,—
But one remembers yet.
Spring 1884.

WHO SHALL SAY?

I TOILED on, but thou
   Wast weary of the way,
And so we parted: now
   Who shall say
Which is happier—I or thou?

I am weary now
   On the solitary way:
But art thou rested, thou?
   Who shall say
Which of us is calmer now?

Still my heart's love, thou,
   In thy secret way,
Art still remembered now:
   Who shall say—
Still rememberest thou?

Circa 1884.

ONE SWALLOW DOES NOT MAKE A SUMMER

A ROSE which spied one Swallow
Made haste to blush and blow:
   'Others are sure to follow':
     Ah no, not so!
The wandering clouds still owe
A few fresh flakes of snow,
Chill fog must fill the hollow,
Before the bird-stream flow
In flood across the main,
   And Winter's woe
End in glad Summer come again.
Then thousand flowers may blossom
   by the shore,—
     But that Rose never more.

Before 1886.

A FROG'S FATE

CONTEMPTUOUS of his home b—
The village and the village-po— .
A large-souled Frog who s;.-
   each byeway
Hopped along the imperial hi;!

Nor grunting pig nor barking .
Could disconcert so great a Fr .
The morning dew was lingerir..
His sides to cool, his tong—
   wet:
The night-dew, when the : .
   should come,
A travelled Frog would send '
   . home.

Not so, alas! The wayside g—
Sees him no more: not so, alas .
A broad-wheeled waggon unawar—
Ran him down, his joys, his care—
From dying choke one feeble cro;
The Frog's perpetual silence broke,-
'Ye buoyant Frogs, ye great a:
   small,
Even I am mortal after all!
My road to fame turns out a w—
   way;
I perish on the hideous highway;
Oh for my old familiar byeway!'

The choking Frog sobbed and w.—
   gone;
The Waggoner strode whistling or
Unconscious of the carnage done.
Whistling that Waggoner stro.ie
   on—
Whistling (it may have happened so
'A froggy would a-wooing go.'
A hypothetic frog trolled he,
Obtuse to a reality.

ich and poor, O great and small,
h oversights beset us all.
₂ mangled Frog abides incog,
₂ uninteresting actual frog :
e hypothetic frog alone
the one frog we dwell upon.
Before 1886.

'THERE IS A BUDDING
MORROW IN MIDNIGHT'

WINTRY boughs against a wintry
   sky ;
  Yet the sky is partly blue
    And the clouds are partly
     bright :—
Who can tell but sap is mounting
   high
    Out of sight,
Ready to burst through ?

Winter is the mother-nurse of Spring,
  Lovely for her daughter's sake,
   Not unlovely for her own :
For a future buds in everything ;
   Grown, or blown,
Or about to break.
Before 1890.

THE WAY OF THE WORLD

A BOAT that sails upon the sea,
  Sails far and far and far away :
Who sail in her sing songs of glee,
  Or watch and pray.

A boat that drifts upon the sea,
  Silent and void to sun and air :
Who sailed in her have ended glee
  And watch and prayer.
Circa 1890.

BROTHER BRUIN

A DANCING Bear grotesque and
  funny
Earned for his master heaps of
  money,
Gruff yet good-natured, fond of
  honey,
And cheerful if the day was sunny.
Past hedge and ditch, past pond and
  wood,
He tramped, and on some common
  stood ;
There cottage children circling gaily,
He in their midmost footed daily.
Pandean pipes and drum and muzzle
Were quite enough his brain to
  puzzle :
But like a philosophic bear
He let alone extraneous care
And danced contented anywhere.

Still, year on year, and wear and
  tear,
Age even the gruffest bluffest bear.
A day came when he scarce could
  prance,
And when his master looked askance
On dancing Bear who would not
  dance.
To looks succeeded blows ; hard
  blows
Battered his ears and poor old nose.
From bluff and gruff he waxed
  curmudgeon ;
He danced indeed, but danced in
  dudgeon,
Capered in fury fast and faster :—
Ah could he once but hug his master
And perish in one joint disaster !
But deafness, blindness, weakness
  growing,
Not fury's self could keep him going.

One dark day when the snow was
  snowing
His cup was brimmed to overflowing:
He tottered, toppled on one side,
Growled once, and shook his head,
  and died.
The master kicked and struck in vain;
The weary drudge had distanced
  pain,
And never now would wince again.
The master growled: he might have
  howled
Or coaxed—that slave's last growl
  was growled.
So gnawed by rancour and chagrin
One thing remained: he sold the skin.

What next the man did is not worth
Your notice or my setting forth,
But hearken what befell at last.
His idle working days gone past,
And not one friend and not one
  penny
Stored up (if ever he had any
Friends, but his coppers had been
  many),
All doors stood shut against him, but
The workhouse door which cannot
  shut.
There he droned on—a grim old
  sinner,
Toothless and grumbling for his
  dinner,
Unpitied quite, uncared for much
(The ratepayers not favouring such),
Hungry and gaunt, with time to
  spare.
Perhaps the hungry gaunt old Bear
Danced back, a haunting memory.
Indeed I hope so: for you see
If once the hard old heart relented
The hard old man may have re-
  pented.
Before 1891.

A HELPMEET FOR HIM

WOMAN was made for man's de...
  Charm, O woman, be not afr...
His shadow by day, his moo...
  night,
Woman was made.

Her strength with weakness is o...
  laid;
Meek compliances veil her m...
Him she stays by whom she is sta...

World-wide champion of truth a...
  right,
Hope in gloom and in danger a...
Tender and faithful, ruddy a...
  white,
Woman was made.
Before 1891.

EXULTATE DEO

MANY a flower hath perfume for ...
  dower,
And many a bird a song,
And harmless lambs milkwh...
  beside their dams
Frolic along;
Perfume and song and whiteness
  offering praise
In humble peaceful ways.

Man's high degree hath will and
  memory,
Affection and desire,
By loftier ways he mounts of prayer
  and praise;
Fire unto fire,
Deep unto deep responsive, height
  to height,
Until he walk in white.
Before 1891.

TO MY FIOR-DI-LISA

THE Rose is Love's own flower, and
    Love's no less
      The Lily's tenderness.
Then half their dignity must Roses
    yield
      To Lilies of the field?
Nay, diverse notes make up true
    harmony;
      All-fashioned loves agree:
Love wears the Lily's whiteness, and
    Love glows
      In the deep-hearted Rose.
1892.

TO-MORROW

PASSING away the bliss, .
The anguish passing away:
    Thus it is
      To-day.

Clean past away the sorrow,
The pleasure brought back to stay:
    Thus and this
      To-morrow.
Before 1893.

SLEEPING AT LAST

SLEEPING at last, the trouble and
    tumult over,
  Sleeping at last, the struggle and
    horror past,
Cold and white, out of sight of friend
    and of lover,
      Sleeping at last.

No more a tired heart downcast
    or overcast,
No more pangs that wring or shifting
    fears that hover,
  Sleeping at last in a dreamless
    sleep locked fast.

Fast asleep. Singing birds in their
    leafy cover
  Cannot wake her, nor shake her
    the gusty blast.
Under the purple thyme and the
    purple clover
      Sleeping at last.

Circa 1893.

POEMS FOR CHILDREN
AND MINOR VERSE

SONNETS

WRITTEN TO BOUTS-RIMÉS

I

AMID the shades of a deserted hall
  I stand and think on much that
    hath been lost.
  How long it is since other step
    has crost
This time-worn floor! This tapestry
    is all
Worm-eaten; and these columns
    rise up tall
  Yet crumbling to decay; where
    banners tost
  Thin spiders' webs hang now;
    the bitter frost
Has even killed the flowers upon
    the wall.

Yet once this was a home brimfull of
  life,
  Full of the hopes and fears and
    love of youth,
  Full of love's language speaking
    without sound :
Here honour was enshrined and
  kindly truth ;
Hither the young lord brought his
  blushing wife,
  And here the bridal garlands
    were unbound.

II

I SIT among green shady valleys
  oft,
  Listening to echo-winds sighing
    of woe ;
  The grass and flowers are strong
    and sweet below ;
Yea I am tired, and the smooth turf
  is soft.
I sit and think, and never look
  aloft,
  Save to the tops of a tall poplar-
    row
  That glisten in the wind, whisper-
    ing low
Of sudden sorrow reaching those
  who laught.
A very drowsy fountain bubbles
  near,
  Catching pale sunbeams o'er it
    wandering ;
  Its waters are so clear the stones
    look through :
Then, sitting by its lazy stream, I
  hear
  Silence more loud than any other
    thing,
  What time the trees weep o'er
    me honey-dew.

III

WOULDST thou give me a heavy
  jewelled crown
  And purple mantle and em-
    broidered vest?
  Dear Child, the colours of the
    glorious West
Are far more gorgeous when the
  sun sinks down.
The diadem would only make me
  frown
  With its own weight ; nay give
    me for my crest
  Pale violets dreaming in perfect
    rest,
Or rather leaves withered to autumn
  brown.
A purple flowing mantle would but
  hinder
  My careless walk, and an em-
    broidered robe
  Would shame me. What is
    the best man who stept
On earth more than the naked
  worm that crept
  Over its surface ? Earth shall be a
    cinder ;
  Where shall be then the beauty
    of the globe ?

IV

I SAID within myself : ' I am a fool
  To sigh ever for that which being
    gone
  Cannot return : the sun shines as
    it shone ;
Rejoice.'—But who can be made
  glad by rule?
My heart and soul and spirit are no
  tool
  To play with and direct ; my
    cheek is wan

With memory; and ever and anon
I weep, feeling life is a weary school.
There is much noise and bustle in
    the street;
  It used to be so, and it is so now;
    All are the same, and will be
      many a year.
Spirit that canst not break and
    wilt not bow,
Fear not the cold, thou who hast
    borne the heat;—
  Die if thou wilt, but what hast
    thou to fear?

V

I SOUGHT among the living, and I
    seek
  Among the dead, for some to
    love; but few
  I found at last, and those had
    quite run through
Their store of love; and friendship
    is too weak,
Too cold for me; yet will I never
    speak,
  Telling my heart-want to smooth
    listeners who
  Would wonder smiling; I can
    bear and do—
Hot shame shall dry no tears upon
    my cheek.
So, when my dust shall mix with
    other dust,
  When I shall have found quiet in
    decay,
  And lie at ease and cease like
    a mere thought,—
Those whom I loved, thinking
    on me, shall not
  Grieve with a measure, saying, 'Now
    we must
  Weep for a little ere we laugh
    to-day.'

VI

AH welladay and wherefore am I
    here?
  I sit alone all day, I sit and think—
  I watch the sun arise, I watch it
    sink,
And feel no soul-light, though the
    day is clear.
Surely it is a folly, it is mere
  Madness, to stand for ever on the
    brink
  Of dark despair, and yet not break
    the link
That makes me scorned who cannot
    be held dear.
I will have done with it; I will not
    stand
  And fear on without hope, and
    tremble thus,
  Look for the break of day and
    miss it ever.
Although my heart be broken,
    they shall never
  Say, 'She was glad to sojourn
    among us,
  Thankful if one would take her by
    the hand.'

VII

AND is this August weather? Nay,
    not so.
  With the long rain the cornfield
    waxeth dark.
  How the cold rain comes pouring
    down! and hark
To the chill wind whose measured
    pace and slow
Seems still to linger, being loth to go.
  I cannot stand beside the sea and
    mark
  Its grandeur—it's too wet for that:
    no lark

In this drear season cares to sing or
    show.
And, since its name is August, all
    men find
  Fire not allowable; winter foregone
    Had more of sunlight and of
      glad warmth more.
    I shall be fain to run upon the
      shore
  And mark the rain.   Hath the
    sun ever shone?
Cheer up! there can be nothing
    worse to mind.

VIII

METHINKS the ills of life I fain
    would shun;
  But then I must shun life, which
    is a blank.
  Even in my childhood oft my
    spirit sank,
Thinking of all that had still to be
    done.
Among my many friends there is
    not one
  Like her with whom I sat upon
    the bank
  Willow-o'ershadowed, from whose
    lips I drank
A love more pure than streams that
    sing and run.
But many times that joy has cost a
    sigh;
  And many times I in my heart
    have sought
    For the old comfort and not
      found it yet.
Surely in that calm day when I
    shall die
  The painful thought will be a
    blessèd thought,
    And I shall sorrow that I must
      forget.

IX—THE PLAGUE

'LISTEN, the last stroke of death
    noon has struck—
  The plague is come,' a gnashing
    Madman said,
  And laid him down straightway
    upon his bed.
His writhèd hands did at the linen
    pluck;
Then all is over. With a careless
    chuck
  Among his fellows he is cast.
    How sped
  His spirit matters little: many
    dead
Make men hard-hearted. — 'Place
    him on the truck.
Go forth into the burial-ground and
    find
  Room at so much a pitful for so
    many.
    One thing is to be done; one
      thing is clear:
Keep thou back from the hot un-
    wholesome wind,
  That it infect not thee.' Say, is
    there any
    Who mourneth for the multi-
      tude dead here?
August 1848.

Xa

WOULD that I were a turnip white,
    Or raven black,
    Or miserable hack
  Dragging a cab from left to
      right;
Or would I were the showman of a
    sight,
  Or weary donkey with a laden
    back,
  Or racer in a sack,

Or freezing traveller on an Alpine
    height ;
Or would I were straw-catching as
    I drown
(A wretched landsman I who cannot
    swim),
    Or watching a lone vessel sink,—
Rather than writing: I would change
    my pink
Gauze for a hideous yellow satin
    gown
With deep-cut scolloped edges and
    a rim.

X*b*

I FANCY the good fairies dressed in
    white,
    Glancing like moonbeams through
      the shadows black,
      Without much work to do for king
        or hack.
Training perhaps some twisted
    branch aright ;
Or sweeping faded autumn-leaves
    from sight
    To foster embryo life ; or binding
      back
      Stray tendrils ; or in ample bean-
        pod sack
Bringing wild honey from the rocky
    height ;
Or fishing for a fly lest it should
    drown ;
    Or teaching water-lily heads to
      swim,
      Fearful that sudden rain might
        make them sink ;
        Or dyeing the pale rose a
          warmer pink ;
Or wrapping lilies in their leafy
    gown,
    Yet letting the white peep beyond
      the rim.

X*c*—VANITY FAIR

SOME ladies dress in muslin full and
    white,
    Some gentlemen in cloth succinct
      and black ;
    Some patronize a dog-cart, some
      a hack,
Some think a painted clarence only
    right.
Youth is not always such a pleasing
    sight,
    Witness a man with tassels on
      his back ;
    Or woman in a great-coat like a
      sack
Towering above her sex with horrid
    height.
If all the world were water fit to
    drown,
    There are some whom you would
      not teach to swim,
      Rather enjoying if you saw
        them sink ;
      Certain old ladies dressed in
        girlish pink,
With roses and geraniums on their
    gown :
    Go to the Bason, poke them o'er
      the rim.

Circa 1848.

TO LALLA

READING MY VERSES TOPSY-TURVY

    DARLING little Cousin,
      With your thoughtful look
    Reading topsy-turvy
      From a printed book

    English hieroglyphics,
      More mysterious
    To you than Egyptian
      Ones would be to us ;—

Leave off for a minute
  Studying, and say
What is the impression
  That those marks convey.

Only solemn silence
  And a wondering smile :
But your eyes are lifted
  Unto mine the while.

In their gaze so steady
  I can surely trace
That a happy spirit
  Lighteth up your face ;

Tender happy spirit,
  Innocent and pure,
Teaching more than science,
  And than learning more.

How should I give answer
  To that asking look ?
Darling little Cousin,
  Go back to your book.

Read on : if you knew it,
  You have cause to boast :
You are much the wiser
  Though I know the most.
24 *January* 1849.

TWO ENIGMAS

I

NAME any gentleman you spy,
And there's a chance that he is I.
Go out to angle, and you may
Catch me on a propitious day.
Booted and spurred, their journey
    ended,
The weary are by me befriended.
If roasted meat should be your wish,
I am more needful than a dish.
I am acknowledgedly poor ;
Yet my resources are no fewer
Than all the trades—there is not one
But I profess, beneath the sun.
I bear a part in many a game ;
My worth may change, I am the same.
Sometimes, by you expelled, I roam
Forth from the sanctuary of home.

2

Me you often meet
  In London's crowded street,
And merry children's voices my
    resting-place proclaim.
Pictures and prose and verse
  Compose me—I rehearse
Evil and good and folly, and call
    each by its name.
I make men glad, and I
  Can bid their senses fly,
And festive echoes know me of Isis
    and of Cam.
But give me to a friend,
  And amity will end,
Though he may have the temper
    and meekness of a lamb.
Spring 1849.

TWO CHARADES

I

MY first is no proof of my second,
  Though my second's a proof of
    my first.
If I were my whole, I should tell you
  Quite freely my best and my worst.

One clue more : — If you fail to
    discover
  My meaning, you're blind as a
    mole ;
But, if you will frankly confess it,
  You show yourself clearly my
    whole.

2

How many authors are my first!
    And I shall be so too
Unless I finish speedily
    That which I have to do.

My second is a lofty tree
    And a delicious fruit;
This in the hot-house flourishes—
    That amid rocks takes root.

My whole is an immortal queen
    Renowned in classic lore:
Her a god won without her will,
    And her a goddess bore.
Spring 1849.

A BOUTS-RIMÉS SONNET

So I grew half delirious and quite sick,
    And through the darkness saw strange faces grin
Of monsters at me. One put forth a fin,
    And touched me clammily. I could not pick
A quarrel with it: it began to lick
    My hand, making meanwhile a piteous din,
    And shedding human tears: it would begin
To near me, then retreat. I heard the quick
Pulsation of my heart, I marked the fight
    Of life and death within me. Then sleep threw
    Her veil around me; but this thing is true.
When I awoke the sun was at his height;
    And I wept sadly, knowing that one new
Creature had love for me, and others spite.
24 *September* 1849.

PORTRAITS

An easy lazy length of limb,
    Dark eyes and features from the South,
A short-legged meditative pipe
    Set in a supercilious mouth:
Ink and a pen and papers laid
    Down on a table for the night,
Beside a semi-dozing man
    Who wakes to go to bed by light.

.   .   .   .   .

A pair of brothers brotherly,
    Unlike and yet how much the same
In heart and high-toned intellect,
    In face and bearing, hope and aim:
Friends of the selfsame treasured friends
    And of one home the dear delight,
Beloved of many a loving heart,
    And cherished both in mine, Good-night.
9 *May* 1853.

CHARON

In my cottage near the Styx
Co. and Charon still combine
Us to ferry o'er like bricks
In a boat of chaste design.
Cerberus, thou triple fair,
Distance doth thy charms impair:

Let the passage give to us
Charon, Co., and Cerberus

CHORUS

Now the passage gives us to
Charon, Cerberus, and Co.
June 1853—Frome Selwood.

THE P.R.B.

1

THE two Rossettis (brothers they)
And Holman Hunt and John Millais,
With Stephens chivalrous and bland,
And Woolner in a distant land—
In these six men I awestruck see
Embodied the great P.R.B.
D. G. Rossetti offered two
Good pictures to the public view;
Unnumbered ones great John Millais,
And Holman more than I can say.

William Rossetti, calm and solemn,
Cuts up his brethren by the column.
19 *September* 1853.

2

THE P.R.B. is in its decadence:
  For Woolner in Australia cooks his chops,
    And Hunt is yearning for the land of Cheops;
    D. G. Rossetti shuns the vulgar optic;
While William M. Rossetti merely lops
  His B's in English disesteemed as Coptic;
  Calm Stephens in the twilight smokes his pipe,
    But long the dawning of his public day;
And he at last the champion great Millais,
Attaining academic opulence,
  Winds up his signature with A.R.A.
So rivers merge in the perpetual sea;
So luscious fruit must fall when over-ripe;
And so the consummated P.R.B.
10 *November* 1853.

CHILD'S TALK IN APRIL

I WISH you were a pleasant wren,
  And I your small accepted mate:
How we'd look down on toilsome men!
  We'd rise and go to bed at eight
  Or it may be not quite so late.

Then you should see the nest I'd build,
  The wondrous nest for you and me;
The outside rough perhaps, but filled
  With wool and down; ah you should see
  The cosy nest that it would be.

We'd have our change of hope and fear,
  Small quarrels, reconcilements sweet:
I'd perch by you to chirp and cheer,
  Or hop about on active feet,
  And fetch you dainty bits to eat.

We'd be so happy by the day,
  So safe and happy through the night,
We both should feel, and I should say,

It's all one season of delight,
And we'll make merry whilst we may.

Perhaps some day there'd be an egg
  When spring had blossomed from
    the snow:
I'd stand triumphant on one leg;
  Like chanticleer I'd almost crow
    To let our little neighbours know.

Next you should sit and I would sing
Through lengthening days of sunny
    spring;
  Till, if you wearied of the task,
I'd sit; and you should spread your
    wing
    From bough to bough; I'd sit
      and bask.

Fancy the breaking of the shell,
  The chirp, the chickens wet and
    bare,
The untried proud paternal swell;
  And you with housewife-matron
    air
    Enacting choicer bills of fare.

Fancy the embryo coats of down,
  The gradual feathers soft and
    sleek;
Till clothed and strong from tail to
    crown,
  With virgin warblings in their
    beak,
    They too go forth to soar and
      seek.

So would it last an April through
And early summer fresh with dew,—
  Then should we part and live as
    twain:
Love-time would bring me back to
    you,
  And build our happy nest again.
8 *March* 1855.

WINTER

SWEET blackbird is silenced with
    chaffinch and thrush,
Only waistcoated robin still chirps
    in the bush:
Soft sun-loving swallows have
    mustered in force,
And winged to the spice-teeming
    southlands their course.

Plump housekeeper dormouse has
    tucked himself neat,
Just a brown ball in moss with a
    morsel to eat:
Armed hedgehog has huddled him
    into the hedge,
While frogs scarce miss freezing
    deep down in the sedge.

Soft swallows have left us alone in
    the lurch,
But robin sits whistling to us from
    his perch:
If I were red robin, I'd pipe you a
    tune
Would make you despise all the
    beauties of June.

But, since that cannot be, let us
    draw round the fire,
Munch chesnuts, tell stories, and
    stir the blaze higher:
We'll comfort pinched robin with
    crumbs, little man,
Till he sings us the very best song
    that he can.
28 *November* 1856.

LOVE'S NAME

LOVE hath a name of Death.
  He gives a breath

And takes away.
Lo we, beneath his sway,
Grow like a flower;
To bloom an hour,
To droop a day,
And fade away.

Circa 1869.

GOLDEN HOLLY

COMMON Holly bears a berry
To make Christmas Robins merry:—
Golden Holly bears a rose,
Unfolding at October's close
To cheer an old Friend's eyes and nose.

Circa 1872.

SING-SONG

A NURSERY RHYME BOOK

[N.B.—*The date of Sing-song as a whole is 'Before 1873': but a few of the compositions were written and inserted at a much later date. Those few are marked 'Before 1894.'*]

RHYMES DEDICATED
WITHOUT PERMISSION
TO THE BABY
WHO SUGGESTED THEM

ANGELS at the foot,
And Angels at the head,
And like a curly little lamb
My pretty babe in bed.

LOVE me,—I love you,
Love me, my baby;
Sing it high, sing it low,
Sing it as may be.

Mother's arms under you,
Her eyes above you;
Sing it high, sing it low,
Love me,—I love you.

MY baby has a father and a mother,
Rich little baby!
Fatherless, motherless, I know another
Forlorn as may be:
Poor little baby!

OUR little baby fell asleep,
And may not wake again
For days and days, and weeks and weeks;
But then he'll wake again,
And come with his own pretty look,
And kiss Mamma again.

'KOOKOOROOKOO! kookoorookoo!'
Crows the cock before the morn;
'Kikirikee! kikirikee!'
Roses in the east are born.

'Kookoorookoo! kookoorookoo!'
Early birds begin their singing;
'Kikirikee! kikirikee!'
The day, the day, the day is springing.

BABY cry—
Oh fie!—
At the physic in the cup:
Gulp it twice
And gulp it thrice,
Baby gulp it up.

EIGHT o'clock;
The postman's knock!
Five letters for Papa;

One for Lou,
  And none for you,
And three for dear Mamma.

BREAD and milk for breakfast,
  And woollen frocks to wear,
And a crumb for robin redbreast
  On the cold days of the year.

THERE'S snow on the fields,
  And cold in the cottage,
While I sit in the chimney nook
  Supping hot pottage.

My clothes are soft and warm,
  Fold upon fold,
But I'm so sorry for the poor
  Out in the cold.

DEAD in the cold, a song-singing thrush,
Dead at the foot of a snowberry bush,—
Weave him a coffin of rush,
Dig him a grave where the soft mosses grow,
Raise him a tombstone of snow.

I DUG and dug amongst the snow,
  And thought the flowers would never grow;
I dug and dug amongst the sand,
  And still no green thing came to hand.

Melt, O snow! the warm winds blow
To thaw the flowers and melt the snow;
But all the winds from every land
Will rear no blossom from the sand.

A CITY plum is not a plum;
A dumb-bell is no bell, though dumb;
A party rat is not a rat;
A sailor's cat is not a cat;
A soldier's frog is not a frog;
A captain's log is not a log.

YOUR brother has a falcon,
  Your sister has a flower;
But what is left for mannikin,
  Born within an hour?

I'll nurse you on my knee, my knee,
  My own little son;
I'll rock you, rock you, in my arms,
  My least little one.

HEAR what the mournful linnets say:
'We built our nest compact and warm,
But cruel boys came round our way
And took our summerhouse by storm.

'They crushed the eggs so neatly laid;
So now we sit with drooping wing,
And watch the ruin they have made,
Too late to build, too sad to sing.'

A BABY'S cradle with no baby in it,
  A baby's grave where autumn leaves drop sere;
The sweet soul gathered home to Paradise,
  The body waiting here.

HOP-O'-MY-THUMB and little Jack
   Horner,
What do you mean by tearing and
   fighting?
Sturdy dog Trot close round the
   corner,
   I never caught him growling and
     biting.

HOPE is like a harebell trembling
   from its birth,
Love is like a rose the joy of all the
   earth;
Faith is like a lily lifted high and
   white,
Love is like a lovely rose the world's
   delight;
Harebells and sweet lilies show a
   thornless growth,
But the rose with all its thorns excels
   them both.

O WIND, why do you never rest,
   Wandering, whistling to and fro,
Bringing rain out of the west,
   From the dim north bringing
     snow?

CRYING, my little one, footsore and
   weary?
   Fall asleep, pretty one, warm on
     my shoulder:
I must tramp on through the winter
   night dreary,
   While the snow falls on me colder
     and colder.

You are my one, and I have not
   another;
   Sleep soft, my darling, my trouble
     and treasure;

Sleep warm and soft in the arms
   your mother,
Dreaming of pretty things, drea
   ing of pleasure.

GROWING in the vale
   By the uplands hilly,
Growing straight and frail,
   Lady Daffadowndilly.

In a golden crown,
   And a scant green gown
     While the spring blows ch...
Lady Daffadown,
   ·Sweet Daffadowndilly.

A LINNET in a gilded cage,—
   A linnet on a bough,—
In frosty winter one might doubt
   Which bird is luckier now.

But let the trees burst out in leaf,
   And nests be on the bough,—
Which linnet is the luckier bird,
   Oh who could doubt it now?

WRENS and robins in the hedge,
   Wrens and robins here and the
Building, perching, pecking, flut
   ing,
     Everywhere!

MY baby has a mottled fist,
   My baby has a neck in creases
My baby kisses and is kissed,
   For he's the very thing for kis

WHY did baby die,
   Making Father sigh,
   Mother cry?

Flowers, that bloom to die,
  Make no reply
Of 'why?'
  But bow and die.

IF all were rain and never sun,
  No bow could span the hill;
If all were sun and never rain,
  There'd be no rainbow still.

O WIND, where have you been,
  That you blow so sweet?
Among the violets
  Which blossom at your feet.

The honeysuckle waits
  For Summer and for heat;
But violets in the chilly Spring
  Make the turf so sweet.

BROWNIE, Brownie, let down your milk,
White as swansdown and smooth as silk,
Fresh as dew and pure as snow:
For I know where the cowslips blow,
And you shall have a cowslip wreath
No sweeter scented than your breath.

Before 1894.

ON the grassy banks
  Lambkins at their pranks;
Woolly sisters, woolly brothers
  Jumping off their feet
While their woolly mothers
  Watch by them and bleat.

RUSHES in a watery place,
  And reeds in a hollow;
A soaring skylark in the sky,
  A darting swallow;
And where pale blossom used to hang
  Ripe fruit to follow.

MINNIE and Mattie
  And fat little May,
Out in the country,
  Spending a day.

Such a bright day,
  With the sun glowing,
And the trees half in leaf,
  And the grass growing.

Pinky white pigling
  Squeals through his snout,
Woolly white lambkin
  Frisks all about.

Cluck! cluck! the nursing hen
  Summons her folk,—
Ducklings all downy soft,
  Yellow as yolk.

Cluck! cluck! the mother hen
  Summons her chickens
To peck the dainty bits
  Found in her pickings.

Minnie and Mattie
  And May carry posies,
Half of sweet violets,
  Half of primroses.

Give the sun time enough,
  Glowing and glowing,
He'll rouse the roses
  And bring them blowing.

Don't wait for roses
  Losing to-day,

O Minnie, Mattie,
  And wise little May.

Violets and primroses
  Blossom to-day
For Minnie and Mattie
  And fat little May.

HEARTSEASE in my garden bed,
  With sweetwilliam white and red,
Honeysuckle on my wall :—
  Heartsease blossoms in my heart
When sweet William comes to call ;
  But it withers when we part,
And the honey-trumpets fall.

'IF I were a Queen,
  What would I do?
I'd make you King,
  And I'd wait on you.'

'If I were a King,
  What would I do?
I'd make you Queen,
  For I'd marry you.'

WHAT are heavy? sea-sand and sorrow :
What are brief? to-day and to-morrow :
What are frail? Spring blossoms and youth :
What are deep? the ocean and truth.

STROKE a flint, and there is nothing to admire :
Strike a flint, and forthwith flash out sparks of fire.

Before 1894.

THERE is but one May in the year
  And sometimes May is wet and cold ;
There is but one May in the year
  Before the year grows old.

Yet though it be the chilliest May,
  With least of sun and most of showers,
Its wind and dew, its night and day
  Bring up the flowers.

THE summer nights are short
  Where northern days are long
For hours and hours lark after lark
  Trills out his song.

The summer days are short
  Where southern nights are long
Yet short the night when nightingales
  Trill out their song.

THE days are clear,
  Day after day,
When April's here,
  That leads to May,
And June
Must follow soon :
  Stay, June, stay !—
If only we could stop the moon
  And June !

'TWIST me a crown of wind-flowers ;
  That I may fly away
To hear the singers at their song,
  And players at their play.'

'Put on your crown of wind-flowers :
  But whither would you go ? '
'Beyond the surging of the sea
  And the storms that blow.'

'Alas! your crown of wind-flowers
  Can never make you fly:
I twist them in a crown to-day,
  And to-night they die.'

BROWN and furry
Caterpillar in a hurry
Take your walk
To the shady leaf, or stalk,
Or what not,
Which may be the chosen spot.
No toad spy you,
Hovering bird of prey pass by you;
Spin and die,
To live again a butterfly.

A TOADSTOOL comes up in a
    night,—
  Learn the lesson, little folk:—
An oak grows on a hundred years,
  But then it is an oak.

A POCKET handkerchief to hem—
  Oh dear, oh dear, oh dear!
How many stitches it will take
  Before it's done, I fear.

Yet set a stitch and then a stitch,
  And stitch and stitch away,
Till stitch by stitch the hem is done—
  And after work is play!

IF a pig wore a wig,
    What could we say?
  Treat him as a gentleman,
    And say 'Good-day.'

  If his tail chanced to fail,
    What could we do?—
  Send him to the tailoress
    To get one new.

SELDOM 'can't,'
  Seldom 'don't';
Never 'shan't,'
  Never 'won't.'

---

1 and 1 are 2—
That's for me and you.

2 and 2 are 4—
That's a couple more.

3 and 3 are 6
Barley-sugar sticks.

4 and 4 are 8
Tumblers at the gate.

5 and 5 are 10
Bluff seafaring men.

6 and 6 are 12
Garden lads who delve.

7 and 7 are 14
Young men bent on sporting.

8 and 8 are 16
Pills the doctor's mixing.

9 and 9 are 18
Passengers kept waiting.

10 and 10 are 20
Roses—pleasant plenty!

11 and 11 are 22
Sums for brother George to do.

12 and 12 are 24
Pretty pictures, and no more.

HOW many seconds in a minute?
Sixty, and no more in it.

And takes away.
Lo we, beneath his sway,
Grow like a flower;
To bloom an hour,
To droop a day,
And fade away.

Circa 1869.

GOLDEN HOLLY

COMMON Holly bears a berry
To make Christmas Robins merry:
Golden Holly bears a rose,
Unfolding at October's close
To cheer an old Friend's eyes and nose.

Circa 1872.

SING-SONG

A NURSERY RHYME BOOK

[N.B.—*The date of Sing-song as a whole is 'Before 1873': but a few of the compositions were written and inserted at a much later date. Those few are marked 'Before 1894.'*]

RHYMES DEDICATED
WITHOUT PERMISSION
TO THE BABY
WHO SUGGESTED THEM

ANGELS at the foot,
And Angels at the head,
And like a curly little lamb
My pretty babe in bed.

———

LOVE me,—I love you,
Love me, my baby;
Sing it high, sing it low,
Sing it as may be.

Mother's arms under you,
Her eyes above you;
Sing it high, sing it low,
Love me,—I love you.

———

MY baby has a father and a mother,
Rich little baby!
Fatherless, motherless, I know another
Forlorn as may be:
Poor little baby!

———

OUR little baby fell asleep,
And may not wake again
For days and days, and weeks and weeks;
But then he'll wake again,
And come with his own pretty look,
And kiss Mamma again.

———

'KOOKOOROOKOO! kookoorookoo!'
Crows the cock before the morn;
'Kikirikee! kikirikee!'
Roses in the east are born.

'Kookoorookoo! kookoorookoo!'
Early birds begin their singing;
'Kikirikee! kikirikee!'
The day, the day, the day is springing.

———

BABY cry—
Oh fie!—
At the physic in the cup:
Gulp it twice
And gulp it thrice,
Baby gulp it up.

———

EIGHT o'clock;
The postman's knock!
Five letters for Papa;

One for Lou,
　　　And none for you,
　　　And three for dear Mamma.

BREAD and milk for breakfast,
　　　And woollen frocks to wear,
And a crumb for robin redbreast
　　　On the cold days of the year.

THERE'S snow on the fields,
　　　And cold in the cottage,
While I sit in the chimney nook
　　　Supping hot pottage.

My clothes are soft and warm,
　　　Fold upon fold,
But I'm so sorry for the poor
　　　Out in the cold.

DEAD in the cold, a song-singing thrush,
Dead at the foot of a snowberry bush,—
Weave him a coffin of rush,
Dig him a grave where the soft mosses grow,
Raise him a tombstone of snow.

I DUG and dug amongst the snow,
And thought the flowers would never grow;
I dug and dug amongst the sand,
And still no green thing came to hand.

Melt, O snow! the warm winds blow
To thaw the flowers and melt the snow;
But all the winds from every land
Will rear no blossom from the sand.

A CITY plum is not a plum;
A dumb-bell is no bell, though dumb;
A party rat is not a rat;
A sailor's cat is not a cat;
A soldier's frog is not a frog;
A captain's log is not a log.

YOUR brother has a falcon,
　　　Your sister has a flower;
But what is left for mannikin,
　　　Born within an hour?

I'll nurse you on my knee, my knee,
　　　My own little son;
I'll rock you, rock you, in my arms,
　　　My least little one.

HEAR what the mournful linnets say:
　'We built our nest compact and warm,
But cruel boys came round our way
　And took our summerhouse by storm.

'They crushed the eggs so neatly laid;
　So now we sit with drooping wing,
And watch the ruin they have made,
　Too late to build, too sad to sing.'

A BABY'S cradle with no baby in it,
　A baby's grave where autumn leaves drop sere;
The sweet soul gathered home to Paradise,
　The body waiting here.

And takes away.
Lo we, beneath his sway,
Grow like a flower;
To bloom an hour,
To droop a day,
And fade away.

Circa 1869.

GOLDEN HOLLY

COMMON Holly bears a berry
To make Christmas Robins merry:
Golden Holly bears a rose,
Unfolding at October's close
To cheer an old Friend's eyes and nose.

Circa 1872.

SING-SONG

A NURSERY RHYME BOOK

[N.B.—*The date of Sing-song as a whole is 'Before 1873': but a few of the compositions were written and inserted at a much later date. Those few are marked 'Before 1894.'*]

RHYMES DEDICATED
WITHOUT PERMISSION
TO THE BABY
WHO SUGGESTED THEM

ANGELS at the foot,
And Angels at the head,
And like a curly little lamb
My pretty babe in bed.

———

LOVE me,—I love you,
Love me, my baby;
Sing it high, sing it low,
Sing it as may be.

Mother's arms under you,
Her eyes above you;
Sing it high, sing it low,
Love me,—I love you.

———

MY baby has a father and a mother,
Rich little baby!
Fatherless, motherless, I know another
Forlorn as may be:
Poor little baby!

———

OUR little baby fell asleep,
And may not wake again
For days and days, and weeks and weeks;
But then he'll wake again,
And come with his own pretty look,
And kiss Mamma again.

———

'KOOKOOROOKOO! kookoorookoo!'
Crows the cock before the morn;
'Kikirikee! kikirikee!'
Roses in the east are born.

'Kookoorookoo! kookoorookoo!'
Early birds begin their singing;
'Kikirikee! kikirikee!'
The day, the day, the day is springing.

———

BABY cry—
Oh fie!—
At the physic in the cup:
Gulp it twice
And gulp it thrice,
Baby gulp it up.

———

EIGHT o'clock;
The postman's knock!
Five letters for Papa;

    One for Lou,
    And none for you,
And three for dear Mamma.

BREAD and milk for breakfast,
    And woollen frocks to wear,
And a crumb for robin redbreast
    On the cold days of the year.

THERE'S snow on the fields,
    And cold in the cottage,
While I sit in the chimney nook
    Supping hot pottage.

My clothes are soft and warm,
    Fold upon fold,
But I'm so sorry for the poor
    Out in the cold.

DEAD in the cold, a song-singing thrush,
Dead at the foot of a snowberry bush,—
Weave him a coffin of rush,
Dig him a grave where the soft mosses grow,
Raise him a tombstone of snow.

I DUG and dug amongst the snow,
    And thought the flowers would never grow;
I dug and dug amongst the sand,
    And still no green thing came to hand.

Melt, O snow! the warm winds blow
    To thaw the flowers and melt the snow;
But all the winds from every land
    Will rear no blossom from the sand.

A CITY plum is not a plum;
A dumb-bell is no bell, though dumb;
A party rat is not a rat;
A sailor's cat is not a cat;
A soldier's frog is not a frog;
A captain's log is not a log.

YOUR brother has a falcon,
    Your sister has a flower;
But what is left for mannikin,
    Born within an hour?

I'll nurse you on my knee, my knee,
    My own little son;
I'll rock you, rock you, in my arms,
    My least little one.

HEAR what the mournful linnets say:
    'We built our nest compact and warm,
But cruel boys came round our way
    And took our summerhouse by storm.

'They crushed the eggs so neatly laid;
    So now we sit with drooping wing,
And watch the ruin they have made,
    Too late to build, too sad to sing.'

A BABY'S cradle with no baby in it,
    A baby's grave where autumn leaves drop sere;
The sweet soul gathered home to Paradise,
    The body waiting here.

    And takes away.
    Lo we, beneath his sway,
    Grow like a flower;
    To bloom an hour,
    To droop a day,
    And fade away.

Circa 1869.

GOLDEN HOLLY

COMMON Holly bears a berry
To make Christmas Robins merry:
Golden Holly bears a rose,
Unfolding at October's close
To cheer an old Friend's eyes and nose.

Circa 1872.

SING-SONG

A NURSERY RHYME BOOK

[N.B.—*The date of Sing-song as a whole is 'Before 1873': but a few of the compositions were written and inserted at a much later date. Those few are marked 'Before 1894.'*]

RHYMES DEDICATED
WITHOUT PERMISSION
TO THE BABY
WHO SUGGESTED THEM

ANGELS at the foot,
  And Angels at the head,
  And like a curly little lamb
  My pretty babe in bed.

———

LOVE me,—I love you,
  Love me, my baby;
Sing it high, sing it low,
  Sing it as may be.

Mother's arms under you,
  Her eyes above you;
Sing it high, sing it low,
  Love me,—I love you.

———

MY baby has a father and a mother,
  Rich little baby!
Fatherless, motherless, I know another
  Forlorn as may be:
  Poor little baby!

———

OUR little baby fell asleep,
  And may not wake again
For days and days, and weeks and weeks;
But then he'll wake again,
And come with his own pretty look,
And kiss Mamma again.

———

'KOOKOOROOKOO! kookoorookoo!'
  Crows the cock before the morn.
'Kikirikee! kikirikee!'
  Roses in the east are born.

'Kookoorookoo! kookoorookoo!'
  Early birds begin their singing;
'Kikirikee! kikirikee!'
  The day, the day, the day is springing.

———

    BABY cry—
    Oh fie!—
At the physic in the cup:
    Gulp it twice
    And gulp it thrice,
Baby gulp it up.

———

EIGHT o'clock;
The postman's knock!
Five letters for Papa;

    One for Lou,
    And none for you,
And three for dear Mamma.

BREAD and milk for breakfast,
    And woollen frocks to wear,
And a crumb for robin redbreast
    On the cold days of the year.

THERE'S snow on the fields,
    And cold in the cottage,
While I sit in the chimney nook
    Supping hot pottage.

My clothes are soft and warm,
    Fold upon fold,
But I'm so sorry for the poor
    Out in the cold.

DEAD in the cold, a song-singing thrush,
Dead at the foot of a snowberry bush,—
Weave him a coffin of rush,
Dig him a grave where the soft mosses grow,
Raise him a tombstone of snow.

I DUG and dug amongst the snow,
    And thought the flowers would never grow;
I dug and dug amongst the sand,
    And still no green thing came to hand.

Melt, O snow! the warm winds blow
To thaw the flowers and melt the snow;
But all the winds from every land
Will rear no blossom from the sand.

A CITY plum is not a plum;
A dumb-bell is no bell, though dumb;
A party rat is not a rat;
A sailor's cat is not a cat;
A soldier's frog is not a frog;
A captain's log is not a log.

YOUR brother has a falcon,
    Your sister has a flower;
But what is left for mannikin,
    Born within an hour?

I'll nurse you on my knee, my knee,
    My own little son;
I'll rock you, rock you, in my arms,
    My least little one.

HEAR what the mournful linnets say:
    'We built our nest compact and warm,
But cruel boys came round our way
    And took our summerhouse by storm.

'They crushed the eggs so neatly laid;
    So now we sit with drooping wing,
And watch the ruin they have made,
    Too late to build, too sad to sing.'

A BABY'S cradle with no baby in it,
    A baby's grave where autumn leaves drop sere;
The sweet soul gathered home to Paradise,
    The body waiting here.

'Fling flowers beneath the footsteps
　　Of the bride;
Fling flowers before the bridegroom
　　At her side.

'FERRY me across the water,
　　Do, boatman, do.'
'If you've a penny in your purse
　　I'll ferry you.'

'I have a penny in my purse,
　　And my eyes are blue;
So ferry me across the water,
　　Do, boatman, do.'

'Step into my ferry-boat,
　　Be they black or blue,
And for the penny in your purse
　　I'll ferry you.'

WHEN a mounting skylark sings
　　In the sunlit summer morn,
I know that heaven is up on high,
　　And on earth are fields of corn.

But when a nightingale sings
　　In the moonlit summer even,
I know not if earth is merely earth,
　　Only that heaven is heaven.

WHO has seen the wind?
　　Neither I nor you:
But when the leaves hang trembling
　　The wind is passing thro'.

Who has seen the wind?
　　Neither you nor I:
But when the trees bow down their
　　　heads
　　The wind is passing by.

THE horses of the sea
　　Rear a foaming crest,
But the horses of the land
　　Serve us the best.

The horses of the land
　　Munch corn and clover,
While the foaming sea-horses
　　Toss and turn over.

O SAILOR, come ashore,
　　What have you brought for
　　　me?
Red coral, white coral,
　　Coral from the sea.

I did not dig it from the ground,
　　Nor pluck it from a tree;
Feeble insects made it
　　In the stormy sea.

A DIAMOND or a coal?
　　A diamond, if you please:
Who cares about a clumsy coal
　　Beneath the summer trees?

A diamond or a coal?
　　A coal, sir, if you please:
One comes to care about the coal
　　What time the waters freeze.

AN emerald is as green as grass;
　　A ruby red as blood;
A sapphire shines as blue as heaven;
　　A flint lies in the mud.

A diamond is a brilliant stone,
　　To catch the world's desire;
An opal holds a fiery spark;
　　But a flint holds fire.

BOATS sail on the rivers,
   And ships sail on the seas;
But clouds that sail across the sky
   Are prettier far than these.

There are bridges on the rivers,
   As pretty as you please;
But the bow that bridges heaven,
   And overtops the trees,
And builds a road from earth to sky,
   Is prettier far than these.

THE lily has a smooth stalk,
   Will never hurt your hand;
But the rose upon her briar
   Is lady of the land.

There's sweetness in an apple tree,
   And profit in the corn;
But lady of all beauty
   Is a rose upon a thorn.

When with moss and honey
   She tips her bending briar,
And half unfolds her glowing heart,
   She sets the world on fire.

HURT no living thing:
   Ladybird, nor butterfly,
Nor moth with dusty wing,
   Nor cricket chirping cheerily,
Nor grasshopper so light of leap,
   Nor dancing gnat, nor beetle fat,
Nor harmless worms that creep.

I CAUGHT a little ladybird
   That flies far away;
I caught a little lady wife
   That is both staid and gay.

Come back, my scarlet ladybird,
   Back from far away;
I weary of my dolly wife,
   My wife that cannot play.

She's such a senseless wooden thing
   She stares the livelong day;
Her wig of gold is stiff and cold
   And cannot change to grey.
Before 1873 *and* 1894.

ALL the bells were ringing
And all the birds were singing,
When Molly sat down crying
   For her broken doll:
   O you silly Moll!
Sobbing and sighing
   For a broken doll,
When all the bells are ringing
And all the birds are singing.

WEE wee husband,
   Give me some money,
I have no comfits,
   And I have no honey.

Wee wee wifie,
   I have no money,
Milk, nor meat, nor bread to eat,
   Comfits, nor honey.

I HAVE a little husband
   And he is gone to sea;
The winds that whistle round his ship
   Fly home to me.

The winds that sigh about me
   Return again to him;
So I would fly, if only I
   Were light of limb.
Before 1873 *and* 1894.

THE dear old woman in the lane
  Is sick and sore with pains and
    aches,
We'll go to her this afternoon,
  And take her tea and eggs and
    cakes.

We'll stop to make the kettle boil,
  And brew some tea, and set the
    tray,
And poach an egg, and toast a cake,
  And wheel her chair round, if we
    may.
    Before 1873 and 1894.

SWIFT and sure the swallow,
  Slow and sure the snail :
Slow and sure may miss his way,
  Swift and sure may fail.

'I DREAMT I caught a little owl
And the bird was blue—'

'But you may hunt for ever
And not find such an one.'

'I dreamt I set a sunflower,
And red as blood it grew—'

'But such a sunflower never
Bloomed beneath the sun.'

  WHAT does the bee do?
    Bring home honey.
  And what does Father do?
    Bring home money.
  And what does Mother do?
    Lay out the money.
  And what does baby do?
    Eat up the honey.

I HAVE a Poll parrot,
  And Poll is my doll,
And my nurse is Polly,
  And my sister Poll.

'Polly!' cried Polly,
  'Don't tear Polly dolly'—
While soft-hearted Poll
  Trembled for the doll.
  Before 1873 and 1894.

A HOUSE of cards
  Is neat and small :
Shake the table,
  It must fall.

Find the Court cards
  One by one ;
Raise it, roof it,—
  Now it's done :—
Shake the table !
  That's the fun.

THE rose with such a bonny blush,
  What has the rose to blush about?
If it's the sun that makes her flush,
  What's in the sun to flush about?

THE rose that blushes rosy red,
  She must hang her head ;
The lily that blows spotless white,
  She may stand upright.

  OH fair to see
Bloom-laden cherry tree,
    Arrayed in sunny white,
    An April day's delight ;
  Oh fair to see !

  Oh fair to see
Fruit-laden cherry tree,

With balls of shining red
  Decking a leafy head;
    Oh fair to see!

CLEVER little Willie wee,
  Bright-eyed, blue-eyed little fellow;
Merry little Margery
  With her hair all yellow.

Little Willie in his heart
  Is a sailor on the sea,
And he often cons a chart
  With sister Margery.
Before 1873 and 1894.

THE peach tree on the southern wall
  Has basked so long beneath the sun,
Her score of peaches great and small
  Bloom rosy, every one.

A peach for brothers, one for each,
  A peach for you and a peach for me;
But the biggest, rosiest, downiest peach
  For Grandmamma with her tea.
Before 1873 and 1894.

A ROSE has thorns as well as honey,
I'll not have her for love or money;
An iris grows so straight and fine
That she shall be no friend of mine;
Snowdrops like the snow would chill me;
Nightshade would caress and kill me;
Crocus like a spear would fright me;
Dragon's-mouth might bark or bite me;
Convolvulus but blooms to die;
A wind-flower suggests a sigh;
Love-lies-bleeding makes me sad;
And poppy-juice would drive me mad:—
But give me holly, bold and jolly,
Honest, prickly, shining holly;
Pluck me holly leaf and berry
For the day when I make merry.

Is the moon tired? she looks so pale
  Within her misty veil:
She scales the sky from east to west,
  And takes no rest.

Before the coming of the night
The moon shows papery white;
Before the dawning of the day
She fades away.

IF stars dropped out of heaven,
  And if flowers took their place,
The sky would still look very fair,
  And fair earth's face.

Winged angels might fly down to us
  To pluck the stars,
But we could only long for flowers
  Beyond the cloudy bars.

'GOOD-BYE in fear, good-bye in sorrow,
  Goodbye, and all in vain,
Never to meet again, my dear'—
  'Never to part again.'
'Good-bye to-day, good-bye to-morrow,
  Good-bye till earth shall wane,
Never to meet again, my dear'—
  'Never to part again.'

IF the sun could tell us half
   That he hears and sees,
Sometimes he would make us laugh,
   Sometimes make us cry:
Think of all the birds that make
   Homes among the trees;
Think of cruel boys who take
   Birds that cannot fly.

IF the moon came from heaven,
   Talking all the way,
What could she have to tell us,
   And what could she say?

'I've seen a hundred pretty things,
   And seen a hundred gay;
But only think: I peep by night
   And do not peep by day!'

O LADY MOON, your horns point toward the east;
   Shine, be increased:
O Lady Moon, your horns point toward the west;
   Wane, be at rest.

WHAT do the stars do
   Up in the sky,
Higher than the wind can blow,
   Or the clouds can fly?

Each star in its own glory
   Circles, circles still;
As it was lit to shine and set,
   And do its Maker's will.

MOTHERLESS baby and babyless mother,
Bring them together to love one another.

CRIMSON curtains round my mother's bed,
   Silken soft as may be;
Cool white curtains round about my bed,
   For I am but a baby.

BABY lies so fast asleep
   That we cannot wake her:
Will the Angels clad in white
   Fly from heaven to take her?

Baby lies so fast asleep
   That no pain can grieve her;
Put a snowdrop in her hand,
   Kiss her once and leave her.

I KNOW a baby, such a baby,—
   Round blue eyes and cheeks of pink,
Such an elbow furrowed with dimples,
   Such a wrist where creases sink.

'Cuddle and love me, cuddle and love me,'
   Crows the mouth of coral pink:
Oh the bald head, and oh the sweet lips,
   And oh the sleepy eyes that wink!

LULLABY, oh lullaby!
Flowers are closed and lambs are sleeping;
   Lullaby, oh lullaby!
Stars are up, the moon is peeping;
   Lullaby, oh lullaby!
While the birds are silence keeping,
   (Lullaby, oh lullaby!)
Sleep, my baby, fall a-sleeping,
   Lullaby, oh lullaby!

LIE a-bed,
Sleepy head,
Shut up eyes, bo-peep ;
Till day-break
Never wake :—
Baby, sleep.

AN ALPHABET

A is the Alphabet, A at its head ;
  A is an Antelope, agile to run.
B is the Baker Boy bringing the bread,
  Or black Bear and brown Bear, both begging for bun.

C is a Cornflower come with the corn ;
  C is a Cat with a comical look.
D is a dinner which Dahlias adorn ;
  D is a Duchess who dines with a Duke.

E is an elegant eloquent Earl ;
  E is an Egg whence an Eaglet emerges.
F is a Falcon, with feathers to furl ;
  F is a Fountain of full foaming surges.

G is the Gander, the Gosling, the Goose ;
  G is a Garnet in girdle of gold.
H is a Heartsease, harmonious of hues ;
  H is a huge Hammer, heavy to hold.

I is an Idler who idles on ice ;
  I am I—who will say I am not I ?
J is a Jacinth, a jewel of price ;
  J is a Jay, full of joy in July

K is a King, or a Kaiser still higher ;
  K is a Kitten, or quaint Kangaroo.
L is a Lute or a lovely-toned Lyre ;
  L is a Lily all laden with dew.

M is a Meadow where Meadowsweet blows ;
  M is a Mountain made dim by a mist.
N is a nut—in a nutshell it grows—
  Or a Nest full of Nightingales singing—oh list !

O is an Opal, with only one spark ;
  O is an Olive, with oil on its skin.
P is a Pony, a pet in a park ;
  P is the Point of a Pen or a Pin.

Q is a Quail, quick-chirping at morn ;
  Q is a Quince quite ripe and near dropping.
R is a Rose, rosy red on a thorn ;
  R is a red-breasted Robin come hopping.

S is a Snow-storm that sweeps o'er the Sea ;
  S is the Song that the swift Swallows sing.
T is the Tea-table set out for Tea ;
  T is a Tiger with terrible spring.

U, the Umbrella, went up in a shower ;
  Or Unit is useful with ten to unite.
V is a Violet veined in the flower ;
  V is a Viper of venomous bite.

W stands for the water-bred Whale—
  Stands for the wonderful Waxwork so gay.
X, or XX, or XXX, is ale,
  Or Policeman X, exercised day after day.

Y is a yellow Yacht, yellow its boat:
  Y is the Yacca, the Yam, or the
    Yew.
Z is a Zebra, zigzaggèd his coat,
  Or Zebu, or Zoöphyte, seen at the
    Zoo.
Circa 1875.

HADRIAN'S DEATH-SONG TRANSLATED

SOUL rudderless, unbraced,
  The body's friend and guest,
  Whither away to-day?
Unsuppled, pale, discased,
  Dumb to thy wonted jest.
16 March 1876.

MY MOUSE

A VENUS seems my Mouse
Come safe ashore from foaming
    seas,
Which in a small way and at ease
    Keeps house.

An Iris seems my Mouse,
Bright bow of that exhausted shower
Which made a world of sweet herbs
    flower
  And boughs.

A darling Mouse it is:—
Part hope not likely to take wing,
Part memory, part anything
    You please.

Venus-cum-Iris Mouse,
From shifting tides set safe apart,
In no mere bottle, in my heart
    Keep house.
New Year 1877.

A POOR OLD DOG

PITY the sorrows of a poor old dog
  Who wags his tail a-begging in
    his need;
Despise not even the sorrows of a
    frog,
  God's creature too, and that's
    enough to plead;
Spare puss who trusts us purring on
    our hearth;
  Spare bunny, once so frisky and
    so free;
Spare all the harmless creatures of
    the earth:
  Spare, and be spared—or who
    shall plead for thee?
Circa 1879.

TO WILLIAM BELL SCOTT

MY old admiration before I was
    twenty
Is predilect still, now promoted to
    se'enty.
My own demi-century plus an odd one
  Some weight to my judgment
    may fairly impart.
Accept this faint flash of a smoulder-
    ing fun,
  The fun of a heavy old heart.
Spring 1882.

COUNTERBLAST ON PENNY TRUMPET

IF Mr. Bright retiring does not
    please,
  And Mr. Gladstone staying gives
    offence,
What can man do which is not one
    of these?
  Use your own common sense.

Yet he's a brave man who abjures
    his cause
  For conscience' sake: let bye-
    gones be byegones :
Not *this* among the makers of our
    laws
  The least and last of Johns.

If all our bygones could be piled
    on shelves
  High out of reach of penny-line
    Tyrtæus !
If only all of us could see ourselves
  As others see us !
21 *July* 1882.

MOLE AND EARTHWORM

A HANDY Mole, who plied no shovel
To excavate his vaulted hovel,
While hard at work met in mid-
    furrow
An Earthworm boring out his burrow.
Our Mole had dined, and must grow
    thinner
Before he gulped a second dinner,
And on no other terms cared he
To meet a Worm of low degree.
The Mole turned-on his blindest
    eye,
Passing that base mechanic by.
The Worm, intrenched in actual
    blindness,
Ignored or kindness or unkindness.
Each wrought his own exclusive
    tunnel,
To reach his own exclusive funnel.

A plough, its flawless track pursuing,
Involved them in one common ruin.
Where now the mine and counter-
    mine,
The dined-on and the one to dine ?

The impartial ploughshare of ex-
    tinction
Annulled them all without distinction.
Before 1886.

TO MARY ROSSETTI

YOU were born in the Spring
When the pretty birds sing
    In sunbeamy bowers :
Then dress like a Fairy,
Dear dumpling my Mary,
    In green and in flowers.
Circa 1887.

WHAT WILL IT BE?

WHAT will it be, O my soul, what
    will it be,
To touch the long-raced-for goal, to
    handle and see,
To rest in the joy of joys, in the joy
    of the blest,
To rest and revive and rejoice, to
    rejoice and to rest ?
Before 1893.

SPEECHLESS

LORD, Thou art fullness, I am
    emptiness :
Yet hear my heart speak in its
    speechlessness,
Extolling Thine unuttered loveliness.
Before 1893.

PLEADING

O LORD, I cannot plead my love of
    Thee :
  I plead Thy Love of me :—
The shallow conduit hails the un-
    fathomed sea.
Before 1893.

A SORROWFUL SIGH OF A PRISONER

LORD, comest Thou to me?
    My heart is cold and dead.
Alas that such a heart should be
    The place to lay Thy head!
Before 1893.

SCARLET

'I SIT a queen, and am no widow,
    and shall see no sorrow.'
Yea, Scarlet Woman, to-day, but not
    yea at all to-morrow.
Scarlet Queen on a scarlet throne,
    all to-day without sorrow,
Bethink thee—to-day must end, there
    is no end of to-morrow.
Before 1893.

HOMEWARDS

LOVE builds a nest on earth and
    waits for rest,
Love sends to heaven the warm
    heart from its breast,
Looks to be blest and is already
    blest,
And testifies, 'God's will is alway
    best.'
Before 1893.

ITALIAN POEMS

VERSI

FIGLIA, la Madre disse,
Guardati dall' Amore:
È crudo, è traditore—
    Che vuoi saper di più?
Non fargli mai sperare
D' entrare nel tuo petto,
Chè chi gli dà ricetto
    Sempre tradito fu.

Colla sua benda al ciglio
È un bel fanciullo, è vero:
Ma sempre è menzognero,
    Ma sempre tradirà.
Semplice tu se fidi
Nel riso suo fallace;
Tu perderai la pace,
    Nè mai ritornerà.

Ma vedo—già sei stanca
Del mio parlar prudente;
Già volgi nella mente
    Il quando, il come, e il chi.
Odimi: i detti miei
Già sai se son sinceri—
E se son falsi o veri
    Saprai per prova un dì.
6 Ottobre 1849.

L'INCOGNITA

NOBIL rosa ancor non crebbe
    Senza spine in sullo stelo:
Se vi fosse, allor sarebbe
    Atta immagine di te.
È la luna in mezzo al cielo
Bella è ver ma passeggiera:—
Passa ancor la primavera:—
    Ah l'immagin tua dov' è?
Circa 1850.

NIGELLA

Purpurea rosa,
Dolce, odorosa,
È molto bella—
    Ma pur non è,
    O mia Nigella,
    Rival di te.

Donna nel velo,
Fior sullo stelo,
Ciascun l' amore
    Reclama a sè;
Ma passa il fiore—
    Tu resti a me.

Circa 1850.

CHIESA E SIGNORE

La Chiesa

Vola, preghiera, e digli
    Perchè Ti stai lontano?
Passeggi Tu frai gigli
    Portando rosa in mano?
Non Ti fui giglio e rosa
    Quando mi amasti Tu?
Rivolgiti alla sposa,
    O mio Signor Gesù.

Il Signore

Di te non mi scordai,
    Sposa mia dolce e mesta:
Se Mi sei rosa il sai,
    Chè porto spine in testa.
Ti diedi e core e vita,
Me tutto Io diedi a te,
Ed or ti porgo aita:
    Abbi fidanza in Me.

La Chiesa

Vola, preghiera, a Lui,
    E grida: Ahi pazienza!
Te voglio e non altrui,
    Te senza è tutto senza.
Fragrante più di giglio
    E rosa a me sei Tu,
Di Dio l' Eterno Figlio,
    O mio Signor Gesù.

Circa 1860.

IL ROSSEGGIAR DELL' ORIENTE

Canzoniere all' Amico lontano.

1

Amor dormente?

Addio, diletto amico;
    A me non lece amore,
    Chè già m' uccise il core
        Amato amante.
Eppur per l' altra vita
    Consacro a te speranze;
    Per questa, rimembranze
        Tante e poi tante.

Dicembre 1862.

2

Amor si sveglia?

In nuova primavera
    Rinasce il genio antico;
Amor t' insinua 'Spera'—
    Pur io nol dico.

S' 'Ama' ti dice Amore,
    S' ei t' incoraggia, amico,
Giurando 'È tuo quel core'—
    Pur io nol dico.

Anzi quel cor davvero
    Chi sa se valga un fico?
Lo credo, almen lo spero:
    Ma pur nol dico.

Gennaio 1863.

3

SI RIMANDA LA TOCCA-CALDAJA

LUNGI da me il pensiere
   D' ereditar l' oggetto
   Ch' una fiata in petto
     Destar ti seppe amor.
Se più l' usar non vuoi,
Se pur fumar nol puoi,
   Dolce ti sia dovere
     Il conservarlo ognor.

Circa 1864.

4

BLUMINE RISPONDE

S' io t' incontrassi nell' eterna pace,
   Pace non più, per me saria diletto;
   S' io t' incontrassi in cerchio maledetto,
Te più di me lamenterei verace.
Per te mia vita mezzo morta giace,
   Per te le notti veglio e bagno il letto:
   Eppur di rivederti un dì m' aspetto
In secol che riman, non che in fugace.
E perciò ' Fuggi ' io dico al tempo; e omai
   ' Passa pur' dico al vanitoso mondo.
Mentre mi sogno quel che dici e fai
   Ripeto in me, ' Doman sarà giocondo,
Doman sarem '—ma s' ami tu lo sai,
   E se non ami a che mostrarti il fondo ?

Gennaio 1867.

5

Lassù fia caro il rivederci.

DOLCE cor mio perduto e non perduto,
   Dolce mia vita che mi lasci in morte,
Amico e più che amico, ti saluto.
   Ricordati di me; chè cieche e corte
Fur le speranze mie, ma furon tue :
   Non disprezzar questa mia dura sorte.
Lascia ch' io dica, ' Le speranze sue
   Come le mie languiro in questo inverno '—
Pur mi rassegnerò, quel che fue fue.
   Lascia ch' io dica ancor, ' Con lui discerno
Giorno che spunta da gelata sera,
   Lungo cielo al di là di breve inferno,
Al di là dell' inverno primavera.'

Gennaio 1867.

6

Non son io la rosa ma vi stetti appresso.

CASA felice ove più volte omai
   Siede il mio ben parlando e ancor ridendo,
   Donna felice che con lui sedendo
Lo allegri pur con quanto dici e fai,
Giardin felice dove passeggiai
   Pensando a lui, pensando e non dicendo,—
   Giorno felice fia quand' io mi rendo
Laddove passeggiando a lui pensai.
Ma s' egli vi sarà quand' io vi torno,
   S' egli m' accoglie col suo dolce riso,

Ogni uccelletto canterà dintorno,
  La rosa arrossirà nel vago viso :—
Iddio ci dia in eternità quel giorno,
  Ci dia per quel giardino il
    paradiso.
Aprile 1867.

7

Lassuso il caro Fiore.

SE t' insegnasse Iddio
  Il proprio Amor così,
Ti cederei, cor mio,
  Al caro Fiore.
Il caro Fior ti chiama,
  ' Fammi felice un dì ' ;—
Il caro Fior che t' ama
  Ti chiede amore.

Quel Fiore in paradiso
  Fiorisce ognor per te ;
Sì, rivedrai quel viso,
  Sarai contento :
Intorno al duol ch' è stato
  Domanderai ' Dov' è ? '
Chè passerà il passato
  In un momento.

Ed io per tanta vista
  In tutta eternità,
Io qual Giovan Battista
  Loderò Dio :
L' Amata tanto amata
  Tuo guiderdon sarà,
E l' alma tua salvata
  Sarammi il mio.
Aprile 1867.

8

SAPESSI PURE

CHE fai lontan da me,
  Che fai, cor mio ?
Quel che facc' io
È ch' ognor penso a te.

Pensando, a te sorrido,
  Sospiro a te :
    E tu lontan da me
  Tu pur sei fido ?
Maggio 1867.

9

IDDIO C' ILLUMINI

QUANDO il tempo avverrà che parti-
    remo
  Ciascun di noi per separata via,
Momento che verrà, momento es-
    tremo
    Quando che fia :

Calcando l' uno inusitata traccia,
  Seguendo l' altro il solito suo corso,
Non ci nasca in quel dì vergogna in
    faccia
    Nè in sen rimorso.

Sia che tu vada pria forte soletto,
  O sia ch' io ti preceda in quel
    sentiero,
Deh ricordiamci allor d' averci detto
    Pur sempre il vero.

Quanto t' amavo e quanto ! e non
    dovea
  Esprimer quell' amor che ti
    portavo :
Più ma assai più di quel che non
    dicea
    Nel cuor ti amavo.

Più di felicità, più di speranza ;
  Di vita non dirò, chè è poca cosa :
Dolce-amaro tu fosti in rimembranza
    A me gelosa.

Ma a me tu preferisti la virtute,
  La veritate, amico : e non saprai
Chi amasti alfin ? Soltanto il fior si
    schiude
    D' un sole ai rai.

Se più di me la Veritade amasti,
  Gesù fu quel tuo sconosciuto
    Amore :—
Gesù, che sconosciuto a lui parlasti,
  Vincigli il core.

Maggio 1867.

10

AMICIZIA

Sirocchia son d' Amor.

VENGA Amicizia e sia la benvenuta,
  Venga, ma non perciò sen parta
    Amore :
  Abitan l' uno e l' altra in gentil
    core
Che albergo ai pellegrini non rifiuta.
Ancella questa docile e compiuta,
  E quei tiranno no ma pio signore :
  Regni egli occulto nè si mostri
    fuore,
Essa si sveli in umiltà dovuta.
Oggi ed ancor doman per l' amicizia,
  E posdomani ancor se pur si vuole,
    Chè dolci cose apporta e non
      amare :
  E venga poi, ma non con luna o
    sole,
Giorno d' amor, giorno di gran delizia,
    Giorno che spunta non per
      tramontare.

Agosto 1867.

11

Luscious and sorrowful.

UCCELLO delle rose e del dolore,
  Uccel d' amore,
Felice ed infelice, quel tuo canto
  È riso o pianto?
Fido all' infido, tieni in freddo lido
  Spina per nido.

Agosto 1867.

12

O forza irresistibile
Dell' umile preghiera.

CHE Ti darò, Gesù Signor mi
  buono?
Ah quello ch' amo più, quello T'
  dono:
Accettalo, Signor Gesù mio Dio,
Il sol mio dolce amor, anzi il co
  mio;
Accettalo per Te, siati prezioso ;
Accettalo per me, salva il me
  sposo.
Non ho che lui, Signor, nol di
  prezzare,
Caro tienlo nel cor fra cose care.
Ricordati del dì che sulla croce
Pregavi Iddio così, con flebil voce.
Con anelante cor : ' Questo ch'
  fanno,
Padre, perdona lor, ch' essi n
  sanno.'
Ei pur, Signor, non sa Quello c
  sdegna,
Ei pure T' amerà s' uno gl' insegna
Se tutto quanto appar, che a Te ne
  piace,
Fugace spuma in mar, nebbia fugace
Successo o avversità, contento
  duolo,
Se tutto è vanita fuorchè Tu solo:
Se chi non prega Te nel vuoti
  chiama ;
Se amore amor non è che Te no
  ama ;—
Dona Te stesso a noi, ricchi saremo
Poi nega quanto vuoi, chè tutt
  avremo :
Di mel più dolce Tu, che ben c
  basti ;
D' amore amabil più, Tu che c
  amasti.

Settembre 1867.

13

FINESTRA MIA ORIENTALE

[IN MALATTIA]

VOLGO la faccia verso l' oriente,
  Verso il meriggio, ove colui
    dimora:—
Ben fai che vivi ai lati dell' aurora;
Chi teco vive par felice gente.
Volgo verso di te l' occhio languente,
  Lo spirito che teme e spera
    ancora;
Volgiti verso quella che ti onora,
T' ama, ti brama, in core e colla
    mente.
Debole e stanca verso te mi volgo:
  Che sarà mai questo che sento,
    amico?
Ogni cara memoria tua raccolgo,—
  Quanto dirti vorrei! ma pur nol
    dico.
Lungi da te dei giorni me ne
    dolgo:
  Fossimo insieme in bel paese
    aprico!

    Fossimo insieme!
    Che importerebbe
      U' si facesse
      Il nostro nido?
    Cielo sarebbe
      Quasi quel lido.
      Ah fossi teco,
      Col cor ben certo
      D' essere amato
    Come vorrebbe!
      Sì che il deserto
      S' infiorirebbe.

Ottobre 1867.

14

EPPURE ALLORA VENIVI

O TEMPO tardo e amaro!—
  Quando verrai, cor mio,
  Quando, ma quando?
Siccome a me sei caro
  Se cara a te foss' io,
  Ti andrei cercando?

Febbrajo 1868.

15

PER PREFERENZA

FELICE la tua madre,
  Le suore tue felici,
Che senton quanto dici,
  Che vivono con te,
Che t' amano di dritto
D' amor contento e saggio:
Pur questo lor vantaggio
  Non lo vorrei per me.

Quel grave aspetto tuo
Veder di quando in quando,
Frattanto andar pensando
  'Un giorno riverrà';
Ripeter nel mio core
(Qual rosa è senza spine?)
'Ei sa che l' amo alfine—
  M' ama egli ancor?' Chi sa?

È questo assai più dolce
Dell' altro, al parer mio:
Essere in ver desio
  O tutto o nulla[1] a te;
Nè troppo vo' lagnarmi
Ch' or stai da me diviso,
Se un giorno in Paradiso
  Festeggerai con me.

Marzo 1868.

---

[1] Ma no; se non amante siimi amico:
Quel ch' io sarò per te non tel predico.

16
OGGI

POSSIBIL non sarebbe
   Ch' io non t' amassi, O Caro :
Chi mai si scorderebbe
   Del proprio core ?
Se amaro il dolce fai,
   Dolce mi fai l' amaro ;
Se qualche amor mi dai,
   Ti do l' amore.

Marzo 1868.

17

TI do l' addio,
   Amico mio,
Per settimane
   Che paion lunghe :
Ti raccomando
Di quando in quando
Circoli quadri,
   Idee bislunghe.

Marzo 1868.

18
RIPETIZIONE

CREDEA di rivederti e ancor ti
   aspetto ;
   Di giorno in giorno ognor ti vo
   bramando :
Quando ti rivedrò, co. mio diletto,
   Quando ma quando ?

Dissi e ridissi con perenne sete,
   E lo ridico e vo' ridirlo ancora,
Qual usignol che canta e si ripete
   Fino all' aurora.

Giugno 1868.

19
Amico e più che amico mio.

COR mio a cui si volge l' altro
   core
Qual calamita al polo, e non
   trova,
La nascita della mia vita nuova
Con pianto fu, con grida, e c.
   dolore.
Ma l' aspro duolo fummi precursor
   Di speranza gentil che canta e
   cova ;
Sì, chi non prova pena amor n
   prova,
E quei non vive che non prov.
   amore.
O tu che in Dio mi sei, ma dop
   Iddio,
   Tutta la terra mia ed assai c.
   cielo,
Pensa se non m' è duol disotto
   un velo
Parlarti e non ti dir mai che t
   bramo :—
Dillo tu stesso a te, dolce cor mio.
   Se pur tu m' ami dillo a te ch' .
   t' amo.

Agosto 1868.

20
Nostre volontà quieti
Virtù di carità.

VENTO gentil che verso il mezzodì
   Soffiando vai, deh porta un mi.
   sospir,
   Dicendo ad Un quel che non
   debbo dir,
Con un sospir dicendogli così :
Quella che diede un 'No' volendo
   un 'Sì'

(Volendo e non volendo—a che ridir?)
Quella ti manda : È vanità il fiorir
Di questa vita che meniam costì.
Odi che dice e piange : È vanità
    Questo che nasce e muore amor mondan ;
    Deh leva gli occhi, io gli occhi vo' levar,
    Verso il reame dove non in van
    Amasi Iddio quanto ognun possa amar
Ed il creato tutto in carità.
Agosto 1868.

21
Se così fosse.

Io più ti amai che non mi amasti tu :—
    Amen, se così volle Iddio Signor ;
    Amen, quantunque mi si spezzi il cor,
    Signor Gesù.

Ma Tu che Ti ricordi e tutto sai,
    Tu che moristi per virtù d' amor,
    Nell' altro mondo donami quel cor
    Che tanto amai.
Agosto 1868.

L' UOMMIBATTO

O UOMMIBATTO,
    Agil, giocondo,
Che ti sei fatto
    Irsuto e tondo !
Deh non fuggire
    Qual vagabondo,
Non disparire
    Forando il mondo :
Pesa davvero
    D' un emisfero
    Non lieve il pondo.
1869.

COR MIO

COR mio, cor mio,
    Più non ti veggo, ma mi rammento
    Del giorno spento,
    Cor mio.
Pur ti ricordi del lungo amore,
    Cor del mio core,
    Cor mio ?
Circa 1870.

ADRIANO

ANIMUCCIA, vagantuccia, morbiduccia,
    Oste del corpo e suora,
    Ove or farai dimora ?
Palliduccia, irrigidita, svestituccia,
    Non più scherzante or ora.
16 *Marzo* 1876.

NINNA-NANNA

1
[ANGELS AT THE FOOT]

ANGELI al capo, al piede ;
    E qual ricciuto agnello
    Dormir fra lor si vede
    Il bel mio bambinello.

2
[LOVE ME, I LOVE YOU]

AMAMI, t' amo,
    Figliolin mio :
Cantisi, suonisi,
    Con tintinnio.

Mamma t' abbraccia,
    Cor suo ti chiama ;
Suonisi, cantisi,
    Ama chi t' ama.

3
[MY BABY HAS A FATHER AND A MOTHER]

E BABBO e mamma ha il nostro
    figliolino,
    Ricco bambino.
Ma ne conosco un altro senza padre
    E senza madre—
    Il poverino!

4
[OUR LITTLE BABY FELL ASLEEP]

S' ADDORMENTÒ la nostra figliolina,
    Nè si risveglierà
Per giorni e giorni assai sera o mat-
    tina.
    Ma poi si sveglierà,
E con cara ridente bocchettina
    Ribacerà Mammà.

5
[KOOKOOROOKOO, KOOKOO-ROOKOO]

CUCCURUCÙ—cuccurucù—
    All' alba il gallo canta.
Chicchirichì—chicchirichì—
    Di rose il ciel s' ammanta.
Cuccurucù—cuccurucù—
    Comincia un gorgheggiare.
Chicchirichì—chicchirichì—
    Risalta il sol dal mare.

6
[BABY CRY]

OHIBÒ piccina
    Tutto atterrita!
La medicina
    Bever si de':
Uno, due, tre,
    Ed è finita.

7
[EIGHT O'CLOCK]

OTTO ore suonano—
    Picchia il postino:
Ben cinque lettere
    Son per Papà;

    Una per te,
    Nulla per me;
E un bigliettino
    V' è per Mammà.

8
[BREAD AND MILK FOR BREAKFAST]

NEL verno accanto al fuoco
    Mangio la mia minestra,
    E al pettirosso schiudo la finestra
Ch' ei pur ne vuole un poco.
[OVVERO]
S'affaccia un pettirosso alla fi-
    estra—
Vieni vieni a gustar la mia minestra.
Lana ben foderata io porto addosso,
Ma tu non porti che un corpetto
    rosso.

9
[THERE'S SNOW ON THE FIELDS]

GRAN freddo è infuori, e dentro è
    freddo un poco:
Quanto è grata una zuppa accanto
    al fuoco!
    Mi vesto di buon panno—
    Ma i poveri non hanno
Zuppa da bere e fuoco a cui sedere,
O tetto o panni in questo freddo
    intenso—
Ah mi si stringe il cor mentre io ci
    penso.

10
[I Dug and Dug Amongst the Snow]

Avai la neve—sì che scavai—
a fior nè foglia spuntava mai.
avai la rena con ansia lena,
a fior nè foglia spicca da rena.
vento aprico, con fiato lieve
,eglia i fioretti, sgela la neve !
a non soffiare su quella rena :
hi soffia in rena perde la lena.

11
[Your Brother has a Falcon]

ìl che il fratello s' ha un falconcello,
E tiene un fior la suora :
Ma che, ma che riman per te,
Il neonato or ora ?
Vo' farti cocchio del mio ginocchio,
Minor mio figliolino :
Da capo a piè ti stringo a me,
Minimo piccino.

12
[Hear what the Mournful Linnets Say]

Udite, si dolgono mesti fringuelli:—
Bel nido facemmo per cari gemelli,
Ma tre ragazzacci lo misero in stracci.
Fuggì primavera, s'imbruna la sera,
E tempo ci manca da fare un secondo
Niduncolo tondo.

13
[A Baby's Cradle with no Baby in it]

Ahi culla vuota ed ahi sepolcro pieno
Ove le smunte foglie autunno
getta !

Lo spirto aspetta in paradiso ameno,
Il corpo in terra aspetta.

14
[O Wind, why do you never rest ?]

Lugubre e vagabondo in terra e in mare,
O vento, O vento, a che non ti posare ?
Ci trai la pioggia fin dall' occidente,
E la neve ci trai dal nord fremente.

15
[O Wind, where have you been ?]

'Aura dolcissima, ma donde siete ?'
'Dinfra le mammole—non lo sapete ?
Abbassi il viso ad adocchiar l' erbetta
Chi vuol trovar l' ascosa mammoletta.
La madreselva il dolce caldo aspetta :
Tu addolci un freddo mondo, O mammoletta.'

16
[If I were a Queen]

'Foss' io regina,
 Tu re saresti :
  Davanti a te
   M' inchinerei.'
'Ah foss' io re !
 Tu lo vedresti :
  Sì che regina
   Mi ti farei.'

17
[What are heavy ? Sea-sand and Sorrow]

Pesano rena e pena :
Oggi e doman son brevi :

La gioventude e un fior son cose
    lievi :
Ed han profondità
Mar magno e magna verità.

18

[A Toadstool comes up in a Night]

Basta una notte a maturare il fungo ;
Un secol vuol la quercia, e non par
    lungo :
Anzi il secolo breve e il vespro lungo,
Chè quercia è quercia, e fungo è
    sempre fungo.

19

[If a Pig wore a Wig]

'Porco la zucca fitta in par-
    rucca ! . . .
    Che gli diresti mai ? '
' M' inchinerei, l' ossequierei—
    " Ser Porco, come stai ? " '
' Ahi guai per caso mai
Se la coda andasse a male ? ' . . .
' Sta tranquillo—buon legale
Gli farebbe un codicillo.'

20

[Hopping Frog, hop here and be seen]

Salta, ranocchio, e mostrati ;
    Non celo pietra in mano :
Merletto in testa e verde vesta,
    Vattene salvo e sano.
Rospo lordo, deh non celarti :
Tutto il mondo può disprezzarti,
Ma mal non fai nè mal vo' farti.

21

[Where innocent bright-eye Daisies are]

Spunta la margherita
    Qual astro in sullo stelo,
E l' erbetta infiorita
    Rassembra un verde cielo.

22

[A Motherless soft Lambkin]

Agnellina orfanellina
Giace in cima alla collina,
Fredda, sola, senza madre,
    Senza madre ohimè !
Io sarotti e madre e padre,
Io sarò tua pastorella ;
Non tremar, diletta agnella,
    Io ci penso a te.

23

[When Fishes set Umbrellas up]

Amico pesce, piover vorrà ;
Prendi l' ombrello se vuoi sur
    secco.
    Ed ecco !
Domani senza fallo si vedra
    Lucertolon zerbino
Ripararsi dal sol coll' ombrellino.

24

[A Ring upon her Finger]

Sposa velata,
Inanellata,
Mite e sommessa :
    Sposo rapito,
    Insuperbito,
    Accanto ad essa.

  Amici, amori,
   Cantando a coro
  Davanti a loro
   Spargete fiori.

25
[THE HORSES OF THE SEA]

  CAVALLI marittimi
   Urtansi in guerra,
  E meglio ci servono
   Quelli di terra.
  Questi pacifici
   Corrono o stanno ;
  Quei rotolandosi
   Spumando vanno.

26
[O SAILOR, COME ASHORE]

' O MARINARO, che mi apporti tu?'
' Coralli rossi e bianchi tratti in su
  Dal mar profondo.
Piante non son nè si scavar da mina :
Minime creature in salsa brina
  Fecerne mondo.'

27
[THE ROSE WITH SUCH A BONNY BLUSH]

ARROSSISCE la rosa—e perchè mai ?
A cagione del sol : ma, sol, che fai ?
  E tu, rosa, che t' hai
Che ti fai rosea sì se bene stai ?

28
[THE ROSE THAT BLUSHES ROSY RED]

LA rosa china il volto rosseggiato,
  E bene fà :
Il giglio innalza il viso immacolato,
  E ben gli stà.

29
[OH FAIR TO SEE]

O CILIEGIA infiorita,
La bianco-rivestita,
  Bella sei tu.
O ciliegia infruttata,
La verde-inghirlandata,
La rosso-incoronata,
  Bella sei tu.

30
[GOOD-BYE IN FEAR, GOOD-BYE IN SORROW]

' IN tema e in pena addio,
  Addio ma in van, tu sai ;
Per sempre addio, cor mio.'
  ' E poi più mai.'
' Oggi e domani addio,
  Nel secolo de' guai
. A tutto tempo addio.'
  ' E poi più mai.'

31
[BABY LIES SO FAST ASLEEP]

' D' UN sonno profondissimo
  Dorme la suora mia :
Gli angeli bianchi aligeri
  Verranno a trarla via ?'
' In sonno profondissimo
  Calma e contenta giace :
Un fiore in man lasciamole,
  Un bacio in fronte—e pace.'

32
[LULLABY OH LULLABY]

NINNA-NANNA, ninna-nanna,
  Giace e dorme l' agnellina.
Ninna-nanna, ninna-nanna,
  Monna Luna s' incammina.

Ninna-nanna, ninna-nanna,
   Tace e dorme l' uccellino.
Ninna-nanna, ninna-nanna,
   Dormi, dormi, o figliolino.
Ninna-nanna, ninna-nanna.

33

[LIE A-BED]

CAPO che chinasi,
Occhi che chiudonsi—
A letto, a letto,
Sonnacchiosetto!
Dormi, carino,
Fino al mattino,—
Dormi, carino.

Circa State 1878.

SOGNANDO

NE' sogni ti veggo,
   Amante ed amico;
Ai piedi ti seggo,
     Ti tengo tuttor.
Nè chiedi nè chieggo,
   Nè dici nè dico,
   L' amore ab antico
     Che scaldaci il cor.

Ah voce se avessi
   Me stessa a scoprire—
Ah esprimer sapessi
   L' angoscia e l' amor!
Ah almen se potessi
   A lungo dormire,
   Nè pianger nè dire,
     Mirandoti ognor!

Circa 1890.

NOTES BY W. M. ROSSETTI

DEDICATORY SONNET, p. lxxiii.—This sonnet formed the inscription or dedication of the volume published in 1881, *A Pageant and other Poems*. Christina Rossetti's books were, with few exceptions, dedicated to her mother; therefore the present inscription can very properly be removed from the position which it would occupy in order of date, and may form the dedication to the entire body of her poems.

The Longer Poems, p. 1.—Christina Rossetti never wrote a poem which could rightly be called long. I have thought it desirable to begin the collection with those few compositions which have some moderate degree of length, not excluding devotional poems. I transgress, in this section, the order of date, for the purpose of putting *Goblin Market* foremost. It has always held a certain primacy amid Christina's poems, and the strict order of date would have brought to the front a poem whose merit by no means qualifies it for such a position—*Repining*.

Goblin Market, p. 1.—The original title of this poem was *A Peep at the Goblins—To M. F. R.*—*i.e.* Maria Francesca Rossetti. I have more than once heard Christina say that she did not mean anything profound by this fairy tale—it is not a moral apologue consistently carried out in detail. Still the incidents are such as to be at any rate suggestive, and different minds may be likely to read different messages into them. I find at times that people do not see the central point of the story, such as the authoress intended it: and she has expressed it too, but perhaps not with due emphasis. The foundation of the narrative is this: That the goblins tempt women to eat their luscious but uncanny fruits; that a first taste produces a rabid craving for a second taste; but that the second taste is never accorded, and, in default of it, the woman pines away and dies. Then comes the central point: Laura having tasted the fruits once, and being at death's door through inability to get a second taste, her sister Lizzie determines to save her at all hazards; so she goes to the goblins, refuses to eat their fruits, and beguiles them into forcing the fruits upon her with so much insistency that her face is all smeared and steeped with the juices; she gets Laura to kiss and suck these juices off her face, and Laura, having thus obtained the otherwise impossible second taste, rapidly recovers.—This poem was skilfully translated into Italian by our cousin, Teodorico Pietrocola-Rossetti, under the title of *Il Mercato de' Folletti*, and was published in Florence (Pellas) in 1867. A cantata was made of the English words towards 1872 by Mr. Emanuel Aguilar.

Maids heard the Goblins cry, p. 1.—Various designations are given to the goblins; they are 'goblin men, little men, merchant men, fruit-merchant men.' They certainly had tails, for one merchant was 'whisk-tailed,' and they went 'lashing their tails' when baffled. Then there is the passage, 'One like a wombat prowled obtuse and furry,' etc. The authoress does not appear to represent her goblins as having the actual configuration of brute animals; it was Dante Rossetti who did that in his illustration to the poem (he allows human hands, however). I possess a copy of the *Goblin Market* volume, 1862, with marginal water-colour sketches by Christina—extending up to the poem *Spring* on p. 51 of that volume, but not farther. She draws several of the goblins,—all very slim agile figures in a close-fitting garb of blue; their faces, hands, and feet are sometimes human, sometimes brute-like, but of a scarcely definable type. The only exception is the 'parrot-voiced' goblin who cried 'Pretty goblin.' He is a true parrot (such as Christina could draw one). There are thirty-five such illustrations to *Goblin Market*—the simplest, as of fruit-branches, being the prettiest. When the special edition of *Goblin Market*, with designs by Mr. Laurence Housman, came out in 1893, Christina, although aware that the drawings possess superior artistic merit (a point, however, as to which she was no *judge*), did not exactly take to them as carrying out her own notion of her own goblins.

For there is no friend like a sister, etc., p. 8.—These lines are clearly connected with the original inscription of the poem, 'To M. F. R.' Christina, I have no doubt, had some particular occurrence in her mind, but what it was I know not. The two poems which immediately precede *Goblin Market* in date show a more than normal amount of melancholy and self-reproach; they are *L. E. L.* (p. 344) and *Ash Wednesday* (p. 217).

Repining, p. 9.—This poem was published in *The Germ*, 1850. It is, of all the poems by Christina Rossetti which appeared in that short-lived magazine, the only one which she did not afterwards reprint. No doubt it is far from being excellent; yet it cannot be called bad. In her MS. it is named *An Argument,* and is very considerably longer than in

The Germ, or hence in the present v the curtailment was a highly ja: act. The reader will readily per that this poem is to some extent moc. upon Parnell's *Hermit*. The c however, is different. Parnell ai: show that the dispensations of Provi: though often mysterious, are just. C tina's thesis might be summarized : Solitude is dreary, yet the life : = among his fellows may easily be drea: therefore let not the solitary rebel.

Three Nuns, p. 12.—The second s: tion of this poem was the first w r standing then as a separate compo: The united poem was inserted in: prose tale *Maude*, with the observa: : 'Pray read the mottoes; put toge: they form a most exquisite little s : which the nuns sing in Italy.' *Ma* was written towards 1850—pen: earlier. It was published in 1897. the poem of *Three Nuns* was exc from it on copyright grounds. T meaning of the mottoes runs thus: I heart sighs, and I know not where' It may be sighing for love, but to : it says not so. Answer me, my h. wherefore sighest thou? It answers : want God—I sigh for Jesus.

The Lowest Room, p. 16.— T original title of this poem was *A Fi; over the Body of Homer*—perhaps t better title of the two; it contains. MS., various stanzas which were omit:. in publication. This is the poem o which Dante Gabriel Rossetti, in published letter to his sister, dated 187; made the following remarks:—' A rea taint, to some extent, of modern vicious style, derived from that same source [Mrs. Browning]—what might be called a falsetto muscularity—always seemed to me much too prominent in the long piece called *The Lowest Room*. This I think is now included for the first time, and ' am sorry for it. . . . Everything i. which this tone appears is utterly foreign to your primary impulses. . . . If I were you, I would rigidly keep guard on this

t t er if you write in the future; and
rnately exclude from your writings
rything (or almost everything) so
ted.' Christina, on receiving this
er, did not acquiesce in its purport,
. later on seemed a little more inclined
do so. However, she always retained
e Lowest Room in succeeding editions.
me it hardly appears that my brother's
w can be pronounced correct. The
l gist of *The Lowest Room*—*i.e.* the
l acceptance, by the supposed speaker,
n subordinate and bedimmed position—
clearly the very reverse of 'falsetto
scularity'; if anything of that kind
ows in the earlier part of the poem, it
ows only to be waved aside.

From House to Home, p. 20.—I have
ways regarded this poem as one of
ly sister's most manifest masterpieces;
ough it is true that the opening of it
ould perhaps not have taken its present
orm had it not been for the precedent
f Tennyson's *Palace of Art*. In this
espect resemblances are obvious; but
divergencies also are of the very essence
f the poem. When a question arose as
o publishing it (in the *Goblin Market*
volume) my brother called attention to
he point, penciling on the MS. note-
book, 'This is so good it cannot be
omitted; but could not something be
done to make it less like *Palace of Art*?'
Christina, however, did nothing at all
in that direction; she substituted the
present title for the original one, *Sorrow
not as those who have no hope*. The
essence of the poem is the severance of
a human heart from the joys and the
loves of earth, to centre in the joys and
the loves of heaven; that it is in part a
personal utterance is a fact too plain to
need exposition. The three poems which
in date immediately precede *From House
to Home* are *The Love of Christ which
passeth Knowledge*, *A Shadow of Dorothea*,
and *By the Sea* (or rather a more personal
and melancholy lyric poem from which
By the Sea is extracted); next after
From House to Home comes *New Year's*

Eve. If the reader cares to turn to these
several poems, he will see in all of them
evidence of a spirit sorely wrung, and
clinging for dear life to a hope not of this
world. As elucidating this phase of feeling, so prominent in many of Christina
Rossetti's poems, I may refer to the
Memoir, p. lii.

The Prince's Progress, p. 26.—The
original nucleus of this poem is the
dirge-song at its close—'Too late for
love, too late for joy,' etc. This was
written in 1861, and entitled *The Prince
who arrived too late*. When Christina
Rossetti was looking up, in 1865, the
material for a fresh poetical volume, it
was, I believe, my brother who suggested to her to turn the dirge into a
narrative poem of some length. She
adopted the suggestion—almost the only
instance in which she wrote anything so
as to meet directly the views of another
person.

A Royal Princess, p. 35.—This poem
was first printed in 1863, in a small
volume named *Poems: an Offering to
Lancashire*, which was got up 'for the
relief of distress in the cotton-districts,'
i.e. the 'Cotton Famine,' consequent upon
the civil war in the United States. The
volume contained contributions by other
writers as well—George MacDonald,
Allingham, Mary Howitt, Isa Craig, Lord
Houghton, Locker-Lampson, Dante Rossetti, etc. That first printed form of the
poem contains some variants from the
present form, which is the same as in
the *Prince's Progress* volume. It is
rather singular that Christina should have
written in October 1861, before any
suggestion of the Cotton Famine began,
a poem which, when she was soon afterwards asked to contribute something for
this object, came in so markedly appropriate.

Maiden-Song, p. 38.—This simple
light-hearted poem—a kind of cross
between the tone of a fairy-tale and that
of a nursery-song, each of them sweetened

into poetry—was deservedly something of a favourite with its authoress.

The Iniquity of the Fathers upon the Children, p. 41.—This title formed at first, in the volume of 1866, the motto of the poem, its title then being *Under the Rose*. The change was made in the re-edition of 1875. In a copy of that re-edition I find a note by Christina as follows: 'This was all fancy, but Mrs. [W. Bell] Scott afterwards told me of a somewhat similar fact.' It seems to me that the 'fancy' may have been partly guided by a leading incident in Dickens's *Bleak House*.

The Months: A Pageant, p. 48.— This *Pageant*, which was written at Seaford, has been acted more than once, at any rate in girls' schools. I remember an instance reported from America not long before the authoress's death. Indeed this was partly in her view in writing the poem.

OCTOBER.
Here comes my youngest sister looking dim
And grim,
With dismal ways.—p. 54.

Christina had a considerable spice of fun in her composition, as well as profound seriousness and rooted melancholy. She wrote these lines regarding November with a side-glance at herself—or at any rate quoted them sometimes as a telling self-description.

A Ballad of Boding, p. 55.—I give to this the date 'before 1882,' on the ground that it was published in the *Pageant* volume, 1881. The MSS. of Christina Rossetti's poems, up to 11 June 1866, are, with few exceptions, extant and dated in notebooks; but after that time, although several MSS. exist, few precise dates are traceable. Christina published the *Prince's Progress* volume in 1866—the *Pageant* volume in 1881. The reader will understand that, in saying 'before 1882'—in this instance, and the like in several others—I do not imply that the composition was written shortly before 1882, for it may date any time between June 1866 and 1881. I am seldom, in such cases, able to approximate the true date nearer than this.

Monna Innominata, p. 58.—To one to whom it was granted to be behind the scenes of Christina Rossetti's life, and to how few was this granted—it is not merely probable but certain that this 'sonnet of sonnets' was a personal utterance—an intensely personal one. The introductory prose-note, about 'many a lady sharing her lover's poetic aptitude,' etc., is a blind—not an untruthful blind, for it alleges nothing that is not reasonable, and on the surface correct, but still a blind interposed to draw off attention from the writer in her proper person.

Sonnet 1, p. 58.—Some English reader may like to see the mottoes of this sonnet and of its successors anglicized. I give them so here; the reader will observe for himself that in every instance the first sentence comes from Dante, and the second from Petrarca: 1. The day that they have said adieu to their sweet friends. Love, with how great a stress dost thou vanquish me to-day!—2. I was already the hour which turns back the desire. I recur to the time when I first saw thee.—3. Oh shades, empty save in semblance! An imaginary guide conducts her.—4. A small spark fosters a great flame. Every other thing, every thought, goes off, and love alone remains there with you.—5. Love, who exempts no loved one from loving. Love led me into such joyous hope.—6. Now canst thou comprehend the quantity of the love which glows in me towards thee. I do not choose that Love should release me from such a tie.—7. Here always Spring and every fruit. Conversing with me, and I with him.—8. As if he were to say to God, 'I care for nought else.' I hope to find pity, and not only pardon. —9. O dignified and pure conscience!

⸮irit more lit with burning virtues.—
⸮. With better course and with better
⸮r. Life flees, and stays not an hour.—
⸮. Come after me, and leave folk to
lk. Relating the casualties of our life.
—12. Love, who speaks within my mind.
ove comes in the beautiful face of this
dy.—13. And we will direct our eyes
⸮ the Primal Love. But I find a burden
⸮ which my arms suffice not.—14. And
[is will is our peace. Only with these
houghts, with different locks.

An Old-World Thicket, p. 64.—This
oem bears a certain analogy to the
arlier one, *From House to Home*. I
hink it sustains the comparison, though
itched in a lower key. The essence of
From House to Home is unison with the
Church Triumphant, through self-abnega-
ion. The essence of the *Old-World
Thicket* might be expressed in a quotation
rom St. Paul: 'The creature itself also
hall be delivered from the bondage of
corruption into the glorious liberty of the
children of God. For we know that the
whole creation groaneth and travaileth
n pain together until now.' The poem
loes not, as I read it, relate to the
Church Triumphant, nor in a very express
orm to the Church Militant; rather, at
he close of the poem, to the scheme of
redemption, and the flock of Christ.

All Thy works praise Thee, O Lord,
p. 68.—In 1897 Prebendary Glendinning Nash, the Incumbent of Christ
Church, Woburn Square (the church frequented by Christina Rossetti in all her
closing years), adapted a portion of this
poem for a harvest festival under the name
A Processional of Creation. It was set
to music by Mr. Frank T. Lowden, and
sung at the evening service in that church,
21 October.

Later Life, p. 73.—The authoress
terms this 'a double sonnet of sonnets';
and I apprehend that the majority of it
must have been written with a definite
intention that its various constituent parts
should form one whole. Probably, when
the general framework was getting into
shape, two or three outlying sonnets were
pressed into the service.

Sonnet 17, 'Past certain cliffs,' etc.,
p. 78.—I consider that the beach of
Hastings and St. Leonard's is here intended.

Sonnet 18, p. 79.—This sonnet is
altered—*i.e.* its octave is entirely different
—from the sonnet named *Cor Mio* (p. 389).

Sonnet 21, p. 79.—The reference to
foreign travel in this sonnet and its suc-
cessor relates to the year 1865, when
Christina, along with our mother, accompanied me to North Italy through
Switzerland.

Sonnet 22, 'Struck harmonies,' etc.,
p. 80.—I think this is spoken figu-
ratively—not as implying that my sister
actually wrote or even composed 'a
song' concerning the Alps. If she
composed any such, it seems to have
remained unpublished and untraced.

Sonnet 25, p. 81.—This sonnet,
being written before 1882, cannot relate
in part to the death of Dante Gabriel or
of our mother. So far as it relates to
any particular death, that of our sister
Maria may have been mainly in the
writer's thought—assuming (that is) that
the sonnet was written after November
1876.

Sonnet 27, p. 81.—This forecast of
death came singularly true; for, if one
had been writing a condensed account
of Christina Rossetti's last days and hours
in December 1894, one might have
described them very nearly in these terms.
Perhaps, however, few among her Christian readers will suppose that she 'may
have missed the goal at last.' The
reference to a 'saint rejoicing on her
bed' may glance at Maria.

Juvenilia, p. 82.—When I was
editing, soon after my sister's death,
those compositions of hers which were
published as *New Poems* in 1896, I put

at the end of the volume all the *Juvenilia*, *i.e.* all the poems written before she completed, on 5 December 1847, her seventeenth year. My object naturally was to set a certain stamp of inferiority on the *Juvenilia*, lest readers of that volume should suppose that these compositions were accepted or presented by me as standing on a footing of equality with work of a less immature age. In the present complete edition of the Poems I do not see that any such precaution can be necessary; and I therefore place the *Juvenilia* immediately after *The Longer Poems*, in the position which belongs to them according to order of date.

To my Mother, on the Anniversary of her Birth, p. 82.—These are the first verses that Christina ever produced; written as they were on 27 April 1842, she was then aged eleven years and a third. I presume that we were all a little surprised at her 'coming out' in this line, but have no express recollection of details. Our grandfather, Gaetano Polidori, who kept a private printing-press, printed the lines at once on a card; he afterwards, 1847, included them in the small volume named *Verses*. I need not say that the lines are regarded by me as in no sense approaching towards excellence. In the first of Christina's note-books these two quatrains appear, and the dates for later productions go on to 3 December 1845; and my mother has written on the flyleaf the following 'N.B.,' which may be worth quoting:—' These verses are truly and literally by my little daughter, who scrupulously rejected all assistance in her rhyming efforts, under the impression that in that case they would not be her own.' At some date—it may have been towards 1850—Christina took it into her head to make some little coloured illustrations to that printed volume of *Verses*; they are slight and amateurish—one might indeed say childish. There is a certain degree of fancy in them, however; and Dante Gabriel always considered that our sister, had she chosen to study and take pains, might have done something as an artist. To the present small poem, emblem is two sprigs of heartsease. I proceed I shall mention other de.... whenever they seem to present any p.. of interest. I may also mention t that there is another copy of the *Ve* illustrated with pencil designs by D.. Gabriel: they must have been made e.r soon after the booklet was printed certainly before the autumn of 184.. The frontispiece is a very truthful pr..l.. likeness of Christina. Then fol designs to *The Ruined Cross* (which p.. I have not thought good enough for .... printing here), *Tasso and Leonora*, *I..* *Isabella*, and *The Dream*. This o..y, neatly bound, was presented by ou. grandfather to the authoress: on the f.. leaf he wrote some verses of his own : her, which had accompanied a bunch .. red and white roses. The profile likene.. of Christina, mentioned above, is the o.. whence was taken a tracing which h.. been reproduced in the published volum.. of *Letters by Dante G. Rossetti to Willia.. Allingham.*

The Chinaman, p. 82.—This trif.. had not hitherto been printed amon.. Christina's compositions, only in th.. book published in 1895—*Dante Gabr.. Rossetti, his Family-letters, with a Memoir* by myself. The account whi.. I there give of the verses is substantia..y as follows:—The year 1842 was the ye.. of the Anglo-Chinese Opium War. I was told by one of my schoolmasters .. make an original composition on th.. subject of China, and I think the com position had to be in verse. What I wrote I have totally forgotten. Christin.. saw me at work, and chose to enter the poetic lists. She produced the present lines.—So far as I can trace, this wa.. quite, or very nearly, the first thing that Christina wrote in verse, after the two stanzas *To my Mother*. About three months before her death I happened to be talking to her as to this and other old family reminiscences, and I found her to under the impression that, by the time then she wrote *The Chinaman*, she had ready done various other small things. ill, looking to known and probable ates, I cannot make it out to be so. uckily the question is not of high aportance to the literary world.

Charity, p. 84.—Christina's note to ese lines in MS. is as follows : 'The regoing verses are imitated from that eautiful little poem *Virtue* by George Ferbert.'

Love Ephemeral, p. 84. — Device : e crescent moon, with a lunar (more ke a solar) rainbow.

Burial Anthem, p. 84.—I have an npression that this was written in elation to the death of some young lergyman esteemed in our household ; here was not any death in our imediate family about that date. Device : sprig of blue and pink forget-me-not.

Lines to my Grandfather, p. 85.— This trifling performance is included mong the *Juvenilia*, not because it is good, but because it has a personal lavour. My sister was at the time, I think, staying with some friends in the country not far from London. Two hyme-words in the final stanza are obviously rhymes, not sense.

The End of Time, p. 87.—Device : a ose crossing a scythe ; within the angle of the scythe, an hour-glass.

Couplet, p. 88.—This was an oral mprovise. As I found occasion to ntroduce it into my Memoir of Dante Rossetti (1895), I may as well repeat the trifle here. Of course, the first line of the *Couplet* comes from a well-known old-fashioned song.

Amore e Dovere, p. 88.—There is a letter from Christina to Dante Gabriel, 1865, saying that the second stanza should be cut out. She assigns no reason, and I think best to leave it in : the reader can give it any consideration

he likes. In stanza 3 no rhyme is supplied to 'lagni'—seemingly an oversight.

Mother and Child, p. 88. — Mr. William Sharp published in *The Atlantic Monthly* for June 1895 a very sympathetic and interesting article, *Some Reminiscences of Christina Rossetti*. Here he says that on one occasion Dante Gabriel 'pointed out that Blake might have written the four verses called *Mother and Child*.' It would seem truer to say that Blake might have written a lyric of higher quality, embodying much the same conception. Device : some flowers of undefined genus, with sun-rays behind them.

Mary Magdalene, p. 89. — As the date shows, these simple and somewhat touching verses were written on 8 February 1846. On 30 March Christina wrote a different poem, *Divine and Human Pleading*—of a slightly 'preachy' kind, dissuading from the invocation of saints. Then, in the printed volume *Verses*, the two compositions, under the second title, were joined together. I am certain that the *Mary Magdalene* is better singly ; and I so give it, omitting the *Divine and Human Pleading*.

On the Death of a Cat, p. 89.—This cat belonged to our aunt, Eliza Harriet Polidori. Device : a cat, in a rather sentimental attitude of languor, extending its right arm over a kitten. The cat is sandy and white, the kitten tabby.

To Elizabeth Read, with some Postage-stamps for a Collection, p. 90.— Miss Read was a young lady under the tuition of our sister Maria : she is now Mrs. Bull, widow of a leading physician in Hereford. Christina had a most cordial liking for her. The design to this trifle is a human personation of one of the stamps, bowing in the character of a 'humble servant,' and wearing the 'livery of red and black,' of a sort of mediæval cut.

Love Defended, p. 90.—Device : a

blind man (stanza 3) groping, with trees in the background.

The Martyr, p. 91.—Device: the soul of the martyr received into heaven by an angel. Between the angel's wings are a series of red and white curves, symbolizing (I suppose) the nine heavens, as in Dante.

The Dying Man to his Betrothed, p. 92.—Device: a rosebush intertwined by a snake.

Gone for Ever, p. 95.—This comes properly among the *Juvenilia*, according to the order of date. It was written before Christina was sixteen years of age, and was included in the privately printed *Verses*. Device: a moss-rose, not fully blown. When she was preparing the *Prince's Progress* volume, 1866, she considered the present lyric good enough to be published—and I suppose no one has questioned her discretion in this respect; and published it was, without any change of diction at all. I have felt some doubt whether, under these circumstances, I ought to include it among the *Juvenilia* or not. On the whole I have thought it best to do so; it gains rather than loses in interest by this observance of the order of date.

The Time of Waiting, p. 95.—Device: a damsel on a steep green slope, stretching her arms up longingly; from the sky a black-hooded woman, or spectre, addresses her with an action of admonition. This seems to be apposite chiefly to triplet 2.

Tasso and Leonora, p. 96.—Device: the shooting star in a female form.

Love, p. 97.—In February 1847 Christina wrote a weak affair, four stanzas, which she entitled *Praise of Love*. This is the final stanza (much superior to the others), and got at last published in *Time Flies*. It was not reproduced in the *Verses* of 1893.

Resurrection Eve, p. 98.—Device: a white grave-cross, two palm-shrubs inter-lacing above it; in the sky, cresc[ent] moon and star.

The Dead City, p. 99.—This w[as] originally called *The City of Sta[tues]*. In point of length it ranks among [the] *Longer Poems*, but my arrangem[ent] retains it among the *Juvenilia*. T[he] reader will, no doubt, perceive th[at it] bears a certain relation to a story in [the] *Arabian Nights*, which was one [of the] comparatively few books which my si[ster] from a very early age, read freque[ntly] and with delight. Beyond this, ta[ken] along with what is obviously indica[ted] in the poem itself, I cannot say whe[ther] any particular intention was presen[t in] her mind.

Came and stole them from their m[ates], p. 99.—This has been remarked up[on] as a palpable make-rhyme, on the a[s]sumption that (if either of the two) [the] word ought to be 'mistress.' But ther[e] is no clear reason why the 'I' of t[he] narrative should be a woman; a phras[e] a little further on strongly suggests th[e] contrary—'Before me the birds ha[d] never Seen a *man*.'

Spring Quiet, p. 103.—As in the cas[e] of *Gone for Ever*, this is a very earl[y] poem, included in the *Prince's Pr[ogress]* volume.

The Dream, p. 104.—I am not sur[e] whether the first short quatrain her[e] printed is an integral portion of th[e] poem, or rather a quotation from som[e] other writer; I fancy the latter.

Eleanor, p. 105.—This may be [a] portrait from the life—I know not no[w] of whom.

Isidora, p. 106.—Maturin's roman[ce] *Melmoth the Wanderer* is, I suppos[e,] still known to several readers; it wa[s] republished some few years ago. Yet [it] may be as well to say, in explanation [of] the present poem, that Melmoth is [a] personage who has made a compact with the Devil, thereby securing an enormous length of life (say at least a century and alf), and the power of flitting at will m land to land. At the end of the m, Melmoth's soul is to be forfeited, less he can meanwhile induce some e else to take the compact off his nds. Melmoth makes numerous efforts this direction, but all abortive. One his intended victims is a beautiful girl med Immalee, a child of Nature in an dian island—a second Miranda. She comes deeply enamoured of Melmoth, it resists his tamperings with her soul. ie is finally identified as the daughter a Spanish Grandee, and is then ptized as Isidora. At one point of e story she espouses Melmoth, and ars him a child. Christina's poem is r deathbed scene. The last line is uly a fine stroke of pathos and of effect; it it is not Christina's—it comes *verttim* out of Maturin.

Zara, p. 107.—See the note on the oem *Look on this picture, and on This* . 323). In the novel of *Women*, Zara the rival (she finally turns out to be ie mother) of Eva; she is a shining ader of society. In the same year, 847, when she wrote *Zara*, my sister rote a separate composition, *Eva*. Its ierit is but middling, and I do not reprouce it here. The device to *Zara* is a oxglove plant, with insects sucking its oison-honey.

Immalee, p. 108.—See the note (p. .66) on *Isidora*.

Heart's Chill between, p. 109.—This oem, called at first *The Last Hope*, was ublished under its present title in *The Athenæum*, 14 October 1848, being the irst poem by Christina that got published. t was reprinted in Mr. Mackenzie Bell's ook, 1898. When I was compiling, in 1895, the volume named *New Poems*, I mitted this composition, thinking that, is it comes, in point of date, near the lose of the *juvenilia*, it ought to have een better than it is, and was hardly good enough for re-publication. The evival of the poem by Mr. Bell alters the conditions somewhat, so I now put it in.

Lady Isabella, p. 109.—This was Lady Isabella Howard, a daughter of the Earl of Wicklow; she was a pupil of my aunt, Charlotte Polidori. My sister entertained an ardent admiration for the loveliness of character and person which marked this young lady, who died of a decline at the age of eighteen or thereabouts.

Night and Death, p. 109.—It may reasonably be assumed that this lyric also has some reference to the death of Lady Isabella Howard.

Death's Chill between, p. 110.—See the preceding note upon *Heart's Chill between*. *Death's Chill between* was published in *The Athenæum*, 21 October 1848. It was originally named *Anne of Warwick*, and was intended to represent (in a rather 'young-ladyish' form) the dolorous emotions and flitting frenzy of Anne, when widowed of her youthful husband, the Prince of Wales, slain after the battle of Tewkesbury. If I remember right, this poem was offered to *The Athenæum* at the same time as *Heart's Chill between;* and my brother then substituted these titles for the original ones, so as to establish between the two a certain relation of contrast in similarity. At the present distance of date, it might perhaps have served better to preserve the first titles. My observations as to the exclusion of *Heart's Chill between* from the *New Poems* apply to this composition as well.

The Lotus-Eaters, p. 111.—Of course the sentiment here, as well as the title, comes to some considerable extent out of Tennyson.

One Certainty, p. 119.—This appears to have been written during a period of illness. In the MS. notebook, the next preceding poem is the sonnet *Rest*, in Christina's own handwriting (15 May); then the present sonnet and *Looking Forward* (8 June) are in our mother's handwriting. Again, on 31 August, *A Testimony* is in Maria's. Towards this period, and even before, Christina's state of health gave rise to serious anxiety. See the *Memoir*, p. l.

Songs for Strangers and Pilgrims, p. 120.—This series of poems continues inclusively up to the verses *Looking back along life's trodden way*, p. 145. It consists of lyrics out of three volumes—those which are named respectively *Called to be Saints* (1881), *Time Flies* (1885), and *The Face of the Deep* (1892). They were reprinted in the *Verses* (1893) published by the Society for Promoting Christian Knowledge; and then, for the first time, they were ordered under one general heading, as given above. In this instance, and in others ensuing later on, I, as a matter of course, follow the arrangement made by my sister, although it entails a certain interference with the order of date. The *Songs for Strangers and Pilgrims* form the eighth and last (not the first) section of those which make up the volume *Verses*; I place it here first because one of its compositions dates as early as 2 March 1850. In the present complete edition, this point, rather than the sequence of sections in the previously issued volume, seems to govern the question. The eight sections (which will be found reproduced one by one as we proceed) take the following order in the *Verses*: (1) *Out of the Deep have I called unto Thee, O Lord*; (2) *Christ our All in All*; (3) *Some Feasts and Fasts*; (4) *Gifts and Graces*; (5) *The World—Self-destruction*; (6) *Divers Worlds—Time and Eternity*; (7) *New Jerusalem and its Citizens*; (8) *Songs for Strangers and Pilgrims*.

Her Seed: It shall bruise thy head, p. 120.—This poem comes from *The Face of the Deep*, and would, in ordinary course, stand dated by me 'before 1893.' But a note made in that book by Christina shows that it was written before the date of our mother's death (which was in April 1886), so I name a date to correspond. The note in question runs: 'This one dearest mamma heard and liked.'

Judge nothing before the time, p.
—From *Time Flies*. The line
the entry for 16 January, and appe
be intended to be read as a sequel
entry for the 15th, which is on the
'In the beginning God created the he
and the earth,' followed by a re
that 'Adam's initial work of pr
(so far as we are told) was sin,
hell, for himself and his posterity

Man's life is but a working i
121.—This stanza is modified fr
conclusion of the little poem *In F*
(p. 238). In its present form it bel
to *Time Flies*.

Marvel of marvels, etc., p. 12
will be observed that this poem
the *Passing Away*, at p. 191—is
up of one sole rhyme-sound; I th
holds an equally high rank amo
authoress's verses. Its principal re
is, no doubt, to the deaths of her s
and mother.

Afterward he repented, and we
123.—In *Time Flies* this lyric, w
has an energetic personal tone, st
without any title, as the entry for 11 M
I do not remember that any salient e
of Christina's life was associated w
that particular day, but may men
that 12 May was the birthday of D
Gabriel, and the prose entry for this l
day might, without much straining,
supposed to have a certain referenc
him; he had died three years b
Time Flies was published. It may
that the two entries were, in some degr
'read together' in their author's mi
as having a relation to him.

Are they not all Ministering Spiri
p. 124.—The precise bearing of t
poem becomes clearer when we obser
its context in *The Face of the Deep*.
comes in after the text—'And the
came unto me one of the seven an
which had the seven vials full of t
last seven plagues, and talked with m
saying, Come hither, I will shew th
the Bride, the Lamb's wife.' T

it specially raised in the prose com-
t, which leads up to the poem, is
this gracious and joyful message is
vered by one of those same angels
) poured forth the plagues.

)ur life is long, etc., p. 124.—This
:e appeared in *Time Flies*, and I date
ccordingly 'Before 1886.' But, on
:rence to p. 185, it will be seen that
; is a modification of a much earlier
:m, *How Long?*—dated 14 April
56. As there are some fundamental
ferences between the two pieces, I
nt both here.

Lord, what have I to offer? etc., p. 124.
The reference to 'a heart-breaking loss'
ems to indicate that these lines refer
some particular event in my sister's
e. They appear in *Time Flies*, under
e date 24 April; I do not identify any
ch event with that day, but can easily
nceive a relation in the poem to some
fferent day.

Can I know it?—Nay, p. 125.—This
omposition (from *The Face of the Deep*)
rms a sort of meditation on the words
ddressed by Christ to the Church of
'hiladelphia. Amid those words comes
he expression 'Thou hast a little
trength.' On this the authoress com-
nents (in prose)—'Why not much
trength? God knoweth.' And soon
fterwards the poem ensues.

What is it Jesus saith unto the soul?
p. 127.—This sonnet, in its first form,
was written on 2 March 1850. As
printed, the octave is not much altered,
but the sextett is entirely recast. The
title used to be *Blessed are they that
mourn, for they shall be comforted*. The
first form of the sonnet appears printed
in the prose tale *Maude*, published in
1897.

'The sinner's own fault,' etc., p. 128.
--Stanza 1 is a modification of stanza 7 in
Margery (p. 360).

Who would wish back the saints, etc.,
p. 129.—These three stanzas, now altered
in metre and diction, formed at first a
portion of the poem *Better so* (see p. 351).

*Where shall I find a white rose blow-
ing?* p. 131.—This was first printed for
a bazaar, held in June 1884, for the
Boys' Home at Barnet, founded by
Colonel Gillum. It was then named
Roses and Roses.

Now they desire a Better Country,
p. 132.—In a copy of *Time Flies*,
Christina marked this as 'my first
roundel.'

These all wait upon Thee, p. 132.—
This stanza comes (with some verbal
modifications) out of the poem *To what
purpose is this Waste?* (see p. 305).

Doeth well . . . doeth better, p. 132.—
I consider that this poem relates to Maria
Francesca Rossetti, who had died in
1876. Christina often called her play-
fully 'Moon' or 'Moony.'

Vanity of Vanities, p. 133.—These
stanzas, altered in diction, come out of
the poem *Yet a Little While* (p. 342).

*Scarce tolerable Life, which all life
long*, p. 133.—I date this sonnet '*circa*
1884,' because I find the rough draft of
it written upon a scrap of paper which
bears the date 'Easter Eve 1884.'

Alleluia! or Alas! my heart is crying,
p. 135.—This little poem comes from *The
Face of the Deep*. It depends immediately upon those texts of *The Apocalypse*
which purport that 'the kings of the
earth' were 'saying, Alas, alas, that great
city Babylon!' on the same occasion
when 'much people in heaven' were
'saying, Alleluia! Salvation and glory
and honour and power unto the Lord
our God.' From this consideration the
authoress proceeds to reflect upon the
alternative in her own spiritual state.

The Flowers appear on the Earth,
p. 135.—Originally these two stanzas
formed a part of the poem *I have a
Message unto Thee*, p. 316. Their
diction has been slightly altered, but
only slightly.

Bury Hope out of sight, etc., p. 137.—In *Time Flies* this forms the entry for 5 December, which was the authoress's birthday. I assume that it was purposely inserted in relation to that anniversary, and probably to the death of Charles Bagot Cayley on the same day.

A Churchyard Song of Patient Hope, p. 138.—Christina, in placing this poem in the *Verses* next after the last-named, seems to have intended that the two should be read together. The original framework of the *Churchyard Song* was quite different: it formed in *The Face of the Deep* part of the reflections upon the Apocalyptic text, 'And God shall wipe away all tears from their eyes,' etc.

One woe is past, etc., p. 138.—Naturally this poem belongs, in *The Face of the Deep*, to the same words in chap. ix. of *The Apocalypse*. As arranged in the *Verses*, I think Christina intended it to be read in association with the preceding two compositions.

Thus I sat mourning, etc., p. 139.—I have seen these two lines objected to as being somewhat ludicrously grotesque. Christina Rossetti did not think any part of the Bible ludicrous, and she found in the prophet Micah, 'I will make a wailing like the dragons, and mourning as the owls.'

Behold, I stand at the Door and Knock, p. 147.—These verses were published in some magazine. I fancy it may have been one named *Aikin's Year*, with which Mary Howitt was connected. If so, I think the publication must be not later than 1854; and these would be (apart from the *Versi*, etc., see p. 446) the first verses by Christina which got into print after the cessation of *The Germ* in 1850.

St. Elizabeth of Hungary, p. 150.—I take it that this lyric received its immediate inspiration from the picture of like subject painted by James Collinson.

A Harvest, p. 153.—In the MS. notebook the title is *Annie*, and the ... extends to twenty stanzas. It the.. the form of an address to 'Annie ... husband or lover; possibly the pu... pathetic lines of Edgar Poe, *For* ... were partly in my sister's mind. some later date she numbered five ... the twenty stanzas, evidently conten... ing to retain those five alone. I ... her lead, and supply a new title. poem as it originally stood is, how... by no means a bad one.

Sleep at Sea, p. 154.—Was at ... named *Something like Truth*.

Some Feasts and Fasts, p. 156.—... general heading continues up to the ... *Sunday before Advent* (p. 179).

Embertide, p. 163.—This poem ... *The Face of the Deep*) takes occasi... from the passage of *The Apoca...* 'And one of the elders saith unto ... Weep not.' The prose comment ... the passage contains the followi... 'What we know with certainty of th... beatified elder is not his name, but ... Christ-likeness. As once his Master on earth, so now he in heaven saith, Weep not. The one and only aspect high ... low need desire to be known by ... Christ-likeness. Thus the saints are stamped, thereby they become recogni... able.' And then follows the present poem.

Monday in Holy Week, p. 165.—T... short piece was originally entitled *...* *under a Crucifix*. Written in 1853, ... was first published in 1885, in *Time Flies*.

Ascension Day, p. 170.—To the last two lines in this poem (ending, 'Is that His cloud?') Christina wrote, in a copy of *Time Flies*, the note: 'An idea picked up, I cannot remember where.'

There remaineth therefore a Rest, p. 180.—In the notebook this composition numbers twelve stanzas; two of them, under the title *The Bourne*, were eventually published ('Underneath the growing grass,' etc.). The remaining ten were unworthy to pair with those two, I think it best to use only five of m.

Paradise, p. 180.—The first title of ; poem was *Easter Even*. In a printed >y of her *Poems*, wherein Christina de a few jottings, she has here noted [ot a real dream.'

Ye have forgotten the Exhortation, 181.—Our father having died on , April 1854, it is not unnatural to ink that this poem, dated 10 May $ 54, bears some direct relation to that .ss. There had been two other deaths the family, May and December 1853— lose of our maternal grandparents; to er grandfather especially Christina was iost warmly attached. The title, *Ye ive forgotten the Exhortation*, standing y itself, does not seem to be specially pposite to this poem. It becomes so vhen read with its context (*Hebrews* xii. ;, 6): 'And ye have forgotten the ::xhortation which speaketh unto you as into children, My son, despise not :hou the chastening of the Lord, nor faint when thou art rebuked of him: for whom the Lord loveth he chasteneth, and scourgeth every son whom he receiveth.'

The World, p. 182.—This is one of Christina Rossetti's most energetic utterances, and a highly characteristic one. She had in fact a great horror of 'the world,' in the sense which that term bears in the New Testament; its power to blur all the great traits of character, to deaden all lofty aims, to clog all the impulses of the soul aspiring to unseen Truth. I recollect her once saying to me with marked emphasis, when my children were past their very earliest years, 'I hope they are not *worldly*.' It ،·is an interesting observation of the great poet Leopardi, in one of his prose writings, that this sense of 'the world' appears to have been entirely unknown to antiquity, and to have formed one of the most potent messages of Jesus Christ.

In Christina's sonnet the opposite aspects of the world by day and by night may call for a little reflection. The primary sense (of course subsidiary to some spiritual meaning) appears to be that the world—like other devils, spectres, and hobgoblins—appears *in propriâ personâ* in the night-hours only; it is then that she is recognized for the fiend she actually is.

Zion Said, p. 183.—As in a previous instance, the context makes this heading more significant,—*Isaiah* xlix. 13, 14: 'The Lord hath remembered his people, and will have mercy upon his afflicted. But Zion said, The Lord hath forsaken me, and my Lord hath forgotten me.' This quotation appears in a condensed form in the poem *Christian and Jew* (p. 203).

Hymn after Gabriele Rossetti, p. 183. —In our father's volume of religious poems, *L'Arpa Evangelica* (1852), there is a composition named *Nell' Atto della Comunione*, in three parts. The third begins with the words—'T' amo, e fra dolci affanni,' and is the one which Christina here translates in two separate versions. The date which I give is conjectural; I assume the translation to have been made not long after our father's death. The copy of the *Arpa Evangelica* into which these verses were inserted is profusely illustrated with pencil-designs by Christina.

I will lift up mine Eyes unto the Hills, p. 184.—In MS. the title of this poem (viewed with predilection by its authoress) was *Now they desire a better Country*. It was printed in the *Lyra Eucharistica*, 1864, as *Conference between Christ, the Saints, and the Soul* (this must, I think, have been a title proposed by the editor of the selection); in 1875, under its present title, it was included in Christina's collected *Poems*.

A Christmas Carol for my Godchildren, p. 187.—Christina, from time to time, acted as godmother to various children—

mostly, I think, children of poor people in the neighbourhood of Christ Church, Albany Street, Regent's Park. It may be worth noting that this carol was written not at Christmas time, but early in October; and in many instances a reference to dates would show that poems about festivals of the Church, or about seasons of the year, were written at dates by no means corresponding.

After this the Judgment, p. 188.—This composition in *terza rima*, written immediately after Christina Rossetti had completed her twenty-sixth year, was at first named *In Advent*, and it began with eight *tersine*, evidently prompted by a sense of the waning of early youth, and of melancholy at present and prospective conditions of life. These opening *tersine* had not any distinctly devotional character, and Christina, when she published her poem, excluded them. They are little or not at all less good than the rest of the composition, so I give them separately (p. 328), supplying a title—*Downcast*, for *In Advent* would no longer have any adequate application to them.

Old and New Year Ditties, p. 190.—It will be observed that these three lyrics were written in three several years. They used to be called—(1856) *The End of the Year*; (1858) *New Year's Eve*; (1860) *The Knell of the Year*. I have always regarded this last as the very summit and mountain-top of Christina's work. I will not say, nor indeed think, that nothing besides of hers is equal to it; but I venture to hold that, while she never wrote anything to transcend it in its own line, neither did any one else. The poem depends for its effect on nought save its feeling, sense, and sound; for the verses avoid regularity of the ordinary kind, and there is but one single rhyme throughout. The note is essentially one of triumph, though of triumph through the very grievousness of experience past and present. In framing the section of her *Devotional Poems*, 1875 and 1890,

Christina used to put these *Ditties* followed only by *Amen* and *The L— Place*. In reading them together, natural for her brother to reflect whe they indicate any special occurrence the years to which they relate. I ca— remember that they do — cannot, instance, say that in 1856 she was in express sense 'stripped of favourite th— she had'; however, the year 186 (besides being the year of Dante Gabri— marriage) was that in which Christina, few days before she wrote *The K—* attained the age of thirty, and h— thoughts as to the transit of years n— have been more than ordinarily solemn. Her reference to her having 'won neither laurel nor bay' has also its interest. The bay began sprouting soon afterwards with the appearance, in *Macmillan Magazine* for February 1861, of the poem *Up-hill*, which at once commanded a considerable share of public attention. It is quite possible that Christina—the most modest of poets, but by no means wanting in the self-consciousness of poetic faculty—thought in 1860 that the bay had been kept waiting quite long enough; and it is a fact that, between 24 July 1860, the date of *The Lambs of Westmoreland*, and 23 March 1861, the date of *Easter Even*, she wrote no verse whatever except this *Knell of the Year*.

The Heart knoweth its own Bitterness, p. 192.—Few things written by Christina contain more of her innermost self than this. In her volume *Verses* (published by the Society for Promoting Christian Knowledge) she took the first and last stanzas of this vehement utterance, and, altering the metre observably, and the diction not a little, she published them with the title, *Whatsoever is right, that shall ye receive* (see p. 194). I think it only right to give the poem in full, as well as the extracted portion of it.

Divers Worlds—Time and Eternity, p. 193.—This series of poems continues up to the verses *For All*. For some eneral remarks on the series see the note (p. 468) upon *Songs for Strangers and Pilgrims*.

Earth has clear call of daily bells, p. 93.—These two stanzas (first printed in *Time Flies*) are modified from two out of the eight which compose the poem *Yet a Little While* (p. 342). That poem has no connection with a stanza which bears the same title (p. 193).

Whatsoever is right, that shall ye receive, p. 194.—See the note (p. 472) to *The Heart knoweth its own Bitterness*.

'*Was Thy Wrath against the Sea?*' p. 195.—These lines from *The Face of the Deep* relate to the text, 'There was no more sea,' after the creation of 'a new heaven and a new earth.' This text dwelt much in Christina's mind, and prompted various allusions in her writings.

And there was no more Sea, p. 195.—See the preceding note. Notwithstanding the title which the present piece bears in the volume *Verses*, it comes in *The Face of the Deep* in connection with a very different passage of *The Apocalypse*—' And every creature which is in heaven and on the earth and under the earth, and such as are in the sea, and all that are in them, heard I saying, Blessing and honour and glory and power be unto Him that sitteth upon the throne, and unto the Lamb, for ever and ever.'

Roses on a brier, p. 196.—Another variation on the same theme. It comes from *Time Flies*, being the entry (without any associated prose) for 9 June.

Parting after parting, p. 200.—This little poem is made up from two separate stanzas first published in *Time Flies*. Stanza 1 forms the entry for 30 May; stanza 2 belongs to 10 August, and in *Time Flies* it relates to the parting and reunion of two martyrs—Laurence and Pope Sixtus. Stanza 1 (ten lines) is condensed from fourteen lines, named *Good-bye*, which were written on 15 June 1858, and (as marked in the MS. note-book) 'in the train from Newcastle.' This implies that Christina was then 'parting' from her friends the Bell Scotts of Newcastle, and, her visit being then terminated, was returning home to London. It will thus be seen that the intensity of feeling here expressed really originated in a very slight occurrence— the occurrence itself merely served the poet's turn as a suggestion of highly serious matters. Stanza 2 used to be the conclusion of the lyric *Meeting*, written on 11 June 1864 (see p. 366).

Advent, p. 202.—In the annotated copy of her *Poems* Christina wrote against this one: ' Liked, I believe, at East Grinstead '—which one may well credit. The liking is shared, by the ' Wise Virgins ' of that establishment, with the greatest living British (or European) poet, Mr. Swinburne, who has fixed upon this composition as about the crown of Christina's devotional work. The greater part of it was set to music for Christina's funeral service at Christ Church, Woburn Square, by the organist, Mr. Lowden. I heard the music sung, and can testify to its beautiful and touching effect.

Only Believe, p. 205.—There were originally some other lines concluding this poem. They appear under the title *What good shall my Life do me?* (p. 215).

New Jerusalem and its Citizens, p. 206.—This heading (from the *Verses*, 1893) extends on to the poem just aforenamed, *What good shall my Life do me?*

Who is this that cometh up not alone? p. 207.—In a copy of *Time Flies* I find the following note by my sister : ' These lines were suggested by a sermon I heard from the Rev. Marshall Turner in Christ Church, Woburn Square.'

Antipas, p. 208.—This poem (which comes from *The Face of the Deep*) is founded upon those words which, in *The Apocalypse*, Christ speaks in addressing the church of Pergamos : ' Thou hast not denied my faith, even in those days wherein Antipas was my faithful martyr, who was slain among you.' And in the prose commentary Christina said: 'Men know him not now, how he lived or how he died. God alone knows him. Enough for blessed Antipas.'

As cold waters to a thirsty soul, etc., p. 209.—These three stanzas are partly identical with the five stanzas which compose *A Shadow of Dorothea* (p. 216). The present three, having been published by my sister, cannot here be omitted. I think it would be a pity to omit the other five, and they therefore figure here as well.

'*Our Mothers*, etc.,' p. 214.—Christina evidently associates together, in the *New Jerusalem* series, this piece and the following one, as having a bearing personal to herself. They both come from *The Face of the Deep*, but from very different contexts there.

Is it well with the Child? p. 214.— This small lyric appeared in *Time Flies*, as being related to the martyrdom of St. Faith (supposed to be 'a noble maiden of Aquitain' in the third century). Her feast is 6 October. The verses formed originally a part of a longer composition named *Young Death*—date, 3 November 1865—and obviously relating to some very youthful person known to the authoress. Who this may have been I cannot now say. The portion of *Young Death* which was not included in the *Verses* has thus a certain personal interest. It is marked by a union of devoutness with quaint *naïveté* characteristic of Christina's verse in some moods; and, as I should not wish the lines to be totally lost, I give them separately under their proper date and title (see p. 244).

What good shall my life do me? p. 215.—See the note (p. 473) on *Only Believe*.

A Shadow of Dorothea, p. 216.—I do not find in the legend of St. Dorothea any incident corresponding closely to this. I understand that, in the poem, the speaker is a human soul, not as confirmed in saintliness, appealing to the flower-bearing Angel of the legend, rather indeed to the Saviour Christ. See the note above on the poem *Cold Waters*, etc.

For Henrietta Polydore, p. 217.— Christina's title only says 'H. P.,' but the lines are certainly intended for Henrietta Polydore, our cousin (see note to p. 421). She was born in England and brought up a Roman Catholic. By a curious train of circumstances she was at one time, while still a child, in Salt Lake City with the Mormons. Her father recovered her thence, at a time when a military expedition was sent by the Federal Government to control affairs in the Territory of Utah; and the present lines were presumably written by Christina when she heard that her youthful cousin was about to re-embark for England.

Ash Wednesday, p. 217.—These verses —bearing no title beyond *Jesus, do I love Thee?*—were printed in the *Lyra Eucharistica*, 1864. *Ash Wednesday* is the authoress's own title in her MS. notebook; I retain it, as the lines were evidently written towards the date of that fast. Preceding the last quatrain, the MS. gives six verses of ecstatic religious appeal which, as they were not printed, I with some hesitation omit.

A Christmas Carol, p. 217.—This was in the *Lyra Messianica*, 1865, named simply *Before the paling of the stars*. I retain my sister's own title.

Christ our All in All, p. 218.—This general heading continues up to the poem *The Chiefest among Ten Thousand* (p. 232). See the note (p. 468) to *Songs for Strangers and Pilgrims*.

An exceeding bitter cry, p. 218.—The phrase 'too late for rising from the dead' may ask a word of explanation. The poem comes from *The Face of the Deep*, and relates to Christ's address to the Church of Sardis, in which occur the

NOTES 475

words, 'Thou hast a name that thou livest, and art dead.'

Thy Friend and thy Father's Friend forget not, p. 226.—This poem is based upon one which was written as far back as 26 August 1859, entitled *Then they that feared the Lord spake often one to another*. The printed version is the shorter of the two, and is modified throughout, the closing lines being quite different.

'*And now why tarriest thou?*' p. 228.—This was set to music (like *Advent*—see the note on p. 473) by Mr. Frank Lowden, and was sung at Christina's funeral service.

Within the Veil, p. 234.—From the *Lyra Messianica*. These verses would seem to refer to the recent death of some religious and cherished young friend ; I cannot say who it was. In MS. the title of the verses is *One Day*.

For a Mercy Received, p. 235.—I am unable to say what the 'mercy' was.

The Lowest Place, p. 237.—As an expression of her permanent attitude of mind in the region of faith and hope, Christina evidently laid some stress on this little poem. She made it the concluding piece in the *Prince's Progress* volume, and also in the combined form of that volume with the *Goblin Market* one. Hence I thought the second stanza of this poem the most appropriate thing that I could get inscribed upon her tombstone in 1895. In the sequence of compositions in her MS. notebook there is nothing to show any exceptional degree of devout absorption towards this date. *The Lowest Place* bears the same date as *The Ghost's Petition*, and comes immediately after the sunny playful-minded *Maiden Song*.

Come unto Me, p. 237.—This is the title given to the sonnet when first published in the *Lyra Eucharistica*; in MS. it stands as *Faint yet Pursuing*. It belongs to a knot of pieces showing some dejection and self-reproach, from 20 January to March 1864. The next following lyrics, *Patience* and *Easter*, have a less disconsolate tone. The other pieces in question are *Beauty is vain*, *What would I give? Who shall deliver me?*

By the Waters of Babylon, p. 239.—*In Captivity* was the first name of this forcible piece of *terza rima*.

Despised and Rejected, p. 241.—The point of view in this poem is rather remarkable. To some extent it pairs with the earlier composition (p. 147), *Behold I stand at the Door and Knock*. That, however, is obviously addressed to the prosperous and callous—the Dives who will not take count of Lazarus. Here we have a different situation. The supposed speaker is clearly a person who has been rather hardly treated by the world, and who determines that henceforth he will be left alone. The message addressed to him is : 'Whatever you exclude, through condonable disgust with the world and its ways, don't exclude Christ, nor yet the poor and suffering, who are Christ's representatives here.' Thus the poem bears some faint analogy (yet not the least resemblance) to *The Poet's Vow* of Mrs. Browning.

Birds of Paradise, p. 242.—This was printed in *Lyra Messianica*, under the title *Paradise in a Symbol*. In that volume the substituted title is appropriate, because another poem by Christina is there, named *Paradise in a Dream* ('Once in a dream I saw the flowers,' etc., see p. 180). For the present poem her own title in MS. was *Birds of Paradise*, which I prefer to retain here. In the MS. the last line of stanza one stands 'Windy-winged they came.' I reproduce the printed phrase, yet am sorry to lose the written one.

I know you not, p. 243.—From *Lyra Messianica*. Date conjectural.

Young Death, p. 244.—This is only a portion of the poem, as first written. See the note (p. 474) on *Is it well with the Child?* The gaps left by the extraction of the latter lyric are indicated here by asterisks.

A Christmas Carol, p. 246. This was first published in *Scribner's Monthly*, January 1872. It was republished, 1875, in the volume of united poems, being then made to open the series of Devotional Poems.

Wrestling, p. 247.—This is the introductory poem to Christina Rossetti's volume of prayers named *Annus Domini*, published by Messrs. James Parker and Co. in 1874. It had not hitherto been reproduced in any volume of her poems. In *Annus Domini* the composition stands untitled. I supply a title of my own. Stanza 7 was not printed in *Annus Domini*. Christina (as notified in Mr. Mackenzie Bell's book) wrote it afterwards, and I find it in the copy which she inscribed to our mother for her birthday, 27 April 1874.

The Master is come and calleth for Thee, p. 248.—In the annotated copy of Christina's poems I find a note as follows: 'Dr. Littledale wanted a hymn—for a "Profession," I think; so I wrote this. But I think it was not adopted.'

Saints and Angels, p. 249.—On this poem Christina made a rather quaint note, personal to myself: 'William aptly remarked that this contains nothing about angels.'

A Rose Plant in Jericho, p. 250.—This sweet little poem has (it would seem) less of personal intensity of emotion than a reader might surmise from its terms. It stands annotated by Christina thus: 'Written once when Mr. Shipley wanted something' (the Rev. Orby Shipley, who edited more than one volume of devotional verse). The precise bearing of the title is not clear to me.

Patience of Hope, p. 250.—This comes from *The Children's Hymn-book*, edited by Mrs. Carey Brock, Bishop How, and others, and published by Messrs. Rivington. The date of publication appears to be 1881, and I therefore date this '*circa* 1880.' The words are set sung to the tune 'Grasmere' by Cameron W. H. Brock. In *Children's Hymn-book* the composition was named *Thou art the same, and Years shall not fail*: when it was printed in the volume of 1891, present title was substituted.

I will Arise, p. 251.—To this some other poems I give the date 'before 1882,' on the ground that they were published in the *Pageant* volume, 1881.

'*Behold, a Shaking*,' p. 255.—The first of these two sonnets is an eve recasting of the third sonnet in the serie (p. 384), named *By Way of Remembrance*. I much prefer that third sonnet. It was not published by Christina herself, and I give both forms of the composition.

Why? p. 260.—It will be seen this sonnet bears some relation to another sonnet, *If only* (p. 244), and to the lyric *When my heart is vexed I will complain* (p. 248).

If thou sayest, etc., p. 261.—The whole context may as well be quoted here: 'If thou forbear to deliver them that are drawn unto death, and those that are ready to be slain; if thou sayest, Behold, we knew it not; doth not He that pondereth the heart consider it? and He that keepeth thy soul, doth not He know it?'

A Sick Child's Meditation, p. 263.—Comes from a little Church serial named *New and Old*.

Out of the Deep have I called unto Thee, O Lord, p. 264.—This section of the *Verses* continues on to the sonnet, *Light of Light*. See the note (p. 468) to *Songs for Strangers and Pilgrims*.

Gifts and Graces, p. 270.—Continues on to the verses which begin, '*Lord, grant us grace to rest upon Thy word*.'

Christmas Carols, p. 278.—It is reasonable to suppose that these three carols were written in different years.

am not aware of the correct dates. e first carol was published (in *The ntury-Guild Hobby-horse*) in 1887, and I give a general date, '*circa* 1887.'

A Hope Carol, p. 280.—I give here e date 'before 1889,' on the ground at the verses were first published in he *Century-Guild Hobby-horse*, 1888.

Yea I have a Goodly Heritage, p. 280. —As to the date, I only know that this as published in October 1890 (in *Italanta*).

Mary Magdalene and the other Mary : Song for all Maries, p. 281.—Perhaps he authoress meant something special by the sub-title. She may have been thinking of her mother's second name Mary, and her sister's name Maria.

A Death of a First-born, p. 282.— Relates to the death of the Duke of Clarence and Avondale.

Faint yet Pursuing, p. 282.—These sonnets were published in *Literary Opinion*, April 1892. Date conjectural.

The World—Self-destruction, p. 283. —This series of poems, lasting up to the lines which begin, 'Toll, bell, toll,' come from *The Face of the Deep*, reprinted in the *Verses*, 1893.

All Things, p. 285.—This short piece belongs also to *The Face of the Deep*. I have given a title, for clearness' sake. My sister did not reproduce the piece in the *Verses* of 1893. I cannot discern any reason for the omission, unless it be that she thought the lines too brief to hold their place in that volume.

Heaven Overarches, p. 286.—When I was looking through my sister's effects, shortly after her death in 1894, I found these verses rather roughly written in a little memorandum-book. Their date must, I think, be as late as 1893. Except *Sleeping at Last* (p. 417), they appear to be about the last lines produced by my sister.

A Portrait, p. 286.—The reader will observe that the second of these two sonnets belongs, in point of date, to the *Juvenilia*. It was written for the death of Lady Isabella Howard. See the note (p. 467) upon *Lady Isabella*. The sonnet which here stands first was meant for Saint Elizabeth of Hungary, and was so entitled ; Christina had before then read with interest Kingsley's drama, *The Saint's Tragedy*. The name *A Portrait* is intended, I assume, to reidentify the brace of sonnets with Lady Isabella Howard. I question, however, whether some of the stronger expressions in the first sonnet are wholly applicable to this young lady.

Three Stages, p. 288.—This triple poem was written, as the reader will perceive, at three very different dates, ranging between 1848 and 1854. The first section was originally named *Lines in Memory of Schiller's Der Pilgrim ;* but, when published by my sister, it received the altered title, *A Pause of Thought*. She did not see fit to publish sections 2 and 3 ; not, I am convinced, that she thought them below the mark, but because of their intimately personal character. I published them in the volume of *New Poems*, keeping them separate, and naming No. 3 *Restive*. As I mentioned at that time, I think the proper ultimate treatment for the three sections is to keep them united, as Christina herself united them in MS. ; and this I now effect.

Lady Montrevor, p. 290.—This sonnet applies to a personage in Maturin's novel, *The Wild Irish Boy*. Christina, as well as her brothers, was in early youth very fond of Maturin's novels, and more than one of her poems relate to these. Lady Montrevor is possibly now almost forgotten. She is a brilliant woman of the world who fascinates 'the Wild Irish Boy,' and leads both him and herself into grave dilemmas.

Song ('When I am dead, my dearest '), p. 290.—This celebrated lyric (which has perhaps been oftener quoted, and certainly oftener set to music, than anything else by Christina Rossetti) was, except for one composition, her only production in December 1848. The other, so far from being of any the like calibre, is so indifferent that it has never been published: it bears the rather odd title, *What Sappho would have said, had her leap cured instead of killing her*—and its date is 7 December 1848. The next poem after *When I am dead* is the *Symbols*, 7 January 1849 (p. 116). The reader may perhaps not object to see here a few particulars about musical settings of Christina's works. *Goblin Market* and *Songs in a Cornfield* are referred to in other notes; also some composed by Mr. Lowden. I myself possess musical settings as follows, but no doubt there are several others. *When I am Dead*, by Mary Carmichael and ten other composers; five from *Singsong*, by Mary Carmichael, and four by Schlesinger; *Up-hill*, four settings; *A Birthday* and *Bird Raptures*, two each; *Hope is like a Harebell*; *First Spring Day*; *If*; *The Skylark*; *Dreamland*; *A Summer Wish*; *Echo*, by Virginia Gabriel; *Yea or Nay*; *I bore with Thee*; *Advent*; *Two Doves*.

An End, p. 292.—This is one of the poems published in *The Germ*, 1850. The others were—*Dreamland*, *A Pause of Thought*, *Song* (Oh roses for the flush of youth), *A Testimony*, *Repining*, and *Sweet Death*.

Dream land, p. 292.—Christina made three coloured designs to this lyric. In the first we see the 'She' of the poem journeying to her bourne. She is a rather sepulchral-looking, white-clad figure, holding a cross; the 'single star' and the 'water-springs' are apparent, also a steep slope of purplish hill which she is leaving behind. The second design gives the night'ngale singing on a thorny rose-bough. In the third, 'She' is rising and ascending winged; her pinions are golden, of butterfly-form.

Looking Forward, p. 293.—The tone of this lyric suggests that it was written in expectation of seemingly imm??? death; in the MS. notebook it st?? in my mother's handwriting (quite c?? trary to wont), and so does another p??? dated in the same month, *One Certain* (p. 119).

Queen Rose, p. 295.—Christina s?? often—possibly too often—the prais?? the rose; she regarded it not merely ?? its own beauty, but as the symbol ?? love, whether construed as deep hum?? affection or as union with the Divi?? The lily stood with her (as with so mary another) for faith.

Endurance, p. 297.—This sonnet does not appear in Christina's MS. note-boo??. It was inserted into the prose tale *Mau..* (published in 1897) as being a mor?? effusion of 'Maude.' As the M?. c? that tale was done in 1850, I presum? that the sonnet may have been writt?? towards that date. It is not very go??, but could scarcely (I think) be omitt?? here. The same remarks (save as t? demerit) apply to the next ensuing lyric. *Withering*. In both cases the titles are mine.

Twilight Calm, p. 297.—This poem looks like a direct transcript from nature, as if the authoress had observed the particular features of the scene one by one, and had noted them down at the moment. And yet it cannot have been so; unless indeed one supposes that it was mainly written at one season, and only concluded at another. Its recorded date, 7 February, is inconsistent with several of the details described—bees, leafy wood, lilies and roses shutting, etc.

Is and Was, p. 300.—The last line of this poem, 'Doing all from self-respect,' may be worth a moment's comment. Much about the time when the poem was written, a lady told my sister that the latter seemed to 'do all from self-respect,' not from fellow-feeling with others, or from kindly consideration for them. Christina mentioned the remark, with an admission that it hit a blot in character, in which a certain amount reserve and distance, not remote from *hauteur*, was certainly at that date perceptible. She laid the hint to heart, and, I think, never forgot it. A like phrase appears in a poem of much later date, July 1865, *Enrica* (see p. 377).

Annie, p. 301.—Christina, the most scrupulous of women and of writers, put to this lyric a note—'query Borrows.' She meant that there may, or possibly may not, be here some unconscious reminiscences from other poems.

Books in the Running Brooks, p. 303.—This, in MS., stands entitled *After a Picture in the Portland Gallery*. What this picture may have been I cannot now say; not one by Dante Rossetti, who did not exhibit in that gallery after 1850.

To what purpose is this Waste? p. 305.—The reader will observe, on p. 132, the composition, *These all wait upon Thee*, extracted with modified diction from the present poem.

Next of Kin, p. 307.—This might appear to be a personal address to some very youthful relative; if so, it can only be intended for the 'Lalla' named on p. 421, for Christina had no other relative younger than herself. But perhaps no personal reference is really intended.

For Rosaline's Album, p. 307.—Rosaline was Miss Orme, who, not long after the date of these verses, married Professor David Masson, now King's Historiographer for Scotland. These sepulchral verses are perhaps not quite the staple for a very youthful (and I might add charming) lady's album.

Dead before Death, p. 313.—I am unable to say what gave rise to this very intense and denunciatory outpouring. It was written three days before the authoress completed her twenty-fourth year; and possibly it may be regarded as an address to herself—not indeed as she was, or even supposed herself to be, but as she might become if 'Amor Mundi' were to supersede the aspiration after divine grace.

The First Spring Day, p. 314.—In a copy of her *Poems*, 1875, Christina made the following note: 'I was walking in the Outer Circle, Regent's Park, when the impulse or thought came.'

My Dream, p. 315.—If anything were needed to show the exceptional turn of mind of Christina Rossetti—the odd freakishness which flecked the extreme and almost excessive seriousness of her thought—the present poem might serve for the purpose. It looks like the narration of a true dream; and nothing seems as if it could account for so eccentric a train of notions, except that she in fact dreamed them. And yet she did not; for, in a copy of her collected edition of 1875, I find that she has marked the piece 'not a real dream.' As it was not a real dream, and she chose nevertheless to give it verbal form, one seeks for a meaning in it, and I for one cannot find any that bears development. She certainly liked the poem, and in this I and others quite agreed with her; I possess a little bit of paper, containing three illustrations of her own to *The Dream*, and bearing the date 16 March '55. There is (1) the dreamer slumbering under a tree, from which the monarch crocodile dangles; (2) the crocodile sleeping with 'unstrung claw,' as the 'winged vessel' approaches; and (3) the crocodile as he reared up in front of the vessel, and 'wrung his hands.' I may add that, for some reason as untraceable perhaps as that which guided Christina in the writing of *The Dream*, Dante Gabriel bestowed the name of 'the prudent crocodile' (from this poem) upon Mr. William Morris, and the nickname found favour with some other members of our circle. Perhaps it will one day turn up in correspondence, and will remain unfathomable to persons who do not read this note.

I have a Message unto Thee, p. 316.—After the sixth stanza of this poem came

480 POETICAL WORKS OF CHRISTINA ROSSETTI

two other stanzas here omitted. My sister used them, with slight verbal alterations, as a separate composition, *The Flowers appear on the Earth* (see p. 135).

To the End, p. 319.—The last quatrain of this poem seems to present a certain reminiscence (yet far from being a plagiarism) from Dante Rossetti's early achievement, *The Blessed Damozel*.

Shut Out, p. 320.—In MS. this piece bears the too significant title, *What happened to Me*.

Acme, p. 323.—In point of sentiment, not at all in the form of treatment, this sonnet bears some analogy to one by Dante Rossetti, *A Superscription*. The latter was written in January 1869, long after Christina's sonnet: the resemblance must be fortuitous.

Look on this Picture and on This, p. 323.—In my sister's MS. this poem is a rather long one, forty-six triplets; I have reduced it to twenty-three—omitting those passages which appear to me to be either in themselves inferior, or adapted rather for spinning out the theme than intensifying it. Longer or shorter, the poem is perhaps hardly up to the writer's mark; but there is a degree of peculiarity about it which disinclines me to drop it out. Were it not for the name 'Eva,' I should be embarrassed to guess what could have directed my sister's pen to so singular a subject and treatment; but that name satisfies me that she was here recurring to a favourite romancist of her girlhood, Maturin (see note to p. 107). In Maturin's novel entitled *Women* there is a personage Eva, and a situation which must certainly have prompted the present poem.

Downcast, p. 328.—This is in strictness a fragment, and its full rhyme-system, as *terza rima*, is necessarily uncompleted. See the note (p. 472) to *After this the Judgment*.

A Triad, p. 329.—This very fine sonnet was published in the volume of 1862, *Goblin Market and other Poems*, but was omitted in subsequent issues. I presume that my sister, with overstrained scrupulosity, considered its moral tone to be somewhat open to exception. In such a view I by no means agree, and I therefore reproduce it here, as I did in the volume of *New Poems*, 1896.

Love from the North, p. 329.—Was originally named *In the Days of the Six Kings*, which is perhaps the better title of the two.

In an Artist's Studio, p. 330.—The reference is apparently to our brother's studio, and to his constantly-repeated heads of the lady whom he afterwards married, Miss Siddal.

In the Round Tower at Jhansi, p. 332.—On hearing this tragic episode of the Indian Mutiny, my sister composed the poem, which I always rate among her masterpieces; and she published it in the *Goblin Market* volume, 1862. In a subsequent reissue she added the following note: 'I retain this little poem, not as historically accurate, but as written and published before I heard the supposed facts of its first verse contradicted.' In that copy of the *Goblin Market* volume in which Christina drew a few coloured designs, she has put a head- and tail-piece to the Jhansi poem. The former is a flag displayed—pink field, with a device of two caressing doves. The latter is the same flag, drooping from its broken staff, and seen on the reverse side, besmeared with blood.

A Nightmare (Fragment), p. 333.—In my sister's note-book this composition begins on p. 25, and ends on p. 27; the intermediate leaf has been torn out. Mere scrap as it is, I should be sorry to lose it quite.

For One Sake, p. 333.—The precise bearing of this sonnet may admit of some uncertainty. It would seem that some woman known to the authoress (I cannot at all say who it was) had died, and was regarded by her as now a saint in heaven, the 'imperishable bride' of Christ. Or possibly the 'imperishable bride' is the Christian Church in the abstract. The phrase as to 'wars and rumours of your wars' seems to be anything but germane to such a theme. The war of the Indian Mutiny was then raging; and it may be that the writer intended to express the opinion—which she certainly entertained —that any such turmoil is a very little thing, in comparison with the question whether the human soul is to be saved or lost to all eternity.

Memory, p. 334.—It will be observed that this remarkable utterance is made up of two separate poems, written at a rather wide interval of dates. No. 1 was originally named *A Blank;* No. 2, *A Memory*.

A Birthday, p. 335.—I have more than once been asked whether I could account for the outburst of exuberant joy evidenced in this celebrated lyric; I am unable to do so. Its correct sequence is shown in these pages, between Part I. of *Memory* and *An Apple Gathering*—poems neither of which is at all in the like strain. It is, of course, possible to infer that the *Birthday* is a mere piece of poetical composition, not testifying to any corresponding emotion of its author at the time; but I am hardly prepared to think that.—In some illustrated comic paper a parody of the lyric was printed; it amused Christina, who pasted it into a copy of her *Poems*, 1875. It may perhaps amuse other people, and I give it here :—

AN UNEXPECTED PLEASURE
(*After Christina G. Rossetti*)

My heart is like one asked to dine
  Whose evening dress is up the spout ;
My heart is like a man would be
  Whose raging tooth is half pulled out.
My heart is like a howling swell
  Who boggles on his upper C ;
My heart is madder than all these—
  My wife's mamma has come to tea.

Raise me a bump upon my crown,
  Bang it till green in purple dies ;
Feed me on bombs and fulminates,
  And turncocks of a medium size.

Work me a suit in crimson apes
  And sky-blue beetles on the spree ;
Because the mother of my wife
  Has come—and means to stay with me.

Winter, My Secret, p. 336.—This was at first named *Nonsense;* but, if there is method in some madness, there may be nous in some nonsense.

My Friend, p. 336.—One can scarcely doubt that this refers to the death of some person known to and beloved by the writer. Perhaps at one time I knew who it was, but do not now.

Maude Clare, p. 337.—This poem was originally much longer than it is now. It numbered forty-three stanzas or thereabouts (there is a gap in the MS. note-book just before its close). It was first published in *Once a Week*, 5 November 1859, with a design by Millais—far from being among his best. There were then sixteen stanzas—now only twelve. I am not sure that the omission of the opening stanza was an advantage ; here it is :—

The fields were white with lily-buds,
  White gleamed the lilied beck ;
Each mated pigeon plumed the pomp
  Of his metallic neck.

Autumn, p. 337.—Was at first entitled *Ding Dong Bell*.

Up-hill, p. 339.—This was, I believe, the first poem by Christina which excited marked attention ; it was published in *Macmillan's Magazine* for February 1861, and was at once accepted by poetical readers as an observable thing. The like had, in its small degree, been the case with the verses printed in *The Germ;* but then *The Germ* had next to no circulation.

At Home, p. 339.—Was originally called *After the Picnic*, and was written (as a pencil-note by the authoress says) 'after a Newcastle picnic,' which must no doubt have been held in company with the Bell Scotts. This, however, was a trivial title, to which my brother raised some objection. He considered this to be about the best of all Christina's poems, and was not (I conceive) far wrong, though there are others equally good. It will be perceived that 29 June 1858 was a red-letter day in Christina's poetic calendar. She produced on that day (or else she simply completed) *Up-hill*, *At Home*, and the ensuing *To-day and To-morrow*, which, though left unpublished during her lifetime, appears to me only a trifle less masterly than the other two. She illustrated *At Home* with two coloured designs, which, inefficiently done as they are, carry a certain imaginative suggestion with them. No. 1 shows the blanched form of the ghost in a sky lit with cresset flames. On one side the sky is bright blue, the flames golden; on the other side, dark twilight grey, and the flames red. No. 2 is the globe of the earth, rudely lined for latitude and longitude. The equator divides it into a green northern and a grey-purple southern hemisphere. Over the former flare sunbeams in a blue sky; below the latter the firmament is dimly dark, and the pallid moon grey towards extinction.

The Convent Threshold, p. 340.—The authoress seems to have combined in this impassioned poem something of the idea of an Héloïse and Abélard with something of the idea of a Juliet and Romeo. The opening lines, *There's blood between us*, etc., clearly point to a family feud, as of the Capulets and Montagues; but it is difficult to believe that the passage beginning 'A spirit with transfigured face' would have been introduced unless the writer had had in her mind some personage, such as Abélard, of exceptionally subtle and searching intellect. It may be observed moreover that (as with the letters of Héloïse to Abélard) this seems to be intended for a written outpouring, not a spoken one: see the line on p. 342, 'I cannot write the words I said.'

Yet a Little While, p. 342.—Stanzas 3, 4, 7, and 8 are used, with modifications, in other poems; the first pair in *Vanity of Vanities* (p. 133), and the second pair in the opening lyric (p. 193) of *Divers Worlds, Time and Eternity*. Nevertheless I have thought it undesirable to cut them out of the present poem.

Father and Lover, p. 343.—These two songs—the first spoken by the Father, and the second by the Lover—come from a prose fairy-tale named *Hero*, which was printed in the volume entitled *Commonplace and Other Stories*, 1870—long out of print. I am not sure as to when my sister wrote *Hero*; it was before 1866, and I think some years before.

By the Sea, p. 343.—This lyric of three stanzas was taken out of one of six stanzas, named *A Yawn*. The longer poem has a much more decided personal note in it.

Winter Rain, p. 344.—There is hardly any poem by my sister, other than this, evincing a certain pleasure in the phenomena of winter. She was rather lavish of her coloured illustrations to it, giving no less than four. These are the 'bower of love for birds,' and the 'canopy above nest and egg and mother,' and the 'meadow-grass pied with broad-eyed daisies,' and the lines on land and water.

L. E. L., p. 344.—This poem was at first entitled *Spring*, and a note was put to the title, '*L. E. L.* by E. B. B. The note must refer to Mrs. Browning's poem named *L. E. L.'s Last Question*; but it is not entirely clear what relation Christina meant to indicate between that poem and her own *Spring*. Apparently she relied either upon L. E. L.'s phrase, which was, 'Do you think of me as I think of you?'—or else upon a phrase occurring in Mrs. Browning's lyric, 'One thirsty for a little love.' It will be clear to most readers that Christina's poem *Spring* relates to herself, and not at all to the poetess L. E. L. (Letitia Elizabeth Landon). I suppose that, when the publishing-stage came on, Christina preferred to retire behind a ud, and so renamed the poem *L. E. L.*, if it were intended to express emotions >per to that now perhaps unduly fortun poetess. The poem, as it stands my sister's MS. note-book, has lines and 3 of each stanza unrhymed, and ≥ has pencilled a note thus: 'Gabriel ed the double rhymes as printed, with brotherly request that I would use ≥m'; and elsewhere she adds, 'greatly proving the piece.' In other respects e printed *L. E. L.* is nearly identical th the MS. *Spring*.

Spring, p. 345.—In that copy of the *oblin Market* volume to which Christina pplied some coloured designs, this poem rinted on p. 51) is the latest, in order pagination, to be thus distinguished. er illustration is rather curious: it >plies to the line 'Life nursed in its ave by Death.' We see Death, a white 1d sufficiently 'bogyfied' personage, olding on her lap a motionless female rm, with yellow hair and pink drapery. markedly leafless tree rises above the roup.

Cousin Kate, p. 347.—Like *A Triad* see the note on p. 480), this poem was ublished by my sister in a volume, but ithdrawn in subsequent issues. The ke was the case with the ensuing poem, *ister Maude*, which seems to show a ertain reminiscence from Tennyson's omposition, *The Sisters*.

No, thank you, John, p. 349.—In the opy of my sister's combined *Poems* 1895), in which she made a few jottings, find this rather amusing entry: 'The original John was obnoxious, because he never gave scope for "No, thank you."' I think I understand who John was; he lated, so far as my sister was affected, it a period some years prior to 1860.

, *The Lambs of Grasmere*, p. 350.—In the above-named copy of the *Poems* Christina has written of the lambs, 'Mrs. Ruxton talked about them.' I still remember the occasion well. Mrs. Ruxton (the 'Mary Minto' mentioned in a published letter of Mrs. Browning) was married to a retired captain in the army, and for a brief while they lived at Grasmere. She was a lady of very dignified character and aspect, whom my sister both liked and respected in no common degree.

Wife to Husband, p. 351.—I am not aware that this poem has any individual application. If any, it might perhaps be to my brother's wife, whose constant and severe ill-health permitted no expectation of her living long. Her death took place in February 1862.

Better So, p. 351.—This poem consisted at first of six stanzas. The 3rd, 4th, and 6th, were extracted by my sister, and, with some modification of diction and metre, were published in *Time Flies*, and in the *Verses* of 1893. The remaining three stanzas seem to me to be of much the same degree of merit; they are complete enough in themselves, so I publish them here. It seems probable that the whole poem was written upon the death of some cherished friend; I do not remember who it was. The date is not consistent with any death in our own family. The next poem relates of course to the decease of the Prince Consort. It might be possible (not, I think, probable) to suppose that Christina wrote the present lines as an appropriate utterance for 'Our Widowed Queen.' The Prince indeed died on 14 (not 13) December, but on the 13th his death was clearly anticipated.

In Progress, p. 352.—The expressions in this sonnet, if used by some one else, might have been not far from apposite to Christina herself. I do not, however, consider that she wrote the verses with any such reference. Clearly the sonnet describes some particular person; I can think of two ladies not wholly unlike this touching portrait—one more especially whom Christina first knew in Newcastle-on-Tyne. But any such guess may be quite wrong.

Seasons, p. 354.—These lines show

a shrinking from winter-time, apparent in several other compositions. Italian blood may partly account for this; yet, after all, there is plenty of beauty in an ordinary winter, English or other, and the sensations of an invalid (troubled up to early middle age with many symptoms which seemed to point towards consumption) may have had more to do with the feeling.

A Ring Posy, p. 354.—Was published in the *Prince's Progress* volume, but omitted by the authoress from later reprints. Possibly she thought the poem to be marked by an unchristian shade of self-complacency.

A Year's Windfalls, p. 355.—A note written by my sister says, 'This was written for the Portfolio Society.' I have not any distinct recollection about this Society; possibly Mrs. Bell Scott had something to do with it.

Twilight Night, p. 359. Part 2 of this compound poem was the earlier written. Part 1 formed at first a chaunt in *Songs in a Cornfield*: see the note below to that poem.

What would I Give! p. 363.—In the sequence of dates there is evidence of a period of spiritual depression and self-reproof. The present poem is followed immediately by *Come unto Me* (which was originally called *Faint yet Pursuing*) (p. 237), and *Who shall Deliver Me* and *In Patience* (p. 238). The last-named is dated 19 March; next comes *Easter*, 9 April. The *Come unto Me*, though in a different metrical form, may almost be regarded as continuous with *What would I Give*.

The Ghost's Petition, p. 364.—Used to be called *A Return*, and had four concluding stanzas following the twenty-five which stand in print. Possibly they are better out; but several readers may have felt a certain abruptness in the present termination. In a copy of Christina's *Poems*, 1875, I find that she has altered line 1 of stanza 5 thus—'Sleep, sister, and wake again.' This alteration, however, does not appear in print in any later edition; and being uncertain as to the date when it was written, I leave aside. My own preference is for the original line.

Hoping against Hope, p. 365.—This was published in *The Argosy*, March 1866, under the title *If*. It was afterwards reprinted with the title which I give, sanctioned (I presume) by my sister. Mr. Frederick A. Sandys made a very able design to it, engraved on wood able, but (to my thinking) not in character with the poem.

A Sketch, p. 368.—These humorous verses (I am perfectly convinced, though their authoress never enlightened me on the subject) relate to a matter which was from the first highly serious to her, and became hardly less than tragic. It is clear to me that the person here banters was Charles Bagot Cayley, a man eminently unpractical in habit of mind, and abstracted and wool-gathering in his meanour. It is equally clear that, by the date when the verses were written August 1864, Christina, though the least forward of women, had evinced towards him an amount of graciousness which a man of ordinary alertness would not have overlooked. This *Sketch* might apparently be interpolated, by a reader of *Il Rosseggiar dell' Oriente*, between Nos. 2 and 3 of that series.

Songs in a Cornfield, p. 369.—In the pathetic poem the names of the singers were at first Lettice, Marian, May, and Janet. Afterwards Marian was turned into Rachel, and Janet into Marian. The original Marian (now Rachel) sang the second song; but this was a different lyric—the one which now forms No. in *Twilight Night*. Also there were dozen concluding lines to the whole poem, left out in printing. *Songs in a Cornfield* was set to music by Sir G. A. Macfarren as a cantata, which was performed more than once. To me the

...sic appeared truly beautiful; but I ...ieve it did not take much with the ...blic, perhaps because of its extremely ...lancholy tone at the close. I some... ...es fancied that, to avoid this objection, judicious move would have been to ...ce the swallow-song last in the ...tata.

Fear an unked strain, etc., p. 372.— ...uppose this provincial word 'unked' ...r unkid) is familiar to several readers: ...stands for 'grim, uncanny, dismal.' ...y sister got hold of it thus. Our uncle ...enry Polydore told us (possibly in some ...ch remote year as 1840) that the old ...untry-woman with whom he was lodg... ...g used to keep a brief diary; and he ...ad noticed that the entry made in it for ...e night of unusual storm was, 'Oh ...hat an unkid night!' This may have ...een in Buckinghamshire, or perhaps ...a Gloucestershire. The small anecdote ...mused us all in its way, and the phrase ...ecame a sort of catchword among us, ...nd, when the occasion offered, Christina ...nshrined the word in a poem.

Amor Mundi, p. 374.—This justly celebrated poem appeared first in *The Shilling Magazine*, with a fine illustration by Mr. Frederick Sandys. It has also been made the subject of an oil-picture by Mr. Edward Hughes. Mr. Sandys showed a group of two lovers—the man guitar-playing and singing, the woman pleasing herself with a hand-mirror. I do not perceive, however, that such was exactly the authoress's intention. I take it that both her personages are female: one of them a woman, the other the World in feminine shape. The first speaker is the woman, who inquires of the World whither she is going: it is the World who is figured with 'love-locks,' and as 'dear to doat on,' and who is afterwards pronounced 'false and fleetest.' The reader can take or reject this opinion as he likes, for I do not remember ever hearing the point settled by Christina. In her arrangement of her poems when collected, she put *Up-hill* next after *Amor Mundi*; a significant juxtaposition, done no doubt with intention. That she thought well of the latter may easily be conjectured; none the less I find in one of her editions the following note on the poem: 'Gabriel remarked very truly, a reminiscence of *The Demon Lover*.' This remark would refer more directly to stanza 3.

From Sunset to Star Rise, p. 375.— This very impressive sonnet was at first entitled *Friends*. In the note-book containing the MS. of the sonnet I find a pencil note, 'House of Charity,' written against the title. The House of Charity was, I think, an Institution at Highgate for reclaiming 'fallen' women; and it may perhaps be inferred that Christina wrote this sonnet as if it were an utterance of one of these women, not of herself. Yet one hesitates to think so, for the sonnet has a tone which seems deeply personal. 'Christina' (thus wrote Mrs. William Bell Scott in 1860) 'is now an associate, and wore the dress—which is very simple, elegant even; black with hanging sleeves, a muslin cap with lace edging, quite becoming to her with the veil.'

En Route, p. 377.—Under this heading I find three pieces in MS. which seem to have little connection one with the other. Presumably they were all written while my sister, along with my mother and myself, was making a flying visit to North Italy (through France and Switzerland). She was never there at any other time. The passionate delight in Italy to which *En Route* bears witness suggests that she was almost an alien—or, like her father, an exile—in the North. She never perhaps wrote anything better. I can remember the intense relief and pleasure with which she saw lovable Italian faces and heard musical Italian speech at Bellinzona after the somewhat hard and nipped quality of the German Swiss. I now give only one piece under the name *En Route*. The first piece and the third were used by my sister in her poem named *An Immurata Sister* (see p. 380).

Enrica, 1865, p. 377.—This poem was first published, under the name of *An English Drawing-room*, in a selection entitled *Picture Posies, Poems chiefly by Living Authors*, 1874, with an illustration by Houghton. I remember perfectly well the lady to whom the verses refer—an interesting person, anything but kindly treated by fate. She was Signora Enrica Barile ; her husband had taken the fancy of altering his name to Filopanti, so she was called Signora Filopanti. Her husband (whom I never saw) had some pretensions as an Italian patriot, an adherent of Mazzini and Garibaldi—the latter indeed, in his *Memoirs*, has spoken of him very highly. He also dabbled in the doctrine of metempsychosis, and would have it that Dante and Beatrice were reincarnated in himself and his wife. The general love of humankind which impelled him to rename himself as Filopanti was, unfortunately, unpropitious to a normal affection for his spouse ; so after a while he gave her notice that she had better look out for some separate means of subsistence. She came to London—a very agreeable bright-natured lady, still perhaps under thirty, personable and comely, and not far from handsome—of course, as the poem shows, eminently Italian in character and manner. It was through Mrs. Bell Scott that our family knew her. Signora Filopanti was the lady who, upon Garibaldi's visit to London in 1864, delivered a brief and extemporized harangue to him in public, as he stood before a vast concourse *en route* from the railway station to the heart of London. The Signora tried to establish a teaching connection in London, with only indifferent success. After a time she left, and I heard little or nothing further about her until 1902 ; she was then living, and in Italy. Here, as in the preceding piece, *En Route*, we can discern the strong Italian sympathies and affinities of Christina.

Husband and Wife, p. 378.—This was published in a book called *A M— of Poets* ; I do not recollect the de— It appears to be the same poem w— (as shown in a letter from my bro— 5 January 1866, published in his *F— Letters*) Mr. F. A. Sandys was think— of illustrating, and for which my bro— proposed the title *Grave-clothes and R— clothes*.

An Immurata Sister, p. 380.—T— poem is constructed out of two co— positions which my sister wrote in l— 1865, and which she at first associa— with the one which is termed *En R—* (see p. 485). The quatrain beginning 'Hearts that die,' and the one beginning 'Sparks fly upward,' were added at som— later date ; and the one beginning 'T— world hath sought' is different from i— first form. The title, *An Immura— Sister*, may be open to some uncertain—. The lines are clearly a personal utter— ance ; and I suppose that my sister mean— to indicate that, by essential condition of soul, she was not unlike one of those nuns whose rule keeps them severely immured.

Once for all (Margaret), p. 380.—Th— name Margaret was added when m— sister printed this sonnet. The perso— whom she meant by it was the first Mr— James Hannay—as I learn from a n— pencilled in one of her editions. Pr— sumably the sonnet was written when M— Hannay contracted a second marriage.

Song, p. 382.—This song (which i— MS. bears a title, *What Comes ?*) is th— last piece entered in Christina's series of note-books, seventeen in number. As I have said before, precise dates are seldom traceable henceforward.

From Metastasio, p. 382.—These lines form a paraphrastic translation from — lyric ('Amo te solo') in Metastasio's *Clemenza di Tito*. I found them as a scrap of MS., pencilled by Christina thus : 'I must have done this for Traventi, who wanted English words to set to music.' Traventi was a Neapolitan musical composer and teacher; the date of the translation may be 1868 or rather earlier.

By Way of Remembrance, p. 384.—To this quartett of sonnets I find the date 1870 appended. To one of them, the third, there is (in a different MS.) the precise date '23.10.70.'

An Echo from Willow-wood, p. 385. —The title indicates that this sonnet by Christina is based on those sonnets by our brother, named *Willow-wood*, which were first published in 1869. Christina's sonnet may possibly be intended to refer to the love and marriage of my brother and Miss Siddal, and to her early death in 1862; or it may (which I think far more probable) be intended for a wholly different train of events. The verses were printed in *The Magazine of Art*, with an illustration by Mr. C. Ricketts. This was in 1890; but, from the association of the sonnet with *Willow-wood*, I give conjecturally the date '*circa* 1870.'

The German-French Campaign, p. 386.—The notice prefixed by the authoress to these two poems is no doubt correct in saying that they were not intended to express 'political bias.' It is none the less true that she had incomparably more general and native sympathy with the French nationality than with the German.

'*The King of Sheshach*,' p. 386.—It is not every one who has the Bible so much at his fingers' ends as my sister had. The king of Sheshach, a potentate obscure to several of us, is discoverable in the book of *Jeremiah*, ch. xxv.

To-day for me, p. 387.—Dante Rossetti considered this to be among Christina's noblest productions, and he has probably been not alone in that opinion. This is one more instance of her marked success in carrying one rhyme from end to end of a poem.

Venus's Looking-glass, p. 387.—Mr. Cayley sent to my sister a short MS. poem named *The Birth of Venus*, and soon afterwards, 13 October 1872, another shorter poem on the same argument. Upon the latter poem she wrote the following note: 'The longer of these two poems was sent me first. Then I wrote one which the second rebuts. At last I wound up by my sonnet *Venus's Looking-glass*.' In a copy of her collected *Poems*, 1875, there is also the following note: 'Perhaps "Love-in-Idleness" would be a better title, with an eye to the next one '—*i.e.* to *Love lies Bleeding*.

Love lies Bleeding, p. 388.—As Christina associated this sonnet with the preceding one, *Venus's Looking-glass*, I have kept them together, dating the second '*circa* 1872.' All that I really know of its date, however, is that it got published in 1875.

Days of Vanity, p. 388.—Appeared in *Scribner's Monthly* for November 1872. Thus I am enabled to fix the date as 'before 1873.' Some other cases of the same sort, not always specified in my notes, occur.

Cor Mio, p. 389.—I find this sonnet in my sister's handwriting, endorsed by her 'the original version of my sonnet.' The reference is to No. 18 in the series named *Later Life*. In that version the octave (beginning 'So late in autumn half the world's asleep') is entirely changed, while the sextett remains the same. The present form of this sonnet, being a more directly personal utterance, seems worth preserving.

A Green Cornfield, p. 389.—This and some other compositions are dated by me 'before 1876,' on the ground that they were first printed in the collected volume of 1875.

Valentines to my Mother, p. 391.—I am probably not alone in considering these as very charming compositions of their simple intimate kind. Christina left a pencilled note about them thus: 'These Valentines had their origin from my dearest mother's remarking that she had never received one. I, her C. G. R., ever after supplied one on the day; and (so far as I recollect) it was a surprise every time, she having forgotten all about it in the interim.' Our mother was born in April 1800, so she was nearly seventy-six when the first Valentine was written; she died in April 1886.

Valentine for 1877, p. 391.—The signature 'C. G. for M. F. R.' means that these verses are spoken as in the person of Maria Francesca (our elder sister) in heaven; she had died in November 1876.

Valentine for 1878, p. 392.—This is marked on the back 'To the Queen of Hearts,' and the like with all the ensuing Valentines.

Valentine for 1883, p. 393.—Here is an evident reminiscence as to the death of Dante Gabriel in April 1882; probably also as to the death of my infant son Michael in January 1883.

Freaks of Fashion, p. 395.—I understand that this was first published in a so-called *Girls' Annual*, 1878. I date it accordingly.

Parted, p. 397.—In 1880 a volume of poems by Mr. C. B. Cayley was privately printed. One of its items was entitled *Moor and Christian*, purporting to be 'taken from a Spanish source,' and expressing the emotion of a Moslem woman severed from her Christian lover. Christina, using the same metre and number of lines, wrote the present composition—of course from a very diverse point of view.

To-day's Burden, p. 397.—Comes from Mr. Hall Caine's compilation, *Sonnets of Three Centuries*, 1882. Date conjectural, but probably not far wrong.

The Key-note, p. 397.—The title is to be understood as meaning that this sonnet was prefixed to the volume *A Pageant and other Poems* (1881), to serve as its key-note.

'*Luscious and Sorrowful*,' p. 398.—These words, 'Luscious and sorrow[...] are borrowed from a little lyric by C[...] named *Noli me tangere*, which was [...] lished in *The Nation*, 1866. In [...] lyric the epithets are applied to the [...] of the nightingale. See also the l[...] poem (p. 450), headed *Luscious Sorrowful*.

Johnny, p. 399.—Christina got [...] pretty anecdote from a book in my [...] session. The copy is imperfect and [...] less, but I have reason to think it [...] named *Recueil d'Actions Héroïque [...] Républicains Français, par* L[...] Bourdon. It contains coloured p[...] by Labrousse, and explanatory text. [...] precise account given of 'Johnny' i[...] follows: He was named Locquet, a[...] eight, and was born in Paris; his 'trait [...] piété filiale' occurred on 15 pluviôse, [...] 7. His mother being very ill and alm[...] penniless, he ran off to a wig-maker priced his fine head of hair at twel[...] francs, received the money, and hande[...] it to his mother, whose illness howe[...] proved rapidly mortal. A soldier t[...] adopted young Locquet, in the Decad[...] Temple of Gratitude. This 'estimab[...] militaire' refused to allow his name [...] appear in the narrative.

Hollow-sounding and mysterious, p[...] 400.—Some readers will recognize th[...] title as being a phrase applied to the s[...] in a poem by Mrs. Hemans.

Sœur Louise de la Miséricorde, 1674 p. 411.—Perhaps it is superfluous to s[...] that this Sœur Louise was the loving a[...] lovely Duchesse de la Vallière, the m[...] tress of Louis XIV. The year 1674 appears to be that in which she retired into a Carmelite Convent; she did n[...] assume the veil, and become Sœur Louise, until 1675.

Birchington Churchyard, p. 412.— The churchyard in which Dante Gabri[...] Rossetti was buried in the same month when this sonnet was written.

One Seaside Grave, p. 413.—It would seem to most people that these lines als[...]

' relate to Birchington; my belief, however, is that they relate to Hastings, where Charles Cayley lies buried.

Who shall say? p. 414.—The date *circa* 1884 is presumed, owing to the rough draft of the poem coming on the back of the sonnet, ' Scarce tolerable life,' etc. See the note (p. 469) to that sonnet.

One Swallow does not make a Summer, p. 414.—Was printed in *Time Flies*, but not reprinted in the *Verses*, 1893. No doubt my sister considered that it was not admissible into that series of exclusively devotional poetry. The like course was pursued with a few other items of *Time Flies*.

A Frog's Fate, p. 414.—Was printed as the preceding item. No title was given to the piece by my sister, so I have supplied one.

The Way of the World, p. 415.—Comes from *The Magazine of Art*, July 1894, and must be the latest printed of any verse compositions within my sister's lifetime. Mr. Britten made an illustration to the stanzas. When they were written is quite uncertain to me—possibly at a date even later than that which I have noted.

Brother Bruin, p. 415.—I think this may probably have been written in consequence of a letter I sent, enclosing for Christina a 'history of a maltreated bear, from yesterday's *Daily News*.'

To my Fior-di-lisa, p. 417.—One of the friends who saw my sister most frequently and affectionately in her closing years was Miss Lisa Wilson. Christina sometimes called her Fior-di-lisa (which is the same as Fleur-de-lys). Miss Wilson, who has a graceful touch of her own both in published verse and in painting, presented to Christina in 1892 a little illuminated book of poems by herself; my sister inserted into it the present lines of response.

To-morrow, p. 417.—This little poem (the title is mine) comes from *The Face of the Deep*; it was not reprinted in the *Verses* of 1893—I hardly see why. It might readily have found a niche in that shrine of sacred song; but, taken singly, it seems more apposite to the section of *General Poems* than to that of *Devotional Poems*.

Sleeping at Last, p. 417.—I regard these verses (the title again is mine) as being the very last that Christina ever wrote; probably late in 1893, or it may be early in 1894. They form a very fitting close to her poetic performance, the longing for rest (even as distinguished from actual bliss in heaven) being most marked throughout the whole course of her writings. I found the lines after her death, and had the gratification of presenting them, along with the childish script of her very first verses *To my Mother*, to the MS. Department of the British Museum.

Poems for Children, and Minor Verse, p. 417.—The term *Poems for Children* explains itself. By *Minor Verse* I designate some few things written by my sister which, while I consider them to be well worthy of preservation, are nevertheless of a slight and casual kind, and hardly fitted for being mixed up among her *General Poems*. In the *Poems for Children* the principal item is the series named *Sing-song* (a title which was proposed by our mother, and immediately adopted, and no doubt liked owing to its origin, by Christina). This series, as it here stands, was compiled by Christina herself, and brought out in 1872 as a separate volume, charmingly illustrated by that fine artist and most estimable and lovable man, Mr. Arthur Hughes. I do not, of course, interfere here with the arrangement adopted by my sister, and therefore the whole of *Sing-song* has to go among the *Poems for Children*. But I cannot help regarding this with some regret, as the series includes various lyrics which, though not unadapted for children, are truly in a high strain of poetry, and perfectly suited for figuring among her verse for adults, and even for taking an honoured place as such. It may perhaps be as well to specify which are the items that I more especially regard in this light. They are the items which respectively begin (1) 'Dead in the cold, a song-singing thrush'; (2) 'I dug and dug amongst the snow'; (3) 'A baby's cradle with no baby in it'; (4) 'Hope is like a harebell trembling from its birth'; (5) 'Growing in the vale'; (6) 'O wind, where have you been'; (7) 'What are heavy? Sea-sand and sorrow'; (8) 'The summer nights are short'; (9) 'Twist me a crown of wind-flowers'; (10) 'Dancing on the hill-tops'; (11) 'If hope grew on a bush'; (12) 'Under the ivy-bush'; (13) 'Sing me a song'; (14) 'The wind has such a rainy sound'; (15) 'Three little children'; (16) 'Rosy maiden Winifred'; (17) 'Roses blushing red and white'; (18) 'When a mounting skylark sings'; (19) 'Who has seen the wind?' (20) 'O sailor come ashore'; (21) 'The lily has a smooth stalk'; (22) 'Oh fair to see'; (23) 'Is the moon tired? she looks so pale'; (24) 'Good-bye in fear, good-bye in sorrow'; (25) 'Baby lies so fast asleep.' These, however, are not the only compositions which might, without any impropriety (but for the original form of their publication), be transferred to the class of *General Poems*.

Sonnets written to Bouts-rimés, p. 417.—Our brother Dante Gabriel and myself were, towards 1848, greatly addicted to writing sonnets together to *bouts-rimés*; most of my verses published in *The Germ*—and this remark applies not to sonnets alone—were thus composed. Christina did not do much in the like way; but, being in my company at Brighton in the summer of 1848, she consented to try her chance. Like her brothers, she was very rapid at the work. The first sonnet in this present series was done in nine minutes; the ninth in five. After the Brighton days she renewed this exercise hardly at all. A few of *bouts-rimés* sonnets, after the first scribbling of them, were retouched to some but only a small, extent.

Sonnet vii, p. 419.—This sonnet a chilly August is certainly not a marked success; but it pictured with some truth the day on which it was written, and allow it to pass muster.

Sonnet viii, p. 420.—Dante Rossetti writing on 30 August 1848, said in relation to one of Christina's *bouts-rimés* sonnets (I am not certain which): 'He other is first-rate. Pray impress up her that this, and the one beginning "Methinks the ills of life" [*i.e.* No. 8], are good as anything she has written, and well worthy of revision.'

The Plague, p. 420.—Dante Rossetti's letter above mentioned says of this sonnet: 'I grinned tremendously over Christina's *Plague*, which however is forcible, and has something good in it.'

Sonnets xa, b, and c, pp. 420, 421.— The sonnet marked *c* was, like 1 to 9, written at Brighton. At a later date— 1850, or perhaps earlier—Christina wrote the prose story for girls entitled *Maude* (published in 1897). An incident in this story is the competition of three young ladies composing *bouts-rimés* sonnets: *c* is pronounced to be the best of the three. The sonnet *a* (it will at once be observed) is not a true sonnet at all, having lines of unequal length. This was, of course, intentional on Christina's part, to mark the inaptitude of the young lady who is supposed to have indited it None the less I give the three sonnets together, as showing how readily Christina could utilize the same rhymes for three entirely distinct lines of thought or subject. Two of the phrases in *c* are thus commented in *Maude*: 'I have literally seen a man in Regent Street wearing a sort of hooded cloak with one tassel. Of course every one will understand "the Bason" to mean the one in St. James's Park.'

To Lalla, p. 421.—This was a pet name given to Henrietta Polydore, daughter of our Uncle Henry. The name was her own baby invention, I think. She became consumptive, and died in America in 1874, aged about twenty-eight.

Two Enigmas, p. 422.—The answer to the first of these enigmas is 'Jack.' It was published in a little pocket-book named *Marshall's Ladies' Daily Remembrancer* for 1850, and must apparently (according to the conditions laid down) have been sent in before June 1849. One copy of the *Remembrancer* was awarded as a prize to the authoress; some other more admired contributors received two copies. The second enigma means 'Punch,' which was another of the subjects for the *Remembrancer* of 1850. This second enigma has reached me only in a manuscript copy made by one of our aunts.

Two Charades, p. 422.—The first means 'Candid,' the second 'Proserpine.' The latter was published in the *Remembrancer* aforenamed. There was another unpublished charade, *Ægisthus*; but I have not thought it deserving of type.

Portraits, p. 423.—This warm-hearted though light effusion is meant for myself in the first stanza, and for Dante Gabriel and myself in the last. There used to be an intermediate stanza, characterizing *him*; it is torn out (by his rather arbitrary hand, beyond a doubt), and I do not remember its terms. Many readers now will agree with me in thinking this a great pity. A laudatory phrase or two regarding myself ought possibly to have induced me to exclude the verses, but I cannot make up my mind to do that.

Charon, p. 423.—These sportive lines take their cue, of course, from the old song, 'In my cottage near the wood.' They tickled our sister Maria uncommonly. I had totally forgotten them; Christina on her deathbed (9 October 1894) happened to recite them to me—for she was often extremely conversible up to and beyond that date, spite of her pain and languor—and I wrote them down from her lips. When first published (1896), the verses were entitled by me *Near the Styx;* but I now gather that Christina's own name for them was *Charon.*

The P. R. B. (1), p. 424.—These lines were sent to me in a letter from Christina (then settled with our parents at Frome, Somerset), saying: 'This morning I commenced a remarkable doggerel on the P. R. B.,' etc. And then, after copying out the lines, 'You may guess that at this point of my letter I came to a stand, from the extra finish bestowed on the three last asterisks.' For a few remarks on the substance of the lines, see the following note.

The P. R. B. (2), p. 424.—Was first published in my *Memoir* of Dante G. Rossetti, 1895. The sonnet was written soon after the election of Millais as A.R.A. The allusions to Woolner, then in Australia; Holman-Hunt, who was projecting to visit Egypt and Palestine; Dante Rossetti, who had ceased to exhibit his paintings; and Stephens, who had scarcely come forward as an exhibiting artist at all, can be readily understood. The allusion to myself is less perspicuous. It means that I, as art-critic of *The Spectator*, abused in that paper my fellows in the Præraphaelite Brotherhood, and that no one heeded my reviews. This joke was not historically true; I upheld, with such vigour as was in me, the cause of the Præraphaelites, and my articles, being at first solitary in that tone of criticism, passed not wholly unobserved.

Winter, p. 425.—Mr. Swynfen Jervis, a friendly acquaintance of our father, wrote a quatrain and a half entitled *Sir Winter;* and he appears to have got Christina to complete the little poem. Christina finished quatrain two, and wrote five others. The third of these five reverts to the idea of '*Sir* Winter'; so I omit it, as being extraneous to the character of her own composition: it has no poetical value.

Love's Name. p. 425.—This small ditty is introduced into the prose tale named *Commonplace*, finished in 1870, and published in the same year. It is supposed to be sung by certain young ladies in Greek costume, enacting a charade upon the word 'Love-apple.'

Golden Holly, p. 426.—This trifle, owing to its associations of old and uninterrupted friendship, I was unwilling in 1896 to omit: and I know now that I ought not to have omitted it, for Mr. Swinburne pronounced it an excellent thing. It was addressed to Holman [Holly] Frederic Stephens, then a little boy, son of our constant friend, Frederic George Stephens (one of the seven members of the 'P. R. B.'). Tennyson once saw the child in the Isle of Wight, and pronounced him (not unreasonably) to be 'the most beautiful boy I have ever seen.' Mr. Stephens senior, in sending me the verses at my request, wrote that they refer 'to H. F. S.'s frequent pet name of "The Golden Holly," given because of the brightness of his long hair, as well as his birthday being on October 31. He had sent a tea-rose to C. G. R.'

Sing-song, p. 426.—The items of this series continue down to the one which begins *Lie a-bed* (p. 443). In the MS. of *Sing-song* Christina made a series of pen-and-ink sketches—slight and primitive of course, but not without suggestiveness. The MS., after lying *perdu* for a long time, has returned to my possession.

Rhymes Dedicated to the Baby who suggested them, p. 426.—The baby son of Professor Arthur Cayley of Cambridge, the celebrated mathematician. The lines, 'I know a baby, such a baby,' were, I think, intended for this dedicatee.

Kookoorookoo—Kikirikee, p. 426.—I may perhaps be pardoned for saying that these poultry-noises form a reminiscence from Christina's own childhood. Our father was in the habit of making the noises to amuse his bantlings.

Willie Wee, p. 441.—This was my mother's pet name for me in childhood: a second reminiscence.

An Alphabet, p. 443.—This was printed in 1875, with some woodcuts, in some magazine; the headline of the pages is *For Very Little Folks*, which may or may not be the title of the magazine itself. It must be an American publication, as the verses are headed *An Alphabet from England*.

Hadrian's Death-Song Translated, p. 444.—In 1876 Mr. David Johnston, of Bath, formed the project of collecting various translations of the famous lines—'Animula vagula blandula,' etc., and issuing them in a volume, which was privately printed. He looked up old translations, and invited new ones. Christina became one of his contributors; also our sister Maria and myself; Christina making an Italian as well as an English translation (see p. 453).

My Mouse, p. 444.—This was not a 'mouse' in the ordinary sense, but a '*sea*-mouse.' Mr. Cayley had picked it up on the seashore, and presented it to my sister, preserved in spirits. The sea-mouse was with her to the end, and may remain with me to the end; its brilliant iridescent hues are still vivid. The scientific name of this creature is *Aphrodita aculeata*; hence the allusion to 'Venus.'

A Poor Old Dog, p. 444.—My sister was a very staunch supporter of the Anti-Vivisection Movement. In a letter to our brother (dated perhaps in 1879) she sent the present verses, with the following remarks: 'There has just been held a fancy sale at a house in Prince's Gate for the Anti-Vivisection cause, and, having nothing else to contribute, I sent a dozen autographs as follows [then come the verses]. Of these, nine on the first day fetched 2s. 6d. or 3s., while one even brought in 10s.! The remaining three, I hope, were disposed of on the closing day.'

To William Bell Scott, p. 444.—These verses were sent to Mr. Scott in acknowledgment of a copy of his volume, *A Poet's Harvest-Home*, issued in April 1882. The reference to 'a heavy old heart' has no doubt to do with the death of Dante Rossetti, 9 April 1882. The verses were first published in Mr. Scott's *Autobiographical Notes*.

Counterblast on Penny Trumpet, p. 444.—These rather neat lines are entirely out of my sister's ordinary groove, which fact (trifling as they are) makes me the more unwilling to leave them out. They stand signed 'C. G. R.: see *St. James's Gazette*, 21 July 1882: motive, a Poem.' I infer (for I have not been at the pains of looking up the *St. James's Gazette*) that that newspaper contained some effusion censuring Mr. Bright for having quitted the Ministry after the bombardment of Alexandria, and also censuring Mr. Gladstone for continuing in the Ministry. My sister knew and cared next to nothing about party politics (apart from questions having a religious bearing); in all her later years, however, her feeling leaned more towards the Conservative than the Liberal cause.

Mole and Earthworm, p. 445.—Here the title is mine. The lines were published in *Time Flies*, but not reproduced in the *Verses* of 1893, where they would have been quite inappropriate.

To Mary Rossetti, p. 445.—These slight lines were addressed to my daughter Mary, probably when aged from five to six.

What will it be? p. 445.—This snatch of verse, and the five following, come from *The Face of the Deep*; they were omitted from the *Verses* of 1893, presumably as being too slight to figure apart from their context. In each instance, except the third, the title is added by me.

Versi, p. 446.—In 1851-52 some young ladies (mostly living in the Regent's Park neighbourhood) had a fancy for getting up a little privately-printed magazine, which was termed *The Bouquet from Marylebone Gardens*. My sister was invited to contribute, and she consented to do so, writing always in Italian. Each contributor adopted some floral name as a signature; Christina was 'Calta.' These *Versi*, and also the following two compositions, come from this rather obscure source. Christina's principal contribution was in prose, not verse—a *Corrispondenza Famigliare* between two supposed young ladies, Italian and English, the former being at school. There are eight of these letters, rather neat performances in their way; and, no doubt, others would have followed but for the early decease of the magazine, the withering of the *Bouquet*.

Nigella, p. 447.—In the *Corrispondenza* above named these verses are introduced as being written by the Italian damsel to accommodate her English friend, who had been asked to produce some Italian lines for a lady's album.

Chiesa e Signore, p. 447.—These lines appear in a scrap of MS. which is thus inscribed: 'Written out at Folkestone 6 August 1871, but date of composition not recollected by C. G. R.' I infer that the date of composition was then rather remote, pehaps towards 1860.

Il Rosseggiar dell' Oriente, p. 447.— For any quasi-explanation as to these singularly pathetic verses—'Love's very vesture and elect disguise,' the inborn idiom of a pure and impassioned heart— I refer the reader to the Memoir. The verses were kept by Christina in the jealous seclusion of her writing-desk, and I suppose no human eye had looked upon them until I found them there after her death.

Si rimanda la Tocca-caldaja, p. 448. —The phrase here, 'Se pur fumar noi puoi,' sounds odd. The lines were written in reply to other lines by Cayley named *Si scusa la Tocca-caldaja.* His final line contains the phrase, 'S'ei mi fumma,' and hence Christina's words in reply.

Blumine risponde, p. 448.—In 'Blumine' the reader will recognize a name used by Carlyle in *Sartor Resartus.*

Lassuso il caro Fiore, p. 449.—The main topic in this little poem must have some relation to what is touched upon in No. 3 of the series.

Per Preferenza, p. 451.—To the first of these stanzas Christina has written the word 'Supposto'; to the second, 'Accertato'; to the third, 'Dedotto.' There must have been in her head some whimsical notion of logical sequence, or what not. I can understand it to some extent, without discussing it.

L' Uommibatto, p. 453.—Christina took it upon her to Italianize in this form the name of the *Wombat,* which was a cherished pet animal of our brother. It will be understood that she is exhorting the Wombat not to follow (which he was much inclined to do) his inborn propensity for burrowing, and not to turn up in the Antipodes, his native Australia. As a motto to these verses Christina wrote an English distich:—

> When wombats do inspire,
> I strike my disused lyre.

Adriano, p. 453.—See the note to p. 444.

Ninna-nanna, p. 453.—The following snatches of Italian verse are translations or paraphrases made by Christina from her own volume *Sing-song.* Our cousin Teodorico Pietrocola-Rossetti first made some translations from that book, whose title he rendered as *Ninna-nanna*: herein I follow his lead. His translations were felicitous. Inspirited by his example, Christina made other—and, I conceive, in poetic essentials still better —translations. Readers familiar with *Sing-song* will perceive that numerous compositions in that volume remain untranslated.

Sognando, p. 458.—I give this title to two stanzas which I find written by Christina into a copy of our father's book of sacred poems—*Il Tempo, ovvero Dio e l' Uomo, Salterio,* 1843. The copy is one which he gave in the same year to his sister-in-law, Charlotte Polidori; as the latter lived on till January 1890, this copy would only at that date, most likely, have become Christina's property. This consideration and also the look of the handwriting induce me to suppose that the verses were written not earlier than 1890; they would thus be the last Italian verses which my sister produced. She has signed them thus: 'C. G. R., fired by papa's calling this metre difficult' —the metre being the one adopted throughout the whole book *Il Tempo* in its original form. This MS. note might suggest a far earlier date for the lines; but, on the whole, I abide by my own view as just expressed.

INDEX TO FIRST LINES

A Baby is a harmless thing, 158
A baby's cradle with no baby in it, 427
A blue-eyed phantom far before, 330
A boat amid the ripples, drifting, rocking, 411
A boat that sails upon the sea, 415
A burdened heart that bleeds and bears, 276
A chill blank world, yet over the utmost sea, 232
A city plum is not a plum, 427
A cold wind stirs the blackthorn, 122
A cup for hope, she said, 308
A dancing bear, grotesque and funny, 415
A diamond or a coal? 438
A dream that waketh, 388
A fool I was to sleep at noon, 379
A frisky lamb, 435
A garden in a garden, a green spot, 291
A glorious vision hovers o'er his soul, 96
A handy mole who plied no shovel, 445
A heavy heart if ever heart was heavy, 126
A holy heavenly chime, 279
A holy Innocent gone home, 412
A house of cards, 440
A hundred, a thousand to one: even so, 332
A is the alphabet, A at its head, 443
A life of hope deferred too often is, 131
A linnet in a gilded cage, 428
A lovely city in a lovely land, 208
A lowly hill which overlooks a flat, 412
A merry heart is a continual feast, 142
A million buds are born that never blow, 410
A moon impoverished amid stars curtailed, 272
A motherless soft lambkin, 433
A night was near, a day was near, 280
A pin has a head but has no hair, 432

A pocket handkerchief to hem, 431
A ring upon her finger, 437
A robin said, The spring will never come, 413
A rose, a lily, and the Face of Christ, 226
A rose has thorns as well as honey, 441
A rose which spied one swallow, 414
A smile because the nights are short, 380
A song in a cornfield, 369
A toadstool comes up in a night, 431
A Venus seems my mouse, 444
A voice said Follow follow, and I rose, 118
A white hen sitting, 436
A windy shell singing upon the shore, 305
A world of change and loss, a world of death, 393
Addio, diletto amico, 447
After midnight in the dark, 126
Agnellina orfanellina, 456
Ah changed and cold, how changed and very cold, 313
Ah Lord, Lord, if my heart were right with Thine, 267
Ah Lord, we all have pierced Thee, wilt Thou be, 137
Ah me that I should be, 219
Ah well-a-day, and wherefore am I here? 419
Ah woe is me for pleasure that is vain, 267
Ahi culla vuota ed ahi sepolcro pieno, 455
Alas alas for the self-destroyed, 285
Alas my Lord, 247
All beneath the sun hasteth, 273
All heaven is blazing yet, 134
All her cornfields rippled in the sunshine, 386
All tears done away with the bitter unquiet sea, 138
All that we see rejoices in the sunshine, 274
All the bells were ringing, 439

All the Robin Redbreasts, 393
All the world is out in leaf, 339
All things are fair if we had eyes to see, 194
All things that pass, 410
All through the livelong night I lay awake, 112
All weareth, all wasteth, 173
Alleluia or Alas my heart is crying, 135
Alone Lord God in Whom our trust and peace, 264
Am I a stone and not a sheep, 234
Amami, t' amo, 453
Amico pesce, piover vorrà, 456
Amid the shades of a deserted hall, 417
An easy lazy length of limb, 423
An emerald is as green as grass, 438
And is this August weather? Nay, not so, 419
And who is this lies prostrate at thy feet? 94
Angeli al capo, al piede, 453
Angels at the foot, 426
Animuccia, vagantuccia, morbiduccia, 453
Annie is fairer than her kith, 301
Another year of joy and grief, 393
Arise, depart, for this is not your rest, 397
Arrossisce la rosa—e perchè mai? 457
As dying, and behold we live, 213
As eager home-bound traveller to the goal, 188
As flames that consume the mountains, as winds that coerce the sea, 210
As froth on the face of the deep, 285
As grains of sand, as stars, as drops of dew, 178
As many as I love. Ah Lord Who lovest all, 170
As one red rose in a garden where all other roses are white, 226
As rivers seek the sea, 390
As the dove which found no rest, 226
As the voice of many waters all saints sing as one, 211
As violets so be I recluse and sweet, 276
Astonished Heaven looked on when man was made, 120
At morn I plucked a rose and gave it thee, 250
At sound as of rushing wind and sight as of fire, 170
Aura dolcissima, ma donde siete? 455
Awake or sleeping, for I know not which, 64

Baby cry, 426
Baby lies so fast asleep, 442
Basta una notte a maturare il fungo, 457
Be faithful unto death. Christ proffer thee, 277
Beautiful, tender, wasting away for sorrow, 398
Because one loves you, Helen Grey, 355
Because Thy Love hath sought me, 230
Because you never yet have loved me, dear, 403
Before the beginning Thou hast foreknown the end, 145
Before the mountains were brought forth before, 73
Before the paling of the stars, 217
Behold in heaven a floating dazzling cloud, 136
Behold the Bridegroom cometh—go ye out, 156
Beloved, let us love one another, says St. John, 159
Beloved, yield thy time to God, for He, 197
Beyond the sea in a green land, 295
Beyond this shadow and this turbulent sea, 282
Blessed Dear and Heart's Delight, 392
Blind from my birth, 437
Boats sail on the rivers, 439
Bone to his bone, grain to his grain of dust, 215
Bread and milk for breakfast, 427
Bring me to see, Lord, bring me yet to see, 212
Brown and furry, 431
Brownie, Brownie, let down your milk, 429
Bury Hope out of sight, 137
Bury thy dead, dear friend, 181
By day she woos me, soft, exceeding fair, 182
By the waters of Babylon, 233
By Thy long-drawn anguish to atone, 165

Can I know it? Nay, 125
Can man rejoice who lives in hourly fear? 273
Can peach renew lost bloom, 136
Capo che chinasi, 458
Care flieth, 310
Casa felice ove più volte omai, 448
Cast down but not destroyed, chastened not slain, 209
Cavalli marittimi, 457
Centre of Earth, a Chinaman he said, 82

INDEX TO FIRST LINES

...i lontan da me, 449
I'i darò, Gesù Signor mio buono? 450
ry-red her mouth was, 105
mi il mio core, 88
e not—let me breathe a little, 110
st rnas hath a darkness, 158
st's Heart was wrung for me, if mine is sore, 227
er little Willie wee, 441
her of the lily, Feeder of the sparrow, 227
l the day and cold the drifted snow, 48
ne back to me, who wait and watch for you, 58
ne blessed sleep, most full, most perfect, come, 153
ne cheer up, my lads, 'tis to glory we steer, 88
ne, cuckoo, come, 354
ne, Thou dost say to Angels, 148
me to me in the silence of the night, 314
me, wander forth with me: the orange flowers, 87
mmon holly bears a berry, 426
nsider, 237
ntempt and pangs and haunting fears, 218
ntemptuous of his home beyond, 414
itent to come, content to go, 277
r mio a cui si volge l' altro mio core, 452
r mio, cor mio, 453
eden di rivederti e ancor ti aspetto, 452
rimson as the rubies, crimson as the roses, 210
rimson curtains round my mother's bed, 442
roak, croak, croak, 357
rocuses and snowdrops wither, 310
rying, my little one, footsore and weary, 428
uccurucù cuccurucù, 454
urrants on a bush, 436

)ancing on the hill-tops, 434
)arkness and light are both alike to Thee, 227
)arling little Cousin, 421
)ay and night the accuser makes no pause, 229
)ay that hath no tinge of night, 126
Dead in the cold, a song-singing thrush, 427
Dear angels and dear disembodied saints, 214

Dear Grandpapa,—To be obedient, 85
Dear Lord, let me recount to Thee, 254
Did any bird come flying? 369
Ding a ding, 437
Do you hear the low winds singing, 307
Does that lamp still burn in my Father's house, 251
Does the road wind up-hill all the way? 339
Dolce cor mio perduto e non perduto, 448
Downstairs I laugh, I sport and jest with all, 344
D' un sonno profondissimo, 457

E babbo e mamma ha il nostro figliolino, 454
Earth cannot bar flame from ascending, 159
Earth grown old yet still so green, 157
Earth has clear call of daily bells, 193
Eight o'clock, 426
Every valley drinks, 344
Everything that is born must die, 141
Experience bows a sweet contented face, 272
Eye hath not seen, yet man hath known and weighed, 129

Fade, tender lily, 297
Faint and worn and aged, 154
Fair the sun riseth, 150
Fairer than younger beauties, more beloved, 391
Fast asleep, mine old familiar friend, 351
Fear, Faith, and Hope, have sent their hearts above, 277
Felice la tua madre, 451
Ferry me across the water, 438
Figlia, la Madre disse, 446
First, last, and dearest, 382
Flesh of our flesh, bone of our bone, 84
Flowers preach to us if we will hear, 156
Fly away, fly away over the sea, 436
Forget me not, forget me not, 83
Foss' io regina, 455
Foul is she and ill-favoured, set askew, 284
Friends, I commend to you the narrow way, 226
From depth to height, from height to loftier height, 412
Frost-locked all the winter, 345

Gazing through her chamber window, 332
Give me the lowest place, not that I dare, 237

Go from me, summer friends, and tarry not, 375
God strengthen me to bear myself, 238
Golden haired, lily white, 209 ; 216
Golden-winged, silver-winged, 242
Gone were but the Winter, 103
Good Lord, to-day, 163
Good-bye in fear, good-bye in sorrow, 441
Gran freddo è infuori, e dentro è freddo un poco, 454
Grant us, O Lord, that patience and that faith, 278
Grant us such grace that we may work Thy will, 276
Great or small below, 127
Green sprout the grasses, 316
Growing in the vale, 428

Had Fortune parted us, 397
Hail, garden of confident hope, 135
Hark, the Alleluias of the great salvation, 179
Hark to the song of greeting ! The tall trees, 86
Have dead men long to wait? 215
Have I not striven, my God, and watched and prayed ? 228
Have mercy, Thou my God—mercy, my God, 234
He bore an agony whereof the name, 177
He died for me: what can I offer Him? 188
He resteth—weep not, 98
Hear now a curious dream I dreamed last night, 315
Hear what the mournful linnets say, 427
Heart warm as summer, fresh as spring, 109
Heartsease I found where Love-lies-bleeding, 134
Heartsease in my garden bed, 430
Heaven is not far though far the sky, 193
Heaven overarches earth and sea, 286
Heaven's chimes are slow, but sure to strike at last, 200
Her face was like an opening rose, 316
Her heart that loved me once is rottenness, 298
Here, where I dwell, I waste to skin and bone, 239
Herself a rose who bore the Rose, 174
Hidden from the darkness of our mortal sight, 208
Home by different ways, yet all, 129
Hope is like a harebell trembling from its birth, 428

Hope is the counterpoise of fear, 271
Hope newborn one pleasant morn, 377
Hop-'o-my-Thumb and little Jack Horn 428
Hopping frog, hop here and be seen, 439
How can one man, how can all men 21
How comes it, Flora, that whenever 353
How great is little man, 121
How know I that it looms lovely, that I have never seen, 231
How many authors are my first, 423
How many seconds in a minute? 431
Hurt no living thing, 439

I a Princess king-descended, deckt with jewels, gilded, drest, 35
I All-creation sing my song of praise 28
I am a king, 434
I am a star dwelling on high, 97
I am pale with sick desire, 184
I bore with thee long weary days and nights, 215
I cannot tell you how it was, 318
I caught a little ladybird, 439
I did not chide him though I knew, 100
I do not look for love that is a dream, 36
I dreamed and did not seek : to-day I see 397
I dreamt I caught a little owl, 440
I dug and dug amongst the snow, 427
I dwell alone—I dwell alone, alone, 337
I fancy the good fairies dressed in white 420
I followed Thee, my God, I followed Thee 176
I found Love in a certain place, 381
I gather thyme upon the sunny hills, 136
I had a love in soft south land, 329
I have a friend in ghostland, 333
I have a little husband, 439
I have a Poll parrot, 440
I have but one rose in the world, 437
I have desired and I have been desired 411
I have done I know not what—what have I done, 261
I have no wit, no words, no tears, 101
I have not sought Thee, I have not found Thee, 261
I know a baby, such a baby, 442
I laid beside thy gate am Lazarus, 130
I lift mine eyes and see, 164
I lift mine eyes to see : earth vanisheth 1;
I long for joy, O Lord, I long for gold, 2

INDEX TO FIRST LINES 499

ooked for that which is not nor can be, 288
Lord, Thy foolish sinner low and small, 224
love and love not : Lord, it breaks my heart, 242
love one and he loveth me, 108
loved my love from green of Spring, 373
marked where lovely Venus and her court, 387
never said I loved you, John, 349
nursed it in my bosom while it lived, 334
peered within, and saw a world of sin, 193
planted a hand, 434
planted a young tree when I was young, 358
plucked pink blossoms from mine apple-tree, 335
praised the myrtle and the rose, 84
rose at the dead of night, 321
said good-bye in hope, 389
said of laughter : it is vain, 119
said : This is a beautiful fresh rose, 380
said within myself, I am a fool, 418
sat beneath a willow-tree, 406
saw a bird alone, 322
saw a saint. How canst thou tell that he, 163
sit a queen, and am no widow, and shall see no sorrow, 446
sit amid green shady valleys oft, 418
sought among the living, and I seek, 419
stood by weeping, 205
tell my secret? No indeed, not I, 336
think of the saints I have known, and lift up mine eyes, 213
thought to deal the death-stroke at a blow, 289
I thought your search was over.' 'So I thought,' 304
toiled on, but thou, 414
took my heart in my hand, 366
was a cottage-maiden, 347
was hungry and Thou feddest me, 225
watched a rosebud very long, 116
weary of my life, 382
will accept Thy will to do and be, 150
will not faint but trust in God, 238
will tell you when they met, 330
wish I were a little bird, 309
wish it were over, the terrible pain, 331
wish we once were wedded—then I must be true, 323
wish you were a pleasant wren, 424

I wonder if the sap is stirring yet, 314
I would have gone : God bade me stay, 242
I would not if I could undo my past, 383
If a mouse could fly, 435
If a pig wore a wig, 431
If all were rain and never sun, 429
If he would come to-day, to-day, to-day, 365
If hope grew on a bush, 434
If I had words, if I had words, 371
If I might see another Spring, 333
If I should say, my heart is in my home, 220
If I were a Queen, 430
If love is not worth loving, then life is not worth living, 127
If Mr. Bright retiring does not please, 444
If not with hope of life, 121
If only I might love my God and die ! 244
If stars dropped out of heaven, 441
If that's water you wash your hands in, 381
If the moon came from heaven, 442
If the sun could tell us half, 442
If thou be dead, forgive, and thou shalt live, 273
If underneath the water, 343
If we shall live, we live, 366
If you'll busk you as a bride, 410
In a far distant land they dwell, 111
In my Autumn garden I was fain, 395
In my cottage near the Styx, 423
In nuova primavera, 447
In Springtime when the leaves are young, 309
In tema e in pena addio, 457
In tempest and storm blackness of darkness for ever, 285
In that world we weary to attain, 197
In the bleak mid-winter, 246
In the grave will be no space, 180
In the meadow—What in the meadow? 435
In weariness and painfulness St. Paul, 172
Inner not outer, without gnash of teeth, 257
Innocent eyes not ours, 132
Io più ti amai che non mi amasti tu, 453
Is any grieved or tired? Yea, by God's will, 164
Is love so prone to change and rot, 323
Is the moon tired? She looks so pale, 441
Is this that name as ointment poured forth, 222
Is this the end, is there no end but this? 284

Is this the Face that thrills with awe, 254
It is a land with neither night nor day, 317
It is enough, enough, one said, 303
It is good to be last not first, 163
It is not death, O Christ, to die for Thee, 266
It is not for her even brow, 302
It is over, the horrible pain, 186
It is over. What is over? 186
It is the greatness of Thy love, dear Lord, that we would celebrate, 164
'It's a weary life, it is,' she said, 312
It's a year almost that I have not seen her, 388
It's oh in Paradise that I fain would be, 249
It seems an easy thing, 140
It was not warning that our fathers lacked, 141

January cold desolate, 432
Jerusalem is built of gold, 206
Jerusalem of fire, 207
Jess and Jill are pretty girls, 354
Jessie, Jessie Cameron, 371
Jesus alone: if thus it were to me, 285
Jesus, do I love Thee? 217
Jesus, Lord God from all eternity, 220
Johnny had a golden head, 399
Joy is but sorrow, 125

Keep love for youth, and violets for the spring, 383
Kookoorookoo kookoorookoo, 426

La rosa china il volto rosseggiato, 457
Laughing Life cries at the feast, 128
Launch out into the deep, Christ spake of old, 175
Leaf from leaf Christ knows, 221
Lie a-bed, 442
Lie still, my restive heart, lie still, 123
Life flows down to death; we cannot bind, 380
Life is fleeting, joy is fleeting, 95
Life is not sweet: one day it will be sweet, 358
Life that was born to-day, 271
Lift up thine eyes to seek the invisible, 209
Lift up your hearts. We lift them up. Ah me! 130
Light colourless doth colour all things else, 143
Light is our sorrow for it ends to-morrow, 122

Like flowers sequestered from the sun, 6
Listen, the last stroke of death's noon has struck, 420
Little lamb, who lost thee? 223
Live all thy sweet life through, 302
Lo newborn Jesus, 279
Long ago and long ago, 38
Long and dark the nights, dim and short the days, 172
Long have I longed, till I am tired, 402
Looking back along life's trodden way, 143
Lord Babe, if Thou art He, 160
Lord, by what inconceivable dim road, 208
Lord, carry me. Nay, but I grant thee strength, 221
Lord, comest Thou to me? 446
Lord, dost Thou look on me, and will not I, 229
Lord, give me blessed fear, 271
Lord, give me grace, 278
Lord, give me love that I may love Thee much, 270
Lord God of Hosts, most holy and most high, 220
Lord, grant me grace to love Thee in my pain, 268
Lord, grant us calm if calm can set forth Thee, 141
Lord, grant us eyes to see and ears to hear, 266
Lord, grant us grace to mount by steps of grace, 228
Lord, grant us grace to rest upon Thy word, 278
Lord, grant us wills to trust Thee with such aim, 265
Lord, hast Thou so loved us, and will not we, 225
Lord, I am feeble and of mean account, 275
Lord, I am here. But, child, I look for thee, 221
Lord, I am waiting, weeping, watching for Thee, 253
Lord, I believe; help Thou mine unbelief, 266
Lord, if I love Thee and Thou lovest me, 260
Lord, if Thy word had been, 'Worship Me not,' 123
Lord Jesu, Thou art sweetness to my soul, 224
Lord Jesus Christ, grown faint upon the cross, 167

INDEX TO FIRST LINES

ord Jesus Christ, our Wisdom and our Rest, 171
ord Jesus, who would think that I am Thine? 219
ord, make me one with Thine own faithful ones, 269
ord, make me pure, 274
ord, make us all love all, that when we meet, 265
ord, purge our eyes to see, 231
ord, Thou art fulness, I am emptiness, 445
ord, to Thine own grant watchful hearts and eyes, 177
ord, we are rivers running to Thy sea, 218
ord, what have I that I may offer Thee? 220
ord, what have I to offer? Sickening fear, 124
ord, when my heart was whole I kept it back, 123
Lord, whomsoever Thou shalt send to me, 124
Love brought me down, and cannot love make thee, 281
Love builds a nest on earth, and waits for rest, 446
Love came down at Christmas, 159
Love doth so grace and dignify, 270
Love for ever dwells in heaven, 83
Love hath a name of Death, 425
Love is all happiness, love is all beauty, 97
Love is alone the worthy law of love, 162
Love is more sweet than flowers, 90
Love is sweet, and so are flowers, 84
Love is the key of life and death, 179
Love loveth Thee, and wisdom loveth Thee, 270
Love me, I love you, 426
Love said nay while Hope kept saying, 132
Love still is love, and doeth all things well, 223
Love, strong as death, is dead, 292
Love, that is dead and buried, yesterday, 388
Love, to be love, must walk Thy way, 274
Love understands the mystery whereof, 121
Love whom I have loved too well, 106
Lovely Spring, 399
Lugubre e vagabondo in terra e in mare, 455

Lullaby oh lullaby, 442
Lungi da me il pensiere, 448
Lying a-dying, 214; 244

Maiden May sat in her bower, 401
Man rising to the doom that shall not err, 255
Man's harvest is past, his summer is ended, 202
Man's life is but a working day, 121
Man's life is death, yet Christ endured to live, 166
Many a flower hath perfume for its dower, 416
Many have sung of love a root of bane, 405
Margaret has a milking-pail, 435
Marvel of marvels if I myself shall behold, 122
Me and my gift: kind Lord, behold, 223
Me you often meet, 422
Methinks the ills of life I fain would shun, 420
Minnie and Mattie, 429
Minnie bakes oaten cakes, 436
Mix a pancake, 436
More shower than shine, 392
Morning and evening, 1
Mother mine, 392
Mother shake the cherry-tree, 432
Motherless baby and babyless mother, 442
My baby has a father and a mother, 426
My baby has a mottled fist, 428
My blessed mother dozing in her chair, 392
My first is no proof of my second, 422
My God, my God, have mercy on my sin, 163
My God, Thyself being Love, Thy Heart is Love, 171
My God, to live: how didst Thou bear to live, 238
My God, wilt Thou accept, and will not we, 231
My happy happy dream is finished with, 288
My harvest is done, its promise is ended, 201
My heart is like a singing bird, 335
My heart is yearning, 231
My life is long. Not so the Angels say, 185
My Lord, my Love, in love's unrest, 183
My Lord, my Love, in pleasant pain, 184

My love whose heart is tender said to me, 132
My mother said, The Child is changed, 296
My old admiration before I was twenty, 444
My sun has set, I dwell, 241
My vineyard that is mine I have to keep, 280

Name any gentleman you spy, 422
Ne' sogni ti veggo, 458
Nel verno accanto al fuoco, 454
Nerve us with patience, Lord, to toil or rest, 264
Never on this side of the grave again, 405
New creatures, the Creator still the same, 222
New Year met me somewhat sad, 190
Ninna-nanna, ninna-nanna, 457
No Cherub's heart or hand for us might ache, 167
No hope in life, yet is there hope, 346
No more! While sun and planets fly, 130
No thing is great on this side of the grave, 139
Nobil rosa ancor non crebbe, 446
None other Lamb, none other Name, 226
Not for me marring or making, 409
Now did you mark a falcon, 348
Now the pain beginneth and the word is spoken, 107
Now the sunlit hours are o'er, 109

O blessed Paul elect to grace, 172
O Christ my God, Who seest the unseen, 144
O Christ, our All in each, our All in all, 230
O Christ our Light Whom even in darkness we, 269
O Christ the Life, look on me where I lie, 136
O Christ the Vine with living fruit, 242
O ciliegia infiorita, 457
O earth, lie heavily upon her eyes, 293
O fallen star, a darkened light, 284
O First-fruits of our grain, 172
O foolish soul, to make thy count, 144
O gate of death, of the blessed night, 153
O happy rose, red rose that bloomest lonely, 97
O happy rosebud blooming, 95
O Jesu, better than Thy gifts, 232

O Jesu, gone so far apart, 175
O Lady Moon, your horns point tow. the East, 442
O Lord Almighty who hast formed u weak, 169
O Lord, fulfil Thy Will, 140
O Lord God, hear the silence of each s 267
O Lord, how canst Thou say Thou lov me? 248
O Lord, I am ashamed to seek Thy Fa. 265
O Lord, I cannot plead my love of Thee 445
O Lord on Whom we gaze and dare n. gaze, 267
O Lord, seek us, O Lord, find us, 283
O Lord, when Thou didst call me dids Thou know, 218
O love, love, hold me fast, 326
O marinaro, che mi apporti tu? 457
O mine enemy, 229
O my love and my own own deary, 379
O rose, thou flower of flowers, thou fragrant wonder, 103
O sailor come ashore, 438
O Shepherd with the bleeding feet, 223
O slain for love of me, canst Thou be cold. 183
O tempo tardo e amaro! 451
O unforgotten, 182
O Uommibatto, 453
O weary Champion of the Cross, lie still 280
O wind, where have you been, 429
O wind, why do you never rest, 428
O ye who are not dead and fit, 131
O ye who love to-day, 271
Of all the downfalls in the world, 133
Of each sad word, which is more sorrowful, 129
Oh fair Milly Brandon, a young maid fair maid, 403
Oh fair to see, 440
Oh for the time gone by when thought of Christ, 237
Oh happy happy land! 203
Oh kiss me once before I go, 378
Oh knell of a passing time, 198
Oh listen, listen, for the Earth, 112
Oh lost garden Paradise, 318
Oh pleasant eventide! 297
Oh roses for the flush of youth, 292
Oh sad thy lot before I came, 327
Oh tell me once and tell me twice, 409

INDEX TO FIRST LINES

Oh the cheerful Budding-time, 354
Oh the rose of keenest thorn, 41
Oh what comes over the sea, 382
Oh what is earth, that we should build, 197
Oh what is that country, 245
Oh whence do you come, my dear friend, to me, 359
Oh where are you going with your love-locks flowing, 374
Oh why is heaven built so far, 398
Oh would that I were very far away, 104
Ohibò piccina, 454
On the grassy banks, 429
On the land and on the sea, 217
On the wind of January, 355
Once again to wake nor wish to sleep, 130
Once I ached for thy dear sake, 165
Once I rambled in a wood, 99
Once I thought to sit so high, 233
Once in a dream, for once I dreamed of you, 352
Once in a dream I saw the flowers, 180
Once like a broken bow Mark sprang aside, 174
Once slain for Him Who first was slain for them, 178
Once within, within for evermore, 211
One and one are two, 431
One face looks out from all his canvases, 330
One passed me like a flash of lightning by, 333
One sorrow more : I thought the tale complete, 140
One step more and the race is ended, 161
One woe is past : come what come will, 138
One word—'tis all I ask of thee, 92
One young life lost, two happy young lives blighted, 282
Otto ore suonano, 454
Our feet shall tread upon the stars, 148
Our heaven must be within ourselves, 133
Our life is long. Not so, wise Angels say, 124
Our little baby fell asleep, 426
Our Master lies asleep and is at rest, 281
Our mothers, lovely women pitiful, 214
Our wealth has wasted all away, 151
Out in the rain a world is growing green, 168
Out of the church she followed them, 337
Own mother dear, 391

Pain and weariness, aching eyes and head, 263
Pardon the faults in me, 351
Parting after parting, 200
Passing away, saith the world, passing away, 190
Passing away the bliss, 417
Patience must dwell with Love, for Love and Sorrow, 274
Perdona al primo eccesso, 93
Pesano rena e pena, 455
Piteous my rhyme is, 163
Pity the sorrows of a poor old dog, 444
Playing at bob-cherry, 436
Poor the pleasure, 409
Porco la zucca fitta in parrucca ! 456
Possibil non sarebbe, 452
Promise me no promises, 350
Purity born of a maid, 173
Purpurea rosa, 447
Pussy has a whiskered face, 434

Quando il tempo avverrà che partiremo, 449

Remember, if I claim too much of you, 384
Remember me when I am gone away, 294
Rest remains when all is done, 200
Rest, rest, the troubled breast, 104
Roses and lilies grow above the place, 294
Roses blushing red and white, 437
Roses on a brier, 196
Rosy maiden Winifred, 437
Rushes in a watery place, 429

S' addormentò la nostra figliolina, 454
S' io t' incontrassi nell' eterna pace, 448
Safe where I cannot lie yet, 214
St. Barnabas with John his sister's son, 174
St. Peter once—'Lord, dost Thou wash my feet ?' 175
Saints are like roses when they flush rarest, 179
Salta, ranocchio, e mostrati, 456
Scarce tolerable life which all life long, 133
Scavai la neve—sì che scavai, 455
Se t' insegnasse Iddio, 449
See, the sun hath risen, 91
Seldom ' can't,' 431
Service and strength, God's angels and archangels, 177
Seven vials hold Thy wrath, but what can hold, 264
Shadow, shadow on the wall, 12

Shadows to-day while shadows show God's will, 142
Shall Christ hang on the cross, and we not look? 254
Shall I forget on this side of the grave? 374
Shall not the Judge of all the earth do right, 223
She came among us from the South, 377
She came in deep repentance, 89
She fell asleep among the flowers, 145
She gave up beauty in her tender youth, 286
She holds a lily in her hand, 234
She listened like a cushat dove, 313
She sat alway through the long day, 9
She sat and sang alway, 290
She sitteth still who used to dance, 387
She stands as pale as Parian statues stand, 311
She turned round to me with her steadfast eyes, 113
She was as sweet as violets in the spring, 301
She was most like a rose when it flushes rarest, 325
She was whiter than the ermine, 300
Short is time and only time is bleak, 201
Should one of us remember, 398
Sì che il fratello s' ha un falconcello, 455
Sing me a song, 435
Sing of a love lost and forgotten, 309
Slain for man, slain for me, O Lamb of God, look down, 224
Slain in their high places, fallen on rest, 210
Sleep, let me sleep, for I am sick of care, 293
Sleep, little baby, sleep, 309
Sleep, unforgotten sorrow, sleep awhile, 323
Sleeping at last, the trouble and tumult past, 417
So brief a life, and then an endless life, 200
So I grew half delirious and quite sick, 423
Soft white lamb in the daisy meadow, 310
Solomon most glorious in array, 138
Some are laughing, some are weeping, 295
Some ladies dress in muslin full and white, 421
Somewhere or other there must surely be, 362

Sonnets are full of love, and this my tome, lxxiii
Sooner or later, yet at last, 157
Sorrow hath a double voice, 142
Sorrow of saints is sorrow of a day, 141
Soul rudderless, unbraced, 444
Sound the deep waters, 154
Sposa velata, 456
Spring bursts to-day, 255
Spunta la margherita, 456
Still sometimes in my secret heart of hearts, 389
Strengthening as secret manna, 308
Strike the bells wantonly, 331
Stroke a flint, and there is nothing to admire, 430
Such a hubbub in the nests, 395
Such is love it comforts in extremity, 272
Summer is gone with all its roses, 290
Sweet blackbird is silenced with chaffinch and thrush, 425
Sweet life is dead. Not so, 320
Sweet sweet sound of distant waters falling, 117
Sweet, thou art pale. More pale to see, 146
Sweetest Elizabeth, accept I pray, 90
Sweetness of rest when Thou sheddest rest, 144
Swift and sure the swallow, 440

Tell me, doth it not grieve thee to lie here, 114
Tempest and terror below, but Christ the Almighty above, 229
Ten years ago it seemed impossible, 352
Thank God, thank God, we do believe, 117
Thank God who spared me what I feared, 235
That Eden of earth's sunrise cannot re 162
That song of songs which is Solomon's, 134
The blindest buzzard that I know, 368
The buttercup is like a golden cup, 399
The child said, 'Pretty bird,' 299
The city mouse lives in a house, 433
The curtains were half drawn, the floor was swept, 292
The days are clear, 430
The dear old woman in the lane, 440
The dog lies in his kennel, 434
The door was shut: I looked between, 320

INDEX TO FIRST LINES 505

The earth was green, the sky was blue, 389
The end of all things is at hand; we all, 179
The fields are white to harvest, look and see, 125
The first was like a dream through summer heat, 20
The flowers that bloom in sun and shade, 250
The goal in sight! Look up and sing, 145
The goblets all are broken, 291
The great Vine left its glory to reign as Forest king, 166
The half moon shows a face of plaintive sweetness, 198
The half was not told me, said Sheba's Queen, 134
The hills are tipped with sunshine while I walk, 133
The hope I dreamed of was a dream, 350
The horses of the sea, 438
The Husband of the widow care for her, 352
The irresponsive silence of the land, 262
The jessamine shows like a star, 295
The joy of saints like incense turned to fire, 212
The King's daughter is all glorious within, 207
The least if so I am, 144
The lily has a smooth stalk, 439
The lily has an air, 435
The lowest place. Ah Lord, how steep and high, 128
The mystery of Life, the mystery, 393
The night is far spent, the day is at hand, 196
The P. R. B. is in its decadence, 424
The Passion Flower hath sprung up tall, 135
The peach tree on the southern wall, 441
The peacock has a score of eyes, 434
The rose is Love's own flower, and Love's no less, 417
The rose that blushes rosy red, 440
The rose with such a bonny blush, 440
The roses bloom too late for me, 114
The roses lingered in her cheeks, 83
The sea laments with unappeasable, 195
The shadows gather round me while you are in the sun, 307
The shepherds had an angel, 187

The shout of a king is among them. One day may I be, 210
The sinner's own fault? So it was, 128
The soonest mended, nothing said, 408
The splendour of the kindling day, 407
The spring spreads one green lap of flowers, 402
The stream moaneth as it floweth, 112
The summer nights are short, 430
The sunrise wakes the lark to sing, 391
The sweetest blossoms die, 116
The tempest over and gone, the calm begun, 167
The twig sprouteth, 143
The two Rossettis (brothers they), 424
The upland flocks grew starved and thinned, 350
The white dove cooeth in her downy nest, 152
The wind has such a rainy sound, 436
The wind shall lull us yet, 304
The world—what a world, Ah me! 283
The year stood at its equinox, 367
There are lilies for her sisters, 319
There are rivers lapsing down, 321
There are sleeping dreams and waking dreams, 55
There is a sleep we have not slept, 186
There is but one May in the year, 430
There is nothing more that they can do, 232
There is one that has a head without an eye, 435
There is silence that saith, Ah me! 406
There she lay so still and pale, 93
There's a footstep coming; look out and see, 364
There's blood between us, love, my love, 340
There's little sunshine in my heart, 366
There's no replying, 400
There's snow on the fields, 427
These days are long before I die, 342
These roses are as perfect as of old, 328
They are flocking from the East, 256
They have brought gold and spices to my King, 148
They lie at rest asleep and dead, 204
They lie at rest, our blessed dead, 127
They made the chamber sweet with flowers and leaves, 308
They scarcely waked before they slept, 159
They throng from the East and the West, 198

This Advent moon shines cold and clear, 202
This near-at-hand land breeds pain by measure, 194
Thou sleepest where the lilies fade, 309
Thou who art dreary, 87
Thou who didst hang upon a barren tree, 244
Thou whom I love, for whom I died, 257
Three little children, 436
Three plum buns, 433
Three sang of love together—one with lips, 329
Through burden and heat of the day, 142
Through the vales to my love! 390
Thy cross cruciferous doth flower in all, 167
Thy fainting spouse, yet still Thy spouse, 230
Thy lilies drink the dew, 275
Thy lovely saints do bring Thee love, 218
Thy name, O Christ, as incense streaming forth, 223
Ti do l'addio, 452
Till all sweet gums and juices flow, 26
Time lengthening, in the lengthening seemeth long, 199
Time passeth away with its pleasure and pain, 199
Time seems not short, 198
To come back from the sweet South to the North, 378
To the God who reigns on high, 83
To think that this meaningless thing was ever a rose, 411
To-day's your natal day, 82
Together once, but never more, 201
Together with my dead body shall they arise, 169
Toll, bell, toll—for hope is flying, 285
Too cold almost for hope of spring, 392
Treasure plies a feather, 140
Tremble, thou earth, at the presence of the Lord, 199
Trembling before Thee, we fall down to adore Thee, 161
Tumult and turmoil, trouble and toil, 230
Tune me, O Lord, into one harmony, 275
Twist me a crown of wind-flowers, 430
Two days ago with dancing glancing hair, 336
Two doves upon the self-same branch, 353
Two gazed into a pool, he gazed and she, 385

Uccello delle rose e del dolore, 450
Udite, si dolgono mesti-fringuelli, 455
Under the ivy bush, 434
Under willows among the graves, 368
Underneath the growing grass, 311
Unmindful of the roses, 413
Unripe harvest there hath none to reap, 132
Unspotted lambs to follow the one Lamb, 160
Up, my drowsing eyes, 178
Up Thy hill of sorrows, 166

Vanity of vanities, the Preacher saith, 111
Venga amicizia e sia la benvenuta, 450
Vento gentil che verso il mezzodì, 452
Voices from above and from beneath, 17
Vola, preghiera, e digli, 447
Volgo la faccia verso l' oriente, 451

Watch with me, men, women, and children dear, 190
Watch yet a while, 121
Water calmly flowing, 84
We are of those who tremble at Thy word, 196
We buried her among the flowers, 301
We know not a voice of that river, 171
We know not when, we know not where, 196
We meet in joy though we part in sorrow, 236
We met hand to hand, 359
Wearied of sinning, wearied of repentance, 252
Weary and weak—accept my weariness, 251
Wee wee husband, 439
Weep yet awhile, 152
Weigh all my faults and follies righteously, 268
What are heavy? Sea-sand and sorrow, 430
What are these lovely ones, yea what are these? 212
What art thou thinking of, said the mother, 88
What can lambkins do, 362
What do the stars do? 442
What does the bee do? 440
What does the donkey bray about? 433
What is it Jesus saith unto the soul? 127
What is life that we should love it, 95
What is pink? A rose is pink, 432

INDEX TO FIRST LINES 507

What is the beginning? Love. What the course? Love still, 274
What is this above thy head, 283
What shall we do with Margery? 360
What will it be, O my soul, what will it be, 445
What will you give me for my pound? 432
What would I give for a heart of flesh to warm me through, 363
When a mounting skylark sings, 438
When all the over-work of life, 192; 194
When Christ went up to heaven the Apostles stayed, 170
When fishes set umbrellas up, 434
When I am dead, my dearest, 290
When I am sick and tired it is God's will, 156
When I was dead my spirit turned, 339
When if ever life is sweet, 150
When my love came home to me, 322
When sick of life and all the world, 197
When the cows come home the milk is coming, 437
When the eye hardly sees, 313
When wickedness is broken as a tree, 206
When will the day bring its pleasure? 252
Where are the songs I used to know? 398
Where innocent bright-eyed daisies are, 433
Where love is, there comes sorrow, 137
Where my heart is, wherever that may be, 359
Where never tempest heaveth, 122
Where shall I find a white rose blowing? 131
Where sunless rivers weep, 292
Where were you last night? I watched at the gate, 361
Wherefore art thou strange and not my mother? 377
Whereto shall we liken this blessed Mary Virgin, 173
While Christ lay dead the widowed world, 168
While I sit at the door, 373
While roses are so red, 363
While we slumber and sleep, 410
Whiteness most white. Ah to be clean again, 275
Who art thou that comest with a steadfast face, 103
Who calleth?—Thy Father calleth, 248
Who cares for earthly bread though white, 128
Who extols a wilderness? 90

Who has seen the wind? 438
Who is this that cometh up not alone, 207
Who knows? God knows, and what He knows, 138
Who scatters tares shall reap no wheat, 169
Who shall tell the lady's grief, 89
Who sits with the King in His throne? 207
Who standeth at the gate? A woman old, 147
Who told my mother of my shame? 348
Who would wish back the saints upon our rough, 129
Whoso hath anguish is not dead in sin, 271
Whoso hears a chiming for Christmas at the nighest, 278
Why did baby die, 428
Why does the sea moan evermore? 343
Why has Spring one syllable less, 408
Why should I call Thee Lord who art my God? 246
Why were you born when the snow was falling? 379
Winter is cold-hearted, 363
Winter's latest snowflake is the snowdrop flower, 393
Wintry boughs against a wintry sky, 415
Wisest of sparrows that sparrow which sitteth alone, 143
Woe for the young who say that life is long, 287
Woman was made for man's delight, 416
Words cannot utter, 168
Would that I were a turnip white, 420
Wouldst thou give me a heavy jewelled crown, 418
Wreathe no more lilies in my hair, 304
Wrens and Robins in the hedge, 428

Yea blessed and holy is he that hath part in the First Resurrection, 211
Yea if Thou wilt Thou canst put up Thy sword, 144
Yes I too could face death and never shrink, 297
Yet earth was very good in days of old, 161
You must not call me Maggie, you must not call me Dear, 375
You tell me that the world is fair, in spite, 302
You were born in the Spring, 445
Young girls wear flowers, 135
Young Love lies sleeping, 312
Your brother has a falcon, 427

Printed by R. & R. CLARK, LIMITED, *Edinburgh.*

Milton Keynes UK
Ingram Content Group UK Ltd.
UKHW021441121223
434238UK00012B/248